ZOMBIES:
MORE RECENT DEAD

Other Anthologies Edited by Paula Guran

ZOMBIES:
MORE RECENT DEAD

Edited by Paula Guran

PRIME BOOKS

ZOMBIES: MORE RECENT DEAD

Prime Books
www.prime-books.com
Germantown, Maryland

For more information, contact Prime Books:
prime@prime-books.com

ISBN: 978-1-60701-433-1

Also available in ebook format:
ISBN: 978-1-60701-417-1

CONTENTS

Return of the Preshamble

Paula Guran

A little over four years ago, I started compiling *Zombies: The Recent Dead*. Published in October 2010, I hoped it was a zombie anthology that not only included outstanding stories, but could serve as an entertaining guide (of sorts) and "historical documentation" to zombie fiction written in the first decade of what had already turned into the Zombie Century.

I was very fortunate to be able to republish an updated version of David J. Schow's introduction and afterword from his collection *Zombie Jam* (Subterranean Press, 2003). Schow wrote of the impact of George A. Romero's films on him personally as well as the rest of us culturally. He also explained how the modern archetype of the living dead is derived from cinematic rather than literary roots.

I added two other short introductory essays. The first, "Preshamble," dealt with the earlier "traditional" zombie mythos (and its one-time popularity). The other, "Deaditorial Note," briefly covered the rise of the living dead in twenty-first century popular culture, including its literature, and the themes most often explored. (You can find them online here: paulaguran.com/zombies-the-recent-dead-intro).

At the time, I wondered if the demand for all things zombie had peaked, if *Zombies: The Recent Dead* was a last chance at doing an anthology of great fiction about the living dead.

I shouldn't have worried.

The Walking Dead premiered on 31 October 2010 on AMC.

The series' popularity either kept the living dead alive or proved they were even more embedded in our pop cultural brains than ever.

By 2013, *The Walking Dead* averaged 5.6 million viewers per episode: the highest audience ratings in the United States for any television show, broadcast or cable. It was also the most popular TV show with advertiser-preferred viewers between the ages of eighteen and forty-nine. Its fifth season will air this fall.

The summer of 2013 brought the movie *World War Z*: big budget ($190 million for production), big star (Brad Pitt), biggest hordes of zombies ever seen, and at this writing, more than $540 million worldwide gross. Biggest z-movie ever and Brad Pitt's biggest grosser.

The Max Brooks novel the film was loosely based on—Brooks freely admitted the only thing his novel and the movie had in common is the title—had been one of two books that truly set off twenty-first century zombiemania: *The Zombie Survival Guide: Complete Protection from the Living Dead* (2003), a parody of a survival guide, and *World War Z* (2006), a serious novel documenting a worldwide zombie pandemic. Both by Brooks, these books brought zombies out of the horror genre and into the mainstream.

How far into the mainstream?

The Walking Dead is not the only hit television series about the living dead. BBC Three's mini-series *In the Flesh* began airing in the UK on 17 March 2013 with three hour-long episodes. (It won the BAFTA Award as best mini-series of 2014 and its leading actor, Luke Newberry, was also honored in his category.) A second season of six hour-long episodes began on 4 May 2014 in the UK and on 10 May 2014 in the U.S. (carried by BBC America). Rather than focusing on humans making violently sure the living dead are dead dead, *In The Flesh* offers a more compassionate view emphasizing the difficulties of "living" as one of the dead.

Eight episodes of a French series, *The Returned* (*Les Revenants*), based on the 2004 film *They Came Back* (also titled, in French, *Les Revenants*) aired in 2012 on Canal+. It became the pay-TV broadcaster's most popular original series ever and won an International Emmy for Best Drama Series. A second season followed. It was aired in the UK in 2013. In the U.S., Sundance Channel aired the first season of *Les Revenants* as *The Returned*. Now, A&E has fast-tracked a ten-episode version, also titled *The Returned*, to air fall 2014. Like *In the Flesh*, the undead are humanized in the series while investigating the effect on the living when those from the not-always-resolved past abruptly show up.

The dead return to life in the French series, but it is closer to ABC's 2013 unrelated series *Resurrection* (based on the novel *The Returned* by Jason Mott) than typical zombie fare. In *Resurrection,* the dead mysteriously appear, look and act as they did while among the living, and have no apparent memory of their deaths or what has passed since then. Perhaps these aren't zombies? Don't be so sure. By the end of *Resurrection*'s first season earlier this year, the undead were at least becoming a major problem that was going to have to be dealt with by the living. ABC has renewed *Resurrection* for a second season.

The BBC has commissioned a zombie "reality" game show, *I Survived a Zombie Apocalypse*. BBC Three—set to go online-only in late 2015—will air the show. The premise: eight contestants are trapped in a shopping mall surrounded by the (supposedly) walking dead. Contestants must use urban survival tactics and their wits to avoid being bitten by the "zombies." Dark humor seems to be intrinsic to the show as a network news release promises that once bitten, contestants "will leave the show in grisly style." An executive producer is quoted as saying, "It's nice to finally have a game show where if you get a challenge wrong, you get your arms ripped off and your brains eaten out."

As for *The Walking Dead,* AMC has announced an as-yet untitled "companion series." Originally (in late 2013) slated to launch in 2015, the network has not offered any details lately on when it will premiere.

Syfy recently announced a thirteen-episode series, *Z Nation,* which "will follow the struggle for humans to survive post-zombie apocalypse." It will premiere fall 2014.

World War Z? Paramount has announced a sequel with Pitt starring, Juan Antonio Bayona directing, and Steven Knight as screenwriter. No date is set, but release in 2016 is expected.

The Lively Living Dead Thriving Elsewhere

Picture books for children featuring zombies (usually light-heartedly) had proliferated by the time *ParaNorman*, a 2012 zombie movie for kids, received nominations for the Academy Award for Best Animated Feature and BAFTA Award for Best Animated Film. So had chapter books for older children and young adult novels. All continue to do so.

In the colorful kids' game *Plants vs. Zombies*, according to the description, a "mob of fun-loving zombies is about to invade your home, and your only defense is an arsenal of 49 zombie-zapping plants . . . Each zombie has its own special skills, so be careful how you use your limited supply of greens and seeds . . . as you battle the fun-dead . . . " There's a large line of toys to match—including plush toys for infants—and a comic book series.

Or, you can try the more generic "Glow in the Dark Flesh Eating Zombies Play Set." (Nine three-inch-tall vinyl glow-in-the-dark flesh-eating zombies. "Turn off the light to see their eerie glow!") Nerf makes a "Zombie Crossfire Bow Toy," and, instead of little plastic army figures, you can now buy a bag of zombies (neon green) and zombie hunters (bright blue, includes Swat/Hazmat units).

When it comes to the undead devouring our kids, I could go on . . .

Oh, hold on to your decaying flesh, I won't.

There are also plenty of zombie comic books, graphic novels, and (yes) manga intended for those a bit older. According to Diamond Comic Distributors, the top-selling comic book of 2013 (not surprisingly) was *The Walking Dead No. 115* and *Walking Dead* volumes accounted for five of the Top Ten graphic novels. But the TV-related franchise isn't the only comic series, published (or, in some cases, were published until recently.) Along with various graphic versions of z-movies old and new and some novels, there are series like *The New Deadwardians, iZombie, Fanboys vs. Zombies, Revival,* and *Afterlife with Archie* (yes, *that* Archie). Even George Romero returned to the zombie genre this year with comic *Empire of the Dead*, illustrated by Alex Maleev and published by Marvel.

Despite the plethora of already-existing zombie videogames, many gamers found *The Last of Us*—with its realistic post-apocalyptic storyline and uncomfortable moral choices—to be one of the best titles of 2013. Also recently popular is *DayZ,* a multiplayer open world survival game test-released in December 2013 for Windows, and still in alpha-testing stage. Noted for its particularly horrific scenarios, the *DayZ* player is a survivor of a zombie virus who must forage for basic needs while killing or avoiding zombies, as well as killing, co-opting, or avoiding other players.

Among z-games to come: *Dead Island 2* is scheduled for a spring 2015 release on Xbox One, PlayStation 4, and PC. *Dying Light*, another action game with zombies will also launch for the Xbox One, Xbox 360, PS3, PS4, and PC sometime in 2015. Zombie survival game *H1Z1* (the name of yet another zombie-making virus) has a tentative release date of the end of 2014 for PC.

For those inclined to at least shamble rather than remain rotting on the couch, there are zombie walks. A combination of flash-mob/cosplay, these events have been around since 2003 and are now documented in more than twenty countries. The largest gathering, so far, according to Guinness World Records, is 8,027 at Midway Stadium in St. Paul, Minnesota, on 13 October 2012. (A pub crawl following the zombie event involved more than thirty thousand more-or-less zombified participants.)

The living imitating the undead have also raised money for various charities.

Live roleplaying games, most notably *Humans vs. Zombies*, have proliferated on college campuses and elsewhere. *HvZ* humans defend themselves against a growing zombie horde with Nerf or other soft-dart guns and rolled-up socks. It is played on six continents and locations including Australia, Denmark, Namibia, and Spain.

Zombie-only versions of "haunted attractions" are beginning to appear as well. Locations are turned into zombie lairs full of the hungry undead and visitors try to survive the flesh-eaters.

The undead are even helping the United States government. In 2012, about a thousand military, law enforcement, and medical personnel participated in a first-responder seminar subsidized by the United States Department of Homeland Security that included a rampaging horde of zombies as part of their emergency response training. It was only a small, tongue-in-cheek part of the training, but using a zombie virus outbreak scenario to train participants for a global pandemic—in which they would need to deal with violent, crazed, and fearful people—proved to be a valuable teaching tool.

That same year, the United States Centers for Disease Control and Prevention began a whimsical emergency preparedness campaign blog—*Preparedness 101: Zombie Apocalypse*—which turned into a very effective platform (so many people accessed the once-bland website, it crashed) to reach and engage a wide variety of audiences on hazard preparedness in general. CDC Director Dr. Ali Khan has noted, "If you are generally well equipped to deal with a zombie apocalypse you will be prepared for a hurricane, pandemic, earthquake, or terrorist attack."

There's more evidence, of course, of our cultural love for these fictional creatures, but to get back to the written word—which is, after all, what *we* are concerned with here . . .

There's No Such Thing as Dead Words in Z-Lit

Other than Quirk Books' 2009 Jane Austen/zombie mash-up *Pride and Prejudice and Zombies*, "coauthored" by Seth Grahame-Smith, no novel since *World War Z* has had anywhere near its impact. (And although *Pride and Prejudice and Zombies* launched a mostly unfortunate subgenre, it now appears to be short-lived and unlikely to crawl forth from its tomb.)

This is not to say there have not been some excellent and/or popular novels since 2006 (I already mentioned some in *Zombies: The Recent Dead*.) Here is a 2009-2014—admittedly incomplete—selection (alphabetically by author's last name; U.S. publisher listed unless published significantly earlier elsewhere):

- Amelia Beamer: *The Loving Dead* (Night Shade, 2010)
- Alden Bell: *The Reapers Are the Angels* (Holt, 2010) and *Exit Kingdom* (Holt, 2012)
- Mira Grant: Newsfeed trilogy (*Feed*, 2010; *Deadline*, 2011; *Blackout*, 2012—all from Orbit)
- Daryl Gregory: *Raising Stony Mayhall* (Del Rey, 2011)

• John Ajvide Lindqvist: *Handling the Undead* (as *Hanteringen av ödöda* in Sweden in 2005; English translation: Quercus, UK, 2009; Thomas Dunne, U.S., 2010)
• Jonathan Maberry: Joe Ledger series (*Patient Zero*, 2009; *The Dragon Factory*, 2010; *The King of Plagues*, 2011; *Assassins Code*, 2012; *Extinction Machine*, 2013; *Code Zero*, 2014; with two more forthcoming in 2015 and 2016, all from St. Martin's Griffin)
• Jonathan Maberry (also from St. Martin's Griffin): *Dead of Night*, (2011) and *Fall of Night* (2014)
• Colson Whitehead: *Zone One* (Doubleday, 2011)

And, just a few of many, for Young Adult readers:

• Sean Beaudoin: The Infects (2012, Candlewick)
• Charlie Higson: Enemy Series: [*The Enemy* (Puffin, 2009), *The Dead* (Hyperion, 2010), *The Fear* (Disney-Hyperion, 2011); *The Sacrifice* (2012), *The Fallen* (2013), *The Hunted* (Puffin, UK, 2014, no U.S. edition as yet)]
• Jonathan Maberry: Benny Imura series (*Rot & Ruin*, 2010; *Dust & Decay*, 2011; *Flesh & Bone*, 2012; *Fire & Ash*, 2013: from Simon & Schuster for Young Readers)
• Carrie Ryan: The Forest of Hands and Teeth series (*The Forest of Hands and Teeth*, 2009; The *Dead-Tossed Waves*, 2010; *The Dark and Hollow Places*, 2011: all Delacorte Press Books for Young Readers)
• Darren Shan: Zom-B series: *Zom-B*, 2012; *Zom-B Underground*, 2013; *Zom-B City*, 2013; *Zom-B Angels*, 2013; *Zom-B Baby*, 2013; *Zom-B Gladiator*, 2014; *Zom-B Mission*, 2014: all Simon & Schuster. *Zom-B Clans*, 2014: Simon & Schuster UK)

During the first decade of the twenty-first century, zombie fiction became even more of a force to contend with in the short form than previously. Now, in the last few years, creative short stories seem to be appearing more frequently in periodicals both online and off, and the walking dead continue to fill anthologies. There don't seem to be as many compilations these days from the very small presses and fewer of the "intended-to-gross-out" variety, but among those from trade publishers (alphabetically by editor):

• Steve Berman: *Zombies: Shambling Through the Ages* (Prime, 2013; mix of reprinted and original stories)
• Holly Black & Justine Larbalestier: *Zombies vs. Unicorns* (Margaret K. McElderry Books, 2010; half zombie, intended for YA)

• John Joseph Adams: *The Living Dead 2* (Night Shade, 2010, mostly reprints)

• Christopher Golden: *The New Dead: A Zombie Anthology* (St. Martin's Griffin, 2010)

• Christopher Golden: *21st Century Dead: A Zombie Anthology* (St. Martin's Griffin, 2012)

• Paula Guran: *Extreme Zombies* (Prime Books, 2012; reprints and *only* for fans of the extreme)

• Stephen Jones: *Zombie Apocalypse!* (Running Press, 2010)

• Stephen Jones: *Zombie Apocalypse! Fightback* (Running Press, 2012)

• Silvia Moreno-Garcia: *Dead North: Canadian Zombie Fiction* [Exile Editions (Canada, but distributed in US), 2013]

• Otto Penzler: *Zombies! Zombies! Zombies!* (Vintage, 2011; aka as *Zombies: A Compendium of the Living Dead*; historical overview; reprints)

Check the acknowledgments at the back of this volume, and you'll discover a broad range of sources of zombie stories from the past few years. You might also note that all but seven of the thirty-six entries collected here were published in 2010 or after. Of those seven: two are poems (which I did not consider for the 2010 volume), one has been published only in Australia, two were not then available for reprint, and the other two I was simply unaware of.

So What Makes Your Crypt So Special?

One thing I noticed as I discovered (or rediscovered) these very recent zombie stories: in our fictional worlds, we seem to accept that zombies exist or will exist far more readily than we did a decade ago. They are almost considered inevitable. Their fictional popularity is even sometimes referenced. This, perhaps, allows the writer to venture further from the generic trope and deal more with dead that live in different ways rather than adhere to the more common ideations—including the more fantastic. It may also allow the authors to be either more compassionate with the undead or even less understanding of the once-human monsters. We've known all along the living dead are really us, but authors seem to be using the metaphor of the zombie in ever more creative ways.

Usually, of course, the stories are more about living humans than the living dead—if and how they remain human after the world is utterly, irrevocably, (but not always horribly) changed. Our reaction to zombies is far more telling than the existence of the dead that walk and prey on the living—if they pose a threat to the living at all.

I won't name titles, so as not to spoil any plots, but among these thirty-six stories you will find both the humorous and the achingly serious. Naturally, using tales of the living dead to comment on culture as a whole, religion, and politics are still fair game, and—

Zombies, along with other apocalyptic events, are used purely as a metaphor for personal pain . . .

The affliction is not immediate onset, you gradually get "sicker" until you are an "end-stager" . . . or the infection comes on in a hour—there is time to record your turning from a thinking person to a brain-eater . . .

Instead of a mass event, returning from the dead can be individual happenstance: a spouse comes back from the grave, a guy at the office shows up after he's dead, through strange science one explores the liminal spaces that separate life from death . . .

The living dead are part of history, and the world has put itself back together one way or another. Zombies, like disease, are just another truism or merely something else that messes your life up . . .

The dead are raised for convenience, through inadvertent or intentional science or even necromancy. Society has contrived ways to deal with them . . .

Zombies are revived in various alternate histories: a pre-Roman Britain . . . First Nation legends . . . ancient Babylon . . . among nineteenth-century pox-ridden cadavers . . . during World War Two . . .

The dead return to life and nothing has changed for them or anyone else . . .

A few *zombis,* with roots in a mixture of Afro-Caribbean lore and the religion of voudou, appear . . . as well as other dead things commanded by more fantastic magic . . .

There is an outbreak of zombism in a posthuman far-future (complete with all the trappings of hard science fiction) on a spaceship traveling to distant stars . . .

Of course there are a variety of gritty futures where civilization has turned into an environment worse than any primitive jungle and one must fight the dead to live . . . and much more.

Are these all truly zombie stories? To me, they are: all deal with the dead coming back to some semblance of physical life. At the very least, they are worthy of your perusal and debate. The zombie subgenre, as I mentioned four years ago, is a hardy virus and continues to mutate and thus thrive.

So, once again, dear readers—*BONE appetit!*

Paula Guran
18 June 2014
International Panic Day

The Afflicted

Matthew Johnson

In the end I managed a bit of sleep, wedged between the trunk and branches of the oak, before dawn came. My knees and elbows ached as I lowered myself to the ground and I could feel a blister forming on my shoulder where the strap of my .30-06 Winchester had rubbed against my oilskin all night. I went over the previous day's events in my mind, walking myself carefully through every mundane moment from when I woke up to when I climbed into the tree to sleep; then I looked down at my watch, waited for the minute to turn over and started to rattle off words that started with *L: life, leopard, lizard, loneliness* . . . Twenty words and thirty seconds later I took a breath and started down the train tracks.

It was about an hour's walk to the camp, my last stop on this circuit. The clearing was packed with tents, their walls so faded by years of sun I could hardly make out the FEMA logo on the side; here and there ripped flaps of nylon fluttered in the breeze. The camps, cramped to begin with, were made even tighter by the lean-tos that had been built to expand the tents or shore them up, so that in places I had to turn sideways to squeeze my way toward the center of the camp.

As I got deeper into the camp, pale figures began to emerge from the tents, most of them dressed in filthy pajamas and bathrobes and nearly all bearing scars or fresh wounds on whatever flesh was exposed. I kept my .30-06 at my side and quickened my pace as they began to shuffle after me on slippered feet.

A single tent stood in the middle of the camp, as worn as the rest but bearing a faded Red Cross logo. When I reached it, I turned around and shrugged out of my backpack one arm at a time. All the narrow paths that led here were now blocked by the shambling forms that had come out of the tents: they paused as they reached the clearing, watching me carefully as I cradled my rifle.

After a few moments, one of them stepped forward. He was bald, save for a fringe of white hair, and he had a bloody gash down the side of his face. Unlike most of the others he was still in reasonably good shape, his skin the color of a walnut. I leveled my rifle at him; he took another shambling step and then stopped.

"Hey, Horace," I said. I gestured at the cut on his face. "That looks bad."

He shrugged. "There's worse off than me."

"I know," I said, lowering my rifle, "but we'll start with you. Then you tell me who's worst off."

He looked back at the others. "There's a lot that are bad off, Kate," he said. "How long do you have today?"

I leaned the rifle in a spot where I could reach it in a hurry if I needed to. "You're my only stop."

He nodded, though he knew as well as I did that even in a full day I only had time to see the very worst off. Their affliction aside, my patients' age and the conditions they lived in meant that each of them had a host of issues for me to deal with. I counted on Horace to keep an eye on who was seriously injured, who had developed anything infectious, and who was showing signs of going end-stage. Everything else—minor illnesses and injuries, the frequent combination of scurvy and obesity caused by their diet of packaged food—I couldn't even hope to treat.

I glanced up at the sky, saw just a few white clouds. "Let's set up outside today," I said. "Sunshine and fresh air ought to do everyone some good."

"Sure. At least we've got plenty of those." Horace gestured to two of the waiting patients and they came up to the tent, giving me a wide berth, and hauled out the exam bed. He turned to the others. "You might as well get on with your day. I'll come get you when she's ready for you."

A few of the waiting patients wandered off when he said this, but most stayed where they were. The line was mostly silent, with little chatter: the camp residents were used to isolation, many of them only coming out of their tents when I visited or to take care of bodily necessities.

I patted the exam table and Horace sat down on it stiffly. I unzipped one of the pockets on my backpack, drawing out my checkup kit, then held his wrist in my hand to take his pulse and slipped the cuff around his arm and inflated it. "Any cough?" I asked.

He shrugged. "Little bit now and then," he said. "I used to smoke. Guess I'm better off now, huh?"

I nodded. A lot of my patients were former smokers: when they were kids everyone had been, and they had grown up watching cigarette ads on TV. I got the TB kit and a pair of gloves out of my pack, pulled on the gloves, and tapped a syringe of PPD into his forearm. "Let's hope it's just that," I said.

He scowled. "Does it matter?" he asked.

I shook my head. "TB's a bad way to go. You remember how this works?"

He nodded.

"Tell me anyway."

"Watch where you pricked me for three days. If there's a spot, stay out of camp until you get back."

"Good. Hey, do you remember what we were talking about last time I was here? You never finished that story."

"You wanted to know how Adele and I met. Right?" I nodded. "Well, she used to work in the corner store. I would go in every day to buy something, just to see her. Of course all I could afford was a Coke, so she started to wonder—"

I reached out to tap him on the lips, right under his nose, and nodded with relief when he didn't react. "Horace, that thing you pull to open a parachute—what's that called?"

"It's a—damn it, that's, I know it . . . " He closed his eyes, frowning. "I don't remember."

"Never mind," I said. "How'd you get the cut?"

He was silent for a moment. "You know how it is."

I opened a steri-wipe and washed his wound; he flinched as I ran my fingers along the edges of the cut. "Does it hurt?"

He shrugged, gritting his teeth and hissing as I pressed a chitosan sponge into the wound and then covered it with plaskin, running my fingers along the edge to make the seal. He jerked his head suddenly and I pulled my hand back. "What is it?" I asked. "Did I hurt you?"

"Rip cord!" He broke into a broad grin. "Rip cord. Right?"

"That's good, Horace," I said. "No progression since last time. Anybody else I should know about?"

"What do you mean?"

"Your cut," I said. "Those are bite marks. Who was it?"

"Jerry," he said after a moment. "He didn't—I didn't know he'd gone end-stage."

"I'm sorry," I said. One of the things that makes the affliction so terrifying is how rapidly and unpredictably it can progress, smoldering like an ember in some and burning like a brush fire in others. That's why it has to be dealt with when the first symptoms surface, when they're still the parents and grandparents we had known in spirit as well as in body. "I don't suppose he's in the dog cage?"

Horace shook his head. "Ran off. Guess he's out in the woods somewhere." He was quiet for a moment. "Am I going to . . . will I . . . ?"

For a moment I said nothing, trying not to look him in the eyes. The fact is that nobody knows for sure what causes the affliction, or even how it spreads: it could be that it's lurking in all of us, waiting for us to grow old. It seemed to me that the ones who had friends or spouses in the camps stayed well longer—but when one went, the others almost always followed soon.

"I can tell that's paining you," I said. "Say no to a little morphine?"

"I guess not."

"Arms up, then," I said, and fished out a syringe. He held his arms up in front of him so that the sleeves of his bathrobe fell to reveal his bare forearms. I drew a finger over his papery skin, tapped the syringe on a good vein. "How does that feel? Better?"

"One of those and I don't feel much of anything," he said. He took a breath, then smiled weakly. "What do you suppose two would do for me? Or three?"

"I don't aim to find out," I said.

"Damn it, Kate—if I'd gone end-stage, you wouldn't hold a moment's thought before you dropped me."

I shook my head. "I'll put down an animal in pain, but you're still a man."

"You won't feel that way when you're my age."

Even just the worst cases took most of the day, and after that I still had the public health work—checking that the rain barrels storing the water supply weren't contaminated, and that the honey buckets were being emptied far enough from the camp—so it was already dark when I finished up, and too late to head to my cabin. I crashed in the Red Cross tent, sleeping on the exam table.

The next morning I rose a bit after dawn and started back to the tracks. My joints were stiff from being on my feet the day before, my skin itched sympathetically from all the scabies cases I had seen, and my stomach was still leaden with the camp ice cream—sugar, wild berries, and Crisco whipped together—one patient had insisted on giving me. (Crisco is a big part of camp cooking, which goes a long way toward explaining the chronic obesity in the camps; the other factor is that, for the most part, the residents have absolutely nothing to do, no motivation even to get out of their tents. The end-stagers, of course, don't have access to the camp food and usually become malnourished soon after they turn.)

Once I had finished my self-check I headed off again, along the train tracks. When I was about halfway to the station I saw that someone else had broken a trail out from the tracks, into the woods: there were a lot of confused footprints in the mud there, and what looked like blood on some thorns. I followed the trail for a little while, keeping a careful pace, then sped up when I heard the shrieks.

The trail led me into a small clearing in the shade of a tall willow. A man and two women, all clearly end-stage, were standing at the foot of the tree. There was a tension among the three of them, like cats facing off over a fallen baby bird, and when I got a bit nearer I could see the cause: a young girl, maybe ten years old, was up in the tree.

I fished my glasses out of my coat pocket, put them on, and then raised the .30-06 to my shoulder. The broad trunk of the tree made it hard for me to line up my shots, and I was worried that dropping the first one would break the tension between them and send the other two up the tree after the girl.

"Are you all right?" I called to her. The end-stagers turned at the sound but stayed where they were, still eyeing each other carefully.

"Who's there?"

"My name is Kate. I'm here to help you. What's your name, honey?"

"I'm Sophie," the girl said after a moment.

The end-stagers were starting to fidget, my presence disrupting the tension that had been holding them back. Whatever I was going to do, I had to do it soon. "How old are you, Sophie?"

"I'm, I'm eleven years old," she said. "Can you get me down?"

"I will, honey, but first I need you to climb higher up. Can you do that? I need you to climb as high as you can."

"I'm—I don't like going high."

I lowered my rifle slowly, aiming just short of the end-stager nearest to me. "Go as high as you can, Sophie. It's really important."

She started to squirm upward, hugging the thick branches tightly. "Is this high enough?"

"High as you can." I kept a close eye on the three end-stagers as she rose, watching to see if any of them would make a break for her or for me. When one of them took a step I fired, sending a shot into the ground next to the male. The crack of the rifle made him jump and destroyed the last of his self-restraint: he started to climb up after the girl, now heedless of the other two. They followed him, more intent now on denying him the prize than on getting it for themselves, and I forced myself to breathe slowly as all three of them went up the trunk. "I can't go any higher!" Sophie shouted.

The male had almost reached her when I was finally able to line the three of them up: I hit him high in the back, just below his neck, and he toppled backward, knocking into one of the others as he fell. By the time I had recovered from the recoil I had the next round chambered and was trying to get a bead on the second one. She was clinging to the tree trunk, frozen between rising higher and heading after me, and I forced myself to slow down and take aim.

I usually prefer body shots—a head shot is better if you make it, but there's too much risk of missing entirely—but she was a difficult target, rail-thin and wearing a ratty brown housecoat that faded into the tree bark, so I had to aim for her white hair. I peered down the rifle sight, took a slow breath in, and then let it out as I squeezed the trigger: a burst of red covered the old woman's head and she slumped, sliding down the tree trunk.

The third one, the heavy woman, had been chewing on the male that had fallen on her, but the sound of my gunshot made her look my way: a few moments later she was up and heading toward me in a stumbling run. She was faster than I had expected and blurred as she neared me. I peered over my glasses to get her back in focus and then fired; the shot took her in the stomach, a fair bit left of center, and turned her to the side but didn't stop her. I chambered another round, squinted, and fired again. My aim was better this time and she fell, first to her knees and then onto her face.

I began to cough, fighting to keep a bead on the fallen end-stager as I gagged and finally spat up a mouthful of greasy vomit. I wiped my mouth with my sleeve and then looked around, hoping the noise hadn't drawn any other company.

"Are you okay?" Sophie called from up in the tree. "Can I come down now?"

"Just take a look around first. Can you see anyone else?"

"No," she said after a few seconds. "There's just you."

"Okay, come on down."

"Okay." She didn't move for a minute or so, then started to inch slowly down the trunk. "Are they—are they all dead?"

I took off my glasses and moved toward the tree. The woman I had hit in the head was gone, but the man was still breathing: I slung my rifle over my shoulder, drew my knife, and rolled him over with my foot. He was better dressed than many of them, in heavy green cotton pants and a blue checked shirt instead of a gown or pajamas: I remembered him telling me that before coming to the camp he had lived on his own, rather than in a home. His skin was thin like an onion's, and white where it wasn't covered with scratches and bruises. My knees protested as I crouched down and slit his throat.

The girl dropped the last few feet and landed next to me. After a moment she threw her arms around my waist; I reached around her and drew her close, feeling her shake as she sobbed silently. "It's all right," I said quietly, and after a few minutes she stepped back, leaving a trail of snot and tears on my oilskin.

She looked from side to side, over her shoulder and then back at me. "Thank you," she said.

"It's all right," I said again. She was dressed in dark blue jeans that showed little wear, a T-shirt, bright red fleece, a yellow plastic windbreaker over that and red sneakers covered in little stickers and doodads. There was some bark and leaf litter stuck to her, but her shoes were mostly clean: she hadn't been in the woods for long. "How did you get here, honey?"

"I was on the train," she said. "I was going to live with my uncle and his wife and his kids." She looked straight at me for a moment, then glanced away. "I was by myself. My grandma . . . "

"So what happened?"

"I was . . . we were going around a bend and something bumped the train. I got knocked into a door and it just opened. I tried to wave at the train but it was too far away by the time I got up and my phone doesn't work here."

"We're a ways from the tracks."

"I got lost. I guess I should have stayed by the tracks, but I didn't know how long it was going to be until the next train came, and I thought if I got higher up I could maybe get a signal on my phone. Then those—those people found me and when I knew what they were I went up the tallest tree I could find." She paused for a breath. "I'd been up there since yesterday."

"Are you okay to walk?" I asked. "We need to get you someplace safe."

She nodded. "Where are we going?"

"I'm going to take you to the Ranger station. They have a radio—they can let the next train know to stop for you."

"How far is it?"

I shrugged. "A bit more than a day."

I handed her a handful of dry breakfast biscuits. She took a bite of one, chewed it slowly, swallowed, and said "Thanks."

"No problem," I said. "I can stock back up when we get to the station."

"No, I mean—thanks. For what you're doing. I didn't—I didn't think there was anyone, I mean anyone not—you know, anyone not *sick* out here." She was silent for a moment. "What—why *are* you out here? Are you—"

"No," I said. I ran my hand through my hair, held it out so she could see the gray starting to speckle the black. "Not yet, anyway."

"So do you—do you, like, *hunt* them or something?"

I shook my head. "That was—I try not to do that. Unless I have to."

"Then why *are* you here?"

I slung my rifle over my shoulder. "I'm a nurse."

At first they thought the homes were the vector. The affliction had spread all through them by the time anybody noticed it; the upticks in violence and dementia were noted but unremarked upon, hardly unusual in the overcrowded facilities, the larger pattern only visible if you saw what was happening with your own eyes. By that point nearly all the work was automated, done either by social robots or remote workers; few homes had more than the one Nurse of Record the law demanded.

So they emptied the homes, setting up the tent cities in National Park campgrounds across the country. None of us who had worked in the homes had shown any symptoms, but that didn't matter. Whether or not we were infected, or infectious, we were seen as tainted—and few of us could find many reasons to disagree with that judgment. So we were each given a choice: a comfortable quarantine, or life in the camps with our former patients. I never found out what any of the other nurses chose, but I can't imagine many of those quarantine apartments were ever occupied.

It wasn't long after I had moved into my cabin that cases began showing up outside of the homes, and everyone over sixty became a presumed latent and carrier. There was never any word about bringing us back, though, just the intermittent shipments of food and medicine and the trains carrying more and more of the afflicted.

It was maybe an hour before she started talking again: just small talk at first, like what my last name was and where I had come from, and telling me a little bit about her life. When she talked about herself I let her lead: I didn't know yet whether her past had made her resilient or if she was just riding on shock and adrenaline, and I couldn't afford to let her crash.

We reached the tracks in good time and followed them east, toward the Ranger station; after an hour or so I stopped.

"What is it?" she asked.

I held a finger to my lips, turned around slowly. "Someone's tracking us," I said quietly.

"Oh," she said after a second. "Do you—is it one of the, the end-stagers, do you think?"

I raised my rifle and began to turn slowly from left to right, watching for movement in the trees. "I don't think so," I said. "Whoever it is has been following us since you came down from the tree. End-stagers don't have that kind of attention span."

Sophie put a hand on my arm: when I glanced at her I saw that she wasn't looking at me, or in the direction my rifle was pointed, but just to the right. Her grip tightened as I turned.

"Sophie," I said, "did anyone else fall off that train?"

For a long moment nobody said anything; then there was a rustling in the bushes, right where I was pointing my rifle. I kept my finger near the trigger but waited as I heard Sophie's breathing get faster and faster. After a few seconds a woman stepped out from behind a tree, dressed in black pants and a jean jacket. Her black hair had hints of white in it, like mine, only hers was white at the roots.

"Don't," Sophie said in a tiny voice.

I took a breath, kept her in my sights. "Are you with her?" I asked.

"Yes," the woman said.

"She's my grandma," Sophie said. "You're right. She was on the train with me." She pulled harder at my arm. "Please don't shoot her."

"I won't," I said, though I didn't lower my rifle. "What's your name?"

"Peggy. Perkins." She raised her hands. "I just—I just wanted to make sure Sophie was all right."

"You shouldn't have been on that train," I said. I glanced at Sophie, then back at Peggy. "They found out, didn't they?"

Peggy nodded. "I couldn't stop her," she said. "They were holding me, and then she just jumped off the train. I didn't want . . . "

There was silence for a moment as she trailed off. I turned to Sophie. "That was a very, very foolish thing to do," I said. "Your grandma is . . . she can't come with us."

"No," Sophie said. "I couldn't. I can't just leave her alone."

"Your grandma is sick, Sophie," I said. "She can't get on the train with you, and they won't let her into the Ranger station."

Sophie crossed her arms. "Then I don't want to go," she said. She scowled, her jaw quivering, and tears were appearing in the corners of her eyes.

Peggy crouched down to look Sophie in the eyes. "Honey, you have to," she said, then turned her head to look up at me. "But I'm not sick yet. I can come with you—as far as the Ranger station. To help keep her safe."

I took a breath. "What's the last meal you ate on the train?"

Peggy frowned. "I don't—"

"I need to know how far along you are. Do you remember what the last thing you ate on the train was?"

She stood up and closed her eyes for a moment. "Ham and cheese sandwich," she said. I watched Sophie's expression, to see if she remembered the same thing. "Little crackers, but I didn't eat them; Sophie had mine."

"All right," I said. "Give me five words that start with R, fast as you can."

"Rainbow. Rutabaga. Rooster. Red . . . Red light."

I nodded, then reached out to tap her on the lips. She drew back but made no other response. "Okay," I said. "You're not showing any definite symptoms yet. But this thing can go very, very quickly."

Peggy's whole body relaxed as she let out a breath. "I promise, I—if you ever think I'm a danger to her, I'll just . . . go away, I'll go into the woods and never come back."

"If you turn," I said, "I'll put you down myself."

We walked for the rest of the day, mostly in silence. Sophie stayed close to Peggy; I felt an absurd jealousy as she held her grandmother's hand and cast occasional glances up at her. We got back to the train tracks after another hour or so, and followed them westward until it began to get dark. I found a suitable tree to sleep in, and after a meager supper of jerky and biscuits, we made our way into its branches.

When I woke up I was alone: Sophie wasn't on her branch, though the bungee cord that had held her there lay on the ground. I loosened my own cord and carefully lowered myself to the ground. My knee locked as I touched: I took a half-dozen deep breaths, straightened my leg and looked around. There was no sign of either of them, nor any sound but the usual noise of the forest in the morning.

"Sophie?" I called quietly. I started back to the tracks, just a few yards away, then stopped when I heard a noise coming from behind me.

"It's us," Sophie called. She emerged from the brush with Peggy trailing behind. Sophie was holding her windbreaker in her hands. "We went to get berries. For breakfast."

"I suppose it wasn't a very good idea," Peggy said, "but I made sure she stayed close."

"No, it's all right," I said. "I was just . . . " I reached up to rub my eyes. "Did you find any?"

Sophie held the hood of her windbreaker up to me: it was about half full of tiny wild raspberries and blackberries. "Look," she said.

"We had a cottage when she was little," Peggy said. She shrugged. "Back before . . . "

We divided the berries between us, and then the remaining breakfast biscuits; Sophie tucked her last one in the pocket of her windbreaker and then looked at her grandmother, who put on a smile.

"Is there any way I can take some of that?" Peggy asked when I lifted my pack.

I shook my head. "It's all right."

"We might go faster."

"I don't remember you having to wait for me yesterday," I said.

"No, I know. I just meant I'd like to, well, carry my weight."

I looked over at Sophie: she was watching us carefully, an expression of concern on her face. "Sure," I said. I separated the zipsack from my backpack, reached inside to take out the box of cartridges, and then handed the sack to her. She swung it over one shoulder as we headed off, first going back to the train tracks and then following them to the Ranger station. I kept my hand on my rifle and watched the woods.

"Hey, I see smoke," Sophie said, pointing ahead of us. "Is that the station?"

I could just see the station's fence and gate, and beyond that a wisp of smoke rising up into the air. "We're almost there," I said. "They wouldn't usually have a fire this time of year, though."

"Do you think something's wrong?" Peggy asked.

I held up my hand, then reached into my jacket pocket for my glasses. Once I had them on I could see that the gate across the tracks was open.

"Get off the tracks," I said, looking back at them. "Come on, now."

"Is there a train coming?" Peggy asked as she stepped carefully over the rail. "Don't they blow a, you know, make a noise? So you know they're coming?"

"Yeah, they do," I said. "But maybe . . . " I waited for a minute, glancing back and forth between the station and the woods. Suddenly my pack felt very, very heavy.

"What are we going to do?" Sophie asked.

"I don't know. I don't understand—they wouldn't open the gate except to let a train through, but that's not long enough for . . . " I turned to look at Peggy and Sophie. "You said your train stopped when they threw you off. How long?"

"I don't know," Peggy said, frowning. "Maybe ten, fifteen minutes."

"Which way was it going?"

"To San Diego," she said. "Why does it matter?"

"I think somebody else got on that train when you got off," I said. I lifted my glasses and rubbed my eyes. "Not on the train, but hanging onto the outside. They must have seen that the trains could get through the fence."

"So what happened to the Rangers?" Sophie asked. "Do you think they're all . . . ?"

"I don't know. I guess they might not bother closing the gate if the station was already compromised . . . " I took a breath, folded my glasses and put them back in my jacket pocket. "We have to get to their radio so that we can tell someone about Sophie, get her out of here."

"Couldn't we just stay here, wait for the next train?" Peggy asked. "I'm sure if you explained . . . "

I shook my head. "The trains that stop here don't let people on," I said. "You're right about one thing, though. You're staying here, but she has to come with me."

"No," Sophie said. She squeezed Peggy's hand in hers. "I, I'll come. I'm not scared, but Grandma has to come too."

"I'm fine," Peggy said. "That's just, my mind is fine. A whistle, the word I was looking for is whistle. There, you see? You just forget things sometimes, at my age. Doesn't that ever happen to you?"

"What did we have for breakfast, Peggy?" I asked.

"Berries," she said.

"What kind of berries?"

She rolled her eyes. "It was . . . well, summer berries. What you pick in the summer, in brambles with, with prickers." She looked away and then back at me: her face was red, her eyes glistening.

"There's a camp just a few hours that way," I said, pointing the way we had come and off to the left. "You'll be all right there, and I'll check on you when I can."

"No," Peggy said. "I'm not going. Not until she's safe."

For a moment I looked at the two of them standing together, then shrugged. "Fine," I said. I slid open the bolt of my rifle, making sure there was a cartridge in the chamber. "Let's go, then, while we've still got some light."

"Should we wait till morning?" Peggy asked.

I shook my head. I had seen too many shapes moving in the bushes, heard too many footsteps and rustling branches. I chewed my lip for a moment, guessing at the distance between the gate and the station—a hundred yards, maybe? "Let's get through that gate as fast as we can—I don't want to get caught in a choke point."

"I haven't seen any—"

"They're there," I said, trying to keep my voice too low for Sophie to hear. "Maybe a lot of them."

As we neared the gate I fought the urge to run: I could hear the end-stagers in the woods around us, feel their eyes on us as we passed through the narrow space. The fence around the Ranger compound was solid steel, with razor wire along the top to keep end-stagers from climbing over it. The open gate, just wide enough for a train to pass through, let us see glimpses of the other side but concealed much more. I slowed my pace as we reached the gate, letting my finger curl around the trigger of my rifle.

Sophie reached the gate and broke into a trot as she passed through, moving out of view. I caught up with her just as she ran into a man in dark clothes who had been moving in front of the gate on the other side. For a moment I thought he might be a Ranger, until I saw his white hair; he turned toward me and opened his mouth to reveal two rows of teeth, like a shark's, perfectly white and gleaming.

I raised the barrel of my rifle, getting ready to shoot and run—the sound of the shot would surely bring all the other end-stagers from the woods—but before I could fire Sophie reached into the pocket of her windbreaker, pulled out the biscuit she had saved from that morning, and held it out to the man.

For a moment he just looked at her, his double teeth grinning obscenely; then he took the biscuit and began to chew it carefully, barely able to get it in his mouth. I stood there, watching as he chewed contentedly on the biscuit, and I saw that he was wearing dentures over his own teeth, which were sliding in and out of his mouth each time he moved his jaw.

After a few moments, Peggy tugged on my sleeve and led me away. The cabin was about fifty yards off the tracks, the firewatch tower a short distance beyond that. Once we had passed the chewing end-stager we broke into a run, crossing the distance between the tracks and the cabin as quickly as we could.

The outside of the cabin was not much different than it had been before it was repurposed—there was not much you could do to make a wall of stacked logs more defensible—but the windows and doors had been replaced with shatterproof Plexiglas and steel, the wood-shingle roof long gone in favor of aluminum. I used my momentum to launch myself up onto the cement platform that stood before the door, the only reminder of the screened porch that had once covered the whole front of the building. Peggy hesitated as she neared it and stumbled; Sophie slowed to help her, the two of them awkwardly levering themselves up onto the platform with their hands.

"Stay close," I said. "We're just going to find the radio and get out."

"Don't you know where it is?" Sophie asked.

"I've never been inside," I said. I took a step back, raised my rifle and waved Peggy forward. "Push it open, then step away."

"What if it's locked?" Peggy said.

"Then we knock very politely and ask the Rangers to let us in," I said, glancing back at the gate.

Sophie grabbed my arm as her grandmother stepped past us, putting a hand on the door handle and turning it tentatively. Peggy leaned into the heavy door, pushing it with her shoulder, and as she did I moved my sights off her and onto the opening doorway. Once she had it fully open I stepped in and then waved the others in after me. When they were both inside, Peggy released the door and it swung back, slamming shut with a heavy thud that made me wince.

The door led into a small foyer that opened into a larger room to the left. I stepped into the room and swung my rifle at the other three corners. Fading light from the window showed a brown leather couch, much-patched with silver duct tape, facing a fireplace on the far wall that held some smoldering logs: in front of it was a wagon-wheel coffee table, its glass top lying in shards on the floor all around, and an eyeless moose head hung on the wall above.

Peggy held her hand to her mouth. "That smell . . . " she said.

"They've been here," I said. An open doorway in the wall to our right led to a hallway, but it was too dark within to see anything. "Let's hope they ran out of toys to play with."

We crossed the room, stepping carefully to avoid the shards of glass, until we stood at the doorway. I took my flashlight from my jacket pocket and handed it to Sophie. "Stay right in front of me," I said quietly.

"I should go first," Peggy said.

I shook my head. "You're too tall. I need to be able to shoot over her."

She opened her mouth, shut it, and nodded. Sophie and I counted a silent *one, two, three* together and then stepped into the doorway, swinging the flashlight and rifle together to the left and then the right. There was a door, half-open, almost directly across from us, and another to the left of it; beyond that the left-hand hallway opened into a room that looked like it spanned the breadth of the cabin. To the right I could see three doors, all on the facing wall, before the corridor faded into darkness.

Peggy pressed against the back of my jacket, trying to squeeze into the doorway with us. "Which way?" she asked.

I nodded at the door across the hall and Sophie and I moved forward together. The wooden door swung inward as she kicked it. The room lit up as she pointed the flashlight inside, with mirror, tile, and porcelain bouncing the light back at us.

"Let's try to the left," I said. "It's not as far from the front door in that direction—maybe we'll get lucky."

The smell we had noticed earlier grew stronger as we opened the next door on the left. It was a smell I had known before I ever came here: every home I ever worked in had it, no matter how hard it had been scrubbed.

The flashlight's beam picked up a carpet, dresser, and two single beds, on each of which lay an unmoving body. I started to cover Sophie's eyes with my hand, but the smell had already reached her: she spat up water and half-digested berries and dropped the flashlight onto the floor. It rolled into the room, and Sophie reached down to pick it up; as her hand closed on it, something seized her and pulled her forward. I took a step, trying to get a bead on the end-stager who had grabbed her, but Peggy rushed past me, knocking me to my knees. In the dim light I saw her grabbing Sophie's other arm, pulling hard, and I heard Sophie scream.

I didn't bother to stand but instead rose to one knee and tried to sight the end-stager. All I could see, though, was Peggy: she had knocked Sophie aside and leapt onto the one who had grabbed her, clawing at him with a savagery that was, I was sure, entirely foreign to her nature.

"Grandma?" Sophie asked.

Peggy turned back to us; her face was chalk-white, her eyes wild. I kept my rifle where it was, watching her carefully.

"Sophie, go," I said. "The way we were going."

Peggy looked from me to Sophie and then back again. She opened her mouth but remained silent, a perplexed look on her face. She took a step toward Sophie and my finger curled inward, touching the cold metal of the trigger.

"*No*," Sophie said. "Don't . . . "

Peggy froze. I rose to my feet, keeping her in my sights. "We have to go now," I said. I backed up toward the door, putting myself between Sophie and Peggy. Sophie reached from behind me and grabbed my arm, pulling it down until the .30-06 was pointed at the floor.

I took a step back out into the hall, still watching Peggy, and glanced to my left. Two end-stagers had emerged from the large room at the end of the corridor. One was a bald male in faded blue pajamas, his bare feet trailing blood; the other was a female dressed in just a dirty, pilly gray bra who had a halo of frizzy gray hair and little round bumps all over her body, like someone had slipped a sheet of bubble wrap under her skin.

"*Go.*"

Sophie looked at her grandmother for a moment before heading down the long corridor, the flashlight's beam jumping around the walls as she ran. I took a step backward, trying to keep both Peggy and the two end-stagers within my arc of fire, then turned and ran after her. I could hear the male and female pick up their pace behind me and swore under my breath, cursing myself for triggering their instincts by running.

Sophie looked back at me, slowing her pace to let me catch up. We were already past the doorway to the room we had come in, so we ran until we could see the end of the hallway. There was a door on the left, just before the furthest wall; beyond it the hallway turned left, with a hint of light visible at its end. The exposed logs on our right showed that we were following the outer wall, and ahead of us we could see light coming through a transom over a wooden door. When we got closer, though, we saw that the door handle had been removed and nails driven through the door into the frame.

I took my jackknife from my pocket and tried to work the blade into the empty socket where the handle had been, thinking that if I could get the latch free I might be able to force the door open.

"Can you use your gun?" Sophie asked.

I took a step back and raised my rifle, aiming at where the handle had been. "I don't know," I said.

"No, the other end—bang it on the hinges."

I nodded, then handed her my knife. "You keep working on the handle." I slid open the bolt and let the cartridge fall to the ground, then turned the rifle around and slammed the butt into the upper hinge. I could see the screws pulling out of the frame, but just barely.

Sophie was kneeling in front of the door handle, trying to disengage the latch with the knife. She glanced behind us, saw the two end-stagers rounding the corner, and screamed.

"Just keep trying," I said. "We can get out of this—"

When I moved to hit the hinges again, though, something was pulling the other way: I turned to see the bubble-wrap woman's hands on the barrel. My finger went to the trigger, but by the time it had gotten there I remembered I had taken out the cartridge.

The bubble-wrap woman had both hands on the barrel now and was trying to pull the rifle away from me. The bald man crouched down, trying to creep past the woman and me to get at Sophie, who screamed again.

Suddenly the bald man's head flew forward, slamming into the door. I glanced away from the woman to see Peggy stumbling back from where she had collided with him. The bubble-wrap woman looked at her, too, and that gave me enough of a chance to pull the barrel out of her grasp; I swung the stock forward and it hit her head with a crunch, knocking her back into the wall. Sophie was curled up into a ball, covering her face with her hands, but the bald man had forgotten about her and was struggling with Peggy, scratching her face with long, dirty fingernails.

I turned back to the hinge and hit it again, saw the ends of the screws come loose from the doorframe. "The doorknob," I said to Sophie.

She moved her hands from her face, then froze as she saw her grandmother struggling with the bald man.

"Sophie, the doorknob," I said again. "If you can get that, I think I can open it."

She nodded and turned back to the door, sticking the point of the knife between the door and the frame. A few moments later the whole door moved slightly within the frame and I lowered the rifle, took a half-step back and slammed my shoulder into the door. The top half of the door pulled free of the nails holding it to the frame and with another slam the whole door came loose and fell onto the ground.

I stepped outside but Sophie didn't follow. "Come on," I said, but she was frozen. Peggy was still wrestling with the bald man, his teeth sunk into her shoulder as she punched him in the stomach. I took the box of cartridges from my pocket, loaded one into the rifle, and drew a bead on the man's bald head. "Don't look, Sophie," I said, then pulled the trigger. The shot drove the man into Peggy, knocking them both over.

"Come on." I grabbed Sophie's wrist and pulled her after me. "There should be another radio up in the firewatch tower."

"No," Sophie said. "My grandma's hurt."

"Oh, honey," I said. "She's not your grandma anymore."

Sophie said nothing as she moved to pull the dead end-stager off her grandmother. Peggy was in bad shape, but still moving; there were cuts and bruises all over her face, and bright red blood was oozing out of the tooth marks on her shoulder. I fumbled with another cartridge, loaded it into the chamber.

"Is she going to die?" Sophie asked.

I raised my rifle and tried to sight Peggy, who was rising stiffly to her feet. "Come on, Sophie," I said. "Get away from her. We have to go."

Sophie turned back to look at me, frowning deeply. "Is she going to die?"

"Yes," I said. "Not right away, but yes, she probably is. Bite wounds are bad—they get infected, and the blood she's lost is going to make it worse."

"Tell me what to do. To help her."

I took a step forward, nudging Sophie aside with the rifle barrel. Peggy looked up at me, silent, her face unreadable. "There's nothing you can do to help her. Your grandma is gone."

"No, she isn't," Sophie said. She turned to Peggy and looked her in the eyes. "You're sick, I know that. But you aren't going to hurt me, and I'm going to help you."

Peggy's ragged breathing slowed as Sophie held her, becoming more regular. After what felt like a long time I took a breath, looked right and left, and then dropped my rifle. I unshouldered my pack, took out some steri-wipes, two syringes of my moxifloxacin/clindamycin bite mix, and one of morphine. "Give me her arm," I said.

Sophie took Peggy's right hand in hers and straightened her arm. I found a good vein, wiped it clean and tapped the three syringes, one after the other. "That should help with infection," I said. "Do you want to do the bandages?"

Sophie's mouth quirked up into a tiny smile, and she nodded. "How do I do it?" she asked.

I handed her a steri-wipe, tore open a pack of chitosan sponges, and handed it to her. "Clean your hands first, then press these into each of the wounds." I held my breath as she touched the first sponge to Peggy's bite marks. "Careful, it might hurt her," I said.

Peggy flinched as Sophie applied the sponges, but did not move. "Now what?" Sophie asked.

"Here," I said, passing her the bandage. "Wrap this around the wounds five or six times, nice and tight."

When she was done she looked back at me. "Is that it?"

"That's everything we can do," I said. I put a hand on her shoulder. "We have to go."

She looked her grandmother in the eyes for another few moments, then stood and turned. "All right," she said. "Let's go."

The firewatch tower stood a few hundred feet down a path past the cabin, silhouetted in the evening light. A narrow wooden staircase zigzagged inside the tower's timber frame, up to the observation post and radio tower at the top.

I paused at the bottom of the staircase, letting Sophie go ahead of me as I watched to see if anyone was coming after us. Peggy was sitting where we had left her, watching us, more still than I had ever seen an end-stager. We climbed up carefully, the stairs creaking and groaning as we rose, and by the time we got to the top the sun had nearly set.

Sophie had said nothing since we started up the stairs. She stopped a few steps below the platform and looked down at me: the stairs reached the platform on the west side of the tower, so we could just see each other in the pale pink light of the setting sun. Down below I could see the whole Ranger compound and I understood why it had angered the end-stagers so much, looking so mockingly like a home.

"What do we do now?" she asked.

"Find the radio," I said. "See if it still works."

"And then?"

"We let people know you're here."

"Do you really think they'll come and get me?"

I took a deep breath, let it out slowly. "We'll tell them what happened. To the Rangers. They'll have to do something about that, and . . . "

After a few seconds she nodded and climbed up onto the platform. There was a small shed there, with a narrow walkway around it and a metal antenna on top. Sophie opened the unlocked door to the shed and we slipped inside.

The small room had an air of long disuse: the flashlight's beam revealed a narrow cot, a folding wire-and-nylon chair, and a desk on which sat a pair of binoculars and a radio and microphone. The radio was old and bulky, a black box with a front panel covered with switches, and even before I reached the desk I knew it was broken. I flicked the on switch up and down a few times, but nothing happened.

Sophie sat down on the cot, saying nothing. I sat down next to her, and as I did the flashlight flickered and died. In the darkness I could hear her banging the butt-end of the flashlight; a few moments later I felt her shifting her weight and then a tiny blue square of light appeared in front of her, just enough for us to see each other's faces.

"Hey, my phone works up here," she said. "Two bars, that's not bad. Should I . . . should I call somebody? Who should I call?"

"Nine one one, I guess," I said. "That's got to do something."

We sat there a while longer, neither of us moving or speaking. "Are you going to come?" she asked finally.

"I can't," I said. "I'm here for good, like everyone else."

"The Ranger that was . . . one of the ones in the room, she looked a lot like you. You could pretend you're her. You could come with me."

"No," I said after a long moment. "I have too many people counting on me." I took a breath. "More than I thought, maybe."

Sophie nodded slowly. "I think I need to stay here too," she said. "To take care of my grandma. And I think maybe you need someone to take care of you, too."

"Maybe," I said, and reached out to take her hand. She smiled, and then we both zipped our jackets and went to sleep sitting up.

Dead Song

Jay Wilburn

The man walked into the dark room and closed the door behind him. He put on the headphones and sat down on the stool. Images of zombies flashed on the screen in front of him. He ignored them and opened the binder on the stand. He pulled the microphone a little closer and waited.

In the darkness, a voice came over the headphones and said, "Go ahead and read the title card again for us slowly so we can set levels."

The man read with particular slowness and articulation, "Dead Doc. Productions presents *The Legend of Tiny 'Mud Music' Jones* in association with After World Broadcasters and Reaniment America, a subsidiary of the Reclaiment Broadcasters Company, with permission of the Reformed United States Federal Government Broadcasters Rights Commission."

He waited silently after he finished.

The voice finally came back on, "Sounds good. We're going to get coverage on the main text for alternate takes. We're also going to have you read the quotes as placeholders until we get character actors to replace them. Read them normally without any affected voice. If we need another tone or tempo, we'll let you know and we'll take another pass at that section. There is also some new material we are adding into the documentary."

"Okay," the man answered.

The voice ordered, "When you're ready, go ahead with section one, then stop."

The man took a drink of water, swallowed, and then waited for a couple beats. He began, "Dead World Records was one of the first music companies to come online after order was restored. They were recording and signing artists during the height of the zombie plague. Tobias Baker and Hollister Z are credited with founding the company.

"They operated from a trailer and storage building on Tobias's family farm, surviving off the land, and clearing zombies from the property between recording and editing."

A black and white image of zombie pits scrolled across the screen as the guys in the booth ran the images to check timing. The man ignored it.

He continued, "They do deserve credit for recognizing the continued value of musical culture and history while everyone else was focused purely on survival. They had the vision to gather and record the unique musical evolution of the Dead Era which shaped all music that came after it."

A grainy video of the men working in their studio rolled on the screen. The man stopped and watched as he waited.

The video froze and the voice said, "Skip to section four. The text is edited from the last time you read it. Read it over once and tell us when you are ready."

The man obliged them by scanning it over. He said, "Ready."

The voice said, "We're rolling on section four."

The man took another drink before he began, "The real unsung heroes of the rise of Dead World Records Incorporated are clearly the collectors that agreed to bring the recordings back to the studio. Many of them were musicians themselves and trekked hundreds of miles through zombie-infested territory to find musical gatherings of the various unique pockets of survivors."

A picture of Tiny flashed on the screen with his name under it. He was wearing shorts, hiking boots, and holding a walking stick. A picture of another man wearing a helmet and carrying a bat replaced it. The name below it was Satchel Mouth Murderman.

The man continued, "Music from this period is clearly defined by both isolation and strange mixtures of people and cultures. The gatherings of these musical laboratories (many of which were destroyed and lost long before the zombies were) is the legacy of men like Tiny 'Mud Music' Jones."

Stills of Tiny with arrows pointing him out passed over the screen.

The man read on, "Tiny traveled farther and gathered more than any other collector. His introverted style and musical talent won trust and entry into enclaves of people no one else could penetrate. Some historians believe much of what we know of Dead Era culture is built off the exploration of Tiny Jones."

The man stopped.

The voice ordered, "Go with section six when ready."

The man began as soon as he had the page, "Tiny was so named due to his four-foot-eleven-inch stature. Even Tobias Baker and Hollister Z didn't know him by any other name besides Tiny. He carried a pack that looked heavier than him with more instruments and recording equipment than food and clothes. He usually played for his supper and, in turn, got others to play for him with tape rolling."

After a short pause, the voice said, "Section seven needs to have a foreboding tone. It's going to be over some heavy music. Articulate it well. Go when ready."

The man read, "He is also the source of the Mud Music legend making three infamous trips into Dead Era Appalachia in search of it."

The voice said, "Let's do that again. Try a little more flow, but a darker tone."

The man read it again. The voice acknowledged, "That was good. Go with section ten now when you're ready."

The man began, "Tiny discovered Donna Cash, whereabouts unknown. Donna Cash is the most quoted artist on the Tribute Wall on Survivor Book. Bootleg recordings of her work are still in the top one hundred downloads each year. Donna Cash was best known for mash-ups of Madonna and Johnny Cash on the drag queen circuit. She was touring when doing so was deadly even for individuals not in drag.

"Tiny is responsible for the only known original recordings of 'True Folsom Blues,' 'Vogue the Line,' 'When the Ray of Light Comes Around,' 'Like a Ring of Fire,' and many other songs that have been covered thousands of times by both straight and drag acts in the Recovery Era. Donna Cash has also been documented more times on the missing person Sighting Wall on Survivor Book than any other person. Mr. S. Parker, the current CEO of Survivor Book, has put a permanent block on Donna Cash sightings.

"Other popular artists on the Dead Era drag circuit that were first recorded by Tiny included Pink Orbosin, Ms. Britt Britt Rotten, and Jerri Leigh Lopper."

The man stopped again and took a drink of water. The voice said, "Let's go with section fourteen."

The man scanned the first few lines before he started, "Tiny Jones recorded examples of New Swing from Pittsburgh, Philadelphia, and Cincinnati. The music was originally used as a distraction for zombies while scavengers went out into the cities for supplies. Traditionally, it is played on rooftops. New Swing is a blend of Big Band, modern Jazz, fifties Rock, and R-and-B. It is defined by a reverb off of buildings. Most modern New Swing musicians create the sound electronically. Tiny recorded P. City Warriors, The Big Bloods led by the late Cap Kat Krunch, and the New Philly Phunk which still plays in Las Vegas with a new lineup.

" 'We let Tiny record after he fought his way to the building and knocked on the door holding two zombie heads in his hands. Would you say no to a cat that showed up like that?'—Miles Diddy, P. City Warriors original line-up."

The man paused again.

The voice asked, "Do you need a break?"

"No, I'm fine," the man answered.

The voice said, "Turn to section twenty-one and start from the third line on to the end of that section."

The man recited, "Glam Grass was discovered outside of Nashville. A tour group of old eighties metal stars ended up in a militia compound with a religious cult. After the fire, Tiny's recordings were the only record of the founders of this musical form. It was defined by electric guitars accompanied by traditional blue grass instruments. The Glam Grass artists usually sang about religious subject matter, often out of the book of Revelation. The style is described as typically heavy, but surprisingly upbeat."

The voice said, "Now section twenty-seven."

The man read, "Across the South, a style known as Death Gospel emerged from places where churches became the refuge of nonbelievers. It was a movement where metal influence came against traditional hymns. Unlike Glam Grass, Death Gospel was darker, slower, featuring minor chords, and was usually played acoustically. This style was documented by several collectors and is still a staple of churches in the Deep South."

The voice directed, "Section twenty-nine."

The man turned one page and found his place, "Tiny was involved in spreading the music and not just recording it. This is noticed most in the style known as Cherokee R-and-B or Red Blues. Tiny is credited with moving the music from North Carolina all the way to Oklahoma.

" 'The day he came to the fences, the zombies parted and allowed him through. He was the first white man admitted to the Cherokee Nation Compounds.'—Chief Blue Wolf Pine, rhythm guitar and vocals, The Silent Dead Players.

"With variations across the South and West, Red Blues included Native American chants combined with tradition blues instrumentation and riffs. Later, Red Blues diverged more from this original formula. The later style was sometimes referred to as Blue Sioux."

After a longer pause, the voice came back and said, "Section thirty-five has been rewritten. Start that from the beginning."

The man read it silently, then began, "Shock-a-Billy was one of Tiny Jones's favorite collections. It featured shock rocker make-up, dark subjects, and Punk/Country combinations. It was mostly advanced by touring acts. Tiny expressed that he felt a kinship with the traveling musicians. Shock-a-Billy artists that stayed in one place were looked on as cowards within the community, posers. The tour busses were often dragsters pulled by animals.

" 'There were competitions between the Shockers to see who could get the most elaborate dragster. At one point, my band had the three-story "Tarmansion." It was built on the chasse of a tractortrailer and was pulled by twenty-six horses. It's a wonder we didn't get eaten by zombies trying to put on a show just traveling from point A to point B.' – Big Bubba Tarmancula, Big Bubba Tarmancula and the Tarmen, Rock and Roll Hall of Fame.

"Shock-a-Billy T-shirts, tour posters, and images are infused in pop culture throughout the Recovery Era."

The voice said, "Read section forty now."

The man drank the rest of his water and then read, "Several styles of urban infusion developed during the Dead Era and were all connected by and counter-influenced by one another through Tiny's travels.

"Gangster and Western was defined by rivalry as opposed to isolation. Vocals are considered more melodic than traditional BZ Era rap. There were often references to local blood feuds between ranches that don't make much sense to modern listeners.

"The ranchers herded animals for food and herded zombies between ranches to foil rustlers and to threaten rival ranches. The results were often quite bloody and costly to human life. Tiny was the only collector to ever go to certain sections of Texas, Arizona, and New Mexico.

"The most infamously violent ranch war was between Big Daddy Bronco and His Boys versus the Lincoln County OGs. Tiny was the only one who succeeded in recording music from both camps.

"Hip Bach is the tag given to another style of music Tiny documented where inner city orchestras and concert halls became the shelters for local populations.

" 'In all the history of time, you have never heard a style as close to God and as close to the street as this. This music allowed people to transcend the situation and see the secrets of life while being surrounded by the walking dead.'—Mr. Butter Hands, Low Town Symphony.

"Tiny Jones often traced music back to its source as he did with Slam Jo. Tiny traveled all the way to the Lud Mine Camp in the Sierra Nevada Mountains. Slam Jo featured spoken word over banjo. New Wave Slam Jo documented by Tiny and other collectors began to incorporate other instruments.

"Tiny Jones was a legend in the Zed Head community. He was deeply involved in documenting the evolution of this daring style of music which mixed techno and house music over recordings of zombies.

"The most famous story of Tiny's involvement was the two weeks he accompanied DJ RomZom out in the open in a gathering expedition through Los Angeles.

"Many fans question modern Zed Head since most DJ's don't gather their own moan tracks anymore.

"The recent release of the alleged 'final recording' of Tiny 'Mud Music' Jones has resulted in a rebirth of the Zed Head movement. Border Patrol forces and security have been increased to discourage Zed Head gatherers from attempting to perform unauthorized expeditions into the uncleared, gray zones."

The voice clicked back into the headphones, "You're doing a great job. Turn to section sixty-four. This is all new material."

The man turned to the page.

"Go when ready," the voice requested.

The man read, "'Tiny and the Mud Music Legend is the modern Area Fifty-one, Brown Mountain Lights, and Kennedy Assassination rolled into one. How do you tell a ghost story to a generation of people that either witnessed Z-Day and survived all the way to the Recovery or that were born in the world after the Dead Era began? What are you going to say that can scare a generation that treats the zombie drills in school like a tornado drill? You tell them about Tiny and the Mud Music. I hadn't stopped being scared since that day.'—Kidd Banjo, former Dead World Records collector and solo artist."

A map of the BZ Era United States with red lines drawing themselves across it appeared on the screen and distracted the man for a split second, but he found his place in the script and continued like a professional, "The first expedition Tiny Jones made into the Appalachian territory took him into the area that today roughly constitutes the border of Gray Zone Three. This collection exposed him to traditional, mountain music not unlike recordings from the early nineteen-twenties' BZE from the same area. Tiny described trailers with wooden add-ons and trinket trash, folk art he saw on the expedition that expressed the same style, character, and sentiment of the music that had managed to stay unchanged through a century and a zombie invasion."

The map now had blue lines appearing and drawing deeper into the mountains. The man read, "The second expedition into the infamous region known as Gray Zone Four came back with a corrupted recording that could not be found later.

"'Something was different about Tiny after that second trip. He was devastated by the recording being garbled. He had me and Hollis drop what we were doing and immediately sit down in a closed, locked room to play it for us. He had whispered the words 'Mud Music' like it was something akin to voodoo. When it started out, it gave me chills because the sound was all fucked up and unearthly. I thought it was the music at first because of course this was Tiny and there was no telling what he might bring back. Then, I saw him crying like he had just watched his newborn child get torn apart by the zombies. He was shaking and beating his fists against his head. Hollis had to hold his hands down to stop him. Believe it or not, that's the last time I ever saw Tiny.'—Tobias Baker, co-founder Dead World Records Incorporated; former CEO D.W. Farms; deceased.

" 'Tiny was changed. He was the most enthusiastic lover of music I had ever known. He was tough as a block of oak. I believe every story I ever heard of him parting seas of zombies, cutting off their heads and carrying them in to impress musicians, and walking right through them to find the music. He was fearless because he loved the music so much. After that trip, he was obsessed. He sat and listened to that recording over and over and over and over and over. After he left, we never found that recording again, but I still hear that shit in my nightmares because of him repeating it and repeating it those last few nights. He sat with his ear to the speaker swearing that it was under the interference. That it was under that ruined recording. Then, he said he heard the voices of the singers speaking to him. He tried to describe the instruments they built. I can't remember now, but I wish I had recorded him talking. I didn't know that when he left that last time that that was it. I would have tried to stop him, if I had known, but he was Tiny Jones. I don't think I could have stopped him, if I had tried.'—Hollister Z, co-founder Dead World Records Incorporated."

The man stopped and looked up to see a blown-up, color photo of Tiny Jones leaning over with his ear to a speaker.

When his headphones crackled, it made the man jump a little. The voice just said, "Section sixty-five."

The man collected himself and began, "He did not return from his third expedition. There were no other confirmed sightings either. Only Donna Cash has more unconfirmed sightings on Internet America.

"As witnessed by Tobias Baker and Hollister Z, Kidd Banjo returned to the farm with a cassette he claimed was given to him by Tiny Jones. Kidd Banjo was a collector for Dead World and in the Recovery Era he rose to prominence as a Shock-A-Billy Revival artist. Cassettes were not in common use at the time and there are no other Tiny Jones recordings on a cassette tape. Kidd claimed he was in the Fort Guilford Colony in western Virginia near the

North Carolina border. Somehow Tiny had entered his room in the fort, had awakened him without disturbing the other men in the bunks, and had given him the tape without being detected by the guards either entering or leaving the heavily secure fort.

"Kidd Banjo insisted it was Tiny and that he was covered in cuts and bruises. He told Kidd to take it directly to D.W. Farms. He said it was the only way he could record it and get out. He said he had to go back or they would know what he had done and they would come looking for him. Kidd asked who 'they' were, but Tiny shushed him and left without answering.

"The following is an excerpt of the recording that was recently released by Dead World Records and has been heavily sampled in recent Zed Head tracts. Please be warned that the sounds are disturbing—including apparent zombie attacks and human screams.

"There is only one section that has distinguishable words near the end of the thirty-eight-minute, twenty-second recording. The voice has not been definitively identified to be Tiny Jones. The two most common interpretations of the section you are about to hear is either 'The horror of it. They obey the mud music. Death is beautiful.' Or 'The whores they obey. The mud music death is beautiful.' "

The man stared at the words he had just read for a long moment. When he looked up, there was a black-and-white photo of the side of a trailer. There were painted words on the side that read, "Don't come looking for us again or we'll come back for you." There was an arrow superimposed over the photo pointing at something under the words.

The voice came back on and said, "Section sixty-six."

The man turned the page and read on, "The following vandalism was found on the trailer on the D. W. Farms property about a week after Kidd Banjo delivered the cassette he claimed was from Tiny Jones. Hollister Z claims the medicine bag hanging from the nail at the bottom of the photograph contained a pair of human testicles among other items such as teeth and fingernails. This was never confirmed and there was no indication of whether or not Tiny died as a result of foul play or from any other cause.

"Other collectors did go into the Appalachian region in search of the secret of the 'last recording' of Tiny Jones and the legendary Mud Music despite the sinister warning. Those who claimed to know of the Mud Music told the collectors stories of mystical powers including the power to tame or command zombies with it, of deals with the devil-god of the walking corpses, and of the fact that the source was always to be found somewhere deeper in the hills. No other collectors were able to bring back any recordings of this legendary music either."

The man stopped and saw a shot of a newspaper with a file picture of Tobias Baker under the headline: *Dead World Records Exec Found Butchered in Gray Zone.*

The voice said, "Section sixty-seven."

The man actually said, "When did this happen?"

The voice came back on, "Stop there. I think you're in the wrong section. Sixty-seven starts with 'recently.' See if you can find the spot again."

The man turned the page, "I have it."

The voice said, "Begin when ready."

The man reached for his glass, but realized it was empty. He went ahead and started. "Recently, Tobias Baker, cofounder of Dead World Records Incorporated, was granted an unprecedented clearance for a manned expedition into Gray Zone Four, one of two uncleared areas deep in the Appalachian Mountains. Contact with radio and GPS were lost on the second day of the expedition. Aerial searches did not reveal the location of the expedition nor evidence to their whereabouts. Three days after the expedition was scheduled to end, Border Patrol claims seven men began approaching the gates from inside Zone Four. It wasn't until they were within ten feet and had not identified themselves that they were identified as zombies. The guards opened fire. The Border Patrol claims the zombies placed one severed head each on the ground by the gate. The seven zombies then returned to the woods despite taking heavy fire. Cameras at the gate malfunctioned before this alleged event and sources asked to remain unnamed.

"Upon inspection, the seven heads proved to be zombified and active. Officials were called in. The heads were deactivated using surgical lasers. They were then placed in secure cases using robots.

"It has been confirmed that six of the heads belonged to the members of the ill-fated D. W. R. expedition including Tobias Baker. The seventh head, which was considerably more decayed and missing all its teeth, has not.

"An unconfirmed rumor on Internet America claims the head is that of Tiny Jones. DNA samples are unavailable and the R. U. S. agency involved has not commented.

"Hollister Z, cofounder of Dead World Records Incorporated, has been unavailable for comment.

"The following is an unconfirmed voice-mail recording that surfaced on Internet America two days before the heads were found. Be warned that this recording contains graphic details of decapitation and dismemberment. It is quite disturbing."

The man stopped and looked up at a picture of a decayed, severed head in a thick plastic case.

The voice said, "Begin with section sixty-eight when you are ready."

"I think I need a break. I'm out of water," the man said as he stared at the screen.

There was a long pause. He was about to repeat his request when there was a click in his headphones and a drawn out hiss of an open mic. He waited a little longer and then thought he heard distant whispers in the background. He listened as he looked at the severed head on the screen in front of him. Then a voice came on and said, "When it is time, we will get you."

The screen went blank and the room was completely dark.

"What?" the man asked with a rush of fear.

The voice repeated, "We will break for about ten minutes. When it is time, we will come get you."

After another couple seconds, his eyes adjusted to the darkness in the room.

The man removed his headphones and walked toward the door in the dark.

Iphigenia in Aulis

Mike Carey

Her name is Melanie. It means "the black girl," from an ancient Greek word, but her skin is mostly very fair so she thinks maybe it's not such a good name for her. Miss Justineau assigns names from a big list: new children get the top name on the boys' list or the top name on the girls' list, and that, Miss Justineau says, is that.

Melanie is ten years old, and she has skin like a princess in a fairy tale: skin as white as snow. So she knows that when she grows up she'll be beautiful, with princes falling over themselves to climb her tower and rescue her.

Assuming, of course, that she has a tower.

In the meantime, she has the cell, the corridor, the classroom and the shower room.

The cell is small and square. It has a bed, a chair and a table in it.

On the walls there are pictures: in Melanie's cell, a picture of a field of flowers and a picture of a woman dancing. Sometimes they move the children around, so Melanie knows that there are different pictures in each cell. She used to have a horse in a meadow and a big mountain with snow on the top, which she liked better.

The corridor has twenty doors on the left-hand side and eighteen doors on the right-hand side (because the cupboards don't really count); also it has a door at either end. The door at the classroom end is red. It leads to the classroom (duh!). The door at the other end is bare gray steel on this side but once when Melanie was being taken back to her cell she peeped through the door, which had accidentally been left open, and saw that on the other side it's got lots of bolts and locks and a box with numbers on it. She wasn't supposed to see, and Sergeant said, "Little bitch has got way too many eyes on her," but she saw, and she remembers.

She listens, too, and from overheard conversations she has a sense of this place in relation to other places she hasn't ever seen. This place is the block.

Outside the block is the base. Outside the base is the Eastern Stretch, or the Dispute Stretch. It's all good as far as Kansas, and then it gets real bad, real quick. East of Kansas, there's monsters everywhere and they'll follow you for a hundred miles if they smell you, and then they'll eat you. Melanie is glad that she lives in the block, where she's safe.

Through the gray steel door, each morning, the teachers come. They walk down the corridor together, past Melanie's door, bringing with them the strong, bitter chemical smell that they always have on them: it's not a nice smell, but it's exciting because it means the start of another day's lessons.

At the sound of the bolts sliding and the teachers' footsteps, Melanie runs to the door of her cell and stands on tiptoe to peep through the little mesh-screen window in the door and see the teachers when they go by.

She calls out good morning to them, but they're not supposed to answer and usually they don't. Sometimes, though, Miss Justineau will look around and smile at her—a tense, quick smile that's gone almost before she can see it—or Miss Mailer will give her a tiny wave with just the fingers of her hand.

All but one of the teachers go through the thirteenth door on the left, where there's a stairway leading down to another corridor and (Melanie guesses) lots more doors and rooms. The one who doesn't go through the thirteenth door unlocks the classroom and opens up, and that one will be Melanie's teacher and Melanie's friends' teacher for the day.

Then Sergeant comes, and the men and women who do what Sergeant says. They've got the chemical smell, too, and it's even stronger on them than it is on the teachers. Their job is to take the children to the classroom, and after that they go away again. There's a procedure that they follow, which takes a long time. Melanie thinks it must be the same for all the children, but of course she doesn't know that for sure because it always happens inside the cells and the only cell that Melanie sees the inside of is her own.

To start with, Sergeant bangs on all the doors, and shouts at the children to get ready. Melanie sits down in the wheelchair at the foot of her bed, like she's been taught to do. She puts her hands on the arms of the chair and her feet on the footrests. She closes her eyes and waits. She counts while she waits. The highest she's ever had to count is 4,526; the lowest is 4,301.

When the key turns in the door, she stops counting and opens her eyes. Sergeant comes in with his gun and points it at her. Then two of Sergeant's people come in and tighten and buckle the straps of the chair around Melanie's wrists and ankles. There's also a strap for her neck: they tighten that one last of all, when her hands and feet are fastened up all the way, and they always do it from behind. The strap is designed so they never have to put their hands in front of Melanie's face. Melanie sometimes says, "I won't bite." She says it as a joke, but Sergeant's people never laugh. Sergeant did once, the first time she said it, but it was a nasty laugh. And then he said, "Like we'd ever give you the fucking chance, sugarplum."

When Melanie is all strapped into the chair, and she can't move her hands or her feet or her head, they wheel her into the classroom and put her at her desk. The teacher might be talking to some of the other children, or writing something on the blackboard, but she (unless it's Mr. Galloway, who's the only he) will usually stop and say, "Good morning, Melanie." That way the children who sit way up at the front of the class will know that Melanie has come into the room and they can say good morning, too. They can't see her, of course, because they're all in their own chairs with their neck-straps fastened up, so they can't turn their heads around that far.

This procedure—the wheeling in, and the teacher saying good morning, and then the chorus of greetings from the other kids—happens seven more times, because there are seven children who come into the classroom after Melanie. One of them is Anne, who used to be Melanie's best friend in the class and maybe still is except that the last time they moved the kids around (Sergeant calls it "shuffling the deck") they ended up sitting a long way apart and it's hard to be best friends with someone you can't talk to. Another is Steven, whom Melanie doesn't like because he calls her Melon-Brain or M-M-M-Melanie to remind her that she used to stammer sometimes in class.

When all the children are in the classroom, the lessons start. Every day has sums and spelling, but there doesn't seem to be a plan for the rest of the lessons. Some teachers like to read aloud from books. Others make the children learn facts and dates, which is something that Melanie is very good at. She knows the names of all the states in the United States, and all their capitals, and their state birds and flowers, and the total population of each state and what they mostly manufacture or grow there. She also knows the presidents in order and the years that they were in office, and she's working on European capitals. She doesn't find it hard to remember this stuff; she does it to keep from being bored, because being bored is worse than almost anything.

Melanie learned the stuff about the states from Mr. Galloway's lessons, but she's not sure if she's got all the details right because one day, when he was acting kind of funny and his voice was all slippery and fuzzy, Mr. Galloway said something that worried Melanie. She was asking him whether it was the whole state of New York that used to be called New Amsterdam, or just the city, and he said, who cares? "None of this stuff matters anymore, Melanie. I just gave it to you because all the textbooks we've got are twenty years old."

Melanie persists, because New Amsterdam was way back in the eighteenth century, so she doesn't think twenty years should matter all that much. "But when the Dutch colonists—" she says.

Mr. Galloway cuts her off. "Jesus, it's irrelevant. It's ancient history! The Hungries tore up the map. There's nothing east of Kansas anymore. Not a damn thing."

So it's possible, even quite likely, that some of Melanie's lists need to be updated in some respects.

The children have classes on Monday, Tuesday, Wednesday, Thursday, and Friday. On Saturday, the children stay locked in their rooms all day and music plays over the PA system. Nobody comes, not even Sergeant, and the music is too loud to talk over. Melanie had the idea long ago of making up a language that used signs instead of words, so the children could talk to each other through their little mesh windows, and she went ahead and made the language up, or some of it anyway, but when she asked Miss Mailer if she could teach it to the class, Miss Mailer told her no really loud and sharp. She made Melanie promise not to mention her sign language to any of the other teachers, and especially not to Sergeant. "He's paranoid enough already," she said. "If he thinks you're talking behind his back, he'll lose what's left of his mind." So Melanie never got to teach the other children how to talk in sign language.

Saturdays are long and dull, and hard to get through. Melanie tells herself aloud some of the stories that the children have been told in class.

It's okay to say them out loud because the music hides her voice. Otherwise Sergeant would come in and tell her to stop.

Melanie knows that Sergeant is still there on Saturdays, because one Saturday when Ronnie hit her hand against the mesh window of her cell until it bled and got all mashed up, Sergeant came in. He brought two of his people, and all three of them were dressed in the big suits, and they went into Ronnie's cell and Melanie guessed from the sounds that they were trying to tie Ronnie into her chair. She also guessed from the sounds that Ronnie was struggling and making it hard for them, because she kept shouting and saying, "Let me alone! Let me alone!" Then there was a banging sound that went on and on and Sergeant shouted, "Shut up shut up shut up shut up shut up!" and then other people were shouting, too, and someone said, "Christ Jesus, don't—" and then it all went quiet again.

Melanie couldn't tell what happened after that. The people who work for Sergeant went around and locked all the little doors over the mesh windows, so the children couldn't see out. They stayed locked all day.

The next Monday, Ronnie wasn't in the class anymore, and nobody seemed to know what had happened to her. Melanie likes to think that Ronnie went through the thirteenth door on the left into another class, so she might come back one day when Sergeant shuffles the deck again.

But what Melanie really believes, when she can't stop herself from thinking about it, is that Sergeant took Ronnie away to punish her, and he won't let her see any of the other children ever again.

Sundays are like Saturdays except for the shower. At the start of the day the children are put in their chairs as though it's a regular school day, but instead of being taken to the classroom, they're taken to the shower room, which is the last door on the right, just before the bare steel door.

In the shower room, which is white-tiled and empty, the children sit and wait until everybody has been wheeled in. Then the doors are closed and sealed, which means the room is completely dark because there aren't any lights in there. Pipes behind the walls start to make a sound like someone trying not to laugh, and a chemical spray falls from the ceiling.

It's the same chemical that's on the teachers and Sergeant and Sergeant's people, or at least it smells the same, but it's a lot stronger. It stings a little, at first. Then it stings a lot. It leaves Melanie's eyes puffy, reddened and half-blind. But it evaporates quickly from clothes and skin, so after half an hour more of sitting in the still, dark room, there's nothing left of it but the smell, and then finally the smell fades, too, or at least they get used to it so it's not so bad anymore, and they just wait in silence for the door to be unlocked and Sergeant's people to come and get them.

This is how the children are washed, and for that reason, if for no other, Sunday is probably the worst day of the week.

The best day of the week is whichever day Miss Mailer teaches. It isn't always the same day, and some weeks she doesn't come at all. Melanie guesses that there are more than five classes of children, and that the teachers' time is divided arbitrarily among them. Certainly there's no pattern that she can discern, and she's really good at that stuff.

When Miss Mailer teaches, the day is full of amazing things. Sometimes she'll read poems aloud, or bring her flute and play it, or show the children pictures out of a book and tell them stories about the people in the pictures. That was how Melanie got to find out about Agamemnon and the Trojan

War, because one of the paintings showed Agamemnon's wife, Clytemnestra, looking really mad and scary. "Why is she so mad?" Anne asked Miss Mailer.

"Because Agamemnon killed their daughter," Miss Mailer said. "The Greek fleet was stuck in harbor on the island of Aulis. So Agamemnon put his daughter on an altar, and he killed her so that the goddess Artemis would give the Greek fleet fair winds and help them to get to the war on time."

The kids in the class were mostly both scared and delighted with this, like it was a ghost story or something, but Melanie was troubled by it. How could killing a little girl change the way the winds blew? "You're right, Melanie, it couldn't," Miss Mailer said. "But the Ancient Greeks had a lot of gods, and all kinds of weird ideas about what would make the gods happy. So Agamemnon gave Iphigenia's death to the goddess as a present, and his wife decided he had to pay for that." Melanie, who already knew by this time that her own name was Greek, decided she was on Clytemnestra's side. Maybe it was important to get to the war on time, but you shouldn't kill kids to do it. You should just row harder, or put more sails up. Or maybe you should go in a boat that had an outboard motor.

The only problem with the days when Miss Mailer teaches is that the time goes by too quickly. Every second is so precious to Melanie that she doesn't even blink: she just sits there wide-eyed, drinking in everything that Miss Mailer says, and memorizing it so that she can play it back to herself later, in her cell. And whenever she can manage it, she asks Miss Mailer questions, because what she likes most to hear, and to remember, is Miss Mailer's voice saying her name, Melanie, in that way that makes her feel like the most important person in the world.

One day, Sergeant comes into the classroom on a Miss Mailer day.

Melanie doesn't know he's there until he speaks, because he's standing right at the back of the class. When Miss Mailer says, " . . . and this time, Pooh and Piglet counted three sets of footprints in the snow," Sergeant's voice breaks in with, "What the fuck is this?"

Miss Mailer stops, and looks round. "I'm reading the children a story, Sergeant Robertson," she says.

"I can see that," Sergeant's voice says. "I thought the idea was to educate them, not give them a cabaret."

"Stories can educate just as much as facts," Miss Mailer says.

"Like how, exactly?" Sergeant asks, nastily.

"They teach us how to live, and how to think."

"Oh yeah, plenty of world-class ideas in *Winnie-the-Pooh*." Sergeant is using sarcasm. Melanie knows how sarcasm works: you say the opposite of what you really mean. "Seriously, Gwen, you're wasting your time. You want to tell them stories, tell them about Jack the Ripper and John Wayne Gacy."

"They're children," Miss Mailer points out.

"No, they're not," Sergeant says, very loudly. "And that, that right there, that's why you don't want to read them *Winnie-the-Pooh*. You do that, you start thinking of them as real kids. And then you slip up. And maybe you untie one of them because she needs a cuddle or something. And I don't need to tell you what happens after that."

Sergeant comes out to the front of the class then, and he does something really horrible. He rolls up his sleeve, all the way to the elbow, and he holds his bare forearm in front of Kenny's face: right in front of Kenny, just an inch or so away from him. Nothing happens at first, but then Sergeant spits on his hand and rubs at his forearm, like he's wiping something away.

"Don't," says Miss Mailer. "Don't do that to him." But Sergeant doesn't answer her or look at her.

Melanie sits two rows behind Kenny, and two rows over, so she can see the whole thing. Kenny goes real stiff, and he whimpers, and then his mouth gapes wide and he starts to snap at Sergeant's arm, which of course he can't reach. And drool starts to drip down from the corner of his mouth, but not much of it because nobody ever gives the children anything to drink, so it's thick, kind of half-solid, and it hangs there on the end of Kenny's chin, wobbling, while Kenny grunts and snaps at Sergeant's arm, and makes kind of moaning, whimpering sounds.

"You see?" Sergeant says, and he turns to look at Miss Mailer's face to make sure she gets his point. And then he blinks, all surprised, and maybe he wishes he hadn't, because Miss Mailer is looking at him like Clytemnestra looked in the painting, and Sergeant lets his arm fall to his side and shrugs like none of this was ever important to him anyway.

"Not everyone who looks human is human," he says.

"No," Miss Mailer agrees. "I'm with you on that one." Kenny's head sags a little sideways, which is as far as it can move because of the strap, and he makes a clicking sound in his throat.

"It's all right, Kenny," Miss Mailer says. "It will pass soon. Let's go on with the story. Would you like that? Would you like to hear what happened to Pooh and Piglet? Sergeant Robertson, if you'll excuse us? Please?"

Sergeant looks at her, and shakes his head real hard. "You don't want to get attached to them," he says. "There's no cure. So once they hit eighteen . . ."

But Miss Mailer starts to read again, like he's not even there, and in the end he leaves. Or maybe he's still standing at the back of the classroom, not speaking, but Melanie doesn't think so because after a while Miss Mailer gets up and shuts the door, and Melanie thinks that she'd only do that right then if Sergeant was on the other side of it.

Melanie barely sleeps at all that night. She keeps thinking about what Sergeant said, that the children aren't real children, and about how Miss Mailer looked at him when he was being so nasty to Kenny.

And she thinks about Kenny snarling and snapping at Sergeant's arm like a dog. She wonders why he did it, and she thinks maybe she knows the answer because when Sergeant wiped his arm with spit and waved it under Kenny's nose, it was as though under the bitter chemical smell Sergeant had a different smell altogether. And even though the smell was very faint where Melanie was, it made her head swim and her jaw muscles start to work by themselves. She can't even figure out what it was she was feeling, because it's not like anything that ever happened to her before or anything she heard of in a story, but it was like there was something she was supposed to do and it was so urgent, so important, that her body was trying to take over her mind and do it without her.

But along with these scary thoughts, she also thinks: Sergeant has a name, the same way the teachers do. The same way the children do.

Sergeant has been more like the goddess Artemis to Melanie up until now; now she knows that he's just like everyone else, even if he is scary.

The enormity of that change, more than anything else, is what keeps her awake until the doors unlock in the morning and the teachers come.

In a way, Melanie's feelings about Miss Mailer have changed, too.

Or rather, they haven't changed at all, but they've become stronger and stronger. There can't be anyone better or kinder or lovelier than Miss Mailer anywhere in the world; Melanie wishes she was a Greek warrior with a sword and a shield, so she could fight for Miss Mailer and save her from Heffalumps and Woozles. She knows that Heffalumps and Woozles are in *Winnie-the-Pooh*, not the *Iliad*, but she likes the words, and she likes the idea of saving Miss Mailer so much that it becomes her favorite thought. She thinks it whenever she's not thinking anything else.

It makes even Sundays bearable.

One day, Miss Mailer talks to them about death. It's because most of the men in the Light Brigade have just died, in a poem that Miss Mailer is reading to the class. The children want to know what it means to die, and what it's like. Miss Mailer says it's like all the lights going out, and everything going real quiet, the way it does at night—but forever. No morning. The lights never come back on again.

"That sounds terrible," says Lizzie, in a voice like she's about to cry.

It sounds terrible to Melanie, too; like sitting in the shower room on Sunday with the chemical smell in the air, and then even the smell goes away and there's nothing at all forever and ever.

Miss Mailer can see that she's upset them, and she tries to make it okay again by talking about it more. "But maybe it's not like that at all," she says. "Nobody really knows, because when you're dead, you can't come back to talk about it. And anyway, it would be different for you than it would be for most people because you're . . . "

And then she stops herself, with the next word sort of frozen halfway out of her lips.

"We're what?" Melanie asks.

"You're children," Miss Mailer says, after a few seconds. "You can't even really imagine what death might be like, because for children it seems like everything has to go on forever."

There's a silence while they think about that. It's true, Melanie decides. She can't remember a time when her life was any different from this, and she can't imagine any other way that people could live. But there's something that doesn't make sense to her, in the whole equation, and so she has to ask the question.

"*Whose* children are we, Miss Mailer?"

In stories, she knows, children have a mother and a father, like Iphigenia had Clytemnestra and Agamemnon. Sometimes they have teachers, too, but not always, and they never seem to have Sergeants. So this is a question that gets to the very roots of the world, and Melanie asks it with some trepidation.

Miss Mailer thinks about it for a long time, until Melanie is pretty sure that she won't answer. Then she says, "Your mom is dead, Melanie. She died before . . . She died when you were very little. Probably your daddy's dead, too, although there isn't really any way of knowing. So the army is looking after you now."

"Is that just Melanie," John asks, "or is it all of us?"

Miss Mailer nods slowly. "All of you."

"We're in an orphanage," Anne guesses. The class heard the story of Oliver Twist once.

"No. You're on an army base."

"Is that what happens to kids whose mom and dad die?" This is Steven now.

"Sometimes."

Melanie is thinking hard, and putting it together, inside her head, like a puzzle. "How old was I," she asks, "when my mom died?" Because she must have been very young, if she can't remember her mother at all.

"It's not easy to explain," Miss Mailer says, and they can see from her face that she's really, really unhappy.

"Was I a baby?" Melanie asks.

"A very tiny baby, Melanie."

"How tiny?"

"Tiny enough to fall into a hole between two laws."

It comes out quick and low and almost hard. Miss Mailer changes the subject then, and the children are happy to let her do it because nobody is very enthusiastic about death by this point. But Melanie wants to know one more thing, and she wants it badly enough that she even takes the chance of upsetting Miss Mailer some more. It's because of her name being Greek, and what the Greeks sometimes used to do to their kids, at least in the ancient times when they were fighting a war against Troy. At the end of the lesson, she waits until Miss Mailer is close to her and she asks her question really quietly.

"Miss Mailer, were our moms and dads going to sacrifice us to the goddess Artemis? Is that why we're here?"

Miss Mailer looks down at her, and for the longest time she doesn't answer. Then something completely unexpected and absolutely wonderful happens. Miss Mailer reaches down and she strokes Melanie's hair.

She strokes Melanie's hair with her hand, like it was just the most natural and normal thing in the world. And lights are dancing behind Melanie's eyes, and she can't get her breath, and she can't speak or hear or think about anything because apart from Sergeant's people, maybe two or three times and always by accident, nobody has ever touched her before and this is Miss Mailer touching her and it's almost too nice to be in the world at all.

"Oh, Melanie," Miss Mailer says. Her voice is only just higher than a whisper.

Melanie doesn't say anything. She never wants Miss Mailer's hand to move. She thinks if she could die now, with Miss Mailer's hand on her hair, and nothing changed ever again, then it would be all right to be dead.

"I—I can't explain it to you," Miss Mailer says, sounding really, really unhappy. "There are too many other things I'd have to explain, too, to make sense of it. And—and I'm not strong enough. I'm just not strong enough."

But she tries anyway, and Melanie understands some of it. Just before the Hungries came, Miss Mailer says, the government passed an amendment to the Constitution of the United States of America. It was because of something called the Christian Right, and it meant that you were a person even before you were born, and the law had to protect you from the very moment that you popped up inside your mom's tummy like a seed.

Melanie is full of questions already, but she doesn't ask them because it will only be a minute or two before Sergeant's people come for her, and she knows from Miss Mailer's voice that this is a big, important secret. So then the Hungries came, Miss Mailer said—or rather, people started turning into Hungries. And everything fell to pieces real fast.

It was a virus, Miss Mailer says: a virus that killed you, but then brought you partway back to life; not enough of you to talk, but enough of you to stand up and move around and even run. You turned into a monster that just wanted to bite other people and make them into Hungries, too. That was how the virus propagated itself, Miss Mailer said.

So the virus spread and all the governments fell and it looked like the Hungries were going to eat everyone or make everyone like they were, and that would be the end of the story and the end of everything. But the real people didn't give up. They moved the government to Los Angeles, with the desert all around them and the ocean at their back, and they cleared the Hungries out of the whole state of California with flamethrowers and daisy cutter bombs and nerve gas and big moving fences that were on trucks controlled by radio signals. Melanie has no idea what these things are, but she nods as if she does and imagines a big war like Greeks fighting Trojans.

And every once in a while, the real people would find a bunch of Hungries who'd fallen down because of the nerve gas and couldn't get up again, or who were stuck in a hole or locked in a room or something.

And maybe one of them might have been about to be a mom, before she got turned into a Hungry. There was a baby already inside her.

The real people were allowed to kill the Hungries because there was a law, Emergency Ordnance 9, that said they could. Anyone could kill a Hungry and it wouldn't be murder because they weren't people anymore.

But the real people weren't allowed to kill the unborn babies, because of the amendment to the Constitution: inside their moms, the babies all had rights. And maybe the babies would have something else, called higher cognitive functions, that their moms didn't have anymore, because viruses don't always work the same on unborn babies.

So there was a big argument about what was going to happen to the babies, and nobody could decide. Inside the cleared zone, in California, there were so many different groups of people with so many different ideas, it looked like it might all fall apart and the real people would kill each other and finish what the Hungries started. They couldn't risk doing anything that might make one group of people get mad with the other groups of people.

So they made a compromise. The babies were cut out of their mommies. If they survived, and they did have those function things, then they'd be raised, and educated, and looked after, and protected, until one of two things happened: either someone came up with a cure, or the children reached the age of eighteen.

If there was a cure, then the children would be cured.

If there wasn't . . .

"Here endeth the lesson," says Sergeant.

He comes into Melanie's line of sight, right behind Miss Mailer, and Miss Mailer snatches her hand away from Melanie's hair. She ducks her head so Melanie can't see her face.

"She goes back now," Sergeant says.

"Right." Miss Mailer's voice is very small.

"And you go on a charge."

"Right."

"And maybe you lose your job. Because every rule we got, you just broke."

Miss Mailer brings her head up again. Her eyes are wet with tears.

"Fuck you, Eddie," she says.

She walks out of Melanie's line of sight, very quickly. Melanie wants to call her back, wants to say something to make her stay: *I love you, Miss Mailer. I'll be a warrior for you, and save you.* But she can't say anything, and then Sergeant's people come. Sergeant's there, too. "Look at you," he says to Melanie. "Fucking face all screwed up like a tragedy mask. Like you've got fucking feelings."

But nothing that Sergeant says and nothing that Sergeant does can take away the memory of that touch.

When she's wheeled into her cell, and Sergeant stands by with his gun as the straps are unfastened one by one, Melanie looks him in the eye. "You won't get fair winds, whatever you do," she tells him. "No matter how many children you kill, the goddess Artemis won't help you." Sergeant stares at her, and something happens in his face. It's like he's surprised, and then he's scared, and then he's angry. Sergeant's people can see it, too, and one of them takes a step toward him with her hand halfway up like she's going to touch his arm.

"Sergeant Robertson!" she says.

He pulls back from her, and then he makes a gesture with the gun.

"We're done here," he says.

"She's still strapped in," says the other one of Sergeant's people.

"Too bad," says Sergeant. He throws the door open and waits for them to move, looking at one of them and then the other until they give up and leave Melanie where she is and go out through the door.

"Fair winds, kid," Sergeant says.

So Melanie has to spend the night in her chair, still strapped up tight apart from her head and her left arm. And it's way too uncomfortable to sleep, even if she leans her head sideways, because there's a big pipe that runs down the wall right there and she can't get into a position that doesn't hurt her.

But then, because of the pipe, something else happens. Melanie starts to hear voices, and they seem to be coming right out of the wall. Only they're not: they're coming down the pipe, somehow, from another part of the building. Melanie recognizes Sergeant's voice, but not any of the others.

"Fence went down in Michigan," Sergeant says. "Twenty-mile stretch, Clayton said. Hungries are pushing west, and probably south, too. How long you think it'll be before they cut us off?"

"Clayton's full of shit," a second voice says, but with an anxious edge. "You think they'd have left us here, if that was gonna happen? They'd have evacuated the base."

"Fuck if they would!" This is Sergeant again. "They care more about these little plague rats than they do about us. If they'd have done it right, we didn't even need to be here. All they had to do was to put every last one of the little bastards in a barn and throw one fucking daisy cutter in there. No more worries."

It gets real quiet for a while after that, like no one can think of anything to say. "I thought they found a cure," a third voice says, but he's shouted down by a lot of voices all at the same time. "That's bullshit." "Dream on, man! Onliest cure for them fuckin' skull-faces is in this here clip, and I got enough for all,"

"They did, though," the third voice persists. "They isolated the virus. At that lab in Houston. And then they built something that'll kill it. Something that'll fit in a hypo. They call it a *phage*."

"Here, you, skull-face." Sergeant is putting on a funny voice. "I got a cure for you, so why'n't you come on over here and roll up your sleeve? That's right. And all you other cannibal motherfuckers, you form an orderly line there."

There's a lot of laughter, and a lot of stuff that Melanie can't hear clearly. The third voice doesn't speak again.

"I heard they broke through from Mexico and took Los Angeles." Another new voice. "We ain't got no government now. It's just the last few units out in the field, and some camps like this one that kept a perimeter up. That's why there's no messages anymore. No one out there to send them."

Then the second voice comes in again with, "Hell, Dawlish. Brass keep their comms to theirselves, like always. There's messages. Just ain't any for you, is all."

"They're all dead," Sergeant says. "They're all dead except us. And what are we? We're the fucking nursemaids of the damned. Drink up, guys. Might as well be drunk as sober, when it comes." Then he laughs, and it's the same laugh as when he said, "Like we'd ever give you the chance." A laugh that hates itself and probably everything else, too.

Melanie leans her head as far to the other side as it will go, so she can't hear the voices anymore.

Eddie, she tells herself. Just Eddie Robertson talking. That's all.

The night is very, very long. Melanie tells herself stories, and sends messages from her right hand to her left hand, then back again, using her sign language, but it's still long. When Sergeant comes in the morning with his people, she can't move; she's got such bad cramps in her neck and her shoulders and her arms, it feels like there's iron bars inside her.

Sergeant looks at her like he's forgotten up until then what happened last night. He looks at his people, but they're looking somewhere else.

They don't say anything as they tie up Melanie's neck and arm again.

Sergeant does. He says, "How about them fair winds, kid?" But he doesn't say it like he's angry, or even like he wants to be mean. He says it and then he looks away, unhappy, sick almost. To Melanie, it seems like he says it because he has to say it; as though being Sergeant means you've got to say things like that all the time, whether that's really what you're thinking or not. She files that thought next to his name.

One day, Miss Mailer gives Melanie a book. She does it by sliding the book between Melanie's back and the back of the wheelchair, and tucking it down there out of sight. Melanie isn't even sure at first that that's what just happened, but when she looks at Miss Mailer and opens her mouth to ask her, Miss Mailer touches a finger to her closed lips. So Melanie doesn't say anything.

Once they're back in their cells, and untied, the children aren't supposed to stand up and get out of their chairs until Sergeant's people have left and the door is closed and locked. That night, Melanie makes sure not to move a muscle until she hears the bolt slide home.

Then she reaches behind her and finds the book, its angular shape digging into her back a little. She pulls it out and looks at it.

Homer. The *Iliad* and *The Odyssey*.

Melanie makes a strangled sound. She can't help it, even though it might bring Sergeant back into the cell to tell her to shut up. A book! A book of her own! And *this* book! She runs her hands over the cover, riffles the pages, turns the book in her hands, over and over. She smells the book.

That turns out to be a mistake, because the book smells of Miss Mailer. On top, strongest, the chemical smell from her fingers, as bitter and horrible as always: but underneath, a little, and on the inside pages a lot, the warm and human smell of Miss Mailer herself.

What Melanie feels right then is what Kenny felt, when Sergeant wiped the chemicals off his arm and put it right up close to Kenny's face, but she only just caught the edge of it, that time, and she didn't really understand it.

Something opens inside her, like a mouth opening wider and wider and wider and screaming all the time—not from fear, but from need. Melanie thinks she has a word for it now, although it still isn't anything she's felt before. Sometimes in stories that she's heard, people eat and drink, which is something that the children don't ever do. The people in the stories need to eat, and then when they do eat they feel themselves fill up with something, and it gives them a satisfaction that nothing else can give. She remembers a line from a song that Miss Justineau sang to the children once: *You're my bread, when I'm hungry.*

So this is hunger, and it hurts like a needle, like a knife, like a Trojan spear in Melanie's heart or maybe lower down in her stomach. Her jaws start to churn of their own accord: wetness comes into her mouth. Her head feels light, and the room sort of goes away and then comes back without moving.

The feeling goes on for a long time, until finally Melanie gets used to the smell the way the children in the shower on Sunday get used to the smell of the chemicals. It doesn't go away, exactly, but it doesn't torment her in quite the same way: it becomes kind of invisible just because it doesn't change. The hunger gets less and less, and when it's gone, all gone, Melanie is still there.

The book is still there, too: Melanie reads it until daybreak, and even when she stumbles over the words or has to guess what they mean, she's in another world.

It's a long time after that before Miss Mailer comes again. On Monday there's a new teacher, except he isn't a teacher at all: he's one of Sergeant's people. He says his name is John, which is stupid, because the teachers are all Miss or Mrs. or Mister something, so the children call him Mr. John, and after the first few times he gives up correcting them.

Mr. John doesn't look like he wants to be there, in the classroom. He's only used to strapping the children into the chairs one by one, or freeing them again one by one, with Sergeant's gun on them all the time and everything quick and easy. He looks like being in a room with all the children at the same time is like lying on an altar, at Aulis, with the priest of Artemis holding a knife to his throat.

At last, Anne asks Mr. John the question that everybody wants to ask him: where the real teachers are, "There's a lockdown," Mr. John says. He doesn't seem to mind that the children have spotted him for a fake. "There's movement west of the fence. They confirmed it by satellite. Lots of Hungries coming this way, so nobody's allowed to move around inside the compound or go out into the open in case they get our scent. We're just staying wherever we happened to be when the alarm went. So you've got me to put up with, and we'll just have to do the best we can."

Actually, Mr. John isn't a bad teacher at all, once he stops being scared of the children. He knows a lot of songs, and he writes up the words on the blackboard; the children sing the songs, first all at once and then in two-part and three-part harmonies. There are lots of words the children don't know, especially in "Too Drunk to Fuck," but when the children ask what the words mean, Mr. John says he'll take the Fifth on that one. That means he might get himself into trouble if he gives the right answer, so he's allowed not to; Melanie knows this from when Miss Justineau told them about the Bill of Rights.

So it's not a bad day, at all, even if they don't have a real teacher. But for a whole lot of days after that, nobody comes and the children are alone. It's not possible for Melanie to count how many days; there's nothing to count. The lights stay on the whole time, the music plays really loud, and the big steel door stays shut.

Then a day comes when the music goes off. And in the sudden, shocking silence the bare steel door slams open again, so loud that the sound feels like it's shoving its way through your ear right inside your head. The children jump up and run to their doors to see who's coming, and it's Sergeant—just Sergeant, with one of his people, and no teachers at all.

"Let's do this," Sergeant says.

The man who's with him looks at all the doors, then at Sergeant.

"Seriously?" he says.

"We got our orders," Sergeant says. "What we gonna do, tell them we lost the key? Start with this bunch, then do B to D. Sorenson can start at the other end."

Sergeant unlocks the first door after the shower room door, which is Mikey's door. Sergeant and the other man go inside, and Sergeant's voice, booming hollowly in the silence, says, "Up and at 'em, you little fucker."

Melanie sits in her chair and waits. Then she stands up and waits at the door with her face to the mesh. Then she walks up and down, hugging her own arms. She's confused and excited and very, very scared.

Something new is happening. She senses it: something completely outside of her experience. When she looks out through the mesh window, she can see that Sergeant isn't closing the doors behind him, as he goes from cell to cell, and he's not wheeling the children into the classroom.

Finally her door is unlocked. She steps back from it as it opens, and Sergeant and the other man step inside. Sergeant points the gun at Melanie.

"You forget your manners?" he asks her. "Sit down, kid." Something happens to Melanie. It's like all her different, mixed-up feelings are crashing into each other, inside her head, and turning into a new feeling. She sits down, but she sits down on her bed, not in her chair.

Sergeant stares at her like he can't believe what he's seeing. "You don't want to piss me off today," he warns Melanie. "Not today."

"I want to know what's happening, Sergeant," Melanie says. "Why were we left on our own? Why didn't the teachers come? What's happening?"

"Sit down in the chair," the other man says.

"Do it," Sergeant tells her.

But Melanie stays where she is, on the bed, and she doesn't shift her gaze from Sergeant's eyes. "Is there going to be class today?" she asks him.

"Sit in the goddamn chair," Sergeant orders her. "Sit in the chair or I swear I will fucking dismantle you." His voice is shaking, just a little, and she can see from the way his face changes, suddenly, that he knows she heard the shake. "Fucking—fine!" he explodes, and he advances on the chair and kicks it with his boot, really hard, so it flies up into the air and hits the wall of the narrow cell. It bounces off at a wild angle, hits the other wall and crashes down on its back. Sergeant kicks it again, and then a third time. The frame is all twisted from where it hit the wall, and one of the wheels comes right off when Sergeant kicks it.

The other man just watches, without saying a word, while Sergeant gets his breath back and comes down from his scary rage. When he does, he looks at Melanie and shrugs. "Well, I guess you can just stay where you are, then," he says.

The two of them go out, and the door is locked again. They take the other kids away, one by one—not to the classroom, but out through the other door, the bare steel door, which until now has marked the farthest limit of their world.

Nobody comes, after that, and nothing happens. It feels like a long time, but Melanie's mind is racing so fast that even a few minutes would feel like a long time. It's longer than a few minutes, though. It feels like most of a day.

The air gets colder. It's not something that Melanie thinks about, normally, because heat and cold don't translate into comfort or discomfort for her; she notices now because with no music playing and nobody to talk to, there's nothing else to notice. Maybe it's night. That's it. It must be night outside. Melanie knows from stories that it gets colder at night as well as darker.

She remembers her book, and gets it out. She reads about Hector and Achilles and Priam and Hecuba and Odysseus and Menelaus and Agamemnon and Helen.

There are footsteps from the corridor outside. Is it Sergeant? Has he come back to dismantle her? To take her to the altar and give her to the goddess Artemis?

Someone unlocks Melanie's door, and pushes it open.

Miss Mailer stands in the doorway. "It's okay," she says. "It's okay, sweetheart. I'm here."

Melanie surges to her feet, her heart almost bursting with happiness and relief. She's going to run to Miss Mailer. She's going to hug her and be hugged by her and be touching her not just with her hair but with her hands and her face and her whole body. Then she freezes where she is.

Her jaw muscles stiffen, and a moan comes out of her mouth.

Miss Mailer is alarmed. "Melanie?" She takes a step forward.

"Don't!" Melanie screams. "Please, Miss Mailer! Don't! Don't touch me!"

Miss Mailer stops moving, but she's so close! So close! Melanie whimpers. Her whole mind is exploding. She drops to her knees, then falls full-length on the floor. The smell, the wonderful, terrible smell, fills all the room and all her mind and all her thoughts, and all she wants to do is . . .

"Go away!" she moans. "Go away go away go away!" Miss Mailer doesn't move.

"Fuck off, or I will dismantle you!" Melanie wails. She's desperate.

Her mouth is filled with thick saliva like mud from a mudslide. She's dangling on the end of the thinnest, thinnest piece of string. She's going to fall and there's only one direction to fall in.

"Oh God!" Miss Mailer blurts. She gets it at last. She rummages in her bag, which Melanie didn't even notice until now. She takes something out—a tiny bottle with yellow liquid in it—and starts to spray it on her skin, on her clothes, in the air. The bottle says *Dior*. It's not the usual chemical: it's something that smells sweet and funny. Miss Mailer doesn't stop until she's emptied the bottle.

"Does that help?" she asks, with a catch in her voice. "Oh baby, I'm so sorry. I didn't even think . . . "

It does help, a little. And Melanie has had practice at pushing the hunger down: she has to do it a little bit every time she picks up her book.

This is a million times harder, but after a while she can think again and move again and even sit up.

"It's safe now," she says timidly, groggily. And she remembers her own words, spoken as a joke so many times before she ever guessed what they might actually mean. "I won't bite."

Miss Mailer bends down and sweeps Melanie up, choking out her name, and there they are crying into each other's tears, and even though the hunger is bending Melanie's spine like Achilles bending his bow, she wouldn't exchange this moment for all the other moments of her life.

"They're attacking the fence," Miss Mailer says, her voice muffled by Melanie's hair. "But it's not Hungries, it's looters. Bandits. People just like me and the other teachers, but renegades who never went into the western cordon. We've got to get out before they break through. We're being evacuated, Melanie—to Texas."

"Why?" is all Melanie can think of to say.

"Because that's where the cure is!" sobs Miss Mailer. "They'll make you okay again, and you'll have a real mom and dad, and a real life, and all this fucking madness will just be a memory!"

"No," Melanie whimpers.

"Yes, baby! Yes!" Miss Mailer is hugging her tight, and Melanie is trying to find the words to explain that she doesn't want a mom or a dad, she wants to stay here in the block with Miss Mailer and have lessons with her forever, but right then is when Sergeant walks into the cell.

Three of his people are behind him. His face is pale, and his eyes are open too wide.

"We got to go," he says. "Right now. Last two choppers are loaded up and ready. I'm real sorry, Gwen, but this is the last call."

"I'm not going without her," Miss Mailer says, and she hugs Melanie so tight it almost hurts.

"Yeah," Sergeant says. "You are. She can't come on the transport without restraints, and we don't got any restraints that we can use. You come on, now."

He reaches out his hand as if he's going to help Miss Mailer to her feet. Miss Mailer doesn't take the hand.

"Come on, now," Sergeant says again, on a rising pitch.

"I'm not leaving her," Miss Mailer says again.

"She's got no—"

Miss Mailer's voice rises over Sergeant's voice, shouts him into silence. "She doesn't have any restraints because you kicked her chair into scrap metal. And now you're going to leave her here, to the mercy of those animals, and say it was out of your hands. Well damn you, Eddie!" She can hardly get the words out; she sounds like there's no breath left in her body. "Damn—fuck—rot what's left of your miserable fucking heart!"

"I've got to go by the rules," Sergeant pleads. His voice is weak, lost.

"Really?" Miss Mailer shouts at him. "The rules? And when you've ripped her heart out and fed it to your limp-dick fucking rules, you think that will bring Chloe back, or Sarah? Or bring you one moment's peace? There's a cure, you bastard! They can cure her! They can give her a normal life! You want to say she stays here and rots in the dark instead because you threw a man-tantrum and busted up her fucking *chair*?"

There's a silence that seems like it's never going to end. Maybe it never would, if there was only Sergeant and Miss Mailer and Melanie in the room: but one of Sergeant's people breaks it at last. "Sarge, we're already two minutes past the—"

"Shut up," Sergeant tells him. And then to Miss Mailer he says, "You carry her. You hold her, every second of the way. And you're responsible for her. If she bites anyone, I'm throwing you both off the transport."

Miss Mailer stands up with Melanie cradled in her arms, and they run. They go out through the steel door. There are stairs on the other side of it that go up and up, a long way. Miss Mailer is holding her tight, but she rocks and bounces all the same, pressed up against Miss Mailer's heart. Miss Mailer's heart bumps rhythmically, as if something was alive inside it and touching Melanie's cheek through her skin.

At the top of the stairs, there's another door. They come out into sudden cold and blinding light. The quality of the sound changes, the echoes dying suddenly. Air moves against Melanie's bare arm. Distant voices bray, almost drowned out by a mighty, droning, flickering roar.

The lights are moving, swinging around. Where they touch, details leap out of the darkness as though they've just been painted there. Men are running, stopping, running again, firing guns like Sergeant's gun into the wild, jangling dark.

"Go!" Sergeant shouts.

Sergeant's men run, and Miss Mailer runs. Sergeant runs behind them, his gun in his hand. "Don't waste rounds," Sergeant calls out to his people. "Pick your target." He fires his gun, and his people fire, too, and the guns make a sound so loud it runs all the way out into the dark and then comes back again, but Melanie can't see what it is they're firing at or if they hit it. She's got other stuff to worry about, anyway.

This close up, the smelly stuff that Miss Mailer sprayed on herself isn't strong enough to hide the Miss Mailer smell underneath. The hunger is rising again inside Melanie, filling her up all the way to the top, taking her over: Miss Mailer's arm is right there beside her head, and she's thinking *please don't please don't please don't* but who is she pleading with? There's no one. No one but her.

A shape looms in the darkness: a thing as big as a room, that sits on the ground but rocks from side to side and spits dirt in their faces with its deep, dry breath and drones to itself like a giant trying to sing. It has a door in its side; some of the children sit there, inside the thing, in their chairs, tied in with straps and webbing so it looks like a big spider has caught them. Some of Sergeant's people are there, too, shouting words that Melanie can't hear. One of them slaps the side of the big thing: it lifts into the air, all at once, and then it's gone.

Sergeant's arm clamps down on Miss Mailer's shoulder and he turns her around, bodily. "There!" he shouts. "That way!" And they're running again, but now it's just Sergeant and Miss Mailer. Melanie doesn't know where Sergeant's people have gone.

There's another one of the big rocking things, a long way away: a *helicopter*, Melanie thinks, the word coming to her from a lesson she doesn't even remember. And that means they're outside, under the sky, not in a big room like she thought at first. But even the astonishment is dulled by the gnawing, insistent hunger: her jaws are drawing back, straining open like the hinges of a door; her own thoughts are coming to her from a long way away, like someone shouting at her through a tiny mesh window: *Oh please don't please don't!*

Miss Mailer is running toward the helicopter and Sergeant is right behind. They're close to it now, but one of the big swinging lights turns and shows them some men running toward them on a shallow angle.

The men don't have guns like Sergeant does, but they have sticks and knives and one of them is waving a spear.

Sergeant fires, and nothing seems to happen. He fires again, and the man with the spear falls. Then they're at the helicopter and Miss Mailer is pulled inside by a woman who seems startled and scared to see Melanie there.

"What the fuck?" she says.

"Sergeant Robertson's orders!" Miss Mailer yells.

Some more of the children are here. Melanie sees Anne and Kenny and Lizzie in a single flash of one of the swinging lights. But now there's a shout and Sergeant is fighting with somebody, right there at the door where they just climbed in. The men with the knives and the sticks have gotten there, too. and the sticks have gotten there, too.

Sergeant gets off one more shot, and all of a sudden one of the men doesn't have a head anymore. He falls down out of sight. Another man knocks the gun out of Sergeant's hand, but Sergeant takes his knife from him somehow and sticks it into the man's stomach.

The woman inside the copter slaps the ceiling and points up—for the pilot, Melanie realizes. He's sitting in his cockpit, fighting to keep the copter more or less level and more or less still, as though the ground is bucking under him and trying to throw him off. But it's not the ground, it's the weight of the men swarming on board.

"Shit!" the woman moans.

Miss Mailer hides Melanie's eyes with her hand, but Melanie pushes the hand away. She knows what she has to do, now. It's not even a hard choice, because the incredible, irresistible human flesh smell is helping her, pushing her in the direction she has to go.

She stops pleading with the hunger to leave her alone; it's not listening anyway. She says to it, instead, like Sergeant said to his people, *Pick your target.*

And then she jumps clear out of Miss Mailer's arms, her legs propelling her like one of Sergeant's bullets.

She lands on the chest of one of the men, and he's staring into her face with frozen horror as she leans in and bites his throat out. His blood tastes utterly wonderful: he is her bread when she's hungry, but there's no time to enjoy it. Melanie scales his shoulders as he falls and jumps onto the man behind, folding her legs around his neck and leaning down to bite and claw at his face.

Miss Mailer screams Melanie's name. It's only just audible over the sound of the helicopter blades, which is louder now, and the screams of the third man as Melanie jumps across to him and her teeth close on his arm. He beats at her, but her jaws are so strong he can't shake her loose, and then Sergeant hits him really hard in the face and he falls down.

Melanie lets go of his arm, spits out the piece of it that's in her mouth.

The copter lifts off. Melanie looks up at it, hoping for one last sight of Miss Mailer's face, but it just disappears into the dark and there's nothing left of it but the sound.

Other men are coming. Lots of them.

Sergeant picks up his gun from the ground where it fell, checks it.

He seems to be satisfied.

The light swings all the way round until it's full in their faces.

Sergeant looks at Melanie, and she looks back at him.

"Day just gets better and better, don't it?" Sergeant says. It's sarcasm, but Melanie nods, meaning it, because it's a day of wishes coming true.

Miss Mailer's arms around her, and now this.

"You ready, kid?" Sergeant asks.

"Yes, Sergeant," Melanie says. Of course she's ready.

"Then let's give these bastards something to feel sad about." The men bulk large in the dark, but they're too late. The goddess Artemis is appeased. The ships are gone on the fair wind.

Pollution

Don Webb

For centuries Nagoya has been known for its mechanized puppets or karakuri ningyô. It was no surprise that Nagoya leads the world with both roboto and kyonshi technologies.

—Nagoya Handbook, 2035 Edition

Billy Parsons had never seen an American *kyonshi*. He had been living in Nagoya for four months as an English teacher. It was an unsteady job, employment mavens were predicting English would soon be on the way out replaced by the winner's language in the Chinese-Brazilian War. Billy didn't care, he was a Nippophile of the first water. He was living in Japan, damn it, Japan, and every step was a movement toward some Rising Sun moment. Every sushi roll, every cup of *matcha*, every recording of a mournful *samisen* brought him that much closer to what he wanted to be.

The *kyonshi* (Billy would never use the cruder term *zombi*) pushed a broom down the school's corridor. The winking lights of his headgear were as Japanese as could be. Billy knew his school had money, but a job like this was commonly done by a *roboto*. Billy pulled out a phone and snapped a picture. All of his friends back in Patterson would be jealous. He wondered from whom the school had bought the *kyonshi*. In life, he would have been middle-aged. His white skin was tanned and leathery and disfigured with several hairy moles, the robotic eyes had been made to look blue. The shambling figure reminded him of a businessman, partly because he was dressed in a pinstriped Western business suit (albeit of a much stronger/thicker fabric) and partially because it resembled Billy's dad. A *kyonshi*! A real live *kyonshi*! Well maybe "live" is not the best choice of terms. Billy was something of a klutz in the sciences. He thought of the zombies as undead. Something his mom would have liked like vampire novels or Hip-Hop. He remembered his great disappointment when

Mom had given him the George Romero film collection for his thirteenth birthday. "You're a boy aren't you? Boys love zombies!" she had said. Billy did not understand that his lack of love for American horror might indicate a taste for other boys in his mom's eyes. She was so relieved later when she found his collection manga focused on tentacle rape. Thank Jesus he's normal.

Billy's dad had passed last year. Weeks of sitting in the hospital in Patterson, watching the nurses stripping the brown clotted blood from the drainage tubes on his chest, smelling the fake pine forest smell of the air freshener, listening to the old man lapse into diatribes against the government's failure to prevent Texan secession, hate-filled rants against his mother adultery, tasteless jokes about the Great Wall of Canada. Billy had felt so glad and so guilty that day Dad had tried to stand without warning and began the pouring out of the last of his tired and toxic blood. As the dangerous chemical splashed on the tiles, Billy thought of the red rays of the Rising Sun. His dreams had come true at last, as his family conveniently left the stage. It was a great and Shakespearean moment. Of course had lived anywhere else—any civilized place—even Texas, he could have sold Dad's dying body to the zombie makers. He could have left that day for his spiritual homeland and lived like the Mikado. Seeing the *kyonshi* was a sign—his father's ghost had joined him in Japan. All was well. All was good. Everything was tending toward its *kami* state.

The class bell broke this anti-Hamlet reverie, and he hurried to his class to teach English to students who were doing what their parents had done for six generations since Pearl Harbor, learning the language of power. Today's lesson: an infinitive can be used just like a noun in all cases save for the possessive. *To err* is human. Mr. Parsons loves *to read*.

Three hours later Billy knelt on his *tatami* mats practicing sitting Zen. His computer screen simulated the meditation master. His randomly selected koan: "Hogen pointed to the bamboo blinds with his hand. At that moment, two monks who were there went over to the blinds and rolled them up. Hogen said, 'One has gained, one has lost.'" Billy had no idea what that meant, but it was so damn Japanese! He focused his mind attentively on the koan, and attended to his breath. Fifteen minutes later he began to nod off, and as his head bent toward the floor, the computer made a booming noise awakening him. His neighbors pounded his wall and yelled in Japanese. Billy did not know if he were closer to enlightenment. He would have to buy better software to detect that, and such modern (or was it postmodern) touches seemed to Billy to be cheating. Enlightenment should come the old fashioned way.

Later he updated his status on the social networks. His old friends in the

Patterson Ottaku Club were suitably impressed. Nothing said Japan more than a *kyonshi*.

Four bestselling manga were devoted to *kyonshi: Kyonshi Love, Reverend Deadman, Kyonshi Girl*, and *Air Raid Siren. Kyonshi Love* featured Katsumi, who intentionally exposed himself to the virus so that he could track his childhood sweetheart Kasumi—it was a retelling of the Robert Silverberg novella "Born with the Dead." *Reverend Deadman* was a zombie Lutheran minister that had broken free from his controller and ran a church in Tokyo by day and fought alien sex fiends by night. His "undead" status gave him limitless energy and immunity from the aliens' sex rays. *Kyonshi Girl* was a schoolgirl, who despite the fact her family had sold her as a *kyonshi,* sought the love of a demon prince and kept losing her underwear in interesting and creative ways. *Air Raid Siren* paid homage to a popular conspiracy theory that the virus was not man-made at all but had appeared at the Hiroshima blast. Billy loved them all. Of course they had nothing to do with the actual biology and economics of *kyonshis.*

When Billy was in high school, Dr. Kenta Sasaki developed the "zombie virus." He had been working with artificial viruses that slow down and stabilize human metabolic functions. His initial work drew from the same reasoning as Western cryonics. If you give a terminal patient a few more years, a cure might be found. Dr. Sasaki's own brother had died a few years before the AIDS cure. The virus stabilized tissue, but like other filoviruses—say, Ebola and Marburg—it showed a great affinity for the cells of the brain, eyes, and reproductive organs. Dr. Sasaki had been very careful in his design, the zombie virus did not share its sisters' ability to infect rapidly. In fact the virus only infected one in ten people it was tried on in the best of circumstances. It was easy to cure, that is eliminate from the system—but the damage it did (especially to the brain) proved irreversible.

Some wealthy people underwent the infection as their only hope. Maybe their rare cancer, maybe their unidentifiable disease would be cured, *and* a cure found for the zombie virus. Their shambling state, their pale skin might be ended in some happy future. But given their looks and the years of zombie mythology in popular culture—they were seen as grade-A George Romero living dead. Although their tasteless food was made by baby food manufacturers, any number of brain-eating jokes came into being in the early years.

Soon there were rest homes in Japan, Canada, Dubai, and Italy full of the blind mindless ex-humans that seemed happy to live forever—as long as they didn't wander in front of a speeding car and or disappear into an open elevator shaft. There were human rights debates, tired old clichés about the dignity of human life were traded by both sides. Then Capeksen, a Japanese robotics firm, came up with a solution. Scoop out the eyes and upper brain and put in a few dedicated microprocessors to care of things. The robotic eyes saw and looked better than blackened pustules. The computers used the remaining nervous system to move the "dead" man around. Suddenly the zombies could care for themselves. They could shower, they could fix food, they seemed more human.

At first no one had thought of them as slaves.

The next day Billy wanted to shoot a film of the *kyonshi* washing toilets in his school. He remained after class. The *kyonshi* paid no heed him as he knelt in front of each toilet and washed it clean. Billy thought this guy would get more out of Zen training than he was. He squirted some blue fluid into each bowl, methodically swished its white porcelain interior then flushed. Billy had shot him processing three bowls in a row and was about to leave when the *kyonshi* tripped on a small pencil stub dropped by a careless student. It pitched forward and dunked its head into the water. Billy winced at the cracking sound of the control unit hitting the bowl, and thought of getting swirlies in the eight grade. Emergency programs went into play and it pulled itself out. The crown-like controller on its head blinked on and off and on and off. The zombie sat with its back against the stall. It looked at Billy and said in toneless Japanese, "An accident has occurred. Please call a Capeksen technician. An accident has occurred, please call a Capeksen technician. Thank you for your aid in maintaining this expensive Kyonshi Mark IV." The *kyonshi* cradled its head in its pale hands like a human with a bad headache. All of the lights went out. Billy's instinctive programing as a human being took over, and forgetting that he was watching a zombie ran to what seemed to be a dying man. The *kyonshi* breathed slowly and evenly. It must be in some sort of sleep mode, thought Billy. He ran to the headmaster's office.

Since Billy had reported the problem (with typical Japanese management style) it became his to oversee. As he waited in the restroom for the technician to arrive, Billy became an average American for a few minutes—underpaid, working in a humiliating environment, hating his boss. He was his father's son for perhaps for the last time. He needed to comfort the zombie. It was like taking care of Dad after Mom left in his ninth-grade year. At least there was no vomit to clean up. Billy got a few stiff brown paper towels and dried the toilet water off of his suit. He pulled the zombie from the stall and laid it out on the green and brown tiles of the restroom. He was making a little pillow for it out of copies of *To Kill a Mockingbird* from his class. As he waited for the technician, he kept telling the *kyonshi* it would be all right, and cussing his asshole boss for making him wait in an unheated restroom. He was patting the cold brow of the *kyonshi*, when the restroom door swung open.

"Please stand away from the Kyonshi Mark IV," said the white-coated technician.

It was an awkward moment. The technician lived in the the apartment next to his. This man or his wife had pounded on Billy's wall many times when his Zazen program would loudly awaken him.

"I tried to make him comfortable," said Billy.

"The Kyonshi Mark IV has no software appreciating comfort. Please explain the accident to me."

The technician showed no signs of recognition, but how many six-foot-eight chubby red-haired Irish-Americans lived in Nagoya? From the small high windows, Billy saw that night had fallen. He had probably pulled this poor man from his apartment—once again disturbing his night.

Watching the man work on the fallen zombie looked like that robot repair scene from a dozen cheap movies. The technician popped the controller open and was removing a small box from behind the *kyonshi's* right eye. He took a small unit from his belt, and connected it to the fallen zombie. He pushed buttons, the *kyonshi* sat up. More buttons, it stood up. The technician pushed more buttons, watched indicator lights and said, "I will have to take him home for repair. I will need you to sign him over to me."

"Home?" said Billy, "Not to a factory or office?"

"I am the Capeksen representative of the area. Many people do not like having the *kyonshi* near them. But I live in an apartment full of Koreans and other foreign devils."

Billy looked down. He had suddenly become Japanese again—not really Japanese of course, but the fantasy Japanese he had hoped to be. Billy Parsons felt loss of face. He bowed, and said quietly, "I am sorry to have disturbed the harmony of your home."

The technician looked like he might laugh. Twice he started to speak, trying to find the right words, finally he spoke in English. "Mr. Parsons, you cannot understand, but you have given my wife and I someone we can yell at. It is a rare gift."

Billy stared. The man was right. He didn't understand. He looked at the bathroom floor again.

The technician said, "Would you like a ride to our home? I have brought my van, and I will have room for your bicycle as well, my friend."

The technician had installed a device with longer cables by the time Billy brought his bike around. He walked the *kyonshi* to the van and stepped him in.

Conversation was limited on the way home. Eventually Billy managed to get the technician to talk about the mechanized puppets that Nagoya was famous for. Robotics had started here long before the West had dreamed of such toys. Billy asked if the technician's family had made the puppets. The technician grimaced and said that his family had been butchers and leather workers. Then the man had laughed as though Billy was the funniest foreign devil of all time.

Billy learned that Capeksen did have a factory here. In fact most of the newly infected were shipped to that factory. The technician was a sort of contractor—much as Billy's grandfather had installed cable TV. Billy guessed the job didn't pay much. When the van had been finally been parked, Billy asked, "Please forgive this one's ignorance of Japanese culture, but why did you say that it is rare you and your wife can yell at anyone?"

The technician looked at him and said, "*Burakumin*." and shrugged. Billy had no idea what he was talking about, so he bowed. The technician laughed again.

When he got to his apartment he asked his phone what *Burakumin* meant. It said, "Village people." He asked his phone to show him "village people," and it showed him a photo of an American disco music group from his grandmother's time. The technician did not look like the cop, the construction worker, or the Indian chief.

He nuked some yakitori, and when it was time to run his zazen program he turned off the "Awakening" feature. His koan for the night was, "A student asked Joshu, 'If I haven't anything in my mind, what shall I do?' Joshu replied: 'Throw it out.' 'If I haven't anything, how can I throw it out?' continued the questioner. 'Well,' said Joshu, 'then carry it out.' "

He nodded off and woke about 8:00 to call Suzi. Suzi had been his Japanese girlfriend. All nippophiles get a Japanese girlfriend. It comes with the small apartment and the visit to fertility shrines. Suzi had ended his dreams about being Japanese. They had dated for three months. One day he had mentioned his hope of marriage. "I cannot marry you." she said, "My family would never speak to me. They want to me marry a Japanese man."

"But I want to live here all of my life." said Billy, "I want to be Japanese."

"If you want to be Japanese, die and be reborn as a Japanese. I date you because you are a foreigner. Last week you told me you loved me. My Japanese boyfriends never say that. You are the same thing for me that I am for you. A fantasy of not being myself."

Billy did not speak to her for a week. When he started talking to her again, it was as a friend, which was his first woman who was a friend. She found another foreigner to date.

"Suzi, what is a *Burakumin?*"

"Have you been talking to old people?"

"No, my neighbor said it. I think it means 'village person.'"

"It does mean 'village person.' That's the literal meaning, but it is really a derogatory term—like some Americans calling Arabs 'towel heads.' In the old days some trades were considered polluted—butchers, leather workers, people who wash corpses, some sexual entertainers. They are separate like a caste. Pollution beliefs are very strong in Shinto."

"But they are Japanese, aren't they? He looks Japanese."

"Of course he *looks* Japanese, he is Japanese by DNA. It's a taboo—your neighbor will make less money, live in bad places, marry into his own kind. The notion of pollution runs deep. Companies used to keep illegal lists of the *Burakumin*. In the beginning of this century they were almost mainstreamed. Then when *kyonshi* technology showed up, they were the only ones who could risk the pollution. You aren't Japanese, you wouldn't understand."

Billy remembered his dad railing against the Italians and the Poles. His mom's maiden name was Polish. Dad explained to him many drunken times, that Mom looked white but . . .

He knew about the human need to hate. His body was full of memories. When he was a geeky teenager obsessed with Japanese pop culture, he was hated. He was *marked*. In sixth grade two junior high boys beat him yelling that he should have learned karate from his comic books. In seventh grade he was tossed headfirst into the girl's bathroom. The impact with the door actually knocked him out, so he arrived unconscious. When he came to in the nurse's office, the principal sent *him* home because of *his behavior*. He had to come the next day with his parents to be reinstated. That led to his Dad's first burning of his manga. Later that year at Halloween he had engaged in cosplay—he was the evilest "hero" of them all: Lelouch Lamperouge. Everyone made fun of him, the dark and interesting antihero of *Code Geass* was called a "Fag Vampire." Some kids caught him in a park. He called his parents and his drunk dad drove up in his small tan Toyota pickup. It began all heroic-like. Dad drove into the park, across the football field toward the white bandstand. The Hulks, the Spider-men, the one Wonder Woman fled from his dad's headlights. Billy ran to Dad. Dad got out of the truck and picked him like a trash-bag and threw him in the back of the truck. Billy heard a rib crack when he landed.

But he stood his ground, he watched anime on his computer, and kept his manga under his bed, took Japanese in high school. He swore a samurai oath to help the downtrodden, yet by his senior year he was making fun of the childish tastes of the new members of the Patterson Ottaku Club. "You like Sinji? And you're potty-trained?" He taunted kids that liked *G-force* or (Buddha help them!) *Speed Racer.*

In college he passed his larva stage as a worm-like *ottaku* and gained the wings of a true Nippophile. He learned Japanese literature, studied Zen, wrote haiku. He majored in English because English teachers can always get crummy apartments. Who cares how bad your apartment is if you can see Nagoya Castle? Of course he had first seen it in *Godzilla vs. Mothra* or had it been *Gamera vs. Gaos?*

No one had saved him, no human had reached out to him, so he choose reading over life, the fantasy of Japan over the reality of Patterson.

Tomorrow he would reach out to his neighbor. He would bridge the gap that surrounded the *kyonshi* workers. His own quest to be Japanese was nothing compared to the *Burakumin*. He surfed the web into the night learning the history of the *kyonshi*.

After Capeksen designed the controllers, a major scandal shook the industry. The promise was that somehow cures would come for the wealthy dead. The controlling units enabled them to live with some measure of dignity—which they did when their families visited. But the zombies also worked well as lawn mowers, gardeners, car washers, and—for some people with a taste for geriatric porn—they became sex slaves. An unscheduled visit by a reporter ended the appeal. No one wanted their grandmother blowing programmers who couldn't get laid otherwise. It did not matter that new safeguards could eliminate this semi-sentient slavery; stock in Capeksen fell like Lucifer from heaven.

It took murder to change the fate of Capeksen again. When the Toronto cannibal, Robert "Taco Time" LeBlanc's infamous Mexi-Cali Grill had been less than careful with the meat grinder and the mangled diamond wedding ring of Mary Casutto wound up in a food critic's mouth, a new "crime of the century" dominated the newsfeeds for months. Who can forget the angry, crying Robert Casutto begging the white-wigged judge to sentence LeBlanc to zombie status? Owning a slave became a statement that one stood for Justice, Liberty, and the Canadian way. Humanity's age-old fascination with slavery re-manifested. At first, zombiehood was reserved for the worst offenders. But the status symbol of owning a (former) human being as a slave began filling the newsfeeds. Every star, every pop singer had a zombie in tow. The Electric

Luddites had an entire zombie road crew with their neon orange logo tattooed
on their pasty faces.

Soon there weren't enough criminals to meet the demand. But people still died.
What if you elected to be infected? What if you could pay off your huge hospital
bills, end debts, put grandchildren through college? Humans have always made
greet sacrifices for their families. The peace of mind that came by selling your
body into thralldom was immense. Poor families dreading the cost of Granddad's
funeral now had a marketable resource. It was a great deal: the living would collect
a huge fee for their loved one's attempt to become infected. Ninety percent of the
time, the infection didn't occur. For the ten percent who made the transition, it
meant no more pain (at least this was what was believed), and even more money.
The sale of one walking zombie paid more than most average humans made in a
year. Japan led the world in *kyonshi* manufacture. Very few countries opposed the
zombies. The Islamic world held out, as did the United States (which had always
been based on flesh-worship). From an American point of view, zombies were as
bad as abortion, euthanasia, and stem-cell research.

Billy biked to school the next morning. There was a hint of frost in the air,
but warmth in his heart. This was the day he would become a man. He would
undo the bullying that had haunted his childhood. This was his day to pay
Japan back.

When the technician arrived with the *kyonshi* following along, Billy almost
ran from his class to meet him. The technician regarded him dully. Billy offered
to take him to lunch. With obvious regret the technician accepted.

It was awful. Over the sweet chicken wings Billy ran through every cliché
that American public education had given him about diversity, the brotherhood
of mankind, the humanness of us all. The technician nodded absently. Billy
began to get it. The man did not want Billy's approval or acceptance. If he
had wanted the acceptance of foreigners he could have moved to the United
States or Brazil. He wanted to be Japanese. His father's generation had seen the
prejudice against the *Burakumin* almost vanish. But Billy couldn't reach out
to the technician any more than a white child could have to his black friend in
the American South in the bad old days. No one is welcomed by someone who
stoops to shake his hand. Toward the end of the meal, as each was eating his
red bean jelly tofu ice cream, Billy tried talking about the *kyonshi*.

"Do you think they remember their former lives?"

"The upper sections of their brains are gone. I doubt they remember anything."

"But they could remember."

"Perhaps. That is why my family is hated. Imagine if you were trapping the soul of someone's relative for generations—*kyonshi* have great vitality. Once the virus is in place, the body has immunity to almost all diseases. Even if the *kyonshi* has a cut, it does not become infected. With care, their useful work-span could be sixty or seventy years."

"The *kyonshi* at my school. I assume he was American?"

"I would have no idea. Did you guess he was American because all of you people look alike?" The technician smiled at his own joke.

"Who sold his body?" Billy asked.

"He may have been dying without heirs. Sometimes a foreigner passes away, and the state steps in to administer the virus before he or she dies. If heirs show up later the *kyonshi* passes to them."

Lunch ended. Billy went back to school. For some weeks he would greet the technician or his wife in the hallway. Then he learned to look away. He bought a new zazen program that administered electric shocks when the novice nodded off. He briefly dated a Japanese-American woman. Spring came. Cherry trees blossomed. Billy wandered slowly through his life in love with all he saw, a cousin of Tantalus. He saw the world he wanted but could not touch it. More or less.

Then, without drama, he overslept a few minutes one day. He rushed to get ready, and slipped in the shower. He lay paralyzed with the warm water rushing over him. His overuse of water triggered an alarm system. The building superintendent found him, shut off the shower, and medical *robotos* took his pruney body to the hospital. There were shocks, and heart massage, and stimulants shot into his bloodstream. A Catholic priest read him his last rites. Billy could hear, but not move, not blink. He heard the saws biting into his skull.

Days, weeks, months later—he came to. His eyesight was much better. He saw the toilets he cleaned, the halls he swept, the walls he repainted every seven years. He saw his neighbor, who had strangely grown old. He felt nothing when his neighbor slapped him. Felt nothing when his neighbor spit upon him.

Thoughts slowly came back to him. He would see Nagoya Castle through the windows of the building he worked in. Nothing had changed for Billy Parsons. The world he wanted was still as remote. He still silently watched Japan. After sixty years of janitorial service, his bones wore too thin to be of use. At the behest of his programmers he walked to the crematorium. There was a flash of light and his soul passed beyond the bounds of this story.

Becca at the End of the World

Shira Lipkin

I nestle the video camera on its makeshift tripod, carefully centering my daughter's image. She tucks her hair behind her ear and gives a strained smile. She is sixteen, and that hair is long and golden-kissed light brown and straight; she has the gangly grace only teenagers have, that sleek gazelle form. She is wearing khaki shorts and a striped tank top, and the bite mark on her arm is already putrefying.

She has about an hour, we think. And I have about an hour on this camera, an obsolete Flip mini. I guess all cameras are obsolete now. I don't know if I'll ever have a device on which to play this. But she wants to do it. And right now, Becca gets anything she wants. Ice cream or a visit to the zoo, a stolen car or a cliff dive; for the next hour, Becca gets anything and everything she wants.

She crosses her legs and leans forward. Her hair falls over the wound, and she winces. "Does it hurt?" I ask. I'm not in the frame. This video is only her.

"A little. It's not a sharp pain anymore. It's a dull ache. Mom, when I'm ready, I'll tell you, and you have to—"

"I know." I have the camera in one hand and the gun in the other, and when my daughter turns, I need to put a bullet in her brain.

We are in an abandoned preschool. It was closed when the dead rose, so there's no gore here; it's eerie in its silence. There should be children here. There should be cacophony. Becca smiles. "Remember my old preschool?"

"I was just thinking about it. So much screaming all the time!"

"Well. So much screaming all the time everywhere now."

"Oh, Becca. You know what I—"

"I know." She looks down; when she looks back up, her eyes are bright. She addresses the camera. "So hi. My name is Becca Martin. I have been bitten by a damn zombie. My mom is going to be taping this because we don't know if anyone has any data on what happens exactly and, like, mental changes . . . and also I just wanted to talk. I'm sixteen. I'm going to die in probably about an hour. Maybe less. And if anyone survives this, I guess I just want you to know that I existed." She lifts a stack of wooden beads on the tangled wire maze and lets them clack down, *clackclackclack*. "Do I have to give the history of the outbreak or anything? Anyone who gets this is already going to know all that stuff, right?"

"Right. You don't have to go into that."

"Okay. So you already know that we have zombies now. This is day five. And everyone—like, every party I have ever been to, we were joking about zombie apocalypse survival plans, and I think all of those people who had plans? I think they're all dead now. I think all the plans were good for if we knew it was coming, that we could see the news on Twitter and armor up and head for secure locations, but that's not the way it happened. We weren't all together and we didn't have time to call each other, it was just happening. My parents and I were leaving the movie theater and Mom, that was a dumb last movie of my entire life—"

"It sucked. I'm sorry." Some romantic comedy I'd already forgotten, with some famous blonde.

"And so my dad made a sound and I turned around and someone was biting him—" her hand flies to her mouth and she looks down again, hair covering her face.

"Sweetie—Becca, don't. You don't have to do this."

She shook her head violently. "And Mom grabbed me and we ran, because Mom could tell right away that everything was really wrong."

It had been the hardest thing I'd ever done, leaving Dan. But in the instant I'd been turning to see him, I'd seen others, other dead things on the street, other people going down, and something in me had quietly said *this is it*, and I knew I couldn't save him. I knew he was already gone. And I had to help Becca.

"And we got home and secured the house and—I don't want to talk about this part."

"You don't have to."

She looks up, eyes huge. "I don't want to die."

"Oh. God. Becca."

I pull her into my arms and she falls apart, huge gasping gulping sobs, and I fall apart along with her—I don't have to be strong for her this time, not now. This is slow, this is so slow, this is agonizing, but I cannot kill my daughter, not when she is still my daughter. Even though the gray is creeping up to her shoulder, down to her wrist. Even though she has begun to reek.

She pulls back eventually, and in a wavering voice, she just talks. About summer camps and school, best friends and crushes. Becca is my only child. I was young when I had her, and so we have always been friends—parent and child first, but friends second. These are old stories with endings we all know, punch lines that we say in unison. She plays with the wooden beads as she talks, constant punctuation—*clackclackclack*. The room is dusk—dark with primary colors beaming out of the gloom. It's quiet and wrong. Everything is wrong. Everything now will always be wrong.

Becca's hand goes *clackclackclack*, and I stroke the gun every time; our new rhythm. A reminder.

She is trying too hard to be brave. She is shaking. *Clackclackclackplink* as one of her fingernails detaches.

She looks at her hand and looks at me. "Mommy," she whispers.

"I know." I take a deep, shuddery breath. "Do you want to keep talking?"

"Yeah."

Her hands are shaking, and the *clackclackclacks* become more irregular. I am watching her and something is rending my heart, my guts. I struggle for breath, watching my beautiful shining daughter go grey, soften.

I was young when I had her. I didn't know what to do, and I didn't have many people around to help; I had to figure it all out on my own. I had a hard time getting her to latch on properly to breastfeed, so it was a huge victory when I finally did, when she finally did; I would prop myself against pillows and cradle her, her head in the crook of my elbow and her butt nestled in my hand, legs kicking idly, and she would look up at me with those big blue eyes as I learned how to be a mother to her. There were classes and her first library card and parks and swimming pools and she grew up; toy xylophones gave way to cell phones and we were going to go look at colleges this summer. A little early, but she couldn't wait. She was so eager to go out into the world. She had so much she was going to do.

She stops talking. *Clackclackclack*.

Clackclack . . . clack.

Clack . . . clack.

"Becca?"

She looks up. Her face is sagging oddly. She is not simply gray. There's a mottling of yellow, green . . .

"Becca." My hand tightens on the gun.

"Mommy." Her voice cracks. "You should do it now."

I carefully turn off the camera and set it aside without releasing the gun or taking my eyes off her. "Not yet, honey."

"No. Mommy. It's time."

"But you're still *there*!" It's torn from me, almost, that plea, physically wrenched. It can't be time yet. It's only been an hour. It's only been sixteen years. She is still here. My baby is still here. It can't be time.

"Mommy," she pleads, and the anguish in her voice matches mine. I can barely see her through my tears; when did that happen? My throat is sore from holding in the sob that's rising, I can't breathe; absurdly, my nose is running. "Mommy," she says again, her voice softer. " . . . I'm hungry."

Her eyes are still her eyes.

I stand.

I set the gun down on a bookshelf, on top of *Pat the Bunny*.

"Mommy, no, you have to."

I walk to my daughter. I kneel before her and I hold my breath, and I hold her hand. "Eat," I whisper.

She sobs, but the last of Becca slips away with that sob, and I feed my daughter for the last time.

The Naturalist

Maureen F. McHugh

Cahill lived in the Flats with about twenty other guys in a place that used to be an Irish bar called Fado. At the back of the bar was the Cuyahoga River, good for protection since zombies didn't cross the river. They didn't crumble into dust, they were just stupid as bricks and they never built a boat or a bridge or built anything. Zombies were the ultimate trash. Worse than the guys who cooked meth in trailers. Worse than the fat women on WIC. Zombies were just useless dumbfucks.

"They're too dumb to find enough food to keep a stray cat going," Duck said.

Cahill was talking to a guy called Duck. Well, really, Duck was talking and Cahill was mostly listening. Duck had been speculating on the biology of zombies. He thought that the whole zombie thing was a virus, like Mad Cow Disease. A lot of the guys thought that. A lot of them mentioned that movie, *28 Days* where everybody but a few people had been driven crazy by a virus.

"But they gotta find something," Duck said. Duck had a prison tattoo of a mallard on his arm. Cahill wouldn't have known it was a mallard if Duck hadn't told him. He could just about tell it was a bird. Duck was over six feet tall and Cahill would have hated to have been the guy who gave Duck such a shitty tattoo cause Duck probably beat him senseless when he finally got a look at the thing. "Maybe," Duck mused, "maybe they're solar powered. And eating us is just a bonus."

"I think they go dormant when they don't smell us around," Cahill said.

Cahill didn't really like talking to Duck, but Duck often found Cahill and started talking to him. Cahill didn't know why. Most of the guys gave Duck a wide berth. Cahill figured it was probably easier to just talk to Duck when Duck wanted to talk.

Almost all of the guys at Fado were white. There was a Filipino guy, but he pretty much counted as white. As far as Cahill could tell there were two kinds of black guys, regular black guys and Nation of Islam. The Nation of Islam had gotten organized and turned a place across the street—a club called Heaven—into their headquarters. Most of the regular black guys lived below Heaven and in the building next door.

This whole area of the Flats had been bars and restaurants and clubs. Now it was a kind of compound with a wall of rubbish and dead cars forming a perimeter. Duck said that during the winter they had regular patrols organized by Whittaker and the Nation. Cold as shit standing behind a junked car on its side, watching for zombies. But they had killed off most of the zombies off in this area and now they didn't bother keeping watch. Occasionally a zombie wandered across the bridge and they had to take care of it, but in the time Cahill had been in Cleveland, he had seen exactly four zombies. One had been a woman.

Life in the zombie preserve really wasn't as bad as Cahill had expected. He'd been dumped off the bus and then spent a day skulking around expecting zombies to come boiling out of the floor like rats and eat him alive. He'd heard that the life expectancy of a guy in a preserve was something like two and a half days. But he'd only been here about a day and a half when he found a cache of liquor in the trunk of a car and then some guys scavenging. He'd shown them where the liquor was and they'd taken him back to the Flats.

Whittaker was a white guy who was sort of in charge. He'd had made a big speech about how they were all more free here in the preserve than they'd ever been in a society that had no place for them, about how there used to be spaces for men with big appetites like the wild west and Alaska—and how that was all gone now but they were making a great space for themselves here in Cleveland where they could live true to their own nature.

Cahill didn't think it was so great, and glancing around he was pretty sure that he wasn't the only one who wouldn't chuck the whole thing for a chance to sit and watch the Sox on TV. Bullshitting was what the Whittakers of the world did. It was part of running other people's lives. Cahill had dragged in a futon and made himself a little room. It had no windows and only one way in, which was good in case of attack. But he found most of the time he couldn't sleep there. A lot of time he slept outside on a picnic table someone had dragged out into the middle of the street.

What he really missed was carpet. He wanted to take a shower and then walk on carpet in a bedroom and get dressed in clean clothes.

A guy named Riley walked over to Cahill and Duck and said, "Hey, Cahill. Whittaker wants you to go scavenge."

Cahill hated to scavenge. It was nerve-wracking. It wasn't hard; there was a surprising amount left in the city, even after the groceries had been looted. He shrugged and thought about it and decided it was better not to say no to Whittaker. And it gave him an excuse to stop talking to Duck about zombies. He followed Riley and left Duck sitting looking at the water, enjoying the May sun.

"I think it's a government thing," Riley said. Riley was black but just regular black, not Nation of Islam. "I think it's a mutation of the AIDS virus."

Jesus Christ. "Yeah," Cahill said, hoping Riley would drop it.

"You know the whole AIDS thing was from the CIA, don't you? It was supposed to wipe out black people," Riley said.

"Then how come fags got it first?" Cahill asked.

He thought that might piss Riley off, but Riley seemed pleased to be able to explain how gay guys were the perfect way to introduce the disease because nobody cared fuckall what happened to them. But that really, fags getting it was an accident because it was supposed to wipe out all the black people in Africa and then the whites could just move into a whole new continent. Some queer stewardess got it in Africa and then brought it back here. It would kill white people but it killed black people faster. And now if you were rich they could cure you or at least give you drugs for your whole life so you wouldn't get sick and die which was the same thing, but they were still letting black people and Africans die.

Cahill tuned Riley out. They collected two other guys. Riley was in charge. Cahill didn't know the names of the two other guys—a scrawny, white-trash looking guy and a light-skinned black guy.

Riley quit talking once they had crossed the bridge and were in Cleveland.

On the blind, windowless side of a warehouse the wall had been painted white, and in huge letters it said:

> *Hell from beneath is moved for thee to meet thee at thy coming.*
> —Isaiah (ch. XIV, v. 9)

This same quote was painted at the gate where the bus had dumped Cahill off.

There were crows gathering at Euclid, and, Riley guessed, maybe around East Ninth, so they headed north towards the lake. Zombies stank and the crows tended to hang around them. Behind them the burned ruins of the Renaissance Hotel were still black and wet from the rain a couple of days ago.

When they saw the zombie there were no crows but that may have been because there was only one. Crows often meant a number of zombies. The zombie fixed on them, turning her face towards them despite the blank whiteness of her eyes. She was black and her hair had once been in cornrows, though now half of it was loose and tangled. They all stopped and stood stock still. No one knew how zombies "saw" people. Maybe infrared like pit vipers. Maybe smell. Cahill could not tell from this far if she was sniffing. Or listening. Or maybe even tasting the air. Taste was one of the most primitive senses. Primitive as smell. Smelling with the tongue.

She went from standing there to loping towards them. That was one of the things about zombies. They didn't lean. They didn't anticipate. One minute they were standing there, the next minute they were running towards you. They didn't lead with their eyes or their chins. They were never surprised. They just were. As inexorable as rain. She didn't look as she ran, even though she was running through debris and rubble, placing her feet and sometimes barely leaping.

"Fuck," someone said.

"Pipes! Who's got pipes!" Riley shouted.

They all had pipes and they all got them ready. Cahill wished he had a gun but Whittaker confiscated guns. Hell, he wished he had an MK19, a grenade launcher. And a Humvee and some support, maybe with mortars while he was at it.

Then she was on them and they were all swinging like mad because if she got her teeth into any of them, it was all over for that guy. The best thing to do was to keep up a goddamn flurry of swinging pipes so she couldn't get to anyone. Cahill hit other pipe mostly, the impact clanging through his wrist bones, but sometimes when he hit the zombie he felt the melon thunk. She made no noise. No moaning, no hissing, no movie zombie noises, but even as they crushed her head and knocked her down (her eye socket gone soft and one eye a loose silken white sack) she kept moving and reaching. She didn't try to grab the pipes, she just reached for them until they had pounded her into broken bits.

She stank like old meat.

No blood. Which was strangely creepy. Cahill knew from experience that people had a lot more blood in them than you ever would have thought based on TV shows. Blood and blood and more blood. But this zombie didn't seem to have any blood.

Finally Riley yelled, "Get back, get back!" and they all stepped back.

All the bones in her arms and legs were broken and her head was smashed to nothing. It was hard to tell she had ever looked like a person. The torso hitched its hips, raising its belly, trying to inchworm towards them, its broken limbs moving and shuddering like a seizure.

Riley shook his head and then said to them. "Anybody got any marks? Everybody strip."

Everybody stood there for a moment, ignoring him, watching the thing on the broken sidewalk.

Riley snarled, "I said strip, motherfuckers. Or nobody goes back to the compound."

"Fuck," one of the guys said, but they all did and, balls shriveled in the spring cold, paired off and checked each other for marks. When they each announced the other was clear, they all put their clothes back on and piled rubble on top of the twitching thing until they'd made a mound, while Riley kept an eye out for any others.

After that, everyone was pretty tense. They broke into an apartment complex above a storefront. The storefront had been looted and the windows looked empty as the socket of a pulled tooth, but the door to the apartments above was still locked which meant that they might find stuff untouched. Cahill wondered: If zombies did go dormant without food, what if someone had gotten bit and went back to this place, to their apartment? Could they be waiting for someone to enter the dark foyer, for the warmth and smell and the low steady big drum beat of the human heart to bring them back?

They went up the dark stairwell and busted open the door of the first apartment. It smelled closed, cold and dank. The furniture looked like it had been furnished from the curb, but it had a huge honking television. Which said everything about the guy who had lived here.

They ignored the TV. What they were looking for was canned goods. Chef Boyardee. Cans of beef stew. Beer. They all headed for the kitchen and guys started flipping open cabinets.

Then, like a dumbshit, Cahill opened the refrigerator door. Even as he did it, he thought, "Dumbass."

The refrigerator had been full of food, and then had sat, sealed and without power, while that food all rotted into a seething, shit-stinking mess. The smell was like a bomb. The inside was greenish black.

"Fuck!" someone said and then they all got out of the kitchen. Cahill opened a window and stepped out onto the fire escape. It was closest and everyone else was headed out into the living room where someone would probably take a swing at him for being an asshole. The fire escape was in an alley and he figured that he could probably get to the street and meet them in front, although he wasn't exactly sure how fire escapes worked.

Instead he froze. Below him, in the alley, there was one of those big dumpsters, painted green. The top was off the dumpster and inside it, curled up, was a zombie. Because it was curled up, he couldn't tell much about it—whether it was male or female, black or white. It looked small and it was wearing a striped shirt.

The weird thing was that the entire inside of the dumpster had been covered in aluminum foil. There wasn't any sun yet in the alley but the dumpster was still a dull and crinkly mirror. As best he could tell, every bit was covered.

What the fuck was that about?

He waited for the zombie to sense him and raise its sightless face but it didn't move. It was in one corner, like a gerbil or something in an aquarium. And all that freaking tinfoil. Had it gone into apartments and searched for aluminum foil? What for? To trap sunlight? Maybe Duck was right, they were solar powered. Or maybe it just liked shiny stuff.

The window had been hard to open and it had been loud. He could still smell the reek of the kitchen. The sound and the stink should have alerted the zombie.

Maybe it was dead. Whatever that meant to a zombie.

He heard a distant *whump*. And then a couple more, with a dull rumble of explosion. It sounded like an air strike. The zombie stirred a little, not even raising its head. More like an animal disturbed in its sleep.

The hair was standing up on the back of Cahill's neck. From the zombie or the air strike, he couldn't tell. He didn't hear helicopters. He didn't hear anything. He stamped on the metal fire escape. It rang dully. The zombie didn't move.

He went back inside, through the kitchen and the now empty apartment, down the dark stairwell. The other guys were standing around in the street, talking about the sounds they'd heard. Cahill didn't say anything, didn't say they were probably Hellfire missiles although they sure as hell sounded like them, and he didn't say there was a zombie in the alley. Nobody said anything to him about opening the refrigerator, which was fine by him.

Riley ordered them to head back to see what was up in the Flats.

While they were walking, the skinny little guy said, "Maybe one of those big cranes fell. You know, those big fuckers by the lake that they use for ore ships and shit."

Nobody answered.

"It could happen," the little guy insisted.

"Shut up," Riley said.

Cahill glanced behind them, unable to keep from checking his back. He'd been watching since they started moving, but the little zombie didn't seem to have woken up and followed them.

When they got to Public Square they could see the smoke rising, black and ugly, from the Flats.

"Fuck," Cahill said.

"What is that?" Riley said.

"Is that the camp?" "Fuck is right." "One of the buildings is on fire?" Cahill wished they would shut the fuck up because he was listening for helicopters.

They headed for Main Avenue. By the time they got to West 10th, there was a lot more smoke and they could see some of it was rising from what used to be Shooters. They had to pick their way across debris. Fado and Heaven were gutted, the buildings blown out. Maybe someone was still alive. There were bodies. Cahill could see one in what looked like Whittaker's usual uniform of orange football jersey and black athletic shorts. Most of the head was missing.

"What the fuck?" Riley said.

"Air strike," Cahill said.

"Fuck that," Riley said. "Why would anyone do that?"

Because we weren't dying, Cahill thought. We weren't supposed to figure out how to stay alive. We certainly weren't supposed to establish some sort of base. Hell, the rats might get out of the cage.

The little guy who thought it might have been a crane walked up behind Riley and swung his pipe into the back of Riley's head. Riley staggered and the little guy swung again, and Riley's skull cracked audibly. The little guy hit a third time as Riley went down.

The little guy was breathing heavy. "Fucking bastard," he said, holding the pipe, glaring at them. "Whittaker's bitch."

Cahill glanced at the fourth guy with them. He looked as surprised as Cahill.

"You got a problem with this?" the little guy said.

Cahill wondered if the little guy had gotten scratched by the first zombie and they had missed it. Or if he was just bugfuck. Didn't matter. Cahill took a careful step back, holding his own pipe. And then another. The little guy didn't try to stop him.

He thought about waiting for a moment to see what the fourth guy would do. Two people would probably have a better chance than one. Someone to watch while the other slept. But the fourth guy was staring at the little guy and at Riley, who was laid out on the road, and he didn't seem to be able to wrap his head around the idea that their base was destroyed and Riley was dead.

Too stupid to live, and probably a liability. Cahill decided he was better off alone. Besides, Cahill had never really liked other people much anyway.

He found an expensive loft with a big white leather couch and a kitchen full of granite and stainless steel and a bed the size of a football field and he stayed there for a couple of days, eating pouches of tuna he found next door but it was too big and in a couple of days, the liquor cabinet was empty. By that time he had developed a deep and abiding hatred for the couple who had lived here. He had found pictures of them. A dark haired forty-ish guy with a kayak and a shit-eating grin. He had owned some kind of construction business. She was a toothy blonde with a big forehead who he mentally fucked every night in the big bed. It only made him crazy horny for actual sex.

He imagined they'd been evacuated. People like them didn't get killed, even when the zombies came. Even in the first panicked days when they were in dozens of cities and it seemed like the end of the world, before they'd gotten them under control. Somewhere they were sitting around in their new, lovely loft with working plumbing, telling their friends about how horrible it had been.

Finally, he dragged the big mattress to the freight elevator and then to the middle of the street out front. Long before he got it to the freight elevator, he had completely lost the righteous anger that had possessed him when he thought of the plan, but by then he was just pissed at everything. He considered torching the building but in the end he got the mattress down to the street, along with some pillows and cushions and magazines and kitchen chairs and set fire to the pile, then retreated to the third floor of the building across the way. Word was that zombies came for fire. Cahill was buzzing with a kind of suicidal craziness by this point, simultaneously terrified and elated. He settled in with a bottle of cranberry vodka, the last of the liquor from the loft, and a fancy martini glass, and waited. The vodka was not as awful as it sounded. The fire burned, almost transparent at first, and then orange and smoky.

After an hour he was bored and antsy. He jacked off with the picture of the toothy blonde. He drank more of the cranberry vodka. He glanced down at the fire and they were there.

There were three of them, one standing by a light pole at the end of the street, one standing in the middle of the street, one almost directly below him. He grabbed his length of pipe and the baseball bat he'd found. He had been looking for a gun but hadn't found one. He wasn't sure that a gun would make much difference anyway. They were all unnaturally still. None of them had turned their blind faces towards him. They didn't seem to look at anything—not him, not the fire, not each other. They just stood there.

All of the shortcomings of this presented themselves. He had only one way out of the building, as far as he knew, and that was the door to the street where the zombies were. There was a back door but someone had driven a UPS truck into it and it was impassable. He didn't have any food. He didn't have much in the way of defense—he could have made traps. Found bedsprings and rigged up spikes so that if a zombie came in the hall and tripped it, it would slam the thing against the wall and shred it. Not that he had ever been particularly mechanical. He didn't really know how such a thing would work.

Lighter fluid. He could douse an area in lighter fluid or gasoline or something, and if a zombie came towards him, set fire to the fucker. Hell, even an idiot could make a Molotov cocktail.

All three of the zombies had once been men. One of them was so short he thought it was a child. Then he thought maybe it was a dwarf. One of them was wearing what might have once been a suit, which was a nice thing. Zombie businessmen struck Cahill as appropriate. The problem was that he didn't dare leave until they did, and the mattress looked ready to smolder for a good long time.

It did smolder for a good long time. The zombies just stood there, not looking at the fire, not looking at each other, not looking at anything. The zombie girl, the one they'd killed with Riley, she had turned her face in their direction. That was so far the most human thing he had seen a zombie do. He tried to see if their noses twitched or if they sniffed but they were too far away. He added binoculars to his mental list of shit he hoped to find.

Eventually he went and explored some of the building he was in. It was offices and the candy machine had been turned over and emptied. He worried when he prowled the darkened halls that the zombies had somehow sensed him, so he could only bring himself to explore for a few minutes at a time before he went back to his original window and checked. But they were just standing there. When it got dark, he wondered if they would lie down, maybe sleep like the one in the dumpster but they didn't.

The night was horrible. There was no light in the city, of course. The street was dark enough that he couldn't see the short zombie. Where it was standing was a shadow and a pretty much impenetrable one. The smoldering fire cast no real light at all. It was just an ashen heap that sometimes glowed red when a breeze picked up. Cahill nodded off and jerked awake, counting the zombies, wondering if the little one had moved in on him. If the short one sensed him, wouldn't they all sense him? Didn't the fact that two of them were still there mean that it was still there, too? It was hard to make out any of them, and sometimes he thought maybe they had all moved.

At dawn they were all three still there. All three still standing. Crows had gathered on the edge of the roof of a building down the street, probably drawn by the smell.

It sucked.

They stood there for that whole day, the night, and part of the next day before one of them turned and loped away, smooth as glass. The other two stood there for a while longer—an hour? He had no sense of time anymore. Then they moved off at the same time, not exactly together but apparently triggered by the same strange signal. He watched them lope off.

He made himself count slowly to one thousand. Then he did it again. Then finally he left the building.

For days the city was alive with zombies for him although he didn't see any. He saw crows and avoided wherever he saw them. He headed for the lake and found a place not far from the Flats, an apartment over shops, with windows that opened. It wasn't near as swanky as the loft. He rigged up an alarm system that involved a bunch of thread crossing the open doorway to the stairwell and a bunch of wind chimes. Anything hit the thread and it would release the wind chimes, which would fall and make enough noise to wake the fucking dead.

For the first time since he left the loft, he slept that night.

The next day he sat at the little kitchen table by the open window and wrote down everything he knew about zombies:

> 1. they stink
> 2. they can sense people
> 3. they didn't sense me because I was up above them? they couldn't smell me? they couldn't see me?
> 4. sometimes they sleep or something sick? worn down? used up charge?
> 5. they like fire
> 6. they don't necessarily sleep
> 7. they like tinfoil ???

Things he didn't know but wanted to:

> 1. do they eat animals
> 2. how do they sense people

3. how many are there

4. do they eventually die? fall apart? Use up their energy?

It was somehow satisfying to have a list.

He decided to check out the zombie he had seen in the dumpster. He had a backpack now with water, a couple of cans of Campbell's Chunky soups—including his favorite, chicken and sausage gumbo, because if he got stuck somewhere like the last time, he figured he'd need something to look forward to—a tub of Duncan Hines Creamy Homestyle Chocolate Buttercream frosting for dessert, a can opener, a flashlight with batteries that worked, and his prize find, binoculars. Besides his length of pipe, he carried a Molotov cocktail; a wine bottle three-fourths filled with gasoline mixed with sugar, corked, with a gasoline soaked rag rubber-banded to the top and covered with a sandwich bag so it wouldn't dry out.

He thought about cars as he walked. The trip he was making would take him an hour and it would have been five minutes in a car. People in cars had no fucking appreciation for how big places were. Nobody would be fat if there weren't any cars. Far down the street, someone came out of a looted store carrying a cardboard box.

Cahill stopped and then dropped behind a pile of debris from a sandwich shop. If it was a zombie, he wasn't sure hiding wouldn't make any difference, and he pulled his lighter out of his pocket, ready to throw the bottle. But it wasn't a zombie. Zombies, as far as he knew, didn't carry boxes of loot around. The guy with the box must have seen Cahill moving because he dropped the box and ran.

Cahill occasionally saw other convicts, but he avoided them, and so far, they avoided him. There was a one dude who Cahill was pretty sure lived somewhere around the wreckage of the Renaissance Hotel. He didn't seem to want any company, either. Cahill followed to where this new guy had disappeared around a corner. The guy was watching and when he saw Cahill, he jogged away, watching over his shoulder to see if Cahill would follow. Cahill stood until the guy had turned the corner.

By the time Cahill got to the apartment where he'd seen the zombie in the dumpster, he was pretty sure that the other guy had gotten behind him and was following him. It irritated him. Dickweed. He thought about not going upstairs, but decided that since the guy wasn't in sight at the moment, it would give Cahill a chance to disappear. Besides, they hadn't actually checked out the apartment and there might be something worth scavenging. In Cahill's months of scavenging, he had never seen a zombie in an apartment, or even any evidence of one, but he always checked carefully. The place was empty, still stinking a little of the contents of the fridge, but the smell was no worse than a lot of places and a lot better than some. Rain had come in where he'd left the kitchen window open, warping the linoleum. He climbed out onto the fire escape and looked down. The dumpster was empty, although still lined with some tattered aluminum foil. He pulled out his binoculars and checked carefully, but he couldn't really see anything.

He stood for a long time. Truthfully he couldn't be a hundred percent sure it was a zombie. Maybe it had been a child, some sort of refugee? Hard to imagine any child surviving in the city. No, it had to be a zombie. He considered lighting and tossing the Molotov cocktail and seeing if the zombie came to the alley, but didn't want to wait it out in this apartment building. Something about this place made him feel vulnerable.

Eventually he rummaged through the apartment. The bedside table held neither handgun nor D batteries, two things high on his scavenger list. He went back down the dark stairwell and stopped well back from the doorway. Out in the middle of the street, in front of the building to his left but visible from where he stood, was an offering. A box with a bottle of whiskey set on it. Like some kind of perverse lemonade stand.

Fucking dickweed.

If the guy had found a handgun, he could be waiting in ambush. Cahill figured there was a good chance he could outlast the guy but he hated waiting in the stairwell. There were no apartments on the first level, just a hallway between two storefronts. Cahill headed back upstairs. The apartment he'd been in before didn't look out the front of the building. The one that did was locked.

Fuck.

Breaking open the lock would undoubtedly make a hell of a lot of racket. He went back to the first apartment, checked one more time for the zombie, and peed in the empty toilet. He grabbed a pillow from the bed.

Cahill went back downstairs and sat down on the bottom step and wedged the pillow in behind his back. He set up his bottle and his lighter beside him on the step, and his pipe on the other side and settled in to watch. He could at least wait until dark although it wasn't even mid-morning yet. After awhile he ate his soup—the can opener sounded louder than it probably was.

It was warm midday and Cahill was drowsy warm when the guy finally, nervously, walked out to the box and picked up the whiskey. Cahill sat still in the shadow of the stairwell with his hand on his pipe. As best as he could tell, he was unnoticed. The guy was a tall, skinny black man wearing a brown Cleveland football jersey and a pair of expensive looking, olive-green suit pants. Cahill looked out and watched the guy walk back up the street. After a minute, Cahill followed.

When Cahill got out to the main drag, the guy was walking up Superior towards the center of downtown. Cahill took a firm hold of his pipe.

"Hey," he said. His voice carried well in the silence.

The guy started and whirled around.

"What the fuck you want?" Cahill asked.

"Bro," the man said. "Hey, were you hiding back there?" He laughed nervously and held up the bottle. "Peace offering, bro. Just looking to make some peace."

"What do you want?" Cahill asked.

"Just, you know, wanna talk. Talk to someone who knows the ropes, you know? I just got here and I don't know what the fuck is going on, bro."

"This is a fucking penal colony," Cahill said.

"Yeah," the guy laughed. "A fucking zombie preserve. I been watching out for them zombies. You look like you been here awhile."

Cahill hadn't bothered to shave and last time he'd glanced in a mirror he'd looked like Charles Manson, only bearded and taller. "Lie down with your hands away from your body," Cahill said.

The black guy squinted at Cahill. "You shittin' me."

"How do I know you don't have a gun?" Cahill asked.

"Bro, I don't got no gun. I don't got nothin' but what you see."

Cahill waited.

"Listen, I'm just trying to be friendly," the guy said. "I swear to God, I don't have anything. How do I know *you're* not going to do something to me? You're a freaky dude—you know that?"

The guy talked for about five minutes, finally talking himself into lying down on his stomach with his arms out. Cahill moved fast, patting him down. The guy wasn't lying, he didn't have anything on him.

"Fuck man," the guy said. "I told you that." Once he was sure Cahill wasn't going to do anything to him he talked even more. His name was LaJon Watson and his lawyer had told him there was no way they were going to drop him in the Cleveland Zombie Preserve because the Supreme Court was going to declare it unconstitutional. His lawyer had been saying that right up until the day they put LaJon on the bus, which was when LaJon realized that his lawyer knew shit. LaJon wanted to know if Cahill had seen any zombies and what they were like and how Cahill had stayed alive.

Cahill found it hard to talk. He hadn't talked to anyone in weeks. Usually someone like LaJon Watson would have driven him nuts, but it was nice to let the tide of talk wash over him while they walked. He wasn't sure that he wouldn't regret it, but he took LaJon back to his place. LaJon admired his alarm system. "You gotta show me how to unhook it and hook it back up. Don't they see it? I mean, has one of them ever hit it?"

"No," Cahill said. "I don't think they can see."

There were scientists studying zombies and sometimes there was zombie stuff on Fox News, but LaJon said he hadn't paid much attention to all that. He really hadn't expected to need to know about zombies. In fact, he hadn't been sure at first that Cahill wasn't a zombie. Cahill opened cans of Campbell's Chunky Chicken and Dumplings. LaJon asked if Cahill warmed them over a fire or what. Cahill handed him a can and a spoon.

LaJon wolfed down the soup. LaJon wouldn't shut up, even while eating. He told Cahill how he'd looked in a bunch of shops, but most of them had been pretty thoroughly looted. He'd looked in an apartment, but the only thing on the shelves in a can was tomato paste and evaporated milk. Although now that he thought about it, maybe he could have made some sort of tomato soup or something. He hadn't slept in the two days he'd been here and he was going crazy and it was a great fucking thing to have found somebody who could show him the ropes.

LaJon was from Cincinnati. Did Cahill know anybody from Cincinnati? Where had Cahill been doing time? (Auburn.) LaJon didn't know anybody at Auburn, wasn't that New York? LaJon had been at Lebanon Correctional. Cahill was a nice dude, if quiet. Who else was around, and was there anyone LaJon could score from? (Cahill said he didn't know.) What did people use for money here anyway?

"I been thinking," LaJon said, "about the zombies. I think it's pollution that's mutating them like the Teenage Mutant Ninja Turtles."

Cahill decided it had been a mistake to bring LaJon. He picked up the bottle of whiskey and opened it. He didn't usually use glasses but got two out of the cupboard and poured them each some whiskey.

LaJon apologized, "I don't usually talk this much," he said. "I guess I just fucking figured I was dead when they dropped me here." He took a big drink of whiskey. "It's like my mouth can't stop."

Cahill poured LaJon more to drink and nursed his own whiskey. Exhaustion and nerves were telling, LaJon was finally slowing down. "You want some frosting?" Cahill asked.

Frosting and whiskey was a better combination than it had any right to be. Particularly for a man who'd thought himself dead. LaJon nodded off.

"Come on," Cahill said. "It's going to get stuffy in here." He got the sleepy drunk up on his feet.

"What?" LaJon said.

"I sleep outside, where it's cooler." It was true that the apartment got hot during the day.

"Bro, there's zombies out there," LaJon mumbled.

"It's okay, I've got a system," Cahill said. "I'll get you downstairs and then I'll bring down something to sleep on."

LaJon wanted to sleep where he was and, for a moment, his eyes narrowed to slits and something scary was in his face.

"I'm going to be there, too," Cahill said. "I wouldn't do anything to put myself in danger."

LaJon allowed himself to be half-carried downstairs. Cahill was worried when he had to unhook the alarm system. He propped LaJon up against the wall and told him. "Just a moment." If LaJon slid down the wall and passed out, he'd be hell to get downstairs. But the lanky black guy stood there long enough for Cahill to get the alarm stuff out of the way. He was starting to sober up a little. Cahill got him down to the street.

"I'll get the rest of the whiskey," Cahill said.

"What the fuck you playing at?" LaJon muttered.

Cahill took the stairs two at a time in the dark. He grabbed pillows, blankets, and the whiskey bottle and went back down to the sidewalk. He handed LaJon the whiskey bottle. "It's not so hot out here," he said, although it was on the sidewalk with the sunlight.

LaJon eyed him drunkenly.

Cahill went back upstairs and came down with a bunch of couch cushions. He made a kind of bed and got LaJon to sit on it. "We're okay in the day," he said. "Zombies don't like the light. I sleep in the day. I'll get us upstairs before night."

LaJon shook his head, took another slug of whiskey, and lay back on the cushions. "I feel sick," he said.

Cahill thought the motherfucker was going to throw up, but instead LaJon was snoring.

Cahill sat for a bit, planning and watching the street. After a bit, he went back to his apartment. When he found something good scavenging, he squirreled it away. He came downstairs with duct tape. He taped LaJon's ankles together.

Then his wrists. Then he sat LaJon up. LaJon opened his eyes, said, "What the fuck?" drunkenly. Cahill taped LaJon's arms to his sides, right at his elbows, running the tape all the way around his torso. LaJon started to struggle, but Cahill was methodical and patient, and he used the whole roll of tape to secure LaJon's arms. From shoulders to waist, LaJon was a duct tape mummy.

LaJon swore at him, colorfully then monotonously.

Cahill left him there and went looking. He found an upright dolly at a bar, and brought it back. It didn't do so well where the pavement was uneven, but he didn't think he could carry LaJon far and if he was going to build a fire, he didn't want it to be close to his place, where zombies could pin him in his apartment. LaJon was still where he left him, although when he saw Cahill, he went into a frenzy of struggling. Cahill let him struggle. He lay the dolly down and rolled LaJon onto it. LaJon fought like anything, so in the end, Cahill went back upstairs and got another roll of duck tape and duck taped LaJon to the dolly. That was harder than duct taping LaJon the first time, because LaJon was scared and pissed now. When Cahill finally pulled the dolly up LaJon struggled so hard that the dolly was unmanageable, which pissed Cahill off so much he just let go.

LaJon went over, and without hands to stop himself, face planted on the sidewalk. That stilled him. Cahill pulled the dolly upright then. LaJon's face was a bloody mess and it looked like he might have broken a couple of teeth. He was conscious, but stunned. Cahill started pushing the dolly and LaJon threw up.

It took a couple of hours to get six blocks. LaJon was sober and silent by the time Cahill decided he'd gone far enough.

Cahill sat down, sweating, and used his T-shirt to wipe his face.

"You a bug," LaJon said.

Bug was prison slang for someone crazy. LaJon said it with certainty.

"Just my fucking luck. Kind of luck I had all my life. I find one guy alive in this fucking place and he a bug." LaJon spat. "What are you gonna do to me?"

Cahill was so tired of LaJon that he considered going back to his place and leaving LaJon here. Instead, he found a door and pried it open with a tire iron. It had been an office building and the second floor was fronted with glass. He had a hell of a time finding a set of service stairs that opened from the outside on the first floor. He found some chairs and dragged them downstairs. Then he emptied file cabinets, piling the papers around the chairs. LaJon watched him, getting more anxious.

When it looked like he'd get a decent fire going, he put LaJon next to it. The blood had dried on LaJon's face and he'd bruised up a bit. It was evening.

Cahill set fire to the papers and stood, waiting for them to catch. Burnt paper drifted up, raised by the fire.

LaJon squinted at the fire, then at Cahill. "You gonna burn me?"

Cahill went in the building and settled upstairs where he could watch.

LaJon must have figured that Cahill wasn't going to burn him. Then he began to worry about zombies. Cahill watched him start twisting around, trying to look around. The dolly rocked and LaJon realized that if he wasn't careful, the dolly would go over again and he'd faceplant and not be able to see.

Cahill gambled that the zombies wouldn't be there right away, and found a soda machine in the hallway. He broke it open with his tire iron and got himself a couple of Cokes and then went back to watch it get dark. The zombies weren't there yet. He opened a warm Coke and settled in a desk chair from one of the offices—much more comfortable than the cubicle chairs. He opened a jar of peanut butter and ate it with a spoon.

It came so fast that he didn't see it until it was at the fire. LaJon saw it before he did and went rigid with fear. The fire was between LaJon and the zombie.

It just stood there, not watching the fire, but standing there. Not "looking" at LaJon, either. Cahill leaned forward. He tried to read its body language. It had been a man, overweight, maybe middle-aged, but now it was predatory and gracile. It didn't seem to do any normal things. It was moving and it stopped. Once stopped, it was still. An object rather than an animal. Like the ones that had come to the mattress fire, it didn't seem to need to shift its weight. After a few minutes, another one came from the same direction and stopped, looking at the fire. It had once been a man, too. It still wore glasses. Would there be a third? Did they come in threes? Cahill imagined a zombie family. Little triplets of zombies, all apparently oblivious of each other. Maybe the zombie he'd seen was still in the zombie den? He had never figured out where the zombies stayed.

LaJon was still and silent with terror, but the zombies didn't seem to know or care that he was there. They just stood, slightly askew and indifferent. Was it the fire? Would they notice LaJon when the fire died down?

Then there was a third one, but it came from the other side of the fire, the same side LaJon was on so there was no fire between it and LaJon. Cahill saw it before LaJon did, and from its directed lope he was sure it was aware of LaJon. LaJon saw it just before it got to him. His mouth opened wide and it was on him, hands and teeth. LaJon was clearly screaming, although behind the glass of the office building, Cahill couldn't hear him.

Cahill was watching the other zombies. They didn't react to the noise at all. Even when there was blood all over, they didn't seem to sense anything. Cahill reflected, not for the first time, that it actually took people a lot longer to die than it did on television or in the movies. He noted that the one that had mauled and eventually killed LaJon did not seem to prefer brains. Sometime in the night, the fire died down enough that the zombies on the wrong side of the fire seemed to sense the body of LaJon, and in an instant, they were feeding. The first one, apparently sated, just stood, indifferent. Two more showed up in the hours before dawn and fed in the dim red of the embers of the fire. When they finally left, almost two days later, there was nothing but broken bones and scattered teeth.

Cahill lay low for a while after that, feeling exhausted. It was hot during the day and the empty city baked. But after a few days, he went out and found another perch and lit another fire. Four zombies came to that fire, despite the fact it was smaller than his first two. They had all been women. He still had his picture of the toothy blonde from the loft, and after masturbating, he looked out at the zombie women, blank-white eyes and indifferent bodies, and wondered if the toothy blonde had been evacuated or if she might show up at one of his fires. None of the women at the fire appeared to be her, although it wasn't always easy to tell. One was clearly wearing the remnants of office clothes, but the other three were blue jean types and all four had such rat's nests of hair that he wasn't sure if their hair was short or long.

A couple of times he encountered zombies while scavenging. Both times his Molotov cocktails worked, catching fire. He didn't set the zombies on fire, just threw the bottle so that the fire was between him and the zombie. He watched them stop, then he backed away, fast. He set up another blind in an apartment and, over the course of a week, built a scaffolding and a kind of block and tackle arrangement. Then he started hanging around where the bus dropped people off, far enough back that the guys patrolling the gate didn't start shooting or something. He'd scoured up some bottles of water and used them to shave and clean up a bit.

When they dropped a new guy off, Cahill trailed him for half a day, and then called out and introduced himself. The new guy was an Aryan Nation asshole named Jordan Schmidtzinsky who was distrustful, but willing to be led back to Cahill's blind. He wouldn't get drunk, though, and in the end, Cahill had to brain him with a pipe. Still, it was easier to tape up the unconscious

Schmidtzinsky than it had been the conscious LaJon. Cahill hoisted him into the air, put a chair underneath him so a zombie could reach him, and then set the fire.

Zombies did not look up. Schmidtzinsky dangled above the zombies for two whole days. Sometime in there he died. They left without ever noticing him. Cahill cut him down and lit another fire and discovered that zombies were willing to eat the dead, although they had to practically fall over the body to find it.

Cahill changed his rig so he could lower the bait. The third guy was almost Cahill's undoing. Cahill let him wander for two days in the early autumn chill before appearing and offering to help. This guy, a black city kid from Nashville who for some reason wouldn't say his name, evidently didn't like the scaffolding outside. He wouldn't take any of Cahill's whiskey, and as when Cahill pretended to sleep, the guy made the first move. Cahill was lucky not to get killed, managing again to brain the guy with his pipe.

But it was worth it, because when he suspended the guy and lit the fire, one of the four zombies that showed up was the skinny guy who'd killed Riley back the day the air strike had wiped out the camp.

He was white-eyed like the other zombies, but still recognizable. It made Cahill feel even more that the toothy blonde might be out there, unlikely as that actually was. Cahill watched for a couple of hours before he lowered Nashville. The semiconscious Nashville started thrashing and making weird coughing choking noises as soon as Cahill pulled on the rope, but the zombies were oblivious. Cahill was gratified to see that once the semiconscious Nashville got about so his shoes were about four feet above the ground, three of four zombies around the fire (the ones for whom the fire was not between them and Nashville) turned as one and swarmed up the chair.

He was a little nervous that they would look up—he had a whole plan for how he would get out of the building—but he didn't have to use it.

The three zombies ate, indifferent to each other and the fourth zombie, and then stood.

Cahill entertained himself with thoughts of the toothy blonde and then dozed. The air was crisp, but Cahill was warm in an overcoat. The fire smelled good. He was going to have to think about how he was going to get through the winter without a fire—unless he could figure out a way to keep a fire going well above the street and above zombie attention but right now things were going okay.

He opened his eyes and saw one of the zombies bob its head.

He'd never seen that before. Jesus, did that mean it was aware? That it might come upstairs? He had his length of pipe in one hand and a Molotov in the other. The zombies were all still. A long five minutes later, the zombie did it again, a quick, birdlike head bob. Then, bob-bob, twice more, and on the second bob, the other two that had fed did it too. They were still standing there, faces turned just slightly different directions as if they were unaware of each other, but he had seen it.

Bob-bob-bob. They all three did it. All at the same time.

Every couple of minutes they'd do it again. It was—communal. Animal-like. They did it for a couple of hours and then they stopped. The one on the other side of the fire never did it at all. The fire burned low enough that the fourth one came over and worked on the remnants of the corpse and the first three just stood there.

Cahill didn't know what the fuck they were doing, but it made him strangely happy.

When they came to evacuate him, Cahill thought at first it was another air strike operation—a mopping up. He'd been sick for a few days, throwing up, something he ate, he figured. He was scavenging in a looted drug store, hoping for something to take—although everything was gone or ruined—when he heard the patrol coming. They weren't loud, but in the silent city noise was exaggerated. He had looked out of the shop, seen the patrol of soldiers and tried to hide in the dark ruins of the pharmacy.

"Come on out," the patrol leader said. "We're here to get you out of this place."

Bullshit, Cahill thought. He stayed put.

"I don't want to smoke you out, and I don't want to send guys in there after you," the patrol leader said. "I've got tear gas but I really don't want to use it."

Cahill weighed his options. He was fucked either way. He tried to go out the back of the pharmacy, but they had already sent someone around and he was met by two scared nineteen-year-olds with guns. He figured the writing was on the wall and put his hands up.

But the weird twist was that they *were* evacuating him. There'd been some big government scandal. The Supreme Court had closed the reserves, the president had been impeached, elections were coming. He wouldn't find that out for days. What he found out right then was that they hustled him back to the gate and he walked out past rows of soldiers into a wall of noise and light. Television cameras showed him lost and blinking in the glare.

"What's your name?"

"Gerrold Cahill," he said.

"Hey Gerrold! Look over here!" a hundred voices called.

It was overwhelming. They all called out at the same time, and it was mostly just noise to him, but if he could understand a question, he tried to answer it. "How's it feel to be out of there?"

"Loud," he said. "And bright."

"What do you want to do?"

"Take a hot shower and eat some hot food."

There was a row of sawhorses and the cameras and lights were all behind them. A guy with corporal's stripes was trying to urge him towards a trailer, but Cahill was like someone knocked down by a wave who tries to get to their feet only to be knocked down again.

"Where are you from?" Tell us what it was like!"

"What was it like?" Cahill said. Dumbshit question. What was he supposed to say to that? But his response had had the marvelous effect of quieting them for a moment, which allowed him to maybe get his bearings a little. "It wasn't so bad."

The barrage started again but he picked out "Were you alone?"

"Except for the zombies."

They liked that and the surge was almost animalistic. Had he seen zombies? How had he survived? He shrugged and grinned.

"Are you glad to be going back to prison?"

He had an answer for that, one he didn't even know was in him. He would repeat it in the interview he gave to *The Today Show* and again in the interview for *20/20*. "Cleveland was better than prison," he said. "No alliances, no gangs, just zombies."

Someone called, "Are you glad they're going to eradicate the zombies?"

"They're going to what?" he asked.

The barrage started again, but he said, "What are they going to do to the zombies?"

"They're going to eradicate them, like they did everywhere else."

"Why?" he asked.

This puzzled the mob. "Don't you think they should be?"

He shook his head. "Gerrold! Why not?"

Why not indeed? "Because," he said, slowly, and the silence came down, except for the clicking of cameras and the hum of the news vans idling, "because they're just . . . like animals. They're just doing what's in their nature to be doing." He shrugged.

Then the barrage started again. *Gerrold! Gerrold! Do you think people are evil?* But by then he was on his way to a military trailer, an examination by an army doctor, a cup of hot coffee and a meal and a long hot shower.

Behind him the city was dark. At the moment, it felt cold behind him, but safe, too, in its quiet. He didn't really want to go back there. Not yet. He wished he'd had time to set them one last fire before he'd left.

Selected Sources for the Babylonian Plague of the Dead (572-571 BCE)

Alex Dally MacFarlane

Letter (clay tablet) found in the property of Kaššaya, daughter of King Nabu-kudurri-usur, in Uruk. Cuneiform inscription dating to the neo-Assyrian Empire:

To the king, my lord: your servant Nabu'a. May Nabu and Marduk bless the king, my lord! On the 7th of Kislev a fox entered the Inner City, and fell into a well in the garden of Aššur. It was hauled up and killed.

Later annotation on the letter of Nabu'a in Aramaic, using ink:

What omen is this? What did Nabu'a prevent? It is a time of terrible plague in Babylon. With your wisdom, perhaps this tablet will help to explain one of the omens presaging the events here: the dead fox seen walking into the temple of Marduk.

Letter (clay tablet) found in the property of Kaššaya:

Innin-Etirat to Kaššaya, my sister, may Anu keep you well in this time of plague! May the plague that afflicts us in Babylon never reach the great city of Uruk!

I send this letter with four tablets that have been brought from the ruins of Nineveh in the north. Everyone in Babylon with the wisdom to understand these tablets—the omens and the measures taken as a result of them—is dead. They are dead, but they walk, they eat the flesh of living people, who then sicken and die and walk through the city, spreading the illness further. Before this terrible plague, there were four omens here in Babylon: the right-hand quadrant of the sun darkened without the moon passing across it, the king dreamed of a dead woman with teeth as sharp as knives, a dead fox was seen walking into the temple of Marduk, bones fell from the noon sky like rain.

Kaššaya, my sister, if you or your scholars can interpret the past omens described in the tablets and whether they relate to our omens, then you will know what measures to take to prevent this plague from reaching Uruk.

I have sent this letter and these tablets with a soldier I know well. I will remain within Babylon, unless the palace becomes unsafe.

Letter (clay tablet) found in the property of Kaššaya, either an archival copy or the unsent original:

Kaššaya to Innin-Etirat, my sister, may Anu keep you safe! May Nabu and Marduk keep Nabu-kudurri-usur, the king, our father, safe! May the great city of Babylon be unharmed by this calamity! Your letter arrived with only one tablet, carried by a woman fleeing Babylon, who tells me that she found your soldier dying on the road. I have given her food. I have ensured that she is watched for signs of this sickness.

You write: "the right-hand quadrant of the sun darkened without the moon passing across it, the King dreamed of a dead woman with teeth as sharp as knives." I too have dreamed this. I too have witnessed this brief darkening of the sun.

I have been to every temple to report the news you have sent me. Offerings are being made to every god in my name and the king's name. The signs of plague are being watched for in Uruk.

Innin-Etirat, my sister, may you remain safe in the palace of Babylon!

Tablet found in the Eanna temple in Uruk:

Eight minas and five shekels of blue-colored wool for an ullakku garment, the property of Innin-Etirat, the king's daughter, brought to Eanna by Innin-Etirat herself on the day she arrived in Uruk, after the outbreak of the plague. Month Šabatu, 7th day, 33rd year of Nabu-kudurri-usur, King of Babylon.

A story passed orally among the women of Uruk (now in southern Iraq) and surviving to this day in several variants (including a Safavid Dynasty manuscript, the only written variant), from which this original has been tentatively constructed:

Long ago there was a terrible plague in the city of Uruk. Can you imagine! The dead in the streets of Uruk, attacking those who still lived. Feasting on those who were too slow. Even the animals could get this sickness: dead dogs and foxes ran through the city, biting the legs of the living. No offering to the gods could end this plague. No medicine could cure it.

All of Uruk's men were given bows and swords to fight the dead, but even this was not enough. Many were bitten. Many found that the dead would not die again no matter how many arrows sank into their chests—even the headless would still stumble, even the teeth would still try to bite them from the ground!

At this time lived three women, daughters of the king, called Kaššaya, Innin-Etirat, and Ba'u-Asitu, who all owned land in Uruk.

It is said of Kaššaya that she was wise, of Innin-Etirat that she was determined, of Ba'u-Asitu that she was bold.

During the time of the plague, each of the daughters gathered all of the women and children working for her into her main property, each well provisioned with water and grain and dates, and built sturdy defences. There they planned to wait until the plague passed, as all terrible illnesses eventually do. They sought to keep everyone from dwelling on the horrors beyond their walls: Kaššaya organized storytelling competitions, Innin-Etirat led the women and children in song, Ba'u-Asitu invented a new dance every morning.

It was Ba'u-Asitu who noticed three foxes below the walls of her home.

A dead fox, its legs shattered, unable to walk but biting out at anything that passed. Two living foxes pinned it down and ate the remnants of its flesh. You wince, but such is the nature of foxes.

Ba'u-Asitu observed that when the living foxes had torn the flesh from the dead fox, it stopped trying to bite. It lay still, a skeleton, truly dead.

Being bold, she darted from the security of her walls with two other women and with great care and stealth took one of the walking dead men from outside. They covered his head with thick cloth so that he could not bite, and secured the door once they brought him inside. Then with tools they stripped the rotting flesh from him.

The bared skeleton of the man stopped moving. The teeth lay in their sockets like needles in a pouch: sharp but unused.

Ba'u-Asitu sent letters to her sisters, to the temples and to the leaders of the soldiers, telling them of this discovery. Letters were also sent to Babylon and the other cities. From then on, the living were able to fight the dead, although it was not easy and many more died.

The flesh of the dead was immediately burnt. The stench filled the city for weeks. The bones were buried far from the cities, in tracts of desert where none lingered long. The teeth were not touched with bare hands.

Eventually the plague passed, as all terrible illnesses do.

In one oral version of this tale, Ba'u-Asitu becomes so famed for her skill at stripping the flesh from the dead that she is known as Ba'u-Asitu the Fox-Woman: an immortal figure who still hunts under an occluded moon with an army of foxes. Screams in the night are attributed to her work. The plague has never spread far again.

Letter (clay tablet) found in the property of Kaššaya:

To Kaššaya, my lady, and Innin-Etirat, my lady: your servant Šamaš-ereš. May Anu and Ishtar keep you both well!

You write: "No one in Uruk or Babylon can say whether the omens we saw before the plague have appeared before. Is there anything in the ruined cities of the north that will help us understand these omens and how to respond to them?"

Nothing I have found yet will help. I do not think that this plague ever afflicted these old cities. The fox in the well of Aššur may have been alive, signifying a different omen. The omens described on the tablets found by Innin-Etirat's servant and lost between Babylon and Uruk may have been the same. Nothing I have found suggests that they were important.

I will continue to search the ruins.

Let us hope that this plague never afflicts Babylon again!

Saying uttered by Uruk women when falling ill with any ailment, recorded on a tablet in Eanna temple:

Let the foxes of Ba'u-Asitu watch over us!

What Maisie Knew

David Liss

There was never a time when keeping Maisie in the apartment felt right to me.
It was always a bad deal, right from the get-go, but there were no good deals,
and this was the least-bad deal going. I couldn't let her stay out in the world,
knowing what she knew, blurting out what she did. It probably would have
been fine if I'd left it alone, but I could not live with such a flimsy guarantee.
It was the chance that things would not be fine that nagged at me, that kept
me awake at night, that made me jump every time the phone rang. I had a wife
I loved, and we had a child on the way. I had a *life*, and I wanted to keep it. A
person can't live like that, waiting for the other shoe to drop, and so I did the
only thing I could do—the only thing I could think of. It was the right call,
but it just so happened that it didn't turn out the way I wanted.

It should have been fine. Everything I knew about reanimates told me it
should be fine. I'd been around them almost all my life. My parents could barely
make car payments, but they rushed out to buy a Series One from General
Reanimation when they first came on the market. Kids growing up today can't
even imagine what those early models were like—buggy and twitchy, with
those ugly uniforms, like weird green tuxedos. I was only five at the time, and
the reanimate creeped the hell out of me when it would lumber into my room
to check on me at night or when it would babysit while my parents were out. I
still remember watching it shamble toward me, a TV dinner clutched hard in
its shaky hands. I wasn't phobic the way some people are. I simply didn't like
them. Dead people should remain dead. That's one of those things that always
made sense, maybe now more than ever.

So I hated going to that apartment where I kept my dead girl, which, on top
of everything else, was hard to afford and which I had to hide from my wife,
who managed most of the household finances.

I'd have rather been anywhere else—at the dentist, the DMV, a tax audit, a
prostate exam. But I was there, at the apartment. I opened the front door and

walked in, smelled the weird chemical smell that reanimates emitted, and the feeling washed over me that I had no business being there. My name was on the lease, but I felt like an intruder.

It was a crappy apartment on the cusp of the very wrong side of town, cheap, but not too dangerous. The place was a one bedroom—more space than Maisie needed, since she supposedly didn't need any space at all. She wasn't supposed to, but I always wondered. Sometime when I came to check on her, the chairs around the cheap kitchen table would look out of place. I always pushed my chairs in, but these were pulled out at odd angles or even halfway across the floor, as though advertising that they'd been moved. I supposed there was nothing wrong with her taking a seat or moving things around if that was what she wanted to do, but she wasn't *supposed* to want to do it. That's what bothered me.

When I went in that day, she was standing precisely where I last left her, her back to the far wall of the living area, her face to the door, light from the slightly parted curtains streaming over her. I watched the dust motes dance around her eyes, visible through the mask, wide and doll-like and unblinking.

Maisie was a black-market reanimate, but she wore the green-and-white uniform of a licensed General Reanimation unit, and of course she wore that matching green-and-white mask, which made her look, to my eyes, like a Mexican wrestler. Plenty of people, even people who liked having reanimates around, found the mask a bit disconcerting, but they all admitted it was better than the alternative.

No one wants to check into a hotel and discover that the reanimate bellboy is one's own dead relative. No one wants to go to a cocktail party and see a dead spouse offering a tray of shrimp pâté on ciabatta.

I hated the uniform—slick and stain resistant, made of some sort of soft plastic. It was oversized and baggy, making it almost impossible to tell that Maisie was female. I hated the full-face mask, but I had her wear it in case there was a fire or the building manager had to send in a repairman to fix something or even if there was a break-in. I didn't want anyone knowing I owned an illegal reanimate. I didn't need that kind of trouble.

I stepped into the apartment and closed the door behind me.

"Hello, Maisie. You may take off the mask if you like."

She remained motionless, as still as a mannequin.

"Maisie, please take off the mask."

With her left hand, she reached up and pulled it off but held on to it. I hadn't told her to put it anywhere, and so letting it go would not occur to her dead brain. Underneath the mask, I saw her face, pale and puffy, hanging loose from her skull, but strangely still pretty.

She had long, flowing curls of reddish blond hair, her pale blue eyes—I'm sure very arresting in life—dull and cloudy in un-death.

I came to check in on Maisie maybe once a week. I should not have to, of course. I ought to have been able to leave her alone for months, but I knew it was a good idea for reanimates to get some exercise lest they gum up. That was part of it. The other part was that I wanted to be sure she wasn't up to no good. Renanimates weren't supposed to have it in them to be up to no good, but if she hadn't been Maisie, had not acted like herself, she wouldn't be in the apartment to begin with.

"How have you been, Maisie?"

Of course there was no response. What was left of her brain couldn't process so abstract a question. That's what Ryan said, and he seemed to think he knew what he was talking about.

"Maisie, get me a beer from the refrigerator.

I could get my own beer, of course, but I needed to find excuses to make her move. I had to specify one from the refrigerator, because otherwise she might get me a warm one from the pantry or she might end up looking for a beer in the medicine cabinet.

Maisie walked off to the kitchen. I followed but only for something to do. I was always bored and uneasy when I came to the apartment. I felt strange, like I was playacting for some invisible audience, like I was a grown-up furtively trying to recapture the magic of childhood toys. Nothing I said to her or did with her felt natural. Christ, I could talk to a dog and feel less like I was talking to myself.

That's why I kept the visits so short. I would drink the beer, order her to do some light cleaning, and then get out of there.

I was thinking about how much I wanted to leave, how much I wanted to get back to my wife, when I walked into the kitchen and saw the fresh-cut flowers on the kitchen table. They were a gaudy assortment of cheap dyed daisies, but they were bright and fresh, very new. They'd been arranged carelessly, and water from the vase puddled on the table. Here's the thing: I had not put the flowers there.

No one else had a key—no one other than the apartment-complex manager or the super. Neither of them had any business in my apartment, and if they did have something important to do, they would have called first. (They had my cell-phone number, since I sure as hell didn't want my wife to know I had an apartment, let alone an apartment where I kept my black-market reanimate.) Even if they had not called first, neither the manager nor the super was about to leave a vase filled with flowers on my kitchen table.

Maisie was now closing the refrigerator and handing me a beer. She did not open the bottle, because I had not asked her to open it. That was how they worked. They did not do anything you did not ask them to do. So where had these flowers come from?

I twisted the cap off the beer and looked at Maisie, who, in the absence of orders, remained perfectly still. "Maisie, where did these flowers come from?"

She stared at me. It was a difficult question for a reanimate, I realized, even as I spoke it. Too abstract. I tried again.

"Maisie, did you put the flowers there?"

It was a yes-or-no question, and she should have been able to answer it, but she said nothing.

"Maisie, answer the question. Did you put those flowers there?" Again, silence. Dark, looming, unblinking silence. It was like demanding answers from a stuffed animal. No; our genetic, animistic impulses gave speaking to a stuffed animal a sort of logic. This was like demanding answers from a bowl of rice.

I took a long drink from my beer and sighed. This was serious.

More than serious. It wasn't just that maybe my reanimate, which wasn't supposed to want anything, somehow wanted flowers. It meant that she had somehow gotten out of the apartment, gone to the store, spent money—money she'd earned from what or stolen from whom? Had she managed to bring it with her from the Pine Box? It meant a whole spiraling vortex of Maisie chaos, and I had to know. I had to.

"Maisie," I said. "Go into the bedroom, remove your clothes, and lie on your back on the bed."

The first thing I need to make clear is that I am not a pervert. I don't have any desire to have sex with reanimates. Given the choice between sex with a reanimate or sex with a real woman, I'll take the real woman every time. Hell, given the choice between sex with a reanimate and no sex, I'd go without sex—at least for a good long while. Like S&M or rubber fetishes or whatever, if you're not into it naturally, it's hard to fake the enthusiasm. If you meet some amazingly hot woman, and she says, "Sure, let's have sex, only I want to tie you up and stick needles in your dick," you're probably going to, with however much regret, take a rain check. Unless you like that sort of thing. Plenty of guys like sex with reanimates. They prefer them to real women. It floats their boat. It does not float mine.

That said, I should point out that in most ways it's kind of like sex with anyone else. It has some unique qualities but also lacks some things that make sex with a living woman enjoyable—for example, that unique sensation of having sex with someone you know is alive.

So, if you are looking at it objectively, it's a trade-off. That day, I looked at it objectively. I didn't want to have sex with her. I wanted to have sex with my wife and no one else. I *liked* sex with my wife. Sure, I would look at an attractive woman when I saw one on the street, but I wasn't about to make any moves. There had been some parties, some business trips, where I'd felt opportunities opening, but I never pursued them. I was in love with Tori. I was happy and I didn't need complications and problems and guilt and lies.

If you are like most people, there are probably a lot of things you don't know about reanimates. Ryan says you are happier that way.

He says the less you have to think about what they are, the easier it is to ignore them, to enjoy the convenience. Ryan says you probably don't know much about their history, for example, because there's no percentage in knowing the history. You also probably don't know much about their nature, and that's a whole other thing. There's a percentage in that one for you. The key thing that I'm getting at is that reanimates have a greater clarity of thought when their feelings are intensified. You can tease out this clarity either with pain or with sex—at least with the females. I'm told it is impossible for the males to have sex, not unless the penis is artificially inflated. There are rumors of male reanimate sex slaves with permanent, surgically crafted boners, but I'm not entirely sure this is true.

Reanimates are totally different creatures during sex. This is a big part of why guys who like to sleep with them get off on it. Also, probably because they are willing and compliant sex slaves whose needs and preferences can be handily dismissed. Then again, some guys just dig the fact that they're dead. But for most of the true enthusiasts, the main thing is that reanimates are hungry for it. They start to feel things, they start to remember themselves, and they—well, I hate to be crass, but the bottom line is that they fuck hungry and hard, and some guys just love it. Not me. It made me feel unclean, like I'd been exposed to something vile and rotting. Even now I don't like thinking about it in too much detail, and the less I say about the particulars, the better.

Adulthood, however, means doing things you don't want to do. So I had sex with Maisie. As soon as I slid into her, it was like a switch flipped inside her soul. She was something else, something vibrant and powerful something that felt not alive but rather *live*, like a storm of a mass of building electricity. That was how she'd been when I'd had sex with her at the Pine Box. She groaned and moaned and murmured. She thrust her hips up at me with a shocking, awkward violence. I didn't want to be there any longer than I had to, so I waited until she seemed good and worked up, and then I asked, "Maisie, did you get those flowers?"

"Fuck off, you asshole."

I guess saying that she surprised me is an understatement. I leaped off of her in astonishment and fear, and I lost shall we say my will to continue. She, in turn, fell back on the bed like a puppet with her strings cut. Just like that, she faded back to her normal, stupefied, lifeless self—still and naked and slightly bloated, not breathing hard like I was, since reanimates did not respirate looking at nothing, and thinking, I was sure, about nothing.

I began to gather up my clothes. "Maisie, get dressed," I said, "and come sit at the kitchen table."

She complied.

I am a nice guy. I like children and animals. I don't especially like violent movies, so what came next wasn't something I enjoyed. It wasn't something that came naturally to me. It was, however, something I had to do. I thought it over. I looked at all sides of it and tried to find another way, but it just wasn't there.

When Maisie sat at the kitchen table, I told her to place her right arm on the table, on top of a thick bathroom towel. Then I asked her to roll up the sleeve of her uniform. With the puffy, pale flesh of her forearm exposed, I grabbed her wrist in one hand and, with the other, thrust a sharp kitchen knife into her arm, just below the elbow.

I've never stabbed a living person, but I'm pretty sure it feels different. Her flesh offered almost no resistance. It was like stabbing wet dough. I felt the knife nick the bone, but it kept going, all the way through, and I felt the tip of the blade make contact with the towel.

Ryan says that pain works as well as sex, but sex, troubling though it is, bothers me less than torture. Anyone who might begin to think that I was a bad person should keep that in mind. I went for pain only when I had no choice.

Maisie did not scream. She did not stand or pull away or fight.

Instead, she looked at me and winced. "You asshole motherfucker."

"Maisie, did you put those flowers there? How did you get them? How did you pay for them?"

Her eyes were now wide and moist, almost clear, almost like a living woman's. The lids fluttered in something like a blink. Her mouth was slightly open, and her usually gray lips were taking on some color.

"Fuck you, Walter," she said without much inflection.

I twisted the knife in the wound. I could feel the flesh pulling and tearing, twisting along with the knife. "Maisie, how did you do it? How did you get the flowers?"

She let out a cry of pain, and then gritted her teeth together in a sick smile. "The more you fuck me, the more you torture me, the more I can think, and all I think about is giving you what you deserve. And it doesn't all go away. Each time I get a little stronger." I yanked out the knife.

Eight months earlier, I was a different man. I was, at least, not a man who could have imagined he would someday soon be torturing his illegal reanimate just after having sex with her, but life throws you curveballs. That's for sure.

Things were pretty good, and they were getting better. I was married to a woman more wonderful and clever and creative than I ever thought would look twice at me. I swear I'd fallen in love with Tori the first time I saw her at a birthday party for a mutual friend, and I could never quite believe my good fortune that she'd fallen for me.

Tori was a cellist with the local symphony. How's that for cool? She was not, perhaps, the most accomplished musician in the world, which was fine by me. I did not want her perpetually on the road, receiving accolades wherever she went, being adored by men far wealthier, better looking, and more intelligent than I. She'd long since given up on dreams of cello stardom and was now happy to be able to make a living doing something she loved. And Tori was pregnant. We'd only just found out, and it was too early to tell anyone, but we were both excited. I was apprehensive too. I think most men are more uneasy about their first child than they like to admit, but I also thought it would be an adventure. It would be an adventure I went through with Tori, and surely that was good enough for me.

Work was another matter. It was okay, but nothing great. I was an account manager at a fairly large advertising agency, one that dealt exclusively with local businesses. There was nothing creative or even challenging about my job, and the pay was no better than decent.

Mostly I tried to get new clients and tried to keep the clients we had happy. It was a grind, trying to convince people to keep spending money on sucky radio advertising they probably didn't need. Most of my coworkers were okay, the atmosphere was congenial enough.

My boss was a dick if my numbers slackened, but he stayed off my case if I hit my targets. Mostly I hit my targets, and that was all right.

The job paid the bills, so we could get good credit and, consequently, live way beyond our means, just like everyone else. We'd bought a house we could hardly afford, and we had two SUVs that together retailed for about half as much as the house. We usually paid our monthly balance on our credit cards, and if we didn't, we got to it soon enough.

It all changed on a Saturday night. It was the random bullshit of the universe. One of the guys at my office, Joe, was having a bachelor party. He was one of those guys I couldn't stand: He had belonged to a fraternity, called everyone "dude," lived for football season and to tell dirty jokes. I don't think he really wanted me there or at his party, but he'd ended up inviting me, and I'd ended up going. Frankly, I had no desire to drop a bunch of money to get him drunk, but it would have been bad office politics to say no.

It started out in a bar and inevitably moved on to a strip club. We went through the obligatory bullshit of lap dances and stuffing G-strings with bills and drinking too many expensive drinks. I guess it was an okay time, but nothing I couldn't have done without.

Hanging out with Joe and his knuckleheaded friends at a strip club or spending an evening in front of the TV with Tori I'd have taken the night at home in a heartbeat.

Ryan was one of the guys there. I'd never met him before, and I couldn't imagine I would want to meet him again. He was tall and wore his blondish hair a little too long to look rakishly long, I guess—and had the body of a guy who spends too much time in the gym. He'd grown up with Joe, and the two of them were pretty tight.

He was the one that suggested we go to the Pine Box. He said he knew a place that was just *insane*. We wouldn't believe how *insane* it was. We had to check out this *insanity*.

It was a bachelor party, so we were drunk and tired and disoriented from an hour and a half in close proximity to tits. We were all, in other words, out of our right minds, and no one had the will to resist. We drunkenly piled into our car and followed Ryan to his insane place about three amazingly cop-less miles away.

The Pine Box had no markings outside to indicate it was anything, let alone a club. It looked like a warehouse. We parked in the strip mall parking lot across the street Ryan said we had to and then crossed over to the unlit building. Ryan knocked on the door, and when it opened, he spoke in quiet tones to the bouncer. Then we were in.

None of us knew what we were getting into, and in all likelihood, none of us would have agreed if we had, but we were now fired by the spirit of adventure, and so we went into the warehouse, which had been turned into a makeshift club. There were flashing red lights and pounding electronic music and the smell of beer in plastic cups.

Tables had been set up all around a trio of ugly, slapped-together stages, and atop them danced strippers. Reanimate strippers.

"Dude, no way!" Joe cried drunkenly but not without pleasure.

"This shit is sick." Even while he complained, he forced his way deeper into the crowd. Had anyone else spoken first, had anyone objected, we might have all left. But Joe was in, and so we all were.

He found a large table and sat himself down and called over to a waitress. You could tell he was loving it—the pulsing music, the lights, the smell of beer spilled on the concrete floor.

The waitress, I saw after a few seconds, was a reanimate—not as pretty as the strippers but wearing a skimpy cocktail dress and no mask. Somehow I hadn't noticed that the strippers weren't wearing masks, because they were wearing nothing, but this waitress, with its brittle blond hair and dead, puffy face exposed, seemed to me inexpressibly grotesque. It had not been terribly old when it died, but it had been fat. Now it moved in a slow, lumbering gait, like a mummy from an old horror movie. It took our order and served our drinks without eagerness or error.

The music was loud, but not so loud that you couldn't talk, and I had the feeling that was important. People came here to look, but also to make contact with each other. They were reanimate fetishists.

I'd never heard of them or knew they existed before that night, but as Ryan told us about his friends, about his Internet groups, about the other underground places in town, I became aware of this entire subculture. There were guys out there who were just into reanimates. Go figure.

Joe seemed drunkenly amused, but Ryan was in heaven. He went up to the stage and put money in their G-strings. He paid for a blocky, jerky reanimate lap dance. He had reanimates shake their reanimated tits in his face.

I thought he was the biggest asshole I'd ever met, and I thought the Pine Box was disgusting. I hated looking at the pale, bloated, strangely rubbery bodies. Even the ones who had been beautiful at the time of death were grotesque now, and many of them bore the scars of the injuries that had taken their lives. One was a patchwork of gashes and rips. One of them, perhaps the one who had been most beautiful in life, had vicious red X-marks on its wrists. It was monstrous and disrespectful and wrong beyond my ability to articulate. I'd never liked dead things, and I knew full well that we only tolerated reanimates because they were hidden behind masks and uniforms that allowed us to forget what they really were.

Ryan saw my mood and tried to get me into the spirit of things.

He offered to buy me a lap dance, but I was a bad sport. I wasn't having fun, and I wasn't going to pretend to have fun.

I stared into space and tried not to look at the dancers, though once in a while I would sneak a look just to make sure it was as bad as I thought. It was. But then, out of the corner of my eye, I saw one of the dancers stop. It caused a little commotion, and so I turned to it. A dancer stood on the edge of the stage, its arms slack by its side, slouching and staring out into the audience. Staring, I saw, at me. At least I thought it was me. Its left hand was weirdly angled, and it took a few seconds for me to notice that it was pushing its long fingernails into the soft skin of its palm. Dark and watery reanimate blood dripped onto the stage. A couple of men in jeans and T-shirts came up to it, shouting orders and gesturing violently, but it remained still, its dead, pale eyes locked on mine.

And then I knew it—I knew *her*, knew who she was or who she had been. It was Maisie Harper. Knowing that felt like falling, felt like a plummet toward my doom. I remembered that face, and, more horribly, she remembered mine. She had taken her secret to the grave, but then she had left the grave and brought the secret with her. She stared, and her eyes locked with mine, and I could not turn away.

And then she opened her mouth and said one word. Even from a distance I could see what she said: "You." That's when I knew I was in trouble. It was when I knew things would never again be the same.

In the apartment kitchen, I sat staring at that weird, unclotting reanimate black blood drying on the towel. Some of the drops had gotten onto my pants. After I'd stabbed her and Maisie had openly defied me, I'd wrapped up her arm and told her I was done with her.

She had gone to stand in the living area, in that spot where she seemed most contented—or whatever passed for contentment with reanimates. Ryan said they couldn't process much information. They had very low brain activity, and their ability to feel or experience from moment to moment was very limited.

That was what Ryan said, but I was beginning to get the feeling that Ryan might not know precisely what the fuck he was talking about.

I cleaned up as best I could and went home. It was a Saturday afternoon, and Tori had been out shopping for baby things with a friend, spending more than we could probably afford, which might once have bothered me, but now I had other things on my mind.

She'd been long home by the time I got there, and she wanted to know where I'd been. She stood there, still strangely thin despite her advanced pregnancy, looking like a toothpick that had swallowed a grape. She wanted to know what I'd been doing to get blood all over my jeans. I was too uneasy even to lie to her, and so I got angry. I hated to get angry with her, but I was frustrated. I might have told her to fuck off. I was not patient, that much is certain. There was some screaming and crying. She accused me of being insensitive, and I told her she was being irrational because she was pregnant and hormonal. As a rule, pregnant women don't respond well to that sort of thing.

The bottom line is that we didn't usually fight like that. I didn't usually speak to her that way, and it left her confused and angry.

Sunday was no better, and Monday at work was a disaster. I hadn't been sleeping well, and when a client called in with a complaint, I probably wasn't as sympathetic or attentive as is appropriate for a competitive industry like advertising. There was an argument with my boss, who acted like a total asshole, even though he was probably right in this case. Things were falling apart, and I was going to have to figure out what I could do to put them back together.

The Pine Box had a website with a password. You got the password for the site at the club, and you got the password for the club at the site. The passwords changed every two weeks or so. It was a clever system designed both to keep the circle of information tight and to insure that regulars kept coming back.

I became a regular. I kept coming back. I had to know just how much Maisie could recall.

Almost every time I went I saw Ryan. It wasn't like we were friends or anything, because I couldn't stand him and thought he was a dick, but he didn't have to know that. Truth was, I needed him or someone like him to guide me though this fucked-up world, and if buying him a few drinks and pretending to laugh at his jokes was what I had to do, then I was willing to take my lumps.

He was into reanimates. That much was probably obvious, but he was into them not just in some weird sexual way. It was the whole package, and he was into them the way some guys are into Hitler or the Civil War. He loved the information most people didn't want. He read books and blogs and articles in scholarly journals. He liked facts and dates and statistics and hidden histories.

We would sit at the bar with nearly naked dead women dancing around us, and Ryan would go on and on about reanimate history.

Some of it was stuff I already knew, and other things I'd never heard before.

"Were you old enough to remember when they first began to capture pictures of the soul leaving the body?" he asked me. "You're a few years younger than me, I guess. I was six. It was amazing." I was too young to remember it, but we'd all seen the pictures, watched documentaries on late-night television. The first pictures were taken by an MIT grad student whose grandfather was dying, and he set up his modified camera in the hospital room. When the pictures first came out, everyone thought it was a hoax, but then they found the process could be repeated every time. Suddenly people knew the soul was a real thing and that it left the body upon death.

It changed the way we thought about life, the afterlife, dead bodies—the whole deal. In some way, it changed the nature of humanity. Our mortality defined us, but with that mortality seriously in question, no one was really sure what we were anymore.

"It was all a crock of shit, anyhow," Ryan was saying. "No one knew where the soul went, did they? It could just go up to the clouds and disappear or turn into rain or whatever. Maybe everyone goes on to eternal suffering more horrible than anything we can imagine.

"No way to tell, but all those assholes imagined they had angels and harps and heavenly choirs sewn up, and that's what opened the door for all this. Soul photography was in 1973, and by 1975 the first-generation reanimates began appearing on the market."

"I always wondered about that," I said. "It only took them two years to figure out how to turn dead people into product."

"That's because they already knew. Here's what they don't teach you in Sunday School: The technique was actually developed by the Nazis during World War II. They were plotting some huge offensive in which they would overwhelm the Allies with an army of the dead, but fortunately the war ended before they had a chance. Americans had the secret for years but knew they could never do anything with it, that the public would flip out. But after the soul photography began, they saw an opening. Christ, do you have any idea how much money the government has made by licensing the procedure? And then there are all the regulations, you know?"

"The regulations," I echoed. "What was that, like the Alabama Accord or something?"

"The Atlanta Convention—a big meeting between industry and government to set the ground rules. When you buy a reanimate from one of the Big Three, they'll warn you never to remove the mask, that it messes up the preservative process, and I think just about everyone obeys. No one wants their reanimate to fall apart on them. And then there are the quarterly servicings. If you miss even one of them, your reanimate becomes unlicensed and can be confiscated by the cops." Ryan was also very interested in where the reanimates come from.

"They pay you, like, what? Seven or eight thousand to sign up, but not a whole lot of people in this country are willing to sell their bodies for eternal slavery, so most of the reanimates come from Africa or Asia. I always thought that was one of the reasons for the masks and the uniforms. I think a lot of white Americans might be more uncomfortable if they had to stare into a black reanimate face. More zombie-ish, I guess."

"So where do these come from?" I asked. Most of the strippers at the club were young white women.

Ryan shrugged. "Some are from Eastern Europe, though those are hard to get because you need ones that spoke English when they were alive. Still, you have any idea how many poor assholes in Latvia are trying to learn English just so they can sell their bodies? But the Americans? They're drug addicts, people with terminal diseases who want something for their families, whatever. A lot of them sell their bodies on the black market. They get less, but there are no taxes. Some young hottie gets pregnant and can't afford an abortion? Maybe she hocks her body, hoping to buy it back. That's the teaser, you know.

"You can always buy it back. How many reanimates out there do you think were convinced they could get their bodies out of hock before they died? Even the black-market dealers let you do it, because they know people can convince themselves that they'll be able to redeem their bodies. Almost no one ever does."

I wondered if that was what happened to Maisie Harper—some crisis she couldn't tell her parents about, so she pawned her body, sure she would have time to buy it back.

"Bunch of morons," Ryan said. "Convince yourself of anything. It's crazy to think that because some chick believed she would always have more time, you can walk in here and just fucking buy her like you would buy a loaf of bread."

Until that moment, I'd had no idea you could buy a reanimate from the
Pine Box. This changed everything. "You mean I could—a person could—buy
one of these girls?"

"You thinking about it? Be hard to explain to your wife, but yeah. I mean,
it's not like a showroom. You can't just point and say, 'I'll take that one,' but
they are sometimes willing to sell if they have extra or if one of them isn't
working out." He now waved his fingers at Maisie. "Like that one. I guess
you've thought about it."

I turned to him. "What do you mean?"

He grinned. "Oh, I don't know. It seems to have a particular interest in you,
and you in it. I've fucked it, you know." He grinned at me again. "It's good
stuff. I bet you they would let it go cheap. I mean, if you wanted a messed-up
reanimate, that is."

I felt as though I were floating outside my body. Was Ryan hinting that he
knew about me and Maisie? How was such a thing possible? But if he did, so
what? We were brothers in sick, fucked-up, reanimate enthusiasm, weren't we?
And even more importantly, he raised this new thought: They sold reanimates
here.

Buying Maisie. It seemed too good to be true. It seemed like all the stars were
lining up to make my life easy, or at least to give me an out from unbearable
complications. They sold the reanimates, and they might be willing to sell
Maisie in particular.

Ryan must have noticed how thoughtful I looked. He laughed.

"Before you do something rash like buy, you might want to sample the
goods."

"Sample the goods?"

He nodded. "It's only a hundred dollars. They have rooms in the back, and
you get a full hour. You can pick any girl you want. If she's on the stage, she's
available, but if you are thinking of buying that one, you should check her out
first."

I looked over at Maisie. She was dancing around a pole very slowly, and
she was looking at me. The idea of having sex with her, with any of them, was
utterly repulsive to me. "No way," I said.

"Don't knock it. If you've never had sex with a reanimate, you have no idea
what you are missing. They *love* it, man. You wouldn't believe how into it they
are. It's like they feel alive when they're doing it. They talk, almost like normal
people. Sex and pain do that." "How do you know about pain?" I asked.

He shrugged. "Different guys have different interests. You meet all sorts of reanimate enthusiasts here. Some are into sex, some are into . . . crazy things."

I was already dismissing this. If people wanted to torture the dead, that was their own business. I was thinking about Maisie and sex. I was thinking about what Ryan had said, that they seemed more human during sex, and they spoke. That meant that Maisie could be telling anyone anything. I really didn't want to try it myself, but I had to know.

I paid my hundred dollars to Yiorgio, one of the Pine Box's owners.

He was a good-looking Greek guy with long hair in a ponytail and a linebacker's physique. He looked like someone who would be curt and dismissive, but he was actually very friendly. He spoke with a heavy accent, but he was very gregarious and casual, like paying to have sex with a reanimate was no big deal. He made his customers feel at home, which I supposed made him a good businessman.

The thing with Maisie was awkward. Wearing nothing but a G-string, she came over to stand in front of us. "You want to go with Mr. Walter Molson?" Yiorgio asked her. "He is true gentleman." I winced when he spoke my name. I didn't want her to know it.

She recognized my face, but until that moment, I don't see how she could have known my name. She did not react, and I hoped that maybe the information was lost on her dead brain.

She followed me to the room Yiorgio had given us. I was expecting something unspeakably seedy—a dusty room with cinder-block walls and a stained mattress on the floor—but the space was actually very neat and pleasant, with a bed and some chairs. The room was well lit, the walls newly wallpapered and with paintings of landscapes and fruit and the kind of bland things you see in hotel rooms. The bed looked freshly made. Yiorgio was clearly a class act.

I closed the door, and Maisie stood there looking at me, not blinking. Yiorgio had told me that whenever I spoke to her, I needed to begin the command with her name or she might not listen. I said, "Maisie, sit down on the bed."

She sat.

There I was in that small room with Maisie. She sat on the side of the bed, her face empty and her eyes as unblinking as a doll's. She was all but naked, but totally oblivious. She'd been beautiful when she was alive, I knew, and she was still beautiful in death if you liked that sort of thing. But even though I felt the surprising heat of her proximity, I had no intention of having sex with her—with it. She was a dead thing, a corpse made active by some mysterious mad science, and that did not get me all worked up. Plus there was the guilt, I didn't want to be the sort of person who would both kill a woman and then fuck her dead body. That wasn't how I saw myself.

"Maisie," I said. "Do you know who I am?"

She did not react.

"Maisie, do you remember ever seeing me before?" Again, nothing. It was better than getting an answer, but it didn't put my fears to rest. Ryan said it all came out during sex, and I knew I was procrastinating. I was looking for some other way to find out what I wanted to know, but I didn't see it. Taking in a long, deep breath, I told her to take off her G-string and lie on the bed. She did that.

I took off my clothes. I'd been afraid I was not going to be able to perform, but I think her nudity and mine were enough to get things going. Her body was strangely warm, almost hot, but it didn't feel like body heat. It was more like there was a chemical reaction happening just below her skin. And the texture was all wrong. It didn't feel like skin, and her flesh didn't feel like flesh. Lying on top of her felt like lying on top of a water balloon. I didn't want to lick or suck or bite or even run my hands over her. I just wanted to do what I had to do and see what happened.

It was like Ryan had said: She was into it. Really into it. She bucked wildly, grabbed onto me, she grunted, groaned, and murmured. And in the middle, she began to speak. "God damn it," she said, "you killed me. I'm fucking you, and you killed me. Walter Molson, you killed me."

I pushed myself off her and staggered backward to the wall. It was worse than I thought. Far worse. By arranging to have sex with her, by putting her in a position where she could learn my name, I had made it worse. I was going to have to do something about this, and I was going to have to do it soon.

The real beginning of the story was two years before all this. Tori's sister was going through a bad patch with her husband, was maybe thinking of getting divorced, and Tori wanted to go out to California to be with her for a few days. We hadn't been married all that long, and this was going to be my first time alone in the new house. I loved my wife, and I loved living with her, but I was also excited for the solitude, which I missed sometimes. You get to thinking about it and you realize you can't remember the last time you spent more than an hour or two without someone else around.

The first night she was gone I was exhausted from work, and basically fell asleep right away. The second night, a Saturday, was something else. I thought about calling up a couple of friends and going out, but somehow it seemed a waste of an empty house to leave it. I was in it for the quiet, for the privacy, and I didn't want to waste it with socializing. I ordered a pizza, turned on a baseball game, and prepared to enjoy a night of not picking up after myself, of leaving the pizza box on the coffee table until morning.

I took out my bottle of Old Charter, and I swear I only planned to do one shot. Two at the most. I wasn't interested in getting drunk, and I was sure that drinking too much would put me right to sleep.

But somehow I didn't stop. The game on TV was exciting, and one shot followed the next with an unremarked ferocity. Come eleven o'clock, I was good and drunk.

Come one o'clock, it seemed to me like a crime against humanity that there was no ice cream in the house, like the UN Office on Desserts was going to come gunning for me if I didn't take care of things.

I understood that I was drunk, very drunk, and that driving under those conditions was somewhere between ill advised and fucking moronic. I also understood that there was a convenience store not half a mile from my house. A straight shot out of my driveway, past four stop signs, and there you are. No need even to turn the wheel. I might have walked. The air would have done me good, but since the idea didn't occur to me, it saved me the trouble of deciding I was too lazy to walk. Something else never occurred to me—turning on my headlights.

That was bad enough, but running that second stop sign was worse. I wasn't fiddling with the radio or distracted by anything. I just didn't see it, and I didn't remember it. With no headlights to reflect against it, the sign was invisible. I had a vague sense that I ought to be slowing down somewhere around there, which was when I felt my car hit something. Sometime thereafter, I knew I had to stop, and after spending a little bit of time trying to find the brake pedal, I did in fact stop. I was a drunk moron, no doubt about it, and I realized I ought to have turned on my headlights before, but I knew enough not to turn on my headlights now.

I grabbed the emergency flashlight from the glove compartment, spent a little while trying to remember how to turn it on, but soon enough everything was under control. I got out of the car and stumbled the hundred or so feet since I hit the thing. My worst fear, I swear it, was that I had hit a garbage can, maybe a dog or cat, but when I approached the stop sign I saw her lying on the side of the road, her eyes open, blood pooling out of her mouth. There was a terrible rattling in her breath, and her upper body twitched violently.

And then I saw the damage to her skull. I saw blood and hair and exposed brain. She raised one limp hand in my direction and parted her lips as if to speak. I looked away.

You never know who you are until you are tested. I'd always thought of myself as the guy who does the right thing, but it turned out I wasn't that guy at all. In that moment I understood that I was drunk, I'd been driving without headlights, and this girl was going to die. I could see her brain, and I could hear her death rattle. Nothing I was going to do could save her, and that was a good thing too, because if I'd thought I could save her, I can't say for sure I would have. Even so, I ought to have called 911—I had my cell phone on me—but if I had, my life would have been over. I would have been looking at jail and disgrace. Everything I was and wanted to be would have been done.

All around me it was dark. No lights were on. No dogs barked.

No one knew I was there. In an instant both clear and decisive, I got back into the car, turned around, drove past the girl I had broken, and managed to navigate my way into the garage. Amazingly, I could find no sign of damage on the car. I was drunk as hell, and I knew it, which meant I could not trust my judgment, but to my foggy eyes, everything looked good. So with nothing else to think about, I went upstairs, got undressed, made a vague gesture toward brushing my teeth, and went to bed.

In the morning, hungover and panicked, I went out and looked at my car. Nothing. No blood, no scratches, no dents. To be certain, I took my car to an automated car wash. Then I began to relax.

The murder, as they called it, of Maisie Harper was a big story for about a day, but then there was that category-4 hurricane that started heading our way, and no one much cared about Maisie Harper anymore. The hurricane missed us, but it hit about two hundred miles north of here, and that generated enough media attention to keep Maisie's name, if not her body, pretty well buried.

Of course, the cops kept working it, and the story made the paper, though only small stories in the back. At first they had no clue who would kill the twenty-one-year-old college student, home for the summer, out for a late-night stroll because she could not sleep. Then the police began to suspect it was her boyfriend. They arrested him, and it looked like I'd caught a break and this guy would take the fall. I cheered the cops on. I didn't bother to think that he hadn't done it, that he was mourning for this girl he possibly loved and very probably liked. All I could think about was that if they nailed him, I could exhale. But they didn't nail him. They let him go, and they made some noise about pursuing more leads. Every day I would look out the window expecting to see cop cars pulling up, waiting to cart me off in shame. The cars never came. They never suspected me, never came to talk to me. There were no witnesses. No one had seen or heard a thing, and eventually the story blew over. In the process, I learned a very important thing about myself. I could do something terrible and live with it, and when the going got tough, I could keep my cool.

When I was done with my hour, I went to see Yiorgio in his office behind the stages.

"You had good time, my friend?"

"I'd like to buy her," I said.

He laughed. "You did have good time. Ryan, he tells me you have never before been with reanimate girl, yes? Maybe you should try some others before you are so sure."

"I don't want to try others. I like that one. How much?"

"You've been good customer, so I don't want trick you. Maisie is difficult girl. She does not always listen. She becomes maybe a problem for you, and I do not want that you come back and tell me you no longer like so difficult a girl. You maybe tell me you want your money back."

"It won't happen," I said. "No returns. I understand the rules going in."

He shrugged. "So long as you understand. Let me tell you something, though. The reanimates, we give them whatever name we want. This one come, she tell us her name. Would not listen to any other name. Very willful."

I nodded. All of this was making me even more convinced I had to get her out of circulation. She knew who she was. She knew who I was. I didn't know if a reanimate's testimony had any legal standing, but I didn't want to find out.

"I want to buy her," I said.

"Okay, my friend. You are very determined, yes? You may buy her for eight thousand dollars. I hope you know this is cash, and all up front. But it includes lifetime servicing."

Eight thousand dollars was a good price. An economy reanimate from one of the Big Three would cost at least fifteen thousand dollars. Even so, I did not know how I was going to get that kind of money. We had no real savings, no more than a fifteen-hundred dollar cushion at any given time. But I had some ideas.

"I'll get you the money," I said. "Soon. Don't sell her to anyone else until I do."

"Who am I to break up true love?" Yiorgio asked.

I blundered my way back to my chair. I hardly noticed Ryan was still sitting there until he started to punch my arm and ask me how I'd liked it.

He was joined by another guy now, a regular named Charlie—older and almost entirely bald but for a strip of white hair and a very white goatee. He was well dressed and spoke very deliberately. He spoke like a rich man.

"This is Walter," Ryan told Charlie. "He and Maisie have that thing."

I was not about to ask what he meant. Better to just be cool, be one of the guys.

We sat around and talked and drank, and then finally, Charlie turned to me. "I'm having a party at my house tomorrow night. Ryan knows about it, but I think it's time you joined our circle. It's the sort of thing a hobbyist like you shouldn't miss."

I was going to have a hard time explaining to Tori where I was going without her. She was about five months pregnant now, starting to show in earnest—not as big as she was going to get, but still new enough to being big to be sensitive about it. You try telling your pregnant wife not to get all worked up about it. You try telling her that she desperately wanted to be pregnant, and now she *was* pregnant, so maybe she should stop complaining about it. Dealing with a touchy pregnant woman who is self-conscious about her appearance makes negotiating with North Korea seem like a pretty sweet deal. There was something about the way Ryan and Charlie spoke that told me that if I skipped the party, they wouldn't quite trust me, wouldn't quite consider me one of them. I didn't know what Ryan might already suspect about me and Maisie, and I didn't want to give him any reason to worry about me.

Tori was furious with me, of course. I was always going out, she said. I was being secretive, she said. I was one of those asshole husbands who cheats on his pregnant wife because she is now fat and ugly. Of course I told her I had never touched another woman, but she didn't believe me, which bothered me. I ended up leaving for Charlie's party with her shouts ringing in my ears and the thin satisfaction of slamming the door.

Charlie lived in a verdant old neighborhood, and his house was massive to the point of being intimidating, probably five thousand square feet and gloriously appointed. Ryan was there, and I recognized quite a few people from the Pine Box, but even so, it was hard at first to shake off the feeling that everyone was judging me for my creepy interests. I drank too much beer too fast, but that made me sociable, and that made things easy. The beer was served by unmasked reanimates in tuxedos. All of them, I soon learned, were black market. And that began to put me at ease. Charlie had illegal reanimates. Why shouldn't I have one?

The party had gone on for a couple of hours, and it seemed like just a regular party to me—people talking and eating, taking hors d'oeuvres from trays. Ryan had promised something wild, but I began to think I was missing something. Then, at about ten at night, we all went outside to the fenced-in, private yard. The mood changed at once. It was tense and charged, full of an almost sexual expectation.

Everyone spoke in low whispers. A couple of men even giggled nervously. I asked them what was going to happen, but they wouldn't tell me. "Better to be surprised," one said, and then his friend gave him a high five.

There was a big sheet of heavy plastic set out in the middle of the backyard, and Charlie ordered one of his reanimate servants to go stand on it. The thing lumbered onto the plastic and stopped. Charlie told him to turn to face the crowd, and it did so. It looked like it had died when it was in its forties or so. It was a slightly heavyset white man with thinning reddish hair and sad gray eyes.

Charlie turned to his guests.

"Hey, guys," he said, "this is Johnny Boy."

"Hi, Johnny Boy!" the crowd shouted.

"Johnny Boy has been a little slow to obey orders lately," Charlie said. "He's not disobedient, but he's getting a little old."

"Awww!" cried Charlie's guests.

"What do you think? Should we retire him?"

Charlie's guests cheered.

Charlie turned to the animate. "Johnny Boy, would you be so good as to remove your clothes for us?"

With the fumbling and mechanical efficiency of its kind, Johnny Boy began to remove its clothes. Perhaps out of habit or training, it folded each piece of clothing, and it left them piled on the plastic sheet. When it was done, it turned back to us, entirely naked. Johnny Boy looked like it'd been killed in some sort of accident: Its torso was all messed up, not exactly scarred, but exposed and purpled in places. Its belly was distended, its flesh swollen, its penis and testicles so shriveled as to be almost invisible. Charlie's guests raised their drinks and toasted it.

"Johnny Boy," Charlie cried, "be so good as to hold out your arms."

Johnny Boy held out its arms.

Now another reanimate arrived with what looked like an old stained butcher's apron, which he handed to Charlie. After putting it on, Charlie lifted an ax he'd clearly had nearby, though I had not seen it until this moment.

Charlie turned to the crowd, brandishing the ax. "You boys ready to send Johnny Boy off in style?"

The guests made it known that they were ready. I took a step back.

I understood now what was happening, the weird grotesqueness of it all. What did it mean? Was it a crime? Was it even cruel? I didn't know, but I didn't *want* to know, I didn't want to see. Yet I knew it would be a mistake to leave or even to show my feelings, to make these guys feel like I thought I was better than they were—which I did, by the way. I stood there and made myself watch.

Charlie, after taking a moment to flash a wolfish grin at his guests, brought the ax up and then swung it down on one of Johnny Boy's outstretched arms. The limb tumbled down to the plastic sheet, continuing to move, and the stump remained outstretched, oozing a slow and steady flow of black, watery liquid. Johnny Boy began to scream.

It did not move its legs. It barely moved its head, but it screamed and shrieked and wailed. The guests cheered. People hooted and clapped and drank to its suffering.

"My brakes!" Johnny Boy cried out. "Oh, my god, the truck, the fucking truck!"

The crowd cheered again.

Charlie handed the ax to Ryan, and he cut off the other arm in a quick, clean stroke. Johnny Boy still screamed, sometimes just noise, sometimes about the impending head-on collision with the truck. Its stumps continued to produce their black blood, like a kitchen faucet left running just a little. Then the ax was handed to another friend, and he cut off one leg. The body tumbled over, but this didn't slow the screaming. It seemed not to know or care what was happening now, but the past, its death, was vivid and real and immediate. The crowd loved it.

I stood there feeling nauseated and horrified while the last leg was cut off and the crowd gathered around to laugh and point and cheer on the dismembered torso. I could not have held my breath all that time, but if anyone had asked, I would have sworn I didn't breathe between the time they started hacking up the reanimate until the time they finally put the pieces on the fire and burned them into stillness and silence.

The party began to clear out after that, but it was still too early and I was too shaken to go home. I wanted to make sure Tori was asleep when I got there, so I wouldn't have to deal with her. I went to a bar and drank too much, but I'd learned my lesson. Even though I now drove a car with headlights that went on automatically, I still checked them before driving home at almost 1:00 a.m.

The lights were out, so I thought I was safe, but when I walked through the door, she was waiting for me, sitting in the dark.

"What is going on, Walter?"

"I don't know what you mean," I said. "I wanted to hang out with some friends. Christ, you are the only wife in America that doesn't want to let her husband out of the house once in a while."

"You got a call while you were out," she said.

"A call! Oh, my God, a fucking call! No wonder you are so upset." I stumbled past her.

"I don't know who it was. It was a woman. She sounded, I don't know, retarded or something. I think she was saying your name, but I couldn't understand the rest."

"Jesus Christ, Tori," I shouted. "A wrong number? You are giving me shit about a wrong number? Have you lost your mind?" I stormed upstairs, and she didn't follow. After fifteen or twenty minutes, I figured she was going to sleep on the couch. Just as well. It gave me time to figure out what the hell I was doing to do with Maisie, who was now calling my house. She must have done it during sex or right after sex or while stabbing herself or something. The point was that someone might have seen her do it. This someone might not have understood this time, but what about the next time or the one after?

Two days later I went to the Pine Box and paid for Maisie. I brought her over to the apartment, and I left her there. Everything was fine for about two months. Then it fell apart.

After the incident with the flowers, I decided I needed to visit more regularly. The next time I went over, she had newer flowers, and on the mantel she'd placed a goldfish bowl with two fish. There was a little tube of fish food next to it. Maisie herself was still and lifeless, as she usually was when I walked in.

"Maisie," I said, "do you want something? Do you need something? Is there anything I can get you that will make you happy?"

She didn't answer.

"I like your fish," I tried.

Nothing.

"Maisie, I order you not to leave this apartment."

Her head moved, just a little. Nothing else, but I knew that deep down she was laughing at me. This dead thing was laughing at me, and she meant to fuck up my life any way she could. Christ, the flowers, the fish—she was toying with me, torturing me. She could ruin me any damn time she wanted to, but she wanted to draw it out. She wanted revenge.

The next day at work was a nightmare. Crap from my boss, fatigue from lack of sleep. As soon as I got out I drove over to Maisie's apartment. Nothing new happened. Maisie seemed like any ordinary reanimate, and I began to think that maybe I had panicked for nothing. Maybe it was a bad patch and now everything had blown over.

Then, on Tuesday, everything changed.

I was halfway through another crappy day when the receptionist rang. "Um, Walter, you need to get out here. There is someone here for you."

"Who is it?"

"Christ, Walter, just get out here."

I went to the reception area, and there was Maisie, uniform on, mask off, her hair and eyes wild. She stood in front of the receptionist's desk, one palm out, raw and bloodied. The other hand held a piece of glass. She brought the glass down into her palm. Around her were the receptionist, one of the agency creatives, and a guy from the mail room. They were just staring.

"Ahh," she cried. "Walter. Walter Molson. Walter Molson." Now here was Xander, my boss.

"What the hell is this, Walter?"

"I don't know," I said. "I don't know."

"Get that thing out of here," he said. "I don't know what you're into, but take your perverted, illegal shit somewhere else."

I managed to get her into the elevator—empty, thank God—and into my car. I shoved her in the back and drove her to her apartment.

I put her in the bedroom, and I called a locksmith to change the locks to the kind that had to be opened with a key even from the inside. I wasn't supposed to change the locks on these doors, but I didn't give much of a shit at this point. We were into the endgame now. I knew it. I had to get rid of Maisie, and I knew just how to do it.

Once the locks were taken care of, I called Ryan to get the number, and then I called Charlie.

"Hey," I said to him. "How often do you have those little parties?" I could hear cloth scraping as he shrugged against the phone.

"Two or three times a year, I guess."

"The thing is," I said, "I have a unit—" I didn't want to talk about reanimates over the phone. You never knew who might be listening. "I need to get rid of it."

"Maisie, huh?" I could practically hear the grin in his voice. "I wondered if things weren't going to come to this. Now, we don't need a full-blown party to have a good time. Something more casual can be whipped up pretty easily. You bring her over Saturday night; we'll fix things up for you."

I didn't go into work for the rest of the week. I didn't call the office, and the office didn't call me. I guessed that job was done. On Saturday night I went out, and Tori didn't bother to argue. Things had never been the same since that fight we'd had after Charlie's last party. They would get better, I knew. Things would improve once I'd dealt with Maisie. Everything would be patched up very, very soon.

I picked up Maisie and brought her to Charlie's house. I was expecting just a half dozen guys or less, but there were twenty-five or thirty people there—almost as big as the last party. I brought Maisie out of the car and led her inside.

"Christ," said Charlie. "You sure you want to get rid of it? It's pretty sweet."

"Trust me," I said. "It's gone haywire. You don't want it."

That was good enough for him. We ordered Maisie to stand in the middle of the living room, and we all got beers from a big bucket in the kitchen. A couple of the guys, including Ryan, said they wanted to taste her before the end, and I knew it would be ungracious to refuse. I just nodded and let them take her into the bedroom. There were probably eight guys in all who went with her. I was worried she would speak, but these were not exactly the sort of people who go to the police with their suspicions.

It was maybe eleven before they brought her outside to stand on the plastic sheeting. She was still naked from the antics in the bedroom, and I arranged her so that she was facing the crowd. I knew this was something I had to do, but I didn't feel right about it. I mean, it didn't matter. It shouldn't matter. She'd been stripping long before I stumbled into that club, and she'd been subjected to far more degrading things. I'd subjected her to them myself. What did one more indignity matter to an animated corpse running on some kind of weird biological batteries? But I knew that she wasn't as oblivious as we'd always thought they were. I knew that it would be an indignity, that whatever Maisie was now, I thought she deserved to end this miserable existence with whatever measure of respect I could provide.

Unfortunately, I couldn't provide any. I needed her destroyed, and I didn't have the guts to do it myself. I knew that much. I needed these guys to do my dirty work, and I would give them whatever they wanted, let them take their pleasure with her any way they chose, if only they would get rid of her for me. Anyhow, I knew that Maisie had some kind of will of her own. She could refuse if she wanted to.

I wished she would. It would make me feel better, and it would demonstrate to the others why she needed to be destroyed.

Charlie stepped forward with the hatchet, and though I meant to turn away, I could not resist taking one last look at Maisie as she stood naked in the night air. She looked in my direction, but her glassy eyes did not meet mine; they aimed themselves instead at nothingness.

In that moment, I felt justified. It really just was some sort of misfiring biological machine. This wasn't murder. It wasn't anything like it. It was a mercy, really.

Then Charlie handed me the ax. "You first," he said.

I shook my head.

He thrust the ax forward again. "No way, bucko. You have to get this party started."

Well, *fuck*, I thought. I was just standing on ceremony now. I'd already killed her once. There was no point in being squeamish. I told her to hold out her arm, and she did. She didn't look at me, and there was no expression on her face. *Maybe she wants this*, I thought.

Maybe she doesn't want to be a reanimate anymore. I sucked in my breath, and I tried to think about nothing as I swung the ax.

It was like slicing butter. The arm came right off. It was so easy. I probably would have gone for the other arm, but Maisie started screaming, and that distracted me. It wasn't like a normal scream, like a human scream. She opened her mouth wide, impossibly wide, like a snake unhinging its jaws to swallow a rat. Her eyes went wide and wild. There was a pause, only a beat, but it felt long and unnatural, and then she began to let out a long, loud, unnatural scream, not of pain, but of anguish, unimaginable anguish.

With Johnny Boy, the guests had loved the shrieking, but there was something different here, something conscious, and we all knew it. Everyone remained still in a moment of stunned confusion, and then, snapping out of his daze, Charlie took the ax from my hands.

He swung with a kind of madness, as though he recognized that Maisie was not a plaything but an abomination, something that had to be destroyed before he was forced to consider what she was, what she meant by her mere existence.

The second arm came off. She had not raised it, and Charlie swung at it as it hung by her side, slicing through just above the elbow and slashing deep into her body.

Maisie screamed again, and Charlie this time swung at her leg. It was a clean cut, and her torso tumbled to the ground, twisting and turning spraying blood in a sickening, black ooze. Still she screamed.

She would not stop screaming.

It was my mess, but I could not bear it any longer. I ran to my car, and I drove home and came crashing through the door like a man possessed. I found my bottle of Old Charter and filled half a water glass and drank it down. Only when I was done gagging on its burn did I realize Tori was awake and on the couch. She'd barely noticed my commotion. She was sitting in front of the TV, and she was talking to me.

"I can't believe how sick some people are," she was saying. "I've never heard of anything like it."

And there it was on the TV. The local news anchor was talking, and the words *Reporting Live* flashed over and over again. I saw Charlie's house in the distance behind the reporter, who spoke about shocking scenes of carnage, a twisted sex cult devoted to the rape and mutilation of reanimates. He could barely restrain his disgust as he spoke. In the picture I could see police cars, their lights flashing, and a figure too dim and distant to recognize being pushed into the back.

Would they mention me to the police? I had no idea. I didn't know these guys, not really. They were well and truly fucked, and so maybe they didn't have any reason to betray anyone else. Charlie owned the house, and he would seem like the big fish to the cops. Maybe they wouldn't ask too many questions.

I looked at Tori, so disgusted by the scene before her. She glanced at me, and as saddened as she was by this spectacle of human depravity, something passed between us, some sort of unspoken code, communicated only with our eyes. It said that we were a team, we were alike. People like this were practically of a different species, and they had nothing to do with us.

Maybe I should have confessed everything then. Maybe I should have come clean. I was never one of those guys. Not really. I was drawn in by circumstance. A terrible accident, a split-second decision to do the wrong thing, and then the terrible fallout. But I wasn't one of those monsters. I didn't *like* mutilating or having sex with reanimates. I thought it was sick, beyond sick. So maybe Tori would understand if I controlled the story.

I said nothing, though, because I held on to the belief that there would be no story to control. Maybe the guys at the party would keep their mouths shut and this horrible chapter of my life would finally be closed. In fact, maybe this was the best thing that could happen. Maisie was gone, and the people who knew about me and Maisie were gone. It was perfect.

I went to bed with Tori, and enflamed by this mutual bond of righteousness, she made it clear she wanted to make love. I felt too disgusting to violate her pregnant body. I felt like a polluter. Afterward, however, I was glad we'd done it. One last, sweet memory to hang on to.

The next day when the phone rang, I was sure it was my doom calling. It was, but doom rarely takes the shape we most fear.

"Mr. Molson," said a voice on the other end in tones of practiced official blandness. "This is Detective Mike Gutierrez. I need you to come speak to us, today if you can."

My heart pounded so hard I feared it would burst, but my brain was racing. If they wanted to arrest me, they would not call. Maybe I was safe.

"Regarding what?" I asked.

"Well, it's an unusual matter. I suppose you saw on the TV about the raid on the reanimate mutilators last night?"

"I saw something about that, yes," I said.

"Well, in addition to the arrests, we confiscated the, urn, remains of one of their, well, victims, I suppose. Thing was all hacked to bits, but the torso and head were still there. And the thing is, the head is still talking. You see, the damn thing is still alive—or animated or whatever—and it's mentioning a name. Mr. Molson, it's mentioning your name, and you are the only person with that name in this city."

I tried to sound casual. "How odd. What is it saying?"

"I think it's best to discuss that in person. Can you come in today at, say, noon?"

I nodded, but then realizing that he could not hear me, I told him it would be fine. I then hung up the phone and sat very, very still.

This was it, then. They had me. They didn't know it yet, or they would be coming for me instead of asking me to come to them, but it was only a matter of time. Maisie's dismembered body would very likely never testify in a court of law, but the cops would come after me if they could, and at the very least, Tori would leave me and I would be ruined with lawyers' fees. I would become an object of scandal and horror. That was the best-case scenario. The worst—jail, where everyone inside would know what I had done. I would be one of those perverts who would be found murdered after a few months of unimaginable torment.

I could not face any of that. I was ruined, but I did not have to live with the ruin. And why should I? We all knew the soul left the body at death. I'd seen a hundred movies of departing souls. Unlike some cynical people, I didn't think the soul departed only to fade into nothingness. This life was just one part of the journey, and it was time for me to get a move on.

I am not a brave man. I did not own a gun and could not have used it if I had. I did not have the courage or the strength to cut my wrists. Instead, I went back to that bottle of bourbon, and I collected some very strong pain pills Tori had gotten but not really used after she'd broken her wrist last year. I drank all the whiskey and swallowed all the pills. I looked for more pills. I found some muscle relaxers, Ambien, Xanax, and a few others things to throw into the mix. Some probably did nothing, but the whole cocktail ought to be pretty lethal.

It was. I was probably dead within an hour, though time is hard to measure now. Only when I was twinkling out did it occur to me how horribly I'd screwed up. I'd forgotten how I'd raised the money to pay for Maisie in the first place. The offices of General Reanimates had given me almost ten thousand dollars to sign the contract, and that seemed like a good short-term solution. I would buy it back eventually. I didn't see any reason why I couldn't. I had plenty of time. It didn't weigh on me at all, and at the moment when I should have been thinking of nothing else, I was thinking only of escape.

Somehow I'd simply forgotten.

I suppose a pill overdose must be a good deal for General Reanimates. No cosmetic work to be done. Not that it much matters. I wear the uniform, and I don't see many living people at all these days. I'm out in the desert, working on an alternative-energy project, setting out solar panels. At least I am making myself useful.

I cannot speak. I cannot will myself even to move, only to follow orders. My mind is mostly still there, though I do not feel entirely like myself. Maybe it is because my soul is gone, and maybe it is because I am dead. I don't know. I don't remember dying, don't remember my soul leaving. I only remember falling asleep and then waking up in the General Reanimates lab. I cannot even wiggle a finger of my own free will. I've given up trying. I cannot imagine how Maisie did it.

There is nothing for me to do but endure my lot and think. It is hot here, and I feel it. We are not insensible. Our uniforms don't breathe, and we cannot sweat. I am miserable and I itch, and every movement is painful. My bones feel like they are scraping together, rubbing, chipping, grinding down. I work twenty-four hours a day.

There is no rest and no end. I can do nothing but what I am told, and I have no escape but my memories. I have told my story to myself I don't know how many hundreds of times. I pretend there is an audience, but there is none, and there never will be. Someday, I hope, I will wear out, but for all I know, this torment, with regular servicing, will last a hundred years. A thousand.

Somehow Maisie could break through, if only a little. Maybe it was anger or the sense of being wronged. Maybe if my end were not so fitting, I could find the will, but I doubt it. I have tried. I don't think anyone could try more than I have, but then I suppose we all try. The man right next to me must be trying, too, but he cannot tell me about it. I think it was just that Maisie was exceptional. Maybe in life, certainly in death. She was, and the rest of us are not, and that is what I must endure over the long, unending horizon.

Rocket Man

Stephen Graham Jones

The dead aren't exactly known for their baseball skills, but still, if you're a player short some afternoon, just need a body to prop up out in left field—it all comes down to how bad you want to play, really. Or, in our case—where you can understand that by "our" I mean "my," in that I promised off four of my dad's cigarettes, one of my big brother's magazines, and one sleepover lie—how bad you want to impress Amber Watson on the walk back from the community pool, her lifeguard eyes already focused on everything at once.

Last week, I'd actually smacked the ball so hard that Rory at shortstop called time, to show how the cover'd rolled half back, the red stitching popped.

"You scalped it," he said, kind of curling his lip in awe.

I should mention I'm Indian, except everybody's always doing that for me.

The plan that day we pulled a zombie in (it had used to be Michael T from over on Oak Circle, but you're not supposed to call zombies by their people names), my plan was to hit that same ball—I'd been saving it—even harder, so that there'd just be a cork center twirling up over our diamond, trailing leather and thread. Amber Watson would track back from that cracking sound to me, still holding my follow-through like I was posing for a trophy. And then of course I'd look through the chain link, kind of nod to her that this was me, yeah, this was who I really am, she's just never seen it, and she'd smile and look away, and things in the halls at school would be different between us then. More awkward. She might even start timing her walks to coincide with some guess at my spot in the batting order.

Anyway, it wasn't like there was anything else I could ever possibly do that might have a chance of impressing her.

But first, of course, we needed that body to prop up out in left field. Which, I know you're thinking "right, *right* field," these are sixth graders, they never wait, they always step out, slap the ball early, and, I mean, maybe the kids from Chesterton or Memphis City do, I don't know. But around here, we've been taught to wait, to time it out, to let that ball kind of hover in the pocket before we launch it into orbit. Kids from Chesterton? None of them are ever going pro. Not like us.

It's why we fail the spelling test each Friday, why we blow the math quiz if we're not sitting by somebody smart. You don't need to know how to spell "homerun" to hit one. You don't have to add up runners in your head, so long as you knock them all in. Easy as that.

As for Michael T, none of us had had much to do with him since he got bit, started playing for the other team. There were the lunges from behind the fence on the way to school, there was that shape kind of scuffling around when you took the trash out some nights, but that could have been any zombie. It didn't have to be Michael T. And, pulling him in that day to just stand there, let the flies buzz in and out of his mouth—it's not like that's not what he did *before* he was dead. You only picked Michael T if he was the only one to pick, I'm saying. You wouldn't think that either, him being a year older than us and all, but he'd always just been our size, too. Most kids like that, a grade up but not taller, they'd at least be fast, or be able to fling the ball home all the way from the center fence. Not Michael T. Michael T—the best way to explain him, I guess, it's that his big brother used to pin him down to the ground at recess, drop a line of spit down almost to his face, the rest of us looking but not looking. Glad just not to be him.

That day, though, with Amber Watson approaching on my radar, barefoot the way she usually was, her shoes hooked over her shoulder like a rich lady's purse, that day, it was either Michael T or nobody. Or, at first it *was* nobody, but then, just joking around, Theodore said he'd seen Michael T shuffling around down by the rocket park anyway.

"Michael *T*?" I asked.

"He still can't catch," Theodore said.

"That was all the way before lunch, though, yeah?" Rory said, socking the ball into his glove for punctuation.

It was nearly three, now.

"Can you track him?" Les said, falling in as we rounded the backstop.

"Your nose not work?" I asked him back.

Just another perfect summer afternoon.

We kicked a lopsided rock nearly all the way to where Michael T was supposed to have been, and then we turned to Theodore. He shrugged, was ready to fight any of us, even tried some of the words he'd learned from spying on his uncles in the garage. He wasn't lying, though. Splatted all over the bench were the crab apples him and Jefferson Banks had been zinging Michael T with.

"Jefferson," I said, "what about him?"

"Said he had to go home," Theodore shrugged, half-embarrassed for Jefferson. "His mom."

Figured. The one time I can impress Amber Watson and Jefferson's cleaning out all the ashtrays in the house then reading romance novels to his mom while she tans in the backyard.

"Who then?" Les asked, shading his eyes from the sun, squinting across all the glinty metal of the old playground.

None of us came to this one anymore. It was for kids.

"He's got to be around," Theodore said. "My dad said they like beef jerky." I seconded this, had heard it as well.

You could lure a zombie anywhere if you had a twist of dried meat on a long string. It was supposed to be getting bad enough with the high schoolers that the stores in town had put a limit on beef jerky, two per customer.

I kicked at another rock that was there by the bench. It wasn't our lopsided one, was probably one Jefferson and Theodore had tried on Michael T. There was still a little bit of blood on it. All the ants were loving the crab apple leftovers, but, for them, there was a force field around where that rock had been. Until the next rain, anyway.

"She's never going to see me," I said, just out loud.

"Who?" Theodore asked, studying the park like Amber Watson could possibly be walking through it.

I shook my head no, never mind, and, turning away, half-planning to set a mirror up in right field, let Gerald just stand kind of by it, so it would seem like we had a full team, I caught a flash of cloth all the way in the top of the rocket.

"It's not over yet," I said, pointing up there with my chin.

Somebody was up there, right at the top where the astronauts would sit if it were a real rocket. The capsule part. And they were moving.

"Jefferson?" Theodore asked, looking to us for support.

Like monkeys, Les and Rory crawled up the outside of the rocket, high enough that their moms had to be having heart attacks in their kitchens.

When they got there, Rory had to turn to the side to throw up. It took that loogey of puke forever to make it to the ground. We laughed because it was throw-up, then tracked back up to the top of the rocket.

"It's Michael T!" Les called down, waving his hand like there was anywhere else in the whole world we might be looking.

"What's he doing?" I asked, not really loud enough, my eyes kind of pre-squinted, because this might be going to mess our game up.

"It's Jefferson," Theodore filled in, standing right beside me, and he was right.

Instead of going home like his mom wanted, Jefferson had spiraled up into the top of the rocket, probably to check if his name was still there, and never guessed Michael T might still be lurking around. Even a first grader can outrun or outsmart a zombie, but, in a tight place like that, and especially if you're in a panic, are freaking out, then it's a different kind of game altogether.

"Shouldn't have thrown those horse apples at him," Gerald said, shaking his head.

"Shouldn't have been stupid, more like," I said, and slapped my glove into Gerald's chest, for him to hold.

Ten minutes later, Les and Rory using cigarettes from the outside of the rocket to herd him away from his meal, Michael T lumbered down onto the playground, stood in that crooked, hurt way zombies do.

"Hunh," Theodore said.

He was right.

In the year since Michael T had been bitten, he hadn't grown any. He was shorter than all us now. Rotted away, Jefferson's gore all drooled down his front side, some bones showing through the back of his hand, but still, that we'd outgrown him this past year. It felt like we'd cheated.

It was exhilarating.

One of us laughed and the rest fell in, and, using a piece of a sandwich Les finally volunteered to open his elbow scab on—we didn't have any beef jerky—we were able to lure Michael T back to the baseball diamond.

After everybody'd crossed the road, I studied up and down it, to be sure Amber Watson hadn't passed yet.

I didn't think so.

Not on an afternoon this perfect.

So then it was the big vote: whose glove was Michael T going to wear, probably try to gnaw on? When I got tired of it all, I just threw mine into his chest, glared all around.

"Warpath, chief," Les said, picking the glove up gingerly, watching Michael T the whole time.

"Scalp *your* dumb ass," I said, and turned around, didn't watch the complicated maneuver of getting the glove on Michael T's left hand, and only casually kept track of the stupid way he kept breaking position. Finally Timmy found a dead squirrel in the weeds, stuffed it into the school backpack that had kind of become part of Michael T's back. The smell kept him in place better than a spike through his foot. He kept kind of spinning around in his zombie way, tasting the air, but he wasn't going anywhere.

And then—this because my whole body was tuned into it, because the whole summer had been pointing at it—the adult swim whistle went off down at the community pool. Or maybe I was tuned into the groan from all the swimmers. Either way, this was always when the lifeguards would change chairs, was always when, if somebody was going off-shift, they would go.

"Amber," I said to myself, tossing my ragged, lucky ball to Les then tapping my bat across home plate, waiting for him to wind up.

"Am-*what*?" Theodore asked from behind the catcher's mask his mom insisted on.

I shook my head no, nothing, and, because I was looking down the street, down that tunnel of trees, Les slipped the first pitch by me.

"That one's free," I called out to him, tapping my bat again. Licking my lips.

Les wound up, leaned back, and I stepped up like I was already going to swing. He cued into it, that I was ahead of him here, and it threw him off enough that he flung the ball over Theodore's mitt, rattled the backstop with it.

"That one's free too," he called out to me, and I smiled, took it.

Just wait, I was saying inside, sneaking a look up the road again, and, just like in the movies, the whole afternoon slowed almost to a stop right there.

It was her. I smiled, nodded, my own breath loud in my ears, and slit my eyes back to Les.

He drove one right into the pocket, and if I'd wanted I could have shoveled it over all of their heads, dropped it out past the fence, into no man's land.

Except it was too early.

After it slapped home, I spun out of the box, spit into the dirt, hammered my bat into the fence two times.

And it was definitely her. Shoes over her shoulder, gum going in her mouth, nose still zinced, jean shorts over her one-piece, the whole deal.

I timed it perfect, getting back to the box, was wound up to *launch* this ball just at the point when she'd be closest to me.

So of course Les threw it high.

I could see it coming a mile away, how he'd tried to knuckle it, had lost it on the downsling like he always did, so there was maybe even a little arc to the ball's path. Not that it mattered, it was too high to swing at, but still—now or never, right? This is what all my planning had come down to.

I stepped back, crowding Theodore, who was already leaned forward to catch the ball when it dropped, and I swung at a ball that was higher than my shoulders, a ball my dad would have already been turning away from in disgust, and knew the instant my bat cracked into it that there wasn't going to be any lift, that it was a line drive, an arrow I was shooting out, blind. One I was going to have to run faster than, somehow.

Still, even though I didn't scoop under it like I would have liked, and even though I was making contact with it earlier than I would have wanted, I gave it every last thing I had, gave it everything I'd learned, everything I had to gamble.

And it worked. The cover flapping behind it just like a comet tail, it was a thing of beauty.

Les being Les, of course he bit the dirt to get out of the way, and Gerald and Rory—second and short—nearly hit each other, diving for what they knew was a two-run hit. A ball that wasn't even going to skip grass until—

Until left field, yeah.

Until Michael T.

And, if you're thinking he raised his glove here, that some long-forgotten reflex surfaced in his zombie brain for an instant, then guess again.

Dead or alive, he would have done the same thing: just stood there like the dunce he was.

Only, now, his face was kind of spongy, I guess.

The ball splatted into his left eye socket, sucked into place, stayed there, some kind of dark juice burping from his ears, trickling down along his jaw, the cover of the ball pasted to his cheek.

For a long moment we were all quiet, all holding our breaths—this was like hitting a pigeon with a pop-fly—and then, of everybody, I was the only one to hear Amber Watson stop on the sidewalk, look from the ball back to me, exactly like I'd planned.

I smiled, kind of shrugged, and then Gerald called it in his best umpire voice: "*Out!*"

I turned to him, my face going cold, and everybody in the infield was kind of shrugging that, yeah, the ball definitely hadn't hit the ground. No need to burn up the baseline.

"But, but," I said, pointing out to Michael T with my bat, to show how obvious it was that that wasn't a catch, that it didn't really count, and then Rory and Theodore and Les all started nodding that Gerald was right. Worse, now the outfield was chanting: "Mi-chael, Mi-cheal, Mi-chael." And then my own dugout fell in, clapping some Indian whoops from their mouths to memorialize what had happened here, today. How I was the only one who could have done it.

But I wasn't out.

Michael T wasn't even a real player, was just a body we'd propped up out there.

I looked back to Amber Watson and could tell she was just waiting to see what I was going to do here, waiting to see what was going to happen.

So I showed her.

I charged the mound, and, when Les sidestepped, holding his hands up and out like a bullfighter, I kept going, bat in hand, held low behind me, Rory and Gerald each giving me room as well, so that by the time I got out to left field I was running.

"You didn't catch it!" I yelled to Michael T, singlehandedly trying to ruin my whole summer, wreck my love life, trash my reputation—"Even a zombie can get him out"—and I swung for the ball a second time.

Instead of driving it off the T his head was supposed to be, I thunked it deeper, into his brain, I think, so that the rest of him kind of spasmed in a brainstemmy way, the bat shivering out of my hands so I had to let it go. And, because I hadn't planned ahead—charging out of the box isn't exactly about thinking everything through, even my dad would cop to this—the follow-through of my swing, it wrapped me up into Michael T's dead arms, and we fell together, me first.

And, like everything else since Les's failed knuckle ball, it took forever to happen. Long enough for me to hear that little lopsided plastic ball rattling in Amber Watson's whistle right before she set her feet and blew it. Long enough for me to see the legs of a single fly, following us down. Long enough for me to hear my chanted name stop in the middle.

This wasn't just a freak thing happening, anymore.

We were stepping over into legend, now.

Because the town was always on alert these days, Amber Watson's whistle was going to line the fence with people in under five minutes, and now everybody on the field and in the dugout, they were going to be witness to this, were each going to have their own better vantage point to tell the story from.

Meaning, instead of me being the star, everybody else would be.

And, Amber Watson.

It hurt to even think about.

We were going to have a special bond, now, sure, but not the kind where I was ever going to get to buy her a spirit ribbon. Not the kind where she'd ever tell me to quit smoking, because it was bad for me.

If I even got to live that long, I mean. If the yearbook staff wasn't already working my class photo onto the casualties page.

I wasn't there yet, though.

This wasn't the top of a rocket, I mean.

Sure, I was on my back in left field, and Michael T was over me, pinning me down by accident, the slobber and blood and brain juice stringing down from his lips, swinging right in front of my face so that I wanted to scream, but I could still kick him away, right? Lock my arms against his chest, keep my mouth closed so nothing dripped in it.

All of which would have happened, too.

Except for Les.

He'd picked up the bat that I guess I'd dragged through the chalk between second and third, so that, when he slapped it into the side of Michael T's head, a puff of white kind of breathed up. At first I thought it was bone, powdered skull—the whole top of Michael T's rotted-out head *was* coming off—but then there was sunlight above me again, and Les was hauling me up, and, on the sidewalk, Amber Watson was just staring at me, her whistle still in her mouth, her hair still wet enough to have left a dark patch on the canvas of the sneakers looped over her shoulder.

I put two of my fingers to my eyebrow like I'd seen my dad do, launched them off in salute to her, and in return she shook her head in disappointment. At the kid I still obviously was. So, yeah, if you want to know what it's like living with zombies, this is it, pretty much: they mess everything up. And if you want to know why I never went pro, it's because I got in the habit of charging the mound too much, like I had all this momentum from that day, all this unfairness built up inside. And if you want to know about Amber Watson, ask Les Moore—that's his real, stupid name, yeah. After that day he saved my life, after Les became the real Indian because *he'd* been the one to scalp Michael T, he stopped coming to the diamond so much, started spending more time at the pool, his hair bleaching in the sun, his reflexes gone, always thirty-five cents in his trunks to buy a lifeguard a lemonade if she wanted.

And she did, she does.

And, me? Some nights I still go to the old park, spiral up to the top of the rocket with a "Bury the Tomahawk" or "Circle the Wagons" spirit ribbon, and I let it flutter a bit through the grimy bars before letting it go, down through space, down to the planet I used to know, miles and miles from here.

The Day the Music Died

Joe McKinney

"But this changes everything," Isaac Glassman said. "You see that, right? I mean you gotta see that. We can't . . . I mean, Steve, you can't . . . I mean, shit, he's dead. Tommy Grind is *dead*! How can you say nothing's changed?"

"Isaac," I said. "Calm down. This isn't that big of a deal."

He huffed into the phone. "Great. You're making fun of me now. I'm talking about the death of the biggest rock star since The Beatles, and you're cracking jokes. I'm telling you, Steve, this is fucking tragic."

I let out a tired sigh. I should have known Isaac was going to be a problem. Lawyers are always a problem. He'd been with us since Tommy's first heroin possession charge back in 2002. That little imbroglio kept us in the LA courts for the better part of a year, but we got *The Cells of Los Angeles* album out of it and that went double platinum, so at least it hadn't been a total disaster. And Tommy was so happy with Isaac Glassman that he added him to the payroll. I objected. I looked at Isaac and I saw a short, unkempt, Quasimodo-looking guy in a cheap suit in the midst of a schoolgirl's crush. "He's in love with you," I told Tommy. "And I mean in the creepy way." But Tommy laughed it off. He said Isaac was just star struck. It'd wear off after a few months.

I knew he was wrong about Isaac even then.

Just like I knew Isaac was going to be trouble now.

Behind me, closed up behind the Plexiglas screen I'd hastily installed across the entrance to Tommy's private bedroom after he'd overdosed and died from whatever the hell kind of mushroom it was he took, Tommy was finishing up on the arm of a groupie I'd brought him. The girl was a seventeen-year-old nobody, a runaway. I'd met her outside a club on Austin's 6th Street two nights earlier. "Hey," I asked her, "you wanna go get high with Tommy Grind?" The girl nearly beat me to my car. And now, after two days of eating on the old long pig, Tommy was almost done with her. There'd be some cleanup: femurs, a skull, a mandible, stuff like that, but nothing a couple of trash bags and some cleaning products wouldn't be able to handle. Long as the paparazzi didn't go through the garbage, things'd be fine.

I turned my attention back to the phone call with Isaac.

"Look," I said. "This isn't a tragedy, okay? Stop being such a drama queen. And secondly, The Beatles weren't *a* rock star. They were *four* rock stars. A group, you know? It's a totally different thing."

"Jesus, this really is a joke to you, isn't it?" Now he sounded genuinely hurt.

"No, it's not a joke." I looked over my shoulder at Tommy. He was at the barrier, looking at me, bloody hands smearing the Plexiglas, a rope of red muscle—what was left of the girl's triceps—hanging from the corner of his mouth. I said, "I'm deathly serious about this, Isaac."

"Yeah, well, that's comforting."

"It should be. Look, I'm telling you, I got this under control."

"He's a zombie, Steve. How can you possibly have that under control?"

Tommy was banging on the Plexiglas now. One hand slapping on the barrier. I could hear him groaning.

"He's a rock star, Isaac. Nothing's changed. He's a zombie now, so what? Hell, I bet Kid Rock's been a zombie since 2007."

"So what? *So what?* Steve, I saw him last night, eating that girl. He looked horrible. People are gonna know he isn't right when they see him."

For the last three years or so, Tommy Grind and Tom Petty had been in a running contest to see who could be the grungiest middle-aged rock star in America. Up until Tommy died and then came back as one of the living dead, I would have said Tom Petty had him beat. But now, I don't know. They're probably tied.

"Nobody's gonna know anything," I said into the phone. "Look, I've been his manager for twenty years now, ever since he was a renegade cowboy singing the beer joints in South Houston. I sign all the checks. I make all the booking arrangements and the recording deals and handle the press and get him his groupie girls for him to work out his sexual frustrations on. I got this covered. The show'll go on, just like it always has."

"Yeah, except now he's eating the groupies, Steve." I thought I heard a wounded tone in his voice. He didn't like to hear about Tommy's other playthings, even before he started eating them.

"True," I said.

"How're you gonna cover that up? I mean, there's gonna be bones and shit left over."

"We'll be careful," I said.

"Careful?"

"Get him nobodies, like this girl he's got now. Girls nobody'll miss. The streets are loaded with 'em."

I turned and watched Tommy picking the girl's hair out of his teeth with a hand that wouldn't quite work right. No more guitar work, that's for sure. But then, that was no big deal. I had got him a cameo in *Guitar Hero XXI* the year before. Tommy Grind's reputation was secure, even if he never played another note.

Finally, Isaac said, "Did he finish that girl yet?"

Good boy, Isaac, I thought.

"Yeah," I said. "Just a little while ago."

"Oh." He hesitated, then said, "And you're sure we can do this? We can just go on like nothing's happened?"

"Absolutely," I said.

Tommy was always prolific. He wasn't much for turning out a polished product—that part we left to the session musicians and the Autotuner people to clean up—but the man had the music in him. He'd spent fifteen hours a day playing songs and singing and just banging around in the studio we built for him in the west wing of the mansion. Just from what I'd heard walking through the house recently, I figured we had enough for three more full-length albums.

It'd just be a matter of having the studio people clean it up. They were used to that. Business as usual when you work for Tommy Grind.

Isaac said, "Steve?"

"Yeah?"

"Can I . . . can I come over and see him?"

"You're not gonna screw this up, are you? No whistle blowing, right?"

"Right," he said. "I promise. I just want to see him."

"Sure, Isaac. Come on over any time."

"And this is how he's gonna live? I mean, I know he's not alive, but this is how it's gonna be?"

"For now," I said.

Isaac didn't look too happy about that. He was watching Tommy Grind through the Plexiglas, bottom lip quivering like he was about to cry. He put his fingers on the barrier and sniffled as Tommy worked on another groupie.

"He looks kind of . . . dirty."

"He's a rock star, Isaac. That's part of the uniform."

"But shouldn't we keep him clean or something. I mean, he's been in those same clothes since he died. I can smell him out here."

He had a point there, actually. Tommy was really starting to reek. His skin had gone sallow and hung loose on his face. There were open sores on his hands and arms. The truth was I was just too scared to change his clothes for him. I didn't want to catch whatever that mushroom had done to him.

"How many girls are in there with him?" Isaac asked.

"Two."

"Just two?" Isaac said, shaking his head in disbelief. "But there's so many, uh, body parts."

"His appetite's getting stronger," I agreed. "He regularly takes two girls at a time now, sometimes three. So, when you think about it, he's actually back to where he was before he died."

"That's not funny, Steve."

I didn't like the milquetoast look he was giving me. I said, "Don't you dare flake out on me, you hear? Between the record sales and the movie deals and video game endorsements and all the rest of it, Tommy Grind is a one hundred and forty million dollar a year corporation. I'm not about to let that fall apart because of this."

"Is that what this is about to you, the money? That's all you care about? What about Tommy? What about what he stood for?"

I laughed.

"Tommy stood for sex, drugs, and rock and roll. That was the world to him."

"His music was the soundtrack for my life, Steve. It means something."

"Bullshit," I said. "It means he liked his women horny, his drugs psychotropic, and his music loud. That was all Tommy Grind ever wanted. Now, all he wants is food. We're good the way I see it."

"We should let him out. Let him get some sunshine."

"Yeah, right," I said. "Isaac, the paparazzi hide in the bushes across the street just praying for a chance to shoot Tommy Grind while he's smoking a joint on the lawn. You have any idea how bad that would be to take him out for a stroll? No, if we're gonna bring him out into the world, we need to do it under controlled circumstances."

He nodded, then leaned his forehead against the barrier and watched the love of his life pop a finger into his mouth. Smaller parts like that he could eat whole.

"Listen," I said, "you want a drink?"

"No, thank you. You go ahead. I'm just gonna sit here for a while and watch him."

I shrugged. "Whatever. I'll be out in the hot tub."

I made myself a whiskey over shaved ice and dropped in an orange slice for garnish. Then I stripped and climbed into the hot tub and let the jets massage my back. The hot tub was outside, but the little courtyard where it was located was covered with ivy to prevent helicopters from peaking in on Tommy's private parties, which were the stuff of legend. One of last year's parties had included half a dozen A-list porn stars and a pile of cocaine the size of an old lady's hat.

I took a couple of phone calls and arranged for a cover of Eddie Money's "I Think I'm In Love" that Tommy had done in his studio a month before he died to appear on *That's What I Call Music, Volume 153*.

As was I finishing, I heard screams coming from the front lawn. I told the guy from Capitol I had to go, hung up, and jumped out of the hot tub.

Fucking Isaac, I thought. *You better not have . . .*

But he had. The little idiot had gone and let Tommy out of his bedroom and taken him for a walk down on the front lawn.

When I got there, clothes soaked through and my feet squishing in my shoes, Tommy was staggering around in the middle of the street, a team of terrified paparazzi gathered around him, snapping pictures. The flashes were making Tommy disoriented and he was swiping the air in a futile attempt to grab the photographers.

I waded into the crowd and grabbed Tommy by the back of his black t-shirt and guided him toward the lawn. I looked around and saw Isaac standing on the curb, a drooping question mark in a cheap blue suit.

"You get him inside," I growled at Tommy.

"I'm sorry," he said. "I just wanted to—"

"Go!" I said. "Now."

He led a reluctant Tommy back to the house. I watched him get most of the way to the front door, my mind scrambling for a way to explain all this, then I turned to the crowd and said, "Okay, people, listen up. Come on, gather around."

Thirty photographers just looked at me.

"What the hell, people? You don't recognize a press conference when you see one? Gather around."

That did it. Soon I was standing in the middle of a tight ring of bodies, cameras rolling.

"All right," I said, "we were hoping to save this announcement for the Grammy's, but clearly Tommy Grind wanted to give you guys a sneak peak. Tommy has just completed his first screenplay. It's called *The Zombie King* and I've just got word from our people in Hollywood that it's a go for next fall. We'll be shooting here in Austin starting around the end of next September."

"A horror film?" one of the paparazzi said.

"That's right. And it's gonna be Tommy's directorial debut, too."

"So, that was . . . what? A costume?"

"Look," I said, and sighed for effect, "what do you think is gonna happen when you give a rock star access to a stable full of professional makeup artists? I mean, we've all seen Lady Gaga, am I right?"

That got a few laughs. I passed out business cards to everybody and told them to send me an email so I'd have their addresses for future press releases.

They scattered after that to email their photos to their contacts and I went inside to kick Isaac's ass.

A few weeks later, in early February, I was back in the hot tub, helping another untraceable young lady out of her bikini for a little warm up before she went in to see Tommy. I was sitting on the edge of the tub, and the girl came over and positioned herself between my legs and put her cheek down on my thigh. The drugs in her drink were already starting to take effect, and I had to nudge her a little to get her to pay attention to what she was supposed to be doing.

She had just gotten to it when Isaac Glassman walked through the sliding glass door.

"Jesus, Isaac," I said, covering up my junk. "What the hell, man?"

"Sorry," he said. "But we have to talk."

The girl had pulled away from me and sunk down to her chin in the water. She wouldn't look at either one of us, even though it was a day late and a dollar short for any pretense at modesty at that point.

"Do you mind?" Isaac said, and pointed at the girl with his chin.

"Just wait for it," I said.

The girl's eyelids were drooping shut. I jumped in, caught her just as her face slid under the water, and pulled her out.

"Help me get her out of here," I said to Isaac.

He reached in and took one arm and I took the other. We pulled her onto her back on the side of the tub. She had great tits, I thought absently. A pity.

I climbed out and slid into my trunks.

"This better be good," I said.

"What are you gonna do with her?"

"What do you think? You're gonna help me drag her into Tommy's room. Then he's gonna eat her."

"But you were gonna have her first?"

"I think Tommy's past the point of jealousy," I said.

He was uncomfortable, stared at his shoelaces, then at the ivy-covered walls behind me. Then, finally, at me. "That's what I want to talk to you about," he said.

"Oh?"

"Yeah. I don't . . . I don't like the direction you're taking Tommy's career. The Eddie Money cover— "

"Has been number one on the Billboard charts for two weeks in a row. What are you trying to say?"

"That's not the point," he said.

Not the point? *Not the point!* I couldn't believe it. The little geek had the gall to stand there and tell me he didn't like my decisions. Christ, what did he know? The song was doing great. The critics were calling its stripped down acoustic arrangement and gravelly-voiced lyrics a masterstroke from one of rock's greatest performers. Industry experts were already anticipating Tommy Grind's fourteenth Grammy, which I would accept on his behalf in just a few weeks.

"Tell me, Isaac. What is the point? I gotta hear this."

"It's a cover song, Steve."

"Yeah, a fucking successful one, too."

"But it's a cover song. Tommy Grind never did cover songs. It was always *his* music, *his* vision. That's what made him so special. That's why people loved him."

"Oh Jesus," I said.

"Seriously, Steve."

"You're so full of shit, you know that? You don't live in the house with him, Isaac. You never heard him playing in there in his studio. The guy would sit in there and play cover tunes all day long. He loved 'em."

"That's because he loved the music, Steve. He played what made him feel good. But when he put his music out there for the world, it was always his own stuff. Don't you see?"

No, you little dweeb, I don't see.

I had managed to get together a lot more original songs off of Tommy's studio tapes than I first thought. We had enough for another eight, maybe nine albums. More if I included the cover tunes he loved so much. And it was good stuff, too. Plus, he had tons of live recordings from the heavy touring he did from 2003 to early 2008. I was thinking of putting together a double live album to go along with a DVD release of his Hollywood Bowl concert last August, maybe a viral marketing campaign on the web. Michael Jackson had been a bigger hit dead than alive, and it was looking like Tommy Grind was going to be even bigger.

"What is it you're accusing me of?" I said. "You think I'm selling him out? Is that it?"

It took him a moment to work up the courage, but finally he squared his shoulders at me and said, "Well, yeah, I do. I guess that's exactly what I'm saying."

It took all the self-control I had to keep from killing him right there where he stood. I felt my face flush with anger.

Maybe he saw it too, because he took a step back.

"You listen to me," I said. "Nobody accuses me of selling Tommy Grind out. Nobody. You don't have that right. You jumped on this gravy train after it had already worked itself up to full speed. But me, I've been with him since the beginning. I was with him in Houston when he was working two daytime jobs and playing all night long in the clubs. I'm the one who got him his first radio time. I'm the one who made the club owners pay up. And when he got drunk and wanted to fight the cowboys who threw beer bottles at him in the middle of his sets, I was the one who stood back to back with him and got my knuckles bloody. So don't you stand there and think you know more about Tommy Grind's vision than I do. I'm the one who told him what his fucking vision was."

That cowed him. He stood there with his eyes fixed on his shoes and it looked like he was about to cry. For a second there I thought he was going to run from the room like a scalded hound. But he suddenly showed more backbone than I knew he possessed. He raised his almost non-existent chin and looked me square in the eyes.

"What?" I said.

"You're the one telling Tommy what his vision is?"

"That's right."

"Well, good. Because I just talked to Jessica Carlton's attorney over lunch. She heard your bit about *The Zombie King*, and she wants in."

"*The Zombie King . . . ?*"

"Yeah. The movie you told the press Tommy had just written. Remember that?"

"Yeah," I said, and looked down at the naked girl at my feet. I had almost forgotten she was there.

Jessica Carlton, damn. The bubble-headed blonde who broke onto the scene a few years back claiming to be as virginally pure as Amy Grant, but had no qualms whatsoever shaking her ass for every camera from L.A. to Hamburg. The claims to virginal purity passed away unnoticed right about the time her first movie came out, and she rose to the status of tabloid cover starlet, which if you ask me was a brilliant piece of marketing. Now she was on the cover of just about every magazine in the grocery store checkout line. The last I heard she was dating an NFL quarterback, was doing a new album, and even had another movie deal on the table. She had the goods, definitely. And if she said she wanted to be in Tommy's movie, well, there was no easy way to refuse that. People would ask questions. *People Magazine* would ask questions.

"That's a problem, right?"

"Yeah," I said. "That's a problem."

And a week later, I still didn't have a solution. The Eddie Money cover had slipped down to number fourteen on the countdown, but we were prepping a new single—a Tommy Grind original—and that would be out in another three weeks, so at least his name would stay out there.

But the Jessica Carlton thing was bothering me. She had come to Texas to see her jock boyfriend, and her people had been calling to set up a meeting. No surprise there. I just didn't know what to tell them.

I started smoking again. Cigarettes, I mean. I never quit weed. That was almost impossible when you hung around Tommy Grind. I quit cigarettes back in 1998, and never felt better. But the stress of dealing with Tommy's unique needs—he was up to four girls a week now, and it was getting increasingly difficult to dispose of the garbage in a way that didn't attract dogs of both the canine and human variety—and the Jessica Carlton situation conspired against me. In a weak moment, I bummed a smoke off of Isaac and within a week was back up to a pack a day.

It made me feel ashamed every time I lit up. Like I was some kind of pansy or something, but, to quote Tommy, a need is a need and it has to feed, like it or not.

The situation reached a head on the night of February 14th—Valentine's Day.

I was in Tommy's fully restored 1972 Triumph TR-6, headed back to the mansion from the store where I'd gone to buy another carton of smokes. It was a cool, crisp night, full of stars, and I had the top down and Tommy's 2003 album *Desert Nights* cranked up on the CD player. The night was cool and clear, and the little Triumph handled the Hill Country roads like a dream. Any other night, I would have been in heaven.

But, like I said, I was troubled.

The feeling got worse when I pulled into the driveway and saw the lights on upstairs.

I had turned them off when I left. Tommy was usually calmest when the lights were off.

"Fuck," I said, and in my mind I was already throttling Isaac.

I parked and went inside, just to make sure. But I wasn't surprised to find Tommy gone. Isaac hadn't even done a half-assed job of cleaning up Tommy's latest meal. Nice enough girl. Said she was from Kentucky, I think.

I went to the security room and replayed the tape. There was Isaac, talking to Tommy through the Plexiglas, opening the door, coaxing him outside. Tommy staggering toward Isaac, hands raised in a gesture that almost looked like supplication.

And then they were off camera until they got downstairs and out the front door.

I turned on the GPS tracker—basically a glorified version of what veterinarians use to track the family pet—that I had injected into Tommy's ass after the last time Isaac walked him outside. Then I called the signal up on my iPad and got a good fix on him.

He was heading down to the west point of Lake Travis. There was a secluded little pocket of vacation homes down there for the uber wealthy. Sandra Bullock and Matthew McConaughey both had houses there not too far from Tommy's. It was his private little retreat from the world. Tommy didn't often like to disconnect, but when he did, that was where he went.

And then, a terrible thought.

Please dear God. Tell me he's not taking her to meet Jessica Carlton. He can't be that stupid.

I called Isaac's cell, and to my surprise, he answered.

"What the hell are you doing?" I said.

"Can't talk," he answered. I could hear Tommy moaning in the background. Car noises. Isaac struggling to keep Tommy off him.

"Isaac. Isaac, don't you dare hang up on me!"

But he did.

Damn it.

I got in my Suburban—the one I'd specially modified with a police prisoner barrier in the back so I could transport Tommy if I needed to—and headed after them.

Thirty minutes later, I was looking up at an eight thousand square foot mansion done up like a Mediterranean villa—red tile roof, white adobe walls, fountains and hibiscus everywhere. I had parked off the main road, in a small gap in a cedar thicket that concealed the Suburban just perfectly, and tried to figure what Isaac was doing. What possible reason could he have for bringing Tommy here? If Jessica Carlton saw him, we were done for. Despite the constant upkeep, Tommy was looking pretty rough these days. Worse than Willie Nelson after a three-day whiskey binge. Which I've seen, by the way. It ain't pretty.

And then it hit me. Valentine's Day. Today was Valentine's Day. Isaac Glassman had no chance of ever becoming Tommy Grind's lover. Not anymore anyway. The pathetic bastard's heart was probably breaking. He couldn't give Tommy flowers, or candy, or stuffed animals, or any of that worthless shit people give each other on Valentine's Day. But he could give him something pretty. Something that Tommy *did* still care about.

I heard shouting from the house. It was muffled, but definitely shouting.

Then gunfire. Three pistol shots, one after another.

That lit a fire under me.

I reached behind the driver's seat of the Suburban and took out a badly scuffed Louisville Slugger, the one with nicks in the business end that went back to the Houston beer joint days.

Old School persuader in hand, I advanced up the driveway and tried the doors and windows until I found an unlocked servant's door off the kitchen.

I looked up and saw a camera in the corner, pointed right at me.

Same system as at Tommy's. I could deal with that.

I looked around and noticed the stove. A huge Viking gas range with a dozen burners.

I cranked them all up to full and walked into the living room, where I could hear a man whimpering.

I didn't recognize him, which probably meant he was part of the legal community. Maybe one of Isaac's lawyer friends. He wore a light gray double-breasted suit with a canary yellow silk shirt and no tie, both of which were torn and splashed with blood. He was clean-shaven and fit looking, but his eyes were crazed. Had to be Jessica Carlton's lawyer. He must have brought her here so the talent could play while the lawyers talked contracts. He turned his insane eyes on me and that's when I saw the pistol in his hand, the slide locked back in the empty position.

"Help me," he pleaded.

I grabbed him by the shoulders. "Who else is in the house?"

"To-Tommy Grind. Oh Jesus. He . . . something's wrong. He attacked Jessica. He bit her leg off. I . . . I think she's . . . I think she's hurt real bad."

Then he held the gun up in front of his face like he had never seen it before.

"I shot him. I emptied the whole magazine into his chest. He just . . . he just kept coming. He's . . . oh Jesus."

"I see. Listen, what's your name?"

"Leslie Gant," he said. He was in deep shock, functioning on autopilot.

"Great. Listen, Leslie . . . you mind if I call you Leslie?"

"Huh?"

"Leslie, I want you to kneel down right here, okay?" He let me guide him to his knees. "That's right," I said. "Just like that. Now put your arms down at your side. Look over there."

"What? Why?"

I pointed his face toward the sliding glass doors that led out to a beautifully dappled swimming pool.

"Perfect," I said. "Now I'm gonna tee off on your head with this bat."

"Wha—"

I swung for the fence. Laid him out like a sack of rocks.

Then I went to find Isaac and Tommy.

Isaac was standing in a hallway outside the master suite. He turned when he heard me approach, and his eyes went wide as the bat came up.

"No!" he said, showing me his palms. "It's okay. Stop, Steve."

"Like hell it's okay. I ain't gonna let you ruin us, Isaac."

"No," he pleaded. "You don't understand."

I was close enough now to see into the master suite. Jessica Carlton, blouse torn off, exposing her absolutely amazing tits, skirt hiked up high enough to give a peek of a white, lacy thong, was pulling herself across the deep pile, honey-colored carpet. There was blood on her face and a huge big bite mark on her right leg. From her expression, I could tell she'd been drugged.

Tommy was staggering towards her, moaning like I'd never heard him do before. There was fresh blood on his face and hands and chest, but if I didn't know better, I'd have sworn he was aroused.

"What the hell?" I said. I turned to Isaac. "Did you drug her?"

"Yeah. GHB."

"How much did you give her?"

"The usual."

"The whole dropper full?"

"Yeah."

"And she's still moving around?"

He shrugged.

"Damn," I said, and whistled. "The girl must be in pretty good shape."

"Yeah."

Tommy caught up with her, fell on her, started to feed. She let out a weak scream, but there was nothing behind it. In less than a minute, she had stopped thrashing.

Feeling stunned, I said, "Isaac, I'm not sure if I'm gonna be able to unfuck this situation."

"I was . . . " he said, and drifted off feebly. "It's Valentine's Day."

I didn't even bother to respond.

"I wanted to give him something, you know? We just take and take and take from his talent. Nobody ever gives back to him. I wanted to give him something special."

"So you gave him Jessica Carlton? Jesus, Isaac, how did you expect to pull that off. This isn't some two-bit groupie chick. People are gonna notice she's gone."

"She wanted to meet Tommy. Leslie Gant called me. He said she was going to be in town. He asked me if we could set up a private meeting between them. You know, a little romantic Valentine's Day dinner the paparazzi wouldn't know about. She's still with that football player guy."

I took a moment to absorb all that. Then, "So no one knows she's here. Is that what you're saying?"

"Leslie Gant knows too."

"I'm not too worried about him," I said.

But I was worried about Isaac. In his mind, he must have felt he was making the supreme lover's sacrifice. He must have felt almost like a martyr, giving someone else to Tommy Grind so that they could satisfy him the way Isaac only wished he could.

"This must have been really hard for you," I said.

He looked at me, a suspicious note of caution in his eye.

"I mean that," I said. "I know you've been in love with him for a long time."

Isaac started to object, but then he hung his head and nodded.

"Listen, come with me. Let's go have a drink and let him eat. What the hell, right? There's nothing more you can do here."

I put my arm over his shoulder and led him back to the living room. He balked at Leslie Gant on the living room floor, but I guided him away from the body.

"Don't worry about him," I said. "Here, we got time for one drink. Then, we got to think about how we're gonna clean all this up. Can't afford any loose ends."

He looked back at Leslie Gant and grunted.

I handed him his drink. "To Tommy Grind," I said. We clanked glasses. I downed mine in one gulp. He sipped his, but managed to get most of it down just the same.

"Hang tight here, okay? I'm gonna go get Tommy and put him in the car."

About five minutes later, I was done with Tommy and back in the living room. Isaac was nearly passed out on the couch.

I slapped his cheeks to rouse him. "Come on," I said. "Don't pass out on me yet."

He stirred.

"Okay," I said, "here's what we're gonna do. You got your lighter on you?"

He reached into his pocket and held up a pink Bic.

"Pink?" I said. "Seriously?"

A corner of his mouth twitched. As close as he was going to get to a smile at this point.

"Well, it'll work. Start lighting those drapes on fire, okay?"

He nodded.

I took the whiskey and a couple of other bottles back to the master suite and lit the bodies on fire. Once I had it going, I came back to the living room and grabbed Isaac by the shoulder.

"Come on," I told him. "Gotta stay on your feet until we get to the car."

We passed his car in the driveway, and though the drugs I had slipped into his drink had made him so groggy he could barely walk, he was still able to point at his car and groan.

"Don't worry about it," I said.

At that very moment—and I mean it was cued like something out of a movie—the house behind us blew up.

And I'm not just talking a part of the house, either.

The whole fucking thing exploded.

The shockwave nearly knocked me down.

Isaac stared at me, stupidly. His mouth was hanging open, a thick rope of drool hanging from the corner of his lips. Some people don't handle the GHB well at all.

"What did you do?" he managed to say, though it came out all as one syllable, slurred together.

"This is your big chance," I said. I leaned him up against the front fender of the Suburban, reached into the driver's side window, and turned up Janis Joplin's "Take Another Little Piece of My Heart."

One of Tommy's favorite songs.

Then I helped Isaac Glassman to the back and balanced him on my hip as I opened the door.

Tommy was waiting inside, watching, his dead eyes locked on Isaac.

Isaac groaned and slapped at my hand in a futile show of resistance. Poor guy, he knew it was coming.

Janis was singing never never never hear me when I cry.

"She's playing your song," I said. "Happy Valentine's Day, Isaac."

Then I chucked him inside, closed the door, and drove out of there before the first sirens sounded in the distance.

I listened to the sounds of weak screams and tearing meat coming from the back seat, but didn't look back.

Instead, I turned up the radio.

It ain't easy being the manager for the biggest rock star on the planet. Sometimes you gotta get your hands dirty. But what the hell? I mean, the show must go on, right?

The Children's Hour

Marge Simon

"You've a whole life ahead of you."
That's what Gramps said
at my birthday party this year.
He gave me a ten dollar bill,
& Momma wouldn't let me
spend it, so it's in the bank.
It's for college, Momma says.

We talk about the good things.
It's Anna's need, not mine,
& she keeps squeezing my hand.

Momma went out for food.
She came back so strange.
Now her face is gray,
& there's blood on her mouth.
It's my fault for crying.

Momma pounds on our door,
but Anna says we can't let her in,
now that she's one of *them*.

Dad's gone, don't know where.
Maybe he'll be home tomorrow,
but Anna doesn't think so.
It was so dark last night,
we couldn't see the moon.

I wonder if there is a moon in the sky
anymore.

Delice

Holly Newstein

The grinding sound of stone on stone was low and muffled by the hot still air. Moments later a stench, so foul as to be almost visible, filled the night like an exhalation. A white-clad figure leaned into the partly opened tomb. A grunt, and the figure pulled something—a something bundled in a stained sheet—out into the heavy air. It slid to the brick pavement with a thud.

The white wraith closed the tomb with another groan of effort. It bent over the bundle and gently pulled a corner of the sheet to one side.

"*Ah me, cette petite. Quelle dommage.*" It picked up the bundle from the bricks. Clutching it closely, it moved away until they were both swallowed up in the inky shadows.

A sickly yellow flash of lightning illuminated the "dead houses" in the cemetery. Thunder sounded a rolling boom in the distance.

The first thing Delice heard was the storm. Fat raindrops thrummed on the tin roof, but it would bring no relief to the stifling August night. "*Ce pauve, ce pauve,*" crooned a strange, soft alto voice. Skirts rustled as the voice's owner moved about the room.

The voice and the rain and the whisper of fabric were very soothing to her. She had not had many peaceful moments in her short life, so she lay quite still, taking small breaths. She did not want the spell broken and the moment lost.

A warm hand touched her cheek.

"*Ma pauve*, wake up now." Delice opened her eyes.

A tall turbaned woman, slender, with café-au-lait skin and slanting black eyes smiled down at her. Deftly she slipped a necklace over Delice's head, placing the cloth amulet on her chest.

"Some *gris-gris* for you. To help Ava Ani. Now we bathe you."

Delice felt a strange energy begin to radiate out from her chest. She watched as the woman filled a basin with warm water. Then she took little ceramic jars from a shelf and began adding things to the water—powders and dried leaves. Fragrance filled the room—a sweet green smell, different from the earthy, mildewy, rotten-meat odor that clung to the inside of Delice's nostrils. While Ava Ani steeped the leaves in the basin of water, she chanted softly, in a language Delice did not quite understand. It was French, to be sure, but it was from the islands—Hispaniola, perhaps. Not the dialect Delice was used to here in New Orleans. The one Madame and Monsieur spoke.

The woman found a clean white cloth and brought it and the basin over to where Delice lay motionless on the table. Ava Ani turned Delice over onto her belly. She gasped as she looked at Delice's back. Delice had never seen her own back, but she knew it was crisscrossed with scars from the whippings Madame had administered over the fourteen years of Delice's life. Madame had a temper, oh yes. Ava Ani traced each scar with a smooth fingertip.

"Each tells a story, no, *ma pauve*? But this one will have a happy ending. Oh yes, Ava Ani will help make it so. And you will help also."

Ava Ani began washing Delice's thin backside with the scented water. Such tenderness! Delice could not remember ever being touched like that. No, she had only been touched to hurt—or worse.

A tiny shudder went down her spine. Ava Ani must have felt it.

"Good, good," she murmured. "The spirits fill you."

When Ava Ani finished bathing Delice, she combed rose oil through her woolly hair, making her matted locks become smooth waves and ringlets. Then she helped Delice sit up and dressed her in a red silk dress that fit her perfectly, even over the chest where Delice's woman-ness was beginning to show. Delice had never owned such a fine dress.

"*Ne pas ce pauve. Maintenant, elle est belle!*" Ava Ani grinned at Delice, showing straight, white teeth. "Now I need a ribbon, a red silk ribbon." As Ava Ani looked for the ribbon, Delice looked around.

She was in a one-room cottage, sitting on a table. There was a bed in one corner and a fireplace in the other. Everything was clean and neat, down to the mysterious bottles and boxes arranged on a shelf over the bed. Hanging down from the shelf was a cloth, embroidered with an intricate, multicolored design. A *veve*.

Delice realized that she was in the house of a *mambo,* a priest of the *voudou.* But how did she get here? Last night she had been home, at the Maison DuPlessis. And something had happened. Something bad. And was it last night? It seemed longer, somehow.

Suddenly it was hard to remember. Hard to think. Madame always called her stupid. Jeannette always said Madame was stupid to think Delice was stupid. But perhaps Madame was right. Right now Delice felt like her head was full of wet cotton.

Ava Ani was back, tying up Delice's new curls with a ribbon."*Non, non, non!*" she exclaimed. "Madame, she is the stupid one. I know, and soon we shall tell Erzulie too. Erzulie is a powerful *djabo* and she will help. Madame will learn, and Monsieur too. No need to look so surprised, *ma petite. Oui*, Ava Ani knows all." She helped Delice down from the table and placed her in a chair in the corner.

"Now, *petite fille*, you sit and rest. Wait until the evening comes."

Delice did as she was told, closing her eyes. She listened to the sounds of the Vieux Carre coming alive as the rain stopped and the clouds gave way to a hot, red, fiery dawn. The fragrance of the bougainvillea hung sweet and heavy in the air.

In front of the Maison DuPlessis, a crowd was gathered. Ava Ani joined them, listening to their conversations and waiting for a glimpse of Monsieur or Madame. The house was still, the shutters tightly closed over the windows as if in shame.

Shame, *vraiment*, thought Ava Ani. She knew the story, perhaps better than anyone in New Orleans. The DuPlessis were a prominent family in society, wealthy and handsome. But their neighbors whispered to each other about the strange sounds that came from the house late at night—screams and inhuman moans, like an animal in distress. Finally the neighbors' curiosity was at last satisfied.

Delphine DuPlessis had chased her maid all through the house until the terrified slave girl had sought refuge on the roof. Madame DuPlessis had followed her onto the roof, and somehow the girl fell off the roof to her death.

A cursory investigation was made, and the DuPlessis were charged a fine for maltreatment. That was the end of that. But, a few hours later, someone deliberately set the kitchen on fire. When the fire department arrived, they made a grisly discovery.

On the third floor, Denis DuPlessis had a private, locked chamber. When the door was opened, the officials found four young slave girls, all under the age of sixteen, chained to the wall. Whips, ropes, iron pokers, and other unspeakable implements were found. All of the girls had had their tongues cut out, so that they could not tell what happened to them in the room, and one had her eyes sewn shut as well. They were horribly scarred and filthy, with deformed limbs and faces from repeated beatings and other abuses.

Delphine had known of her husband's peculiarities, and not only tolerated them but actually acted as a procuress for him. The girl who fell to her death had been selected by Delphine for the chamber, but was able to escape before she was bound and chained.

A shutter flicked open an inch or so, then closed. A barely perceptible movement, but Ava Ani saw. That meant Monsieur and Madame DuPlessis were still there. They would not be for long, Ava Ani knew. No, no, with their money and their position they would make their escape from New Orleans. Back to France, perhaps.

Time is short, thought Ava Ani. Very well. *Ce soir.*

Her hands closed tightly into fists, fingernails digging red crescents into her palms.

While Ava Ani was gone, Delice tried to remember how she got here. She found that her mind worked slowly, so slowly. It took her most of the day to piece it together.

She remembered that Madame had summoned her quite late to Madame's fine, high-ceilinged bedchamber. Madame was thin and pale, with eyes like ice. Madame had looked her up and down. Her eyes lingered on Delice's chest, and the spot where her legs joined her body. Delice wondered if Madame could see through her threadbare calico dress and see the sprouting of soft dark hair that was growing there. Before she left, Jeannette had told her that the hairs meant you could have a baby now. Delice missed Jeannette terribly and wished with all her heart that Madame had not sold her last year.

"It is time." Madame sighed. "Go wash, Delice, and then come back."

"Yes, Madame," Delice had replied. She quickly returned to Madame's chamber, face and hands clean.

"Denis wants you," Madame had said, and then laughed queerly. "Come, we will go upstairs."

Madame's laugh frightened Delice. But she dared not show it lest she be whipped. Maybe she would be whipped anyway, Madame was so strange tonight. She timidly approached the third floor room, her hands twisting in the pockets of her dress. Madame followed her at a distance, her shoes tapping lightly on the floor.

Monsieur opened the door to the room with a big smile and put out a hand to welcome Delice. But then a puff of wind had opened the door wide. The smell of excrement and infection and pure raw fear had filled Delice's nostrils. She saw the bodies of the girls, chained in dumb misery, limbs smeared with feces and blood. One had lifted her head and met Delice's eyes with her own vacant and hopeless ones under a mat of blood-crusted hair.

"Jeannette," Delice breathed, recognizing her girlhood friend. Jeannette was not sold. Jeannette had been here, for almost a year.

Delice wasted no breath screaming. Her muscles jumped to life. She pushed back Monsieur's fat white hand and turned and fled, running. She had thrust Madame out of her way, terrified, and ran to the hall door. She had tugged frantically at the doorknob, but it would not open. Madame and Monsieur were running after her, the shoes tapping out a frantic beat now.

Delice spun around and ran into one of the guest bedchambers. At the far end, a window opened onto the second floor roof. She would run onto the roof and climb down somehow, she thought. She flung the shutters open and crawled out onto the roof. She pressed herself into the shadows, her heart pounding.

She heard Madame say, "Give it to me, Denis, you fool." Then the rustling of Madame's skirts, like a snake's hiss, as she too made her way onto the roof.

Delice tried to make herself small, to inch her way along the sloping, slippery tiles without being seen. Madame's pale eyes were sharp though, and cut through the darkness like a lantern.

"Delice!" she called, and out of habit Delice looked up.

The clouds parted and the moon shone down on Madame. She stood not ten paces' distance. Her dark hair was tumbled and wild, her face ghostly white in the silver light.

In her hand was a pistol.

"Delice, get back inside. Now!" Madame commanded. She raised the pistol, pointing it at her.

Delice had stared at the pistol. Madame would surely kill her. But to go back inside . . . that was worse than death. Suddenly Delice was no longer afraid.

If I am to die, then I will die. But I choose.

She rose up and began to run. She heard a pop, and then a ball sang past her ear. She felt the hot rush of air against her cheek. She ran and ran and suddenly she was flying. Flying . . .

And then there was nothing. Nothing until she had awakened here, at Ava Ani's.

That night, two slender figures moved slowly and silently through the close, black-velvet darkness that enshrouded the city. They disappeared down an alley that ran behind the Maison DuPlessis, and slipped over the fence that enclosed the rear yard. Ava Ani paused as two shiny blue eyes watched her from under the boxwood hedge.

"*Venez ici,*" she whispered, staring back at the eyes. Delice watched as Madame's white Persian cat came out from under the shrubs and approached Ava Ani. It moved slowly and deliberately, like a child's pull toy, straight toward her. Delice watched, fascinated. She hated Henri. She had been bitten and scratched countless times by that ill-tempered cat.

As Henri reached Ava Ani, she reached down and picked him up by the scruff of his neck. A blade flashed, and in a moment Henri was dead, his belly opened. Ava Ani dusted fine powder around him in intricate patterns, and began to chant softly, in a strange dialect.

The chant grew louder and louder, until the sound seemed to come from inside Delice's head. Her ears pounded. Her body no longer felt heavy and clumsy. She felt light and quick—and a fever began boiling in her veins. She rose up on her toes, threw her head back and opened her mouth.

A cool wind, light as a zephyr, sprang up. It circled around the cat, ruffling the blood-caked fur, barely disturbing the *veves* Ava Ani had designed around the sacrifice. It rustled through Delice's red silk skirts. Suddenly Delice's mouth snapped shut, and her body shuddered convulsively. Then she was still, and slowly turned her head toward Ava Ani, who bowed her head in fearful respect before the powerful *djabo*. A fierce, terrible beauty suffused Delice's narrow face.

Delice spoke. "This cat pleases me. I will do as you ask. It will be my pleasure, oh yes indeed." Delice laughed, a merry sound in the darkness, and with a swirl of red skirts was gone.

Ava Ani fled.

The rustle of silk was the only sound in the Maison DuPlessis that night. Silently, something moved through the house like an avenging angel. When the sun came up, the Vieux Carre pulsed with screams as more grotesque discoveries were made at the Maison DuPlessis.

Next to the well behind the house lay the bloody, disemboweled carcass of the DuPlessis' cat. Fine flour had been carefully sprinkled around the body. In the ominous red early morning light, flies were already thick and buzzing on the cat's exposed organs and its sightless china-blue eyes.

Denis DuPlessis was found in his bed. His throat was slashed, his eyeballs cut out and placed neatly, side by side, on his tongue, which had been pulled from his mouth and down over his chin. His hands had been cleanly amputated at the wrists, and lay on the gore-soaked coverlet, palms up as if in supplication.

Madame DuPlessis was also in bed with her throat cut, her nightgown pulled up around her waist, and the murder weapon sheathed to the hilt between her legs. It was a long, exquisitely sharp knife, of the kind used to cut sugar cane. Blood had spattered and splashed all over the walls and the ceiling, making glistening black rivulets as the drops rolled toward the floor.

No one in the house had heard anything except the faint sibilance of silk on the parquet tiles and the oriental carpet. But under the stench of the house, the smell of hot pennies and vomit, and sulfur, was the sweet fragrance of rose oil.

Ava Ani had been waiting. Delice arrived just at dawn, her dress stiff with blood, her eyes gleaming, her hands caked with gore. She had smiled broadly at Ava Ani.

"It was pleasant indeed, *mambo*. Now I return the girl to you." Delice's eyes rolled back and she had fallen to the floor, a limp small bundle.

Ava Ani picked her up and carried her to the fireplace. Even though the morning was stifling hot, a fire burned. In front of the fireplace there was a tub filled with the same scented water she had washed Delice with the night before. Ava Ani pulled off Delice's red silk dress and threw it in the fire, where it smoldered, then suddenly blazed with a bright blue-and-white flame.

Delice's eyes opened again to find herself once more at Ava Ani's. How did she get here from the DuPlessis'? The fire caught her eye. Delice thought the flames looked clean and pure, not smudgy and orange like usual. Then she saw the remnants of her dress burning in the fire. Why was Ava Ani burning her new dress?

It was a shame to burn that pretty red dress, but Delice could not find the words to protest.

Ava Ani bathed Delice again, and the water turned red as it ran down her thin body.

"You see, *ma fille*. Erzulie came when Ava Ani called. Erzulie liked Madame's fine Persian *chat* enough to ride you to justice. Yes, yes, it says in the Catholic Bible, justice, justice shalt thou pursue." She poured clean water over Delice's head as she stood in the tub.

Delice blinked. She remembered nothing of a woman named Erzulie. And what was this about liking Henri? She opened her mouth to ask, but no sound came out. Her voice was gone.

Ava Ani saw Delice's mouth open and close, like a fish. "You cannot speak. But I think you wish to know what has happened. The DuPlessis, *c'est mort*. Erzulie killed them in their beds as they slept the sleep of the damned. And you, *ma fille*, you made a fine *cheval* for her. She used your feet, your hands, to do what needed to be done." Ava Ani helped Delice step out of the tub and wrapped her in a length of white linen. She took Delice's face in her hands and looked into her eyes.

"You remember, do you not? Madame chased you onto the roof. She had a pistol, no? She stopped there and pointed it at you, her hair all tumbling and looking like a devil from hell."

Delice nodded. She was trembling. Her mind was so slow, her body so heavy. Her hands throbbed as though she had used them very hard. Ava Ani's eyes searched her face.

"You ran, *petite fille*. You ran right off the roof and fell. Fell onto the stones in the courtyard. Fell hard."

Delice finally understood. She was a *zombi*. Ava Ani had brought her back to life in order to avenge her own death. Her dark eyes widened in terror.

Now she was enslaved forever, mute and stupid. Ava Ani had stolen the blessed release of death that she had chosen for herself. The one thing she had been able to choose—denied her for eternity.

Delice tried to scream, but all she could do was breathe out a rusty croak. She tried to pull away from Ava Ani, but the *mambo* tightened her grip on Delice's face and shook her head.

"Your work is done here, *ma pauve*. I have no more need for you. Soon you will sing again. This time, with the angels." She began to chant low, swaying with the rhythm of the song. Delice swayed with her, her hands curled around Ava Ani's wrists, her eyes shut. A white fog filled her mind and she thought she heard singing.

"*Mambo* Ava Ani?"

Ava Ani whirled, her white skirts flashing in the darkness. "Who wants to know?" she replied, hiding her fear under anger.

"Philippe LaPlace," came the response. "Why are you here? Did the . . . information I gave you not serve?" Philippe came forth from behind a tomb.

"It served me very well," Ava Ani replied, her teeth clenched. She did not like this *bokor*-man of the Cochon Gris. But she could not be rude. She had come to him, filled with rage and grief for the victims of the DuPlessis. He had helped her in her plan to rid New Orleans of them, and taught her the powerful dark *voudou* she would need to know. She knew Philippe was powerful, and he frightened her. Still, she did not care to be spied on. She turned away from him in order to place a linen-wrapped bundle into the tomb she had just opened.

"So I heard," he said. A low chuckle echoed in the deep indigo shadows. "Erzulie is a creative one, is she not?"

Ava Ani shuddered. Philippe came forward and stood next to her. He ran his hand along the open edge of the tomb. "You sent the little girl back then?" he asked. "Pity."

"Delice did all that was needed. I have no need for a *zombi* to do my bidding. She spent her life enslaved. No need for her to spend her death there too." Ava Ani rolled a length of red ribbon, scented with rose oil, into a small tight coil. She slipped it into the *gris-gris* bag she wore around her neck.

"You are too soft, Ava Ani," scoffed Philippe. "Join with us in the Cochon Gris and find your true power."

"*Non, merci,*" she replied, a bit tartly. Ava Ani leaned her weight against the stone slab. She pushed with every ounce of strength she had, and slowly the slab slid back into place, sealing the tomb. Delice again shared a dead-house with the other dead slaves of the DuPlessis household.

Ava Ani straightened up, wiping the sweat from her forehead. In the faint starlight she saw Philippe scowling at her. Her almond eyes narrowed, but she forced a smile.

"Erzulie liked the fancy white *chat* I fixed for her," Ava Ani said sweetly. "*Mais oui,* she liked it very much. She said to me that she had never had such a fine gift." She watched Philippe's shadowed face. A moment passed—and then a flash of white teeth answered her.

"Very well, *mambo.* I see you made a friend of Erzulie. You go back to your little magic and I will go back to mine."

"*C'est bon,*" Ava Ani said, but he was already gone. She turned back to the dead-house.

"No more *voudou, ma fille.* Now only angel songs." She got down on her knees and fumbled around her neck. Under the *gris-gris* bag that hung between her breasts she found her rosary. She pulled the cross out from the neck of her dress and let her fingers slide along the warm smooth ebony beads. "Now I pray to the Catholic gods for your eternal rest, *ma petite.*" She knelt in front of the dead-house and crossed herself.

"Hail *Marie,* full of grace, the Lord is with thee . . . "

Trail of Dead

Joanne Anderton

You don't realize how many dead things there are out here until you walk over them. Hmm, maybe I should rephrase that. I didn't realize how many dead things there were out here until I walked over them. Yes, that's better. No one else would have this problem.

Most of them are lizards, poor things little more than dried-out skin and tiny bones. They shuffle—why do dead things *shuffle*?—like they're made of cardboard. All stiff legs and flat backs. Snakes too, and they have so much trouble moving on the sand. Then there's the odd, dusty skeleton. People who've been dead for so long they collapse as soon as they've pulled their way out, bones crumbling away in the breeze.

They make me sad, those ones. Really, this is my fault. I know it. And here they are dissolving away like they've never existed, all because of *me*.

I stop for a moment, pull a stolen bottle of water from my tattered backpack and drink quickly. Only takes a sec before I realize there's something buried at my feet. A beak pokes up into the hot, late afternoon air. It's dark, with two large holes near the tip. A thin skull soon slithers after it, a few scraggly feathers attached, sticking up like a demented mohawk.

Emu. Damn. If that thing's still got legs, oh how it will *run*.

I stuff the warm bottle in my bag and start to jog.

There are worse things than emus, to be sure. So the longer I stay out here the better. Away from cities, farms, any kind of human habitation. If I'm lucky no one else will suffer for my mistakes, my damned, drunken pride.

And I just might stay ahead of the old woman and her stones.

"It is conventional wisdom that a bullet to the head will do. Use something with a good amount of kick, like a shotgun." The Hunter did not draw a gun; he balanced a Japanese sword with a woven green hilt and glinting edge in the palm of his hand. "But you know why we shouldn't use those, don't you?"

Chase looked up at him, pimple-ridden face paler than whitewash. "Yes, sir." His voice broke, and he shook his head. "It's not their fault."

"No indeed. And we're here to give them peace, to be dignified about it. Not to have ourselves a good time." Grimly, the Hunter tipped up his wide-brimmed, rabbit-fur hat with his thumb. Dark brown eyes surveyed the park, touching on each of the approaching undead in turn. "Hunting is an old art, boy. You need to remember that." He leaned forward, weight on the balls of his feet, balanced. Fluid. Ready. "A clean cut to the neck, separate head and body. One swipe is all it takes. No mess, no disrespect. No *guns*."

The Hunter leaped forward and cut the undead down. He wasted nothing. Each stroke sliced through a rotting neck, each step took him right to the next cadaver. Slowly, the park emptied. The mass of shambling, rotting corpses became a heap of sprawled, rotting corpses.

Chase watched as the Hunter and the undead danced. He glanced down at the small, ugly-looking gun in his hand. An old-school thing, derringer the Hunter had called it, with a smooth wooden handle and a chrome barrel. Just looking at it made him feel sick. That the Hunter had put a gun instead of a sword into his fumbling, unsure hand said a lot.

"Chase!" The Hunter snapped from across the park. "Watch yourself!"

Chase looked up to a reaching, decayed hand. Yelping, he stumbled backward and lifted the derringer with a reluctant arm. The zombie had not been dead for long. She had hair, it tangled into a bleached-out nest at her shoulders, and most of her face remained intact. There was lipstick on parts of her lips.

She still looked like a person, and that always made it hard.

For one thing, they were quicker. The undead woman knocked Chase's hand to the side even as he tried to aim the gun. She lunged, bloodied mouth snapping in the air like a rabid dog. Chase gave into his shaking legs and fell, leaving her teetering, head swiveling with almost comic confusion.

It helped, in a way. She didn't look human any more, acting like some deranged animal instead of a woman. Chase scooted back, aimed up at her even as she saw him collapsed on the churned-up dirt, and fired. The first shot took her in the shoulder, pushing her back. As Chase fumbled for the spare bullets in his front pocket, dropped one in the mud and scrambled desperately to find it, she righted herself. She reached down.

He didn't need the second shot. With a step and a tight swing of his sword, the Hunter cut her down.

Driza-bone coat flapping in a putrid breeze, the Hunter stared down at his apprentice. He did not offer a hand up. "Knives are too short, close quarters fighting only favors the undead." He pulled a clean, white cloth from his pocket.

Chase had heard this speech before, heard it many times. He guessed it showed just how little regard the Hunter had for him, how much of a disappointment his so-called chosen boy had turned out to be. The man didn't have anything else to say.

"Foils are no good for cutting through necks; you need to be on a horse or a trail bike to make sabres any use. But this—" the Hunter wiped his sword with the cloth, removing flaps of crackly skin and chunks of dry flesh. There was never very much blood. "—this is perfect."

The Hunter looked into the distance, eyes shadowed by his hat, mouth set and serious. "Remember this, and when it is your time, treat her well." Gently, he slid the sword into a lacquered scabbard at his hip. "You will make a Hunter one day. When I am gone."

Chase gave up on the bullet, lost in the mud, and pushed himself to his feet. His pants were plastered with muck, especially around his backside where it clung with an uncomfortable weight. Quickly, before the Hunter could pick him up on it, he bundled up a handful of his navy polo shirt and wiped dirt off his gun. All the while, he tried to get the image of decapitating the Hunter out of his mind. But when you're apprenticed to a Necromancer Hunter, that's part of the deal. The only way to make sure that when they die, they stay dead.

A cold wind whipped clouds into the sky and threatened rain. With the city's undead put down, it was time to leave. The civilian survivors needed to be getting back to their homes, cemeteries would need fixing. A lot of flowers had to be planted. They always planted flowers after a rising. A reminder of life, in all its beauty? Or just to try and cover the smell?

A thin, reedy melody rang through the park and echoed from gray empty buildings. The Hunter dug in his jacket and pulled out a small, silver phone, as clean as his sword and just as shiny. Its ringtone, slow and creepy in the midst of the dead, sent Chase's skin crawling.

"Hunter." The Hunter began to pick his way through the corpses and gestured to the boy to follow. "Another town? Where?"

The streets were sprinkled with abandoned cars, but not as many as other cities the Hunter had cleansed. People were getting warning now. They didn't know *who* the Necromancer was, or even what he was trying to do, but they had been able to predict his movements for a week now and get the civilians out. It made things easier. Zombies on their own could be contained, but zombies with a city-load of fresh people to contaminate? Now that was a national disaster.

"He's still heading west then." The Hunter frowned. "No, I've never seen this kind of thing before. And I've been hunting Necromancers since I was a boy." He glanced meaningfully at his apprentice. "They usually have a goal, concentrate on a particular spot. Seen them raise the dead for revenge, for love. One even tried to make an army out of the things. Damned disrespectful. But raising a city here, a country town there." The Hunter shook his head. "This is strange, and I don't like strange. Especially not from a Necromancer."

Another pause.

"I know. We'll hurry. Just keep your soldiers out of my hair." He tapped fingers on the hilt of his sword. "Because they panicked last time, that's why! Hard enough to dispatch a city of zombies without boys with guns running around screaming. Hunters have always dealt with the living dead. Let us do what we were put on this earth to do!" He snapped the phone together. "*That* is why you don't let the army get involved."

He sighed and glanced over his shoulder. "Time to hurry, boy. The bastard is trying to lose us in the desert."

The Hunter broke into a run, threading his way around bodies and cars, and Chase struggled to follow.

I can't seem to get far enough away. They follow me. People; with their houses and their animals and their damned, walking dead. Didn't think I'd find any out here, where the dirt is a dark orange and the sparse, thicket-y type grass a little gray. But they're here.

I glance over my shoulder, count three lizards, the hindquarters of a roo and two lonesome, struggling human arms. When I look forward again there's a farmhouse. Sudden and close.

I stop, just for a moment, to stare at the falling wooden fence that wasn't there a second ago. At the peeling weatherboard building, half its veranda sunk into dust, wire-mesh door hanging crooked from its hinges. I don't stop long; I am aware of the shuffling behind me. Doesn't look like anyone could live in something so rundown, but that's not really what I'm worried about. Someone lived in this place *once*. Did they die here? Were they buried here? And what if they had a pet, some cattle-dog mutt buried beneath the looming gum. Undead dogs are quick on their rotting little paws, let me tell you.

The house is oddly familiar, in the way all rundown houses are. But in the end, the sun forces my decision. Out here, it always does. The dead things behind me stink. My water is almost gone, so too the packets of junk food I stole from a screaming petrol-station worker while zombies tried to clamber over her counter. At least the farmhouse offers shade. So I hurry.

The screen door opens with a groan that echoes down the dark hallway. Like the house is a zombie itself. It bangs when I shut it, resists when I try to do a rusted latch. In the end I resort to a piece of stiff wire to keep it closed. There are still gaps at the floor and again near the ceiling; the door doesn't line up properly. But they're too small for the roo, the crumbling stairs hopefully too difficult for the lizards and the bony, disconnected arms.

I wonder if there's any water left in an old, dry place like this. Sunlight splinters in through the door, but the details of the house remain in shadow. I can't see the color of the threadbare carpet, I can't make out the photos in frames that hang on the wall. All I can see is an opening at the end, shifting with a curtain of beads that rattle in a warm breeze.

I brush the beads aside, ignoring cobwebs that stick to my hand and shoulder, and step into a kitchen. Dried eucalypt leaves darken the floor, piling up in corners and beneath cabinets. The windows are open, glass smashed and tattered curtains of yellowing lace fluttering.

A long, dark timber table dominates the room; it pushes out over cracked linoleum from a faded green wall. An old woman sits at one end, thin white hair pinned to her head, floral-patterned dress too wide for her skeletal frame. She looks up at me, and she smiles. Unfocused, watery eyes dance, her hands play with sticks and little white stones on the tabletop.

That's when I realize I should never have stepped inside. It is her house, changed, yes, but hers all the same. Older, wider, spread somehow from a city two-bedroom to a farmhouse. But I know that table; I recognize those lacy drapes.

I try to take a step back. Something presses against my back. Large and solid, but damp. Cold fluids soak through my shirt.

I gag as rot washes over me, ripe, strangely sweet and thick. It runs down the back of my throat.

Hands grip my shoulders. They hold me upright and *ooze* against my skin.

"So, dearie." The old woman's voice still sounds like the rattling of bones. Only now, it's a sound I know well. "Have you found what you were looking for?"

"Your Necromancer's a woman. Did you know that?"

The Hunter tipped his hat back and scowled. The only admission of surprise he was likely to give. "Why do you say that?"

The young policeman shifted on his feet, uncomfortable beneath the Hunter's scrutiny. "We have reports . . . ah, sir. From civilians fleeing the area, from the emergency service workers sent in to get them out. A woman, probably early thirties. Medium build, blond—"

"Yes, thank you." The Hunter rolled a cigarette in his hand but didn't take his eyes from the policeman. He lit it, lazily, and let it dangle from the corner of his mouth as he spoke. "It does not matter *what* she looks like. I need to know if she *is* the Necromancer or just some poor girl in the wrong place at the wrong time."

The policeman took off his deep blue cap and ran fingers through sweat-dampened hair. He used the hat to beat at perpetually buzzing flies and leaned back into the shade of the post office's tin roof. The Hunter did not move, and beside him, Chase tried to follow his example. But whatever it was the Hunter possessed that made even the insects respect him, Chase didn't have it. He resorted to waving them away.

Replacing his cap, the policeman nodded. "*They* were following. All of the witnesses were very clear. She had . . . zombies, ah, following her. People from the cemetery." He gestured back along the dirt road and Chase glanced over his shoulder. There wasn't much to this town and it had been almost empty when he and the Hunter drove in. Only a few bony cats and half a dozen lizards. The Hunter had dispatched them with ease. "Not only that. Roos and cattle too. Couple of sheep—"

"Yes, thank you." The Hunter stepped back, into the dirt street and the full blow of the mid-morning sun. Chase followed with reluctance. "I understand."

"Sir?" The policeman reached out, but didn't leave the building's shadow. "We can help—"

"Which way did you say she went?" The Hunter dropped his cigarette and snuffed it into the dust with the heel of his boot.

The young man pointed.

"There, you've helped." With that, the Hunter spun and marched to his car, muttering about who was going to poke their nose into his business next. The car was an old, clunky thing that drunk down petrol and didn't even have air-conditioning. But it got them out of the small town soon enough.

The Hunter drove in silence, following the road, eyes intent. Chase waited until the older man gave a deep sigh. "A woman."

Chase looked at him but did not ask. Whatever the Hunter wanted him to know, the Hunter would say.

Chase had learned the Hunter's quirks quickly, after the weathered, scowling man had taken him away from family and friends. Even got him out of school. All his talk about destiny and the struggle for the future of mankind had impressed his parents well enough. Must have worked on his teachers too.

After two months following the guy around, it would be nice if it had rubbed off on Chase. Would have made things a whole lot easier. But as it was, he couldn't shake the feeling that this apprenticeship was all one big mistake.

"Not many women Necromancers, not many at all." With one hand the Hunter riffled through the glove box and found a glass bottle of lukewarm water. He tossed it into the boy's lap without looking. "Drink, it's hot out here. Easy to get too dry."

Chase obeyed, wrinkling his nose at the stifled taste.

"They just don't have it in them, the *need* for control that drives a man to raise the dead." He shook his head as the boy offered the bottle of water. "No, you don't see many women Necromancers at all, let alone one who would raise so many, so indiscriminately. It doesn't make sense."

Dry, orange earth sped along beneath them. Thin trees, bent and drooping, spotted the side of the road. At one point a small flock of emus ran in the distance. Chase watched the sheer monotony of it all and tried not to breathe too loudly. Not while the Hunter was thinking.

"Why would she have them follow her? She's raised cities and left them there, so why are they following her now? It makes no sense."

The Hunter braked suddenly and turned off the road. The movement threw Chase against the window, and as he rubbed the bump forming on his forehead, he strained to look out the back. Half a kangaroo hopped beside the trunk of a termite-hollowed tree. Wire wrapped around its tail and snagged on the bark.

It was not struggling to hop along the road, instead it headed into the bush. The way the Hunter was driving. Not on any path, over fallen logs, and hard, cracking dirt.

"No sense at all."

He hasn't been dead that long, but it's hard to recognize him. Guess that's what the car did. Took off most of his face, and his body doesn't look the same either. It's missing something in his back that made him stand straight, so he slouches to the side. His remaining green eye has gone cloudy.

He doesn't know me.

The old woman sits me in a chair and pushes a plate of rock cakes at me.

I just stare at him. He stands at the doorway, hands still raised where he had been holding my shoulders, eye looking straight ahead.

"Eat something, dearie. You're looking a little thin."

Finally, I turn to glare at her. Rock cakes and their china plate shatter as I knock them from the table. "Bitch."

"Now, now." The old woman smiles, one hand fiddles with a large silver ring on a knobbly finger. "You shouldn't be speaking to me like that, should you? Or haven't you learned yet?"

I pull back, fold in on myself like she's slapped me.

"*Have* you found what you were looking for?" She collects a small, round stone and strokes it. I feel my back straighten, my knees draw together like a good, polite girl. A great shudder runs through me.

"No. But you know that." I want to turn around, to point. So I do, but only once she's put down the stone. "You had him all along."

The old woman nods. "Convenient, wouldn't you say?"

"Why would you do that?"

She shakes her head. "Maybe you haven't learnt anything after all. You came into my house, *dearie*. You made demands like you owned the place, didn't you?"

When I don't respond she glances at the white stone. I nod, but don't trust myself to speak. I just don't seem to say the right things. "A dead husband's quite an ask, even for an old witch like me."

She cackles her laugh. "You can't have expected it for free."

I look down at my knees. The memory is hazy, mixed with alcohol and grief, and dwarfed by weeks of shuffling undead. I remember stumbling up front stairs, somewhat less rundown than the entrance to *this* house. Slamming an almost empty bottle of vodka—God, I can't even remember if it had a flavor—on the table. Shouting at her, crying at her. Her little, twisted smile. Yes, I remember that.

She gave me a stone, pretty, shaped like a rose but black. And then she asked her price.

"You knew I couldn't give it to you." A life for a life, I guess. But a baby? And someone else's baby at that, because I had none of my own, and she wasn't willing to take the risk.

Her eyes sharpen and pin me down like a butterfly on a board. "It was too late by then." She is disgusted by me; I can see it in the wrinkling of her nose. "And you still used my stone."

I swallow, and for a second consider standing up. How far would I get if I tipped up the chair and ran for the kitchen door? Before she had time to pick up one of her damned stones?

She collects a stick from the table and runs it over her weathered palm.

I don't bother, what's left to fight for anyway? "Yes." My shoulders sag forward, a little more with each word. "I took it to his grave. I placed it there, like you said. Planted it into the earth, as deep as I could dig. But he didn't come out. I waited, I waited until *they* surrounded me and I couldn't breathe for the smell." I had pushed my way through a cemetery's worth of dead to get out of that place, and not even the cold sea spray coming up from the cliffs could clean away the stench. They had watched me, empty eye sockets, sagging skin and gaping, grinning mouths. They followed until I came to the road, until I passed shops and *people*. Then . . . then they had started to feed.

But never on me.

"There is always a price."

"My husband had just died, I was drunk—"

She snorts, very unladylike. "Doesn't give you the right to steal from me." She looks me up and down, out of the corner of her eye. "So you've been walking since then? Coming all the way out here, trying to get away from everyone?"

"Trying to save them." My mouth tastes like orange dust.

"How very noble." Sounding bored, she pushes away from the table. Perfume drapes over me as she rests her cold hand on my head. "I wonder how many people died, before you thought to do that."

She steps back. I raise my head, slowly. Open my eyes and turn to her. Have I been crying? The world between us, between me and *him*, is wavering.

"Now I just have to decide." She folds the last flap of a velvet cloth over her stones and places them gently in a white handbag with a faux-gold clip. "If I want to keep him."

She lifts a hand and my husband, my *dead* husband, leans his cheek against her skin.

I stand, quickly, chair toppling to the floor. Outside, tires skid to a stop over dust and gravel.

The Hunter knew the zombie was there before Chase saw it in the hallway gloom. He grabbed Chase with one hand, pulled him back, forced him behind, and drew his blade with the other. Didn't even give him the chance to find his gun, but then, what was the point?

But the creature didn't rush at them. Stooping in the doorway, it turned and grinned with half a face.

The Hunter breathed in sharply.

"Let him through." A crackly voice commanded, and the zombie stepped aside to reveal a small, ancient-looking woman.

"Who are you?" The Hunter edged forward, sword extended, voice tense and clipped. Chase held back. He fumbled his gun out of its holster and held it high.

The crone laughed. "Come looking for your Necromancer, have you?"

The Hunter stepped onto faded plastic tiles; Chase hung in the darkness of the hallway. One hand clung to the doorframe. The derringer's barrel was cold as he leaned it against his cheek, the only way to ensure he held it steady.

The Hunter's blade twitched between zombie and old woman. "How do you—?"

"She's right here." The old lady gestured. A younger woman stood by a wooden table. Her face was ruddy with sunburn; she was dressed in tattered jeans and a filthy shirt. Her hands shook, and she clasped the edge of the table as though that was all that kept her upright. "That's your Necromancer, Hunter. Aren't you going to do justice for all those her undead killed?"

The young woman shook her head. Straggly blond hair caught in sweat on her forehead and chin. "No."

The Hunter hesitated. His sword pointed at her, and the young woman closed her eyes. Slowly, the Hunter turned back to the little old lady. "I know Necromancers. I can feel them. She is no Necromancer, although she stinks of the dead."

The blond woman's eyes snapped open. They were sharply blue. "Now *you*." The Hunter straightened his arm, leveling his sword with the old woman's smiling face. "*You* I can feel. But . . . you're not quite right." Chase could hear a scowl in the Hunter's voice.

The old woman cackled. "Pity." She clutched at a pale handbag, fiddling with the clasp. "If you don't want to play, Hunter, you should leave. You're out of your depth here. Can you feel that?"

"I do not think so." The Hunter raised his sword. "Tell me what you are."

"Too strong for the likes of you."

The zombie lurched forward, hands outstretched, and the Hunter spun. The young woman screamed as his blade shot out, as the zombie fell, headless. The old woman was laughing again, hand in her bag. She withdrew a single, white stone.

"Don't let her—!" The young woman shouted.

Chase jumped forward, aimed at the small, old woman, and pulled the trigger. The derringer clicked, hollow and empty, and Chase realized he had never reloaded it. He just hadn't remembered.

The Hunter gave a gargling cry as his sword turned back in toward his own, living, neck.

I watch David fall; watch his head hit the ground a moment before his body. Even under all that laughing, I can hear it "splat" against the floor.

I need to go to him. I need to hold him and know that he is truly dead. I hope that he has, perhaps, found a kind of peace now. After I denied it to him.

But I can't. I shout as the old woman pulls a stone from her bag, as the man's solid face breaks into shock. She will not make me responsible for his death too.

The porcelain shard is sharp, it cuts my hand. But as the man slices at his own neck with his long, strange sword, I don't care. I grip it tightly, I feel the blood, and I bring it down into the old woman's shoulder.

Her laughter becomes a shrill scream. The man's sword clatters to the ground and he staggers backward. I cut her again. And again. Until her fingers release the small, white stone, and she doesn't breathe. Doesn't move.

When she is dead she, thankfully, doesn't rise in my presence. I guess she thought I had learnt my lesson after all.

Standing is too hard, so I shuffle over to David's body. He doesn't look right without his head. I arrange it as best I can.

"Who are you?" The man is also on the ground, leaning against the wall while a teenage boy hovers at his side. The boy's face is pale, his eyes terrified, but he doesn't say a word.

"Jane." Not really an explanation.

The man holds a white cloth up to his neck. There is a small nick there, just enough to bleed. I stare down at his discarded sword. So close. "I am the Hunter." He nods to the boy. "My reluctant apprentice."

The boy grimaces.

"We have been tracking you. It was you, wasn't it? Raising the dead."

"It wasn't my fault!" I had only wanted to raise one. Just one. That's okay, isn't it?

The Hunter looks meaningfully at the old woman. "Stone witch, wasn't she?"

I shake my head. I'm not really sure. She was the crazy old woman down the street when we were kids, the one we called a witch. When we grew up she had changed in our eyes, become eccentric and a little sad. But you don't forget those childhood fears, those stories you tell yourself.

And at the worst point in my life, she was there. Door open. Bag of stones in her hand.

"She is. Powerful creatures, much stronger than a Necromancer." He clears his throat, carefully. "I'm not too sure on them myself. Those stones are supposed to be lives, I heard. The younger the better. At any rate, they are not an easy kill." The Hunter is staring at me. Grimly, I meet his gaze. His eyes are hard, but thoughtful. "Pretty good for a first kill. Think you'd like some more?"

I frown. "More?"

"You know what it's like. Seen it first hand now, I'll warrant. You know why the dead should stay dead, why those who raise them should be brought to justice."

I picture the petrol-station worker, backed up against the window as the zombies fed. I only looked back that once. Slowly, I nod. "Yes. I do."

The Hunter smiles. Wrinkles crinkle beneath his stubble, his dark, serious eyes are almost friendly. The boy has gained some color in his cheeks and looks relieved.

"Tell me." The Hunter catches his sword with the tip of his boot and drags it closer. With a wince, he picks it up, turns it around, and holds the handle toward me. "Have you ever held one of these?"

The Death and Life of Bob

William Jablonsky

Bob Jarmush is dead.

We do not even notice Bob's empty chair until Marlene tells us, just after eight, when we are all settled in. It happened early Saturday morning, she says, her thin face devoid of its usual condescending smile. Bob collapsed while pruning his hedges, and by the time the paramedics arrived it was too late.

His funeral is on Thursday; Marlene and her executive assistant Cayla will make a brief, dignified appearance. We may also attend if we wish.

We set about erasing Bob from the office. Jeremy, the IT kid, clears his password from the system; Cayla slides the Star Wars statuettes, R2D2 pencil sharpener, and framed picture with Mark Hamill into an empty office-paper box. Bob has no family, so there will be no awkward, somber-faced presentation of the box of junk at his front door. For this, we are thankful.

His voicemail has forty-seven messages on it—deranged school board members complaining that our science textbooks teach evolution, or that our history texts have too few white people. We decide to leave them to his replacement, whoever that may be.

When we are finished, Cayla bows her head low, says a prayer for Bob. We do not listen; our gaze drifts to the newly embroidered pattern on her brown corduroy skirt—ivy, perhaps, or a giant green centipede—we cannot tell. Her fashion transgressions are many and we have given up trying to decipher them.

She says, "Amen," and we're done.

We stare at Cayla's skirt some more, attempting to make sense of the embroidery before it haunts our dreams.

Tuesday

As we hang our coats on the rack, we hear a piercing scream from outside. We run to the window, thinking we are about to look upon a mugging, or a rape. Nothing so exciting has happened here since Roger's ex-wife caught him with

Charlotte and chased him down the street with a Ginsu knife. But when we reach the window, we see only Cayla on her knees in an empty parking space, an entire tray of her dry, flavorless poppy seed muffins scattered on the blacktop. Someone probably ought to help, but this would require speaking to her.

When we turn around, Bob is standing in the doorway, silent, his face devoid of expression.

His eyes are dull, recessed and deflated in their sockets, lips dry and cracking, skin an indefinable pinkish-bluish-gray. His face sags from his skull as if the skin is detaching from his hairline; his dingy iron-gray mustache clings to his face, and beneath his kelly-green oxford shirt is the shadow of a stapled Y-incision.

For a few seconds, we muse that he doesn't look that different. Then it hits us, and we stand paralyzed at our desks. He lopes toward us across the 60s-era gold diamond rug. Our bodies tense: at the first guttural moan it'll be every man for himself.

Instead, Bob's blank expression explodes into a big sheepish smile.

"Morning, kids," he says, his voice a low raspy whisper. "How was your weekend?"

Someone in the first row of cubicles passes wet gas—probably Roger, who has colitis—and a smell like rotten pork fills the office.

Bob tosses his threadbare tan touring cap and windbreaker on the rack, sits down at his desk, stares at the empty desktop like it's alien for the first time in eighteen years. His eyes are still clouded over, and when he looks up, we cannot bear them upon us. "Anybody know where my stuff is?"

We say nothing; Roger gets up and runs to the bathroom.

"Hello?" Bob says again.

The tense silence is broken when Cayla comes inside, clutching her silver crucifix, her skirt covered in muffin crumbs and parking-lot dirt. She tiptoes up to Bob, as if that will escape his notice; hand quivering, she reaches out and touches Bob's shoulder with one fingertip.

He smiles again. "Good morning, Cayla." She crumples into a ball on the floor, spewing gibberish. (Cayla goes to the church that used to be a Sav-A-Lot, where they speak in tongues, so no one is surprised.)

Finally—because he is the only one who can move—Jeremy runs down the narrow aisle to Marlene's office.

We can only see them through her window—Jeremy's arms flailing, Marlene stoic in her big leather chair, as if she thinks he's just taken a hit of meth. Then she looks, and her eyes go wide. After a long, deep breath, she wills herself to her feet.

Marlene tosses her long, layered, salt-and-pepper locks, pushes her spectacles up her nose. She is beautiful, imperious, more like a museum curator than a textbook sales rep. It is clear that she is the only one capable of handling this.

And so she does. Walks right up to Bob, who is busy trying to log on to the computer. Marlene taps Cayla on the shoulder. "Back to your desk, Cayla," she says. "It's all right." But we can all tell she has steeled herself for the worst. As Cayla creeps away, Marlene and Bob share a long, silent stare.

"Bob?" she says, apprehension in her lilty voice. "This is very unusual."

Bob lifts himself out of his chair, raises his arms; Marlene stands her ground. We are certain he is about to seize her and sink his mangled teeth into the soft flesh of her shoulder. We will certainly leave her to die, but in the aftermath we will speak of her with reverence.

But Bob does not eat her.

Instead he smiles, big and broad, puts his doughy arms around Marlene and hugs her tight.

"It's good to see you again," he says. He looks over her shoulder at all of us on the sales floor. "It's so good to be back."

Marlene gently extricates herself from Bob's embrace. "I'm sure we're all glad to see you alive and well, Bob. But as I said, this is a little unusual."

His dingy gray eyebrows jut upward. "Oh. You've hired someone already?"

"Well, no," Marlene says, disarmed. "But, Bob, you passed away. You were dead."

Bob shrugs. "I came back," he says. "Can't blame you for being nervous, though. Couldn't we just chalk it up to sick leave?"

Marlene looks around the room, then back at Bob, her face relaxing as she exits crisis mode. "Let's talk about it in my office," she says. "Everyone else, back to work."

We stare through Marlene's office window trying to discern what is happening. Both are smiling, with an occasional laugh, and after a few minutes he hoists himself out of the faux-leather chair and they shake hands. Stan the accountant, who is partially deaf, reads her lips as Bob gets up: "Welcome back," Marlene says. "To everything."

Bob lumbers back, sits down at his desk like nothing happened at all. When he sees us staring, he gives us a quick wink.

We hear a burbling sound, hear poor Roger whisper, "Not again."

Bob's fingers move slowly over the dial buttons as he answers his voicemail—not so much like a zombie lacking fine motor control, but stiffly just the same. We watch his doughy torso to see if he is still breathing. He is.

We wonder if his heart is still beating, and email Jeremy to see if he has the stones to check. He does not. Cayla comes over only once, empties the box of knickknacks and Star Wars statuettes on Bob's desk, scurries back to her cubicle with a little cry. She does not speak all day, and for this we are grateful.

He goes to the breakroom at lunchtime; we try not to look at him, pretend to follow the tiny cracks in the yellow plaster wall, take far too long selecting chips and soda from the vending machines. He pulls out a vintage Darth Vader lunchbox—one of the old metal kind we all had in grade school—and a plastic bag. We expect something gray and spongy, but instead he unwraps a cheese and tomato sandwich on an Asiago roll. We watch his teeth as he takes his first bite: a bit yellow, but normal, not jagged and rotten. He chews, slowly.

He sees that we are watching. "Mmmmmm," he moans. "Braaaiiiinnns."

Our jaws drop. Charlotte, the telemarketer, drops her soda on the speckled gray linoleum. Cayla's hands flutter around her face and she runs away. For thirty seconds the breakroom is quiet as death. Then Jeremy starts to laugh—a muffled giggle he tries to control, but he fails and gives in to a full belly laugh.

"You are one sick motherfucker," he says.

Bob salutes. "At your service."

Then everyone laughs, and suddenly we feel better.

Wednesday

Bob looks better this morning, his hue more pink, less like a deflated blue balloon, his movements fluid and normal. Not at all like an undead thing.

At lunchtime, as he plays with his laptop in the breakroom, he sips coffee out of a Yoda-head mug, closing his eyes as if it's the best thing he's ever tasted. He watches the screen for a minute, then launches into a wheezing laugh.

We try not to look. We really do.

"Hey kids," he says. "Want to see something really cool?"

Of course we do, but the adults are not bold enough to say yes. Fortunately, Jeremy is there. "Hell yeah, man!"

Bob hits the mouse pad, turns his laptop toward us. We pull up plastic chairs and gather round like children.

Bob talks with his mouth full of bagel. "Hospital sent me this yesterday with a big settlement check, just for a laugh," he says. "Not for the faint of heart."

He clicks *Play*, and a moment later, there he is, blue-gray on a metal table, his floppy bits hanging out in the open. (We should be offended, but this is too fascinating for propriety.) Next thing we know, a young Asian woman in a white coat and facemask is cutting a deep "Y" into his torso. Just as she inserts the rib-spreader, Bob's limp hand goes stiff, juts out and grabs her by the wrist. She screams, drops the ribspreader. Then Bob's eyes snap open and he too begins to scream, like a lion being stabbed in the gut. He rolls off the table and, for the next two minutes, runs naked and bellowing around the morgue, chest gaping open, chasing away anyone who gets close. Finally a group of orderlies wrestle him to the ground and drape a white sheet over him, and the recording ends.

It is the most spectacular thing we have ever seen.

Bob smiles. "Pretty cool, huh?"

"Did it hurt?" Charlotte asks, pointing toward Bob's chest. (It occurs to us that this is the most any of us have said to Bob in years.)

"Not really," Bob says. "Didn't feel much of anything. Itches like crazy now, though."

"Can we see?" Jeremy asks, giddy.

Bob shrugs, untucks his brown polo, pulls it up over his pudgy body. And there it is: the Y-shaped line of staples running down his entire torso.

Incredible.

"Staples will be out in a few days," he says.

Cayla, standing in the doorway, interrupts our trance. "When you died," she says, saccharine in her smile, "Did you see loved ones? Your family?"

A long silence follows—Cayla is clearly expecting him to say his dear old granddad showed up to lead him to the Pearly Gates. But Bob shakes his head.

"Sorry, kiddo," he says. "One minute I was falling face-first into the hedges, the next I was splayed open on that table. Nothing in between."

Cayla's smile goes taut, like it's been carved into her face. "Well, that can't be," she says. "You weren't really dead."

"As a doornail," Bob replies. "No pulse, no brain activity, nothing."

"Then you must not be Christian," Cayla huffs.

"Catholic, born and raised," Bob says.

Cayla's entire face scrunches up so tight we think it will implode. "I'm confused," she says. "Of all people, why you?"

Bob shrugs. "Couldn't tell you, kiddo. Just glad to be back." He reaches out to pat her shoulder, but she recoils.

"Don't touch me," Cayla whispers, and turns to leave, her frilly, multilayered pink skirt bouncing with each step.

Bob takes another long sip of coffee. "Tell you what, kids—being dead sure does make you appreciate things like a good cup o'Joe."

We nod, suddenly craving coffee. That ancient Bunn churns out a sludge that tastes like it's been squeezed from a wet dishrag, but as the hot liquid touches our lips, it seems richer somehow.

Thursday

For most of the day we stare at Bob, smiling as he takes his calls, waving or winking at us when he senses our eyes on him. The deep lines that etched his face before he died are beginning to disappear, though we can still see pronounced veins on his forehead and forearms. We are almost used to him being back, so much so that on occasion our eyes wander back to Cayla, in her lime-green tunic and skirt and a medallion twice the size of her fist, with a cannon and a cross and the caption, IN THE ARMY OF THE LORD. When she has paperwork for Bob she tries to pass it to one of us to hand him; we pretend to be busy just to watch her slink up to Bob's desk, set the papers on the very edge, and tiptoe away as if he doesn't see.

It is our tradition to do karaoke night at Big Mike's on Thursdays after work, and for the first time since any of us has been here, we invite Bob, who thinks about it for a minute, shrugs, and says, "Don't mind if I do."

Big Mike's is a bar and grill next to the office, built like an oversized Airstream trailer with a little plank for a dance floor and miniature juke boxes at each table. Bob looks around the place as we go in, joy in his eyes. "This place has been here for nine years and I've never even been inside," he says. "Imagine that." We are pleased with ourselves for introducing him to such a treasure, even if a bit late.

For the first half-hour no one steps up—it takes a few beers to lose enough inhibition—but finally Bob gets up from his seat next to Charlotte. He fiddles with the karaoke machine for a minute, presses the button. Horns blast over the PA; Bob seizes the microphone stand like he's about to swing it, and belts out the lyrics to "Mack the Knife" in a velvet baritone you'd never expect to come out of his dumpy body. And he's good.

None of us knew Bob could sing.

When Bob is finished, the half-drunk crowd bursts into applause; he takes a bow and returns to us.

"That was fucking awesome!" Jeremy slurs, slapping Bob on the shoulder.

Later, when Roger gets up to do a spastic rendition of Barbara Mandrell's "Sleepin' Single in a Double Bed," we watch in awe as Bob takes Charlotte's hand

and leads her to the little wooden pallet of a dance floor. At first it's ridiculous, Bob's thin arms flailing about his pudgy torso like no human thing, and it takes every bit of Charlotte's will not to laugh. A few people at the tables near us do, but Bob doesn't care. After a minute or two, he loosens up and starts whipping her all over the floor. When the song ends, he twirls her under his arm; dour, anorexic, alcoholic Charlotte is laughing, but there's no mockery in it, and once she stops twirling she plants a kiss on his neck, right below his ear.

At ten, when we're dried out and tired, we stumble back to the office parking lot. Spent as we are, we still notice Charlotte climbing into Bob's old hatchback, and we smile.

Friday

When we arrive at work, Charlotte's blue Volvo is still in the same space as last night, far from the building near the railroad tracks, and we believe in miracles.

Then we notice the red spray paint on the front door: GOD HATES ZOMBIES.

Of course Marlene asks, and of course Cayla denies it.

Bob and Charlotte arrive together: Bob first, Charlotte thirty seconds later, acting like nothing has happened.

"You old dog," Jeremy says, punching Bob in the shoulder. Bob merely winks and whispers, "Shhh."

It takes Cayla a moment to comprehend the meaning of it, but when she does she cups her hand over her mouth like she's holding in vomit.

Bob actually looks good, better than before he died: eyes full, skin bright and peachy, posture straight and tall. Even his clothes are better: a form-fitting charcoal blazer and smoky gray slacks in place of his usual sagging Henleys and khakis. For most of the morning he softly whistles the synthesizer line from Rod Stewart's "Do Ya Think I'm Sexy," which gets stuck in our heads for the rest of the day. We should be annoyed, but Bob has never seemed so happy—no, *alive*—and we feel strangely elated. Even Charlotte is in a good mood, slapping Bob's flat ass whenever he passes.

But Cayla is here, so there must be drama. Just after ten, she sends Bob the wrong form via Roger. Bob gets up, shuffles over to her little gray cubby near Marlene's office, taps her on the shoulder. When she realizes it's him she pulls back so hard she falls out of her chair and scrapes her face on a cubicle wall. Bob reaches out to help her up, but she grunts like a frightened animal and does a sort of crabwalk out of the cubicle, all the way to the ladies' room.

We hear her mad scrubbing under the faucet, her voice murmuring a prayer in tongues.

Bob finally knocks on Marlene's door. "I think something's wrong with Cayla," he says, and she glides across the office floor to the restroom.

We can't make out what they're saying, other than, "Are you all right?" and Cayla's tearful, "I can't work with that thing around here. You have to fire him." The rest is a low mumble. Finally Cayla bursts out in tears, and before we know it she is out the front door.

Marlene emerges a few seconds later, her face red but expressionless. "Let's get back to work," she says. "Everything's fine."

Over lunch, Bob tells us what he plans to do with the hefty settlement check from the hospital—we are awed that he still comes to work, but he says it gives him a reason to get up in the morning—when Cayla returns with a tall gray-skinned old man in a black camp shirt and white collar, Bible clutched under one arm, cane in the other. He moves slowly, the thin cane barely enough to support him, and she practically drags him to the breakroom.

"That's him, Reverend," she says, pointing at Bob.

"All right," the old man says. "Let's get this over with." He looks around at all of us. "If it's not too much trouble, I'd like everyone to join hands." We look to Bob, not knowing what to do. He nods, and we go along with it.

The old pastor sets down his cane, draws from his breast pocket a small plastic crucifix, and holds it and the Bible at arm's length, inches from Bob's face. "Everybody repeat after me." His voice is a crackly whisper. "Away, undead thing! Back to the grave!"

We repeat his words. Nothing happens.

The old man sighs. "I said, away!" He lunges a little too far the second time, and drops his Bible at Bob's feet. Bob leans over, picks it up, dusts it off, and hands it back.

"Thank you, my boy," the old man says. Then he turns to Cayla. "I don't think it's working, dear. You might need a Catholic for this sort of thing."

Cayla grunts. "You're the only one who'd agree to do this."

"Well, I'm sorry, sweetie," he says as Bob helps him into a chair. "Guess I don't have it like I used to."

Bob hands the old pastor a cup of coffee. "Here you go, Reverend," he says. "Guys," he says to all of us, "Can you give us a minute? Cayla, you stay."

We file out, though those whose desks are near enough listen for any tidbit we can pick up.

After about ten minutes, Bob and the reverend emerge. The old man reaches out and shakes Bob's hand. "You're truly a miracle, son," he says. "Best of luck in your new life."

Bob asks Jeremy to drive the old man back to his retirement home, then turns back to the breakroom. Cayla is sitting in a corner, hands tightly folded in her lap. She stands when Bob enters.

"Stay away." Her voice is mousey.

He approaches her like some creature in a bad movie. For a minute we think he's regressed, and might just dig his teeth into her skull and eat her brain. Not that she'd be much of a meal. Bob stops a few feet from her, just out of arm's reach. She goes rigid.

"I'm not going to hurt you, Cayla. I promise." Bob's voice is soft. Tender.

"You're a monster."

This is too much; a few of us shout back at her, "You're the monster!" But Bob raises his left hand and we fall silent.

"No, Cayla. I'm just Bob. Same as ever. Maybe a little better." He holds his hand out to her, and her face seems to soften. "How 'bout we start over?"

"Okay." She reaches out slowly, shakes his hand, but quickly pulls it back. "Your hand's cold."

"Cayla . . . " Bob starts to say, and steps closer.

Cayla screams like she's being stabbed in the liver, so loud it echoes in the metal beams of the building.

Marlene rushes in to save the day, of course. She points to Cayla and summons her into her office, then closes the door.

Five minutes later Cayla comes out sobbing, walking in slow motion to her desk and clearing off the crucifixes and Jesus statuettes. On her way out, she stops before Bob's desk and glares.

"I'm sorry, Cayla," Bob says.

She pulls a book of matches from the box, lights one, throws it at Bob. It goes out before touching him.

She lights another, flings it. He catches it gracefully, snuffs it out in his closed palm. Then Max, the security guard, steps up behind her and ushers her out.

Cayla stops once more at the door. "You people are in league with the devil!" she shouts, just as Max gives her a little shove, and then she's gone.

Monday

The air smells faintly of smoke as we pull into the parking lot. It is early May, too soon to burn leaves, but we think nothing of it.

When Bob arrives with Charlotte on his arm, he looks like a million bucks: electric blue pinstripe suit with a black button-up shirt and no tie, hair trimmed neatly up around his ears, handlebar mustache close-cropped and sleek, bags gone from under his eyes. There is no sign of the Y-incision scar beneath his collar, as if his transformation into a new man is complete. Charlotte is giddy as she clings to his arm, the smile practically glued in place—a rarity that usually causes us unease, but this time it's . . . nice. Comforting.

By 9:30, we hear chanting in the parking lot. We pay no attention, fixated as we are on Charlotte using her phone-sex voice on sales calls, until Roger finally gets up to investigate.

"Um, guys," he says, peering out the glass door. "You'd better take a look."

Outside on the sidewalk is a crowd of fifty or more, holding homemade signs that read, GOD HATES THE UNDEAD, and ZOMBIE, GO BACK TO THE GRAVE. A few hold makeshift torches—broom handles and baseball bats with flaming rags attached to them. When Bob comes over to see, they shrink back a little, point their torches like spears.

Marlene locks the door. "I'm calling the police." She calls from Roger's phone, then waits.

"I don't think it is a peaceful protest," she says. Another pause. "No, I don't think it can wait until later." She sighs, slams the phone down. "They'll send someone when they can."

A shrill, familiar voice outside echoes through a megaphone. "You know what we want," Cayla shrieks. "Send out the zombie or we torch the building."

Stupid Cayla, we think. This building is made of brick. Then two of her minions lay torches in front of the glass door. The clear pane blackens, then cracks, and black smoke starts seeping in under the door.

The old gold-diamond carpet begins to singe.

"Okay," Marlene says. "Everyone out the back. Calmly."

We rush en masse to the back exit, a metal double-door with a rusty frame and peeling brown paint, nearly trampling one another. All but Bob and Charlotte, that is, who calmly follow Marlene. But when we get there the door is hot, the smell of smoke and kerosene hanging in the air.

We panic. Anyone would.

Our eyes wander to Bob, hanging back behind the throng, holding Charlotte's hand.

Marlene notices. "Absolutely not," she says, voice raised just enough to cut through the noise. "We're not sending Bob out there."

Our shaky chatter stops. Of course not. We have a genuine miracle in our presence.

"I'm calling nine-one-one," Marlene says, and runs to her office.

This, we know, will solve the problem. Sooner or later the firemen and cops will arrive, douse the flames, disperse the mob.

Five minutes later, they have yet to arrive—one of the drawbacks to working in a business park ten minutes outside of town.

"Maybe I should go out and talk to them," Bob says.

"That sounds like a very bad idea, Bob," Marlene says. She is, of course, correct.

Then someone lays a couple more torches by the front door, and the glass goes completely black. In a minute it will shatter, the mob will enter, and the whole place will burn.

Because of the smoke and the panic, it's not clear who is the first to seize Bob. But someone does, and then we all grab hold, and we hoist him over our shoulders and begin to carry him toward the window.

He does not struggle or even object. Charlotte does, screaming and swatting at us from behind. "Stop!" Marlene shouts over and over. We barely hear her.

Someone opens the window and pops the screen, and out he goes.

We close the window and watch.

Bob picks himself up off the ground and limps around to the front of the building, creeping toward the mob with his arms raised, and for a few seconds they just stare. He says something to them. We can't hear, but it's working—people lower their torches and signs, and we swear a few of them smile. Then Cayla grabs a torch from someone and sets him ablaze. His suit goes up like flash paper.

Only Jeremy has the fortitude to watch further, reporting what he sees: the rest of the mob, horrified, like they didn't really expect her to do it; Cayla staring blankly as Bob writhes on the asphalt, as if she doesn't understand what's happened; a state trooper tackling her. The rest is chaos: the parking lot full of squad cars, fire engines, and flashing lights.

Bob isn't moving by the time they put him out. We stare at the smoldering heap until the EMTs zip him into a plastic sack and drive away. Then, we think, when Bob comes back tomorrow he'll have quite the story to tell.

Tuesday

We show up to work uneasy and fretting, though we make no mention of the reason.

Marlene is locked in her office, lights out, head in hands in the shadow of her computer screen. The contractors have already put in a new glass door, and by the time we step over the threshold, two men from Karpet King have almost finished laying down the new rug, a dark jewel-blue number with a bubble pattern. It is, we agree, one hell of a nice carpet. This is what we discuss as we pour our coffee and prepare for the day.

At 7:55, we all look up at the clock. No Bob. No Charlotte, either, though she usually takes her sweet time. For all we know they'll come in together, Charlotte laughing as she drapes her arm over Bob's, singed bits peeling off as they go. We will take comfort in this and forget yesterday's unpleasantness.

By a quarter after, we are still waiting. It is unlike him to be late. Our eyes drift toward the new glass door that Bob will eventually walk through, then down to the new carpet, glistening like a sapphire in the morning sun. We have to remind ourselves to exhale. And we keep thinking, as the seconds tick away, it really is a fine carpet.

Stemming the Tide

Simon Strantzas

Marie and I sit on the wooden bench overlooking the Hopewell Rocks. In front of us, a hundred feet below, the zombies walk on broken, rocky ground. Clad in their sunhats and plastic sunglasses, carrying cameras around their necks and tripping over open-toed sandals, they gibber and jabber among themselves in a language I don't understand. Or, more accurately, a language I don't *want* to understand. It's the language of mindlessness. I detest it.

Marie begged me for weeks to take her to the Rocks. It's a natural wonder, she said. The tide comes in every six hours and thirteen minutes and covers everything. All the rock formations, all the little arches and passages. It's supposed to be amazing. Amazing, I repeat, curious if she'll hear the slight scoff in my voice, detect how much I loathe the idea. There is only one reason I might want to go to such a needlessly crowded place, and I'm not sure if I'm ready to face it. If she senses my mood, she feigns obliviousness. She pleads with me again to take her. Tries to convince me it can only help her after her loss. Eventually, the crying gets to be too much, and I agree.

But I regret it as soon as I pick her up. She's dressed in a pair of shorts that do nothing to flatter her pale, lumpy body. Her hair is parted down the middle and tied to the side in pigtails, as though she believes somehow appropriating the trappings of a child will make her young again. All it does is reveal the graying roots of her dyed hair. Her blouse . . . I cannot even begin to explain her blouse. This is going to be great! She assures me as soon as she's seated in the car, and I nod and try not to look at her. Instead, I look at the sun-bleached road ahead of us. It's going to take an hour to drive from Moncton to the Bay of Fundy. An hour where I have to listen to her awkwardly try and fill the air with words because she cannot bear silence for anything longer than a minute. I, on the other hand, want nothing more than for the world to keep quiet and keep out.

The hour trip lengthens to over two in traffic, and when we arrive the sun is already bearing down as though it has focused all its attention on the vast asphalt parking lot. We pass through the admission gate and, after having our hands stamped, onto the park grounds. Immediately, I see the entire area is lousy with people moving in a daze—children eating dripping ice cream or soggy hot dogs, adults wiping balding brows and adjusting colorful shorts that are already tucked under rolls of fat. I can smell these people. I can smell their sweat and their stink in the humid air. It's suffocating, and I want to retch. My face must betray me; Marie asks me if I'm okay. Of course, I say. Why wouldn't I be? Why wouldn't I be okay in this pigpen of heaving bodies and grunting animals? Why wouldn't I enjoy spending every waking moment in the proximity of people that barely deserve to live, who can barely see more than a few minutes into the future? Why wouldn't I enjoy it? It's like I'm walking through an abattoir, and none of the fattened sows know what's to come. Instead they keep moving forward in their piggy queues, one by one meeting their end. This is what the line of people descending into the dried cove look like to me. Animals on the way to slaughter. Who wouldn't be okay surrounded by that, Marie? Only I don't say any of that. I want to with all my being, but instead I say I'm fine, dear. Just a little tired is all. Speaking the words only makes me sicker.

The water remains receded throughout the day, keeping a safe distance from the Hopewell Rocks, yet Marie wants to sit and watch the entire six-hour span, as though she worries what will happen if we are not there to witness the tide rush in. Nothing will happen, I want to tell her. The waters will still rise. There is nothing we do that helps or hinders inevitability. That is why it is inevitable. There is nothing we can do to stem the tides that come. All we can do is wait and watch and hope that things will be different. But the tides of the future never bring anything to shore we haven't already seen. Nothing washes in but rot. No matter where you sit, you can smell its clamminess in the air.

The sun has moved over us and still the rocky bottom of the cove and the tall weirdly sculpted mushroom rocks are dry. Some of the tourists still will not climb back up the metal grated steps, eager to spend as much of the dying light as possible wandering along the ocean's floor. A few walk out as far as they can, sinking to their knees in the silt, yet none seem to wonder what might be buried beneath the sand. The teenager who acts as the lifeguard maintains his practiced, affected look of disinterest, hair covering the left half of his brow, watching the daughters and mothers walking past. He ignores everyone until the laughter of those in the silt grows too loud, the giggles caused by sand fleas nibbling their flesh unmistakable. He yells at them to get to the stairs. Warns them of how quickly the tide will rush in, the immediate undertow that has sucked even the heaviest of men out into the Atlantic, but even he doesn't seem to believe it. Nevertheless, the pigs climb out one at a time, still laughing. I look around to see if anyone else notices the blood that trickles down their legs.

The sun has moved so close to the horizon that the blue sky has shifted to orange. Many of the tourists have left, and those few that straggle seemed tired to the point of incoherence. They stagger around the edge of the Hopewell Rocks, eating the vestiges of the fried food they smuggled in earlier or laying on benches while children sit on the ground in front of them. The tide is imminent, but only Marie and I remain alert. Only Marie and I watch for what we know is coming.

When it arrives, it does so swiftly. Where once rocks covered the ground, a moment later there is only water. And it rises. Water fills the basin, foot after foot, deeper and deeper. The tide rushes in from the ocean. It's the highest tide the world over. It beckons people from everywhere to witness its power. The inevitable tide coming in.

Marie has kicked off her black sandals, the simple act shaving inches from her height. She has both her arms wrapped around one of mine and is staring out at the steadily rising water. She's like an anchor pulling me down. Do you see anything yet? she asks me, and I shake my head, afraid of what might come out if I open my mouth. How much longer do you think we'll have to wait? Not long, I assure her, though I don't know. How would I? I've refused to come to this spot all my life, this spot on the edge of a great darkness. That shadowy water continues to lap, the teenage lifeguard finally concerned less with the girls who walk by to stare at his athletic body, and more with checking the gates and fences to make sure the passages to the bottom are locked. The last thing anyone wants is for one to be left open accidentally. The last thing anyone but me wants, that is.

The sun is almost set, and the visitors to the Hopewell Rocks have completely gone. It's a park full only with ghosts, the area surrounding the risen tide. Mushroom rocks look like small islands, floating in the ink just off the shore. The young lifeguard has gone, hurrying as the darkness crept in as fast as the water rose. Before he leaves he shoots the two of us a look that I can't quite make out under his flopping denim hat, but one which I'm certain is fear. He wants to come over to us, wants to warn us that the park has closed and that we should leave. But he doesn't. I like to think it's my expression that keeps him away. My expression, and my glare. I suppose I'll never know which. Marie is lying on the bench by now, her elbow planted on the wooden slats, her wrist bent to support the weight of her head. She hasn't worn her shoes for hours, and even in the long shadows I can see sand and pebbles stuck to her soles.

She looks up at me. It's almost time, she whispers, not out of secrecy—because no one is there to hear her—but of glee. It's almost time. It is, I tell her, and try as I might I can't muster up even a false smile. I'm too nervous. The thought of what's to come jitters inside of me, shakes my bones and flesh, leaves me quivering. If Marie notices, she doesn't mention it, but I'm already prepared with a lie about the chill of day's end. I know it's not true, and that even Marie is smart enough to know how warm it still is, but nevertheless I know she wants nothing more than to believe every word I say. It's not one of her most becoming qualities.

The tide rushes in after six hours and thirteen minutes, and though I'm not wearing a watch I know exactly when the bay is at its fullest. I know this not by the light or the dark oily color the water has turned. I know this not because I can see the tide lapping against the nearly submerged mushroom rocks. I know this because, from the rippling ocean water, I can see the first of the heads emerge. Flesh so pale it is translucent, the bone beneath yellow and cracked. Marie is sitting up, her chin resting on her folded hands. I dare a moment to look at her wide-open face, and wonder if the remaining light that surrounds us is coming from her beaming. The smile I make is unexpected. Genuine. They're here! she squeals, and my smile falters. I can't believe they're here! I nod matter-of-factly.

There are two more heads rising from the water when I look back at the full basin, the first already sprouting an odd number of limbs attached to a decayed body. The thing is staggering towards us, the only two living souls for miles around, though how it can see us with its head cocked so far back is a mystery. I can smell it from where we're sitting. It smells like tomorrow. More of the dead emerge from the water, refugees from the dark ocean, each one a promise of what's to come. They're us, I think. The rich, the poor, the strong, the weak. They are our heroes and our criminals. They are our loved ones and most hated enemies. They are me, they are Marie, they are the skinny lifeguard in his idiotic hat. They are our destiny, and they have come to us from the future, from beyond the passage with a message. It's one no one but us will ever hear. It is why Marie and I are there, though each for a different reason—her to finally help her understand the death of her mother, me so I can finally put to rest the haunting terrors of my childhood. Neither of us speak about why, but we both know the truth. The dead walk to tell us what's to come, their broken mouths moving without sound. The only noise they make is the rap of bone on gravel. It only intensifies as they get closer.

For the first time, I see a thin line of fear crack Marie's reverie. There are nearly fifty corpses shambling towards us, swaying as they try to keep rotted limbs moving. If they lose momentum, I wonder if they'll fall over. If they do, I doubt they'd ever right themselves. Between where we sit and the increasing mass is the metal gate the young lifeguard chained shut. More and more of the waterlogged dead are crowding it, pushing themselves against it. I can hear the metal screaming from the stress, but it's holding for now. Fingerless arms reach through the bars, their soundless hungry screams echoing through my psyche. Marie is no longer sitting. She's standing. Pacing. Looking at me, waiting for me to speak. Purposely, I say nothing. I'll let her say what I know she's been thinking.

There's something wrong, she says. This isn't—

It isn't what?

This isn't what I thought. This, these people. They aren't *right* . . .

I snigger. How is it possible to be so naive?

They are exactly who they are supposed to be, I tell her with enough sternness I hope it's the last she has to say on the subject. I don't know why I continue to make the same mistakes. By now, I'd have thought I would have started listening. But that's the trouble with talking to your past self. Nothing, no matter how hard you try, can be stopped. Especially not the inevitable.

The dead flesh is packed so tight against the iron gates that it's only a matter of time. It's clear from the way the metal buckles, the hinges scream. Those of the dead that first emerged are the first punished, as their putrefying corpses are pressed by the throng of emerging dead against the fence that pens them in. I can see upturned faces buckling against the metal bars, hear softened bones pop out of place as their lifeless bodies are pushed through the narrow gaps. Marie turns and buries her face in my chest while gripping my shirt tight in her hands. I can't help but watch, mesmerized.

Hands grab the gate and start shaking, back and forth, harder and harder. So many hands, pulling and pushing. The accelerating sound ringing like a church bell across the lonely Hopewell grounds. I can't take it anymore, Marie pleads, her face slick with so many tears. It was a mistake. I didn't know. I never wanted to know. She's heaving as she begs me, but I pull myself free from her terrified grip and stand up. It doesn't matter, I tell her. It's too late.

I start walking towards the locked fence.

I can't hear Marie's sobs any longer, not over the ruckus the dead are making. I wonder if she's left, taken the keys and driven off into the night, leaving me without any means of transportation. Then I wonder if instead she's watching me, waiting to see what I'll do without her there. I worry about both these things long enough to realize I don't really care. Let her watch. Let her watch as I lift the latches of the fence the dead are unable to operate on their own. Let me unleash the waves that come from that dark Atlantic Ocean onto the tourist attraction of the Hopewell Rocks. Let man's future roll in to greet him, let man's future become his present. Make him his own past. Who we will be will soon replace who we are, and who we might once have been.

The dead, they don't look at me as they stumble into the unchained night. And I smile. In six hours and thirteen minutes, the water will recede as quickly as it came, back out to the dark dead ocean. It will leave nothing behind but wet and desolate rocks the color of sun-bleached bone.

Those Beneath the Bog

Jacques L. Condor
(Maka Tai Meh)

Prunie Stefan, wearing a plaid shirt and men's trousers cinched at her waist with a rope, toiled at flensing a fresh moose skin. Her hair was in two braids tied together across her back so it did not fall in her way. Her husband, Martin, trimmed sinews from a moose carcass hung on a crossbar in the forks of two trees. The work of trimming and flensing was tiresome, but necessary for both of them.

A campfire blocked the entrance to their campsite against marauding bears attracted by the moose kill. Prunie pushed the flensing tool against stretched skin to remove fat and fibers. The final tanned skin would be smooth as the velvet cloth sold at the Nelson River trading post.

Bot flies darted around Prunie's head and arms so she ran to the enveloping alder wood smoke of smudge fires where she was free of the buzzing pests. Prunie used the tail of her blood-spattered shirt to wipe her watering eyes. She left the smoke and walked to the riverbank fifty paces away. Prunie scanned the lake. Something moved far out on the water. She shaded her eyes with her hands to make out the object. A freight canoe with a single sail moved far out on the water. The canoe came closer and she recognized the man at the tiller.

My Uncle Alex from Cranberry Portage, Prunie thought. *Coming to visit his relatives at Reed Lake.*

Wind scudded across the water and threw up spumes of white froth. The man turned the canoe into the sudden gust. The sail lofted. Prunie saw the painted clan symbol on the canvas and recognized several people in the canoe.

"Hey, husband," she called out. "People are coming: Uncle Alex and my aunties. There are other men with him." Martin turned from his butchering. "They smelled my moose meat over there in Cranberry." He laughed. "I know your relatives. They can sniff meat twenty kilometers away. Am I wrong?"

"Yes, wrong. Perhaps they come just to visit," Prunie said. "We'll feed them, no? It's good I shot this moose. You're lucky your husband is a great hunter." He planted a kiss on her nose and laughed. The woman laughed with him and rolled her eyes.

"You should get to cookin'," Martin said. With a knife as long as his wife's forearm, he sliced through the carcass and pried loose a section of ribs.

"I'll roast these over a slow fire," Prunie said. "But I need meat for stew. They'll need hot soup. It's cold on the lake." Martin cut several lean strips from the belly of the moose. Prunie went to her cooking fire with her arms full of meat.

Martin walked to the rock ledge boat landing at the river's mouth and waited for the canoe to nudge into shore. He saw the guns and the backpacks and knew the relatives were not just visiting, but hunting.

Old Alex climbed from the canoe bobbing in shallow water. The old man waded to shore. As tribal elder and leader of a hunting party, it was his duty to be the first ashore.

The old man shook Martin's hand. "Hello, my relative." Prunie's cousins, both in their early thirties, greeted Martin.

"Remember me? I'm Peter and this is my brother, Freddie." Freddie pumped Martin's hand.

"Uncle, good to see you," Prunie embraced the old man. "Good to see you, niece. It has been a year."

Martin waded out to the canoe and picked up an auntie in each arm and carried them to shore. There were squeals and laughter.

"Don't drop them!" Old Alex shouted. "They are the only ones to cook and take care of me."

Peter tried to help the third and eldest of the aunties ashore. The old woman waved him off. She crawled out of the canoe, lifted two layers of long skirts above her knee-high rubber boots and plodded through the water. A large black dog leapt out of the canoe and splashed behind her. One of the strangers whistled a shrill command. The dog dropped on his belly on the gravel shore.

The visitors followed Prunie to her campfire where they drank hot soup and warmed themselves. The oldest woman stirred the ashes of the fire with a willow stick before she dropped in a bundle of tobacco, cedar twigs and red yarn. Her offering flared for a moment and the fire smoldered as before.

"I had to do that, Prunie," the old Auntie Rose said. "That's my prayer offering to Manitou. I been prayin' since we left home. That lake is dangerous with the crosswinds rushin' in."

"Oh, Sister Rose, you worry too much about everythin'. You're always praying for somethin' or other," Alex said.

"Somebody's got to do the prayin' or we wouldn't have any protection at all."

"I'm glad you pray, Auntie Rose. It makes me feel safer," Prunie said. "Do you pray too, Auntie Sophia?"

"I sure do, but when Rose tells me I ought to be prayin' to the Old Ones, I get peevish. I'm a good Catholic, Prunie," Auntie Sophia said.

"Well I wish prayers could kill these pesky bugs!" Young Aunt Nettie swatted at a circling ring of black flies swarming around her head.

"Hard freeze works better than prayers on bugs," Uncle Alex said.

The youngest of the aunties made a sound like "Pish" and walked downwind of a smudge fire and let the smoke discourage the pests.

"We haven't seen moose on our side of the lake. Don't know where they gone to," Alex said.

"Alex is too old to hunt moose." Aunt Sophia said.

"I am not too old," the old man replied.

"If I say you are—then you are," Sophia replied. "That's why these two boys came along—to get some moose meat for us—forgot to introduce them."

"These boys are from our village," Auntie Rose explained. "The tall one is Nikolas. That black dog is his. It's a good duck dog. This skinny one is Ephraim. They is good boys."

"And good hunters, too," Sophia added.

The man called Nikolas whistled again and the black dog came and crouched at his feet. "This is River. I call him River 'cause he takes to water every chance he gets. Never go any place without him," Nikolas said.

"You never go any place without that silly cap either," Auntie Sophia pointed to the leather hat the man wore. It was decorated with fishing lures, bits of shell, dangling beads and animal fetishes. The hat was firmly tied under the man's chin with leather thongs.

"He sleeps in that damned hat," Alex said. "Come on, we got to talk huntin'."

"You're a pushy old man bringing up the main subject without first jest visitin'," Sophia said.

"And you won't let a man talk about huntin' in peace." Sophia kicked at Alex's moccasin-shod foot and missed. She shrugged and walked away to join Prunie and Nettie at the cooking fire. As she passed her eldest sister, Sophia noticed that Rose held a spruce root basket in her hands and a tattered red blanket was draped over her arm.

"What you plannin' to do with that stuff, Rose?" Sophia asked, frowning.

She recognized the divining tools and knew her sister intended to consult the bones and foretell the future.

"Leave me be, Sophia!" Rose croaked. "I'm gonna go off yonder and do me some prayin'."

"Prayin', I don't mind, Rose, but tossin' around them old bones and little colored rocks is the devil's work in my way of thinkin'."

"Then stop thinkin'. Don't pay me any mind and let me do my *niganadjimowin* divinin' in peace."

"Oh go off by yourself and throw them smelly old bones all over the place if you want. My advice is to toss all that evil stuff in the Grassy River." Sophia turned abruptly and went to tend the roasting ribs.

Rose moved several meters farther away and spread her blanket. She peered inside the basket. The bones were there. The porcupine bones would tell her of hunting success and the beaver hipbone foretold the fate of all in the camp. The other tiny bones and colored agate stones and the *pindjigos-san* medicine bag helped old Rose with vague details of her divinations. She covered the opening of the basket with her hand and shook it seven times. She sang divination song-prayers before she turned the basket upside down and let the contents spill on the worn red blanket. Rose bent to study the pattern the bones made. She read the message:

> *Three moose will be taken—not by these hunters but by others. Danger surrounds this camp. Two hunters will die!*

"*Ka! Kawin! Namawiya! Ka! Ka!*" She cried out. "No! Oh my, no! Oh no!" and slumped to the ground.

Prunie saw her old auntie fall and rushed to her side. "What is it, Auntie?" Prunie asked.

"I think she fainted," Nikolas said, hurrying to their side. "I'm all right you two." Rose allowed herself to be raised to a sitting position. "The bones' message scared me. I'm all right, but this camp and two of the hunters are in danger. Two gonna die!"

Nikolas shook his head, eyes growing wide. "Who? Which one of us is it? When? Who will die?" he asked.

"Foolish man!" Rose hissed. "The bones don't give me a time and a place! They don't spell out names if that's what you're thinkin'."

Prunie looked up into Nikolas's worried face and forced a smile. "Sometimes what the bones reveal never come true. Isn't that right, Auntie? Sometimes the bones reveal things that have already happened."

The old auntie did not answer. She gathered her divining items and replaced them in her basket.

Nikolas helped Rose to her feet. "Sometimes things you see don't happen?"

"Prunie said that. *I didn't*," Rose said. "I might read the bones wrong—but it doesn't happen often. I must make prayers to Manitou. The danger is from the dead ones who live. Go away and leave me be."

Nikolas watched the old woman hobble off to pray and turned to Prunie. "What is that old one talking about? You believe in all this stuff?"

"You shouldn't worry about what she saw in the bones. Forget about this, Nikolas. Don't say anything to the others and neither will I." Prunie tried to sound calm. Nikolas hesitated before nodding his agreement.

When she finished her prayers, a grim-faced Auntie Rose joined the other women. When Sophia asked Rose what was wrong, the older sister said nothing, put down the carving knife and walked away. Auntie Rose kept apart from everyone. She stared into space, silent and alone. Prunie felt uneasy and it showed on her face.

Sophia patted her arm and said, "Don't worry, Prunie. Rose is in one of her moods. She always gets that way whenever she messes with them old bones. She calls it *'seein' visions.'* What she imagines she sees, I ignore. She just wants attention. She'll get over her bad mood and be her regular sassy self in a few hours."

Nikolas joined the men at their campfire. Uncle Alex discussed the route from the headwaters of Reed Lake to the west bank, then north where moose were to be found.

"I had good luck up at Rabbit Lake 'bout seven, maybe eight seasons ago," Uncle Alex said.

"Then let's head up there," Martin said.

"We'll need canoes," Peter said. "Can't get the big canoe up there."

"We'll borrow from my relatives," Martin said.

"Good," Alex said. "Here's the plan. Martin and Peter will hunt together with me and Freddie as a second team. Nikolas will be the go-between for the two groups."

That night Prunie walked to the lean-to where Martin rested, puffing on his clay pipe. She crawled into bed.

Martin blew out a puff of smoke, took the pipe from his mouth. "Did you see the look on Auntie Rose's face when she heard we'll go up to Rabbit Lake?" Martin asked.

"I was too busy listening to Uncle's plans to notice," Prunie said. "Auntie Rose has been in a bad mood all day."

Martin gave a big sigh.

"What do you want to tell me?" Prunie asked. "Did Auntie Rose say something to you tonight?"

He phrased his answer carefully. "This is not the first time Rose talked about danger around that lake. When she came here four years ago she told me never to go there if I was alone."

"But you're not going alone," Prunie said. "So what's the problem?"

He rolled on his side and faced his wife. "Auntie Rose said she'd had visions; *warnings*, she called them, about some dead things."

"If she wants to warn you, to protect you, let her do it. Old people, like Auntie Rose, are the only ones who still know how to do such things. If I knew the old protection songs and how to make amulets to protect you, believe me, I'd do it."

"I thought you were a church member."

"I am, but maybe there's something true and powerful in the old ways. I want you back safe and in one piece."

"I'll come back safe. I've not hunted over that way, ever since old Rose spooked me four years ago."

"What did she do?"

"She took me aside and said she wanted to talk. She looked towards Rabbit Lake and started talking to herself as much as to me," Martin explained. "She said the night was full of evil spirits on the other shore; dead things walkin' around and don't I see 'em? I tell her, 'No. I don't see no dead things.' Then she asks, 'Did you ever hear any whistlin' when you was over there at night?'"

"No." I told her. 'You will some day, she said, when you hear the whistlin' you'll know. The *wanisid manitous*, evil spirit things is around. Somebody's gonna die.'"

Prunie lay beside her husband. She felt a chill in spite of the warmth of the heavy quilts and blankets. Memories of old legends; stories of the hairy men; the *wendigo*; wild men of the woods, the *ganibod*; the dead people who walk; the under-the-lake-people; the old tales invaded her brain like misty ghosts that wouldn't take clear shape or form. The fear of something ancient, something terrible and deadly, some- thing she knew existed but had never seen nor heard grew within her. She shuddered and Martin, feeling her tremble, asked if she was cold.

"Yes," she said and snuggled against him. She slept fitfully, awakening suddenly in the late night. She was jolted upright in the bed still feeling the tugging, clawed hands of some nightmare creatures, imagined dream horrors.

The camp came alive with morning activity. Supplies were pushed into backpacks. Freddie and Ephraim carried gear to the lakeshore. Prunie and Sophia helped Nettie pour water on the campfires while they waited for Martin, Peter, and Nikolas to come up the lake with the canoes borrowed from the villagers. Auntie Rose paced back and forth at the far end of the spit of land and muttered her prayers.

Shouts announced Martin's and the boys' arrival with three smaller canoes. Uncle Alex supervised the placement of packs and people in them. He took his Elder's place in the first canoe before they moved towards the north bank several kilometers away.

Before the second night in the new camp, brush lean-to shelters had been fashioned to face a central fire pit where the women prepared the meals. Smaller "bear-fires" burned in outlying pits.

The third night in camp, a despondent group sat around the fire. Two days without moose sign had passed. Nikolas and his dog brought in rabbits and a goose to provide the camp with fresh meat but the moose remained elusive.

The weather stayed warm. The bushes close to camp were heavy with Manitoba *mashkigimin*—high-bush cranberries—and a few late fruiting *pikwadjish*—wild mushrooms—were found on the forest floor. With a supply of walleyes and pike from the lake, the women prepared daily meals. The hunters grumbled as they ate, and complained every night that the moose must have moved farther northwest from Rabbit Lake.

When Auntie Rose heard this, she developed another bout of sulky silence. The women hoped her moody spell would soon end. Such behavior disturbed the harmony of the camp.

Each night, campfires provided a sense of safety, holding the thick darkness of the wilderness at bay. For Rose, the shadowy trees concealed *matchi manadad*—very evil things, the dead who live—watching, waiting to steal forward if the fires died.

The nights in this part of Manitoba were cold, silent, and, to Rose, threatening. She listened for whispering voices or the whistling calls, but heard nothing. Rose pulled her blanket tighter and recited songs of protection for herself and the group. Her repeated chants lasted until the first gray streaks of false dawn.

On the fifth morning, a damp haze of fog hung over the forest and camp blurring the outlines of everything it touched. The men sat huddled around the central fire.

Martin spoke to Peter and Uncle Alex. "Ain't no moose for three-day's walk. I say we go up past Rabbit Lake. What you think?"

Old Alex rubbed his hands together and held them palms outward to the campfire. "Good idea," he said. "That lake has a big bog at the north end. There's a big sinkhole in the middle of the bog you gotta watch out for, but it's a safe enough place to camp and hunt."

Peter said, "I heard nobody goes up there."

"That sinkhole has a bad name, that's why some hunters don't go there," Uncle Alex said. "It's called the 'death hole.' Been there before. It's a strange place."

Auntie Rose stared at Alex and shook her head vigorously in negation. Martin saw the old uncle telegraph a quick message with his eyes.

Auntie Rose slammed her hand down on the earth and shouted, "No! Never—you can't go there. Something bad will happen!"

Prunie was surprised when her auntie spoke out with such emphatic anger. When Rose disagreed with anything or anyone, she usually turned silent and never shouted.

Alex turned to Rose. "Not the time to speak of visions and deaths." To the other men he said, "It is nothing. Get ready to leave."

Uncle Alex acted as if the harsh exchange had not taken place and said, "We will leave when the sun stands directly over us and camp out by Rabbit Lake."

It was obvious that old Rose did not like this plan at all. She went silent in her sulky manner. This time her silence seemed to convey something more than just disapproval.

Prunie saw a different expression on her auntie's face—a look of fear. It flashed quickly like a burst of flame from bear fat dropped in a campfire. The old woman's expression filled Prunie with a sense of dread.

At noon, the men packed their gear into three small canoes. When the hunters started paddling away, Martin shouted to Rose who stood apart from the others.

"Keep prayin' for us and we're all gonna come back." Martin could not hear the words the old woman whispered to the wind.

The hunters arrived at Rabbit Lake before nightfall. Peter built a large fire. The bright blaze illuminated the shelters made from tarps and branches. They ate smoked fish and talked.

Nikolas sat close to the fire ring, squatting on his haunches, his arm draped about his dog. He stared north in the direction of the bog. "Uncle Alex, you said people didn't come up here. Is there something you didn't tell us about this place?"

Alex swallowed the bite of smoked pike before he spoke. "Your Auntie Rose is a superstitious old woman," Alex said.

"There was a flat space where the bog is now, a burial site for murdered Cree and Ojibwe people. Generations ago the Dene people from up north fought our people over that flat place—good hunting land. The Dene pretended to leave but came back before dawn and slaughtered all the men in the camp. Old ones say they left the bodies unburied and put a Dene curse on the corpses. The spirits of the dead were unhappy."

"What did our people do?" Martin asked Alex.

"Stories say our people came up here and buried all they could find and built spirit houses over the graves. Maybe it was too late to calm the spirits of those dead men. I don't know. But no one from our tribes ever came back here much after that."

"But that happened years ago," Nikolas said.

"Yes," Alex said. "Right after the bodies were buried, a big fire came through and burned all the trees and brush as well as the grave houses. The rains and heavy snows created high run-off and filled the creeks to overflowing. Creeks changed course and turned the burial ground into a lake for a few years until most of it dried up. Now it's nothing but a bog with that deep sinkhole in the middle."

Uncle Alex knocked tobacco ash from his pipe. "Now it's grown back. Where there's willows and water, you got moose. We'll have good luck tomorrow."

Martin heard gravel crunch and saw Nikolas and his dog leave the fire and walk to the edge of Rabbit Lake. A swift gust of wind grew the fire's embers into flame. In the sudden fire-flare, Martin saw the man and the dog clearly.

What Martin saw on Nikolas's face was terror. Nikolas returned and knelt beside his dog and stared into the fire.

"What's the matter?" Martin waited for an answer. None came. "You think maybe bad things live up in that bog?" Nikolas still did not answer. The dog crouched at his side whined and shifted his ears.

Peter put his arm around Nikolas and said, "You're not afraid of an old tale about some things that died there a long time ago, are you?"

Again Nikolas did not answer. He pushed Peter's arm from his shoulder and stood up abruptly. Nikolas stepped out of the ring of firelight; his dog followed at his heels, whimpering. They faced the forest and the bog, watching and listening.

"I need some sleep," Martin yawned. "I'm shootin' moose tomorrow." Martin, Peter, and Alex went to the spruce bough shelters.

Freddie stood beside Nikolas. "Don't be payin' any heed to long ago stories. There ain't no such things around today."

"What makes you so sure, Freddie?" Nikolas muttered.

"Because nobody's seen anything for almost a hundred years, that's why I'm sure."

"Maybe they weren't lookin' in the right places, Freddie."

"You're actin' crazy, Nikolas. I'm goin' to bed. Don't let the spooks and *matchi* men get you." Freddie laughed and walked away.

Nikolas stood alone staring into the darkness. The dog growled low in his throat, lifted his ears and pointed his muzzle into the air, sniffing. Nikolas moved back towards the fire. Some innate memory struggled to access ancient warnings. His senses became acute. He heard sounds. They came out of the black night, swirling to his ears on the mists rising from the sinkhole in the bog. The sounds were high-pitched whistles, dropping in tone and fading away to nothingness.

With shaking hands, Nikolas tore open his pouch of sacred tobacco and cedar and offered the contents to the coals. He chanted his prayer so quietly his ears did not hear the words. He prayed, because he now knew the old tales were true. The creatures lived. Dead souls walked the brush forests of Rabbit Lake; the hunting party had invaded their homeland.

Ephraim tended the fires circling the camp while the women talked story by the big campfire. Rose was over her pouting spells. She told stories of family foibles and escapades, which made everyone laugh out loud. The laughter echoed back from the ringing, low hills. The echoes brought a sudden quiet to the gathering of women.

"I think I'd better get to bed before I laugh myself to death," Nettie said.

"Nobody ever dies laughin'," Auntie Rose grumbled. "Death ain't funny at all."

Young Nettie stopped giggling abruptly. "That was a dumb thing to say, Sister Rose." She hurried away.

Prunie put her arm around Rose. "We all say dumb things sometimes."

"You think I'm just a foolish old lady when I tell you what the bones show me. Huh?" Rose sniffed.

"No Auntie. I don't think that."

"You don't believe what I tell you?" Rose followed a spark's skyward flight from the fire with her eyes.

"I didn't say that. It's just that—"

"It's because you're one of these modern Indians hanging around Wekusko or Flin Flon, listening to what white people say. You believe their stories more than our old stories? Our stories kept Ojibwe people protected more than a hundred generations."

"Auntie Rose, it's a different time."

"Don't I know that? Four generations separate you and me." The young girl touched the weathered hand of her old auntie. "But I do listen, Auntie."

"But do you believe? What I'm gonna tell you now, about things in the bog, you gotta believe. They are real livin' creatures out there that are waitin' to kill someone. I had visions. They are dead things but still alive and eatin' living flesh."

Prunie stiffened at the thought.

She paused and formed her words carefully so as not to anger the old woman. "Auntie, those bog things that could kill our men . . . What are they?"

"Like a man, but not a man. They are all *nibo*, dead—for long, long time, but still alive somehow. Got hands like ours, but with claws. They are *mask*, ugly *gi-mask*, disfigured."

"Now you're trying to scare me with those old stories about the *wendigo* boogeymen of the woods," Prunie said.

"I'm not tryin' to scare you, child!" Rose pulled away. "I just want you to know there are dead things that walk."

Prunie whispered, "Auntie, don't you think if something like that *did* exist, we would have seen them?"

"They been seen, but those who saw them never lived to tell about them. The dead men live in the cursed bog by Rabbit Lake."

"Well, every one of the men has a rifle. If they see any of them up there, they can shoot them and kill them."

"There are some things that can't be killed—by guns, anyway. It'll take more than bullets to kill them bog creatures."

"Why do they live in a bog?"

Rose leaned towards Prunie. "They den in the bogs like beavers and muskrats."

"How could they do that?"

"They go down under the water and dig dens into earth banks at the edge of deep water."

"How do they get out in the winter when the ice freezes thick on the bog?" Prunie asked. "Wouldn't they be trapped with nothing to eat?"

"Them creatures take moose and anything else that wanders into their bog, then stores the meat up for winter. Just like a beaver does with green poplar branches.

"They got holes and tunnels dug up into the woods. They sneak out and roam around whenever they want. Don't make no nevermind if the bog is frozen over or not."

"I see," Prunie said. She smiled at her eighty-eight-year-old auntie and leaned over and kissed her on both cheeks and smoothed the old woman's straggles of coarse white hair back under her floral-printed babushka. "I love you, Auntie Rose."

"I love you too, Prunie. I wish you would send Ephraim to talk the men into comin' away from that bog."

"They'd laugh at us for worrying. The men plan to get winter meat and think that's the place to do it." Prunie stood. "I'm going to get us each a mug of hot coffee. It's getting chilly. Aren't you cold, Auntie?"

The old one shook her head. "I will have a cup anyway." Rose reached for the spruce root basket of divining bones.

She shook the basket vigorously before she dumped the bones on the blanket folded into a square.

"Waugh!" the old woman cried out. "Again it is two who will die!"

At daybreak, Martin found Nikolas curled up in a ball, next to his dog, his special hat pulled down over his ears, sleeping by the embers of the fire.

When the group woke him, he seemed to be surprised that he was still in the encampment and said, "Waugh! I am still alive!"

The men chuckled. A light dusting of snow in the earliest hours of the morning powdered Nikolas's clothes.

Nikolas shook his head, brushing off the snow with his hands.

"This is good. Snow helps us track moose now," Alex said. "Today I don't hunt," Nikolas said. "It was foolish of me to fall asleep outside. I couldn't shoot straight today. I'd spoil your hunt. Go without me. Maybe River will help me get some ducks or geese."

"Geese are good eatin', too," Martin offered.

"You get us some geese, Nikolas," Alex said. "We stay with our plan. I go up the east side of the lake with Freddie. Martin and Peter can take the west shore."

Freddie and Alex climbed into their canoe. The pair paddled into fog. Martin and Peter followed in the second canoe. They drew abreast of Uncle Alex's canoe.

"We will return with meat," Peter whispered.

"We'll get two moose apiece," Martin whispered just as Peter had done. Prey could hear a hunter's plans and so they must keep their voices low. The two canoes separated and headed to opposite sides of the lake.

Nikolas sat by the fire and watched the sun dissipate the fog. The sound of geese honking low overhead brought him to his feet. River jumped up, whining and wagging his tail.

"Stragglers heading to the far end of the lake," he told his Labrador. "They're tired. Let's go get us some geese, River." The excitement of a hunt pushed the fears of the night from Nikolas's mind. He slid the canoe into the water and River jumped in. He paddled in the direction the geese had flown. Nikolas pushed his leather hat with all its trinkets and totems firmly on his head and bent into his paddling, propelling the canoe forward.

Peter and Martin paddled the shoreline. No tracks were visible from the shore into the bush. They stopped paddling and let the canoe drift. They searched the willow thickets near a bend. Peter made a sudden hissing sound and pointed to the thick brush near a flat point of beach jutting into the water. The hunter made another sign for "listen" and cupped his hand to his ear. Martin did the same.

Both heard the sound of breaking twigs as something moved quickly away from their canoe. Martin pulled towards the thicket on the shoreline. A louder crashing followed as the something took off running at top speed through the brush.

"Moose," whispered Martin, and beached the prow on the sand. Peter grabbed his rifle and leapt onto the shore. He made signs telling Martin to go upwind and frighten the moose back where he would be waiting. Martin understood and back-paddled. He moved the canoe forward in silence some two hundred meters up the shoreline, jumped from the beached canoe and started inland, making noise to scare the moose back towards Peter.

Taller hemlocks among the spindly spruce created a thick canopy of interlocking branches. There were no tracks. Peter could hear the snapping of branches and crackling of twigs. He thought more than one animal hurried away. Suddenly the sounds stopped. Peter stopped, dropped to one knee and pointed his rifle in the direction where he had last heard sounds. Peter listened. The sounds he heard were like whispers children make. Over the whisperings came a series of short, low whistles.

Martin checked the rifle he had slung over his shoulder. He released the safety and began to walk towards his hunting partner. He saw or heard nothing as he sneaked through the thick brush and deadfalls.

Peter held his rifle at the ready for some time. The animals in front of him had not changed position. He had heard no sounds of movement, just murmurs. The muscles in his left forearm twitched with the strain of holding the heavy weapon. He lowered the rifle to relax his arm.

There was a snap of a twig behind him. Before he could turn something hard and heavy struck the back of his head and he pitched forward, unconscious.

When the hunter came to his senses he was being carried by the grasping hands of many strong creatures that moved at great speed. The creatures held him by the arms and legs and made whispered, lisping sounds and murmurs. As they ran, they called to each other with low whistles.

Martin heard the sounds of running animals directly ahead. They seemed to be going away from him. He heard murmurs, soft burbling sounds and whistles and could not imagine why, or how, any running moose could make such noises.

Alex sat on a fallen log and wondered why he had failed to spot any moose.

"The moose is hidin' from me," he told Freddie. "I'm wonderin' where they went, Uncle Alex."

"Freddie, walk along the shore and see if you can find any tracks. I'll sit here and wait for you."

Minutes passed and Freddie came back. He stood in front of Alex and shrugged his shoulders. "I can't figure it out. I saw moose tracks and they all led up to that bog—the one with the big sinkhole in the middle. Didn't see any moose, though. I did see lots of moose bones and three sets of skulls and antlers all bleached out white."

"Was the tines on the antlers all chewed up by porcupines eatin' on 'em? Was the bones scattered like bears and wolves had got to them?"

"Nothin' like that. They was all stacked up neat-like. The leg bones in one pile, the skulls in another and the ribs in another pile."

"Why'd anybody stack up moose bones like that?"

"Beats me," Freddie said.

At that moment two shots from a twelve-gauge shotgun rang out.

Martin stopped in his tracks. The sound of the gunshots echoed. It was Nikolas's shotgun. He pushed his way through the willows towards the gunshots. Martin heard a muffled scream. The tangled branches pulled at his clothing, as if trying to prevent him from reaching Peter.

Peter could not scream again. One of the creatures pried open his mouth with insistent claws and forced a chunk of lichen-moss into his open mouth. The creatures scurried through the willow and aspen growth towards the bog. Peter's eyes bulged in fear and panic. The choking moss barred the air from his lungs.

Peter heard the whistles grow in volume and the lisping sounds increased to an excited pitch as the creatures dragged Peter into the water. He felt the cold splash against his legs and back as the creatures propelled him feet first into the sinkhole.

The grasping creatures swarmed over his body, forcing him upright in the icy water until only his head remained above surface. Suddenly the whistles reached a crescendo and the things that held him pulled his head under the water. Peter gulped in a last breath of air and choked on the lichen and brackish bog water that rushed in. The grasping claws pulled him down, down . . .

Martin pushed on through old deadfalls to the border of Rabbit Lake. He stopped and listened for sounds that might direct him. He heard a sudden series of whistles from the direction of the bog. The whistling rose in volume and then stopped abruptly.

Loons? Could it be loons so late in the season?

He moved down a slope towards the far end of the lake. The water here was dark and looked deep. Martin experienced a brief jolt of unexplainable fear. The water's surface was still and placid. No loons swam there to disturb the black-mirror surface.

Nikolas heard the gabbling of geese at the far end of Rabbit Lake. He used his canoe paddle to test the depth of the water and found it less than half a meter deep. He pumped the paddle up and down; solid rock was beneath the canoe. He gave his dog a signal to stay.

Nikolas pulled his favorite hat down tight on his head and tied the thongs beneath his chin in a double knot. He did not want to lose the hat when he pushed through brush.

The cackling and the gabbling of the geese lessened. Nikolas crouched low, held aside dangling willow branches and peered through the peephole in the leaves. Nikolas's jaw muscles tightened at what he saw.

A sunken ring of earth, edged with a circle of rock ledges and moss-covered gravel, held a round, dark expanse of water several meters in diameter. A circle of water stared back at him like a giant cycloptic black eye. On the surface, six geese circled in a small bunched flock of frightened birds.

What the hell happened to the rest of the flock? They couldn't have flown away! I would have seen them. He raised his shotgun to fire as he pushed through the willows.

When the remaining birds flapped across the water in rising flight, he fired two shots. Both shots hit the targets and two geese fell into the dark water of the sinkhole.

Nikolas whistled to the waiting dog. River came bounding through the willows and leapt into the water to retrieve the geese. Nikolas watched River swimming at his top speed towards one of the birds.

Now what in the hell happened to the other one? The damned bird is gone. Geese don't sink when you hit them, not right away anyhow. Before Nikolas could concoct an answer, he saw River falter in the middle of the sinkhole. The dog let the bird fall from his mouth and gave a terrified yelp before he was pulled under the surface.

"River!" Nikolas shouted. "River! Hold on, boy!"

The man dropped his gun and slid down the mossy incline across the wet gravel and fell into the water. He swam only three strokes towards where the dog had gone down when something clutched at his ankles. The swimming man was held fast in the water. More and more clutching hands tugged at his legs and lower body.

"Oh God!" he cried out just before he was yanked under the black surface.

When Martin heard yelping and sounds of splashing, he turned to his right towards the sounds. He ran up a slight incline and skidded to a stop. Below him yawned the "death hole." He scanned the area in all directions.

The first thing he saw was Nikolas's hat floating two meters from the pool's edge. Then he saw the dog cowering in a stand of willows. The animal quivered with fright and gave out a keening wail.

Martin hurried around the rim of the sinkhole to the dog. "Hey there, boy. Where's your boss?"

The dog raised itself on its bleeding forepaws and bared its teeth in a menacing snarl.

"River. What's got into you? What chewed you up like this?"

The Labrador dropped on his belly and did a wiggling crawl backwards through the willows. Martin pushed through the brush and saw the dog, tail between his legs, howling and running as fast as his wounded legs could carry him down the trail to the camp.

He moved back to the sinkhole. Nikolas's hat had floated to the very edge. Martin knelt down to retrieve it. It felt heavy in his hand, as if snagged on something. He set down his rifle and used both hands to pull the leather hat from the water.

The hat gave way suddenly, and Martin fell on his backside onto the slick moss and gravel. Nikolas's severed head, the hat still firmly tied to it, fell into his lap. Martin scrabbled sideways away from the horrible object.

He raised his head and yelled as loud as he could. "Peter! Goddammit, Peter, get over here! Quick!"

Martin moved backwards through the willows just as the dog had done and ran as fast as he could down the same trail.

Fifteen minutes later, Freddie and Alex knelt looking at moose tracks leading to the edge of the circle of black water.

"Uncle Alex. This is what I wanted to show you."

The old man looked down at the mud. Freddie pointed. Alex saw three sets of tracks; one set made by a big bull.

"That's a big moose. See how deep he sinks into the mud?" Alex said. "That other set of tracks is a cow moose. Her hooves ain't as pointy as the bull's." He moved a few feet to his left. "Look here, Freddie, the cow had a yearling with her, too."

Freddie studied the bull's tracks. His mouth felt dry and he moistened his lips with his tongue. "Somethin' ain't right here. Come and look at this."

Alex looked where Freddie touched the slurred tracks with a willow stick.

"These tracks are real deep and messed up. See how they are bunched up close together with the dew-claws showin' in the prints?"

"I see that." Alex said. "What does that tell you?"

"It tells me it was a damn big bull moose, and that he was pullin' backwards trying to get away."

"Trying to get away from what?"

"From whatever was tryin' to pull him into the sinkhole."

"Whatever was pulling him in had to be monstrous big," Freddie said.

"Maybe it was several things all pullin' together," Alex replied.

"What?" Freddie scratched his head at the thought.

Alex studied the other tracks. "Something pulled the cow and the yearling calf into the water. Look around, you won't see no tracks comin' out!"

"What do you think happened?"

"I think somethin' got the three moose we been huntin' before we did."

"Whaaat?" Freddie dragged out his question.

"And now I think we best get away from this place fast as we can."

"What about the canoe?"

"Forget about the canoe. What killed them moose will kill us, too. Let's go. Rose knew what she was talkin' about!"

Old Alex started down the trail away from the bog at a wobbly trot.

"What are you talkin' about, Uncle Alex?"

"I'll tell you when we get back to camp. You'd better get a move on if you want to keep livin'."

Martin heard the padding of feet behind him. When he turned, he saw the willows were shaking. He cocked his rifle and held it at waist level, the barrel aimed at the spot where the willows moved.

Alex and Freddie came through the willows and stopped in their tracks when they saw Martin in the trail with his rifle pointed at them.

"Martin! Don't shoot!" Freddie yelled.

Alex saw the fear Martin struggled to hide. "So you know about the bog things?" Uncle Alex said.

"Something killed Nikolas—in the death hole place."

"Let's get as far away from here as we can. Come on. It's a long way to run."

"What about Peter, we can't go off and leave him up there."

"Pretty sure the things got Peter, too."

"Why would you think that? We gotta look for him!" Martin said.

"Old Rose said two people would die on this hunt. It's too late to save Peter. He's gone. Them dead, flesh-eatin' things—those damned creatures took him or we'd have heard from him by now."

"Martin. Let's go! I wanna get outta here." Freddie ran down the trail.

Rose sat staring up the trail. Uncle Alex hobbled to his sister. The others rushed to greet the hunters. The group encircled Auntie Rose. The old woman's eyes were open but not seeing. "Rose," Alex said. There was no response. "Rose?" The old woman's eyes fluttered shut and she began to moan.

Alex shook his sister. "Answer me!"

Sophia explained. "Yesterday, a little time before noon, I heard her scream. Prunie heard it too, and we thought a bear had come into camp."

"About an hour ago, that black dog came runnin' in here. His legs were all chewed up but he wouldn't let anyone get near him," Prunie said.

Ephraim said. "Rose just been sittin' there and mumblin'."

"She began to say words that frightened all of us," Nettie said.

"What in hell did she say?" Alex demanded.

"She called Peter's name. She said. '*Matchi wanisid manitou* got him.' And the words: 'They pulled him under. *Madagamiskwa nibi; gi-nibowiiawima manadas matchi ijiwe-bad—wissiniwin, matchi!* The water is moving, he is dead, just a body now; the evil ones are eating!'

"I thought she'd gone crazy." Sophia swallowed hard and continued. "Next she hollered, 'Nikolas! Look out! Get away from there!'"

"I don't understand what's goin' on," Nettie whimpered.

"I do," Alex said. "What she saw in the bones came true. Peter is dead and Nikolas too. We have to go back to Cranberry and give them the sad news."

Rose exhaled a great breath and shuddered and opened her eyes. "I have seen it all," she said.

"It is finished," the old man said.

"No. It is not finished yet." Rose struggled to her feet. "Are you ready to listen to me now?"

"Say what you want to say, Sister," Sophia said.

"Strike camp and pack up. We must be gone from here before dark comes."

No one doubted the old woman's words. They hiked the trail to Martin's hunting camp, where there was shelter. Uncle Alex and Ephraim coaxed the wounded black dog to follow.

Alex, Freddie, Sophia and Nettie packed the freight canoe for the return trip to their village. Prunie and Martin insisted Old Rose spend the winter at their cabin and Rose agreed.

Two weeks later, a flotilla of seven canoes from Cranberry Portage made their way to Rabbit Lake. Forty men from Prunie's village carried cans of fuel oil and gasoline two miles inland to the sinkhole.

The men did as Old Rose had instructed them. They spread oil and gasoline on the black surface of the death hole, dropped in a sealed case of dynamite with a timed detonator and hurried down the trail. The resulting explosion was heard miles away. The fire burned for several days, but died out beneath the heavy rains of mid-September.

When the first heavy frosts crusted the ground, four young men from Flin Flon appeared at Martin's cabin. They told Prunie and Rose they intended to hike to Rabbit Lake and see what remained of the sinkhole.

"There is nothing there. It is finished," Rose said. "You should not go."

The boys were polite to the old woman but paid no attention to her words. They left that afternoon, promising to return the next day. Snow clouds massed in gray billows overhead began to drop light flurries.

Rose made her way to a dark corner of the cabin.

The boys found the dynamite and fire had obliterated the sinkhole and left meters of burned brush and scorched trees. Farther away from the ruined bog, the taller trees and leafless willows were untouched by the fire. The boys moved into the shelter of the trees and set up a lean-to of canvas and spruce branches before exploring the area.

"Hey, Lucas, look over here. There's a whole bunch of trails and tracks," a slender boy said.

The tracks were barely visible in the quickly melting snow and the slanting late afternoon sun muddled their shape.

"Looks a little like black bear tracks," the slender boy said. "Some prints have claw marks."

"There sure are a lot of them," the boy called Lucas said.

Four days later, the boys had not returned. At Prunie's urging, Martin and a neighboring Cree man went to search for them. The first snows of the season had melted and the tracks and trails in the forests surrounding the old bog were no longer visible.

What the men found was the collapsed and destroyed lean-to shelter. The white of the canvass was spattered with rust-red stains.

The boys' backpacks were ripped and scattered about. Two rifles, their stocks broken and the barrels stuffed with chunks of lichen-moss, lay near the campsite.

Martin and his neighbor searched farther into the forest and found four neat piles of human bones. The skulls in one pile, the leg bones in another and the ribs placed in two mounded stacks.

What Still Abides

Marie Brennan

Let me tell a tale of my father's kin, for in me runs their blood, and so to me falls this burden: to keep the knowledge, the old-thought, the shape of how it began, as my father gave it to me.

Harvest-time it was, the time of reaping and of dying, when his breath stopped and his blood stilled, and they laid his body in the ground. He had a name then, that now is gone; my father knew it but told me not, saying it died with his life, and to speak it now would blight the speaker's tongue.

He died at harvest and they laid him in the ground, axe at his side and barrow built over his head. After that came winter, wolf-cold and sharp. It was a time of hunger, of bellies clenching hard and even kin looking upon one another with an unkind eye. Men tholed ill luck in those long nights: sickness and wound, horses lame and kine lost. Then came spring with storms, grimful rains to drown the fields, and the ground that was his grave became black with mud.

One night a man, Leofnoth by name, son of Leofmaer, hied to the eorl's hall to drink among the thanes, as was his wont, and a shame unto his wife. But when he came there, they saw he was white as bone with fear and his hands shook like leaves in the wind, though he had not yet taken ale. When they asked what had frighted him so, he said he had seen a man standing upon the grave.

For this they laughed at him, and gave him a cup to drink. But rest Leofnoth would not, holding that he told only truth, and furthermore that the man was no thing of this world. And so in the teeth of a storm, three men rode out to see what of what he spake.

Stood a dréag upon the brow of his barrow, feet mud-deep, neither shifting nor breathing.

Warriors they were, bold thanes of the eorl, who had seen that man buried and would swear their oath that he was dead. Yet there stood the lich: frost-shrunken his limbs and grey as old snow, like a curse upon the ground. Bold might they be, but near him none would go, for fear of this unearthly thing. Instead they settled that they would fetch a god-man, whose holy words would lay the wight once more.

But when came the god-man with them to the barrow at the mist-shrouded break of day, cast down he could not what had risen from that earth, for the thing was mightier than he. Whatever words said he, the bone-home neither shifted nor breathed, nor gave any show it saw the thanes and the god-man. Dead had he been, and so was he still, even upon the height of the barrow instead of in its heart.

The first of the thanes set himself to undertake what the god-man could not do, and bring low this weird thing. Fastened he his feet upon the ground, and put the heels of his hands upon the body, throwing against it all his weight. So might he have struggled against the mightiest tree, what little harvest had he for his work. Sought then the next of his fellows, and then the third, and then the three together, but all their strength could not shift the life-left flesh so much as the span of a hair.

Unrestful were their hearts at this, but hid they their fear with laughter, saying that the wight wanted only the freshness of the wind.

And so they left him there, for they could do naught. Came the children of the town to scorn at the thing, daring one another to feel the dréag's dead hand, and their mothers pulled them away.

Seven days after, came there a rider upon a horse, an errand-man for the eorl. As it went by the barrow his horse bolted in fear, dashing up the slope and hurling its burden to the ground. But struck the horse's hoof against the head of the man, and came thus his blood, soaking the loam at the lich's feet.

When came the thanes to gather up the errand-man's body, the dréag was not as he had been. Thick now were the arms withered by winter, ripe as the beginning of rot. But not like life was this; sick-swollen was he, full with the foulness of those who dwell with worms.

Among them were none with will enough to strike the wight. Frightened, left they the errand-man where he lay and rode back to their hall.

Then went out word from the eorl, that he would give rich gold to the man who rid him of this wicked thing. To this call came Aescwulf of the east, a warrior bold whose deeds men heard in tale and song, and said he that his sword would cut down what the god-man's words could not.

Therefore went Aescwulf to the top of the barrow with his sword in his hand, to meet the risen wight. Dry was his mouth and cold his blood at seeing dead flesh stand, but held he to his meaning and his end, lest he shame himself and his good name lose in the eyes of his fellow men.

With keen edge he cut, striking at the sticks of the wight, and meat and bone gave way before his blade. But fell too the sword from Aescwulf's hand: stopped had his heart at the start of his strike, and now he lay dead beside the dréag.

For Aescwulf was great mourning and great thanks, that he had freed the folk from their fear. To his kin gave the eorl the plighted gold and meed besides, for the loss of their fellow in so worthy a work. The wight his men graved in the ground once more, and gave yield to the gods that he should not leave another time.

But when waned the moon, stood the shape again on the height of the hill, the dréag as he had been.

Darker then were the days, gray the sky with clouds, and colder waxed the wind even as the summer grew. Came again the god-man, and four strong men with him, weaponed with whitethorn. For then was it the month of three milkings, and with the wood of that month might they steal the strength that fed his soul. At the god-man's rede bound they the bone-home and broke it from the earth, and once more laid it down where it should keep.

But in this doing, pricked the thorns of the wood into the men's hands, so that their blood fell onto the skin of the wight. Drank the gray flesh these drops and thereafter grew white, shining lich-sick as they steeked the barrow shut.

Still darker dimmed the sun, so that churl and thane and eorl alike dwelt in grave-gloom. Came then the rain almost without halt, drowning the home of seeds, killing the year before it lived. Empty were the keeps of corn after winter's end; hunger was man's dish, and want his drink, and the wolf of death came for many.

Thin grew the sky-sickle and withered into black, and when darkest came the night, rose again the dréag to stand upon the ground.

More gold gave the eorl, and clubs of the crabapple tree, for the boldest men to bear. Now this is the soul-strength of apple: that it is the tree of life, whose wood is bane to things of death. Hewn was this wood from a holy tree, and marked with runes by the god-man, to give it might against the dréag.

Rode forth six men who climbed the hill, and with reckless hearts put themselves against this threat. Scathed their clubs the skin, and with the first blow came the breath of the wolf, the wind of winter, from the wounds they made. Twice struck their arms, and crumbled the blossoms of the hedges into dust. At the last blow, fell the birds from the trees, their feathers breaking against the ground.

From the skin of the dréag wept tears of black blood that froze the hands of the men. Numb-fingered, took they the raven's food and thrust it into the ground, stopping the way with stone. Then came the women and children, half-starved and scared, with shale from their houses and flint from their fields, to roof over the barrow so naught might grow upon it again. But beneath the blood, the hands of the men were white as midwinter snow.

Long then were the nights, though summer should have made sweet the sky. Brought the day little sun and no hope, and dwindled horse and kine for lack of grass. All kept watch for the waning of the moon, and what they knew it must bring.

When saw the watchers the wight again, it was the death of hope. No strength of sinew nor holiness of heart could drive the dréag down whither it should be, and its foulness drained the life from the land. Dim were the days and dead the fields, and the men with white hands walked about with empty eyes, stopping neither for food nor for sleep. Dread they woke in those who saw them, and in fear some sought to fight them; but when their foes their hands met, numb went their limbs, as if winter's cold bent their bones. And so left they such men to wander, and those who had not forsaken hope kept far from their path.

But unaware the eorl was not, and had readied himself for this rising.

On the ground before his hall stood a stone. Into this carved the god-man his strongest runes, and wrote over them with his blood, begging the gods, the great ones of the other worlds, to make the stone the stopping of this bane.

Sent the eorl the last of his thanes to the bone-home's bed, where the wight stood again. Dragged they the dréag thence, the white-handed ones walking after, as if they were the thanes of that thing. But stopped they at the stakes that marked the ground of the eorl's hall.

On that ground one woman came forth, having kissed her kin and bid them farewell; Saehild was her name, and well she knew this work would be her death or worse. But for the well-being of her folk, put she her hands to the lich's flesh, cutting it loose with an iron knife. Ulfcytel, best of the thanes, took the body-sticks she bared and laid them upon the stone, that the god-man had named the grinder of the grave. With other stones he broke them, stones carved also with the runes and blood of the god-man, while put Saehild the flesh into a churn of oak, whose staff then beat it soft. White grew their skin where it met bone and meat, but their word they had given, and break it they would not before they were done.

When ended their work, stood they with the empty-eyed ones; but their word they had kept, and so the eorl gave wergeld to their kin.

What abided still they put into a box, whose lid they nailed down with iron. At ene fell dead the god-man, and his body rotted where it lay. At this ill foretoken, more gave in to fear, but said the eorl that all his strength had gone into the spell, and his death was a mark of its might.

Few then yet stood at the eorl's side. Frost-bitten was the wind and dim the light, and held many to their homes; of those who did not, too many walked about bearing white skin and empty eyes. But yet lived hope in the eorl's heart. Took he the box and rode to the wealth-house of the dead, shifting aside the stone to bury his burden where first they had laid the lich, in harvest-time so long before. Then, having roofed the room anew, set he a watch, to see if things would now be well.

The end of this, all men know. Upon the dark of the moon, rose for the last time what men had thought to rid themselves of, fed full by the blood of the god-man, witlessly given. Came then those who yet lived, herded before the white-handed ones, to see the doom of the eorl, torn asunder for seeking to stop this thing. Fell his wound-flood upon the watching ones, waking hunger in their hearts. Crawled they up the barrow's side to beg the blessing from the dréag; cut he his arm, and from it drank they the wolf-wine, which gave to them knowledge of their wyrd, and new ravening.

And so has it been since that day. Never came the sun over this land after that; dwell we therefore in darkness, that men from without hold in fear. From our new god take we our gift, and do his will however he bids. All hail to the holy one, the bestower of blood, the gainsayer of the grave, whose life and might shall be everlasting.

Jack and Jill

Jonathan Maberry

1

Jack Porter was twelve going on never grow up.

He was one of the walking dead.

He knew it. Everyone knew it.

Remission was not a reprieve; it just put you in a longer line at the airport. Jack had seen what happened to his cousin, Toby. Three remissions in three years. Hope pushed Toby into a corner and beat the shit out of him each time. Toby was a ghost in third grade, a skeleton in fourth grade, a withered thing in a bed by the end of fifth grade, and bones in a box before sixth grade even started. All that hope had accomplished was to make everyone more afraid.

Now it was Jack's turn.

Chemo, radiation. Bone marrow transplants. Even surgery.

Like they say in the movies, life sucks and then you die.

So, yeah, life sucked.

What there was of it.

What there was left.

Jack sat cross-legged on the edge of his bed watching the weatherman on TV talk about the big storm that was about to hit. He kept going on and on about the dangers of floods and there was a continuous scroll across the bottom of the screen that listed the evacuation shelters.

Jack ate dry Honey-Nut Cheerios out of a bowl and thought about floods. The east bend of the river was one hundred feet from the house. Uncle Roger liked to say that they were a football field away, back door to muddy banks. Twice the river had flooded enough for there to be some small wavelets licking at the bottom step of the porch. But there hadn't ever been a storm as bad as what they were predicting, at least not in Jack's lifetime. The last storm big enough to flood the whole farm had been in 1931. Jack knew that because they showed flood maps on TV. The weather guy was really into it. He seemed jazzed by the idea that a lot of Stebbins County could be flooded out.

Jack was kind of jazzed about it, too.

It beat the crap out of rotting away. Remission or not, Jack was certain that he could feel himself die, cell by cell. He dreamed about that, thought about it. Wrote in his journal about it. Did everything but talk about it.

Not even to Jill. Jack and Jill had sworn an oath years ago to tell each other everything, no secrets. Not one. But that was before Jack got sick. That was back when they were two peas in a pod. Alike in everything, except that Jack was a boy and Jill was a girl. Back then, back when they'd made that pact, they were just kids. You could barely tell one from the other except in the bath.

Years ago. A lifetime ago, as Jack saw it.

The sickness changed everything. There were some secrets the dying were allowed to keep to themselves.

Jack watched the Doppler radar of the coming storm and smiled. He had an ear bud nestled into one ear and was also listening to Magic Marti on the radio. She was hyped about the storm, too, sounding as excited as Jack felt.

"*Despite heavy winds, the storm front is slowing down and looks like it's going to park right on the Maryland/Pennsylvania Border, with Stebbins County taking the brunt of it. They're calling for torrential rains and strong winds, along with severe flooding. And here's a twist . . . even though this is a November storm, warm air masses from the south are bringing significant lightning, and so far there have been several serious strikes. Air traffic is being diverted around the storm.*"

Jack nodded along with her words as if it was music playing in his ear.

Big storm. Big flood?

He hoped so.

The levees along the river were half-assed, or at least that's how Dad always described them.

"Wouldn't take much more than a good piss to flood 'em out," Dad was fond of saying, and he said it every time they got a bad storm. The levees never flooded out, and Jack wondered if was the sort of thing people said to prevent something bad from happening. Like telling an actor to break a leg.

On the TV they showed the levees, and a guy described as a civil engineer puffed out his chest and said that Pennsylvania levees were much better than the kind that had failed in Louisiana. Stronger, better maintained.

Jack wondered what Dad would say about that. Dad wasn't much for the kind of experts news shows trotted out. "Bunch of pansy-ass know-nothings."

The news people seemed to agree, because after the segment with the engineer, the anchor with the plastic hair pretty much tore down everything the man had to say.

"Although the levees in Stebbins County are considered above average for the region, the latest computer models say that this storm is only going to get stronger."

Jack wasn't sure if that was a logical statement, but he liked its potential. The storm was getting bigger, and that was exciting.

But again he wondered what it would be like to have all that water, that great, heaving mass of coldness come crashing in through all the windows and doors. Jack's bedroom was on the ground floor—a concession to how easily he got tired climbing steps. The house was a hundred and fifteen years old. It creaked in a light wind. No way it could stand up to a million gallons of water, Jack was positive of that.

If it happened, he wondered what he would do.

Stay here in his room and let the house fall down around him.

No, that sounded like it would hurt. Jack could deal with pain if he had to, but he didn't like it.

Maybe he could go into the living room and wait for it. On the couch, or on the floor in front of the TV. If the TV and the power was still on. Just sit there and wait for the black tide to come calling.

How quick would it be?

Would it hurt to drown?

Would he be scared?

Sure. Rotting was worse.

He munched a palmful of Cheerios and prayed that the river would come for him.

2

"Mom said I can't stay home today," grumped Jill as she came into Jack's room. She dropped her book bag on the floor and kicked it.

"Why not?"

"She said the weatherman's never right. She said the storm'll pass us."

"Magic Marti says it's going to kick our butts," said Jack.

As if to counterpoint his comment there was a low rumble of thunder way off to the west.

Jill sighed and sat next to him on the edge of the bed. She no longer looked like his twin. She had a round face and was starting to grow boobs. Her hair was as black as crow's wings and even though Mom didn't let her wear make-up, not until she was in junior high, and even then it was going to be an argument. Jill had pink cheeks, pink lips, and every boy in sixth grade was in love with her. Jill didn't seem to care much about that. She didn't try to dress like the middle school girls, or like Maddy Simpson, who was the same age but who had pretty big boobs and dressed like she was in an MTV rap video. Uncle Roger had a ten-dollar bet going that Maddy was going to be pregnant before she ever got within shooting distance of a diploma. Jack and Jill both agreed. Everyone did.

Jill dressed like a farm girl. Jeans and a sweatshirt, often the same kind of sweatshirt Jack wore. Today she had an olive drab U.S. Army shirt. Jack wore his with pajama bottoms. Aunt Linda had been in the army but she died in Afghanistan three years ago.

They sat together, staring blankly at the TV screen for a while. Jack cut her a sly sideways look and saw that her face was slack, eyes empty. He understood why, and it made him sad.

Jill wasn't dealing well with the cancer. He was afraid of what would happen to Jill after he died. And Jack had no illusions about whether the current remission was going to be the one that took. When he looked into his own future, either in dreams, prayers, or when lost in thought, there was an end to the road. It went on a bit farther and there were was a big wall of black nothingness.

It sucked, sure, but he'd lived with it so long that he had found a kind of peace with it. Why go kicking and screaming into the dark if none of that would change anything?

Jill, on the other hand, that was different. She had to live, she had to keep going. Jack watched TV a lot, he saw the episodes of Dr. Phil and other shows where they talked about death and dying. He knew that some people believed that the dying had an obligation to their loved ones who would survive them.

Jack didn't want Jill to suffer after he died, but he didn't know what he could do about it. He told her once about his dreams of the big black nothing.

"It's like a wave that comes and just sweeps me away," he'd told her.

"That sounds awful," she replied, tears springing into her eyes, but Jack assured her that it wasn't.

"No," he said, " 'cause once the nothing takes you, there's no more pain."

"But there's no more *you*!"

He grinned. "How do you know? No one knows what's on the other side of that wall." He shrugged. "Maybe it'll be something cool. Something nice."

"How could it be nice?" Jill had demanded.

This was right after the cancer had come back the last time, before the current remission. Jack was so frail that he barely made a dent in his own hospital bed. He touched the wires and tubes that ran from his pencil-thin arm to the machines behind him. "It's got to be nicer than this."

Nicer than this.

That was the last time they'd had a real conversation about the sickness, or about death. That was nine months ago. Jack stopped talking to her about those things and instead did what he could to ease her down so that when the nothing took him she'd still be able to stand.

He nudged her and held out the bowl of cereal. Without even looking at it she took a handful and began eating them, one at a time, smashing them angrily between her teeth.

Eventually she said, "It's not fair."

"I know." Just as he knew that they were having two separate conversations at the same time. It was often that way with them.

They crunched and glared at the TV.

"If it gets bad," Jack said, "they'll let everyone go."

But she shook her head. "I want to stay home. I want to hang out here and watch it on TV."

"You'll be *in* it," he said.

"Not the same thing. It's better on TV."

Jack ate some Cheerios and nodded. Everything was more fun on TV. Real life didn't have commentary and it didn't have playback. Watching a storm beat standing in one while you waited for the school bus to splash water on you. It beat the smells of sixty soaking wet kids on a crowded bus, and bumper-to-bumper traffic waiting for your driveway.

As if in response to that thought there was a muffled honk from outside.

"Bus," said Jack.

"Crap," said Jill. She stood up. "Text me. Let me know what's happening."

"Sure."

Jill began flouncing out of the room, but then she stopped in the doorway and looked back at him. She looked from him to the TV screen and back again. She wore a funny, half-smile.

"What?" he asked.

Jill studied him without answering long enough for the bus driver to get pissed and really lay on the horn.

"I mean it," she said. "Text me."

"I already said I would."

Jill chewed her lip, then turned and headed out of the house and up the winding drive to the road where the big yellow bus waited.

Jack wondered what that was all about.

3

Mom came into his room in the middle of the morning carrying a tray with two hot corn muffins smeared with butter and honey and a big glass of water.

"You hungry?" she asked, setting the tray down on the bed between them.

"Sure," said Jack, though he wasn't. His appetite was better than it had been all summer, and even though he was done with chemo for a while, he only liked to nibble. The Cheerios were perfect, and it was their crunch more than anything that he liked.

But he took a plate with one of the muffins, sniffed, pasted a smile on his mouth, and took a small bite. Jack knew from experience that Mom needed to see him eat. It was more important to her to make sure that he was eating than it was in seeing him eat much. He thought he understood that. Appetite was a sign of health, or remission. Cancer patients in the full burn of the disease didn't have much of an appetite. Jack knew that very well.

As he chewed, Mom tore open a couple of packs of vitamin-C powder and poured them into his water glass.

"Tropical mix," she announced, but Jack had already smelled it. It wasn't as good as the tangerine, but it was okay. He accepted the glass, waited for the fizz to settle down, and then took a sip to wash down the corn muffin.

Thunder rumbled again and rattled the windows.

"It's getting closer," said Jack. When his mother didn't comment, he asked, "Will Jilly be okay?"

Before Mom could reply the first fat raindrops splatted on the glass. She picked up the remote to raise the volume. The regular weatherman was no longer giving the updates. Instead it was the anchorman, the guy from Pittsburgh with all the teeth and the plastic-looking hair.

"Mom?" Jack asked again.

"Shhh, let me listen."

The newsman said, "Officials are urging residents to prepare for a powerful storm that slammed eastern Ohio yesterday, tore along the northern edge of West Virginia and is currently grinding its way along the Maryland-Pennsylvania border."

There was a quick cutaway to a scientist-looking guy that Jack had seen a dozen times this morning. Dr. Gustus, a professor from some university. "The storm is unusually intense for this time of year, spinning up into what is clearly a high-precipitation supercell, which is an especially dangerous type of storm. Since the storm's mesocyclone is wrapped with heavy rains, it can hide a tornado from view until the funnel touches down. These supercells are also known for their tendency to produce more frequent cloud-to-ground and intracloud lightning than other types of storms. The system weakened briefly overnight, following computer models of similar storms in this region, however what we are seeing now is an unfortunate combination of elements that could result in a major upgrade of this weather pattern."

The professor gave a bunch more technical information that Jack was pretty sure no one really understood, and then the image cut back to the reporter with the plastic hair who contrived to look grave and concerned. "This storm will produce flooding rains, high winds, downed trees—on houses, cars, power lines—and widespread power outages. Make sure you have plenty of candles and flashlights with fresh batteries because, folks, you're going to need 'em." He actually smiled when he said that.

Jack shivered.

Mom noticed it and wrapped her arm around his bony shoulders. "Hey, now . . . don't worry. We'll be safe here."

He made an agreeing noise, but did not bother to correct her. He wasn't frightened of the storm's power. He was hoping it would become one of those Category Five things like they showed on Syfy. Or a bigger one. Big enough to blow the house down and let the waters of the river sweep him away from pain and sickness. The idea of being killed in a super storm was so delightful that it made him shiver and raised goose bumps all along his arms. Lasting through the rain and wind so that he was back to where and what he was . . . that was far more frightening. Being suddenly dead was better than dying.

On the other hand . . .

"What about Jill?"

"She'll be fine," said Mom, though her tone was less than convincing.

"Mom . . . ?"

Mom was a thin, pretty woman whose black hair had started going gray around the time of the first diagnosis. Now it was more gray than black and there were dark circles under her eyes. Jill looked a little like Mom, and would probably grow up to look a lot like her. Jack looked like her too, right down to the dark circles under the eyes that looked out at him every morning from the bathroom mirror.

"Mom," Jack said tentatively, "Jill *is* going to be alright, isn't she?"

"She's in school. If it gets bad they'll bus the kids home."

"Shouldn't someone go get her?"

Mom looked at the open bedroom door. "Your dad and Uncle Roger are in town buying the pipes for the new irrigation system. They'll see how bad it is, and if they have to, they'll get her." She smiled and Jack thought that it was every bit as false as the smile he'd given her a minute ago. "Jill will be fine. Don't stress yourself out about it, you know it's not good for you."

"Okay," he said, resisting the urge to shake his head. He loved his mom, but she really didn't understand him at all.

"You should get some rest," she said. "After you finish your muffin why not take a little nap?"

Jeez-us, he thought. She was always saying stuff like that. Take a nap, get some rest. *I'm going to be dead for a long time. Let me be awake as much as I can for now.*

"Sure," he said. "Maybe in a bit."

Mom smiled brightly as if they had sealed a deal. She kissed him on the head and went out of his room, closing the door three-quarters of the way. She never closed it all the way, so Jack got up and did that for himself.

Jack nibbled another micro-bite of the muffin, sighed and set it down. He broke it up on the plate so it looked like he'd really savaged it. Then he drank the vitamin water, set the glass down and stretched out on his stomach to watch the news.

Rain drummed on the roof like nervous fingertips, and the wind was whistling through the trees. The storm was coming for sure. No way it was going to veer.

Jack lay there in the blue glow of the TV and the brown shadows of his thoughts. He'd been dying for so long that he could barely remember what living felt like. Only Jill's smile sometimes brought those memories back. Running together down the long lanes of cultivated crops. Waging war with broken ears of corn, and trying to juggle fist-sized pumpkins. Jill was never any good at juggling, and she laughed so hard when Jack managed to get three pumpkins going that he started laughing, too, and dropped gourds right on his head.

He sighed and it almost hitched into a sob.

He wanted to laugh again. Not careful laughs, like now, but real gut-busters like he used to. He wanted to run. God, how he wanted to run. That was something he hadn't been able to do for over a year now. Not since the last surgery. And never again. Best he could manage was a hobbling half-run like Gran used to when the Miller's dog got into her herb garden.

Jack closed his eyes and thought about the storm. About a flood.

He really wanted Jill to come home. He loved his sister, and maybe today he'd open up and tell her what really went on in his head. Would she like that? Would she want to know?

Those were tricky questions, and he didn't have answers to them.

Nor did he have an answer to why he wanted Jill home *and* wanted the flood at the same time. That was stupid. That was selfish.

"I'm dying," he whispered to the shadows.

Dying people were supposed to get what they wanted, weren't they? Trips to Disney, a letter from a celebrity. All that Make-A-Wish stuff. He wanted to see his sister and then let the storm take him away. Without hurting her, of course. Or Mom, or Dad, or Uncle Roger.

He sighed again.

Wishes were stupid. They never came true.

4

Jack was drowsing when he heard his mother cry out.

A single, strident "No!"

Jack scrambled out of bed and opened his door a careful inch to try and catch the conversation Mom was having on the phone. She was in the big room down the hall, the one she and Dad used as the farm office.

"Is she okay? God, Steve, tell me she's okay!"

Those words froze Jack to the spot.

He mouthed the name.

"Jill . . ."

"Oh my God," cried Mom, "does she need to go to the hospital? What? How can the hospital be closed? Steve . . . how can the damn hospital be—"

Mom stopped to listen, but Jack could see her body change, stiffening with fear and tension. She had the phone to her ear and her other hand at her throat.

"Oh God, Steve," she said again, and even from where Jack stood he could see that Mom was pale as death. "What *happened*? Who did this? Oh, come on, Steve, that's ridiculous . . . Steve . . ."

Jack could hear Dad's voice but not his words. He was yelling. Almost screaming.

"Did you call the police?" Mom demanded. She listened for an answer and whatever it was, it was clear to Jack that it shocked her. She staggered backward and sat down hard on a wooden chair. "*Shooting*? Who was shooting?"

More yelling, none of it clear.

Shooting? Jack stared at Mom as if he was peering into a different world than anything he knew. He tried to put the things he'd heard into some shape that made sense, but no picture formed.

"Jesus Christ!" shrieked Mom. "Steve . . . forget about, forget about everything. Just get my baby home. Get yourself home. I have a first aid kit here and . . . oh yes, God, Steve . . . I love you, too. Hurry!"

She lowered the phone and stared at it as if the device had done her some unspeakable harm. Her eyes were wide but she didn't seem to be looking at anything.

"Mom . . . ?" Jack said softly, stepping out into the hall. "What's happening? What's wrong?"

As soon as she looked up, Mom's eyes filled with tears. She cried out his name and he rushed to her as she flew to him. Mom was always so careful with him, holding him as if he had bird bones that would snap with the slightest pressure, but right then she clutched him to her chest with all her strength. He could feel her trembling, could feel the heat of her panic through the cotton of her dress.

"It's Jilly," said Mom, and her voice broke into sobs. "There was a fight at the school. Someone *bit* her."

"Bit—?" asked Jack, not sure he really heard that.

Lightning flashed outside and thunder exploded overhead.

5

Mom ran around for a couple of minutes, grabbing first aid stuff. There was always a lot of it on a farm, and Jack knew how to dress a wound and treat for shock. Then she fetched candles and matches, flashlights and a Coleman lantern. Big storms always knocked out the power in town and Mom was always ready.

The storm kept getting bigger, rattling the old bones of the house, making the window glass chatter like teeth.

"What's taking them so damn *long*?" Mom said, and she said it every couple of minutes.

Jack turned on the big TV in the living room.

"Mom!" he called. "They have it on the news."

She came running into the room with an armful of clean towels and stopped in the middle of the floor to watch. What they saw did not make much sense. The picture showed the Stebbins Little School, which was both the elementary school and the town's evacuation shelter. It was on high ground and it was built during an era when Americans worried about nuclear bombs and Russian air raids. Stuff Jack barely even knew about.

In front of the school was a guest parking lot, which was also where the buses picked up and dropped off the kids. Usually there were lines of yellow buses standing in neat rows, or moving like a slow train as they pulled to the front, loaded or unloaded, then moved forward to catch up with the previous bus. There was nothing neat and orderly about the big yellow vehicles now.

The heavy downpour made everything vague and fuzzy, but Jack could nevertheless see that the buses stood in haphazard lines in the parking lot and in the street. Cars were slotted in everywhere to create a total gridlock. One of the buses lay on its side.

Two were burning.

All around, inside and out, were people. Running, staggering, laying sprawled, fighting.

Not even the thunder and the rain could drown out the sounds of screams.

And gunfire.

"Mom . . . ?" asked Jack. "What's happening?"

But Mom had nothing to say. The bundle of towels fell softly to the floor by her feet.

She ran to the table by the couch, snatched up the phone and called 9-1-1. Jack stood so close that he could hear the rings.

Seven. Eight. On the ninth ring there was a clicking sound and then a thump, as if someone picked up the phone and dropped it.

Mom said, "Hello—?"

The sounds from the other end were confused and Jack tried to make sense of them. The scuff of a shoe? A soft, heavy bump as if someone banged into a desk. And a sound like someone makes when they're asleep. Low and without any meaning.

"Flower," called Mom. Flower was the secretary and dispatcher at the police station. She went to high school with Mom. "Flower, are you there? Can you hear me?"

If there was a response, Jack couldn't hear it.

"Flower. come on, girl, I need some help. There was some kind of problem at the school and Steve's bringing Jilly back with a bad bite. He tried to take her to the hospital but it was closed and there were barricades set up. We need an ambulance . . ."

Flower finally replied.

It wasn't words, just a long, deep, aching moan that came crawling down the phone lines. Mom jerked the handset away from her ear, staring at it with horror and fear. Jack heard that sound and it chilled him to the bone.

Not because it was so alien and unnatural . . . but because he recognized it. He knew that sound. He absolutely knew it.

He'd heard Toby make it a couple of times during those last days, when the cancer was so bad that they had to keep Toby down in a dark pool of drugs. Painkillers didn't really work at that level. The pain was everywhere. It was the whole universe because every single particle of your body knows that it's being consumed. The cancer is winning, it's devouring you, and you get to a point where it's so big and you're so small that you can't even yell at it anymore. You can curse at it or shout at it or tell it that you won't let it win. It already has won, and you know it. In those moments, those last crumbling moments, all you can do—all you can *say*—is throw noise at it. It's not meaningless, even though it sounds like that. When Jack first heard those sounds coming out of Toby he thought that it was just noise, just a grunt or a moan. But those sounds *do* have meaning. So much meaning. Too much meaning. They're filled with all of the need in the world.

The need to live, even though the dark is everywhere, inside and out.

The need to survive, even though you know you can't.

The need to have just another hour, just another minute, but your clock is broken and all of the time has leaked out.

The need to not be devoured.

Even though you already are.

The need.

Need.

That moan, the one Jack heard at Toby's bedside and the one he heard now over the phone line from Flower, was just that. Need.

It was the sound Jack sometimes made in his dreams. Practicing for when it would be the only sound he could make.

Mom said, "Flower . . . ?"

But this time her voice was small. Little kid small.

There were no more sounds from the other end, and Mom replaced the handset as carefully as if it were something that could wake up and bite her.

She suddenly seemed to remember Jack was standing there and Mom hoisted up as fake a smile as Jack had ever seen.

"It'll be okay," she said. "It's the storm causing trouble with the phone lines."

The lie was silly and weak, but they both accepted it because there was nothing else they could do.

Then Jack saw the headlights on the road, turning off of River Road onto their driveway.

"They're here!" he cried and rushed for the door, but Mom pushed past him, jerked the door open and ran out onto the porch.

"Stay back," she yelled as he began to follow.

Jack stopped in the doorway. Rain slashed at Mom as she stood on the top step, silhouetted by the headlights as Dad's big Dodge Durango splashed through the water that completely covered the road. His brights were on, and Jack had to shield his eyes behind his hands. The pick-up raced all the way up the half-mile drive and slewed sideways to a stop that sent muddy rainwater onto the porch, slapping wet across Mom's legs. She didn't care, she was already running down the steps toward the car.

The doors flew open and Dad jumped out from behind the wheel and ran around the front of the truck. Uncle Roger had something in his arms. Something that was limp and wrapped in a blanket that looked like it was soaked with oil. Only it wasn't oil, and Jack knew it. Lightning flashed continually and in its stark glow the oily black became gleaming red.

Dad took the bundle from him and rushed through ankle-deep mud toward the porch. Mom reached him and tugged back the cloth. Jack could see the tattered sleeve of an olive-drab sweatshirt and one ice-pale hand streaked with crooked lines of red.

Mom screamed.

Jack did, too, even though he could not see what she saw. Mom said that she'd been bitten . . . but this couldn't be a bite. Not with this much blood. Not with Jill not moving.

"*JILL!*"

He ran out onto the porch and down the steps and into the teeth of the storm.

"Get back," screeched Mom as she and Dad bulled their way past him onto the porch and into the house. Nobody wiped their feet.

Roger caught up with him. He was bare-chested despite the cold and had his undershirt wrapped around his left arm. In the glare of the lightning his skin looked milk white.

"What is it? What's happening? What's wrong with Jill?" demanded Jack, but Uncle Roger grabbed him by the shoulder and shoved him toward the house.

"Get inside," he growled. "*Now.*"

Jack staggered toward the steps and lost his balance. He dropped to his knees in the mud, but Uncle Roger caught him under the armpit and hauled him roughly to his feet and pushed him up the steps. All the while, Uncle Roger kept looking over his shoulder. Jack twisted around to see what he was looking at. The bursts of lightning made everything look weird and for a moment he thought that there were people at the far end of the road, but when the next bolt forked through the sky, he saw that it was only cornstalks battered by the wind.

Only that.

"Get inside," urged Roger. "It's not safe out here."

Jack looked at him. Roger was soaked to the skin. His face was swollen as if he'd been punched, and the shirt wrapped around his left arm was soaked through with blood.

It's not safe out here.

Jack knew for certain that his uncle was not referring to the weather.

The lightning flashed again, and the shadows in the corn seemed wrong.

All wrong.

6

Jack stood silent and unnoticed in the corner of the living room, like a ghost haunting his own family. No one spoke to him, no one looked in his direction. Not even Jill.

As soon as they'd come in, Dad had laid Jill down on the couch. No time even to put a sheet under her. Rainwater pooled under the couch in pink puddles. Uncle Roger stood behind the couch, looking down at Mom and Dad as they used rags soaked with fresh water and alcohol to sponge away mud and blood. Mom snipped away the sleeves of the torn and ragged Army sweatshirt.

"It was like something off the news. It was like one of those riots you see on TV," said Roger. His eyes were glassy and his voice had a distant quality as if his body and his thoughts were in separate rooms. "People just going apeshit crazy for no reason. Good people. People we know. I saw Dix Howard take a tire iron out of his car and lay into Joe Fielding, the baseball coach from the high school. Just laid into him, swinging on him like he was a total stranger. Beat the shit out of him, too. Joe's glasses went flying off his face and his nose just bursting with blood. Crazy shit."

" . . . give me the peroxide," said Mom, working furiously. "There's another little bite on her wrist."

" . . . the big one's not that bad," Dad said, speaking over her rather than to her. "Looks like it missed the artery. But Jilly's always been a bleeder."

"It was like that when we drove up," said Uncle Roger, continuing his account even though he had no audience. Jack didn't think that his uncle was speaking to him. Or . . . to anyone. He was speaking because he needed to get it out of his head, as if that was going to help make sense of it. "With the rain and all, it was hard to tell what was going on. Not at first. Just buses and cars parked every which way and lots of people running and shouting. We thought there'd been an accident. You know people panic when there's an accident and kids are involved. They run around like chickens with their heads cut off, screaming and making a fuss instead of doing what needs to be done. So, Steve and I got out of the truck and started pushing our way into the crowd. To find Jill and to, you know, see if we could do something. To help."

Jack took a small step forward, trying to catch a peek at Jill. She was still unconscious, her face small and gray. Mom and Dad seemed to have eight hands each as they cleaned and swabbed and dabbed. The worst wound was the one on her forearm. It was ugly and it wasn't just one of those bites when someone squeezes their teeth on you; no, there was actual skin missing. Someone took a bite *out* of Jill, and that was a whole other thing. Jack could see that the edges of the ragged flesh were stained with something dark and gooey.

"What's all that black stuff?" asked Mom as she probed the bite. "Is that oil?"

"No," barked Dad, "it's coming out of her like pus. Christ, I don't know what it is. Some kind of infection. Don't get it on you. Give me the alcohol."

Jack kept staring at the black goo and he thought he could see something move inside of it. Like tiny threadlike worms.

Uncle Roger kept talking, his voice level and detached. "We saw her teacher, Mrs. Grayson, lying on the ground and two kids were kneeling over her. I . . . I thought they were praying. Or . . . something. They had their heads bowed, but when I pulled one back to try and see if the teacher was okay . . ."

Roger stopped talking. He raised his injured left hand and stared at it as if it didn't belong to him, as if the memory of that injury couldn't belong to his experience. The bandage was red with blood, but Jack could see some of the black stuff on him, too. On the bandages and on his skin.

"Somebody bit you?" asked Jack, and Roger twitched and turned toward him. He stared down with huge eyes. "Is that what happened?"

Roger slowly nodded. "It was that girl who wears all that make-up. Maddy Simpson. She bared her teeth at me like she was some kind of fuckin' animal and she just . . . she just . . . "

He shook his head.

"Maddy?" murmured Jack. "What did you do?"

Roger's eyes slid away. "I . . . um . . . I made her let go. You know? She was acting all crazy and I had to make her let go. I had to . . . "

Jack did not ask what exactly Uncle Roger had done to free himself of Maddy Simpson's white teeth. His clothes and face were splashed with blood and the truth of it was in his eyes. It made Jack want to run and hide.

But he couldn't leave.

He had to know.

And he had to be there when Jill woke up.

Roger stumbled his way back into his story. "It wasn't just here. It was everybody. Everybody was going batshit crazy. People kept rushing at us. Nobody was making any sense and the rain would not stop battering us. You couldn't see, couldn't even think. We . . . we . . . we had to find Jill, you know?"

"But what *is* it?" asked Jack. "Is it rabies?"

Dad, Mom, and Roger all looked at him, then each other.

"Rabies don't come on that fast," said Dad. "This was happening right away. I saw some people go down really hurt. Throat wounds and such. Thought they were dead, but then they got back up again and started attacking people. That's how fast this works." He shook his head. "Not any damn rabies."

"Maybe it's one of them terrorist things," said Roger.

Mom and Dad stiffened and stared at him, and Jack could see new doubt and fear blossom in their eyes.

"What kind of thing?" asked Dad.

Roger licked his lips. "Some kind of nerve gas, maybe? One of those, whaddya call 'em? *weaponized* things. Like in the movies. Anthrax or Ebola or something. Something that drives people nuts."

"It's not Ebola," snapped Mom.

"Maybe it's a toxic spill or something," Roger ventured. It was clear to Jack that Roger really needed to have this be something ordinary enough to have a name.

So did Jack. If it had a name then maybe Jill would be okay.

Roger said, "Or maybe it's—"

Mom cut him off. "Put on the TV. Maybe there's something."

"I got it," said Jack, happy to have something to do. He snatched the remote off the coffee table and pressed the button. The TV had been on local news when they'd turned it off, but when the picture came on all it showed was a stationary text page that read:

WE ARE EXPERIENCING
A TEMPORARY INTERRUPTION IN SERVICE.
PLEASE STAND BY.

"Go to CNN," suggested Roger but Jack was already surfing through the stations. They had Comcast cable. Eight hundred stations, including high def.

The same text was on every single one.

"What the hell?" said Roger indignantly. "We have friggin' *digital*. How can all the station feeds be out?"

"Maybe it's the cable channel," said Jack. "Everything goes through them, right?"

"It's the storm," said Dad.

"No," said Mom, but she didn't explain. She bent over Jill and peered closer at the black goo around her wounds. "Oh my God, Steve, there's something in there. Some kind of—"

Jill suddenly opened her eyes.

Everyone froze.

Jill looked up at Mom and Dad, then Uncle Roger, and then finally at Jack.

"Jack . . . " she said in a faint whisper, lifting her uninjured hand toward him, "I had the strangest dream."

"Jilly?" Jack murmured in a voice that had suddenly gone as dry as bones. He reached a tentative hand toward her. But as Jack's fingers lightly brushed his sister's, Dad smacked his hand away.

"Don't!" he warned.

Jill's eyes were all wrong. The green of her irises had darkened to a rusty hue and the whites had flushed to crimson. A black tear broke from the corner of her eye and wriggled its way down her cheek. Tiny white things twisted and squirmed in the goo.

Mom choked back a scream and actually recoiled from Jill.

Roger whispered, "God almighty . . . what *is* that shit? What's wrong with her?"

"Jack—?" called Jill. "You look all funny. Why are you wearing red makeup?"

Her voice had a dreamy, distant quality. Almost musical in its lilt, like the way people sometimes spoke in dreams. Jack absently touched his face as if it was his skin and not her vision that was painted with blood.

"Steve," said Mom in an urgent whisper, "we have to get her to a doctor. Right now."

"We can't, honey, the storm—"

"We *have* to. Damn it, Steve I can't lose both my babies."

She gasped at her own words and cut a look at Jack, reaching for him with hands that were covered in Jill's blood. "Oh God . . . Jack . . . sweetie, I didn't mean—"

"No," said Jack, "it's okay. We *have* to save Jill. We have to."

Mom and Dad both looked at him for a few terrible seconds, and there was such pain in their eyes that Jack wanted to turn away. But he didn't. What Mom had said did not hurt him as much as they hurt her. She didn't know it, but Jack had heard her say those kinds of things before. Late at night when she and dad sat together on the couch and cried and talked about what they were going to do after he was dead. He knew that they'd long ago given up real hope. Hope was fragile and cancer was a monster.

Fresh tears brimmed in Mom's eyes and Jack could almost feel something pass between them. Some understanding, some acceptance. There was an odd little flicker of relief as if she grasped what Jack knew about his own future. And Jack wondered if, when Mom looked into her own dreams at the future of her only son, she also saw the great black wall of nothing that was just a little way down the road.

Jack knew that he could never put any of this into words. He was a very smart twelve-year-old, but this was something for philosophers. No one of that profession lived on their farm.

The moment, which was only a heartbeat long, stretched too far and broke. The brimming tears fell down Mom's cheeks and she turned back to Jill. Back to the child who maybe still had a future. Back to the child she could fight for.

Jack was completely okay with that.

He looked at his sister, at those crimson eyes. They were so alien that he could not find *her* in there. Then Jill gave him a small smile. A smile he knew so well. The smile that said, *This isn't so bad.* The smile they sometimes shared when they were both in trouble and getting yelled at rather than having their computers and Xboxes taken away.

Then her eyes drifted shut, the smile lost its scaffolding and collapsed into a meaningless slack-mouthed nothing.

There was an immediate panic as Mom and Dad both tried to take her pulse at the same time. Dad ignored the black ichor on her face and arm as he bent close to press his ear to her chest. Time froze around him, then he let out a breath with a sharp burst of relief.

"She's breathing. Christ, she's still breathing. I think she just passed out. Blood loss, I guess."

"She could be going into shock," said Roger, and Dad shot him a withering look. But it was too late, Mom was already being hammered by panic.

"Get some blankets," Mom snapped. "We'll bundle her up and take the truck."

"No," said Roger, "like I said, we tried to take her to Wolverton ER, but they had it blocked off."

"Then we'll take her to Bordentown, or Fayetteville, or any damn place, but have to take her somewhere!"

"I'm just saying," Roger said, but his voice had been beaten down into something tiny and powerless by Mom's anger. He was her younger brother and she'd always held power in their family.

"Roger," she said, "you stay here with Jack and—"

"I want to go, too," insisted Jack.

"No," snapped Mom. "You'll stay right here with your uncle and—"

"But Uncle Rog is hurt, too," he said. "He got bit and he has that black stuff, too."

Mom's head swiveled sharply around and she stared at Roger's arm. The lines around her mouth etched deeper. "Okay," she said. "Okay. Just don't touch that stuff. You hear me, Jack? Steve? Don't touch whatever that black stuff is. We don't know what's in it."

"Honey, I don't think we can make it to the highway," said Dad. "When we came up River Road the water was halfway up the wheels. It'll be worse now."

"Then we'll go across the fields, God damn it!" snarled Mom.

"On the TV, earlier," interrupted Jack, "they said that the National Guard was coming in to help because of the flooding and all. Won't they be near the river? Down by the levee?"

Dad nodded. "That's right. They'll be sandbagging along the roads. I'm surprised we didn't see them on the way here."

"Maybe they're the ones blocked the hospital," said Roger. "Maybe they took it over, made it some kind of emergency station."

"Good, good . . . that's our plan. We find the Guard and they'll help us get Jill to a—"

But that was as far as Dad got.

Lightning flashed as white-hot as the sun and in the same second there was a crack of thunder that was the loudest sound Jack had ever heard.

All the lights went out and the house was plunged into total darkness.

7

Dad's voice spoke from the darkness. "That was the transformer up on the access road."

"Sounded like a direct hit," agreed Roger.

There was a scrape and a puff of sulfur and then Mom's faced emerged from the darkness in a small pool of match-light. She bent and lit a candle and then another. In the glow she fished for the Coleman, lit that and the room was bright again.

"We have to go," she said.

Dad was already moving. He picked up several heavy blankets from the stack Mom had laid by and used them to wrap Jill. He was as gentle as he could be, but he moved fast and he made sure to stay away from the black muck on her face and arm. But he did not head immediately for the door.

"Stay here," he said, and crossed swiftly to the farm office. Jack trailed along and watched his father fish in his pocket for keys, fumble one out, and unlock a heavy oak cabinet mounted to the wall. A second key unlocked a restraining bar and then Dad was pulling guns out of racks. Two shotguns and three pistols. He caught Jack watching him and his face hardened. "It's pretty wild out there, Jackie."

"Why? What's going on, Dad?"

Dad paused for a moment, breathed in and out through his nose, then he opened a box of shotgun shells and began feeding buckshot cartridges into the guns.

"I don't know what's going on, kiddo."

It was the first time Jack could ever remember his father admitting that he had no answers. Dad knew everything. Dad was Dad.

Dad stood the shotguns against the wall and loaded the pistols. He had two nine-millimeter Glocks. Jack knew a lot about guns. From living on the farm, from stories of the army his dad and uncle told. From the things Aunt Linda used to talk about when she was home on leave. Jack and Jill had both been taught to shoot, and how to handle a gun safely. This was farm country and that was part of the life.

And Jack had logged a lot of hours on *Medal of Honor* and other first-person shooter games. In the virtual worlds he was a healthy, powerful, terrorist-killing engine of pure destruction.

Cancer wasn't a factor in video games.

The third pistol was a thirty-two caliber Smith and Wesson. Mom's gun, for times when Dad and Uncle Roger were away for a couple of days. Their farm was big and it was remote. If trouble came, you had to handle it on your own. That's what Dad always said.

Except now.

This trouble was too big. Too bad.

This was Jill, and she was hurt and maybe sick, too.

"Is Jill going to be okay?" asked Jack.

Dad stuffed extra shells in his pockets and locked the cabinet.

"Sure," he said.

Jack nodded, accepting the lie because it was the only answer his father could possibly give.

He trailed Dad back into the living room. Uncle Roger had Jill in his arms and she was so thoroughly wrapped in blankets that it looked like he was carrying laundry. Mom saw the guns in Dad's hands and her eyes flared for a moment, then Jack saw her mouth tighten into a hard line. He'd seen that expression before. Once, four years ago, when a vagrant wandered onto the farm and sat on a stump watching Jill and Jack as they played in their rubber pool. Mom had come out onto the porch with a baseball bat in her hand and that look on her face. She didn't actually have to say anything, but the vagrant went hustling along the road and never came back.

The other time was when she went after Tony Magruder, a brute of a kid who'd been left back twice and loomed over the other sixth graders like a Neanderthal. Tony was making fun of Jack because he was so skinny and pantsed him in the school yard. Jill had gone after him with her own version of that expression and Tony had tried to pants her, too. Jack had managed to pull his pants up and drag Jill back into the school. They didn't tell Mom about it, but she found out somehow and next afternoon she showed up as everyone was getting out after last bell. Mom marched right up to Nick Magruder, who had come to pick up his son, and read him the riot act. She accused his son of being a pervert and a retard and a lot of other things. Mr. Magruder never managed to get a word in edgewise and when Mom threatened to have Tony arrested for sexual assault, the man grabbed his son and smacked him half unconscious, then shoved him into their truck. Jack never saw Tony again, but he heard that the boy was going to a special school over in Bordentown.

Jack kind of felt bad because he didn't like to see any kid get his ass kicked. Even a total jerkoff like Tony. On the other hand, Tony had almost hurt Jill, so maybe he got off light. From the look on Mom's face, she wanted to do more than smack the smile off his face.

That face was set against whatever was going on now. Whatever had hurt Jill. Whatever might be in the way of getting her to a hospital.

Despite the fear that gnawed at him, seeing that face made Jack feel ten feet tall. His mother was tougher than anyone, even the school bully and his dad. *And* she had a gun. So did Dad and Uncle Roger.

Jack almost smiled.

Almost.

He remembered the look in Jill's eyes. The color of her eyes.

No smile was able to take hold on his features as he pulled on his raincoat and boots and followed his family out into the dark and the storm.

8

They made it all the way to the truck.

That was it.

9

The wind tried to rip the door out of Dad's hand as he pushed it open; it drove the rain so hard that it came sideways across the porch and hammered them like buckshot. Thunder shattered the yard like an artillery barrage and lightning flashed in every direction, knocking shadows all over the place.

Jack had to hunch into his coat and grab onto Dad's belt to keep from being blasted back into the house. The air was thick and wet and he started to cough before he was three steps onto the porch. His chest hitched and there was a gassy rasp in the back of his throat as he fought to breathe. Part of it was the insanity of the storm, which was worse than anything Jack had ever experienced. Worse than it looked on TV. Part of it was that there simply wasn't much of him. Even with the few pounds he'd put on since he went into remission, he was a stick figure in baggy pajamas. His boots were big and clunky and he half walked out of them with every step.

Mom was up with Roger, running as fast as she could despite the wind, forcing her way through it to get to the truck and open the doors. Roger staggered as if Jill was a burden, but it was just the wind, trying to bully him the way Tony Magruder had bullied Jill.

The whole yard was moving. It was a flowing, swirling pond that lapped up against the second porch step. Jack stared at it, entranced for a moment, and in that moment the pond seemed to rear up in front of him and become that big black wall of nothing that he saw so often in his dreams.

"Did the levee break?" he yelled. He had to yell it twice before Dad answered.

"No," Dad shouted back. "This is ground runoff. It's coming from the fields. If the levee broke it'd come at us from River Road. We're okay. We'll be okay. The truck can handle this."

There was more doubt than conviction in Dad's words, though.

Together they fought their way off the porch and across five yards of open driveway to the truck.

Lightning flashed again and something moved in front of Jack. Between Mom and the truck. It was there and gone.

"Mom!" Jack called, but the wind stole his cry and drowned it in the rain.

She reached for the door handle and in the next flash of lightning Jack saw Jill's slender arm reach out from the bundle of blankets as if to touch Mom's face. Mom paused and looked at her hand and in the white glow of the lightning Jack saw Mom smile and saw her lips move as she said something to Jill.

Then something came out of the rain and grabbed Mom.

Hands, white as wax, reached out of the shadows beside the truck and grabbed Mom's hair and her face and tore her out of Jack's sight. It was so *fast*, so abrupt that Mom was there and then she was gone.

Just . . . gone.

Jack screamed.

Dad must have seen it, too. He yelled and then there was a different kind of thunder as the black mouth of his shotgun blasted yellow fire into the darkness.

There was lightning almost every second and in the spaces between each flash everything in the yard seemed to shift and change. It was like a strobe light, like the kind they had at the Halloween hayride. Weird slices of images, and all of it happening too fast and too close.

Uncle Roger began to turn, Jill held tight in his arms.

Figures, pale-faced but streaked with mud. Moving like chess pieces. Suddenly closer. Closer still. More and more of them.

Dad firing right.

Firing left.

Firing and firing.

Mom screaming.

Jack heard that. A single fragment of a piercing shriek, shrill as a crow, that stabbed up into the night.

Then Roger was gone.

Jill with him.

"No!" cried Jack as he sloshed forward into the yard.

"Stay back!" screamed his father.

Not yelled. Screamed.

More shots.

Then Dad pulled the shotgun trigger and nothing happened. Nothing.

The pale figures moved and moved. It was hard to see them take their steps, but with each flash of lightning they were closer.

Always closer.

All around.

Dad screaming.

Roger screaming.

And . . . Jill.

Jill screaming.

Jack was running without remembering wanting to, or starting to. His boots splashed down hard and water geysered up around him. The mud tried to snatch his boots off his feet. Tried and then did, and suddenly he was running in bare feet. Moving faster, but the cold was like knife blades on his skin.

Something stepped out of shadows and rainfall right in front of him. A man Jack had never seen before. Wearing a business suit that was torn to rags, revealing a naked chest and . . .

. . . and nothing. Below the man's chest was a gaping hole. No stomach. No skin. Nothing. In the flickering light Jack could see dripping strings of meat and . . .

. . . and . . .

. . . was that the man's spine?

That was stupid. That was impossible.

The man reached for him.

There was a blur of movement and a smashed-melon crunch and then the man was falling away and Dad was there, holding the shotgun like a club. His eyes were completely wild.

"Jack for Christ's sake get back into the house."

Jack tried to say something, to ask one of the questions that burned like embers in his mind. Simple questions. Like, what was happening? Why did nothing make sense?

Where was Mom?

Where was Jill?

But Jack's mouth would not work.

Another figure came out of the rain. Mrs. Suzuki, the lady who owned the soy farm next door. She came over for Sunday dinners almost every week. Mrs. Suzuki was all naked.

Naked.

Jack had only ever seen naked people on the Internet, at sites where he wasn't allowed to go. Sites that Mom thought she'd blocked.

But Mrs. Suzuki was naked. Not a stitch on her.

She wasn't built like any of the women on the Internet. She had tiny breasts and a big scar on her stomach, and her pubic hair wasn't trimmed into a thin line. She wasn't pretty. She wasn't sexy.

She wasn't whole.

There were pieces of her missing. Big chunks of her arms and breasts and face. Mrs. Suzuki had black blood dripping from between her lips, and her eyes were as empty as holes.

She opened her mouth and spoke to him.

Not in words.

She uttered a moan of endless, shapeless need. Of hunger.

It was the moan Jack knew so well. It was the same sound Toby had made; the same sound that he knew he would make when the cancer pushed him all the way into the path of the rolling endless dark.

The moan rose from Mrs. Suzuki's mouth and joined with the moans of all the other staggering figures. All of them, making the same sound.

Then Mrs. Suzuki's teeth snapped together with a *clack* of porcelain.

Jack tried to scream, but his voice was hiding somewhere and he couldn't find it.

Dad swung the shotgun at her and her face seemed to come apart. Pieces of something hit Jack in the chest and he looked down to see teeth stuck to his raincoat by gobs of black stuff.

He thought something silly. He knew it was silly, but he thought it anyway because it was the only thought that would fit into his head.

But how will she eat her Sunday dinner without teeth?

He turned to see Dad struggling with two figures whose faces were as white as milk except for their dark eyes and dark mouths. One was a guy who worked for Mrs. Suzuki. Jose. Jack didn't know his last name. Jose something. The other was a big red-haired guy in a military uniform. Jack knew all of the uniforms. This was a National Guard uniform. He had corporal's stripes on his arms. But he only had one arm. The other sleeve whipped and popped in the wind, but there was nothing in it.

Dad was slipping in the mud. He fell back against the rear fender of the Durango. The shotgun slipped from his hands and was swallowed up by the groundwater.

The groundwater.

The cold, cold groundwater.

Jack looked numbly down at where his legs vanished into the swirling water. It eddied around his shins, just below his knees. He couldn't feel his feet anymore.

Be careful, Mom said from the warmth of his memories, *or you'll catch your death.*

Catch your death.

Jack thought about that as Dad struggled with the two white-faced people. The wind pushed him around, made him sway like a stalk of green corn.

He saw Dad let go of one of the people so he could grab for the pistol tucked into his waistband.

No, Dad, thought Jack. *Don't do that. They'll get you if you do that.*

Dad grabbed the pistol, brought it up, jammed the barrel under Jose's chin. Fired. Jose's hair seemed to jump off his head and then he was falling, his fingers going instantly slack.

But the soldier.

He darted his head forward and clamped his teeth on Dad's wrist. On the gun wrist.

Dad screamed again. The pistol fired again, but the bullet went all the way up into the storm and disappeared.

Jack was utterly unable to move. Pale figures continued to come lumbering out of the rain. They came toward him, reached for him . . .

. . . but not one of them touched him.

Not one.

And there were so many.

Dad was surrounded now. He screamed and screamed, and fired his pistol. Three of the figures fell. Four. Two got back up again, the holes in their chests leaking black blood. The other two dropped backward with parts of their heads missing.

Aim for the head, Dad, thought Jack. *It's what they do in the video games.*

Dad never played those games. He aimed center mass and fired. Fired.

And then the white-faced people dragged him down into the frothing water.

Jack knew that he should do something. At the same time, and with the kind of mature clarity that came with dying at his age, he knew that he was in shock. Held in place by it. Probably going to be killed by it. If not by these . . . whatever they were . . . then by the vicious cold that was chewing its way up his spindly legs.

He could not move if he was on fire, he knew that. He was going to stand there and watch the world go all the way crazy. Maybe this was the black wall of nothing that he imagined. This . . .

What was it?

A plague? Or, what did they call it? Mass hysteria?

No. People didn't eat each other during riots. Not even soccer riots.

This was different.

This was monster stuff.

This was stuff from TV and movies and video games.

Only the special effects didn't look as good. The blood wasn't bright enough. The wounds didn't look as disgusting. It was always better on TV.

Jack knew that his thoughts were crazy.

I'm in shock, duh.

He almost smiled.

And then he heard Jill.

Screaming.

10

Jack ran.

He went from frozen immobility to full-tilt run so fast that he felt like he melted out of the moment and reappeared somewhere else. It was surreal. That was a word he knew from books he'd read. Surreal. Not entirely real.

That fit everything that was happening.

His feet were so cold it was like running on knives. He ran into the teeth of the wind as the white-faced people shambled and splashed toward him and then turned away with grunts of disgust.

I'm not what they want, he thought.

He knew that was true, and he thought he knew why.

It made him run faster.

He slogged around the end of the Durango and tripped on something lying half-submerged by the rear wheel.

Something that twitched and jerked as white faces buried their mouths on it and pulled with bloody teeth. Pulled and wrenched, like dogs fighting over a beef bone.

Only it wasn't beef.

The bone that gleamed white in the lightning flash belonged to Uncle Roger. Bone was nearly all that was left of him as figures staggered away clutching red lumps to their mouths.

Jack gagged and then vomited into the wind. The wind slapped his face with what little he'd eaten that day. He didn't care. Jill wouldn't care.

Jill screamed again and Jack skidded to a stop, turning, confused. The sound of her scream no longer came from the far side of the truck. It sounded closer than that, but it was a gurgling scream.

He cupped his hands around his mouth and screamed her name into the howling storm.

A hand closed around his ankle.

Under the water.

From under the back of the truck.

Jack screamed again, inarticulate and filled with panic as he tried to jerk his leg away. The hand holding him had no strength and his ankle popped free and Jack staggered back and then fell flat on his ass in the frigid water. It splashed up inside his raincoat and soaked every inch of him. Three of the white-faced things turned to glare at him, but their snarls of anger flickered and went out as they found nothing worth hunting.

"Jack—?"

Her voice seemed to come out of nowhere. Still wet and gurgling, drowned by rain and blown thin by the wind.

But so close.

Jack stared at the water that smacked against the truck. At the pale, thin, grasping hand that opened and closed on nothing but rainwater.

"Jack?"

"*Jill!*" he cried, and Jack struggled onto his knees and began pawing and slapping at the water, pawing at it as if he could dig a hole in it. He bent and saw a narrow gap between the surface of the water and the greasy metal undersides of the truck. He saw two eyes, there and gone again in the lightning bursts. Dark eyes that he knew would be red.

"Jill!" he croaked at the same moment that she cried, "Jack!"

He grabbed her hands and pulled.

The mud and the surging water wanted to keep her, but not as much as he needed to pull her out. She came loose with a *glop!* They fell back together, sinking into the water, taking mouthfuls of it, choking, coughing, sputtering, gagging it out as they helped each other sit up.

The white things came toward them. Drawn to the splashing or drawn to the fever that burned in Jill's body. Jack could feel it from where he touched her. It was as if there was a coal furnace burning bright under her skin. Even with all this cold rain and runoff, she was hot. Steam curled up from her.

None curled up from Jack. His body felt even more shrunken than usual. Thinner, drawn into itself to kindle the last sparks of what he had left. He moaned in pain as he tried to stand. The creatures surrounding him moaned, too. Their cries sounded no different from his.

He forced himself to stand and wrapped his arm around Jill.

"Run!" he cried.

They cut between two of the figures, and the things turned awkwardly, pawing at them with dead fingers, but Jack and Jill ducked and slipped past. The porch was close but the water made it hard to run. The creatures with the white faces were clumsier and slower, and that helped.

Thunder battered the farm, deafening Jack and Jill as they collapsed onto the stairs and crawled like bugs onto the plank floor. The front door was wide open, the glow from the Coleman lantern showing the way.

"Jack . . . " Jill mumbled, slurring his name. "I feel sick."

The monsters in the rain kept coming, and Jack realized that they had ignored him time and again. These creatures were not chasing him now. They were coming for Jill. They wanted her.

Her. Not him.

Why?

Because they want life.

That's why they went after Mom and Dad and Uncle Roger.

That's why they want Jill.

Not him.

He wasn't sure how or why he knew that, but he was absolutely certain of it. The need for life was threaded through that awful moan. Toby had wanted more life. He wanted to be alive, but he'd reached the point where he was more dead than alive. Sliding down, down, down.

I'm already dead.

Jill crawled so slowly that she was barely halfway across the porch by the time one of *them* tottered to the top step. Jack felt it before he turned and looked. Water dripped from its body onto the backs of his legs.

The thing moaned.

Jack looked up at the terrible, terrible face.

"Mom . . . ?" he whispered.

Torn and ragged, things missing from her face and neck, red and black blood gurgling over her lips and down her chin. Bone-white hands reaching.

Past him.

Ignoring him.

Reaching for Jill.

"No," said Jack. He wanted to scream the word, to shout the kind of defiance that would prove that he was still alive, that he was still to be acknowledged. But all he could manage was a thin, breathless rasp of a word. Mom did not hear it. No one did. There was too much of everything else for it to be heard.

Jill didn't hear it.

Jill turned at the sound of the moan from the thing that took graceless steps toward her. Jill's glazed red eyes flared wide and she screamed the same word. "*NO!*"

Jill, sick as she was, screamed that word with all of the heat and fear and sickness and life that was boiling inside of her. It was louder than the rain and the thunder. Louder than the hungry moan that came from Mom's throat.

There was no reaction on Mom's face. Her mouth opened and closed like a fish.

No, not like a fish. Like someone practicing the act of eating a meal that was almost hers.

There was very little of Jack left, but he forced himself once more to get to his feet. To stand. To stagger over to Jill, to catch her under the armpits, to pull, to drag. Jill thrashed against him, against what she saw on the porch.

She punched Jack, and scratched him. Tears like hot acid fell on Jack's face and throat.

He pulled her into the house. As he did so, Jack lost his grip and Jill fell past him into the living room.

Jack stood in the doorway for a moment, chest heaving, staring with bleak eyes at Mom. And then past her to the other figures who were slogging through the mud and water toward the house. At the rain hammering on the useless truck. At the farm road that led away toward the River Road. When the lightning flashed he could see all the way past the levee to the river, which was a great, black swollen thing.

Tears, as cold as Jill's were hot, cut channels down his face.

Mom reached out.

Her hands brushed his face as she tried to reach past him.

A sob as painful as a punch broke in Jack's chest as he slammed the door.

11

He turned and fell back against it, then slid all the way down to the floor.

Jill lay on her side, weeping into her palms.

Outside the storm raged, mocking them both with its power. It's life.

"Jill . . . " said Jack softly.

The house creaked in the wind, each timber moaning its pain and weariness. The window glass trembled in the casements. Even the good china on the dining room breakfront racks rattled nervously as if aware of their own fragility.

Jack heard all of this.

Jill crawled over to him and collapsed against him, burying her face against his chest. Her grief was so big that it, too, was voiceless. Her body shook and her tears fell on him like rain. Jack wrapped his arms around her and pulled her close.

He was so cold that her heat was the only warmth in his world.

Behind them there was a heavy thud on the door.

Soft and lazy, but heavy, like the fist of a sleepy drunk.

However Jack knew that it was no drunk. He knew exactly who and what was pounding on the door. A few moments later there were other thuds. On the side windows and the back door. On the walls. At first just a few fists, then more.

Jill raised her head and looked up at him.

"I'm cold," she said, even though she was hot. Jack nodded, he understood fevers. Her eyes were like red coals.

"I'll keep you warm," he said, huddling closer to her.

"W-what's happening?" she asked. "Mom . . . ?"

He didn't answer. He rested the back of his head against the door, feeling the shocks and vibrations of each soft punch shudder through him. The cold was everywhere now. He could not feel his legs or his hands. He shivered as badly as she did, and all around them the storm raged and the dead beat on the house. He listened to his own heartbeat. It fluttered and twitched. Beneath his skin and in his veins and in his bones, the cancer screamed as it devoured the last of his heat.

He looked down at Jill. The bite on her arm was almost colorless, but radiating out from it were black lines that ran like tattoos of vines up her arm. More of the black lines were etched on her throat and along the sides of her face. Black goo oozed from two or three smaller bites that Jack hadn't seen before. Were they from what happened at the school, or from just now? No way to tell; the rain had washed away all of the red, leaving wounds that opened obscenely and in which white grubs wriggled in the black wetness.

Her heart beat like the wings of a hummingbird. Too fast, too light.

Outside, Mom and the others moaned for them.

"Jack . . . " she said, and her voice was even smaller, farther away.

"Yeah?"

"Remember when you were in the hospital in January?"

"Yeah."

"You . . . you told me about your dream?" She still spoke in the dazed voice of a dreamer.

"Which dream?" he asked, though he thought he already knew.

"The one about . . . the big wave. The black wave."

"The black nothing," he corrected. "Yeah, I remember."

She sniffed but it didn't stop the tears from falling. "Is . . . is that what this is?"

Jack kissed her cheek. As they sat there, her skin had begun to change, the intense heat gradually giving way to a clammy coldness. Outside, the pounding, the moans, the rain, the wind, the thunder—it was all continuous.

"Yeah," he said quietly, "I think so."

They listened to the noise and Jack felt himself getting smaller inside his own body.

"Will it hurt?" she asked.

Jack had to think about that. He didn't want to lie but he wasn't sure of the truth.

The roar of noise was fading. Not getting smaller but each separate sound was being consumed by a wordless moan that was greater than the sum of its parts.

"No," he said, "it won't hurt."

Jill's eyes drifted shut and there was just the faintest trace of a smile on her lips. There was no reason for it to be there, but it was there.

He held her until all the warmth was gone from her. He listened for the hummingbird flutter of her heart and heard nothing.

He touched his face. His tears had stopped with her heart. That was okay, he thought. That's how it should be.

Then Jack laid Jill down on the floor and stood up.

The moan of the darkness outside was so big now. Massive. Huge.

He bent close and peered out through the peephole.

The pounding on the door stopped. Mom and the others outside began to turn, one after the other, looking away from the house. Looking out into the yard.

Jack took a breath.

He opened the door.

12

The lightning and the outspill of light from the lantern showed him the porch and the yard, the car and the road. There were at least fifty of the white-faced people there. None of them looked at him. Mom was right there, but she had her back to him. He saw Roger crawling through the water so he could see past the truck. He saw Dad rise awkwardly to his feet, his face gone but the pistol still dangling from his finger.

All of them were turned away, looking past the abandoned truck, facing the farm road.

Jack stood over Jill's body and watched as the wall of water from the shattered levee came surging up the road toward the house. It was so beautiful.

A big, black wall of nothing.

Jack looked at his mother, his father, his uncle, and then down at Jill.

He would not be going into the dark without them.

The dark was going to take them all.

Jack smiled.

In the Dreamtime
of Lady Resurrection

Caitlín R. Kiernan

"Wake up," she whispers, as ever she is always whispering with those demanding, ashen lips, but I do not open my eyes. I do not wake up, as she has bidden me to do, but, instead, lie drifting in this amniotic moment, unwilling to move one instant forward and incapable of retreating by even the scant breadth of a single second. For now, there is *only* now; yet, even so, an infinity stretches all around, haunted by dim shapes and half-glimpsed phantasmagoria, and if I named this time and place, I might name it Pluto or Orcus or Dis Pater. But never would I name it purgatorial, for here there are no purging flames nor trials of final purification from venial transgressions. I have not arrived here by any shade of damnation and await no deliverance, but scud gently through Pre-Adamite seas, and so might I name this wide pacific realm *Womb*, the uterus common to all that which has ever risen squirming from mere insensate earth. I might name it *Mother*. I might best call it nothing at all, for a name may only lessen and constrain this inconceivable vastness.

"Wake up now," she whispers, but I shall rather seek these deeper currents.

No longer can I distinguish that which is *without* from that which is *within*. In ocher and loden green and malachite dusks do I dissolve and somehow still retain this flesh and this unbeating heart and this blood grown cold and stagnant in my veins. Even as I slip free, I am constrained, and in the eel-grass shadows do I descry her desperate, damned form bending low above this warm and salty sea where she has laid me down. She is Heaven, her milky skin is star pierced through a thousand, thousand times to spill forth droplets of the dazzling light which is but one half of her unspeakable art. She would have me think it the totality, as though a dead woman is blind merely because her eyes remain shut. Long did I suspect the whole of her. When I breathed and had occasion to walk beneath the sun and moon, even then did I harbor my suspicions and guess at the blackness fastidiously concealed within that blinding glare. And here, at this moment, she is to me as naked as in the hour of her birth, and no guise nor glamour would ever hide from me that perpetual evening of her soul. At this moment, all and everything is laid bare. I am gutted like a gasping fish, and she is flayed by revelation.

She whispers to me, and I float across endless plains of primordial silt and gaping hadopelgaic chasms where sometimes I sense the awful minds of other sleepers, ancient before the coming of time, waiting alone in sunken temples and drowned sepulchers. Below me lies the gray and glairy mass of Professor Huxley's *Bathybius haeckelii*, the boundless, wriggling sheet of *Urschleim* that encircles all the globe. Here and there do I catch sight of the bleached skeletons of mighty whales and ichthyosauria, their bones gnawed raw by centuries and millennia and aeons, by the busy proboscides of nameless invertebrata. The struts of a Leviathan's ribcage rise from the gloom like a cathedral's vaulted roof, and a startled retinue of spiny crabs wave threatful pincers that I might not forget I am the intruder. For this I *would* forget, and forswear that tattered life she stole and now so labors to restore, were that choice only mine to make.

I know this is no ocean, and I know there is no firmament set out over me. But I am sinking, all the same, spiraling down with infinite slowness towards some unimaginable beginning or conclusion (as though there is a difference between the two). And you watch on worriedly, and yet always that devouring curiosity to defuse any fear or regret. Your hands wander impatiently across copper coils and spark tungsten filaments, tap upon sluggish dials and tug so slightly at the rubber tubes that enter and exit me as though I have sprouted a bouquet of umbilici. You mind the gate and the road back, and so I turn away and would not see your pale, exhausted face.

With a glass dropper, you taint my pool with poisonous tinctures of quicksilver and iodine, meaning to shock me back into a discarded shell.

And I misstep, then, some fraction of a footfall this way or that, and now somehow I have not yet felt the snip that divided *me* from *me*. I sit naked on a wooden stool near *Der Ocean auf dem Tische*, the great vivarium tank you have fashioned from iron and plate glass and marble.

You will be my goldfish, you laugh. *You will be my newt. What better part could you ever play, my dear?*

You kiss my bare shoulders and my lips, and I taste brandy on your tongue. You hold my breasts cupped in your hands and tease my nipples with your teeth. And I know none of this is misdirection to put my mind at ease, but rather your delight in changes to come. The experiment is your bacchanal, and the mad glint in your eyes would shame any maenad or rutting satyr. I have no delusions regarding what is soon to come. I am the sacrifice, and it matters little or none at all whether the altar you have raised is to Science or Dionysus.

"Oh, if I could stand in your place," you sigh, and again your lips brush mine. "If I could *see* what you will see and *feel* what you will feel!"

"I will be your eyes," I say, echoing myself. "I will be your curious, probing hands." These might be wedding vows that we exchange. These might be the last words of the condemned on the morning of her execution.

"Yes, you shall, but I would make this journey myself and have need of no surrogate." Then and now, I wonder in secret if you mean everything you say. It is easy to declare envy when there is no likelihood of exchanging places. "Where you go, my love, all go in due time, but you may be the first ever to return and report to the living what she has witnessed there."

You kneel before me, as if in awe or gratitude, and your head settles upon my lap. I touch your golden hair with fingers that have scarcely begun to feel the tingling and chill, the numbness that will consume me soon enough. You kindly offered to place the lethal preparation in a cup of something sweet that I would not taste its bitterness, but I told you how I preferred to know my executioner and would not have his grim face so pleasantly hooded. I took it in a single acrid spoonful, and now we wait, and I touch your golden hair.

"When I was a girl," I begin, then must pause to lick my dry lips.

"You have told me this story already."

"I would have you hear it once more. Am I not accorded some last indulgence before the stroll to the gallows?"

"It will not be a gallows," you reply, but there is a sharp edge around your words, a brittle frame and all the gilt flaking free. "Indeed, it will be little more than a quick glance stolen through a window before the drapes are drawn shut against you. So, dear, you do not stand to *earn* some final coddling, not this day, and so I would not hear that tale repeated, when I know it as well as I know the four syllables of my own beloved's name."

"You *will* hear me," I say, and my fingers twine and knot themselves tightly in your hair. A few flaxen strands pull free, and I hope I can carry them down into the dark with me. You tense, but do not pull away or make any further protest. "When I was a girl, my own brother died beneath the wheels of an ox cart. It was an accident, of course. But still his skull was broken and his chest all staved in, though, in the end, no one was judged at fault."

I sit on my stool, and you kneel there on the stone floor, waiting for me to be done, restlessly awaiting my passage and the moment when I have been rendered incapable of repeating familiar tales you do not wish to hear retold.

"I held him, what remained of him. I felt the shudder when his child's soul pulled loose from its prison. His blue eyes were as bright in that instant as the glare of sunlight off freshly fallen snow. As for the man who drove the cart, he committed suicide some weeks later, though I did not learn this until I was almost grown."

"There is no ox cart here," you whisper. "There are no careless hooves and no innocent drover."

"I did not say he was a drover. I have never said that. He was merely a farmer, I think, on his way to market with a load of potatoes and cabbages. My brother's entire unlived life traded for only a few bushels of potatoes and cabbages. That must be esteemed a bargain, by any measure."

"We should begin now," you say, and I don't disagree, for my legs are growing stiff and an indefinable weight has begun to press in upon me. I was warned of these symptoms, and so there is not surprise, only the fear that I have prayed I would be strong enough to bear. You stand and help me to my feet, then lead me the short distance to the vivarium tank. Suddenly, I cannot escape the fanciful and disagreeable impression that your mechanical apparatuses and contraptions are watching on. Maybe, I think, they have been watching all along. Perhaps, they were my jurors, an impassionate, unbiased tribunal of brass and steel and porcelain, and now they gaze out with automaton eyes and exhale steam and oily vapors to see their sentence served. You told me there would be madness, that the toxin would act upon my mind as well as my body, but in my madness I have forgotten the warning.

"Please, I would not have them see me, not like this," I tell you, but already we have reached the great tank that will only serve as my carriage for these brief and extraordinary travels—if your calculations and theories are proved correct—or that will become my deathbed, if, perchance, you have made some critical error. There is a stepladder, and you guide me, and so I endeavor not to feel their enthusiastic, damp-palmed scrutiny. I sit down on the platform at the top of the ladder and let my feet dangle into the warm liquid, both my feet and then my legs up to the knees. It is not an objectionable sensation, and promises that I will not be cold for much longer. Streams of bubbles rise slowly from vents set into the rear wall of the tank, stirring and oxygenating this translucent primal soup of viscous humors, your painstaking brew of protéine and hæmatoglobin, carbamide resin and cellulose, water and phlegm and bile. All those substances believed fundamental to life, a recipe gleaned from dusty volumes of Medieval alchemy and metaphysics, but also from your own researches and the work of more modern scientific practitioners and professors of chemistry and anatomy. Previously, I have found the odor all but unbearable, though now there seems to be no detectable scent at all.

"Believe me," you say, "I will have you back with me in less than an hour." And I try hard then to remember how long an hour is, but the poison leeches away even the memory of time. With hands as gentle as a midwife's, you help me from the platform and into my strange bath, and you keep my head above the surface until the last convulsions have come and gone and I am made no more than any cadaver.

"Wake up," she says—*you* say—but the shock of the mercury and iodine you administered to the vivarium have rapidly faded, and once more there is but the absolute and inviolable present moment, so impervious and sacrosanct that I can not even imagine conscious action, which would require the concept of an apprehension of some future, that time is somehow more than this static aqueous matrix surrounding and defining me.

"Do you hear me? Can you not even *hear* me?"

All at once, and with a certitude almost agonizing in its omneity, I am aware that I am being watched. No, that is not right. That is not precisely the way of it. All at once, I know that I am being watched by eyes which have not heretofore beheld me; all along there have been *her* eyes, as well as the stalked eyes of the scuttling crabs I mentioned and other such creeping, slithering inhabitants of my mind's ocean as have glommed the dim pageant of my voyage. But *these* eyes, and this spectator—my love, nothing has ever seen me with such complete and merciless understanding. And now the act of *seeing* has ceased to be a passive action, as the act of being *seen* has stopped being an activity that neither diminishes nor alters the observed. I would scream, but dead women do not seem to be permitted that luxury, and the scream of my soul is as silent as the moon. And in another place and in another time where *past* and *future* still hold meaning, you plunge your arms into the tank, hauling me up from the shallow deep and moving me not one whit. I am fixed by these eyes, like a butterfly pinned after the killing jar.

It does not speak to me, for there can be no need of speech when vision is so thorough and so incapable of misreckoning. Plagues need not speak, nor floods, nor the voracious winds of tropical hurricanes. A thing with eyes for teeth, eyes for its tongue and gullet. A thing which has been waiting for me in this moment that has no antecedents and which can spawn no successors. Maybe it waits here for every dying man and woman, for every insect and beast and falling leaf, or maybe some specific quality of my obliteration has brought me to its attention. Possibly, it only catches sight of suicides, and surely I have become that, though *your* Circean hands poured the poison draught and then held the spoon. There is such terrible force in this gaze that it seems not implausible that I am the first it has ever beheld, and now it will know all, and it shall have more than knowledge for this opportunity might never come again.

"Only tell me what happened," you will say, in some time that cannot ever be, not from *when* I lie here in the vivarium you have built for me, not from this occasion when I lie exposed to a Cosmos hardly half considered by the mortal minds contained therein. "Only put down what seems most significant, in retrospect. Do not dwell upon everything you might recall, every perception. You may make a full accounting later."

"Later, I might forget something," I will reply. "It's not so unlike a dream." And you will frown and slide the ink well a little ways across the writing desk towards me. On your face I will see the stain of an anxiety that has been mounting down all the days since my return.

That will be a lie, of course, for nothing of this will I ever forget. Never shall it fade. I will be taunting you, or through me *it* will be taunting your heedless curiosity, which even then will remain undaunted. This hour, though, is far, far away. From when I lie, it is a fancy that can never come to pass—a unicorn, the roaring cataract at the edge of a flat world, a Hell which punishes only those who deserve eternal torment. Around me flows the sea of all beginnings and of all conclusion, and through the weeds and murk, from the peaks of submarine mountains to the lowest vales of Neptune's sovereignty, benighted in perpetuum—horizon to horizon—does its vision stretch unbroken. And as I have written already, observing me it takes away, and observing me it adds to my acumen and marrow. I am increased as much or more than I am consumed, so it must be a *fair* encounter, when all is said and done.

Somewhen immeasurably inconceivable to my present-bound mind, a hollow needle pierces my flesh, there in some unforeseeable aftertime, and the hypodermic's plunger forces into me your concoction of caffeine citrate, cocaine, belladonna, epinephrine, foxglove, etcetera & etcetera. And I think you will be screaming for me to come back, then, to open my eyes, to *wake up* as if you had only given me over to an afternoon catnap. I would not answer, even now, even with its smothering eyes upon me, *in* me, performing their metamorphosis. But you are calling (*wake up, wake up, wake up*), and your chemicals are working upon my traitorous physiology, and, worst of all, *it* wishes me to return from whence and when I have come. It has infected me, or placed within me some fraction of itself, or made from my sentience something suited to its own explorations. Did this never occur to you, my dear? That in those liminal spaces, across the thresholds that separate life from death, might lurk an inhabitant supremely adapted to those climes, and yet also possessed of its own questions, driven by its own peculiar acquisitiveness, seeking always some means to penetrate the veil. I cross one way for you, and I return as another's experiment, the vessel of another's inquisition.

"Breathe, goddamn you!" you will scream, screaming that seems no more or less disingenuous or melodramatic than any actor upon any stage. With your fingers you will clear, have cleared, are evermore clearing my mouth and nostrils of the thickening elixir filling the vivarium tank. "You won't leave me. I will not let you go. There are no ox carts here, no wagon wheels."

But, also, you have, or you will, or at this very second you are placing that fatal spoon upon my tongue.

And when it is done—if I may arbitrarily use that word here, *when*—and its modifications are complete, it shuts its eyes, like the sun tumbling down from the sky, and I am tossed helpless back into the rushing flow of time's river. In the vivarium, I try to draw a breath and vomit milky gouts. At the writing desk, I take the quill you have provided me, and I write—"*Wake up,*" *she whispers.* There are long days when I do not have the strength to speak or even sit. The fears of pneumonia and fever, of dementia and some heretofore unseen necrosis triggered by my time *away*. The relief that begins to show itself as weeks pass and your fears fade slowly, replaced again by that old and indomitable inquisitiveness. The evening that you drained the tank and found something lying at the bottom which you have refused to ever let me see, but keep under lock and key. And this night, which might be *now*, in our bed in the dingy room above your laboratory, and you hold me in your arms, and I lie with my ear against your breast, listening to the tireless rhythm of your heart winding down, and *it* listens through me. You think me still your love, and I let my hand wander across your belly and on, lower, to the damp cleft of your sex. And there also is the day I hold my dying brother. And there are my long walks beside the sea, too, with the winter waves hammering against the Cobb. That brine is only the faintest echo of the tenebrous kingdom I might have named *Womb*. Overhead, the wheeling gulls mock me, and the freezing wind drives me home again. But always it watches, and it waits, and it studies the intricacies of the winding avenue I have become.

> *She rolls through an ether of sighs—*
> *She revels in a region of sighs . . .*
> —Edgar Allan Poe
> (December 1847)

Rigormarole

Michael A. Arnzen

Don't be afraid, boy—
this here corpse is twice dead.
Come on over to the gurney
and take a gander at that there
shiny yellow knob snuggled in
his Corpus Collosum like
a gawdamn popcorn kernel.
Here, let me use this here probe
to give y'all a better look. See that
ugly thing? That there cluster of
gunk? No, that ain't human at all.
You'll only find 'em in zombies.
I dub it the "Resurrectal Cortex"—
a fancy name for this whole new lobe
that emerges inside what's left of the brains
of the dead like a fetus in a fetid womb.
I reckon that's what they're feeding
when they eat folks dry. And that's
what we're popping when we shoot 'em
in the melon. Here, let me remove it
so we can get a better look. There it is.
Okay, here, hold that. Heavier than you
'spected, ain't it? Feels like a rotten
grapefruit, right? Tastes like one, too.
Sure, I ate one. Go on ahead and try
it yerself. Come on, take a big bite.
And you better get used to it, boy.
Cause the only thing that'll
ever really rid the world

of these undead bastards for good
is a zombie zombie. Dammit,
I said eat it. Sure, I know
it tastes like death warmed over,
but it ain't gonna kill you.
It'll make you one of us—
one of the unundead.
And there's plenty more
where that came from. Plenty.
Eat up. Just close your eyes
and try to think of it as
Communion without all that
high-falutin' ceremony
and fancy rigormarole.

Kitty's Zombie New Year

Carrie Vaughn

I'd refused to stay home alone on New Year's Eve. I wasn't going to be one of those angst-ridden losers stuck at home watching the ball drop in Times Square while sobbing into a pint of gourmet ice cream.

No, I was going to do it over at a friend's, in the middle of a party.

Matt, a guy from the radio station where I was a DJ, was having a wild party in his cramped apartment. Lots of booze, lots of music, and the TV blaring the Times Square special from New York—being in Denver, we'd get to celebrate New Year's a couple of times over. I wasn't going to come to the party, but he'd talked me into it. I didn't like crowds, which was why the late shift at the station suited me. But here I was, and it was just like I knew it would be: 10:00 p.m., the ball dropped, and everyone except me had somebody to kiss. I gripped a tumbler filled with untasted rum and Coke and glowered at the television, wondering which well-preserved celebrity guest hosts were vampires and which ones just had portraits in their attics that were looking particularly hideous.

It would happen all over again at midnight.

Sure enough, shortly after the festivities in New York City ended, the TV station announced it would rebroadcast everything at midnight.

An hour later, I'd decided to find Matt and tell him I was going home to wallow in ice cream after all, when a woman screamed. The room fell instantly quiet, and everyone looked toward the front door, from where the sound had blasted.

The door stood open, and one of the crowd stared over the threshold, to another woman who stood motionless. A new guest had arrived and knocked, I assumed. But she just stood there, not coming inside, and the screamer stared at her, one hand on the doorknob and the other hand covering her mouth. The scene turned rather eerie and surreal. The seconds ticked by, no one said or did anything.

Matt, his black hair in a pony tail, pushed through the crowd to the door. The motion seemed out of place, chaotic. Still, the woman on the other side stood frozen, unmoving. I felt a sinking feeling in my gut.

Matt turned around and called, "Kitty!"

Sinking feeling confirmed.

I made my own way to the door, shouldering around people. By the time I reached Matt, the woman who'd answered the door had edged away to take shelter in her boyfriend's arms. Matt turned to me, dumbstruck.

The woman outside was of average height, though she slumped, her shoulders rolled forward as if she was too tired to hold herself up. Her head tilted to one side. She might have been a normal twenty-something, recent college grad, in worn jeans, an oversized blue T-shirt, and canvas sneakers. Her light hair was loose and stringy, like it hadn't been washed in a couple of weeks.

I glanced at Matt.

"What's wrong with her?" he said.

"What makes you think I know?"

"Because you know all about freaky shit." Ah, yes. He was referring to my call-in radio show about the supernatural. That made me an expert, even when I didn't know a thing.

"Do you know her?"

"No, I don't." He turned back to the room, to the dozens of faces staring back at him, round-eyed. "Hey, does anybody know who this is?"

The crowd collectively pressed back from the door, away from the strangeness.

"Maybe it's drugs." I called to her, "Hey."

She didn't move, didn't blink, didn't flinch. Her expression was slack, completely blank. She might have been asleep, except her eyes were open, staring straight ahead. They were dull, almost like a film covered them. Her mouth was open a little.

I waved my hand in front of her face, which seemed like a really clichéd thing to do. She didn't respond. Her skin was terribly pale, clammy looking, and I couldn't bring myself to touch her. I didn't know what I would do if she felt cold and dead.

Matt said, "Geez, she's like some kind of zombie."

Oh, no. No way. But the word clicked. It was a place to start, at least.

Someone behind us said, "I thought zombies, like, attacked people and ate brains and stuff."

I shook my head. "That's horror movie zombies. Not voodoo slave zombies."

"So you do know what's going on?" Matt said hopefully.

"Not yet. I think you should call nine-one-one."

He winced and scrubbed his hand through his hair. "But if it's a zombie, if she's dead an ambulance isn't—"

"Call an ambulance." He nodded and grabbed his cell phone off the coffee table. "And I'm going to use your computer."

I did what any self-respecting American in this day and age would do in such a situation: I searched the Internet for zombies.

I couldn't say it was particularly useful. A frighteningly large number of the sites that came up belonged to survivalist groups planning for the great zombie infestation that would bring civilization collapsing around our ears. They helpfully informed a casual reader such as myself that the government was ill prepared to handle the magnitude of the disaster that would wreak itself upon the country when the horrible zombie-virus mutation swept through the population. We must be prepared to defend ourselves against the flesh-eating hordes bent on our destruction.

This was a movie synopsis, not data, and while fascinating, it wasn't helpful.

A bunch of articles on voodoo and Haitian folklore seemed mildly more useful, but even those were contradictory: The true believers in magic argued with the hardened scientists, and even the scientists argued among themselves about whether the legends sprang from the use of certain drugs or from profound psychological disorders.

I'd seen enough wild stories play out in my time that I couldn't discount any of these alternatives. These days, magic and science were converging on one another.

Someone was selling zombie powders on eBay. They even came with an instruction booklet. That might be fun to bid on just to say I'd done it. Even if I did, the instruction book that might have some insight on the problem wouldn't get here in time.

Something most of the articles mentioned: Stories said that the taste of salt would revive a zombie. Revived them out of what, and into what, no one seemed to agree on. If they weren't really dead but comatose, the person would be restored. If they were honest-to-God walking dead, they'd be released from servitude and make their way back to their graves.

I went to the kitchen and found a saltshaker.

If she really was a zombie, she couldn't have just shown up here. She had come here for a specific reason, there had to be some connection. She was here to scare someone, which meant someone here had to know her. Nobody was volunteering any information.

Maybe she could tell me herself.

Finally, I had to touch her, in order to get the salt into her mouth. I put my hand on her shoulder. She swayed enough that I thought she might fall over, so I pulled away. A moment later, she steadied, remaining upright. I could probably push her forward, guide her, and make her walk like a puppet.

I shivered.

Swallowing back a lump of bile threatening to climb my throat, I held her chin, tipping her head back. Her skin was waxen, neither warm nor cold. Her muscles were limp, perfectly relaxed. Or dead. I tried not to think of it. She'd been drugged. That was the theory I was going for. Praying for, rather.

"What are you doing?" Matt said.

"Never mind. Did you call the ambulance?"

"They should be here any minute."

I sprinkled a few shakes of salt into her mouth.

I had to tip her head forward and close her mouth for her because she couldn't do it herself. And if she couldn't do that, she surely couldn't swallow. None of the information said she had to swallow the salt, just taste it. In cultures around the world salt had magical properties. It was a ward against evil, protection against fairies, a treasure as great as gold. It seemed so common and innocuous now. Hard to believe it could do anything besides liven up a basket of French fries.

Her eyes moved.

The film, the dullness went away, and her gaze focused. It flickered, as if searching or confused.

Fear tightened her features. Her shoulders bunched, and her fingers clenched into claws. She screamed.

She let out a wail of anguish, bone-leaching in its intensity. A couple of yelps of shock answered from within the apartment. Her face melted into an expression of despair, lips pulled back in a frown, eyes red and wincing. But she didn't cry.

Reaching forward with those crooked fingers, she took a stumbling step forward. My heart racing, my nausea growing, I hurried out of her way. Another step followed, clumsy and unsure. She was like a toddler who'd just learned to walk. This was the slow, shuffling gait of a zombie in every B-grade horror movie I'd ever seen. The salt hadn't cured her; it had just woken her up.

She stumbled forward, step by step, reaching. People scrambled out of her way.

She didn't seem hungry. That look of utter pain and sadness remained locked on her features. She looked as if her heart had been torn out and smashed into pieces.

Her gaze searched wildly, desperately.

I ran in front of her, blocking her path. "Hey—can you hear me?" I waved my arms, trying to catch her attention. She didn't seem to notice, but she shifted, angling around me. So I tried again. "Who are you? Can you tell me your name? How did this happen?"

Her gaze had focused on something behind me. When I got in front of her, she looked right through me and kept going like I wasn't there. I turned to find what had caught her attention.

A man and woman sat wedged together in a secondhand armchair, looking like a Mack truck was about to run them down. The zombie woman shuffled toward them. Now that I was out of the way, she reached toward them, arms rigid and trembling. She moaned—she might have been trying to speak, but she couldn't shape her mouth right. She was like an infant who desperately wanted something but didn't have the words to say it. She was an infant in the body of an adult.

And what she wanted was the man in the chair.

A few steps away, her moaning turned into a wail. The woman in the chair screamed and fell over the arm to get away. The man wasn't that nimble, or he was frozen in place.

The zombie wobbled on her next step, then fell to her knees, but that didn't stop her reaching. She was close enough to grab his feet. Those clawlike hands clenched on his ankles, and she tried to pull herself forward, dragging herself on the carpet, still moaning.

The man shrieked and kicked at her, yanking his legs away and trying to curl up in the chair.

"Stop it!" I screamed at him, rushing forward to put myself between them.

She was sprawled on the floor now, crying gut-wrenching sobs. I held her shoulders and pulled her back from the chair, laying her on her back. Her arms still reached, but the rest of her body had become limp, out of her control.

"Matt, get a pillow and a blanket." He ran to the bedroom to get them. That was all I could think—try to make her comfortable. When were those paramedics going to get here?

I looked at the guy in the chair. Like the rest of the people at the party, he was twenty-something. Thin and generically cute, he had shaggy dark hair, a preppy button-up shirt, and gray trousers. I wouldn't have picked him out of the crowd.

"Who are you?" I said.

"C-Carson."

He even had a preppy name to go with the ensemble. I glanced at the woman who was with him. Huddled behind the armchair, she was starting to peer out. She had dyed black hair, a tiny nose stud, and a tight dress. More like the kind of crowd Matt hung out with. I wouldn't have put her and Carson together. Maybe they both thought they were slumming.

"Do you know her?" I asked him, nodding at the zombie woman on the floor.

He shook his head quickly, pressing himself even farther back in the chair. He was sweating. Carson was about to lose it.

Matt returned and helped me fit the pillow under her head and spread the blanket over her. He, too, was beginning to see her as someone who was sick—not a monster.

"You're lying," I said. "She obviously knows you. Who is she?"

"I don't know, I don't know!"

"Matt, who is this guy?"

Matt glanced at him. "Just met him tonight. He's Trish's new boyfriend."

"Trish?" I said to the woman behind the armchair.

"I—I don't know. At least, I'm not sure. I never met her, but I think . . . I think she's his ex-girlfriend. Beth, I think. But Carson, you told me she moved away—"

Carson, staring at the woman on the floor, looked like he was about to have a screaming fit. He was still shaking his head.

I was ready to throttle him. I wanted an explanation. Maybe he really didn't know. But if he was lying . . . "Carson!"

He flinched at my shout.

Sirens sounded down the street, coming closer. The paramedics. I hoped they could help her, but the sick feeling in my stomach hadn't gone away.

"I'll meet them on the street," Matt said, running out.

"Beth," I said to the woman. I caught her hands, managed to pull them down so they were resting on her chest. I murmured at her, and she quieted. Her skin color hadn't gotten any better. She didn't feel cold as death, but she felt cool. The salt hadn't sent her back to any grave, and it hadn't revived her. I wasn't sure she could be revived.

A moment later, a couple of uniformed paramedics carrying equipment entered, followed by Matt. The living room should have felt crowded, but apparently as soon as the door cleared, most of the guests had fled. God, what a way to kill a party.

The paramedics came straight toward Beth. I got out of the way. They immediately knelt by her, checked her pulse, shined a light in her eyes. I breathed a little easier. Finally, someone was doing something useful.

"What happened?" one of them asked.

How did I explain this? She's a zombie. That wasn't going to work, because I didn't think she was one anymore. *She was a zombie* didn't sound any better.

"She was going to leave," Carson said, suddenly, softly. Responding to the authority of the uniform, maybe. He stared at her, unable to look away. He spoke as if in a trance. "I didn't want her to go. She asked me to come with her, to Seattle—but I didn't want to do that, either. I wanted her to stay with me. So I . . . this stuff, this powder. It would make her do anything I wanted. I used it. But it . . . changed her. She wasn't the same. She—was like that. Dead almost. I left her, but she followed. She kept following me—"

"Call it poisoning," said one paramedic to the other.

"Where did you get this powder?" I said.

"Some guy on the Internet."

I wanted to kill him. Wanted to put my hands around his throat and kill him.

"Kitty," Matt said. I took a breath. Calmed down.

"Any idea what was in this powder?" one of the paramedics said, sounding like he was repressing as much anger as I was.

Carson shook his head.

"Try tetrodotoxin," I said. "Induces a death-like coma. Also causes brain damage. Irreparable brain damage."

Grimacing, the paramedic said, "We won't be able to check that until we get her to the hospital. I don't see any ID on her. I'm going to call in the cops, see if they've had a missing persons report on her. And to see what they want to do with him."

Carson flinched at his glare.

Trish backed away. "If I tried to break up with you—would you have done that to me, too?" Her mouth twisted with unspoken accusations. Then, she fled.

Carson thought he'd make his own zombie slave girlfriend, then somehow wasn't satisfied at the results. She probably wasn't real good in bed. He'd probably done it, too—had sex with Beth's brain-damaged, comatose body. The cops couldn't get here fast enough, in my opinion.

"There's two parts to it," I said. "The powder creates the zombie. But then there's the spell to bind her to you, to bind the slave to the master. Some kind of object with meaning, a receptacle for the soul. You have it. That's why she followed you. That's why she wouldn't stay away." The salt hadn't broken that bond. She'd regained her will—but the damage was too great for her to do anything with it. She knew enough to recognize him and what he'd done to her, but could only cry out helplessly.

He reached into his pocket, pulled something out. He opened his fist to reveal what.

A diamond engagement ring lay in his palm.

Beth reacted, arcing her back, flailing, moaning. The paramedics freaked, pinned her arms, jabbed her with a hypodermic. She settled again, whimpering softly.

I took the ring from Carson. He glared at me, the first time he'd really looked at me. I didn't see remorse in his eyes. Only fear. Like Victor Frankenstein, he'd created a monster and all he could do when confronted with it was cringe in terror.

"Matt, you have a string or a shoelace or something?"

"Yeah, sure."

He came back with a bootlace fresh out of the package. I put the ring on it, knotted it, and slipped it over Beth's head. "Can you make sure this stays with her?" I asked the paramedics. They nodded.

This was half science, half magic. If the ring really did hold Beth's soul, maybe it would help. If it didn't help—well, at least Carson wouldn't have it anymore.

The cops came and took statements from all of us, including the paramedics, then took Carson away. The paramedics took Beth away; the ambulance siren howled down the street, away.

Finally, when Matt and I were alone among the remains of his disaster of a party, I started crying. "How could he do that? How could he even think it? She was probably this wonderful, beautiful, independent woman, and he destroyed—"

Matt had poured two glasses of champagne. He handed me one.

"Happy New Year, Kitty." He pointed at the clock on the microwave: 12:03 a.m.

Crap. I missed it. I started crying harder.

Matt, my friend, hugged me. So once again, I didn't get a New Year's kiss. This year, I didn't mind.

The Gravedigger of Konstan Spring

Genevieve Valentine

There was something more civilized about a town that could bury its dead, if they stayed dead, and so Folkvarder Gray put out the notice for a gravedigger.

John the gravedigger was the best in the Nyr Nord Territory. He dug them narrow and he dug them deep, and when he came to Konstan Spring he provided references from Nyr Odin, where he had been called in to exercise his craft after the second English War for the Territory.

Folkvarder Gray looked over the letters, and then he shook John's hand and took the "Gravedigger Wanted" sign out of the window, and felt very satisfied.

The water in Konstan Spring was warm all year, and it ran clear and pure, and once you drank it all your cuts and aches and pains vanished from you as if they were caught up in the current.

The town was young (everything in that country was young) and did no great business. The land around the spring had to be worked to coax any crops from the dirt, and it was so far from the sea or the railroad or the Nations tribal gatherings that there was no profit in hotels or in trading.

The general store and the saloon, the chemist and the town lodge, the blacksmith and the whorehouse, tended to those who lived there; there was little other need. The folkvarder's office, with its little jail cell, stayed empty. There was no trouble to be had; people only found Konstan Spring by accident, and often hurried through on their way to someplace greater.

All the same, some lonesome souls had found their way to Konstan Spring.

It was a town that suited painstaking people, and when the town gathered for meetings to decide if newcomers should be given the water, the votes were orderly, and there was hardly a raised voice in the lodge.

(Mrs. Domar was sometimes louder than most people cared for, but the town was loyal to its own—where else could someone go, who had tasted the water in Konstan Spring?—and no fuss was made about her.)

The only man to bring the water out of Konstan Spring had been Hosiah Frode, the old chemist. Two years back he had written "KONSTAN'S ALE—MIRACLE TONIC" on his wagon and taken three barrels, early one morning before Folkvarder Gray could stop him.

Everyone waited to see what would happen. No one said it, but they all worried—if the gunslingers and the gamblers and the ill-living folk got wind of Konstan's Ale and came looking for the spring, the town might be overrun with greedy sorts, and they would never be rid of them.

It was a dark winter.

But Konstan Spring was a practical town, and even under the shadow of trouble, they all made do. Kit down at the whorehouse hired a few new girls all the way from Odal in case city men had finer tastes, and she taught Anni the blacksmith's daughter how to cook sturdy food so she could work the kitchen when all the rich, sickly gentlemen came looking for the water.

But the water must not have been such good luck to Hosiah Frode, because he never came back, and no rush of travelers ever appeared.

Secretly, Folkvarder Gray suspected Frode had angered a higher power with his thieving, and been struck down by stronger hands than theirs—the water was a great gift, and Frode should have known better than to abuse it.

It was a shame, Gray thought; Frode was a liar and a thief, but he had been a fine chemist, and Gray respected a man who was able with his work.

Frode never returned.

By spring, the men in town had developed fine enough taste to call on the new whorehouse girls from Odal (Kit had chosen the very best), and Kit sent Anni the blacksmith's daughter over to the chemist's.

No one complained about the change; Anni had been a terrible cook.

When he came into town, John the gravedigger took the room above the chemist shop. Anni lived in back of the shop, so the upstairs had been sitting empty.

The best the room had to offer was the view of the fenced-in graveyard past the new-painted lodge.

The flat, empty ground had never been touched; as yet, no one who lived in Konstan Spring had died.

The room above the chemist was small and Anni was an indifferent hostess, but John didn't move quarters. People figured he was sweet on Anni, or that the view of the graveyard was as close as a gravedigger could come to living above his store like an honest man.

No one minded his reasons. Anni needed the money. In Konstan Spring the chemist never did much business.

The first man John buried was Samuel Ness, who got himself on the losing end of a fight with his horse.

The grave appeared one shovel at a time, sharp-edged and deep as a well. There was no denying John was an artist. The priest thanked John for the grave even before he asked God to commend Samuel's soul.

"Won't work," muttered Mrs. Domar.

Mrs. Domar was Samuel's nearest neighbor. She had come to Konstan Spring already a widow; her husband had fallen ill on the road, and died in an Inuit town just twenty miles from the Spring. She persevered, but the stroke of bad luck had turned her into a pessimist.

Samuel had a young orchard at the edge of his property line, and Mrs. Domar knew that if there was a way Nature could work against her inheriting that little grove of apple trees, it would.

It was the usual funeral, except that the priest, after the service, suggested that John fill in a little of the ground before the body went inside it.

John obeyed. He wasn't one to argue with the clergy.

Two days later, Samuel Ness wriggled his way out of the shallow grave and came home to his farm and his orchard.

"I knew it," muttered Mrs. Domar as soon as she saw him coming.

John, if he was surprised, said nothing. He smoothed down the earth after the priest had taken back the headstone, and for a few nights, if you walked all the way from the outlying farms to the chemist's, you could see John sitting at his window, looking out over the sparse graveyard as if deciding what to do.

Everyone worried. They'd feared a gravedigger would lose the will for it in Konstan Spring, and they worried that if he went out into the world there would be questions about his hardiness. They had been lucky with Frode, but luck gave out any time.

People suggested that the folkvarder meet with him and point out the hundred-year contract John had signed. They suggested the priest give him counsel. Some suggested Anni should. If he was sweet on her, her kind face would do some good.

Philip Prain, who minded the general store, was the brave one who finally asked John what his plans might be, now that everything was in the open and John knew that the water wasn't just for one's health.

John said, "Try harder, I reckon." After a moment he asked, "We see a lot of travelers?"

Folkvarder Gray and Prain and Kit down at the whorehouse held a Town Council meeting to discuss the problem.

They spoke for a long time, and made up their minds on the subject. They planned to put it to a vote before the town, since the town was very strict about having a say, but none of them would object. John was a treasure they couldn't lose, and there were bound to be some drifters coming by sooner or later.

In the normal way of things, strangers would have a drink at the saloon and a girl at the whorehouse and ride out the next day, but there was no record of travelers once they were this far into the wild; not everyone can be missed.

The first drifter came on horseback a few weeks later, before there had been a formal vote.

He ordered liquor all night, and went to bed with one of Kit's girls, and fell asleep without ever having tasted the water from Konstan Spring.

He suffered a horrible attack in his sleep. Some nightmare had troubled him so that he'd twisted his neck up in his blankets and broken it.

Anni brought John the good news.

This time John had a little audience: Folkvarder Gray and Anni came, and Mrs. Domar, who wanted to see how to get that sharp edge in her own flowerbeds.

"You cut the ground so clean," Anni said after a time. "Where'd you learn?"

"Started young," he said. "Buried my ma and pa when I was twelve. Practice."

Anni nodded, and after he was finished they walked home side by side.

She was a quiet sort of girl, and John kept to himself, but Konstan Spring began to lay wagers for the month they'd be married. Anni's father, the old blacksmith, wanted it at once—the gravedigger got a hundred dollars a year. Samuel Ness thought it was too soon for a man to be sure he wanted a wife; he said no one should rightly marry until the spring, when the flowers were out.

Kit at the whorehouse swore they'd never get married, but everyone said it was only because John had never given her any business; she had sour grapes, that was all.

—

For the whole winter it went on that way. The town welcomed four men, each traveling alone, bound for New Freya or Odin's Lake, and one as far south as Iroquois country. Each one had gotten lost in the dark cold, in the snow or the freezing rain, and found themselves outside the saloon in Konstan Spring.

Each one spent the night at the whorehouse—Kit insisted—and of course it was much better to have a hot mug of mead to burn off the frost of a long ride, so there was no occasion to drink the spring-water.

The next morning John got a knock on his door from the Gerder boy who worked at the post office, or Mary the redhead from the whorehouse, to let him know he had a job to be getting on with.

Four travelers was less than it should be, even in winter, and they all worried that a gravedigger of John's skill would tire of having nothing to do. John, however, seemed happy to dig only one perfect grave a month for that whole winter; each one straight as a ruler, crisp edges, ground as smooth as God had ever made it.

People in Konstan Spring began to warm to him. For all they were patient, they were proud, and it was a comfort that the gravedigger of Konstan Spring knew the importance of a job done right.

Finn and Ivar Halfred were clerks who stumbled into Konstan Spring just before the thaw—the last spoils of winter for John the gravedigger.

They were from Portstown, Ivar told the Gerder boy, who took their horses. The Gerder boy didn't have the sense to ask where they were going (he didn't have the sense God gave an apple), so Gerder the father, who tended the saloon, asked instead.

Most of the people in Konstan Spring came out when strangers came into town. It was always interesting to see new people, no matter how briefly they'd be staying.

Anni and John sat at a little table in a corner, set apart from the crowd and noise of the saloon. At the other tables the wagers about their courtship went up and up and up, even in the midst of looking at the strangers; there was always a place for a friendly bet.

At last, old Gerder asked the brothers, "What brings you to Konstan Spring?"

By that time Ivar was already drunk, and he laughed loudly and said, "We were supposed to head south for Bruntofte, but we turned right instead of left!" which was an old joke that no one paid any mind. It was never hard to tell which of two brothers was the fool.

"Bruntofte isn't very welcoming," Gerder said. "Hope you boys plan to do some trade; they don't like people showing up with empty hands. We all saw what happened to the English, before they got driven out."

After a little pause, Finn sighed and said, "Haven't thought that far ahead. We're just looking to start over in a place that has enough room to be lonely in."

You didn't get as far as Konstan Spring unless you were putting something behind you, so no one was surprised to hear it. But the way he spoke must have struck Anni something awful, because she got up from her seat and took a place next to Finn at the bar.

She'd never been pretty (not compared to whorehouse girls from Odal), but the way she looked at him would have charmed a much less lonely man than Finn Halfred.

They talked until late, until everyone had gone home but Kit from the whorehouse, whose girls were working to bring Ivar back and lighten his pockets. They tried to hook Finn, too, but Anni put her hand on his arm, and the girls respected her claim.

Anni brought Finn home with her when she left that night, his arm linked with hers. The girls from the whorehouse thought it was a scandal, but Kit told them to mind their own business and tend to their customer.

Kit was no fool; she knew how slowly time moved in Konstan Spring, and a girl shouldn't be a bad cook and an indifferent chemist year in and year out without anything else happening inside of her. Anni could have a night with a young clerk if she wanted. (It was the first thing Anni had managed well in a long time. Kit was glad to see something worthy from Anni at last.)

The next morning Anni brought Finn out on the little promenade. She told Kit in passing, "He got thirsty—I gave him some water."

Kit told the town.

They held a meeting (in the lodge, safely away from Anni) to discuss what to tell Finn about his brother's sad accident the night before.

Philip Prain said right off that it was a shame about the wagering pool, but Folkvarder Gray called them back to order; all things in their time, gambling had no place in the lodge. They had to decide what would happen now, with their gravedigger.

John was a steady man, but now they weren't sure who would do for him but old Mrs. Domar, who was a widow and too old to be suitable.

"As if I would," sniffed Mrs. Domar.

The only other girl in town was Gerder's daughter Sue, who was only fourteen and couldn't yet go courting. If she got a little older, then perhaps they could consider, but none of them had been in Konstan Spring long enough to really know if the young ever grew older, or if the grown slowly grew old.

(Konstan Spring hadn't been an early settlement by the Longboaters. It hadn't even been in the eyes of the railroad men. It was a town by accident, because the water was of value; a town because the people in it were slow to want change; a town because it was better to live among the same kind forever than to risk going into the wide new country full of strangers.)

The town was like the Ness orchard, whose little apple trees (always saplings and never older) bent their young branches nearly to snapping just to bear their fruit.

It would be the same with Sue, if they let her go courting too early.

Outside, John had turned his hand to his art for poor Ivar Halfred, and one shovelful of dirt after another bloomed from the ground as he worked.

Folkvarder Gray went himself to break the news.

He told Finn that Ivar had drunk himself to death, and his whorehouse girl hadn't been able to wake him no matter what they did. Finn was sorely grieved, and Folkvarder Gray thought it was best to wait for some other day to explain about the water.

On his way out, the folkvarder tipped his hat to John, who was sharpening the edge of his shovel on a boulder that sat beside a wide grave, sharp-edged and deep as a well. John looked as quiet and calm as ever, but Folkvarder Gray had been disappointed in a woman himself, many years back, on his home shores, and he knew the look of a heartbroken man doing a chore just to keep his hands busy.

"No need for all this, John," Folkvarder Gray said. "It'll be weeks yet before the thaw opens the roads, and no knowing when the next one will come."

Folkvarder Gray looked carefully into the thick dark of the grave. "A little steep, my boy," he said after a moment. The warm damp rose up from the ground, sharp-smelling, and he stepped back. That was no smell for the living.

"It's just for practice," said John, turned the shovel on its edge, slid a slender finger along it until he began to bleed.

After the service on Sunday, Anni and Finn went out walking.

Inside the lodge, Samuel Ness started a new wager that they'd come back that same day and ask the priest to marry them. Mrs. Domar, who didn't approve of such suggestions, went to the window and pretended to be deaf.

From the window Mrs. Domar could see Anni and Finn walking on
the lawn behind the lodge, hand in hand toward the chemist's, and John's
silhouette in the upper window, looking out toward the graveyard to admire
his work.

"Finn will come sniffing around after a job," said Philip Prain. "I could
make use of him in the store maybe a month out of the year, but he'll have
to make his money some other way, and I don't see much need for a clerk in
Konstan Spring."

"We have need for him if he does good work," said Folkvarder Gray. "And
who will be the chemist if he takes Anni out to some farm instead of staying in
town? We can't do without a chemist. It's not civilized."

"They'll find some way to scrape by," said Kit. "Young fools like that always
do."

"It's no good," said Mrs. Domar, watching John look over at the cemetery.

No one answered her; Mrs. Domar never saw good in anything.

The wager, sadly for Samuel, came to nothing.

That evening, Finn and Anni disappeared from Konstan Spring, and if
Folkvarder Gray noticed that the chemist's house was quiet, that the boulder in
the yard was gone and the wide deep grave was smoothed over, he said nothing
to John about it.

No town was run well without some sacrifices. Artists had their ways, and
another chemist would be easier to come by than a gravedigger of so much
patience and skill.

The question of Anni and Finn trapped in the grave made the folkvarder
sorry for Anni's sake, but it was what came sometimes of breaking a good
man's heart.

(Not everyone can be missed.)

It was for the best. Anni had never been a good chemist; Konstan Spring
deserved better, he knew.

Samuel Ness paid Kit from the whorehouse two dollars, having been wrong
about both Anni and John, and Anni and Finn.

Mrs. Domar didn't approve of Kit, but she had never forgiven Samuel for
taking back his orchard, and was happy to see him lose a little money.

Kit kept the money in an envelope, for a wedding present in case Anni
should ever come home. (She knew Anni must; she wasn't the type to disappear
on her own.)

After a month of no word, Kit sent redheaded Mary from Odal over to the shop at the edge of the graveyard.

Mary knew a little about the chemist's, and a little about coaxing the hearts of quiet men, and it would be best, Kit figured, to have the gravedigger of Konstan Spring soon settled with a pretty young wife.

Others did not quite agree; against Kit's complaints, Folkvarder Gray put a CHEMIST WANTED sign in the window of his office, and sent young Gerder to town on horseback with another advertisement for the train station wall.

Folkvarder Gray was confident that sooner or later a wonderful chemist would come across the advertisement, when the time was right. The country was still rough and unknown, and brave artists were hard to come by, but he was prepared—he would take nothing but the best.

Konstan Spring could afford to wait, and Folkvarder Gray knew the importance of a job done right.

Chew

Tamsyn Muir

HITLER DEAD! FÜHRER FELL AT REICH CHANCELLERY!

Anton's American soldier had whipped out the torn front page of the newspaper for him to translate the headline. His German was very bad and Anton's English worse, but they worked it out anyhow, repeating it back and forth to each other until they were satisfied with the results. He admired the headline mainly because the American was his friend, then asked for chewing gum.

His American was inclined to be generous with his largesse, so he gave to Anton four pieces of Juicy Fruit wrapped up in a twist of the old wrapper. He also got a pat on the head, which at ten years old was something to resent but he put up with it anyway. He wrapped up the gum in his handkerchief. Anton took only half a piece for himself, chewing it and chewing it on the road home until it lost all of its flavor and was tack in his mouth. He weighed up his options: it was a well-known fact that swallowing it would coat his lungs and almost certainly kill him, but it seemed like such a waste not to.

His father was sitting next to the smuggled radio when he came through the door, crying and laughing and crying again as Radio Hamburg repeated the news: *Attention! Attention! Our Führer is dead*. Bread was burning on the stove, but the pale sour bread he made wasn't much to cry over if it was burnt up. Anton left him with three and a half pieces and his handkerchief and went back out into Stuttgart, rich with time to waste before work.

In the evenings, the house rubble looked like the hills of giant ants. He liked to pretend that they were what had laid waste to so many of them: huge six-legged insects with clacking, dripping mandibles, knocking down chimneys and blackening the walls with their giant ant excretions. It might look like the scorch-mark from a shell, but Anton knew it was the monster ants, fooling everyone else by acting like it was the war. He spent a little time nudging his toe into sooty puddles and watching smoke rise from the American barracks over to the south, and went to loiter by the fences there when the thrill of giant ants palled.

There was a camp there, for Russian prisoners. In the evenings you could hear them arguing in loud Slavic voices, their figures in the prison yard wreathed in darkness as they shouted and sometimes fought. Hitler was dead, but it seemed like they yelled as they always yelled before and wheeled blows at each other with the exact same blind, unhappy aim. Anton decided to go back home by weaving a path behind the empty cloth factory where the tall, frondy weeds grew in the cracks in the path.

In the shadow of the smokestack stood his American soldier and a strange woman, with a headscarf over her head. The soldier had his gloved fingers crammed in her mouth so that the only noises she could make were wet pants, and her skirts were ripped across the breadth at the back. Her legs were naked and white, flashing in the shadows as she struggled, and Anton stared dumbly as the man scraped the woman's forehead up against the factory wall over and over and over again.

He noticed Anton, but didn't even seem to care for either staring boys or blood. Anton could not move. "It's all right," his American assured him in his broken German. *Alles gut.* The woman seemed to be nearly knocked senseless, half-fainted against the cold concrete. "It's all right, son." He dropped his handful of headscarf and rooted around in a pocket instead. "You go home! You have good night!"

Though the flesh was white, the blood on it was purple. Anton had something thrown at him. It slid off his jersey and onto the ground. "You go home," said his American. "You go."

The woman did not make a sound, but every so often she jerked around like a fish on a hook. An unopened packet of chewing gum lay near the frondy weeds. Juicy Fruit. The woman in her headscarf gurgled into those prying fingers, more blood mixing with saliva, and Anton took the gum and ran away; he could think of nothing else to do.

Somebody would know. Somebody would find out. The Juicy Fruit paper crackled in his fingers. When he thought he had run away enough and could not see the cloth factory any more, he sat on a pile of rubble and crammed all of the gum into his mouth. It made a wet and noisy ball as he chewed it. He swallowed, hard, and it made a lump in his throat all the way down.

His father worked in the Red Cross hospital that the French doctors had set up. Well—that wasn't quite true. He did not work in the hospital, but in the basement of the empty bakery next door where they had the morgue. When the doctors and nurses were tired of them and had done all that they could,

Anton's father washed the bodies of the dead. So did Anton, as the hospital was small.

It was an odd occupation and he liked it. He wasn't one of those boys who ran around and shouted; he was a boy who liked looking at things. Looking at the dead people was easy now. His father told him they were all going to Heaven, except maybe the Nazis, so you didn't have to feel bad about them. When he passed by the hospital to go to the bakery morgue, he saw rows of whey-faced women there.

"I don't want you going out at night," said his father, washing toes. "All these Moroccan soldiers, those Tunisians, attacking our girls. It's disgusting. You come here before six o'clock, Anton."

Anton thought about it.

"Why is it only women?"

His father made that *tch!* noise which meant he didn't really want to answer the question. "Your hair's getting too long," he said. "I will cut it."

"They do things to them, don't they?"

Wrong question. Anton was set to wring out sponges.

He kept thinking about the gum in his stomach rather than anything else. Swallowing all those pieces really would kill him. He would drop down dead, which was a relief, because then he wouldn't ever have to meet his American soldier again or think about the woman. He thought about the woman's white, bloodied legs and split lips. He thought about the unbuttoned front of the American's trousers. Sweat prickled on his palms.

"You smell like sweets," said his father, when he was done with the sponges. "No more! Stop annoying the soldiers for them. The Americans, they've liberated us. Stuttgart was proudly outside the Reich for years. Now we have our dignity back—if the Tunisians would just go and stop their disgusting business."

"What if it wasn't Tunisians?" asked Anton, but his father didn't understand.

The next day he found himself by the factory again. His legs took him there, unwilling, and he watched the American soldier fold a woman over some abandoned crates. Anton thought it might have been the same woman. He did not talk to Anton this time, just rummaged in his pocket and tossed chewing gum to him like you would for a clamorous seagull. Then he went back to his work. Anton's mouth tired of chewing by the time he got back home. He had started burying the wrappers in the rubble piles, like they were for the monster ants.

One night, his father washed the body of a woman and he realized with a start it was *his* woman—the American soldier's woman, that was: it had taken him a bit to notice because her throat was torn in a long raggedy line terminating halfway across the neck. His father fancied himself a bit of a coroner. "Suicide," he said, shaking his head. "See how the first hole here is deep, and the rest of the gash is much shallower? See how it is a hole, not a cut? Ah, Anton, what a waste. Commend her to God. "

Her hips and her thighs were all one bruise. Her wrists had bracelets of fat red marks with flecks of dried blood beneath her fingernails. Anton did not breathe.

"Poor lady," his father said. "She is somewhere happy now."

She did not look happy. Her jaw was clenched shut. There was a silvery fleck at the corner of her mouth, and his father reached out to try to wipe it away. It didn't wipe. His fingers were very gentle as he pressed on her lips and opened them up, and took a thin wafer out from underneath the swollen tongue. "Those nurses are being lazy," said Anton's father, and held up the wafer to the light. A striped Juicy Fruit wrapper, oily with blood.

Anton had to close his eyes and count to ten, which he had not needed to do in the morgue since he was eight. His father must have seen, because he said quietly: "Go out and get some air, darling. Not too far. Stay by the door."

The night was dark and cold. From down the street he heard raucous voices, infantrymen. Anton hugged his knees to his chest until his father came outside to take him home.

On the third day his American soldier was smoking indolently by the chimney wall. "What," he said laughingly, "now '*haben Sie cigarette*'?" Anton shook his head. "Good boy," said the American. "Good. No smoke! Makes you sick."

There was only one piece of gum for him now. He clutched it in his fist and saw every policeman on the corner now as he walked, every woman, imagined their staring through his fingers to see what was inside. The giant ants settled in their holes underneath the untidy piles of brick, muttering about chewing gum and Anton, and he took the key from beneath the bakery flowerpot to open up the morgue.

Nobody had come for the woman because nobody knew who she was. There were many people in Stuttgart like that now. She would be written down as *Lieschen* and put at the crossroads grave come Sunday when the priest came. Anton touched her chilly fingers gently, as his father had touched them gently, and then he prized open the mouth to put the piece of chewing gum within. He could hide it there, inside her.

He wet himself when the dead woman began chewing. The soft rectangular strip mulched between her pink-stained teeth as she rolled it around in her mouth, gray eyes flicking open as she spread it on her palate and sucked out the flavour as Anton always did. He was aware of hot trickles down his legs.

When she swallowed, there was a brief flash of pink in that ugly hole at her throat. The dead woman was staring at the ceiling, and he was sure that once she turned that gaze on him he would be killed immediately.

"Tell me how much you got," she said.

Her voice was a little bubbly, whistling through that awful hole, but otherwise sounded perfectly normal. Anton could not speak. She said, "You ate his food. How much did you eat?"

Because his brain would not work, he had to count on his trembling fingers. He had liked math when he had been at school. Five pieces to a packet, which meant—"Ten pieces," he said, and recalled further. "And one half. Ten and a half. Since Tuesday."

She was silent. He tried to be brave about it. "Am I going to die?" he said.

"Ten pieces," she said without answering, "and a half. That will be enough, I think. Go and get me ten pieces and a half as payment for your staring—and change your pants."

Ten (and a half) pieces of chewing gum was an unbelievable amount. For one, he had gotten ten-and-a-half pieces only by accident in the first place, but fear made him trek all over Stuttgart in desperation thinking about how he was going to do it. When the next day his American soldier said, "No rations!" he nearly wept like a baby of five. His soldier must have felt bad, because he ruffled Anton's curls instead. Though he'd had a bath just that week, Anton had to go and wash his hair after.

The next day he got two pieces from the American, and two from a French doctor who knew his father—impertinence his father would have smacked him for, but this was a matter of life and death. Anton snuck down to the morgue and fed them to the dead woman piece by piece.

She spat out the two from the French doctor—"No good," she said—but ate the two from the soldier. Her eyelids fluttered and her fingers twitched, slowly unbending, stiff toes curling inward underneath her sheet. "You're slow."

"He didn't have much. It's hard to get."

"You got it before. You can get it again."

There was nothing he could say to that.

One piece the next day made three, which meant the vastness of seven and a half pieces to go—now the dead woman could sit up and even hobble a little, and he got her a coat and some skirts to hide all the red splotches from where her body had lain on the table. His dread tripled when she said, "It's cold here. Take me home with you."

"You can't. My father will find out."

"This place is full of dead people. I don't like it."

"But *you're* dead," said Anton, nearly crying from frustration.

"Just one night."

There was nothing for it. He went to her late that night, and she leaned on his shoulder through the streets of Stuttgart where nobody noticed them but a policeman who said, "Go home!" when he saw them both. The woman was heavy and smelled a little sickly, that familiar chilly smell of dead body. When they got to Anton's house, she clambered through his window then lay on his bed.

Anton made to sleep on the floor, rolling up his unraveling jersey to put underneath his head. They both lay in awkward, uncomfortable silence.

"I just wanted a cigarette," she said. "I was going to pay him, you know; I don't beg. I had some apples that weren't soft."

He did not know what to say to this, but felt like he had to say something. "Were you very old?" asked Anton.

"Nineteen," said the woman—so, yes, quite old.

The floor was hard, so he was surprised when he did somehow get to sleep. He was woken up by a noise like wet hiccups: the dead woman was crying. "I'm sorry," she said. "I'm sorry." Anton put his clammy hand up into hers. After a little while she stopped crying, but held his hand until he was nearly asleep.

"My name is Elke," she said, startling him awake.

"What?"

"My name is Elke. When they put me away," she said, "don't let them call me anything else."

In the thin morning sunlight she was gone and he was tucked up in the blankets. Truthfully, he was relieved.

Six pieces. His American had given him another three to make him go away when he found him talking to an American girl, one of the ones with stockings and shiny hair who came with the USO. The day after that, Anton couldn't find him, and Sunday would come soon, and he didn't want his dinner because he was too busy thinking about ways to get more chewing gum. That suited

Anton, because when his father found out that he had asked the French doctor for candy he got a wallop. Anton didn't really want to look him in the eye.

He went to the gardens of the houses that had been bombed, picking flowers. It was a sad bunch of woody roses and nosegay, but when he gave it to his soldier, who was still standing in the shadow of the factory wall, he was touched. "Oh, son," he said. He took one of the roses and put it in his buttonhole, waving it to be admired, and Anton smiled wanly. "I have a brother." He fumbled with the German as he said it: *Mein Bruder? Mein kleinen Bruder?* Now Anton felt sick. "Little brother. Just like you."

He pinched Anton's cheek and laughed at his grimace, then gave him a whole packet of Juicy Fruit. "Brush your tooths," he said.

Eleven pieces—that was eleven—he stuffed the packet down his shirt and ran all the way to the bakery. His fingers fumbled with the key. As he flung himself down the stairs, his dead woman was already sitting up, gaunt and waiting, and they ripped open the packet together with impatient hands. The last piece he broke in half with his fingernail. She gobbled it up with the rest.

"All right," she said. "That's good." She swung her legs over the side of the pallet and wrapped herself in the skirt and coat, pulling the collar up over her punctured neck. Anton didn't quite know what he'd been expecting; she was still very dead, though now she walked tall and graceful and smooth. "Let's go, shall we?"

"Where are we going?" he asked.

But he already knew.

Outside in the bustle of Stuttgart nobody looked at them. He held tightly to her hand, the skin slipping a little underneath his palm, past the anthill piles of rubble from the houses and past the camp where the Russian men fought. He led her to the abandoned factory with its thrusting smokestacks, and there was his American soldier: still with the rose tucked inside his buttonhole, grinding out the butt of his cigarette as he prepared to leave.

At first his mouth rounded in a greeting for Anton, but then he saw the dead woman. The coat had slipped open to show her dead and naked throat, the squeezed bruises of her—her chest, her waxen skin.

His American soldier screamed. She was on him even as his gun clattered bullets into her body and she forced his face into the wall—pushed her fingers into his mouth so that his screams spluttered into a wet muffle. Anton thought that she put her mouth to the place between his soldier's neck and shoulder to kiss him, but then there were wet gristly sounds that were definitely not kissing.

He pretended himself into one of the rubble piles safely buried in the rocks. He put himself into a monster ant and walked around in the dark, his bristly body scraping up against the bodies of other monster ants. The dead woman chewed wet, noisy mouthfuls, swallowing in grunts, hand rooting around somewhere at the soldier's belly and into his shirt. Their bodies moved together as one.

When it was over, his dead woman's belly was grossly distended and there were only scraps of cloth left in her hands, and he couldn't believe how she'd done it—and she couldn't either, because she had to be a little sick next to the wall. He did not look. Her mouth was dripping red and she tried in vain to wipe it, but when that didn't work all she did was cry and cry like a child.

"I was always going to be in the ground with him in me," she said. "I just wanted to make sure, that's all. I just wanted to make sure." And then she was a little sick again.

Anton went to see her Sunday when she was buried. Before she was wrapped up in her sheet she said, "You will come and see me, won't you? You don't hate me?" and could only fall asleep when he held her hand. Perhaps it wasn't sleeping. He sewed her up in a grubby shroud as he had seen his father do, and he was there when they put her at the crossroads grave for suicides. Her and the American. With a stone he expended some effort scratching letters onto a piece of wood, and when he was done had some splinters and E-L-K-E for his pains.

When he made the walk back home into Stuttgart and to the bakery next to the Red Cross hospital, he tried to imagine the monster ants again, but they didn't come. It was as though he had thought about them too hard and they had burnt up in his brain.

There must have been something in his face when he met his father at the door of the bakery morgue. "I forgive you, darling," said his father, and put one arm around him. "Just stop acting like one of the beggar-boys from now on. Look! I have something for you."

From one of his capacious pockets, his father drew something thin and silvery. He presented it to Anton with the air of a magician: two sticks of Juicy Fruit in a bit of their wrapper, smelling as sweet and as sickly as they always did. "There," he said proudly. "Since you like it so much."

He did not understand why Anton gagged.

'Til Death Do Us Part

Shaun Jeffrey

"It's her, Dad, I swear it is. Over there, it's Mum."

I exhaled slowly and looked at my fourteen-year-old son, Tim, as he excitedly pointed across the street. Before he could say any more, I took hold of his shoulder and turned him toward me. "You know it isn't her. She's dead. We buried her. You know that."

Tim twisted out of my hands. "I'm not making it up, she's alive. I just saw her."

Before I could stop him, Tim bolted across the road, a car horn blaring in response as the driver of a Honda Civic slammed his brakes on to avoid sending my son to see his mother in a more literal sense, which would have been an ironic twist of fate if he'd died in the same way.

"Come back," I shouted before giving chase.

I couldn't be too angry with him. His mother's death had hit him hard. Probably harder than it had me if I'm honest, but saying he'd seen her in the street, well, it was sad and rather unnerving.

Sure I shed bucketsful of tears when Joanna died, spent days questioning why God was so cruel to take her away from us in the prime of her life, but Tim and his mother, they'd shared a special bond, one that only mothers and sons can share.

I dodged shoppers wandering along the high street and gulped deep breaths, my knees cracking. Although only in my mid-thirties, I was out of shape.

Tim was about forty feet ahead and running like a gazelle, his gangly frame almost as thin as the shadow that trailed in his wake. He got his willowy stature from his mum. Not that I was obese, but my trouser size had outgrown my age by a couple of numbers, giving me a paunch—much of which was a direct result of the alcohol I'd drowned myself in after the funeral. Tim had been my lifeline. When I realized how destructive my drinking had become, I stopped. Had to be strong.

I still hadn't adjusted fully and had taken for granted all that Joanna did around the house. I didn't have a clue how the washing machine worked, couldn't iron to save my life, but I'd had to go on a steep learning curve, if not for my sake, then for Tim's. The house had become a shit hole. I didn't wash or clean for days at a time. Dishes piled up in the sink and once the cupboards were empty we'd relied on takeaway food. The local Chinese restaurant was on speed dial.

For a while Tim became the adult and me the child. But now I was back in control. I'd gone back to work at the bank and Tim had settled back in at school. He'd fallen behind on his work, but he was catching up and the teachers were understanding and weren't on his back about it.

I realized that Tim had stopped running and he was standing in front of a disheveled-looking figure that from behind looked like a homeless person, one of the dispossessed as I liked to think of them.

As I caught him up I could feel a pain in my side and I stood wheezing for a couple of seconds. "Come on, Tim. Let's go home."

"I told you. I told you it was her," Tim said, a smile on his face that I never thought I'd see again.

Confused, I shook my head. "Come on, stop being stupid."

"Look. Look at her." He pointed at the homeless person.

I glanced towards the figure, not really wanting to make eye contact in case I got drawn into conversation with them, but I felt that I should apologize. Instead I stared open-mouthed. Despite the gray skin with the sores and welts, the lopsided mouth and the dead, glassy eyes, there was no mistaking the face. Impossible as it seemed, it was Joanna.

"Mum, it's me, Tim."

I listened to my son as though he was speaking from the end of a tunnel; couldn't take my eyes off Joanna. Her skin looked papery and dry, tendons protruding from the back of her hands where the skin had sunken in. Her fingernails were torn and there was dirt around them as though she had been clawing through the earth.

Joanna didn't respond. She started walking, although it was more of a shuffle.

"Mum. Talk to me, mum." Tim barred her path and Joanna bumped into him, rocking back on her heels.

She was wearing the dress we'd buried her in. Tim had chosen it, saying it was her favorite. I guess he knew her better than me as I didn't have a clue what her favorite piece of clothing had been.

Sunlight glared from the shop window behind Joanna, making me squint. When I looked back it had given her a halo effect, like an angel.

I gulped, tongue a thick slug stuck to the roof of my mouth.

"Jo, is it really you?" I asked, the words coming out in a rush.

Joanna didn't reply.

I cleared my throat and said, "How? I don't understand. You . . . you were dead. They buried you."

Still no response.

Afraid that I may have been caught up in Tim's delusion, I reached out and touched Jo's hand. She was real but her skin was cold and leathery to the touch and I recoiled slightly.

After a moment I realized there was an aroma in the air that originated from Joanna. It was cloying, like spoiled meat that had gone past its sell by date.

"Dad, why isn't she answering?"

I looked at Tim and shook my head. "I don't know." Truth was I didn't know anything anymore. Joanna was dead, and yet here she was, walking.

It just wasn't possible.

"We need to get her home," Tim said.

I watched Joanna keep trying to walk forwards, but Tim kept holding her back. She was like an insistent fly butting into a window and seemed to have no concept of what was happening.

Swallowing to moisten my throat, I tried to think what to do. I noticed a few people staring at us as they walked past and knew that I had to get us off the street to somewhere that we could work this out.

"Okay, give me hand to help her," I said as I grabbed her arm. Tim took hold of her on the other side and we walked her towards the car park where I'd left the car.

Once we arrived I opened the door and bent her joints to allow us to sit her on the front seat. Then I fastened the seat belt, more to secure her in position than for any form of safety, as deep in my heart I knew she was dead.

With us all inside the car the smell was more pungent and it clung to the back of my throat, making me feel a little sick so I lowered the window to let some fresh air in then started the engine.

Joanna sat there, rocking backwards and forwards like a nodding car novelty.

I glanced in the rear view mirror. Tim was still smiling.

Before going home I drove to the cemetery.

"What are we doing here?" Tim asked.

"I need to check that it's really her."

"Of course it's her."

I exhaled slowly. "Well, I just need to check." I exited the vehicle and Tim followed. He grabbed the door handle to help his mother out, but I said, "She'll be better off staying in the car." Tim looked at me for a moment and then nodded.

We followed the path among the gravestones. I tried to swallow as I walked, but couldn't produce any saliva. Dappled sunlight flickered through the surrounding trees. I was hoping to see the grave was undisturbed so that I could say it wasn't Joanna, but even from a distance I noticed a mound of earth like a giant mole had burrowed its way out.

I stood before the mound and stared down into the hole, trying to imagine Joanna clawing at the coffin lid, scraping away for weeks on end until she scratched her way through.

I parked in the driveway and then made sure the coast was clear before leading Joanna out of the car. I didn't want to explain what was going on to the neighbors as I didn't have a clue myself and wouldn't know where to begin. All I knew was that, impossible as it seemed, my wife had returned from the grave.

Tim and I ushered her into the house and I closed the door. Joanna hadn't said a word all the way home. I wondered whether she recognized us. Wondered whether she was cognizant.

"We need to get her cleaned up and then get some fresh clothes on her," Tim said.

I nodded dumbly, happy to let Tim take control of the situation while I tried to think about what the hell was going on. We led Joanna upstairs to the bathroom and I started to undress her while Tim went to fetch some fresh clothes from the ones we hadn't yet been able to throw away. Joanna stood stockstill as I unbuttoned her dress at the back, letting it drop to the floor and I saw she was staring at her reflection in the mirror. Did she recognize herself?

There were signs on her body where the car had struck, deep lesions that had been sewn shut. I tried not to look at them as I removed her bra, her once full breasts now flaps of skin that made me feel a little repulsed to look at.

Tim hurried into the bathroom as I was removing her underwear and I felt a little embarrassed both for Jo and me, but Tim seemed unfazed and was taking it all perfectly in his stride. He got his practicality from his mother.

"I've got her another dress," he said. "It'll be easier to get on and off. I didn't bother with underwear. Do you think she'll need any?"

I shook my head. "I guess not."

Tim had selected a pale blue knee-length dress with large white flowers that he put on the edge of the bath. "She needs a shower," he said.

I ushered her into the shower stall and switched on the spray. Hot steaming water shot out and I tested the temperature before remembering she was dead so probably wouldn't know how hot it was anyway. Once she was underneath the spray she kept walking forwards into the wall, water bouncing off her head. Tim leaned in and grabbed a bottle of shampoo.

"Soon have you looking like your old self," he said as he washed her hair.

I lowered the toilet seat and sat down to watch as Tim lovingly washed his mother like it was the most natural thing in the world. Bits of skin and hair came away in his hands but he didn't seem concerned.

Once he had finished we guided her out of the shower, toweled her dry and then I sprayed her with some of my antiperspirant to mask the smell that still emanated from her. I raised her arms to allow Tim to pull the dress over them and over her head. Tim then combed her tresses, ignoring the fact he was pulling more out than he was straightening.

While he did this I stared into her eyes. They had once been bright blue. Now they looked dead and lifeless. Could she still see? If she did, could she recognize anything?

I felt myself choking up so I swallowed and rubbed my eyes. Steam drifted around the room and I felt hot but didn't know if it was due to the temperature or the circumstances.

"Now what are we going to do?" I asked as I wiped perspiration from my brow.

Tim looked at me. "Well me and Mum are going to go watch telly," he said before leading Joanna away. As he reached the door, Tim turned and looked at me. "I love you, Dad." Then he left the room. A tear rolled down my cheek and I wiped it away. Seconds later I heard the television downstairs and the sound of Tim laughing at something.

I knew I had to find out how she had returned from the grave, so I walked through to the spare bedroom where the computer was and switched it on. If more people had come back to life, surely there would be news of it. After ten minutes of searching I came up with nothing. Perhaps if it had happened to other people, whoever found them wouldn't say anything. Perhaps they were just glad to have their loved ones back. Or perhaps they were afraid someone would come and take their nearest and dearest away to experiment on them to find out how it had occurred and what was making them tick.

Unable to find out whether it had happened elsewhere, my next course of action was to see if I could discern why or how it happened.

After an hour's searching I discovered that zombification, for want of a better word, can supposedly result from parasitic bites like one from a single cell organism called *toxoplasmosa gondii* that infects rats but can only breed inside a cat's intestines. So it takes over the rat's brain and basically programs itself to get eaten by a cat. Then there were neurotoxins, or certain kinds of poisons that slow your bodily functions to the point that you'll be considered dead even though you're not. Or perhaps a virus of some kind. Finally there was neurogenesis, or the method by which scientists can re-grow dead brain tissue.

None of them helped me discover how Joanna had come back, just that it wasn't outside the realms of possibility that she could have done so. And the woman downstairs was proof enough, if any were ever needed, that it certainly was possible.

I switched the computer off and then went downstairs to join my family.

The knock at the door made me jump. I stared across at Tim as he sat reading to his mum. She paid no attention as she staggered around the room. Despite having had her in the house for a couple of days, I still hadn't gotten used to having my wife back.

The knock came again, more insistent, joined by the ringing of the doorbell. I jumped up and walked to see who was there. "Keep quiet," I said as I shut the living room door behind me.

I opened the front door and my jaw dropped when I saw the acne-scarred police officer standing there.

"Mr. White?"

I nodded dumbly, my pulse racing.

"I'm afraid I have some disturbing news for you. There's no easy way to say this, but your wife's grave has been desecrated and her body removed."

I swallowed the lump in my throat. "Desecrated?"

"Don't worry, sir, we're going to do our best to find her body."

I glanced along the hallway before turning back. "Who would do something like that?"

The police officer shrugged and stared at his feet. "I don't know sir. I really don't."

The next few days were spent in a kind of haze as I learned to accept that Joanna was back in our lives. We didn't tell anybody. She was our secret. When

I went to work and Tim went to school, we locked her in the cupboard under the stairs.

Tim seemed to believe that everything was back to normal, and that we should just carry on as though nothing had happened. He even expected me to accept her back into my bed, but certainly for now, that wasn't going to happen and I wrapped her in a sleeping bag at night, pulling the toggle on it tight enough to cocoon her inside. Not that she slept and I could hear her bumping around, shuffling like a giant caterpillar. Even though she was my wife, I still didn't know exactly how I felt about having a dead woman in the house, never mind in my bed. Necrophilia wasn't something I wanted any part of. Not that Joanna would be in the least bit able to reciprocate. She ambled around the house like a robot, bumping into walls and falling over things as though she couldn't see too well. Perhaps that's why she walked along with her arms raised most of the time, sort of like feelers.

She certainly didn't cost much to look after. She didn't eat and she didn't go to the toilet and once you got used to her being around you could almost believe she wasn't dead. I even started talking to her and although she didn't reply, I found her presence comforting.

I will admit that for the first few days I was nervous, as zombies had a reputation for biting people and making them one of the undead, but Joanna didn't seem to have any interest in biting, so I eventually accepted that she wasn't going to eat us.

Tim doted on her. He took over all the chores involved with looking after his mum. Bathing, dressing, and generally taking care of her as though she was an invalid. I gradually accepted the situation.

My main fear—aside from being eaten—had been that Joanna would slowly rot away and we'd lose her all over again, but after a few days she stopped decomposing and reached a point of stasis.

Now I was no artist, but with the use of liberal amounts of makeup my wife could be made to look almost normal (this was the only thing Tim didn't do for her as he accepted Joanna for what she looked like, but he was happy for me to apply foundation, blusher, and rouge as I saw fit). When all of her hair dropped out I bought her a wig and glued it in place. And even though she stopped smelling of decay, I sprayed Jo with her favorite perfume so I could smell her as she shuffled around the room, the scent conjuring a host of memories.

To all intents and purposes we were one big happy family.

Now I was still wondering how Joanna had come back to life, never mind how she'd escaped her coffin under the ground, and I did consider that perhaps she had been the result of some form of experiment. But if that was the case, how had she escaped?

On a regular basis, I sat her down and, for want of a better word, interrogated her with a barrage of questions about what had happened, but she never replied and her dead eyes grew more and more blank, the blue eyeballs now covered by a white film. All she wanted to do was wander around in an aimless daze.

But our secret couldn't last forever and the next thing we knew, a neighbor spotted Joanna through the window. When he recovered from his faint he called the police. At that point he may as well have called the army, navy, and the air force because everyone and his mother descended on our detached house. Reporters set up camp outside and then scientists came. As I'd feared, they wanted to experiment on her to see how she had risen from the dead, even offering vast sums of money, but I declined. Although dead, she was still my wife. In sickness and in health and all that (I didn't like to think about the 'til death do us part as that had already happened.)

Next came the zealots. The religious nutters who claimed that like Jesus, Joanna had risen from the grave, so she must be the new messiah. Well she didn't die for anyone's sins. She died in an accident when hit by a car, but they didn't want to hear the truth. All they wanted was to see their messiah. To be touched by her as she obviously had special powers and could cure all their ailments.

As a result of all this attention we became prisoners in our own house.

I peered through a gap in the curtain. It was like a riot out there. People kept knocking at the door and I'd already taken the batteries out of the doorbell and unplugged the telephone.

Someone banged on the window, and I recoiled and backed away.

"What are we going to do?" Tim asked.

I collapsed onto the settee and cupped my face in my hands.

Tim sat next to me. "We can't stay in here forever. We've already run out of food."

Across the room, Joanna bumped into the wall. I stared at her.

Despite what Tim thought, the person opposite wasn't his mother anymore. It was just an animated shell. We were holding on to a memory of who she once was. But I knew what I had to do. Tim would probably hate me for doing it, but I had no other choice.

"Tim, I want you to go upstairs and pack."

My son looked at me and frowned. "Pack for what?"

"We're leaving."

Tim hesitated as though he sensed something in my words, but after a moment he turned and ran up the stairs. A moment later I heard drawers opening and cupboard doors banging.

With no time to lose I stood and ran into the kitchen and picked up a large kitchen knife with a serrated edge. Then I returned to the living room. I turned Joanna to face me and briefly kissed her on the lips. Words were not necessary, but I had to be strong, both physically and mentally.

I placed the serrated edge against her throat and a tear rolled down my cheek. Hopefully the other information I'd learned about zombies and decapitation were true.

If so, Joanna would live forever, at least in our memories.

There Is No "E" in Zombi Which Means There Can Be No You or We

Roxane Gay

[A Primer]

[Things Americans do not know about zombis:]

They are not dead. They are near death. There's a difference.
They are not imaginary.
They do not eat human flesh.
They cannot eat salt.
They do not walk around with their arms and legs locked stiffly.
They can be saved.

[How you pronounce zombi:]

Zaahhhhnnnnnn-Beee. You have to feel it in the roof your mouth, let it vibrate.
Say it fast.

The "m" is silent. Sort of.

[How to make a zombi:]

You need a good reason, a very good reason.

You need a pufferfish, and a small sample of blood and hair from your chosen candidate.

Instructions: Kill the pufferfish. Don't be squeamish. Extract the poison. Just find a way. Allow it to dry. Grind it with the blood and hair to create your *coup de poudre*. A good chemist can help. Blow the powder into the candidate's face. Wait.

[A Love Story]

Micheline Bérnard always loved Lionel Desormeaux. Their parents were friends though that bonhomie had not quite carried on to the children. Micheline and Lionel went to primary and secondary school together, had known each other all their lives—when Lionel looked upon Micheline he was always overcome with the vague feeling he had seen her somewhere before while she was overcome with the precise knowledge that he was the man of her dreams. In truth, everyone loved Lionel Desormeaux. He was tall and brown with high cheekbones and full lips. His body was perfectly muscled and after a long day of swimming in the ocean, he would emerge from the salty water, glistening. Micheline would sit in a cabana, invisible. She would lick her lips and she would stare. She would think, "Look at me, Lionel," but he never did. When Lionel walked, there was an air about him. He moved slowly but with deliberate steps and sometimes, when he walked, people swore they could hear the bass of a deep drum. His mother, who loved her only boy more than any other, always told him, "Lionel, you are the son of L'Ouverture." He believed her. He believed everything his mother ever told him. Lionel always told his friends, "My father freed our people. I am his greatest son."

In Port-au-Prince, there were too many women. Micheline knew competition for Lionel's attention was fierce. She was attractive, petite. She wore her thick hair in a sensible bun. On weekends, she would let that hair down and when she walked by, men would shout, "Quelle belle paire de jambes," *what beautiful legs*, and Micheline would savor the thrilling taste of their attention. Most Friday nights, Micheline and her friends would gather at Oasis, a popular nightclub on the edge of the Bel Air slum. She drank fruity drinks and smoked French cigarettes and wore skirts revealing just the right amount of leg. Lionel was always surrounded by a mob of adoring women. He let them buy him rum and Cokes and always sat at the center of the room wearing his pressed linen slacks and dark T-shirts that showed off his perfect, chiseled arms. At the end of the night, he would select one woman to take home, bed her thoroughly, and wish her well the following morning. The stone path to his front door was lined with the tears and soiled panties of the women Lionel had sexed then scorned.

On her birthday, Micheline decided she would be the woman Lionel took home. She wore a bright sundress, strapless. She dabbed perfume everywhere she wanted to feel Lionel's lips. She wore high heels so high her brother had to help her into the nightclub. When Lionel arrived to hold court, Micheline made sure she was closest. She smiled widely and angled her shoulders just so and leaned in so he could see everything he wanted to see within her ample cleavage. At the end of the night, Lionel nodded in her direction. He said, "Tonight you will know the affections of L'Ouverture's greatest son."

In Lionel's bed, Micheline fell deeper in love than she thought possible. Lionel knelt between her thighs, gently massaging her knees. He smiled luminously, casting a bright shaft of light across her body. Micheline reached for Lionel, her hands thrumming as she felt his skin. When he was inside her, she thought her heart might stop it seized so painfully. He whispered in her ear, his breath so hot it blistered her. He said, "Everything on this island is mine. You are mine." Micheline moaned. She said, "I am your victory." He said, "Yes, tonight you are." As he fucked her, Micheline heard the bass of a deep drum.

The following morning, Lionel walked Micheline home. He kissed her chastely on the cheek. As he pulled away, Micheline grabbed his hand in hers, pressing a knuckle with her thumb. She said, "I will come to you tonight." Lionel placed one finger over her lips and shook his head.

Micheline was unable to rise from her bed for a long while. She could only remember Lionel's touch, his words, how the inside of her body had molded itself to him. Her parents sent for a doctor, then a priest, and finally a mambo which they were hesitant to do because they were a good, Catholic family but the sight of their youngest daughter lying in bed, perfectly still, not speaking, not eating, was too much to bear. The mambo sat on the edge of the bed and clucked. She held Micheline's limp wrist. She said, "Love," and Micheline nodded. The mambo shooed the girl's parents out of the room and they left, overjoyed that the child had finally moved. The mambo leaned down, got so close, Micheline could feel the old woman's dry lips against her ear.

When the mambo left, Micheline bathed, dabbed herself everywhere she wanted to feel Lionel's lips. She went to Oasis and found Lionel at the center of the room holding a pale, young thing in his lap. Micheline pushed the girl out of Lionel's lap and took her place. She said, "Just one more night," and Lionel remembered her dark moans and the strength of her thighs and how she looked at him like the conquering hero he knew himself to be.

They made love that night, and Micheline was possessed. She dug her fingernails in his back until he bled. She locked her ankles in the small of Lionel's back, and sank her teeth into his strong shoulder. There were no sweet words between them. Micheline walked herself home before he woke. She went to the kitchen and filled a mortar and pestle with blood from beneath her fingernails and between her teeth. She added a few strands of Lionel's hair and a powder the mambo had given her. She ground these things together and put the *coup de poudre* as it was called into a silk sachet. She ran back to Lionel's, where he was still sleeping, opened her sachet, paused. She traced the edge of his face, kissed his forehead, then blew her precious powder into his face. Lionel coughed in his sleep, then stilled. Micheline undressed and stretched herself along his body, sliding her arm beneath his. As his body grew cooler, she kissed the back of his neck.

They slept entwined for three days. Lionel's skin grew clammy and gray. His eyes hollowed. He began to smell like soil and salt wind. When Micheline woke, she whispered, "Turn and look at me." Lionel slowly turned and stared at Micheline, his eyes wide open, unblinking. She gasped at his appearance, how his body had changed. She said, "Touch me," and Lionel reached for her with a heavy hand, pawing at her until she said, "Touch me gently." She said, "Sit up." Lionel slowly sat up, listing from side to side until Micheline steadied him. She kissed Lionel's thinned lips, his fingertips. His cold body filled her with a sadness she could hardly bear. She said, "Smile," and his lips stretched tightly into something that resembled what she knew of a smile. Micheline thought about the second silk sachet, the one hidden beneath her pillow between the pages of her Bible, the sachet with a powder containing the power to make Lionel the man he once was—tall, vibrant, the greatest son of L'Ouverture, a man who filled the air with the bass of a deep drum when he walked. She made herself forget about that power; instead, she would always remember that man. She pressed her hand against the sharpness of Lionel's cheekbone. She said, "Love me."

What Once We Feared
A Forest of Hands and Feet Story

Carrie Ryan

The first time I saw the apartment building I thought it looked like a bunker; it never occurred to me that we'd end up using it as one. Nicky's the one who actually lived there—or at least she and her dad moved in there when her mom kicked them out. She was the one who suggested we take shelter there. It's not like we had a lot of other options and it seemed like a good idea at the time.

But isn't that always the case? The ideas that seem so good in the moment turn out to be the worst when everything is said and done?

The Overlook—that's the name of the apartment building—was a massive chunk of a structure that sat just outside the interstate loop circling Uptown. (How pretentious does a city have to be to call it "Uptown" rather than "Downtown?") It was made of concrete and half dug into a hill so that three sides had a long, thick foundation and the fourth faced the road.

Most importantly, though, it was the closest place we could think to run when the outbreak began raging through the city. We'd been on a senior class field trip to Discovery Place when it happened. I'd just stepped outside with Nicky and I was thinking about how hard I'd worked to make sure I ended up partnered with her for this project and then *BAM!*

Nicky didn't know what made the sound and at first, neither did I. I couldn't place it—it was loud but not a gunshot, solid but not familiar. I was still trying to figure it out when I saw the body lying broken on the ground. Nicky hadn't seen it yet and I tried to keep her turned away. Then there was another *BAM!* and she started screaming.

The man landed not five feet away, one leg completely shattered underneath him from the fall. Another hit right after that, and I swear to God it seemed like it was raining bodies.

(Later, Felipe would start singing "It's Raining Men" whenever Nicky brought this up. It took her a while, but eventually she started laughing at the joke—what else could you do?).

Nicky had already jumped back under the Discovery Place awning, but like a moron I just stood there. "Jonah!" she screamed at me. "What are you doing?"

I was never able to explain it to her in a way she understood, but I couldn't stop staring at that first body. Later I'd realize that bits of his shattered leg had sprayed across my pants. But in that moment I just kept thinking that there are two hundred six bones in the adult human body and I wondered how many of them were broken in the fall and from which story of the skyscraper he'd plummeted.

There was something impossibly beautiful about the moment. All at once I grasped that the man had lived his life and in an instant it was gone—and I'd been there to see it happen. How many people get the experience of watching the moment someone dies? The switch from "something is there" to "something is not?"

I guess now that's kind of a moot question; at the time, though, I remember being awed.

It was looking up that shocked me out of my reverie. There were more of them coming, tumbling through the air like acrobats. I stumbled back and Nicky grabbed my arm and pulled me to safety. No lie—two seconds later a body hit right where I'd been standing.

He was the first to start moving. He was so broken up it was impossible to tell where he'd been bitten, but it was the only explanation. The only way someone who'd just been dead could suddenly be not-dead.

When the first dead guy came back to life—not that guy on the sidewalk, but a man from the West Coast who'd ended up on the news weeks before—we all should have run. That's what I know now.

But when the president goes on TV and tells you that everything's under control, that the disease has been contained, and the best thing you can do is not panic and try to live your life as normally as possible—that's when you're in trouble. That's when your parents send you off to school when they should be packing you up and raiding the grocery store.

That's why your teacher still insists on the senior trip to the Discovery Place: because that's what normal means. And since Uptown was packed with armed reservists and the outbreak hadn't even touched the East Coast, the principal and most of our parents figured we'd be safe.

As it turned out, we weren't.

Half of our class was stuck in the bowels of Discovery Place when the panic began, but Nicky and I were outside with Beatrice, Felipe, and Gregor right behind us. We could hear screams coming from down the block.

The air stank of blood and Felipe had to shout over the sound of the reservists' gunshots. "We should go back in—get to the buses through the rear entrance!"

The guy who'd landed in front of me was so broken there was no way he'd ever be able to stand, but even so, he twitched his fingers against the concrete, splitting his nails as he tried to drag himself closer.

Beatrice began hyperventilating and Nicky's cheeks shone with tears. I hated the indecision of that moment. Even now I wish I could go back there and stop time and just give myself a minute to think.

All around us, people were giving up on their cars, not even bothering to turn them off or to shut their doors after abandoning them in the middle of the road. The streets were gridlocked, horns blaring. We knew then that we'd never get far.

We'd never get home.

That's when Beatrice said: "I want to go home."

I'm pretty sure that's what made Nicky say, "My dad's apartment—it's in the Overlook." And then we started running.

We were like a hive mind—no discussion, no coordination. One of us thought it and so it became. We ran through through the city like a pack, desperate to escape. We learned quickly to stay in the middle of the road—those on the outside were the easiest targets.

Everywhere was madness. Or so I thought. Maybe I didn't truly understand madness yet, because I still felt the compulsion to steady those who stumbled. To pull them free of clawing hands.

I still tried to help.

There were only two entrances to the Overlook: the leasing office, its windows already shattered, and the underground garage, which had a massive, jail-like gate stretched across the ramp.

Nicky pulled a remote from her purse and pointed it at a black box. Slowly, slowly, with a lot of creaking, the gate began to roll open. She was the first through, and then Beatrice and Felipe. They sprinted through the garage for the bank of elevators. I was the one to hold Gregor back.

"It's every man for himself, right?" I asked him.

He didn't get what I was saying.

"Look," I tried again. "We gotta lock this thing down now, right? Is it wrong if we do that? Keep everyone else out?"

Gregor's eyes were wide as he looked from me to the road outside. People were screaming, trying to run. So many of them were smeared with blood that it was impossible to tell who'd been infected already and who was safe.

"Come on, Jonah!" Nicky screamed. Her panic was contagious, and my fingers fumbled as I pried the cover off the electric motor that worked the garage gate.

"Tell her to just hold on a sec," I ordered Gregor, "and get that clicker from her!"

I'd wanted to be all cool and find a way to disable the motor, but in the end I couldn't keep focused on all the wires and gears. I ended up grabbing one of the big metal garbage bins and slamming it against the motor until it was in enough pieces to be unsalvageable. Gregor pointed the clicker at the black box and sure enough, the gate was well and thoroughly broken.

No one was getting in through the garage.

Once we were all piled inside one of the two marble-and-wood elevators, Nicky had to use a special electronic key to access the penthouse level. When she pressed the "P" button Felipe whistled. "Fancy girl, eh?"

She rolled her eyes at him. I remember that so distinctly because I'd been thinking how glad I was that he was such an ass because it made me look better by comparison.

Of course, that only lasted until we reached the top floor and the elevator doors opened. Nicky stepped out into the vestibule first, without even pausing to look around, and I grabbed her hand before she could take off down one of the dim, carpeted hallways.

"What are you doing?" I hissed in her ear. "What if it's not safe?"

Beatrice muffled a cry by pushing her palm against her mouth, and even Felipe's face paled. A long hallway stretched from both sides of the elevator. Gregor took off to the left, but the floor must have been configured in a square or something, because a minute or two later he came sprinting back from the right. "Everything's clear," he reported. The corridors were silent, empty.

"Yeah, but for how long?" Felipe asked.

As if in response one of the elevator engines kicked in, and it whisked away from our floor down into the bowels of the building. There was a distant ding and then the sound of the elevator starting its climb back up.

I held my breath, hoping it stopped before reaching us, and thought of all those people out in the city. They were going to run somewhere, and this place would look pretty good, with its thick walls and proximity to Uptown. It was the closest thing to a fortress our city had.

"Unless we're the ones who called for it," Nicky whispered. "Whoever it is would need to have a key to get to this floor."

Beatrice finally spoke up. "They . . . those things . . . can't . . . " She moved her hand in the air as if it could talk for her. " . . . like, think, can they? You know, press buttons and stuff like that?"

(It's funny how long it took us to start using the word *zombie*. For the longest time we just called them "they" or "those things," because *zombie* was a word that existed in games and movies. It felt stupid saying it, always coming out with a kind of "shit, can you believe I'm actually using this word?" laugh.)

"We shouldn't wait to find out," Felipe suggested, already easing down the hallway. He tugged on Nicky's sleeve and she shrugged him off.

"It could be my *dad*," she said, emphasizing that last word. Felipe flicked his eyes at me, like I was somehow in control of the situation. But none of that mattered because the elevator dinged and my stomach turned over on itself as the doors slid open.

I don't know who was more surprised—us or him. There was a moment where it felt like it could be a normal day and this normal guy with graying hair was getting home from work with his suit a little rumpled, his tie loose around his neck.

But then I saw where his sleeve was torn and how he held his hand against his stomach. There was blood. A *lot* of blood.

It's not like he could think we wouldn't see it, and for a second he had a guilty look on his face. Almost panicked, even. But then he must have remembered that he was an adult and we were just a bunch of teenagers, because he pushed past us and strode down the dim hallway, his keys rattling in his bloody fingers.

And it worked. We stood there like dumb kids and let him do what he wanted, because seriously, who were we to stop him?

Then, to add to our stupefied uselessness, the elevator doors began to slide closed and I couldn't get there in time to stop them. I started pounding the button, trying to call it back. The call light lit up, but I was too late. Behind the double doors, the engine hummed and wires whisked the elevator back down into the building.

There would be more coming—more people. More infected. I'd locked the garage down, but they could still get into the Overlook through the office. We wouldn't stay safe for long if that happened. We had to stop them. Any way we could, we had to keep anyone else from getting up to the penthouse.

We had to stop the elevators from running.

I closed my eyes, trying to concentrate, but every thought was shrouded in a red-tinged panic. "How many elevators are there?"

Nicky didn't answer and I turned to face her. "How many?" I asked again, and she kind of flinched as though my words had been physical.

"Just these two," she finally answered. "Why?"

Behind the metal doors I heard the cables whirring, from the bowels of the building, floor chimes rang one after another, growing louder. Other people were entering the building. Like water rising, they would get to us eventually if we didn't find a way to pull the plug.

On the other side of the vestibule a sign for the billiard room hung on the wall next to a set of double doors. I tried the handles but they were locked. "Can you get me in here?"

Nicky's face was pale, her lips white and dry and the rims of her eyes raw. She was shutting down; my words seemed to be getting trapped in her head in some kind of endless cycle. Instead of answering, she stood there blinking.

Behind her the elevator's engine hummed. Blood roared through me—that feeling of having the perfect strategy for winning a game and just hoping you have the chance to play it out.

And knowing just how many ways it could all go wrong.

A crisp *ding* sounded, and even though we'd been the ones to call the elevator, its arrival startled us. We turned as one, waiting for the doors to slide open. I braced myself for a monster to come stumbling out and felt almost light-headed when I saw that the car was empty.

Except for the glistening pool of blood oozing along the floor.

"Oh my God," Beatrice started mumbling over and over. She backed down the hallway, a low wail building in the back of her throat.

"Don't let it leave!" I called to Gregor as the doors began to slide shut. He had to dive for it, his foot slipping on the blood and his elbow crashing against the wood-paneled wall

I turned to Nicky and wrapped my fingers around her shoulders, forcing her to focus. "I need you to get me in that room."

Her hands shook as she held out the same black electronic key she'd used to access the top floor. I pressed it against the lock and the door opened with a click.

I didn't care anymore about trying to appear smooth and confident. I only cared about what could be coming in that second elevator. Hearing its ascent, the beep of buttons as it climbed past floor five, then six, then seven. Knowing that eventually someone else with a key to the top floor would come home, bringing with them more danger.

Those men who'd dropped from the top of the skyscrapers earlier—the ones who'd stayed dead which meant they were probably uninfected—had to have jumped because that was less terrifying than whatever was coming for them. I didn't want to know what that was. I didn't want to face it up here in this dim hallway.

As I'd hoped, the billiard room had a few heavy comfortable chairs, and I grabbed the closest one, dragging it over the thick carpet into the hallway. Gregor kept having to battle the elevator doors as they tried to close over and over again. The alarm started to buzz, the sound grating and horrible in what had been almost silence before.

Gregor helped me maneuver the chair into place to block the doors, and then he climbed out, cradling his elbow. "Call the other one," I told him as I went back for a second chair.

Nicky tried to stop me. "What are you doing?"

I moved around her. With the alarm going I couldn't hear the cables of the second elevator, couldn't tell how close it was. "Locking it down."

"But my dad . . . " She grabbed my sleeve.

I pulled free. Said nothing. Started dragging another chair out into the hallway.

She jumped in front of me, kneeling on the seat and leaning over the back toward me. "My dad's still out there," she argued.

My hands clenched the armrests. I felt the words rising in my throat, pushing against my vocal cords. "Screw your dad!" I wanted to scream in her face, because seriously, what were we supposed to do? Camp out in the hallway and stand guard? Hope that her dad eventually showed up and wasn't as bloody as the last guy?

Instead, I took a deep breath. "It's not safe." How could she not understand?

The other elevator dinged, and even before the doors opened we heard banging and moaning. "Oh crap," Gregor breathed.

Beatrice took off running down the hallway, and Felipe chased after her. But I didn't follow. I couldn't. We had to block the elevator so more of those things didn't get up here. I kicked the chair I'd been dragging toward Gregor and then grabbed Nicky, throwing her into the billiard room.

When the elevator doors whisked open, I wasn't looking. I was racing toward the row of pool cues hanging on the wall.

It was the first time I'd heard the moaning up close and personal. Not filtered through the TV as background noise in a newscast or as part of the panicked stampede out of Uptown earlier.

This was the sound of something that used to be human and was no more. It was the kind of thing that could make your heart stop, your lungs constrict, your nerves shrivel.

Later the sound would become the backdrop to everyday life, the way the hiss of electronics and the buzz of traffic used to be. But not in that moment. Right then, I realized that death had a sound and it was coming for us.

"No, no no no no nonononono," I kept muttering under my breath. I'd had the winning hand here—I'd known how to keep us safe, and this wasn't part of it.

I swept the pool cues into my arms, hating how flimsy they felt. How in the world could these protect us? Protect me? They'd snap instantaneously. No way could they inflict the damage necessary.

When I got back to the door I saw Gregor in the hallway, holding the chair up like a lion tamer, trying to push back a tall woman in a business suit. One of her sleeves was ripped off and her skirt was twisted. A gash ran the length of her face, flapping open to show her teeth and the bones around her eye. Her hair was drenched with blood. It was still wet, hanging in ropes that splashed against her neck and sent droplets flinging onto the walls and the front of Gregor's shirt.

I could just close the door, I thought. My hand curled around the knob. Nicky and I would be safe locked in here. We could survive.

Behind me, Nicky gurgled in panic, and Gregor must have heard, because he glanced up at me. With that one look he knew. I could see it register in his eyes. I was going to abandon him.

Every man for himself, he was thinking, remembering the way I'd said it earlier.

The thing about decisions is that sometimes you don't make them for the right reasons. Sometimes you have an idea of yourself that isn't real. It's an aspiration; it's the picture you hold in your mind so that you don't weep at all of your failings.

In my head, I was the savior. I was the strong one, the guy in charge who could keep us safe. But I knew standing there that that would never be me. Never *could* be me.

In reality, I was the coward. The one so terrified of dying I'd sacrifice anyone and everyone for the chance to keep my own heart beating for just another second.

With that single glance, Gregor knew this truth about me. It was written in the disappointment that shuddered his breathing with the terror-laced understanding that suddenly, he was alone in his fight.

What's funny is that if I'd just let him die, he'd have taken that knowledge with him. I'd have been safe from his censure. I could have repositioned the mask of competence over my face and stared down the next challenge, hoping not to waver and fall again.

The thing is—I didn't decide to save Gregor because that's the kind of guy I am. I tried to save him because I couldn't stand him knowing the worst of me.

The chair Gregor was using as a weapon was heavy and unwieldy. His arms were tiring and his reactions slowing. I leapt into the fight with a pool cue in each hand. My first swipe went wild, snapping against the woman's shoulder and doing nothing.

"That won't work!" Gregor screamed.

"I know!" I shouted back.

Images from old kung fu movies flashed in my head, but none of them were long or bright enough for me to capture them and figure out what to do. Behind us, Nicky screamed, "Kill it!" as though somehow that would be helpful.

The woman lurched, her teeth snapping at Gregor's fingers. He yanked his hand out of reach, dropping one side of the chair in the process. In that second he was unprotected, and the creature lunged.

I tried to use the cue to push her back, but I was only successful at tilting her off balance, and I quickly shoved the other cue between her legs, tripping her.

She fell to the floor with a thump, something somewhere inside her snapping. Already she was pushing herself to her knees. I didn't know what to do to stop her, so I kicked her in the abdomen, sending her tumbling to the side. Gregor toppled the chair over her, trying to position it so that the crossbars on the legs would pin her down. But it wasn't working.

She grabbed Gregor's pants, yanking hard. He lost his footing and fell, his head smashing the wall as his body went limp. The woman flailed, teeth going straight for Gregor's ankle. Nicky screamed.

If I'd had time maybe I'd have thought to wedge the pool cue in her mouth so she couldn't bite him. I could have rolled the woman onto her stomach and pinned her arms back while the others figured out a way to tie her up.

But I knew nothing except panic; I tasted its bitterness at the back of my throat, the heat of it searing my neurons so that I couldn't think. Instead, I just acted out of pure, blind instinct and kicked the woman, hard, in the face.

The year before I'd been the placekicker on the football team. I knew how to kick a ball, how to gather the power in your legs and transfer it out through the top of your foot.

As I felt her teeth rip free and heard her jaw popping, I thought, *This is a woman's face you're destroying. A human being you're attacking.*

Her head snapped back, her moans choked on shards of teeth now lodged in her throat. But that didn't stop her reaching for Gregor again.

It was like this would never end.

That's the truth I grasped in that moment and never lost again: this was the beginning. I could kill this woman and there would be another behind her. And another behind that. They would come and come and come and eventually I'd have nothing left in me to fight.

It would never be a question of how long *they* could last; it was all about how long *I* could. And I knew, right then, that I would give up. Not now and perhaps not soon, but at some point I would have fight left in me, and I would let it go.

Because I wasn't strong enough for this new world.

In the end, I'm not a survivor.

There was something about embracing my inevitable death, knowing that it would come and it would be my choice, that made it easier to flip the chair over and press the top rail of it against the woman's throat. She was pinned on her back, facing me, her jaw crooked, her mouth a gaping mess.

Her mascara was smeared, dried grayish tears streaking her cheeks. I assumed she'd died in the elevator, alone. Just trying to go home. Later, when we started breaking into apartments looking for supplies, I'd find hers—a tidy corner unit with views of the mountains. Her furniture was modern, her bathroom a mess, and her kitchen had been that of a woman who loved to cook. Cupboards stuffed full, a refrigerator with the first fresh vegetables we'd had in days. She had only one picture frame on her dresser, and in it was a photo of her and another girl who looked just like her. Probably her sister.

Sometimes I wondered what it would be like to find that sister. To have to confess that that woman was the first human being I'd ever purposefully hurt. She was the first I killed.

And it was terrible and impossible.

As I pressed the rail of the chair against her throat I realized that choking her was useless. Decapitation or destruction of the brain—that's what we'd been told on the news—were the only defenses. And yet, no matter how much weight I put behind it, even when I jumped, trying to add pressure, I couldn't sever her neck. I couldn't even crush her spinal cord.

Nicky had pulled a groggy Gregor out of the way, and she cradled his head in her lap as she watched me try to kill this woman. "Oh God," she moaned over and over again. Felipe had come back, and he pulled another chair from the billiard room to finally block off the second elevator. This time, Nicky didn't protest or mention her dad.

Beatrice stood down the hallway, already a dim ghost. I should have realized then that she'd jump, eventually. The first of us to give up.

But not the last.

I'd grown up with the assumption that the human body is fragile. It isn't. "Give me a pool cue," I said, holding out my hand. Nicky traded glances with Felipe, and I could tell she was about to ask why when he shook his head slightly, stopping her.

He picked it up, held it out to me. It wasn't easy to line up the tip of it against the woman's eye. Her lids were open, the irises visible, and I didn't want to see, but I had to.

It took more force than I thought it would, and all the while the woman struggled, snapping her teeth at me. Terror clogged my throat, infiltrated my lungs like smoke. I couldn't breathe, couldn't think, couldn't force my muscles to move the way they needed to.

Her eyeball compressed but held firm. I tried using momentum but I was shaking too hard, and each time I tried to bring the tip of the pool cue down I missed the socket. Nicky was sobbing at this point and the elevator doors were still trying to close; their alarms screamed.

"Just do it!" Nicky screeched.

And I did. Letting go of the chair, I wrapped both hands around the pool cue and I jammed it into the dead woman's eye with all the force of my body weight and then some. There was a sickening pop that I felt more than heard as the tip of the cue jerked down, sinking through the bone of her orbital socket and then her brain.

The woman choked out one last moan as I twisted the cue, moving it back and forth like it was a shovel loosening dirt.

I know there was still sound, but in my head there was silence. A soft, stuffy kind like you see on TV when a character's hearing goes out after an explosion. Everyone else sat stunned, staring at me.

Maybe I expected to see some sort of admiration. A moment of unity that we're all in this together—that it wasn't me alone who'd killed this woman, but me acting on behalf of a team.

Except that wasn't what I found. I knew they were grateful. I knew they understood that I'd saved their lives. But that couldn't keep the horror from their eyes. The disgust.

Later they'd rally around me and Felipe would start joking about it. And once, when we pried open the door to the neighbor's wine closet, he and Gregor would act it all out again and we'd laugh (Beatrice would already be gone by then).

But in that moment there was just a sound-softened silence. All of them staring at me like *I* was the monster.

"Help me get him up," Nicky finally murmured to Felipe, and together they helped Gregor to his feet. A thin trickle of blood smeared the back of his neck, and it took him a minute to become steady.

We left the woman in the little vestibule by the elevators for the time being. It felt strange to abandon her there like that. She looked so exposed—no longer a monster but the victim of some cruel sadistic murder. Before catching up with the others, I flipped the chair over in an attempt to cover her ravaged face.

Nicky's father's place was at the far end of the building, one of a pair of apartments that jutted toward Uptown like a finger pointing at the city. The door opened onto a long rectangular room with the kitchen first, the dining room in the middle, and an awkwardly shaped living room at the other end.

Hardwood gleamed along the floor, the far wall nothing but floor-to-ceiling windows bordering a pair of sliding doors that opened onto a wide balcony. Beyond was a spectacular view of Uptown, the afternoon sun glaring off a sea of office buildings.

A set of double doors off the living room led to the master suite: a massive space with a king-sized bed and full sitting area flanking another wall of windows, a huge walk-in closet, and a marble bathroom that boasted both a Jacuzzi and walk-in shower. Next to the kitchen was a hallway that led to another full bathroom, a bedroom (Nicky's room, I guessed, though it was about as personalized as a hotel), and an office.

Outside was chaos, but inside a sort of odd calm settled around us. The dissipation of adrenaline left us drained and worn. Something inside Nicky must have clicked into "hostess" mode—maybe it made her feel normal to offer us something to drink and eat. As if this were any ordinary day and we were just hanging out after school.

We tried calling home using both our cell phones and the land line, but we could never get through. (Only Gregor would get the chance to speak to his parents again, and he refused to tell us anything about the conversation. He just hung up the phone and stepped out onto the balcony, where he screamed and screamed and screamed).

Beyond that, no one really had much to say. We barely made eye contact as we shuffled through the unfamiliar rooms. Suddenly, we became oddly polite, apologizing in soft voices if we had to maneuver around one another to get to the bathroom or ask for a towel.

As the day wore on, we each retreated to separate areas, as though marking out territory. Gregor lay on the master bed with an ice pack on his head, while Beatrice drifted into the guest room, closing the door behind her. All of us could hear her sobbing, but none of us knew what to say.

Ultimately, Felipe ended up in the office, which looked more like central command than anything else. One wall held four televisions, and he tuned them all to different channels. The computer had three screens, and he quickly filled them with an array of news blogs, obsessively refreshing and following links for more information.

Nicky staked her claim on the balcony outside, tucking herself into an Adirondack chair with a quilt wrapped around her shoulders and her back to the windows. I had no idea how she was doing: if she was awake or asleep, crying or praying.

I couldn't settle anywhere. I tried sitting on the couch, but my mind roared with action plans. So much needed to be done, and every time I thought of something new I added it to my mental list, which was shaped like a pinwheel and kept spinning and spinning and spinning.

There were so many variables, so many calculations to make, that all of it felt like quicksand. We needed to gather food, but how urgent that was depended on how long the electricity lasted and how quickly the food in the fridges spoiled. Nicky had mentioned that some of the building's power came from solar panels mounted on the roof, but who knew how much that would help?

We needed to figure out what to do about the guy down the hall. He was clearly infected, but how long would it be until he turned? How long did we have to figure out how to kill him and build up the nerve to follow through with it?

My mind flicked through possibilities like a deck of cards: we could use a knife, a hammer, a baseball bat. We could search the other apartments for a gun. But how would we get access to the other places? The doors were reinforced with steel. (In the end we cut through the walls, tunneling from room to room. It turned out that the couple down the hall had a loaded revolver in their bedside table, but by the time we found it, it was too late—

Gregor and I had already taken care of the infected guy with a carving knife and a nine iron.)

I needed to find bike chains to double-lock the gates on the stairs, I needed to find buckets and bowls to fill with water, I needed to find a way to paint "5/ Alive" on a sheet and hang it out the window, as the news instructed. I needed to figure out if there were pets in the other apartments and what to do with them.

My mind wheeled down all the various paths our lives were about to take, parsing the possibilities, finding the holes and stuffing them with solutions that were the wrong shape and size no matter how tantalizingly right they appeared. There were so many "if . . . then" possibilities that any attempt to figure out the future fractured under the weight of uncertainty.

And when dawn finally broke, I knew I'd followed the thread of every eventuality and they all led to the same knotted end.

Stepping out onto the balcony was like stepping into another world. This side of the building jutted out from a sloping bank, so the drop to the ground was much farther than I'd expected. At the bottom of the hill sat a concrete barrier topped by a fence that bordered the southern stretch of the interstate loop around Uptown.

Car alarms blared, horns blasted, people screamed. The air smelled of blood and ash, pain and despair. Down the road flames blazed and smoke billowed from a twisted pile of metal that used to be an eighteen-wheeler and who knows how many cars. A few industrious souls tried to thread their way through on foot, bikes, or motorcycles.

But the fences along the interstate were like the walls of the shore, keeping the tide of living dead from escaping. From my vantage point so many stories up, it was easy to recognize that those people trapped on the road had little chance of surviving. But they didn't know that yet. They couldn't see what I did: the churning storm of dead less than a mile away.

I cupped my hands around my mouth and shouted a warning. Nicky stirred behind me: "I tried already—it won't work. Even if they hear you, they won't listen." Her voice was listless, scratchy.

It crawled under my skin. Because I knew she was right and that she wasn't just talking about the poor souls on the road below. She was talking about all of us. We were fooling ourselves into thinking that by continuing the struggle we could somehow survive. That that was all it took, the act of struggle somehow a guarantee of success.

But that didn't mean we didn't have our own storm of dead to face down the road. Just because we were safer didn't mean we were safe.

322   Carrie Ryan

The thing was, Nicky had suddenly stopped playing by the rules, and that made me angry. The rule was that she pretended we could be okay. That was her role in all of this: hopeful survivor.

"What, so you're just gonna give up?" I failed to keep from sneering, and so I kept my back to her, my hands clenched around the wide railing along the balcony. She didn't answer, which made it worse.

I needed a fight. Because of the itch I could never scratch, the need to *do* in a world where doing had become impossible. The rest of them found ways to contend with this new reality (well, until Beatrice jumped and the fall didn't kill her—that was the beginning of the end for Felipe).

For me, I held on by planning the next move and the one after that. And the truth was, I already saw where it ended. In my mind I could picture every path, every eventuality, and they all led to one place: the storm of zombies waiting.

We had no hope. The conclusion was written. The last line had been carved in stone and our judgment handed down. There was no appeal, no do-over. The moment we'd stepped into the Overlook we'd chosen our path, and we'd chosen wrong.

It would take us a long time to get there—longer than I'd even realized at first. The building had an elaborate roof garden with a saltwater pool. Early on we rigged a ladder to get up there, and thanks to a retiree with an odd penchant for collecting seed packets, we were able to plant a vegetable patch that was pretty successful.

But on that first morning at the Overlook there was this moment when I was standing on the balcony with Nicky and the rising sun hit the pink-tinted windows of an apartment building a few blocks south. And suddenly, everything around us turned rosy; the world became soft and beautiful.

Nicky pulled me down into the chair next to her and she tilted her head back and I did the same. "When you only look at the sky," she whispered, "it's like nothing's changed."

And she was right. The wall of the balcony blocked the chaos below—I could no longer see the wrecks or the carnage. In that rose-tinged heartbeat, there existed a flutter of hope. I could see it in Nicky's eyes—that what she'd said earlier wasn't really true. Being the hopeful survivor wasn't just a role. She didn't believe in giving up, which is something I wouldn't come to fully understand until much, much later, when her raw-ribbed chest rattled and wheezed.

I'd come onto the balcony that morning to give her the chance to circumvent it all: change her decision and choose a new path. She could fly over the railing or take the elevator down to the main level or find any other number of ways to determine her own ending.

All I could see were the ways our world had fallen apart, but somehow Nicky had found a way to show me that in some respects it was still the same, and it could be beautiful.

At the very end she would take it all back, of course. When death was no longer a promise but a pressing reality, I asked her if she regretted this dawn-inspired commitment to survival. Her answer had been a simple yes. That if she'd had it to do over again, knowing that rescue would never come, she'd have killed herself on that first morning.

And then she was gone and it was just me. The only one who'd never really hoped. The one who'd never seen the Overlook as some sort of waiting room before life resumed as it had once been. The one who understood that our world hadn't been put on pause but shifted into a new reality and that days would continue to come and go, piling on one another as they always had.

I'd known from the beginning what Nicky had understood only at the very end. But just because I'd seen the truth from day one didn't mean I needed to force her and the others to see it too. Because there's something I learned in that sliver of pink sunrise: we all come into the world knowing we're going to die. And maybe I'd figured out that our death would come sooner and it would come harder, but that didn't make it any more or less inevitable.

And it didn't mean there wasn't something worthwhile about those days in between—the good and the bad of them. The kisses and the fights and the fears and the laughter. I was done with fearing death and I was done with fearing regret. I'd made my choices. Maybe they'd been the wrong ones, but I intended to live them to the end.

The Harrowers

Eric Gregory

The kid didn't have a feed. He glanced over his shoulder and scratched the back of his head, and I saw there was nothing in his neck. You didn't find many folks without feeds in the city. Right away, I knew he'd brought me a problem. "I'm looking for Ez," he said, and I said yeah, I was him.

He looked relieved then lowered his voice. "And you're a guide?"

I wiped grease on the front of my jeans, closed the hood of the 4Runner, and gestured for the kid to follow me. He took the hint, nodding with absurd gratitude, and I led him down past the line of old rigs, all waiting to be stripped. Across the yard, someone cranked up a saw.

"Who gave you my name?" I asked.

"Guy called himself Coroner."

"You don't want to talk to him again."

The kid gave a sad sort of smile. "No. I really don't."

He wasn't the roughneck sort who usually came around looking for a guide. Right age, maybe: Seventeen, eighteen. But the boy had a pressed, conservative look to him. Skinny, clean-shaven, all done up in slacks and suspenders and a white, sweaty shirt. I didn't know what to make of him, and I didn't like that I didn't know.

"You from around here?" I asked.

He shook his head. "No, sir. Lynchburg."

"Nice town," I lied. Hive of fanatics. "How long you been here, then?"

"Not quite a day."

"And you already want to go outside." I grinned. "Jesus."

It wasn't much cooler in the office, but there was beer and shade. The kid settled onto my ratty, floral-print sofa, and I opened two Yanjings, thinking maybe he was used to the fancy stuff. I still couldn't get a fix on him, but he dressed like a big spender. He folded his arms and crossed his legs at the knee, glancing at the old gas station signs on the wall.

"What do I call you?" I said.

He frowned into his beer. "P. K."

"All right, P. K. You want to tell me about your deathwish?"

He shook his head.

"No deathwish. I just want to see my old man again."

My turn to frown. "Your old man."

"Yessir. He's outside."

I slid my bottle across the desk, back and forth from one hand to the other.

"How far outside?"

"Cherokee North. Between here and Johnson City."

"That's a lot of forest."

He shrugged.

Some guides don't like to get nosy. Take the job, don't ask questions. Lot of those guides develop a nasty case of dead.

"You want my help," I said, "you're going to have to tell me what he was doing there." If Coroner had sent him, I didn't have many choices here, but maybe the boy didn't know that. He nodded, answered without hesitation.

"We were out harrowing."

Christ, I thought. And then: Of course—P. K.: Preacher's Kid. Should've caught that earlier. I finished off the Yanjing, then opened the cooler and unscrewed a jar of whiskey. I'd heard of harrowers before, but never met one alive.

"You were with him," I said.

"Yessir."

"He preaches, you shoot. That how it works?"

The kid looked embarrassed. "I haven't learned to bless yet."

"And you got separated?"

He inclined his head. "Pack of wolves surprised us. We were running, and my father—" He paused. "He fell. Over a ledge. I saw him roll, heard him call out, but the slope sharpened and—I didn't see where he landed. I searched until sundown. I love my father, but—" he pursed his lips "—but I'm not stupid."

"You did right." I leaned forward. "But you understand he's dead."

The boy was silent.

"I ain't gonna sell you false hope. Your daddy's gone. I'll take your money, I'll take you out there, and I'll help you make whatever amends you want to make. But I want us both to understand what's going on here. I don't want any confusion between us. You have to show me that you know we're not going to find him smiling."

"I have to find him," he said. "I know the odds."

I wasn't sure he did. "I ain't cheap. And I ain't stupid either." I told him the deposit. "I need to see triple the advance in a credit account, and I need the account linked to my feed. In the event of my death, the triple transfers automatically to my family."

Little joke, there. Family.

"That's fair," he said. "And if I die?"

"We link your feed to my account. The deposit transfers back."

He shook his head. "I don't have a feed."

I'd forgotten. Mark of the Devil. I smiled through a stir of jealousy. The little metal nub in my neck let me work in the city, let me spend and collect credit, but mostly it just felt like a warm seed of debt, always itching beneath my skin, waiting for me to die or default, always threatening to grow.

"We can go to my credit agency and set up a timed withdrawal from my account," I said. "If you're not around to cancel it in three days, the advance'll transfer to the account of your choice."

He nodded. "Works for me."

"I think we understand one another, P. K." I took the Colt from my drawer, set it on my desk. The old, faded sticker on the grip said *Keep Asheville Weird.* "If you got the yuan, I got the yeehaw."

And just like that, we were in business.

No one ran outside the law in Asheville without owing money to Coroner. He found you when you were down, desperate, earthless. He fed you, paid your rent. If you wanted to be a guide, he made it easy: Set you up as a company mechanic, pulled all the right bureaucratic triggers to assign you to truckers on his payroll, to divert shipping routes. Last Christmas, he'd bought me a suit of skintight armor straight out of Cupertino. Sometimes it was hard to figure out where the companies ended and Coroner began, but it was absolutely clear who owned you.

Coroner had placed me and Xin Sun together so often that I could tell you her granddaddy's favorite singer (Johnny Cash) and the city where her mama was born (Raleigh). She was short, wiry, somewhere in her forties, with a line of faded hearts tattooed around her wrist. Her rig was a behemoth, a messy cross between a Humvee and an old furniture truck. I sat in the cab, behind the old automatic rifle mounted on the hood. P. K. huddled in the cargo crawlspace with the liquor.

Xin caught my eye as she eased toward the gate. "You're a bad person, Ez."

"Yeah?"

"The daddy's gone," she said. "Boy don't need to see that."

"I told him. He can make up his own mind."

She shook her head, scratched her neck. "He's green as shit. The dead on the moon can see it. You ought to know better."

"He's shot his share of dead. He don't need a mama, Xin."

She stared straight ahead, gripped the wheel.

Asshole, said the silence.

The traffic light changed, and Xin eased forward again. Bluecoats crowded around us with rifles and pads. My feed ran hot, so I could almost feel their fingers in the back of my neck, sifting through my licenses and permissions, my employers and outstanding debts. The bluecoat captain read through our manifest while his grunts looked over the cargo. Xin ignored me, and I tried not to touch my gun or crack my knuckles or otherwise announce that I was scared turdless. I listened to the clang of footsteps in the back and wondered what the kid was thinking, hidden down there with the liquor.

The footsteps in the back receded. The door slammed shut, and the captain waved us on. I tipped an invisible hat and Xin told him to have a good one.

The gate opened, and we drove outside.

There's something about leaving a city that makes you want to get drunk and scream. You ride out into the emptiness of the frontier and you can feel the weight of gazes falling away with every mile. Debts, shopping centers, manifests—all that headsmoke recedes until it's just you and the quiet, the clouds wrapped around road-carved mountains. I watched the trees as we rode out: The leaves were only just tinged with orange. Ahead, the Interstate wound through the broad swells of the Blue Ridge, all steep slopes and sharp drops. If you rode fifteen miles outside of Asheville, you could hardly tell that anyone had ever bothered to live on the mountains. Even the billboards were scarce and choked by kudzu.

"Want to let him out?" said Xin.

"Guess I ought to."

I pulled myself out of the gunner's seat, grappled my way to the back and ducked past stacked pallets marked in Portuguese, Italian, Chinese. All the world's shit packed up in crates. You couldn't see much by the emergency lights, and as often as I'd navigated Xin's rig, they packed it a little different every time. I pushed a box of canned soup off of the hidden door, rapped three times, waited, rapped again. I heard the door unlatch from his side, and I pulled it open. P. K. stared out from the crawlspace, his arms crossed over his chest like an old-fashioned corpse, mason jars shifting slightly around him. He was red-faced, his hair sweat-wet against his forehead.

"Thank you," he breathed.

I offered my hand. "Everything all right down there?"

He blinked. "Are we out?"

"Yessir."

I helped him up, guided him to the front. "Have a sit-down," I said, waving him into the gunner's seat. Xin glanced over her shoulder and smiled at the boy.

"Hope you didn't sample the whiskey," she said. Gently, teasing. "I don't want Coroner to come knocking."

He flushed. "No, ma'am. I don't drink."

I tried not to imagine Coroner at my door.

Xin laughed. "That so? You're either wise or insane. Not sure which."

"Out here," P. K. ventured, smiling nervously, "I think it's for the best."

"Out here, you may be right."

On the side of the road, empty signs. Words scraped and weathered away. A lone dead woman, one-armed and skeletal, limped along the side of the road, stumbling now and then into the guardrail, threatening to tumble over and down into a far hollow. Xin and P. K. fell silent, and I watched the sky for birds.

I still couldn't work out what Coroner was trying to say, sending me this job. When I'd called to line up the ride, I asked about the kid, but the minder only told me that the operation was important to the boss. "Make sure the boy and his daddy come back with you," he'd said. "Finish the job, you'll be fine."

Coroner wasn't an idiot—he knew the preacher was dead by now. Was he trying to play the kid for money? That didn't make sense; this was small change for him. He wanted the job done, but I didn't understand why. I didn't know the stakes, didn't understand what I stood to lose.

Xin braked hard, lashing me out of my thoughts.

I barely caught myself from toppling headfirst into the windshield. Ahead, an eighteen-wheeler lay on its side, its head curled into the median and its ass blocking half of the Interstate, splayed out like a sleeping cat. The semi's rear turret was shredded, the cow-catcher banged up and twisted into bad art. Gathered around the cab was a cluster of red bears—dead, from the look of them—ripping the skin from the rig. In unison, the bears looked up from their work.

Some people call dead eyes dull, but I've never understood that. You look the dead in the eyes, you see the judgment.

When guides and truckers get together to drink, you hear talk of road churches that worship the red bears. We're not a very spiritual lot, but I believe it. Sometimes you got to pray to the thing that scares you. And if you ain't scared of a twelve-foot, three-thousand-pound monster bred to consume as much flesh as possible, you're already underground. The companies engineered the red bears to clear the forests of the dead, and on paper, it still sounds like a good idea: Carnivorous cyborg weapons, carrion-eaters with titanium-reinforced skeletons. They were supposed to be uninfectable, a walking immune system for the world outside.

Problem was, they got infected anyway.

I grabbed P. K.'s shoulder, tried to pull him out of the seat, but he shook me off. Four of the animals broke off from the pack, loping toward us. Xin gripped the wheel, shifted the truck into reverse. The approaching dead split into two groups, flanking us; the ones that stayed behind tore open the cab of the downed rig—

Crack.

The nearest bear lurched to the right as blood sprayed from the side of its head. His face blank, P. K. swung the barrel of the rifle toward the next animal, then frowned slightly when he noticed that the first bear was still coming, its jaw hanging loose and swinging side-to-side as it ran. Xin watched the mirror and held the wheel steady, pushing the truck backward as fast as it would go, but the bears moved faster, hardly slowing as P. K. shot them in the chest, in the head. Finally, the one with the loose jaw stumbled and fell forward, as if it was dizzy or out of breath. At first, I thought P. K. had worn it down, but no: its hind legs had collapsed.

The other three bears were close enough that I could see the meat between their teeth. I leaned into P. K.'s ear, shouted over the gun: "*Shoot them in the legs.*"

He nodded once and concentrated his fire on the space in front of the animals. There was less flesh around the joints where their forelimbs met their paws; red fur and muscle fell away, and bone-alloy gleamed underneath. P. K. didn't waste a shot, but we'd have to reload soon. The tallest bear staggered and hit the pavement, scraped away its snout as it fell.

The last hurled itself forward and hit our hood. The rig shook, but Xin kept it steady. The bear slumped and fell away then lay still on the road. Xin slowed, and we watched the rest of the dead in the distance. There were seven or eight bears circled there, maybe more. They'd already pulled apart the cab of the fallen truck, and now were eating.

"I can turn us around," Xin said quietly. "Get off the last exit, bypass the Interstate for a couple miles."

I wondered about the folks in the middle of that circle. Other truckers. Other guides, maybe. I wondered if I knew them.

"Yeah," I said. "Let's do that."

"I hope they were Christians," P. K. said softly.

We talked about our families. Xin's mother, half out of her mind in a nursing home in Charlotte. She didn't mention her ex-husband and sons. My daughter, grown and living on a Monsanto farm colony in the Pacific, still writing every couple months for money. Xin had heard the story a dozen times before—often enough that she ought to have pegged it for bullshit—but she still watched me with something between warmth and bitterness.

P. K. told us about his father, Joseph. At first, the kid spoke hesitantly, responding to Xin's questions with short, one-word answers, but finally he relaxed into his story, seeming to surprise himself with the pleasure of the telling.

Joseph hadn't always harrowed souls in the wilderness. As a young man of the Lynchburg Watch, he'd walked the walls and killed the dead. Joseph had mumbled his prayers since he was a boy, the town being what it was, but he didn't find religion until a circuit rider passed through in the summer of his twentieth year. He'd only recently become a father, and the death he'd dealt out weighed on him with new urgency, even if it was only the long-rotted he'd sent to their final repose. The circuit rider preached that the souls of the dead still resided in those wasted bodies, that for all their hunger and decay, they could always receive or reject the love of Christ. He preached that the living death was an opportunity, a flesh limbo, and that it was the duty of all Christians to speak the gospel to lost souls and offer them salvation. Just as Christ had descended to Hell to harrow pagan souls, the faithful were bound to travel the wilderness and minister to the dead.

Joseph found his calling. He rode with the circuit man for three years, preaching in the walled cities and preaching to the dead outside, returning now and then to Lynchburg to give his wife and son the money he'd collected from churches throughout the South. When P. K. was seven, Joseph came home to find his wife lost to pneumonia, his son motherless and afraid. For almost a year, Joseph gave up the circuit and raised the boy, working the wall as he'd done before, now hollering salvation as he delivered bullets into creeping bodies.

It was on the wall that he had his Revelation. As he fired his rifle at a cluster of dead in army camouflage, an angel of the Lord seized his tongue and set it ablaze with the language Enoch knew, the words spoken in the Kingdom of Heaven. The dead paused to hear his ministry, and he saw the light of Christ in their eyes. He killed them all immediately, before they could move or doubt. He was ecstatic.

His fervor restored, Joseph resolved to return to the wilderness, this time with his son. P. K. was already a fine shot, a junior watchman. The circuit rider had traveled in an armored truck, declaiming over loudspeakers, but Joseph now understood that glass and metal separated him from the souls he meant to save; he bought two horses and taught P. K. to ride.

"Wait," I said. "You rode *horses*? Out here?"

P. K. shrugged. "They're fast."

"You're fucking with me now."

"No, sir."

I glanced aside at Xin. She focused on the road, negotiating the sharp, mountainside S-curves of Cherokee North. We had to drive at a crawl, but P. K. said we weren't far from the last place he'd seen Joseph.

"How do you survive something like those bears?"

He smiled tightly. "I got lucky last night. But the dead stand aside for my father. He preaches as he rides."

They stand aside, I thought. *Of course.*

"What happened next?" said Xin. "He taught you?"

P. K. seemed reluctant. "That's all there is to tell. He taught me to ride, and we rode. We visited churches often enough to keep food in our stomachs, but his heart was never much in ministering to the living. We spent more and more time in the wild, released thousands of souls to the Lord. Father's done his best to teach me the tongue of Heaven, but I lack . . . " He trailed off, stared out the window. "The Revelation," he finished quietly.

The tires whined as the road wound back around on itself, almost a three-hundred-sixty degree turn. I gritted my teeth, tried not to see the sheer drop to my left or the rock face to my right. P. K. leaned forward, pointed at a graffiti symbol on the rock. "I recognize—"

Something hit the side of the truck. Hard, on the right side.

We screeched toward the side of the road, mangled the guard-rail. "The *hell*—" Xin shouted. I swung behind P. K.'s seat, pulled on the safety straps and curled into a ball. There was another deep, metal-rending crash, and another, and then the world rolled and blurred. A rank, cloudy explosion as the airbags deployed and then gravity fell out from underneath me, snapped back in brief, vicious cracks against my knees and elbows. I covered my head the best I could, but suddenly it felt *hot*, and then everything was heavy and dark.

Metal ground against metal, keening.

"Wake," shouted Xin, "the fuck up."

Two gunshots. I took a breath like a knife to the chest, opened my eyes. The cab was pillowy and white. Almost heavenly, except for the bent metal and bloodstains. There was a sour stench, piss mixed with sulfur. My feed burned. I moved my fingers, feet, blinked blood out of my eyes. Felt like maybe I'd bruised a rib, but I could sit up, breathe. Limbs intact. Head was wet, but it was a shallow gash.

Xin stood over me, covered in white powder from the airbags. A pleasant, middle-aged phantom with a Desert Eagle. There was a wide hole in the back of the rig. Jeans and soda and high heels, all strewn around like Christmas in the Asheville Mall, not that I'd ever had the yuan or self-loathing to step in there. Three dead men in faded orange jumpsuits peered inside the truck, eager in the instant before Xin shot them down.

"You good?" she asked.

"Golden. P. K.?"

"Up top." She gestured toward the roof with her head. "Looks like they hit us with rocks."

I unbuckled the safety straps, stood up shakily. Almost fell, but steadied myself against the driver's seat.

"Kid have a gun?" I asked, fumbling for my holster.

"He's got the rifle."

"So why isn't he shooting?"

Xin bit her lip. I flicked off the safety on my Colt, and we pressed our way to the back, kicking aside boxes of designer boots, finally stepping outside. It looked like Xin had killed the last of the orange-suited dead: there was nothing but breeze and the glare of afternoon light. The truck was caught between two large trees; we hadn't rolled all the way to the bottom, maybe hadn't rolled that far at all, which meant we were still on a sharp slope.

Also, P. K. wasn't up top.

I ripped the handset from my belt. Prayed it wasn't broken.

"Where the hell are you?" I hissed.

There was a long silence. I wondered what Coroner would do if I lost the boy. Lost the *money*. "Down the hill a bit," P. K. answered at last, his voice crackling on the handset. "To the east. You can probably still see me."

And there he was, through the trees: A dot.

"I already sent the SOS," Xin said, leaning into my handset. "Company's coming. Maybe thirty minutes. We just got to wait here."

P. K. said, "My old man's close. I can find him in half an hour."

"Wait here for the rescue," Xin said. "We'll all go out and look for him."

He gave a sad little laugh. "The company's not going to send out a search party. You know that. All they care about is their cargo and whatever they can salvage from the truck. My father's less than meaningless to anyone but me."

Well, I wanted to say, *he is dead*. Instead, I started down the hill.

"Slow down," I said. "I'm coming with you."

"What?" said Xin.

I took my thumb off the handset.

"Kid can't die," I said, wondering how much honesty I could afford.

"You mean you need the money."

I held on to a low tree limb with my free hand. Moved ahead, grabbed hold of another tree, all the while trying not to slip on leaves or trip on roots.

"Jesus, Ez." Xin was flushed, agitated. She took a step forward, not following me so much as making sure I could hear her. "We *all* need the money. But it's no goddamned good if you're dead."

"Not true. Boy owes me a pile if I die."

"Yeah? What if you both get eaten?"

"That'll be complicated. May have to hire an accountant."

"I save your life and you're going to leave me alone. All those times we rode together, you're going to leave me alone."

I forced myself to keep walking, to fix my eyes on the kid. "You know guilt don't work on me, Xin. Lock yourself in the crawlspace. Pour a few shots, drink to our health, and don't let the rescue team leave without us." I stepped over another corpse in an orange jumpsuit, pale and gaunt and forest-scratched, its face little more than a skull beneath skin. These were the desperate dead, the old and ravenous. The fatter, younger, brighter ones favored the night, when the sun wouldn't rot muscle from their bones.

"Ez," said Xin. "The boy's lying."

I stopped.

"I don't know what's truth and what's lies," she said. "But I seen him before. Back home, at the New French. Playing cards and throwing back shots." She

lowered her voice, spoke in a high-speed hiss. "That no-ma'am-I-don't-drink
business was horseshit, and I reckon he's been in Asheville a lot longer than a
night. I don't know what his game is here, but I don't feel like dying for a lie
today. Just stay back. If the kid gets himself killed, well, we lose a little money.
We'll have another job tomorrow."

Was *she* telling the truth? Or just trying to keep me from getting myself
killed? As long as Coroner was knocking on my door, it didn't really matter.

"Tomorrow's too late," I said.

She shook her head and stepped back. She said, "You stupid asshole."

I worked my way down.

P. K. waited in a hollow where the ground flattened out. There was a creek
nearby, invisible but mumbling. He forced a smile, cradled the M-16. His
clothes were sweat-soaked, weighted down with ammunition. The air smelled
smogless and new. Like God had just invented it and still thought it was good.

"You ain't a tourist," I said.

He shrugged a shoulder, then turned away and raised his rifle toward the
trees. Skipped over a rocky outcrop and made toward the sound of the creek. "I
told you. I've spent every day outside for as long as I can remember. We should
keep our mouths shut."

Ordinarily I'd have welcomed the caution. There was a certain flavor of
tourist who hooted his glee every time he pulled a trigger, or almost pulled a
trigger, or thought about pulling triggers. But silence seemed ridiculous now,
and I didn't appreciate the boy hushing me. "We're the only game in town, kid.
Every corpse for miles around already knows we're here."

He gave another half-shrug.

The creek was low enough that we didn't bother walking on stones. Tadpoles
flitted around our boots. On the other side, we started moving uphill again.
The leaves here were shot through with streaks of red, as if we'd stumbled our
way deep into autumn.

"You're a hell of a good son," I said. "Boy your age usually wants to strangle
his daddy."

He looked back. "Did you strangle yours?"

"Never knew him. But I wanted to." I paused. "Strangle him, I mean."

He chewed that over a while. "Where did you grow up?"

"Richmond."

"Never heard of it."

"That's because it ain't there anymore."

The flutter of birds overhead. You could depend on birds. They died and stayed dead. Twigs snapped underfoot. The climb sharpened.

"I have to be honest with you," he said.

"Okay."

"Sometimes, I think I'm not a good enough person."

"I know *I'm* not."

"I mean to speak the tongue. The angels' language."

"Are you an angel?"

"No."

"There you go."

P. K. pursed his lips, looked like he wanted to say something. Instead, he pointed up. I followed the line of his finger to the purpling sky ahead and the silhouette of an old fire tower. When clients wanted to hunt, I took them to towers like that. Tall, ancient, sturdy. Dead folks are slow climbers.

"That's where he'll be," said the boy. "I should warn you—"

I raised my hand to cut him off. Listened.

"Do you hear that?" I whispered.

The strongest argument against talking when you're outside is that your voice masks important warnings. Like the sound of feet against dirt, running.

We sprinted up the hill. P. K. scanned the woods ahead, his rifle following his eyes, and I glanced back over my shoulder. My lungs felt like someone had balled them up, pissed on them, and stapled them into my ribcage, but I pushed on, legs dragging underneath me. My feed was hot with its broadcast of *I am alive, I am still alive, I will pay my debts*, and a tendril of shame shot through the middle of my fear, because this was the only reason anyone cared that I was alive, to earn and owe money. We made it halfway to the tower before I saw our pursuers, and realized I'd been wrong about the sound.

It wasn't just feet against the dirt.

There were also paws.

The wolves were ragged, skeletal things, ribs half-exposed beneath gray and white fur. They wove like steel needles through the trees. A man and a woman trailed the wolves, wearing tattered green uniforms. I fired at the closest animal. Missed.

"Behind us," I rasped.

P. K. twisted around as he ran, took aim, tore the front legs off the wolf I'd missed. I couldn't tell how many were left—they ducked in and out of sight, gray-green blurs, faces of the forest. One appeared a body's length from P. K.'s left side; I got it in the head, almost fell over the body as it crumpled. Caught my footing and squeezed off a shot at the man in green.

The dead didn't breathe, didn't growl or hiss or groan. They watched and lunged and snapped, silent. Eyes flashed ahead. They flanked us with a kind of brutal grace, closing from every side with each footfall, and I had one of those idiot epiphanies that seem profound when you're dizzy with adrenaline and about to be eaten: *It's like they're dancing.* Every lunge in concert, every bite. We were going to die because the dead were dancers.

The kid stopped.

I was running too fast, too close behind him. We hit the dirt. Someone shouted, but I didn't understand the words. I smelled rotted meat. I tried to stand but my legs were tangled; someone was still shouting. My shoulder throbbed. Each breath was a suckerpunch. I gripped the Colt, braced for the bite, and someone was still shouting. I looked up.

The dead all stared at the man in black.

He was tall, pale. He wore a day's gray-brown stubble and his eyes were hidden by the shadow of his wide-brimmed hat. His voice was hoarse but commanding as hunger—every nonsense syllable he shouted was a slap, a crack, all thunder and hard edges. The dead folks slumped as he spoke, cowed or subdued or enraptured. The wolves pawed the dirt, uncertain, saliva dripping from their mouths, their eyes never leaving the preacher. Joseph took off his hat and stared down at his son, his blue eyes blunt, and then he spoke English instead of the babble of Heaven.

"Go on and shoot 'em," he said. "My throat hurts like a bitch."

When I first came to Asheville, I'd lived for six months with an ex-Pentecostal poet from the mountain collectives south of Blacksburg. Once, after a night of smoke and sweat and Blackjack, she'd given me slurred lessons in glossolalia, giggling as she coached me on tongues. There were, she said, patterns in the babble. Sounds that looped and recurred. Subtle cadences. The language of Heaven was poetry without meaning, empty words taking shapes.

There was an art to it.

Silently, I wrapped my tongue around the syllables of Joseph's sermon. *Nalumasakala, sayamawath,* shit like that. Kidsounds, but they'd tamed the dead. The man had reached out with his tongue and *controlled* them. I tried to memorize his rhythms and words that weren't words. I wanted to beg him to preach again.

Joseph wasn't lost. He wasn't stranded or waiting for saviors. He was at home, at ease.

There was a reinforced steel stable at the base of the tower—a horse grunted inside. After we killed the last of the dead, Joseph lit a cigarette and gestured to a rope ladder. Invited us up for coffee. "I ain't got much to offer," he said, "but I can boil you some beans."

P. K. didn't move. "You need to come with us," he said, terse and low. "Rescue's coming soon, but we have to meet them on the other side of the creek."

"Already told you. I ain't going nowhere."

P. K. gripped his rifle. "Father. You can't live out here."

Joseph snorted. "Missed you too, Christopher. How you like the city? You going to introduce me to your friend?"

"He's a tour guide. He's here to help. You're sick. We want to help you."

Christopher. The kid glanced at me, frowned.

"My name's Ezekiel," I said. Held out my hand. He eyed me carefully, then shook it.

"You from around here?" he asked.

"No, sir. Richmond."

He grimaced, exhaled smoke. "You had people there?"

My joke, my family. "I did."

"I passed through, once. Few months after Christopher left." He flicked ash into the dirt. "You see that place, you have a hard time looking the Lord in the eye."

I didn't know what to say. I said, "Yes, sir."

"Father," Christopher pressed. "You need to come with us now."

Joseph shook his head. "It's good to see you, son. I'm happy to drink a cup of coffee with you, and you can tell me what it is you really want. Grace Baptist took up a collection last month—you need money, we can talk. But I ain't going to live inside of walls for you." He turned around, started to walk back to his ladder.

And P. K.—Christopher—hit him in the head with the butt of his rifle.

The preacher crumpled.

My instinct was to reach for the Colt, but I balled my fist and stood very still. Christopher kneeled and fumbled in his father's jacket, withdrew a ring of keys.

"He doesn't want to leave the wilderness anymore," he said. "He's senile. He needs saving. If you want to help him, the best thing you can do is help me get him on the horse."

You could smell the bullshit in every word. I watched him as he searched through his daddy's keys, and I remembered Xin's story about the New French. I remembered that the minder told me to bring back the old man, and a nasty hunch worked itself out in my head. I would have shaken my head in grudging admiration, but no one had told me, and that left me scratching the nub in the back of my neck. Feeling the dim heat of my feed, the constant heat of debt and return. Coroner had sent me into this blind, and now I was stuck, choiceless. Why had he chosen me? Because I was dependable? Or because he thought I was stupid, expendable?

Finish the job and you'll be fine.

"Okay," I said slowly. "I'll get this arm, we'll hold him up together."

We pulled his father to his feet, draped his arms over our shoulders and carried him to the stable. Christopher unlocked the steel door, and we hauled Joseph inside. The place was cramped and thick with shit-stink. Bars of light slanted through the grates, and the ground was covered with hay. The horse huffed, stepped back. It was gaunt, its fur as black as Joseph's coat. I couldn't remember the last time I'd seen such a large animal alive. Rodents tended to stay dead, but most mammals bigger than cats were liable to come back. You didn't see them much in the cities.

The horse was calm; it let us push Joseph onto its back without much fuss. We swung the preacher around by his legs so that he was sitting more or less upright, his head hanging forward. Christopher climbed onto the horse, inclined his head to me. "Thank you," he said.

Then he shot me in the chest.

The blast knocked me into the dirt. Even with the armor under my coat, it felt like someone had jackhammered the breath out of me, and I fought to suck down air. Christopher's horse charged into the woods, and for a beautiful, adrenaline-soaked moment, I stopped worrying about money and consequences and Coroner. I raised the Colt, fired.

The first shot missed. The second hit its mark, and the boy toppled from the horse. The animal panicked, reared back, and knocked off the preacher, who fell on his side and rolled.

I winced and climbed to my feet. Staggered outside in time to see the kid duck behind a tree, weaving and heavy-breathing but alive, the M-16 in hand. I pulled the trigger again, splintered bark, took cover behind a fallen trunk.

It looked an awful lot like Coroner had bought the kid Californian armor, too.

"So," I called, "You want to sell your old man?"

Christopher coughed. It took me a moment to realize he was laughing. "Is that why you're shooting at me? Because I'm a bad *son*?" His shot grazed bark, burned moss, whistled over my head. "Or do you want to sell him yourself?"

"Didn't plan on it," I said. I slid down the length of the log, listened for footsteps or tells. "I just make a point of shooting folks who shoot me."

He was silent.

"I want to know if I got this right," I shouted. I willed him to make a move while I talked, willed him to peer out and try to find me. "You were sick of it, weren't you? The preaching. The wilderness. You were sick of it, and you were sane, and you wanted to go live with the living, so you ran off to the city and got caught up in cards and whiskey. Do I have it right so far?"

Wind in the leaves. The snap of a reloaded magazine. I focused on the snap, raised the barrel of the Colt over the log.

"You play the tables long enough in the New French, you start owing money around town. Which, in the end, really just means you owe Coroner. I bet it wasn't long before Coroner came calling, and you started to wonder what you could give him to get him off your back. Then you remembered your daddy, and it all—"

He cut me off with a thundercrack. I fired twice over the log.

The Colt clicked.

Christopher must have heard it. He coughed and fired into the dead tree, tearing through moss and bark and wood as if he were hacking with a machete, moving closer and coughing and ripping apart the air—

And then he stopped.

There was a *snap*, and the woods fell silent.

I peered over the log.

She held him like a lover. His head hung limp, twisted. Her forearm was mangled, her mouth bloodstained. She was still covered in the powder from the airbag. Three dead rescue workers in camouflage armor staggered through the trees behind her.

I gave up, then.

Those armor suits, so bulky and futile. Xin Sun with blood in her mouth. Everyone was dead. No one was coming for me. And even if I found my way home, Coroner would be waiting.

Xin pressed her lips against the dead boy's throat. At first, it looked like a kiss. And then it didn't. She opened the artery, ripped away muscle. Her eyes flicked to the side and met mine; she seemed torn between finishing her meal and moving on to me. The boy's blood ran down the front of her shirt. The rescue crew's legs were all bent into painful angles—maybe they'd wrecked—but they still hitched toward us, inch by inch.

"You were right," I said softly. "I'm a stupid asshole."

She watched me, shifted her weight. You look the dead in the eyes, you see the judgment.

"I can't go back to the city. Don't know why I'd go back, anyway. I ain't got no family, no daughter in California. All I got is a landlord and some funerals I ain't paid for."

The rescuers were close now. I opened my fingers, dropped the Colt.

"I don't want to be owned," I said. "I don't want to owe nobody no more. I been stuck a long time."

She was silent. I tried to relax. Tried not to feel the blood drum in my neck, my chest. The air tasted good—I was glad to die outside. It was the best I could hope for, going out where I could see the birds. There was a kind of relief in it, a lightness. *This is how it's going to be.* Feet scuffed the dirt, one step and then another.

"Go on, Xin," I said.

She jerked backward with a *thwip.*

Xin and Christopher fell, tangled together. Before they hit the dirt, the rescue workers' heads shattered in a spray of bone and blood. I spun around, followed the sound of silenced shots. The preacher stood at the base of his tower with a pistol in each hand, his guns raised toward me and the dead, his face empty as an abandoned city.

We burned the bodies in silence. Joseph stood too close to Christopher's pyre, head bowed and lips moving wordlessly. The sun was almost down. I held one of his pistols and watched the woods. Far as I could tell, the preacher didn't know what his son had planned to do. I wasn't going to tell him. I didn't have anything more to say to Xin, and I felt guilty for it. Still, I stood by her pyre, clinging quietly to my only friend at a lonely party.

When the preacher finished his prayers, we climbed the tower and watched the fires burn down. He made bitter coffee, and we drank it slowly as the stars came out, denser and brighter than I'd seen in years. When Joseph spoke, his voice was hoarse and flat.

"You still want to try to take me back to your city?"

I reckoned I could do it. Carry him to Coroner. My debt might not be paid, but the boss would be off my back for another day. He'd have something priceless, something that no thuglord or company—not even the few who could fly over oceans—could buy: words that could hold the dead at bay. Joseph might not cooperate, but Coroner knew how to make a man talk. He'd learn the loops and rhythms, put poets on his payroll, try to vivisect the tongue of Heaven. He'd try to figure out what other things those words could make the dead do.

I swallowed my coffee. "No, sir."

The old man nodded, then unsheathed his knife.

"You were blessing her," he said.

I watched the knife's tip, tried to work out the right answer. He took my silence for confusion.

"The woman. You were blessing her."

The pyre coals glowed below, a constellation of deaths.

"Her name was Xin Sun," I said. "She was the nearest thing to family that I had." I looked up from the knife and met his eyes, willing him to believe me. "I don't know how to save a soul, but I would have liked to have saved hers."

There was nothing about Xin's soul that needed saving. I hoped she would have forgiven the lie. Joseph leaned on the rail and toyed with his knife, moonlight glinting on the blade. My palms were sweaty, my throat tight with unasked questions. I wasn't used to wanting something like this. Wanting to walk in the wilderness, outside of walls. Wanting to ride the roads and forests, far from companies and criminals, free from Coroner and the machinery of obligation. I'd never believed that kind of life was possible, and now I was drunk on the fantasy.

"If you want me to teach you," Joseph said at last, "I'm gonna have to cut out your feed."

I touched the warm nub on my neck and bit back a smile.

Mark of the Devil.

Already, I could feel it. The sting of alcohol. Metal on skin, the knife's edge like nightbreeze. Blood. One drop, and then a trickle. The cut, the last hum of the feed running my numbers.

And then a release, when it tells the world that I'm a dead man.

Resurgam

Lisa Mannetti

"You can't buy human flesh and blood in this country, sir, not alive, you can't," says Wegg, shaking his head. "Then query, bone?"
—*Our Mutual Friend,* Charles Dickens

For most of the nineteenth century, anatomy professors and students could secure bodies only on surreptitious nocturnal visits to a church cemetery or, more likely, a potters field.
—*Dissection*, John Harley Warner and James M. Edmonson

It had happened before and Auden Strothers knew it. So now on an uncharacteristically snowy March night he was in Yale's Cushing Whitney medical library looking for answers that stubbornly evaded him.

This morning at approximately 2:00 a.m. the cadaver (nicknamed Molly until today) he shared with three other fledgling doctors suddenly sat up, hemostats clinging to her open mid-section like long silver leeches, widened her jaws and took a chunk out of Sheri Trent's right shoulder.

Sheri hissed—as much from surprise as pain, Auden guessed—and clamped her left hand against the wound. Auden's own breathing became rapid behind his paper mask, and he found himself staring at the blood that seeped between the fingers of his teammate's pale yellowish latex glove. Sheri's gaze followed his and, for a second (a second too goddamn long, Auden thought), she watched the blood that dripped from her glove and pattered on to the naked woman's waxy thighs.

"Christ, I'm bitten. She bit me!"

At the same time Auden's mind declared: *You've gone crazy! I told you a thousand times to stay the hell away from Gronsky's stupid meth lab* . . . his right hand which held the scalpel that had been so recently and delicately buried inside Molly's exposed liver came up and plunged the knife straight into the corpse's nearest eye.

There was a soft, drawn-out *pffft*—as if he'd let the air out of a mostly deflated party balloon—and Molly collapsed backward against the steel table. *God, they'd only recently unwrapped the woman's head and face (the better to preserve her, my dear) and now he'd absolutely ruined her eye and their other teammates—not to mention Professor Sriskandarajah—were going to have a fit—*

"Help me, Strothers—what should I do?" Sheri pivoted her wrist and peeled her cupped hand back from the wound a few times tentatively, wielding the lunate and scaphoid bones at the bottom of her palm like a hinge.

The bite was a ragged open mouth at the juncture where the fleshy part of her upper arm began. He blinked under the glare of the brilliant overheads and automatically recited as if his professor called on him to evaluate the case and answer up quickly: "Size 4-0 absorbable suture . . . "

"What the *fuck* is wrong with you?" she said. "I'm bleeding!"

Ordinarily on a Thursday night, even this late, there'd be five or six students bent over the semi-flayed bodies on the metal slabs, but the spring holidays were coming and they were the only ones in the dissecting room. Trent was as much a grind as he was.

She couldn't go to the university clinic or the emergency room or the local doc in the box—that much was clear—because how could she explain who had bitten her? The medicos would want to know whose teeth sank into her flesh, would want to set police officers on the trail of the perpetrator. She could use a mirror and stitch herself—awkward, of course, utilizing just the one, left hand—but not impossible.

Sheri started toward him, moving out from her side of the table.

But all Auden Strothers could think about was how the first day his hands probed and dived inside Molly, the skin beneath his gloves had gone numb from contact with the eight gallons of formaldehyde that had been pumped into her—that had been unsettling and nasty—and now Sherri Trent expected him to risk . . . *infection.*

He shot out from the aisle created by the tables, intent on hustling his skinny ass through the nearest door at the rear of the lab.

Still holding her hand against the wound, Sheri closed in on him. Even then Auden realized she might want no more than a brief comforting touch, a friend and colleague's hand laid gently on her good shoulder, but the combination of the crystal he'd snorted two hours earlier and the spectacle of the uprising cadaver rocketed his mind to panic. He meant only to fend her off with out thrust elbows (less chance of contagion, he gibbered inwardly). Instead, he got his back into it and, with his arms extended and his palms upraised, gave her chest a hard shove: Sheri crashed against Team 22's table which lay perpendicular to their own.

Maybe someone on that team planned to come back after a break but fell asleep over a textbook in the lounge, or a Red Bull in the cafeteria; or maybe Sheri Trent had unzipped the black body bag halfway to get a look at her competitors' handiwork. Arms flailing, her hands skittered wetly under the rectangular skin flaps tessellating the corpse's chest and pushed them back like doors on a bulkhead. Auden caught a brief glimpse of both the layer of bright yellow fat and the reddish striated muscle that reminded him of very old skirt steak.

"Strothers!" She sounded shocked and disappointed more than physically hurt.

A few drops of Sheri's blood—no more than a scattering, really—flicked onto the cadaver's pallid torso and blatted against the heavy plastic. The noise seemed preternaturally loud to Auden. He saw the corpse's feet twitch inside the bag.

The last thought he had before he fled the room stripping off his gloves and cramming them into his lab coat pocket was that Team 22's cadaver had been tagged with a blue cloth—which meant the family, if there was any family, didn't want the remains. Instead, when the first year medical students were finished with it, the body would go into a common grave.

Auden sat at one of the heavy wooden reading tables in Cushing Whitney, one hand resting on the opened pages of the nineteenth century facsimile text before him, absently mulling over which disease or condition might hold the key he so desperately needed now. Cholera? Tuberculosis—known as consumption for hundreds of years prior to the twentieth century? Glanders? Leprosy? No, none of them had the right feel; he had no sense of that click he experienced that was part frisson, part lightning-shot inspiration that told him he was dead on. But there had to be something that would help him understand the seemingly spontaneous resurrection of the dead, because he was certain it wasn't a new phenomenon.

He looked past the shaded table lamp, his gaze wandering from the tall arched windows that framed pelting snow, the elegant mahogany paneling, the balcony with its tiered ranks of books, to the canopy-shaped ceiling two stories overhead.

After he'd fled the lab last night leaving Sheri Trent bleeding he'd gone back to his tiny apartment in North Haven, snorted two thick lines of meth, then decided what he really needed was sleep. He rummaged the medicine cabinet and came up with three Percocet—the remains of a battle with an aching molar last summer.

He stayed away from the lab all day, but he'd come to the medical library after darkfall to try and puzzle his way through what precisely had happened to the cadaver inked with identification number C 390160 and what might happen to Sheri Trent.

He'd pored over incunabula, drawings, and historic pamphlets; he'd downloaded digital images and manuscripts. After three frustrating hours and two more lines of meth he snuffled quietly and surreptitiously in the maze of stacks, it occurred to him to hunt through the library's journal resources.

Journals, he knew, could often be highly personal documents . . .

Auden scavenged both printed and online materials for a long time; the library would be closing soon, but he wasn't overly worried—even if Yale had increased security since that kid at NYU suicided the previous November when he clambered up and over Plexiglas shields and plummeted ten stories to the floor of the atrium.

All the grinds had ways and means to access the lab or the library after hours and to hide out from patrolling guards.

It was getting on for 1:00 a.m.—nearly twenty-four hours since the Sheri Trent disaster—and he was about to give up. He toked vapor from a black, electronic cigarette, and the thought crossed his mind that it was ironic that the library addition had been built in the classic Y-shape of an autopsy incision.

Auden fingered the thin leaves of the journal (not an original, but a bound reproduction, he thought) written by a nineteenth century medical student named John Sykes. Glancing at the neatly lettered pages, it occurred to him that the whole thing might be a fabrication . . . dissection humor concocted to amuse fraternity brothers during long winter nights. On the other hand, as he thumbed and scanned and read—not passively, but with verve—his own excitement grew.

Maybe the nicotine jolted the precise synapses he needed to make the mental connections, or maybe it was the result of his hours-long research, or pure dumb luck on a snowy March night; maybe Sykes' journal *was* nothing more than a series of monstrous notations by a man hoping to write a harrowing novel someday.

Whatever it was, it didn't matter; because Auden Strothers realized he'd just found exactly what he needed.

February 26th, 1873

Until tonight I thought I was inured to providing the college with medical specimens. . . . I'd even overcome the resentment I felt about being a "scholarship boy." The sons of Dunham, Wister, Parkerton—those giants of commerce and industry—aren't expected to grub in dirt or hacksaw through metal and marble to produce cadavers the future doctors desperately need to perfect skills they'll use when they treat their patients. Strictly speaking it's not illegal; the law looks the other way in hopes that one of us, or our counterparts here or across the pond, or in Europe will save his life down the line. Books are nothing to bodies.

Each time we go out, we meet by pre-arrangement in front of the lecture hall and shuffle our feet in nervous anticipation and blow on our hands to ward off the chill while Dr. Perry stands on the steps of the lecture hall and gives a little pep talk—part lecture, part plea, part innuendo. "Men," he says, "our duty—unpleasant as it may be—is of the utmost importance. Never forget that for an instant."

Twice the professor slipped up during his standard speech; once last autumn he accidentally inserted the phrase "of gravest importance," and a second time, around the Christmas holidays when brandy-toddies and rum-shrub were abundant, he made reference to "the task that lies ahead." Only a second year student we call "Cruncher" laughed out loud—he was overly familiar with digging down over the head and yanking out a corpse cranium-first.

But tonight's task was supposed to be simpler. After all, the ground is still frozen hard in New England, so we were going to nearby Blue Haven to raid a "receiving vault," where they stack up the dead until the spring thaw permits gravediggers to shovel deeply into the thin stony soil.

There were just four of us and—*quelle luxe*—Dr. Perry brought along his own Miller landau for us to ride in and collect the bodies we'd carry back, instead of sending us off to the dark, wide-scattered cemeteries in groups of two and three.

I was glad for once that more of my fellow resurrection men had not shown up. It's only now that I'm writing these pages that I wonder if they knew what was afoot or if their intuition—or some yet unknown, unmapped sense, or even angel guardians—warned them.

We were seated inside the coach; Perry was upfront alongside his driver. Cruncher sat facing me. "Here, Sykes. You look like you could use a bolt." He extended a flask, and more for the sake of politeness than anything else, I took a swig.

"Have another and pass it around." He nodded toward Freddie O'Rourke and Tom Winterbourne who were both first year students and had only been on one or two other midnight raids. "There's wild work ahead, laddies."

Winterbourne looked uncomfortable and shifted in his seat.

"I've got armlets, you bet," O'Rourke said, "and they're vulcanized, to boot."

Cruncher tilted his head back against the upholstery and laughed. "You're going to need more than a couple of rubber sleeves to grope amongst this lot," he said. "And more than those flimsy cotton butcher aprons Perry's toted along."

The carriage lights were swaying as the horses jigged along and Cruncher studied my face. "Sykes doesn't know."

"Sykes doesn't know what," I said.

"Liked it better when to work off your scholarship, you only had to wait tables or sweep out the lab or set out the gear for the rich boys, Sykes?"

"You're drunk, Cruncher." I turned away. It had been bad when I had to don black tie and serve meals, or clean up blood and vomit in the lab, or lay out everything from yachting togs to surgical notes for the sons of senators and kingmakers. I had actually begged the professor for some job, *any* job where—away from the tonier crowd—I thought it would be easier for me to maintain my dignity, my sense of self.

"Fourth year students—even those with straight A's who have to unbury the dead—think they know everything."

"I know you're an ass, and for the moment, that's enough for me," I said under my breath.

He passed the flask to O'Rourke who drank and handed it to Winterbourne.

"Maybe you imagine you'll be in practice some day," Cruncher said. " 'Mrs. Smythe, it seems poor little Teddy has contracted influ*enza*,' " he said in a stricken voice; then paused. "Only you *won't* be treating the swells on Park Avenue like the rest of your class, *you'll* be seeing a bunch of immigrants and rotters and drunks and ignorant women who haven't gotten their monthlies and are shocked to learn they're expecting another 'blessed event' for the seventh time."

I didn't say a word; there wasn't any point to arguing with Cruncher. He wasn't on scholarship, but it was clear he drank too much and there were rumors he was well-acquainted with opium dens in the city. He wasn't like the swells, but his family had money. He must have wanted to get his medical degree or please a demanding father: why else would he be out after midnight scrabbling in cemeteries?

"No answer, eh, Sykes? Well, here's one for you. Show 'im, Tommy."

Winterbourne reached inside his coat and pulled out a folded sheet of paper and handed it to me.

There wasn't enough light to read it carefully, but it didn't matter because I knew the page from the communicable diseases text book very well:

> **Small pox** *(variola, qv.) Causative organism, not definitely known. More common during the colder seasons. No age exempt. May occur in utero. No preference as to sex. Acquired chiefly by direct contact with patient. Symptoms: Onset abrupt with chills. Headache (usually frontal), intense lumbar pains, elevation of temperature which may rise to 104 or higher, nausea, or more frequently, vomiting. Fever remains high until evening of 3rd or morning of 4th day, when it falls sharply, often to normal.*
>
> *With the drop in temperature, the eruption makes its appearance, coming out as a rule about the face, and soon afterward on extremities and to a lesser extent, the trunk. These lesions pass through a series of well-documented phases: macules, papules (which are raised and filled with fluid), vesicles, pustules (which feel to the touch as if bird shot pellets have been embedded under the skin) and finally, crusts.*
>
> *About the 2nd day of eruption, the macules become papular (raised and filled with fluid) which increase in size and become vesicles. The vesicles increase in size and from the 7th to 8th day well-developed pustules are present, having the appearance of drop-seated or inverted areolae. In some cases, the blisters overlap and merge almost entirely producing a confluent rash, which detaches the outer layer of skin from the flesh beneath it and renders the sufferer more likely to succumb to death. From the 8th to the 11th day, desiccation occurs and by the end of the 21st day, scabs have formed over the lesions and flaked off, leaving permanent, pitted etiolated scars if the patient survives.*
>
> *There is no disease so repulsive, so dirty, so foul smelling, so hard to manage, so infectious as smallpox may be and is . . .*

I felt my face blanch and I suddenly felt light-headed.

"Ho, Winterbourne, hand over the flask. Feeling a trifle peaked, Sykes?"

I was livid all right—with rage. But I made myself sound calm: "The joke's over. How much are you paying them for this little stunt, Crunch—?"

"The name's Van Dyson, Sykes, and you damn well know it—"

Now he was turning red; he wasn't as drunk as I thought, this time he'd caught my sarcasm.

"—and it's no joke."

In the flicker-glow of the carriage lantern his dark eyes met mine. For a second, I thought they were lit with greed—but it was a peculiar kind of avarice: it had nothing to do with money. He was after something and he wanted it badly, but I suddenly knew it wasn't anything as unimportant as recompense or stipends—we really did come from different worlds. But I wouldn't back down. "And I'm no fool," I said. "The nearest outbreak's in Provincetown—eighty miles from here."

"Ever been in a pest house, Sykes? No, I didn't think so." He groped for the flask and drank, wiping his mouth with his sleeve. "The one in Provincetown is fourteen by fourteen feet. Plenty of room for the stricken *and* the nurse—if they can get one." He smirked.

"And your point is?"

"With less than a third of the population vaccinated, why do you think they build pest houses smaller than gazebos?"

"Well, I hardly—"

"You hardly *what*? You hardly know anything but what you've read in books or heard from fringe academics like *Professor* Perry." He leaned forward. "Let me tell you something. People are so afraid of the pox—so afraid of being isolated like lepers and sent to pest houses to rot and die alone—that their fear helps spread the disease."

"The bodies of the dead are supposed to be *burned*," O'Rourke said. "Jesus and Saint Mary." He crossed himself quickly.

"People have been put to death for burning bodies—except during plague times—but Brunetti of Padua is going to unveil a cremation chamber at the Vienna world exposition this summer, Sykes," Cruncher said. "Not that you've seen the piece in the *New York Times*, I'm sure—considering the cost of the subscription these days."

"Being poor doesn't make people stupid, Van Dyson," I said.

"No, but it can send them to a pest house."

"Are you saying the rich don't get reported?"

Cruncher threw back his head and laughed. "Not only do they fail to be reported when they're alive and raging with smallpox and shedding scabs like noxious red confetti, when they're dead their doctors put down the cause to 'heart disease' or 'paralysis of the diaphragm' or 'puerperal—that is, childbed—fever.'" He nodded toward Winterbourne and O'Rourke. "Dirty, ugly way to die—but not as ugly or dirty as smallpox."

"Of course," Winterbourne said.

"Nor does the ego-bloated mayor of Provincetown want his wife burned like a Salem witch or buried in a common grave or consigned for eternity to Pox Acres—which during the winter is merely a hole in the ground in the pest house cellar and, during the rest of the year, some raggedy ground a few hundred yards north. No, the mayor wants to visit his wife's tombstone after church on Sunday mornings wearing his top hat, and ready to shake the hands of the recently bereaved."

"She died from small pox," I said.

"Yes," Cruncher said. "And as long as you brought up Provincetown, Sykes, you might as well know that only eight names out of twenty-seven of people who had small pox were reported in the newspaper—"

"Enough, Cruncher—"

"—and according to the 1870 census, the average income of *those* eight was $547.50; but the average income of the *other* nineteen was $2,300."

"Christ, I said *shut up!*"

"All of the headstones in pox cemeteries face east. Isn't that curious?"

I started to lunge for him, but O'Rourke threw his arm between us and Winterbourne hissed. "Stop it both of you, right now, we're here."

The landau slowed and out the window I saw the curved stony embrasure of the receiving vault.

Dr. Perry's driver had hitched a small cart-like wagon—long enough to accommodate bodies—to the landau, and now he rolled back the canvas tarp and pulled out tools while the rest of us stood just outside the metal door. Winterbourne twirled a hooded lantern and its single ray sparkled against the gravel drive and played over gleaming saw blades and pry bars.

"Many medical men eschew protection," Perry began while Winterbourne held the light and the driver worked at picking the lock. "In my day, surgeons operated in blood-stiffened frock coats—the stiffer the coat, the more it conveyed the expertise of the practitioner. Some still believe there's no object in being clean, that cleanliness is out of place and they consider it finicky and affected—that pus is as inseparable from surgery as blood. An executioner might as well manicure his nails before chopping off a head," he said. "But we've got gloves and armlets and heavy rubber aprons," he glanced at Cruncher. "And we're going to be very careful. We're only going to take the bodies toward the back of the vault—no one's going to miss them, because no one is going to check very closely. Not with a dozen pox victims stashed in the crypt, too." He paused. The lock clattered onto the gravel and Perry's driver stooped to retrieve it and loop it in the staple of the hasp. "All right, we're in," Perry said.

The Blue Haven receiving vault was built into the side of a steep hill. Its façade was typically ornamental: heavy bronze doors fancied with grille-work and set in bricks that rose above the rounded snow-covered hill like crenellated castle walls.

Inside, the ceiling was arched and the bricks were skim-coated with flaking whitewash, but moss grew on the damp walls and the air was dank. Even in this cold weather, you could detect the subtle scent of decay. Perry tied his handkerchief over his mouth and nose, and the others followed his lead. I was too embarrassed to fumble mine out—it was dotted with tiny holes and its edges were badly frayed.

"Let's be quick, gents. Get the lids pried off and hustle the bodies out to the cart. My man will get the coffins nailed shut again."

Either there'd been a hell of a lot of typical deaths that winter in Blue Haven or small pox was more rampant than anyone who lived in the area had been led to believe: There must have been a hundred caskets. Someone (probably the sexton from St. Bartholomew's parish and his crew of gravediggers) had started off packing the coffins onto the heavy wooden shelves that lined three walls, then given up and crammed them in upright like matchsticks. Indeed, one shelf on the western side of the crypt had collapsed under the weight, and the coffins lay helter-skelter, tipped onto their sides and crowding the narrow space between them and their vertical neighbors.

"Standing room only, eh, Sykes?" Cruncher said.

I inserted my crowbar under the wooden lid of a cheap toe-pincher model and put my weight into it.

"C'mon, you're not seriously mad at me, are you?"

The body fell out and smacked headfirst into the back of another coffin. It sounded like a frozen side of beef being hit with a cook's rolling pin. Cruncher steadied the upright casket, so it wouldn't domino the rest.

"I'll help you carry her out to the wagon," Cruncher said, taking the corpse by the shoulders.

I picked up her feet. She was face down and her long brown hair swung against Cruncher's knees. "She must have been young," I said.

Her skirt hung wire-straight and stiff. It creaked like a sail in an ice storm, and a pair of glass beads she'd been decorated with rattled against the brick floor. Her leather shoes chilled my hands even through my gloves.

"Yes, too young to pin up her hair," Cruncher agreed, looking over his shoulder to navigate the maze of coffins and move us toward one of the lanterns resting on a casket near the door.

The moon was barely visible behind heavy cloud cover. Still there was enough light to see the wagon and swing the dead girl into the pile of corpses.

"Christ, I could feel the crystals of ice melting in her hair where my hands touched," Cruncher said. "Here, warm up. Have some brandy."

When I weighed the flask in my hand and hesitated, he said: "Finish it and don't worry. I've got a bottle stashed under the seat in Perry's hearse."

That made me laugh and I snorted and coughed, spraying brandy onto the bodies.

"Hey, don't waste it on the stiffs—they've already been baptized."

That made me laugh harder and bending over, cough more. Cruncher pounded my back.

"All right now, Sykes?"

"Yes," I said, straightening up and giggle-coughing into my fist.

"Good," he said, and gave my shoulder a light squeeze that had, I thought, all the camaraderie in the world behind it.

"We might as well get a good haul," Perry was saying to Winterbourne and O'Rourke as I re-entered the crypt. "We've got the wagon and I know of another medical institution that will pay good money for any left-overs. If there are any . . . "

"Sure, Professor," Winterbourne said. "As many as you like. Me and Freddie are as strong as oxes."

"Freddie and *I*," Perry automatically corrected. "And it's not *oxes*," he paused, catching sight of me. "Never mind. Oh, Sykes, perhaps you could start opening a few crates on the east side of the vault? Where's Van Dyson got to?"

"Right here, Professor," Cruncher said from behind a coffin near the door. He caught my eye and mimed refilling his flask.

"Excellent. Hard as hell to keep track of things with all these caskets lying chockablock about. Well, I was just saying to young Winterbourne and O'Malley here—"

"O'Rourke, sir." Winterbourne took a step sideways and tromped on Freddie's foot.

"What's that?"

"Nothing, sir," O'Rourke said.

"Good. Please don't interrupt. First year students have that habit and it's a bad one. Never learn a damn thing that way. What was I saying?"

"About the haul, Professor," Cruncher said.

"Yes. You partner up with Sykes and get to work on the caskets on my left here. It's better to take a few from each area—less likely the gravediggers will notice. They won't, anyhow—morons, the lot of them."

We snaked toward the eastern wall.

From across the vault, Perry was saying "Now, even if we pick up too many for our own students, we can always render bodies down to bone. There are medical schools in sore need of skeletons. I can show you how to articulate a specimen. It's quite an art,"

"Yes, Professor," O'Rourke said.

"Like to learn that skill, O'Malley?"

"You bet."

"Good lad, you never know if you'll get through all four years and it's good to have a trade—a lucrative trade—to fall back on . . . "

"Did Perry make you learn how to articulate a skeleton?" Cruncher said in a low voice as we started to pry open the first lid.

"No. What about you?"

"No, but I watched—from a distance—but very closely, so I know how it's done. I guess he figures 'O'Malley' doesn't have much chance making it through the program." He dropped a coffin nail in the pocket of his leather apron.

"Or if he does get a degree, Perry thinks he's only going to treat shanty Irish, anyhow," I said.

"God save the Queen," Cruncher said, winking. "Dyson is strictly English. The Van in my name is from my mother's family." Cruncher tilted the flask and took a long swallow; then he passed the brandy across the coffin to me. I had a drink and handed it back.

"Ready?"

He nodded and we lifted the lid away,

"Aaugh!" I stepped back, pressing my sleeve against my nose and mouth. The stench rising out of the casket was unbelievable.

"Not quite frozen yet," Cruncher said.

I felt myself beginning to retch.

"Here, sit down a minute."

I sat on the cold floor and lowered my chin between my knees.

"Put some of this under your nose."

He handed me a small round tin.

"It's camphor ointment with a little peppermint and lavender." He pulled aside his makeshift mask and I saw it gleaming above his upper lip. "Keeps the reek safely at bay."

"She has the pox," I said.

"No question there; her dancing days are done."

I laughed weakly.

"And for godssake, take this handkerchief and tie it on."

Maybe he saw me blush, or maybe it was because I didn't immediately put my hand out for it when he took it from his pocket. "Go on, use it. I don't give a good goddamn if you don't have a handkerchief, Sykes. You're smart. I like intelligent people."

I smeared on a thick dollop of the waxy cream. *He has magic pockets*, I thought irrationally. *What's next? A white rabbit, a flock of parrots?*

"That's right, cover your mustache hole," he said.

I took the handkerchief—heavy linen—and monogrammed JVD, and began to fold it.

"Thanks, Jerry."

"Don't let the monogram show, a gentleman never does." Above the makeshift mask, his eyes were merry.

"I know," I said, tying it on, then standing up again and looking down at the woman's hideously scarred face. "Terrible. Even her eyelids."

"Maybe her eyes, too. She might have died blind." He leaned over and lifted the scabrous flap of flesh and I saw that the sclera of her right eye had gone red from hemorrhage. He whispered, "Let's take her, Sykes . . . think of what we could learn dissecting her."

I realized that avarice I'd seen in his eyes earlier was for knowledge, even forbidden knowledge. But it didn't stop me from interjecting, "Are you mad?"

He held up his gloved hands and waggled his fingers. "Nothing to worry about, Sykes. Seriously."

I put my face up to his until we met like a bridge over the body and were nearly nose-to-nose. "The scabs . . . she'll contaminate all the other bodies . . . "

"Chuck her to one side at the bottom of the wagon, once we're in the lab we can spray 'er and any of the others in proximity with phenol—no one's going to get sick."

"The professor—"

"It's dark, he's old and tired, he won't see a thing. And a little judiciously dispensed cash will keep O'Rourke and Winterbourne shut up if they do notice her; and we make sure we're the ones to haul our specimen out of the cart."

"But in the lab—the others are bound to notice tomorrow when it's daylight . . . "

"We'll start tonight, we'll hide her till we're done. Sykes, this could be the making of our careers."

He didn't say, *Especially yours.* We both knew that medical school scholarship boys were lucky to eke out a living—and they had to compete with midwives and barber-surgeons and even dentists. "What about afterward, Van Dyson?"

I saw the corners of his eyes crinkle and tilt upward and knew he'd smiled behind his mask. "That's pie, Sykes, pure pie. We cut her up, flense and boil her to get rid of the grease; then we can articulate the skeleton."

"And?"

"Keep it for a souvenir in your office or sell it. But I'm betting that when we're done dissecting, neither of us will have to concern ourselves with anything more than where we're going to display our Copley Medals. Just think. We'll be in the company of Franklin and Gauss and Ohm."

We had to shift a few bodies, but we wedged the pox victim on the bottom and against the slats that made up the wagon's side boards. I started to push a corpse on top of her but Van Dyson caught my arm. "One more, Sykes," he pleaded. "A male. It will make our research more complete. And after tonight, neither one of us will have to play at being resurrection men ever again."

I nodded.

He was whistling as we walked back into the crypt for the last time. Cruncher really was an apt nickname, I thought—he wanted knowledge and, like his fictional counterpart, he was going to renounce grave robbing.

I heard the tower clock strike 2:00 a.m. We'd unloaded most of the corpses and dragged them to the lab. There was an oversized dumb waiter to hoist them to the second floor, but it took two men to pull its ropes—especially if there were two bodies on its platform.

"I must be getting old, lads. Can you handle the rest of these?"

"Sure, Professor."

"No problem."

"Certainly."

"Absolutely. Good night, Dr. Perry," I said.

"All right, I'll take the landau and one of the horses, and my man can stay behind till you're done, then drive the wagon back."

"We can handle it, sir, no need for your man to hang about. Winterbourne can drive the wagon back."

"Thanks, Van Dyson. Thank you all. It's been a magnificent catch: An even dozen new specimens."

"G'night, sir."

Winterbourne had hooded the lantern again, and in the semi-dark, Jerry and I loaded the pox victims onto the dumb waiter.

"You go upstairs; shout down when the bodies are level with the floor, and I'll tie off the ropes down here and I'll send O'Rourke up." His hands were clumsy with the thick gloves; he fumbled under his apron, then handed me a five-dollar gold piece. "But don't let him hang around. Give him this. I'll come up and we'll move the bodies into the lab ourselves. All right?"

We shook hands briefly, then he pulled out the silver flask for the last time. "To Van Dyson and Sykes," he said. "To our success."

The anatomy lab was on situated on the second floor to take advantage of the sun that poured in through its skylight. Adjacent and behind a heavy, metal-clad door, was a kind of cold storage unit (also completely lined with metal) stacked with huge blocks of ice procured from the river, where we'd trundled most of the bodies we collected. But Winterbourne and O'Rourke had laid out three or four on vacant tables in the dissection room.

"Even a top-notch school like Yale has a dearth of specimens," I said when we wrestled the male smallpox victim onto the last dissecting table.

"Well, these two won't be occupying valuable space for long," Jerry said. "Get some phenol, alcohol, whatever you can find." He'd pulled down all the dark green shades and lit the room like Christmas—candles and lamps, even a crackling fire.

I went to the glassed cabinets. My hand was on the knob and I turned and said, "Let's just spray them down and cover them up, I'm whipped."

"Not on your life." He was rifling a drawer in the dissection table he normally used and pulled out a syringe and a vial. "Seven-percent solution, cocaine. Nobody will be here before noon, they'll all be in the lecture hall."

I swallowed uneasily.

"Are you sure?"

"Of course I'm sure. How do you think I have the best grades in my class?"

Nightmares come to life. They really do. No one's going to believe this—believe *anything* in these pages, but I'm going to leave them in my room after I flee.

For all I know, they'll be thrown away, but at least I'll have written down what happened. Was it something in the disease itself that initiated the transition? I keep thinking about what Van Dyson said about the segregated pox cemeteries when I'd been about to punch him in Dr. Perry's landau: *All the headstones face east.* And these victims were from the eastern wall of the crypt. It wasn't *folie a deux*, it wasn't the cocaine. *It wasn't.*

We'd sprayed the bodies; perhaps unwittingly we tracked or transferred scabs, carried them on our trouser or shirt cuffs from one corpse to the next. I was chattering away a mile a minute, my mind seemed filled with an exultance that bordered on ecstasy: there was nothing Van Dyson or I couldn't do. He smiled. "Really clears the brain, doesn't it? Let's inject one more hypo each, then get started."

We undressed the body. He lowered the lamp over the male. "Excellent. He's thawing. That will make things easier for us." He handed me the scalpel. "You may have the honor of the first cut, Dr. Sykes."

"I'll start with the classic Y, so we can look at how the organs might have been affected."

He nodded. "I've got a stack of slides ready next to the microscope." He stood opposite me, leaned in.

I pushed down, concentrating on making a straight line, keeping the depth even, and drew the knife upwards toward the sternum.

The man suddenly gave out a groan and his body convulsed.

I stepped back, scalpel in hand.

The corpse lurched upright and before I could react, its hands were around Van Dyson's throat and its mouth . . . dear God, its mouth . . . was buried in the flesh of Van Dyson's cheek. Van Dyson screamed. The thing broke his neck as easily as you'd snap a wishbone. His head hung at peculiar cant, his tongue rolled out between his slack lips and his eyes dulled. The corpse gnawed mouth, nose, the tender skin beneath the chin, grunting. Blood poured down its throat and chest.

I shrieked.

It raised its eyes to look at me and what I saw in them was malice beyond any evil I could ever have imagined. Then it grinned.

Behind me, the female was stirring.

Half-flensed bodies began to tremble on their tables beneath the sheets.

I lunged at the male creature with my scalpel upraised and plunged it into his ear.

The blade snapped off and he fell in a heap onto the wooden boards.

Be quick now, Sykes, aim true, I told myself. *There are knives by the drawer-full here.*

I stabbed eyes, ears, heads. I dismembered as many of the bodies as I could, boiled the parts in a huge black kettle I hung inside the fireplace. I could scarcely keep myself from vomiting a hundred times. It wasn't doctoring, it was butchery.

Then I heard a rattle from behind the metal-clad door. As their bodies thawed—just enough—the time of the others we'd collected had come.

It was already near daylight.

I looked around helplessly at the carnage of the dissection room, then toward the knocking from behind the heavy metal door.

I'd never get all of them rendered quickly enough.

Besides, I mourned inwardly, it was Van Dyson who knew how to articulate them, how to give a corpse a purpose even when its flesh was gone. They'd be harmless when the meat of their brains was gone, I thought; and fire would have to see to the rest.

I raked the logs from the fire, turned over the kerosene lamps.

I heard the wild scream of the rising flames mingling with the guttural cries of the resurrected ones from behind the metal-clad door, and I fled.

Auden Strothers crept stealthily into the darkened anatomy lab. *Not a soul in sight—just whatever's left of their wrecked bodies.*

There was no time to worry about what might have happened to Sheri Trent, he reminded himself. Their cadaver—C 390160—lay under its blue sheet, its punctured eye hanging slightly askew on its cheekbone. *Impossible to think they ever nicknamed the foul thing Molly.* The autopsy students were always roving from table to table, watching a group prepare a slice of pancreas for histology, observing one of the professors work on a delicate area like the tongue and larynx . . . and people got their hands in—even if the cadaver technically belonged to another team.

He carefully unzipped the body bag embracing Team 22's cadaver—the one that Sheri Trent had spattered with her own blood after she'd been bitten. Trent must've gotten her shit together when she saw the thing twitch—it too, had a deflated eye.

But, there were all those daily casual exchanges from table to table . . . and he counted two more blue sheets tagging corpses in the room . . . *and* the common graves where, Strothers had no doubt, the "disease" spread quietly underground and from place to place to place.

He snorted three lines of meth and joked inwardly that dismembering the bodies he was *sure* were infected, was essentially hackwork.

In his mind's eye he saw the dead woman sit up and lunge, yellowed teeth bared. He saw the bloody pocket of the wound in Sheri's arm. He cut and flensed, retching over his shoulder. Strothers picked up a surgical power saw, intent on wresting the femur from the pelvis. "For Christ's sake," he said aloud. He was trained to work carefully, what he was about to do was a waste. Besides, he hated the whine of the saw. If he proceeded cautiously—with precision—the bones could be articulated, he reminded himself, and used in schools and labs and hospitals.

There was a kitchen off the lounge where he could boil up the remains. Hell, if it came to it, he could cart them home in plastic garbage bags and fire up his own stove.

It was going very well, he was whistling when the lab door suddenly burst open.

He started; sure for a brief second that a mindless, shambling corpse that had once been Sheri Trent had come to gnaw his flesh.

"Security!" A female officer with blond hair advanced on him.

More cops piled into the room.

Strothers followed their gaze from the flensed bodies to the baggie spilling white powder cheerily across an empty chrome table.

"You're under arrest!"

"You don't understand—they're infected!" he shouted.

He felt his arms jerked backwards, cold metal handcuffs bit into his wrists.

Outside, through the windows, Strothers could see the flashing red lights of town and state police cars.

He watched the crimson glow play over the pale skin and ruined muscles of the cadavers, giving them an unearthly vibrancy—a warmth, he was certain, that would soon return them to life.

I Waltzed with a Zombie

Ron Goulart

It was the only movie ever made starring a dead man. This was back in the late spring of 1942 and Hix, the short, feisty, and unconquerably second-rate writer of low budget B-movies, was one of the few people who knew about it. He'd hoped to turn the knowledge to his advantage. But that didn't quite work out.

His involvement commenced on an overcast May afternoon. He was pacing, as best he could, his diminutive office in the Writers Building on the Pentagram Pictures lot in Gower Gulch.

Carrying his long-corded telephone in one hand and the receiver in the other, he was inquiring of his newest agent, "In what context did Arthur Freed use the word 'tripe,' Bernie?"

"He applied it to your movie treatment, the one I was foolish enough to let you cajole me into schlepping over to MGM," replied Bernie Kupperman from the Kupperman-Sussman Talent Agency offices over in the vicinity of Sunset Boulevard. "The full sentence was, 'How dare you inflict such a load of tripe on me, Bernie?'"

"That's not so bad. He could have called it crap instead of tripe." Hix, his frizzy hair flickering, halted just short of an unstrung mandolin that lay in his path.

"Actually, Hix, he did, but I never use that kind of language over the phone."

Sighing, the short screenwriter set his telephone down on his wobbly desk atop a scatter of glossy photos of starlets, drafts of scripts, three old issues of *Whiz Comics,* and a paper plate that once had held a nutburger. "Alas, that's the curse of being ahead of my time with my ideas."

"Two weeks ahead isn't that far," suggested his agent. "Oh, and Freed, hardly using any profanity at all, did mention that he'd heard that Val Lewton is planning to do a picture with the same title over at RKO."

"What I hear is that Lewton and his heavy-handed director Tourneur are probably both about to get the bum's rush out of the studio before they have time to make another clinker like *Cat People*." Hix gazed at a spot on the far wall where a window would've been if his office actually had a window. "More importantly, Bernie, Lewton's flicker is entitled *I Walked with a Zombie*, while my proposed blockbuster enjoys the far superior title of *I Waltzed with a Zombie*."

"Even so, Hix, we—"

"Furthermore, pal, Lewton's movie is going to be just another trite lowbrow effort aimed chiefly at the Saturday matinee crowd, mostly pubescent boys who flock into movie palaces to eat popcorn, whistle at Rita Hayworth, and pass gas," he pointed out. "My effort is a big budget musical, the very first horror musical comedy ever conceived by man."

"So far nobody—"

"Face it, buddy, the concept of a Technicolor musical in the horror genre is, well, both brilliant and unique." When Hix's head bobbed enthusiastically, his frazzled hair fluttered. "Were I given to hyperbole, I'd dub it super-colossal."

After a few silent seconds, his agent told him, "Estling over at Star Spangled Studios wants you for another Mr. Woo quickie."

Hix sank down into his slightly unstable swivel chair, sighing again. "As a potential Oscar winner," he complained, "I ought to be working for somebody who's not as big a moron as Estling."

"He's offering five hundred bucks more than you got for *Mr. Woo at the Wax Museum*."

"Okay, tell him I'll write it," said Hix. "But keep pitching *I Waltzed with a Zombie*."

"Only if it doesn't look like it's going to result in my suffering bodily harm."

Hix hung up and slid the phone toward the edge of his desk. "Twenty-nine smash B-movies since I came here six years ago and they still treat me like a hack."

The telephone rang.

"Mr. Hix's private office," he answered in, he was quite certain, a very convincing imitation of a very polite British servant.

"Listen, Hix, I've got to talk to you."

"That can be arranged, Marlys," he assured her. "Still unhappy about how things are going for you at Paramount? You've only been under contract for a little over three months after all."

"I still haven't been cast in one darn movie, Hix," Marlys Regal told him. "But this is something else, something maybe worse. Can you meet me in the Carioca Room at the Hotel San Andreas on Wilshire at five?"

"I can, sure. But what exactly—"

"Listen, besides writing a whole stewpot of movies that are always on the lower half of double bills, I know you've done some amateur detective work now and then."

"I wouldn't apply the word amateur to my work in the 'tec field, kid. In fact—"

"You also know a lot about spooky stuff, occult matters?"

"We've been keeping company for well over a month. In that time you must've deduced that I'm an expert in the field."

"Particularly zombies?"

"Well, sure. My as-yet unsold epic musical is about . . . Whoa now. Are you hinting that you know something about *real life* zombies?"

"I am, yes, and I'm afraid I could be in trouble."

"So, tell me exactly what—"

"Nope, it's too darn risky to say any more from where I am right now. Meet me at the Carioca Room. Bye, darling." She ended the call.

Cradling the receiver, he stood up and lifted his umber-colored sport coat off the eagle-topped coat rack to the left of his desk. As he shrugged his way into it, frazzled hair vibrating, he made his way to the door. "If I crack a zombie case," he said, grabbing the dented doorknob, "I can get some terrific publicity for *I Waltzed with a Zombie*."

The green and scarlet parrot behind the long teakwood bar was alive. He swung on his gilded perch in his gilded cage, now and then squawking out what were probably Brazilian curses. The other parrots, the ones perched high in the fake banana palms that decorated the dim-lit Carioca Room, were stuffed.

Arriving about ten minutes after five, Hix stopped near the bar and scanned the surrounding South American gloom.

"Still busily turning out crap, Hix?" asked an overweight writer who was occupying a nearby stool.

"I've recently been promoted to writing tripe, Arnie." Eyes narrowed, he looked again at the surrounding tables. There was no sign of Marlys.

After swallowing the rest of his Manhattan and plucking the cherry from the bottom of the glass, Arnie said, "Buy you a drink, old buddy?"

"I'm meeting somebody."

"Anybody I know?" he inquired, biting the cherry.

"I'm hoping for Carmen Miranda," Hix answered. "My doctor advised me to get more fruit in my diet. I figure if I eat her hat, I'll—"

"*Marafona*," cried the parrot, agitating his golden cage. "*Marafona*."

Marlys Regal, smiling very faintly, had just entered the cocktail lounge. She spotted Hix, gave him a minimalist wave before crossing to an empty table next to an almost believable palm tree. Before sitting down, she looked back toward the doorway. She was a very pretty young woman in her early twenties, slender and, at the moment, a redhead.

Arnie nodded. "Cute, but a little too skinny for my tastes," he observed. "And obviously too good for you."

"She's lowered her standards because of wartime shortages." Hix, his crinkly hair fluttering, went trotting over to the actress. En route he passed out greetings to some of the other customers. "Hi, Chester, you were great in the new Boston Blackie flicker."

"That crap," said the actor.

"Tripe," corrected Hix. "Howdy, Eleanor, loved you in *Ship Ahoy*."

"Do I know you?"

As he seated himself opposite Marlys, the young actress asked, "Did you notice anybody watching me as I came in, Hix?"

"Sure, each and every guy, with the exception of Grady Sutton. As I've oft told you, kiddo, you're very presentable."

"No, seriously. I'm pretty sure I'm being watched."

He reached across, put his hand over hers. "Okay, so what's going on wrong?"

"Well, I know something and I figured maybe Paramount wouldn't want it known. All I really was after was a chance at a good part, you know."

"Are we talking blackmail?"

"I call it goosing my darn career. Thing is, I'm not sure how they took my proposition and, past couple days, Hix, I have this really spooky feeling they've got a watch on me."

"The time has come, Marlys, for a few more details."

She inhaled slowly, exhaled slowly. "Now this all started before I met you at the Rathbones' party in April, Hix, so don't get jealous or hit the ceiling. You see—"

"What'll you folks have?" asked the buxom blond waitress who materialized out of the shadows.

The red-haired actress said quietly, "I'd like bourbon and water."

"Plain ginger ale," said Hix.

Nodding, the waitress departed.

Resting both elbows on the tropical-patterned tablecloth, Hix suggested, "Get back to your story."

"Well, before I met you I dated other people."

"Sure. I've been known to do the same."

"Well, some four months ago I was seeing Alex Stoner and—"

"Stoner? The grand old man of the silver screen? Ain't he a bit old for you?"

"He was only fifty-six."

Hix straightened. "*Was?* According to Louella, Hedda, and Johnny Whistler, the old boy is still above the ground. Fact is, he's over at your very own Paramount about two-thirds of the way through starring in their big budget historical fillum of the year, *The Holy Grail*. He's cast as King Arthur."

She took another slow breath in and out. "Alex died early in March," she said in a low voice. "Three weeks into *The Holy Grail*."

"So how come he's still acting in the darn film?"

"They brought him back to life," she replied.

It was a little over an hour later that Hix got knocked cold by a conk on the head.

He and Marlys had retreated to the small living room of the small cottage that Hix was renting on the ocean side of Santa Monica. The starlet had become convinced that it wasn't safe to keep talking at a public place like the Carioca.

Pacing the venerable flowered carpet he'd acquired at a rummage sale over in Altadena last fall, Hix was going over what details the young actress had thus far provided. "So you were sleeping with this old coot when he shuffled off?"

Marlys was sitting on the lime-green sofa. "Yes, I woke up at seven in the morning and the poor guy was stone cold dead next to me," she said. "That was really unpleasant."

"Tell me some more about what you did next, kid."

"I was alone at his place in Bel Air. Alex had given his two servants a few days off," she said. "I was darn certain he had kicked off, so there sure wasn't any reason to call an ambulance."

Hix sat on the wobbly arm of his only armchair. "And what about the cops?"

"Spending a night in bed with a dead major movie star doesn't give you the kind of publicity I need," she answered. "Besides which, Alex was already partway through shooting the King Arthur flick and I figured Paramount might not care to have his dying made public right away."

"How come you phoned this guy Wally Needham?"

She looked toward the draped window, frowning. "Did you hear something outside?"

"Relax, kiddo. Nobody followed us here from the Carioca," he assured her. "Having penned a bunch of Mr. Woo pictures, not to mention three Dr. Crimebuster epics, I know a little bit about how to avoid being tailed."

Sighing, Marlys continued. "Well, I first met Wally at Schwab's when I stopped in for a cup of coffee one afternoon a few months ago."

"Another of your beaus?"

"We were friends, sure. It doesn't hurt to have a friend who works in publicity at Paramount Pictures."

"No, that could sure be darn helpful to anybody's career." He stood, crossed to the lemon-yellow drapes, and pulled them a few inches open to look out into the approaching twilight. "Nobody around. By the way, I'm not crystal clear on how I can help you rise in show biz."

"C'mon, Hix," she told him. "I'm simply fond of you."

"Well sir, that's a relief." He turned his back to the window. "Explain to me a bit more about what this publicity lad did."

"Well, he got to Alex's mansion less than an hour after I telephoned him," she said. "After making certain Alex was dead, Wally asked me if I'd like to sign a movie contract with Paramount."

"Provided you kept your mouth shut about Alex Stoner being dead."

She nodded. "Yes, I couldn't very well pass up an opportunity like that to graduate out of Poverty Row quickies," she replied. "Then Wally went into Alex's office and phoned various people, higher-ups at the studio. I heard him tell somebody, 'Dr. Marzloff can do it. We'll use him.'"

"They hired Dr. Sandor Marzloff? Quack physician and phony self-proclaimed sorcerer to the stars?"

"Not so phony, it seems, Hix. He brought Alex back to life, after all," the actress pointed out. "He told me once that he'd lived for several years in Haiti and learned—"

"You dated him, too?

"We had a few drinks a couple of times. Long before I met you, Hix."

"Um," commented Hix.

"I have the impression that Alex Stoner wasn't the first defunct actor he reanimated," she said. "In fact . . . Holy Christ!" She had risen partly off the sofa and was staring past the writer.

Slowly he turned. "Oops."

Two large men, wearing pinstripe suits and with cloth sugar sacks over their heads had silently entered his living room and were pointing large revolvers at him and the young actress.

"You couldn't possibly have tailed us here," Hix told them. "I dodged any—"

"You forget that you're one of the most famous hacks in Hollywood, Hix," explained the larger of the intruders. "One of our people spotted you with this dame at the Carioca. We didn't follow you, we just looked up your address in a phone book."

"Ah, the price of fame. Now, I suggest you—"

That was as far as he got. The other hooded intruder had returned his gun to its shoulder holster, withdrawn a substantial-looking blackjack from a side pocket and lunged to bop Hix on the skull.

He heard Marlys scream as he was dropping down into oblivion.

Birds were twittering and chirping, in a cheerful Disney-like manner, to announce the advent of a new day. Morning sunshine was beaming in through the opening between Hix's tacky yellow drapes. With an awakening groan, he sat up on his living room floor.

"Oy," he observed, feeling suddenly dizzy. "One doesn't usually experience a hangover after two glasses of ginger ale."

Then he recalled that a hooded intruder had conked him on the coco last night. Slowly and carefully, he glanced around the small room. It didn't appear to be in any worse shape than it had been prior to the intrusion.

"Marlys?" he said in a voice that vaguely resembled his own. Clearing his throat, he tried again. "Marlys?"

Tottering some, Hix arose to a standing, albeit wobbly, position. He stumbled through the entire rest of his cottage. Outside of a scraggly stray orange cat who'd snuck in through the open kitchen window to explore the substantial collection of dirty dishes in the lopsided sink, there was nobody else in the entire place.

"Shoo," he suggested half-heartedly as he returned to his living room. "I reckon I better call the police to report—"

His phone rang. It was residing on a sprawling stack of old copies of *Daily Variety* and *The Hollywood Reporter*.

After swallowing and blinking a few times, he made his way to the telephone and snatched up the receiver. "Forest Lawn Annex."

Marlys, somewhat breathlessly, inquired, "Hix, dear, are you okay?"

"I might ask the same of you."

"I'm fine, perfectly fine," said the starlet, inhaling and exhaling. "That whole business last night was simply a misunderstanding."

"Those hoodlums really meant to coldcock somebody down the street from here?"

"No, silly. See, they weren't hoodlums at all. But a couple of Paramount Pictures executives."

"Oh, so? Is that the current style for Paramount execs? Flour sacks over their heads?"

"Actually those were sugar sacks."

"Even so," he said. "What in the hell is going on, kiddo?"

Taking another deep breath, the young actress told him, "See, dear, they got the foolish idea that you had kidnapped me. What happened was a sort of rescue operation."

"Your value to Paramount has apparently increased a lot since yesterday."

"They reconsidered my proposition and decided it was in the best interests of the studio to comply," she said. "It's very exciting."

"Sounds like."

"Oh, and I wanted to let you know, dear, that I won't be able to go with you to that Korngold concert at the Hollywood Bowl on Saturday."

"Are they shipping you off to Guatemala?"

"No, just to Arizona for a few weeks. They're picking me up at noon," she said. "I'm going on location. Paramount wants me to play the dance hall singer in the new Randolph Scott Western. It's a real step up for my career. I get shot in the final reel."

"A painful place to be shot," he said. "Now explain what the devil is going on?"

"It turns out that quite a few people at Paramount were unhappy that I was unhappy. So they—"

"I bet you're going to have to forget all about Alex Stoner and Dr. Marzloff."

"Not exactly forget, just simply keep mum about what I may or may not know," Marlys explained. "Oh, and you don't have to worry, Hix. I convinced everybody at the studio last night that—"

"That's where they dragged you?"

"I went voluntarily once I realized what was up. This is the first time I was at a meeting with so many important movie people," she said, still sounding a bit breathless. "As I was explaining, dear, I convinced them that you and I were simply shacking up for a one-night stand. I never mentioned anything about Dr. Marzloff or poor Alex to you."

"There goes my reputation for celibacy."

"At least you won't get conked on the noggin anymore . . . Gosh, I just looked at the clock, Hix. I really have to finish packing."

"Well, it's been swell having this little chat," he assured the actress. "It's sure taken a load off my mind."

"One other thing," she cautioned. "I don't think it'd be a wise idea for you to talk to anybody about zombies for a while."

"The word *zombies* will never cross my lips again," he promised. "Bon voyage."

"Same to you, darling." She hung up.

Hix cradled the phone, picked up the receiver again, and made a series of calls.

A few minutes past two that afternoon, Hix was seated at one of the huge oaken tables in the vast dining hall of Camelot. He was finishing up the second half of the baloney on rye sandwich he'd found in his box lunch and conversing with the two former chorus girls who were working as extras in *The Holy Grail*. Like the writer, they were dressed as Hollywood's idea of Middle Ages peasant folk.

"I hear," Hix said, setting aside the remnants of his sandwich, "that Alex Stoner has been feeling poorly of late, Exine."

"You can say that again, sweetie," she replied as she scratched at her bosom through the coarse gray material of her tunic. "Yesterday they had to do thirty-seven takes of the scene where he's supposed to be knighting Ray Milland. He kept dropping his goddamn sword."

"Only thirty-three takes," corrected the redheaded peasant girl on Hix's left. "By the way, Hix honey, how come you're working as an extra on this flicker?"

"I'm really not an extra, Mindy," he explained, lying. "I'm doing research for an A-budget Hollywood murder mystery George Marshall wants me to script for Alan Ladd."

Exine observed, yet again scratching her bosom, "That's good news. It's about time you quit writing those crappy Mr. Woo programmers."

"Actually, the Mr. Woo films are considered by many an astute and discriminating critic to be stellar examples of the mystery cinema at its absolute best."

"C'mon, where the hell would an astute and discriminating critic find a job in this pesthole of a town?" asked Mindy, who was now scratching her bosom, too. "Geez, everybody in the Middle Ages must've spent most of their time scratching their boobs."

Before Hix could provide an answer, a uniformed guard came striding into the immense hall, causing some of the colored banners on the imitation stone walls to flutter. "Okay, kids, nobody's supposed to eat their lunch in here," he informed them. "Please, scram."

"As soon as we finish our after-dinner mints," Hix assured him.

The plump guard did a take. "Hix? What the hell are you doing in that getup?"

"I'm going through an unexpected slow period in my usually spectacular writing career, Nick."

"Sorry to hear that, pal. You and the dames better toddle along, though," advised the guard. "Stoner's going to do the scene where he addresses the village peasants in about fifteen."

Hix stood up, gathering the scraps from his meal and dumping them in the white cardboard box. Among the phone calls he'd made earlier was one to a photographer friend at the *L.A. Times*. He'd asked him to use his connections at Paramount to get him a job as an extra in *The Holy Grail* in some scenes featuring Alex Stoner. He wanted to see for himself if Stoner acted any differently now that he was dead.

He soon found out.

The fog machines were sending a gray mist swirling across the wide stone courtyard of Camelot Castle. A young extra put her fist up to her mouth and coughed loudly.

"Don't do that when the damn cameras are rolling, sis," warned a nearby assistant director loudly.

Hix, standing between a redheaded girl in a Gypsy costume and a bearded fat man who was clutching a shepherd's staff, was watching a sort of reviewing stand a few yards away. The stand had a wooden throne in the center of a row of carved chairs and was bedecked with brightly colored pennants. He lifted his weathered peasant cap to scratch his frizzy hair.

One of the director's assistants was assigning some of the bit players to chairs. There were lesser knights wearing chain mail, some ladies-in-waiting, and not one but two jesters.

The door of one of the dressing room trailers that sat just beyond the enormous set now swung open and Queen Guinevere, wearing a low-cut gown trimmed in ermine, regally descended the stairs. The crowd of more than a hundred extras murmured as she was escorted to the stand.

"So that's Sylvia Thompson," observed a pretty blonde milkmaid, shifting her grip on her pail. "Not all that pretty in real life, is she?"

"What makes you think this is real life?" inquired Hix.

The milkmaid glanced back at him. "Hix? Have you sunk even lower?"

"Doing a favor for DeMille."

The door of another one of the other trailers came flapping open. Alex Stoner, a thin white-bearded man, came stumbling out into the misty afternoon. He teetered on the top step, then went tumbling down to land on a tangle of cables and wires at the set edge.

His ornate gilded crown popped free of his gray head and landed on the booted foot of a wide, broad man dressed as a yeoman.

"Drunk again," said a chubby friar.

The milkmaid shook her head. "I think the poor guy's sick. He's looked like crap since Monday."

"Booze can do that. I ought to know," said a husky blacksmith.

Two large men in business suits came hurrying down out of the trailer in the fallen actor's wake.

"Eureka!" said Hix to himself. "I'll wager that these two gents are the same pair that broke in on me and the ambitious Marlys last evening."

They tugged Stoner to his feet, restored his crown.

"Fell . . . down . . . getting worse," muttered the actor.

"Chin up," advised one of the men. He sounded like the one who'd done the talking last night.

Slowly the two alleged studio executives guided Alex Stoner to the stand. "I've got bunions," the actor was saying in a fuzzy voice. "I never had bunions until Dr. Marzloff worked his—"

"Button your lip, sir," advised the one who'd bopped Hix.

When Stoner reached the next to the last step of the wooden stairway, his legs suddenly went limp.

The two executives yanked him upright, hustled him over to the gilded throne he was supposed to sit on.

A lean prop man materialized to hand the swaying actor an Excalibur sword made of balsa wood.

Grabbing the sword, Stoner held it high, tip of the blade pointing skyward. "People of Camelot," he started reciting, "I wish you to join . . . um . . . to join me . . . um . . . Now, what in the hell do I want these halfwits to join me for?"

Excalibur fell from his now shaking hand. He dropped to his knees. He fell forward and hit the planks with his face, producing a resounding smack. The jeweled crown left his head again, rolled off the stage and landed hard on the cobblestones of the courtyard, losing at least three sparkling fake jewels in the process.

The two executives picked up the now unconscious actor. They deposited him, with a thump, on the gilded throne.

The one who did the talking picked up a megaphone. "Mr. Stoner seems to have had a mild fainting spell."

From where Hix was standing it looked as though Stoner had ceased to breathe. "They're going to have to get him back to Dr. Marzloff," he concluded.

The executive said, "We'll be escorting Mr. Stoner to his personal physician. I'm sure it's nothing serious. Today's shooting is canceled. Call casting about what time to show up tomorrow. Thank you one and all."

When night started closing in on the town of Santa Rita Beach, Hix, wearing dark gray slacks and a black pullover, was stretched out on a patch of hillside forest just above Dr. Marzloff's small private sanitarium. The address of the two-story slant-roofed place he found simply by checking a couple of Greater Los Angeles phone books. The floor plans of the joint he borrowed from a former singing cowboy who'd gone into real estate after first Republic and then Monogram had tossed him out on his ear. The infrared camera and the night binoculars he got from the same *L.A. Times* photographer who'd fixed up the extra stint at Paramount. The bagel with cream cheese he'd just finished eating he'd picked up at Moonbaum's delicatessen while passing through Hollywood en route to this beach town.

By the time the screenwriter had gathered up this assortment of stuff it was nearing seven in the evening. As the evening darkened it also grew increasingly overcast. Parked down in the white-graveled parking lot at the back of the sanitarium was a panel truck with the Paramount Pictures logo on the passenger-side door. There was also a big color poster for *The Road to Morocco* on the side of the vehicle, with portraits of Bing Crosby, Bob Hope, and Dorothy Lamour.

Hix, while wiping bagel crumbs off his chin, said to himself, "Dottie Lamour would be perfect for *I Waltzed with a Zombie*. Sure, we could put her in front of a whole chorus line of sexy girl zombies in tight sarongs. Though maybe Paramount wouldn't loan her out to MGM or Twentieth after I expose them as employers of dead actors."

The presence of this Paramount truck indicated to Hix that the defunct actor had indeed been brought back to Dr. Marzloff for a tune-up. The problem was, how many times can you revive the same corpse? Even with voodoo.

There was a large skylight on the slanting left side of the roof. Lights were already on in the room below when Hix had come skulking along to watch the place. According to the floor plans, Marzloff's laboratory and surgery were below that bright-lit skylight.

A dog all at once began barking, barking in a loud chesty way that indicated a large and mean-minded hound.

Hix swung his glasses in the direction of the new sound. "Ah, only a neighbor's animal."

The big Doberman was attached to a log chain on the other side of the high stone wall that surrounded the Marzloff setup.

The night kept getting colder and darker. In another few minutes Hix would make his careful approach. There was a sturdy drainpipe running up the side of the gray building. Having considerable confidence in his stuntman abilities, Hix was certain he could, under the cover of night, scale the seven-foot-high stone wall, then shinny up the pipe to reach the roof. He'd then, unobserved, snap some news-photo-quality shots of Dr. Marzloff reviving the corpse of Alex Stoner.

He'd turn the pictures over to his buddy at the *L.A. Times*. He might also give Johnny Whistler, who was easier to reach than Hedda or Louella, a call. True, Whistler had told him never to phone again with his pathetic attempts to get publicity for his mediocre fleapit movies. But this time he had an earthshaking scoop. The subsequent front-page stories would result in a hell of a lot of publicity for him. And for *I Waltzed with a Zombie*.

"I bet," he said as he rose to start his slow, careful approach to the re-animator's lab, "we can hire Cole Porter or Irving Berlin to write *Zombie Waltz*."

From up on the hillside the darn Doberman had seemed to be securely attached to a sturdy walnut tree at the backside of the stark white Art Deco house of Dr. Marzloff's neighbor.

But just as Hix was scrambling over the stone wall around the sanitarium and realizing that his wall-climbing skills had somewhat diminished since he'd turned thirty, he heard a chain snapping and then became aware of an angry, growly sort of barking. It grew ever louder and closer in the overcast darkness of the night.

"Heel!" he ordered quietly over his shoulder. "Sit! Roll over! Play dead!"

These were the only dog commands he could recall from the script he'd written for *Socko the Wonder Dog Goes to War* last autumn.

None of them made an impression on the angry Doberman. Snarling, he leaped for the climbing writer.

He managed to nip the heel of one of the strange shoes that Hix was pretty certain he'd bought down in Tijuana while hung over a few months ago. The dog took a hunk out of the orange-brown Mexican shoe, but Hix was not hurt.

Hix was able to pull himself to the top of the wall. He stretched out there for a moment, facedown, and caught his breath.

The dog continued to growl and jump down there in the darkness. Apparently everyone at the Marzloff establishment was too busy bringing the late Alex Stoner back to life to notice Hix's less than silent arrival.

The thick drainpipe commenced producing metallic groans when Hix, panting as quietly as he was able, had managed to convey himself up roughly three quarters of its two-story length.

Over on the other side of the stone wall the surly Doberman was continuing to convey his annoyance with a lengthy series of angry barks.

Pausing to again catch his breath, the writer continued his ascent to the slanting roof and the illuminated skylight.

"You're going to have to expand your exercise plan," he advised himself as he labored upward. "Playing volleyball once a week with a gaggle of starlets in the Pentagram Pictures parking lot obviously isn't sufficient."

At long last—it took him nearly ten minutes according to the radium dial on his wristwatch—Hix reached his goal. Clutching the metal edge of the sturdy gutter, he pulled himself up on to the roof.

Sprawling flat, he inched his way over to the edge of the big skylight. Careful not to go sliding back down the incline of the roof, he prepared to take a look down into the lab/surgery.

"Hot dog!" he exclaimed internally upon noticing that one of the large glass panels in the skylight was propped open, thus allowing him to hear what was being said down below.

A voice that must belong to Dr. Marzloff was saying, in a thick accent that sounded like Akim Tamiroff or Gregory Ratoff on a bad day, "I am no longer optimistic, gentlemen."

"He's alive again," pointed out the Paramount exec who'd conked Hix.

"True, but he's passed away twice again since you delivered him here to me."

"I'm not . . . really . . . feeling so . . . hot," admitted Alex Stoner.

Risking a peek downward into the brightly lit room Hix saw the two large Paramount men standing close beside a white operating table, considerable concern showing on their faces.

Stretched out on the table, looking extremely pale and clad in a white hospital gown, was the late actor. He was groaning in his deep, actor's voice.

The squat, thickset Marzloff had on a pale blue medical jacket and a stethoscope dangling around his neck. On his bald head he was wearing a voodoo headdress consisting chiefly of chicken feathers, cat fur, and rat tails. In his right hand he held a large hypodermic and in his left a maraca that had tiny skulls painted on it in bright red lacquer.

Stoner said, "Dying once . . . was bad enough . . . but dying three more . . . "

"Four," corrected the doctor.

The other executive said, "Look, Doc, we only need this guy for one more week and then it's a wrap."

"Don't forget he has to dub a few pieces of dialogue," reminded his colleague.

"We can always get Paul Frees to do that. He can imitate anybody's voice."

"Gentlemen, I very much fear he can't be kept alive for longer than a few more minutes."

"We could settle for *three* days."

"Not even *three* hours. I've been able, as you know, to have some luck with an initial reanimation. But—"

"I have . . . a few . . . " said Stoner, half sitting up on the table, shivering and shaking violently, " . . . last words . . . I'd like to thank the Academy for . . . Aargh!" Falling back with a thud, he died for the fifth time.

"Holy Moley," said Hix, reaching the borrowed camera out from under his sweater. Surreptitiously, he aimed it at what was going on down in the laboratory.

"C'mon," ordered one of the executives. "Revive this guy again."

"I do not believe it would be of any use."

"Try it!"

Sighing, the doctor adjusted his chicken feather headpiece. "My exclusive blending of up-to-date medical expertise and ancient Haitian voodoo can only do so much."

"Get going, Doc!"

After administering the shot in the hypodermic to a thin, pale arm of the dead actor, Marzloff began to dance around the body, shaking the maraca and chanting, "Damballah. Ioa. Damballah-Wedo. Gato Preto. Damballah."

Hix, chuckling silently, clicked off shots. "What an expose this is going to be. I'll be the darling of the press and . . . Oh, crap."

He'd discovered he was swiftly sliding toward the edge of the sharply slanting roof.

Flipping over onto his back as he slid, Hix managed to stuff the big camera under his dark sweater and, at the same time, use his heels to try to brake his descent.

He succeeded with the camera, but he kept sliding ever closer to the drop.

Hix made a grab for the gutter edge as he went over. As he caught it, the jerking halt of his drop sent pain all across his shoulders and back. He hung two stories up for what seemed like more than a minute.

Then he caught hold of the drainpipe and went down to the ground, quite a bit faster than he'd gone up.

Limping, he scurried to the wall. After inhaling enthusiastically a few times, he got himself to the top. He lay stretched out on the stones. Nobody had noticed his departure.

Wheezing, as well as panting, Hix let himself down on the other side.

Waiting for him, silently, was the big mean-minded black and tan dog.

The next morning, the new secretary at his agent's office pretended she didn't know who Hix was. "Who?" she inquired in a voice that was both nasal and snide.

"*Hix*. Bernie's most successful client."

"Surely, you're not John O'Hara."

"Tell him that terrific idea we talked about has come to fruition. We're all in the money."

"I'll try to contact Mr. Kupperman. Hix, was it?"

After three and a half long minutes Bernie came on the line. "Hix, how many times have I warned you about using profanity with my secretaries?"

"I merely stated my name."

"She apparently though Hix was a dirty word."

"A common mistake, yeah. But the purpose of my call is to alert you to dust off my brilliant *I Waltzed with a Zombie* treatment, Bernie."

"Why in the heck would I do something like that?"

"Because I am on the brink of turning into an international celebrity due to my exposure of insidious zombie trafficking in Tinsel Town," he announced. "I'll be exposing a major Hollywood studio that's featured a dead actor in a starring role in their latest Technicolor historical epic."

"Baloney. How can you do that?"

"Soon as I sell my exclusive story to the *L.A. Times.* And possibly give it to my old pal Johnny Whistler, too."

"What sort of proof do you have? Photographs would be nice."

Hix hesitated. "I *had* a whole stewpot of great shots, Bernie," he said. "Unfortunately my camera fell out of my sweater while I was running through a section of Santa Rita Beach."

"Exercising, were you?"

"Well, actually, I was running for my life."

"So why didn't you pick up the camera?"

"The ferocious dog that was chasing me over hill and dale stopped to eat the camera. Or at least take a couple of hefty bites out of it," he explained. "But I can still provide the press with a first-hand account of my witnessing a noted actor being resurrected. An attempted resurrection maybe, because I fell off the roof before—"

"Who was, according to you, being revived? And who was doing this?"

"The actor in question was none other than Alex Stoner, Paramount's star of *The Holy Grail.* The first time this old ham died was back three months ago and they—"

His agent made an exasperated sound. "Don't you read the newspapers, Hix? Don't you listen to Johnny Whistler's seven-thirty a.m. broadcast on Mutual?"

"I overslept because . . . why?"

"Alex Stoner didn't die three months ago. He died last night of a massive heart attack," Bernie told him. "Paramount Pictures announced that early this morning."

"I fell off the roof too soon. Looks like they couldn't revive him this time."

"Actually, Hix, they're burying him at Forest Lawn on Friday," the agent informed him. "Paramount says they've got enough footage in the can to put *The Holy Grail* together."

"*I Waltzed with a Zombie* is still a terrific idea."

"Tell you what, I'll try it on Monogram," said Bernie. "I hear they're thinking of doing some cheapie musicals. Maybe we can get six thousand dollars out of them. What say?"

Hix was silent for a moment. "Sure, give it a try, Bernie," he said, and hung up.

Aftermath

Joy Kennedy-O'Neill

Everybody knows that pestilences have a way of recurring in the world; yet somehow we find it hard to believe in ones that crash down on our heads from a blue sky.

—Albert Camus, *The Plague*

I'm driving to Houston when Def Leppard's "Love Bites" comes on the radio. I have to pull over and watch my hands shake; it's been years since anyone aired anything like that—no "Reality Bites," no "Once Bitten Twice Shy"—although I suppose that playing the song is a sign that the nation is moving on. I sit in the car and tremble, feeling angry and nauseous. *Love bites, love bleeds, love lives, love dies . . .*

After the epidemic, when a few radio stations had finally come back online, it was just news updates, dead lists, and static interrupted by the long silences of power outages. Then when some of the grids got stabilized it was "all Gershwin, all the time," and then last year, when everyone was digging victory gardens to supplement rations, it was big band tunes. Swing, baby, swing. Pull ourselves up by bootstraps, brother. Moving on and moving up. I can hum "Jump, Jive, and Wail" in my sleep now. *When you wake up, will you walk out? It can't be love if you throw it about . . .*

I'm so shaky that I think about turning around for home, but the car has its entire gas ration in the tank and I really need to see an optometrist. I'm starting to squint and tear up when I teach, so my prescription has probably changed. The headaches are awful. They started soon after last year's *Tres de Julio* celebration and feel like an elastic band is wrapping around my forehead, squeezing with every heartbeat. Cal has been kissing each eye when I get home. There are no more eye doctors in Lake Jackson but he said there are a few in the city who are taking appointments as best they can around the rolling blackouts. He even heard that Bausch and Lomb's Argentina plant might be going online again, so there may be contact lenses soon.

I have to pull myself together. An hour's drive is a luxury that I should be savoring; my calves have grown thick from bicycling to work. H-town's skyline ahead of me is lovely under the blue summer sky. Of course, the Chase Tower's top is still left ragged by an airliner's crash; seeing its scarred bone-beams reminds me of 9/11 and a more innocent time. Back then we thought that three thousand Americans dying by terrorists' hands was the most horrific thing we'd ever witnessed. We thought HIV and cancer and SARS were the big bogeymen in the closet. But now, with a planet missing nearly one-third of its population, our fears from the last decade seem glamorously bittersweet. *When you're alone, do you let go?*

A yellow butterfly is perched on top of a bullet-dented road sign. Things seem almost back to normal—there is no smoke on the horizon, the barricades have been removed, and grass and bluebonnets grow on the side of the road. There are birds singing, red-tailed hawks catching the thermals, and the buzzards are only devouring roadkill. It's just a possum. Everything is fine.

So I pull back into the near empty lanes as the song ends and a Britney Spears tune comes on—whatever happened to her? Did she make it?—and I know I can't handle these voices from the past, *my* past, so soon. I still need baby steps with Benny Goodman. And I'm thinking that I must be the last person in the world who is still having a problem getting over *it*, but when I walk into the optometrist's dingy waiting room there are two cases of hysterical blindness waiting patiently for their names to be called.

They now say that the first person who got sick was a sheep herder in Bhutan, which upends everyone's theory of a terrorist's biolab accidental release. The man got flu-like symptoms but still felt well enough to attend a national festival and grand opening of a new railway going over the Black Mountains. Later, hundreds of other people in Bhutan, Nepal, and India got sick with the same bug and recovered. It was what they then called the *ovis* flu, which was supposed to be just a weak cousin of the swine and bird flu. I remember reading about it in *Newsweek*'s science section while sipping coffee at the kitchen table . . . two years ago that feel like two thousand.

Then it mutated. Patient Zero was a grandmother in New Delhi whose lungs filled up with fluid from trying to fight the flu. She succumbed after forty-eight hours and was placed inside the hospital's morgue, but the next day there was pounding from within the cooler. An unnerved hospital worker opened the

door and there she was—naked, pale, blank-eyed, and blinking . . . and hungry.
She had unzipped her body bag and was half out of it. Everyone remembers
where they were when they first saw the YouTube video of her attacking the
nurses. A security camera captured the grainy image of her staggering down
the hospital hallway; one foot was still caught in the body bag and she dragged
it behind her like a wrinkled cocoon. Her breasts were long and dangled like
fleshy pendulums as she lunged for the first nurse. There were sprays of blood
as she bit into the woman's hospital scrubs, and when the second nurse—a
man—tried to intervene, the old woman leaped and threw her whole body on
him. She sat on his chest as he shouted in surprise and tried to flip her over.
She actually ate half of his neck and one cheek—we could see her swallowing.
Her face was devoid of expression.

The video went viral. Most everyone thought it was a hoax but it was hard
to dismiss. Her white haunches and her black pubic hair . . . and the way the
first nurse fell so hard on the floor that we could see her arm breaking and her
pager go flying . . . None of it seemed staged. We supposed it could be CGI'ed
but every time Cal and I watched it together the hair had risen on my arms.
The video had been soundless but I imagined the sound of that body bag
shuffing on the linoleum as she took each step, like a needle off the track of a
turntable. *Ssh. Ssh. Ssh.* The same sound I would later make to Lindy when she
had nightmares about the "sick people" outside our boarded up windows. *Ssh,
ssh, ssh. Go to sleep.*

More incidents like the one in the New Delhi hospital followed: Mumbai,
Singapore, Tokyo, Bangkok. Doctors backpedalled, saying it was physically
impossible for the dead to rise and what we were seeing were patients who had
been prematurely declared dead. Calming sound clips included "Determining
death can be difficult . . . " "The puffer fish, for example, emits a powerful
neurotoxin which can induce a death-like paralysis . . . "

But one beleaguered doctor was adamant. "The patient's heart had stopped.
There was no brain activity. Forty-eight hours later there was *still* no brain
activity, and her tissues had actually started to decay and putrefy." (I remember
his Indian accent and emphasis on pu*trif*y.) "And then the patient rose." This
was the sound bite played round the world.

"What did the optometrist say?" Cal asks when I get home.

I present my new black-rimmed glasses with lenses as thick as Coke bottles,
and wrinkle my nose. "I need a new prescription, but these are the only ones
he had close to it."

He laughs. "Sexy librarian look. How is Houston?"

"Good. Less traffic, that's for sure. Someone in the waiting room said that the museums might reopen for one day a week." I don't tell him about the cases of hysterical blindness, or the new "old" songs playing on the radio.

"I'd love to see the Menil collection again," he smiles hopefully. "How much were the glasses?"

"Eighteen ration points. I'll put in more overtime."

"No worries. I'll do more." Our candles are lit because the power is off again and we share a can of chili that only expired two months ago, along with some sliced cucumbers from our victory garden. I can smell the shadows of the house, dusty and waiting. Their silences press on me as firm as a hand. In the back of the house is Lindy's room, and I suppose her stuffed animals are covered in dust and her plastic fairies all have cobwebbed wings.

The first time I saw a Turner, in real life, was on campus. Cal was teaching his college algebra class in the A-wing and I was downstairs teaching English lit. The black, beetle-like phone mounted on the classroom wall began to ring and I stopped my lecture to stare at it stupidly. I had never heard the classroom phones ring before. Before I could reach for the receiver all the students' cell phones started buzzing and vibrating, and an alarm in the hallway went off and a speaker crackled: "Emergency alert. Please lock all classroom doors and wait for instructions. Do not use emergency exits. Repeat . . . "

I rushed to the back of the room and locked the door. The college had installed the phones, alert systems, and the new door locks soon after the Virginia Tech shootings. I told the students to move away from the windows. I thought we had a shooter, or that maybe there had been an accidental release at the nearby petrochemical plants. But a shadow passed by the window.

A girl shrieked and we saw a man's gaunt face and hollowed eyes. He was shuffling past our classroom to the pavilion outside. There were crusts of blood around his mouth and fingers. A campus security guard cornered him but the man, moving surprisingly fast, rushed towards the guard and bit into his jugular. Both tumbled to the ground and then the man . . . god it's hard to write this . . . the man bit straight down into the guard's belly and shook his head, like a dog does, as he ripped out portions of entrails. The guard's white shirt became blood soaked but it wasn't like the horror movies, not all red and monochromatic; it was red and maroon and dark brown and then bile green when the bowels were pierced. My students were screaming, hysterical.

I was frozen.

Three police officers ran into the pavilion and shot. One of the bullets *ping*ed against a bronze sculpture of cranes, and I remember how dispassionate the regal birds looked. One bird had been sculpted with its foot tucked up against its body, and now it looked as if it was trying to gracefully avoid the bloodshed at its feet. More shots: once, twice . . . at the third we saw shards of pink pieces of bone explode from the man's kneecap but he crawled onward, always reaching for the police. He looked ravenous. He never said anything, just groaned, and his eyes were milky and dead-looking, like a shark's. It wasn't until they shot him right in the head that he stopped for good. I smelled the vomit from one of my students as it seeped into the classroom carpet.

The blood from the two dead men outside was pooling, running through the cobblestones, being funneled straight toward our classroom's baseboard. I stood up shakily and pulled the blinds down. We huddled under the tables in the classroom and listened to the squawk of the police radios outside until the alert system blatted, "Please proceed to emergency exits."

That was our last day at work. Cal and I raced to each other's offices and grabbed tests and papers to grade—isn't that funny? I suppose we were thinking that a few days at home and there would soon be a cure. A final alert was being sent out: "To minimize the threat of contagion, all local school districts will be closing. In the aftermath of today's tragedy . . . "

"Why is it always 'aftermath'?" Cal said as we raced to the car. "They never call it 'after English or after Science.' " It was his math teacher joke, and a really old one. But he was trying to comfort me. We were running so fast that we couldn't hold hands.

"We've got to get Lindy," I said. All I could think about was our daughter.

We saw real horrors on the road getting to her sitter's. I won't write about them . . . I can't; I'll make myself ill. When we got to the sitter's she didn't say anything except "Christ Lord almighty," and deposited our sleepy four-year-old in my arms. Then she slammed her door shut and locked it.

When we made it home, we ran inside and bolted our own door. And that was the last time Lindy and I were ever outside together.

This morning I watch Cal work his Sudoku puzzles and I wonder if it always took him this long to complete them. He doesn't seem as quick-witted. He used to be able to make me laugh with just one dry retort, or one silly pun. I haven't laughed in a long time. Does he have post-traumatic stress? Do I? Does he have permanent cerebral damage from the infection? I listen to him chew his cereal and I feel so grateful he's alive. And furious too.

"What?" he asks, noticing me looking at him.

"Nothing."

"Mmm." He keeps chewing his cereal. He's stopped complaining about the watered-down milk because he knows we're lucky; places in Europe and South America haven't had milk supplies all year. He looks at his watch and pushes his bowl away. "I gotta run. I'll be in late tonight."

"No problem." I start clearing the dishes. "Me too."

There is a lot of work to be done when so many people are gone. We volunteer to deliver mail three times a week; the U.S. mail is starting to creep along but the international deliveries are still dicey. Citizens must mow their yards plus maintain any adjacent abandoned properties. We do pothole repair, trash collection, and food delivery.

There isn't enough demand at the college for Cal to teach algebra again, so he is working at the local airport doing helicopter maintenance. He complained bitterly when he received his Citizen's Orders. "I worked on helicopters twenty years ago! What will I remember?" But the U.S. Council for Recovery must have found his old Army records, and flying workers out to the Gulf's offshore rigs is a top priority.

As he works in the hangers I do street cleaning, dig in our victory garden, and teach basic English at the college. There are no more literature classes; the liberal arts may have gasped their last breath with the plague. English as a Second Language isn't really my field, but since half of the students are now Spanish-speaking, it's needed. Especially after the second *Tres de Julio* celebration and the borders declared open indefinitely. The hot jobs of the future will be elementary ed (for the upcoming baby boom), medical care, and industry. To add to my load, I also take a Spanish refresher course taught by one of my colleagues.

With teaching, volunteering, studying, and digging in the dirt, I'm tired all the time. I crave sleep but it's full of nightmares. Ever since Cal mentioned wanting to see the Menil collection in Houston, I dream of Greco-Roman statues, deathlike in their pale and marbled skin. In my dreams they are cold to the touch, as white as bones.

"You look tired," he says, as if reading my thoughts.

"I'm fine," I lie. "When will you get in?" I run water over the dishes as he gets his toolbox.

"Maybe midnight."

"That *is* late."

"Well, I've got mail deliveries, street repair, then work at the hanger."

"But *midnight*? You're going to the Lazarus meetings, aren't you?" I hadn't planned to ask that, but it just came out and I can't pull the words back into my mouth.

"What? Of course not."

I stop washing the dishes and turn to him. "If you need a support group, I understand. I just want you to be honest with me about it."

"I'm not hanging around with a bunch of Jesus freaks. You know that."

"Do I?" My words can't stop themselves. I think to myself *shut up, shut up, shut up* but I still go on. "Yesterday you said that Revelation had predicted the rising of the dead. And that communion is a type of cannibalism."

"I don't have to go to a meeting to know that."

"But then you were talking about how Christians believe God forgives everything, no matter how horrible, and you seemed to be *admiring* the idea. Don't you remember how you used to laugh at that?"

"Can you blame people for wanting to hear some comforting words now?"

"But you've *never* believed in a god."

"I still don't! Christ, after everything that's happened you think I believe in some white-bearded grandpa in the sky? And just because I'm thinking about some things out loud, trying to wrap my head around what has happened, philosophically, you think I'm going to meetings?"

"I'm sorry."

"Are you mad at me for something?" he asks. "Is there anything you want to talk about?"

His question is so big that my brain turns off.

"No."

"Look," he says. "The only thing that the Lazarus loo-loo's have right is that it's not the Turners' fault what happened. It was the *virus'* fault. Right?"

"Right." I stand with my arms crossed over my chest. I know he thinks that I'm self-righteous, just because I never turned. I was an NI. A Mole. A scared but healthy citizen hiding in the dark with my head between my knees. But even though I was a Non-Infected, I have just as much guilt as anyone else.

"We all have to stand together," he says.

He's echoing the President, the former U.S. Secretary of Education, who seems to channel Abraham Lincoln, Margaret Thatcher, and even Winston Churchill on her good days. *A house divided against itself cannot stand.*

"I'll see you tonight," he says. I expect him to come over and hug me in reconciliation but he doesn't; he just leaves. The front door still has the deep drill bit holes in it left over from the two-by-four bracings. When it slams shut, it looks like it's been crucified.

The first thing Cal did was board up the house. We were lucky that we already had the hurricane plywood and boards in his garage shop; by this time there was already looting at the lumber stores. Then I heard grinding. When Cal came out of the garage he had made arrows for his recurve bow and sharpened an old Civil War sword he had found at a flea market years ago. I kept Lindy occupied and away from the TV, where live reports of outbreaks were showing horrific scenes. Cal said we needed food. I begged him not to go but he took the longest of the kitchen knives and the sword. He was gone for two days. I only allowed myself to be hysterical when Lindy was asleep. Cell phones weren't working and there were sounds of gunfire in the distance. When the car finally screeched back into the driveway, it was full of supplies.

"Cal!" I removed the bracings and let him in. I tried to hug him and Lindy was shouting "Daddy! Daddy!" but he pushed us back. "Stay inside. Let me unload."

He had parked the car as close to the front door as possible, as both a barricade and quick escape. He unpacked bags of cornmeal, rice, beans, flour, bottles of vitamins, cans of Sterno, bags of dog food, and boxes of moist cat food.

"Are we going to eat *pet food*?" I asked.

"There's almost nothing left. But no one has thought of the pet stores yet."

"What's it like out there?"

"It's spreading very fast."

"But what took you so long?"

"The highways are clogged. People are getting trapped inside their cars. I had to go off-road just to get what I could and I got stuck in the baseball field. There were lots of . . . *them*, wandering around, looking for people. I had to hide in the backseat under a blanket until they were gone. Then I dug out the tires."

He had a stuffed toy for Lindy and she danced with it into her room.

"There are people jumping off overpasses," Cal whispered. "There's no place to go right now."

I had never seen my husband's hands shake before.

"We'll be okay here, right?"

"We'll be okay," he kissed me. "We'll hunker down. I'm glad I thought of the pet stores. The animals were locked up and thirsty. I opened the cages and let them go."

"Will they be okay?"

"They're fast; they have instincts. Hell, they probably have a better chance than most of us."

Later that night, I heard him working in the attic.

I think about what Cal said as I bicycle to work. "We all have to stand together." I pedal around the broken-down tank that is left on Main Street. The morning sun glistens on the armor plating but the tank's shadow stretches long and cold. The main gun on the turret points like an accusing finger. How can things get back to normal when there are so many reminders? It's not fair that Turners don't have memories of what happened. It's not fair that they "died" and got to escape, drifting off to some numbing space while their bodies were puppets of the plague. It's too *easy* for them to say that we can stand together and move on. Clasp our hands in friendship. Hurrah.

I get to campus and lock my bike, right by the new hitching posts. A few saddled horses are here already, blithely munching on the grass and swishing their tails. With gas rations being what they are, the rodeo horses have new jobs as commuters. In Australia they are using camels and in India, elephants. I walk down the sidewalk that professors scrubbed clean, past the fields where we buried bodies, and enter through doors that I rinsed free of bloody handprints. The first jobs for returning faculty and staff were to help clean the campus, and I won't describe what we saw. Or smelled.

I walk past the computer lab where the "Campus Eight" held their last stand against Turners. Eight students holed up all winter, using the ceiling spaces to reach food in the bookstore and cafeteria. They nearly made it. But a pack of Turners was always pounding, pounding on the doors and they finally clawed their way in. The president of the college says that the students actually died of dehydration first, and then the Infected broke in and ate the remains. But I helped clear out the lab and I know the truth of the battle that took place in there. I found one of the student's journals and he named, specifically, who was pounding on the doors. Two of the Turners were deans and three were professors.

There will be no engraved memorial plaque for the "Campus Eight." Hell, there probably won't be memorials for *anyone*—that's not how things are done any more. People can't honor people they killed with their bare hands and devoured. There is no precedent—no historical, sociological, or psychological guidebook—for rabid cannibalization on a mass scale. Sure, there are horror films of zombies (a word we don't use) but those were what passed as entertainment and not real life.

In real life we're supposed to forget about it and move on. We're not supposed to use the expression "pack" of Turners, or "hoards," or "murder." It's "groups" and "causalities." The slang terms "Turners" and "Moles" should be the Infected (I) and Non-Infected (NI). As faculty, we can't ask which student was what during the epidemic, nor can we ask who is a legal citizen or not. Students can't wear T-shirts with logos about the plague, such as "Bite Me," "One Bullet—One Brain," "Turner = Turncoat," or "Moles have Souls." One logo has the Christian fish, the *ichthys*, with a bite taken out of it and the words "Fish is Brain Food." Those are worn by the unrepentant eaters. They are a minority, but they are loud. Most of them belong to the anti-Lazarus organizations that suggest the plague absolutely proves there is no God. These are the groups I thought Cal might have joined by now.

In class, I watch my students and I can't help but wonder who turned and who hid. Every closed-lipped smile I see makes me wonder if there are cracked teeth behind it, broken from biting on bones, buttons, and jewelry. I look at fingers, trying to find disfigurements left from clawing through barricades. I wonder who ate their sisters, their parents, their pets. I look at scars. But sometimes I teach an entire class *not* looking at them, simply rolling the chalk through my fingers and feeling the gritty dust on the old chalkboards that were wheeled into the classrooms. (The rolling blackouts often knock out the projectors.) The chalk is as smooth as the Grecian statues in my nightmares. Those marbled feet; those stony veins that I hold in my dreams . . . sometimes I think I'm losing my mind.

But there is one student. Maria. There is something different about her. She is defiant. Her eyes flash and she holds her chin high. Her brown hair is lustrous and her smile is dazzling with white perfect teeth. There is something untouchable about her, as if she has weathered everything with a grace and haughty anger. When she enters the room and says "Hola, profesora"—in a tone both icy and warm—it sounds as if she is saying: "This is nothing to me."

I wish I were more like Maria.

After work I slide my ration card into the scanner at human resources and it adds my daily work points. I immediately type into the keyboard and remove four of the points, sending them directly to the National Institute for Parentless Children.

It is late afternoon when I pedal for home; the shadow of the tank still inks the asphalt on Main Street. I try to veer around it, but I end up wheeling into its darkness, as if I'm rolling into a well.

↶

They came at all hours of the day and night. They scraped along the side of the house, moaned at the doors, ran their fingernails over the boards. Lindy cried and acted out—who could blame her? We had to be quiet. When the power went out we had candles; when the gas went out we had blankets. Our world got smaller and smaller. And colder. By late December, they were breaking in. Cal protected us as best as he could—he aimed for their eyes with his arrows; he aimed for their throats with the sword.

But there were too many of them. And not just the Infected either, there were looters too. The sick and the non-sick alike were trying to kill us. We moved up to the attic.

Cal had already prepared everything. He had made a rain-tight hatch for the roof that we could open and let light in, when the weather wasn't too frigid. He had drilled peepholes and ventilation tubes. He had paints and colors for Lindy to draw on the low-hanging rafters, and he had hidden little toys for her to find in nooks. We had games. The attic stairs could be easily pulled up and secured behind us. He had black-out covers for every hole, window, and gap.

We even had a hand-crank radio that was our only link to the outside. Every nation had the flu. It was a pandemic. That December we learned about the quarantine camps for the Infected. In January we learned about the military bombing those camps: New York, L.A., Chicago, San Antonio . . . We heard about North Korea using a nuclear bomb on China. The dust from the bomb was making the winter even colder.

In February we heard about a rebel group of survivors across the border who were refusing to hide. They were fighting.

Today my student Maria is as haughty and beautiful as ever. After class a man is waiting for her outside and I do a double take. He looks like Felix Narvaez, the leader of the Mexican rebel survivors, the man for whom *Tres de Julio* will forever be known.

"This is mi tío," Maria tells me proudly.

"Hello, pleased to meet you," Felix Narvaez says in perfect English and shakes my hand.

I'm dumbfounded. I had heard rumors that he was setting up a business on the Texas coast, but here? In our town? Students walk by staring at him and tittering. A few people are waiting nearby for autographs.

"My niece tells me that she enjoys your class."

"Thank you."

His dark hair is tinged with gray. His teeth are gleaming and perfect. Like

Maria, he is tall and stands straight. They share the posture of the victorious. It's true—he looks like Zorro. I think of the famous picture of him as he stood his ground on the Reynosa Bridge in McAllen, Texas: his right hand holding a rifle, his left hand making the peace sign. They say his legs straddled the Rio Grande and his heart straddled two worlds: he embraced both the living and dead.

"Mr. Narvaez, it's such an honor to meet you. What are you doing here in Lake Jackson?"

"I am starting my shipping business nearby, in Freeport."

"He knows how to get food and gas," Maria says. "You need anything, he's the go-to hombre."

"I have workers here on campus." He motions to a flatbed truck in the empty parking lot full of cardboard boxes, crates of bottled water, and baskets of fruit. "My people have just signed the contract for food services here, and for the main supply runs in the county."

"That's wonderful."

I've already heard the rumors that Felix Narvaez can get anything; that he used to be a higher-up in the Los Zetas cartel before the epidemic. He claims that he was "a simple farmer," but everyone knows that he had access to weapons, lots of them, and when the plague broke out he saved all the Non-Infected that he found, from Monterrey to Reynosa. They moved as a unit up towards the border on horseback, in ATVS, in trucks towing wagons—mothers, fathers, grandparents, and children, all hungry and dreaming of getting to the Valley, that Eden of grapefruit, oranges, tangelos, melons, and cattle. From there they dreamed of rebuilding San Antonio, Corpus Christi, Houston. In each town along the way it was Felix Narvaez who kicked the doors down, saved the Non-Infected, and fought off the Turners either by hand or by bullet. But when they reached the Rio Grande they were met by four thousand Infected who had shambled from McAllen, Mission, Edinburg, and other border towns until they mindlessly reached the river. The water was a natural barrier that had them shuffling aimlessly along the banks. Aimless, that is, until they smelled the fresh flesh of Narvaez's people. They groaned in hunger. They say that the sound of that groaning hoard shook the walls in McAllen. They say that birds flew away. They say the water in the Rio Grande trembled. It was here where Felix Narvaez met the horde head-on, on the Reynosa International Bridge, on the third of July.

"I saw you on the broadcast from New York," I said. There had been a parade for him on the first anniversary, down what was left of Wall Street. The President had given him a medal.

"Ah," he shrugs modestly. "Sí." He looks at me and it is as though he is looking right into me. I can tell that he has already pegged me for a Mole, and I smile widely so he can see my teeth. I'm blushing. I take off my ugly black-rimmed glasses and pretend to wipe the thick lenses.

"It was nice to meet you," I say, and he actually gives me a short bow. The mayor of the town and college's Board of Regents are clasping his hand, patting his back, moving him towards the college's entrance sign to pose for pictures. The deans smile for the cameras with closed lips. Feliz Narvaez and Maria make the peace sign. I take my bike from the rack and Señor Narvaez is still watching me.

I race home, pedaling like I'm pumping the blood back into my heart.

Winter went on forever. By March it had even snowed. We used the roof's hatch to get fresh air and turn out our buckets of refuse, "night-soil" as they used to call it. When we ran out of water Cal made furtive trips to the pond in the backyard. We boiled a half-gallon at a time using Sterno cans.

The Infected never stopped. They shambled outside and even dug through our shit. We slept a lot and ate very little. Lindy had regressed into speaking baby talk.

"Do you think she'll remember this?" Cal asked.

"I hope not."

"She could turn into a writer and write a book about it. It could be like *The Diary of Anne Frank*."

"There are a million Anne Franks out there right now," I said.

Cal sang to her softly and held her hand. When he finished, he said, "I need to leave for more supplies."

"That's crazy!" I whispered. "You'll never get through the streets."

"I've been thinking I could crawl under them, using the big drainage pipe that runs from the pond over to Second Street. There's a gas station there, and an office supply store. I know the store had vending machines and I bet more food was in the employee lounge."

I begged him not to go. I told him we had enough to last a few more months, and that he was just bored and starting to get careless. But he left.

"I don't get people's fascination with Felix Narvaez," Cal says. "There were hundreds of other people who did similar things: Laurent de Gaulle in France, Anahi Mendez in Bolivia, that Chinese woman who saved all the children in her province . . ."

"But Felix Narvaez is ours. He's *our* country's war hero."

"It wasn't a war. It was a *virus*. Besides, the cure was being distributed that same day. It would have been a national day of celebration with or without him."

I don't argue with him, but I'm annoyed. We have power and I'm at my computer. I don't know why I do it, but I open up a file that has a picture that I took of Cal a few weeks after the cure.

"Who is that?" he asks, leaning over.

"It's you."

Cal jumps. "Bullshit."

The picture shows a gaunt figure on the bed. The eyes are hollow, sunken. The gums are pulled back from the teeth. An IV tube of antibiotics and fluids snakes over his arm. "That's you. That's a few days after I found you at the rescue center."

"It looks like a Civil War soldier," he says, "like one of those daguerreotypes of the dead on the battlefield. Look at that beard! No, that's not me. I never grew a beard."

"Yes you did. In the attic. You stopped shaving because we didn't have any extra water. Remember?"

"No. I always shaved." He looks at the picture. "That's me all right. Look at the tattoo. But if I grew a beard that means I wasn't Infected after all. The Infected were dead—they couldn't grow hair."

"You *were* Infected. I saw you get sick. You grew that beard in the attic, you got sick, and four months later when I found you it was still the same length. It didn't grow any longer because you were . . . " I can't say "dead." It's true, but I can't say it to him. It's too cruel.

"I always shaved."

"Are you crazy? You got sick. You Turned."

Cal jumps up and paces the room. He walks towards Lindy's room but stops himself. "Things happen for a reason!" he says.

"What? Another quote from the Lazarus brochure?"

"Things happen for a reason!" he says again.

"Okay, so what's the reason?"

"If we hadn't had the plague, we wouldn't have had the cure. The cure is likely to prolong human life indefinitely. Just think of it, now we know how it suspends cellular decay and we know how to manipulate it. The bubonic plague had massive benefits in the fourteenth century—there were huge developments in technology, medicine, and mathematics. This plague will be the same. The sacrifice of so many people leads to better lives in the future. This virus may be the promise of an eternal life!"

His hand is resting on the doorknob to Lindy's room.

"Sacrifice? Eternal Life? You *have* been going to the Lazarus meetings." I walk into our bedroom and slam the door.

Cal came back to the attic. He brought some cans of food and all seemed well, but two days later he began coughing. I searched him for scratch or bite marks but he was clean. We didn't know then that the virus was also airborne, and not just transmitted by saliva and bodily fluids. We had heard on the radio that some people were claiming they were bitten and didn't get sick, but we didn't understand what that meant. Now we know that the reason Moles didn't get sick was because many of them had a natural immunity, like me. And Lindy.

It had started with a random mutation that jumped from sheep to human, but who knew that plastics—*plastics* of all things—were responsible for the flu's gruesome effect? It's hard to believe. BPA, the chemical Bisphenol-A that is in everything from plastic bottles to Tupperware, is what the scientists call a "xenoestrogen endrocrine disruptor." It became the catalyst for the prions of the mutated *ovis* flu to hijack the infected brains and circulatory systems.

Our ignorance of the viral nuances proved a disaster. Families let in other survivors, who had unknowingly picked up the bug. Cal had met other people holed up in the office supply store. One of them must have been a carrier.

His fever rose. "It's probably from crawling through that freezing culvert," I said. "It's probably nothing." His face was pale and sweaty; he hadn't shaved in weeks.

"I can't Turn," he said. "I can't hurt you or Lindy. I can't be up here with you."

"You won't Turn. You'll be fine. Hush."

I fell asleep curled against him and Lindy for warmth. Some time that night I heard the attic stairs descend then pop back up.

He was gone. He had written on one of the rafters, right by Lindy's drawings. "I love you."

Cal gets into the bed during the night and holds me. "I don't like it when we fight," he whispers.

Turners say that the first thing they remember is their chest pounding when their hearts started beating again and the cold, quick breath of air back into the lungs. Some say they remember floating to a heavenly white light and being jerked back, but Cal says he remembers nothing. They can't remember the screaming or the taste of blood on their teeth, like warm copper pennies. It's up to the Non-Infected to remember. It's up to me.

The nation's economy is nearly nonexistent, and the only million-dollar selling product is a little plastic bracelet that says, "Jesus rose. Jesus forgives."

I watch Cal in the dark next to me and I want to hit him. I want to smoother him, choke him, bite him, kiss him. I hate him; I love him. He's my husband. He was Lindy's father. He saved us. He was once undead and now he's back.

"What's on your mind? Why don't you ever talk to me?" he whispers.

Surely he must know. But I say nothing and we make love instead. I think of Felix Narvaez.

Cal was gone. One day I heard shuffling below us in the garage and looked through a peephole in the attic's floor. It was him. He was standing in front of his workbench looking blankly, as if he had forgotten something. He moaned. Then he shuffled out through a broken gap in the door and joined the other Turners, slowly walking down the streets looking for blood.

Two months later Lindy and I had eaten all the dog and cat food. Cal's idea had saved our lives so far; there were people starving all over the world. I was going to have a make a plan.

Cal has erased his picture from my computer. I was looking for it this morning but it's gone. I don't blame him for not wanting a reminder of what he looked like post-infection, but it was mine. He had no right to destroy it. I check the message boards and realize that I miss the old Internet, full of silly videos. The U.S. Council for Recovery has set up Neighbor-Board, the only social networking site we have, but it's not the same. There is no YouTube or video sharing. The last thing the Council wanted was someone posting old footage of attacks. The feeling I have knowing that Cal got on my computer and deleted his picture is the same one I have when I use this new "net." It feels likes some sort of violation, or censorship.

I ride my bike to work and it's a fine spring morning. There is even a sprig of green sprouting from the dirt and grit in the tank on Main Street.

I had climbed out of the roof's hatch, screaming for Lindy. The roar in my ears turned out to be planes zooming in from the horizon: crop dusters. A yellow mist came streaming out from them. One of the planes flew so close that the pilot waggled his wing tip at me. He probably thought I had been on the roof, shouting for joy.

At this same time, Felix Narvaez was on the bridge in McAllen, facing the four thousand gruesome hungry dead. He had been listening in on the radio contact between the military and heard the cure was on the way. He refused to fire on the Infected. He stopped right where he was. His people had enough firepower to destroy the whole hoard but he ordered them not to fire. Instead, they fought them off by hand until the planes soared overhead and released their loads. They could have died in their act of compassion, and they nearly did. Narvaez watched the dust settle and the slow shift of consciousness begin.

That was the day I lost Lindy. That was the day the world came back alive. It was the third of July.

This morning when I get to campus I go to the faculty break room first. Sarah, the psychology teacher, is talking with the Spanish teacher, Kay. "It's not anorexia," Sarah says, "but something near to it. I'm sure it's based on guilt and not physiology. Clinically, I'll be interested to see the long-term effects. Some of the people I'm seeing can't keep anything down, and it's not just Turners either. There is a subset of people who didn't get infected at all but are claiming that they did, and that they can't remember anything. They are also vomiting when they think of food."

Poor Sarah. Not only does she teach classes and volunteer like the rest of us, her Citizens Orders have her counseling post-traumatic shock victims. Kay sees me and clears a space for me.

"Buenos días. ¿Cómo estás?"

"Hola. Muy bien. ¿Y tú?

"Así así," Kay smiles. She has always been something of a quiet seer. When Cal and I got married she gave me a beautiful candelabra and her handwritten note said: *Something to help light your way.* Kay has told me that in less than ten years more than half of the country will not speak English. I had asked her what would happen if the borders closed and the English-speakers got ticked off about being outnumbered. She had said, "Perhaps another Civil War, no? Neighbor against neighbor, yet again."

Kay listens quietly while Sarah talks about her patients. I put my lunch in the faculty fridge and excuse myself. "I have to go to the library. Adiós."

I know what I have to do. I dreamed about it last night. I dreamed I was teaching Daniel Defoe's tale of the bubonic plague, Katherine Anne Porter's tale of the 1918 flu, Albert Camus' tale of cholera, Randy Shilts's tale of HIV,

Richard Preston's tale of Ebola . . . There were so many books on the lectern that they spilled over. I leaned against a marble bust of Giovanni Boccaccio and it fell, crashing to the floor. I knelt to retrieve the pieces but found only marble feet instead, tiny and delicate, like a child's. "What will they write of us?" I asked the class. "What will they write of *us*?" The students tried to answer but their voices only beeped and blared like the campus emergency alerts. When I woke, I knew what I needed to do.

I've timed my visit carefully, when I know the head librarian will be there. She was a Mole. She and her husband made it out to their deer lease in West Texas where they survived on venison and canned fruit, but they ran out of heat and nearly froze in the winter. She lost two toes.

"I have something for the library," I tell her. "But not everyone should see this. Not everyone would understand."

I slide her the journal that I found in the computer lab, written by one of the Eight.

Her eyes open wide. "I heard rumors about this!" She fingers the bloodstained pages. "I'll put it in the archive," she whispers. "Only I have the key."

I nod. "Maybe later, people will want to know."

"Does it name names?"

"Yes."

"Was Cal . . . "

"No. He wasn't one of them."

I turn to leave but she has gripped my hand. Her eyes are welling up with tears and we hold hands over the circulation desk top; the granite is as cold as marble. We share the solidarity of the hidden. There is a sentence in the journal where the student wrote, "We know our families are gone but we still love them. We know hope is gone too but we still have it. We're starving. We're too weak to fight them off. Whoever finds this, please know that we were here. We hope the world makes it."

The cure stayed in the air, like magic. The sunlight made it shimmer as golden dust motes. Soon the sprayer trucks used for mosquito repellent were fogging the neighborhoods with it as well. All over the country, the hidden emerged from basements, cellars, attics, safe rooms, and offices. We were skeletal, rib-worn and pale. We squinted in the bright sunlight, like the moles that we were.

I had asked Maria if her uncle could get something for me. I whispered the name of the item in her ear, terribly embarrassed. "No problema," she said.

I thought it would come wrapped in paper or disguised in some way. But when one of Narvaez's workers on the flatbed truck hands it to me, the pink plastic is obvious. I slip the pills in my purse and give my ration card for him to slide through his handheld debit machine. Technically, what I'm doing is wrong. The President has announced a temporary ban on all birth control items, hoping to boost the recovery boom. But Narvaez's worker doesn't bat an eye. I wonder what other things Maria's uncle gets for people, legal or not.

"Hello, professor." I turn around and it is Felix Narvaez himself.

"Hi."

"Have you everything you need?"

He must know what is in my pocket. Probably nothing about his businesses escapes his attention. "Yes, thank you." He is looking at my wedding ring.

"My husband was a Turner," I say, as if that might explain anything. We watch each other and I hold my chin up, like Maria does. I too can be unrepentant.

"It must be difficult sleeping with betrayal, no?" he says.

I was nearly too weak to go find him. To be honest, I was so upset over Lindy that I didn't even look for him; it was a colleague from work who called me, telling me there was someone who looked like Cal at one of the Recovery Centers. I found him lying on an army cot.

The medicine from the planes and foggers had cured the Infected, but many were dying. Once the body was reawakened and the immune system started working, massive infections took over. Turners had broken teeth, with bits of gristle and bone lodged in their gums. Many died from oral infections. There was a shortage of antibiotics. Cal was lucky. He would be okay. Many people had been shot or knifed; some injuries were too horrendous to be cured. People were dying all over. Non-Infected were shooting themselves, jumping off of bridges, hanging themselves in closets—they were wracked by the guilt from "putting down" an Infected loved one. Imagine the ones who had shot their own children in the head and then saw the cure come sprinkling down from the sky, like a prayer answered too late?

In those early weeks of July, the Infected and the Non-Infected looked alike. We were all stuck in the lacuna of being half-alive.

Cal saw me and reached out from his cot. I instinctively backed away. He looked hurt.

"Lindy?" he asked, looking around.

"She's gone."

Cal began to wail and a volunteer nurse rushed over. "Hush," she said sternly. She knew if one person let go it would snowball from cot to cot, town to town, nation to nation—a whole world gone mad with hysteria and grief. Once it started it would never stop.

"Let's go home," I said.

Felix has asked me to dinner. I haven't given him my answer yet.

Summer is coming along nicely and the victory garden outside is producing well. I dreamt of the statues again last night but they turned into Lindy. I had left the attic to find more supplies, but she had followed behind me. I didn't know. She got too close to an opening in a window and something yanked her. I dreamt I'm trying to pull her back inside the house but the thing outside won't let her go. It sounds like an animal. There is blood. The dream goes soundless. I'm holding a statue's feet, no . . . they are Lindy's feet and they are going cold. Her little toes twitch. I feel for a pulse at an ankle. Her feet become drained of blood; they turn as white as bone, as still as stone.

Cal chews his cereal and sees me deep in thought. "What is it?"

"Nothing."

Felix has procured extra gas rations for faculty, so I get to drive the car to work. It's sunny and I put on my sunglasses—I have contact lenses now, also thanks to Felix. When I turn on the radio they are finishing a replay of the President's State of the Union speech: "To persevere is to live—to live together as one country, one nation—together in health, hope, and liberty. Forgiveness is not forgetfulness, but rather an acknowledgement of the innate need for security, survival, and the necessity of recovery. We shall *all* be reawakened to see a new vision of our nation . . . " After she finishes there is applause and then a John Lennon song starts playing. I listen to the chorus: *"And we all shine on . . . "*

I drive slowly around the commuters on bicycles and on horseback; people wave to each other and smile. I pass by the tank on Main Street and there is a tiny tree sprouting up from the turret. A cardinal warbles and sings on the strongest branch, as red as a drop of blood.

Someday maybe the world will "make it," as the writer of the Campus Eight had hoped. I don't know if it will involve remembering or forgetting. I don't know what languages our silences might speak. But maybe it will be okay. Maybe someday I will tell Cal that I dreamed of him crouched over the body of our daughter, taking bite after loving bite.

A Shepherd of the Valley

Maggie Slater

The low-lying fog across the tarmac made it difficult to be certain, but the figure moving toward the tower limped like a roamer. James Shepherd lifted his binoculars—it was a girl, a young girl, wearing a jacket so large its cuffs hung over her hands and the waist almost down to her knees. She favored her left leg, or perhaps her ankle. No doubt she'd been walking on it unconsciously for weeks, maybe even months.

I can fix that, Shepherd thought, and it made him smile. It had been a while since a roamer wandered onto his ground space. He'd have to give her a good name. A sweet name. Perhaps Esther. *Little Esther*, he thought, and tapped in the command for Peter to intercept and incapacitate.

Luke was also in the area, not a hundred meters off by Hanger B.

Adding Esther would make his group an even dozen, and that too made Shepherd smile. He pulled off a piece of masking tape and pressed it beneath the others on the control panel. With a marker, he wrote her name.

Twelve was a good number. A holy number, if the Good Book was right. Peter, Matthew, David, John, Paul, Mary, Luke, Bartholomew, Joseph, Martha, Mark, and now Esther. Yes, twelve was right.

As he watched Peter tromp toward the newcomer, Shepherd heard a strange noise over the radio. At first, he thought it might be a breeze caught in Peter's microphone, but it grew steadily stronger. The moan reached him across the speakers in the air traffic control tower just as the little red button next to Peter's name began blinking ferociously.

Not a moment after that, Luke's light started flashing, too.

Shepherd stared at the lights, hardly remembering what they were meant to indicate. It had been so long since one had flashed.

He snatched up his binoculars and looked out at the three figures, now visible and moving toward one another. As he watched, the girl lifted what he'd mistaken for a long stick at her side and pointed it at Peter's head.

The girl was alive.

Shepherd's hands leapt for the microphone button. "No, wait!"

The blast of a shotgun echoed through his tower speakers.

Panicked, Shepherd twisted the knob for Luke's frequency and slammed the speaker button again. "Wait! Don't shoot." He stabbed his fingers onto the keyboard to command Luke to stand still. "Hold your fire. They won't hurt you. I'm in control."

The speakers buzzed. "Who's talking? Where are you?"

Shepherd froze at the sound of the voice and lifted his face toward the window again. "Penny?" His voice cracked when he said her name.

"Hold on," Shepherd said, ducking under the control panel to plug in the video line for Hanger B's security camera. A flood of gray light filled the dusking room behind him as he scrambled back into his seat.

The girl stood some twenty yards away from the hanger, and Luke was less than half that distance from her, his back and the glint of his bolted metal spine visible on the video feed. The girl's shotgun was leveled at his chest. The video was too grainy to see much else in detail.

Shepherd leaned in until the static from the screen crackled at the tip of his nose. "What's your name?" He couldn't even be sure of her face shape, let alone her features.

"I'm not telling you shit until you tell me where you are."

"Sorry—I just need to fix . . . something." Shepherd squinted and leaned back from the screen, as though blurring the image more would somehow make it sharper.

Is it? He couldn't be sure. He counted off how old Penny would be now, if she was still safe. She'd been fourteen when she left, so she'd be nineteen now.

Over the speakers, Luke's wheezing grew stronger. The muzzle of the girl's shotgun, which had dipped toward the ground as she surveyed the area, snapped back to attention. Shepherd glanced at the light next to Luke's name, but it no longer blinked.

"How are you doing this?" The girl's voice had a husky growl in it, too low for Penny. But the longer he looked at the video, the more the girls seemed alike. "How are you controlling that thing?"

"I'm coming down. Wait there."

"You try to pull any tricks and I'll blow this motherfucker's head off just like the last one."

"No tricks. I'm in the control tower. You'll see me coming."

The girl grunted as Shepherd released the microphone button and headed for the stairs. Bart and Mary stood barring the door out to the tarmac where he'd placed them. Their lips and blood-crusted teeth chewed at him around the edges of the speakers he'd installed in their throats. They gave him a cursory glance as he slipped past them with a light touch to their shoulders and a quiet, "Excuse me."

He'd grown so used to them that he'd forgotten how frightening they must look to a someone who didn't realize the suits prevented them from acting on their feral instincts. Still, his chest tightened as he turned the corner of the tower and saw the three figures in the foggy distance: two standing and one crumpled on the ground.

"Lord, have mercy upon them," Shepherd whispered.

He wanted to run to them, but he fought the urge for fear of making the girl nervous. With each step, he tried to make out the details of her hair, her face, her height—anything to determine with certainty that she was familiar. But as he drew near, and the girl turned toward him, he knew she wasn't Penny. Just a youth alone in a bitter world clutching to her firepower like a security blanket.

He lifted his hands.

"I'm not going to hurt you," he said. "It was me you heard. Please, put the gun down."

"Not on your life," the girl said, glaring at Luke. His exosuit was locked at the joints, but he didn't struggle against the sudden stillness of his limbs. Instead, he twisted his head as a trickle of bloody spittle dribbled down his chin from the side of his mouth.

But then, Luke had always been the quietest of the bunch. Shepherd felt a pang of guilt that he was glad that Peter had taken the shot, and not Luke.

What kind of a father thinks like that? His gaze dropped to the form on the ground collapsed in a pile of awkward angles. A marionette with cut strings and stiff metal joints.

The girl aimed her gun toward him as Shepherd knelt beside what was left of Peter. The left side of Peter's head was gone; pulped gray matter coated the asphalt. The dislodged speaker hung out the open side of his skull. The battery pack strapped to his twisted back hummed.

With a sigh, Shepherd pressed Peter's remaining eyelid shut and flipped the switch on the pack to shut it down. Then he bowed his head and whispered the Lord's Prayer. He wished he knew what pastors used to say over gravesites, but all he could remember—which he added to the end of the prayer he knew—was, "Ashes to ashes. Dust to dust."

The girl shifted her weight on her stronger leg, and the gravel crunched. He could see now that the heel of her favored foot was pushed up and out of the dirty sneaker. There was crusted blood speckled up the ankle.

"You're hurt," he said.

The girl scowled at him. "Who the fuck are you? And what . . . what the *fuck* is that?" Her finger stabbed in Luke's direction.

"That's Luke. And this was Peter. You don't have to be afraid. No one here will hurt you." He began to rise to his feet, but the girl pushed the muzzle of her shotgun into his chest.

"Don't move."

She was younger than he'd first thought, certainly younger than his Penny would be now, but Shepherd knew better than to underestimate the anger of youth, so he sank back down to his heels and lifted his hands again.

"I have a first aid kit in the tower," he said. "And food, if you want it. I'd be happy to share it with you."

"Yeah, right." The girl scoffed, her attention flickering between him and Luke. "You're just going to be a good neighbor and give me medicine, food, and a big damn feather bed for nothing?" She shook her head, and her sneer twisted into something a little like a smile. "You think I don't know how this works?"

The girl took a shuffling, unsteady step back, putting a little more space between them. For a moment, a wince cracked her face. "Are there more of those things around here?"

"Yes. There are nine others."

The girl cursed and reached into a backpack she wore slung over one shoulder. Tucked under her arm and obscured by the bulky jacket, Shepherd hadn't even noticed it until then. She squinted at him as she pulled out a box of shotgun shells and pried it open with one hand while the other remained on the trigger. She glanced at the box—once, twice—mouthing the numbers she counted without seeming to realize it.

"You won't need your weapon here," Shepherd said. "They can't hurt you. Even if they wanted to, I've modified them so that they can't move without my command."

"Oh, yeah?" She stuffed the box of ammo back into her bag. "Prove it."
"How?"

As he stood, she smiled, keeping the shotgun pointed at his chest. "Go up and stick your arm near those nice chompers of his."

Shepherd nodded and walked to Luke's side. He put his hand on the roamer's shoulder, squeezing it. Luke seemed calmer in the eyes today. Perhaps—if he wasn't reading too much into it—even a little sad when his unfocused gaze rolled down to Shepherd. Perhaps he understood what had happened to Peter.

Perhaps.

"It's okay, Luke," he said softly. "It's all right."

"What kind of a sicko are you?" The girl watched him with narrow, red-rimmed eyes. "I mean, hey, don't get me wrong, everyone's got the right to go ape shit these days, and I'm thrilled to pieces to meet you, Mr. Talks-to-Zombies, but . . . *shit* . . . " She shook her head from side to side slowly. "You're fucking insane, you know that?"

It was the rush of blood to his face that made him suddenly realize that he was angry. It had been so long since he'd let himself feel like that, or screamed, or cursed, or broke things, or released all that pent-up energy inside of him. It was a thought that made him close his eyes and will the flames back into submission. Flames unchecked—like tempers, like pride—rose and consumed, driven only by selfish destruction. Tamed fire was much more productive.

Patience, he reminded himself. It wasn't a virtue he'd had to practice lately. His flock of injured souls didn't know what they were doing, and it was easy to forgive them. Years had passed since he'd spoken to someone who could talk back to him, could curse at him, could shout at him. When he opened his eyes, he could see the girl for what she was: alone and scared, just like Penny had been.

"Not insane," he said quietly. "Just . . . " If he listened too closely, he could almost hear Penny's screams still ringing in the dark coils of his inner ear, could almost feel the sting of her fingernails against his arms, his face, and the warmth of her spit in his eye. It made him shiver before he could stop himself.

He looked up into Luke's bruised and bloodied face, the one empty eye socket that oozed milky puss, the broken teeth in his blackened gums, the spidery blue veins webbing his sagging jaw. "How can I not pity them? They're misery incarnate."

The muzzle of the shotgun clicked as it dipped down to the pavement. The girl squinted behind her, at the fringe of trees and the orange haze of the sunset tinting the fog around them. She wobbled on her good leg, and the toes of her injured foot pushed against the ground to stabilize her. She gritted her teeth and sucked a sharp breath through them. She glanced back at him with a softened frown and cleared her throat.

"Look, this is how this is going to work," she said. "I need that first aid kit. And a place to stay for the night. I've got my own food, if you don't want to share. I get that, so don't worry about it. I've got a little ammo I could give you in exchange, or . . . " The frown shifted to a hard, motionless expression that seemed to draw her eyes further back into her skull. "Or maybe we can work out something else."

"I don't want anything from you," Shepherd said. "I don't need anything."

The girl hoisted the shotgun up so that its muzzle pointed toward the darkening sky, resting against her shoulder. "Sure, you don't. Just name it. I'm not a prude, so you don't have to be embarrassed."

Shepherd looked at the scrawny girl and felt a pang in his chest. She'd been alone for a long time. Alone and very conscious of it. Was Penny like this now? Hardened? Ruthless? Did she know how to pull herself back like that, to disconnect, to escape when there was no one to protect her?

"I don't want anything from you," Shepherd said. "Your company is enough. I haven't spoken to anyone in years. It's just nice to hear a voice that isn't my own, and . . . " He wasn't sure if he should say anything, but the girl's doubts shaded her face, and the pang in his chest made him bold. "You remind me of my daughter. That's all. You can keep your gun and your belongings. I won't hurt you or trick you. I can swear that in the Lord's name, if you want. I take my oaths seriously."

The girl watched him beneath her drooping eyelids, but after a moment, her gaze fell to the ground and she nodded. "Fine. But I'm only staying for one night."

Sometime in the slow, hobbling trip back to the tower, the fog dissipated, and the evening's long, wet shadows stretched like steel bars across the asphalt. The girl refused Shepherd's help as she limped along, despite the sweat pearling on her brow and the lancing wince that crossed her face every time she put too much weight on the injured foot. But despite that streak of stubbornness, she seemed to trust him, at least to a degree. She made no protest other than a hunched-shoulder glance at Bart and Mary as he lead her past them and into the tower. She didn't ask about the floors they bypassed, moving up to the second highest, and even allowed him to carry her up the final flight of stairs and into the furnished living room.

Her arm over his shoulder felt like a broken wing—thin and fragile beneath the thick bulk of the jacket she wore. She was light, too, and for a moment he allowed his imagination to think she might be an angel sent to give him some kind of message.

He lowered her on the sofa bed he slept on, and sat down beside her. A sigh whistled through her teeth as she gingerly slid her sneaker off, revealing the heel to ankle gash glistening with dark, oozing blood.

"I was following the river," she said as she settled back and moved her foot onto his lap for closer inspection. "There was a . . . a metal bracket or something. I don't know. It was hidden in the tall grass."

She twitched when he put his finger near the inflamed laceration. The pale skin was red and swollen; grains of dirt lined the tender edges. Yellow bruising spread out and up the leg.

"How long have you been walking on this?" Shepherd asked.

"Two, maybe three days, I think." The girl's face had gone ashen and she swallowed hard. "Do you . . . do you have some water or something? I think I'm going to throw up."

She lay quietly, eyes closed, as Shepherd brought her a cup of water and then retrieved his first aid kit. He put on his reading glasses, the kit's rubber gloves, and carefully lifted her foot back onto his lap.

"I'm going to have to clean this," he said. "It may hurt."

The girl grimaced and shrugged. "I can handle it."

He used the antiseptic wipes to clean out the dirt and gathering puss. The girl's teeth clicked from time to time as she clenched them, but she said nothing—not a curse, not a whine, not a whimper. But when he tossed the first wipe away, he saw that her cheeks were wet.

His heart ached, watching her fluttering, moist eyelashes, her averted gaze. His own foot tingled along the ankle, and his stomach turned. In the semi-light of the room, and with her hair brushed back, her face struck him with its similarity to Penny's. In another life, at another time, she could have been mistaken for a daughter of his. Maybe she and Penny might even have been friends, confused for sisters—or twins—while shopping at the mall or volunteering at the hospital. The angle of her nose was like his; her eyes, slightly wide set and pale, could have been Anne's.

Anne. Shepherd looked down at the blood smeared on the rubber gloves, and the room suddenly spun. The last time he'd had blood that red, that fresh, on his hands . . . His throat tightened. Little trickles of blood dripped down his palms and onto his pants. The antiseptic on the second wipe was wet, and its liquid blurred the red streaks on his fingers, turning them a softer, fading pink.

He tried to be gentle as he continued, but judging from her occasional twitches and hisses of air, he knew he didn't always succeed. When had he last been near someone who could feel anything, could wince, could ache, or sting, or whisper curses under her breath? The skin he worked on blushed deeper with the irritation. His hands trembled. The silence between them, pierced only by her involuntary reactions to his touch against the wound, crept under his skin and festered into a film of nervous energy.

"Where are you from, originally?" he asked, noting the crack in his voice when he spoke. "Around here?"

The fabric of the sofa hissed as she shook her head against it and sighed. "I can't really talk right now," she whispered. "I'm barely holding it in as it is."

"Then I'll talk," Shepherd said. "Sorry, it's just . . . I haven't spoken to anyone in . . . years, I think. I mean, I talk to my flock, but it's . . . " He paused, closed his eyes against the sudden flicker of a headache. He wanted to pinch the bridge of his nose, or press his palms against his suddenly burning eyes, but he could feel the slime of blood on his gloves between his fingers, could smell it thick in his nostrils. He wasn't sure when he'd started sweating, but suddenly he felt clammy and cold, and had to fight back a shiver.

"It's not the same," he said, the words pushing themselves off his tongue and out of his lips before he had time to even think about what he was saying. "And it's just nice to know someone hears you—I mean, really *hears* you—instead of just . . . you know. I don't even know if they can understand me, and sometimes . . . sometimes you just . . . just . . . "

"Hey." He glanced at the girl. She was looking right at him, no hint of smirk or scowl on her face. "I get it," she said, so softly he almost couldn't hear it. "Talk if you need to. It's better than bottling this shit up."

Shepherd sat back and leaned his head against the wall behind him. He closed his eyes and tried to breath slowly, deeply, imagining all the little particles that made up his body, his cells, his molecules, his atoms, his electrons, and the energy that—for the moment—gave him existence. That same energy that gave everything he could see or touch or smell or taste or hear substance, all of life; the same energy that made dirt, made trees, made animals, made Penny, made roamers, and likewise made planets, stars, galaxies—everything. He was awash in a sea of existence, and it was good.

When he opened his eyes, the shivers had passed and he felt calmer. *Though I walk through the valley of the shadow of death*, he thought, *I shall fear no evil, for Thou art with me. Thy rod and thy staff, they comfort me.*

He sighed and shook his head, once more leaning forward to apply the antiseptic wipe to the cut. "I'm sorry," he said, pleased to hear that his voice was steady. "I'm not normally so easily shaken. It's just that at first glance, I really thought you might be my daughter. It got under my skin. That's all."

The girl frowned, eyes closed. "Where is she?"

"I don't know."

"Alive?"

"Don't know." He shook his head and tilted the foot toward him. The girl winced. "I'm sorry. I'm almost done."

Shepherd taped the wound closed with a series of adhesives and pressed a clean square of gauze over the spot, which he bound in place with an ace bandage. The girl sighed as he wrapped up the foot, and rested her head back against the sofa arm. She sniffed and rubbed her jacket sleeve across her face.

"Thanks," she said. "I don't think I could have done that myself."

Shepherd lowered her foot onto the sofa as he stood. "You really should stay off it for a few days. And I'm not just saying that so you'll hang around." He smiled, hoping she could sense his sincerity. "The cut needs to close up a little. The bandages won't hold under too much movement."

The girl smirked. "Lucky you. What'll it cost me?"

Shepherd peeled off the gloves and tossed them into the trash. "Is that what it's like out there now? No one's willing to help each other without a motive?"

"It's the way of the world, Pops. You don't get something for nothing, you know?"

Does Penny think like that, too? He shook his head and sighed, trying not to let his mind carry the thought any further. "Well, I don't believe in that," he said.

"What do you believe in, then?" the girl asked, shifting herself up onto her elbows. "I can't trust you if I don't know what you want."

Shepherd smiled and moved toward the door. "What I want?"

What did he want, really? *Penny,* he thought, but it made him frown. That door had closed a long time ago, and the girl's presence only made that more clear to him. The Penny who lived now—if she lived at all—wouldn't be his Penny, wouldn't be his little girl. She'd be world-hardened, angry, and defensive. He wasn't even sure she loved him anymore, wherever she was, though he thought about her every day, and prayed for her safety, and ached to comfort her, to explain to her, to show her that he'd taken what she said to heart.

"Meaning." Shepherd looked down at his hands. "I want meaning. And that's not something you can give me. That's for the Lord to reveal."

"So you're waiting for a sign? Is that why you take care of those things? Because of some twisted sense of responsibility?"

The gruffness in her tone made him smile despite himself. She sounded like a normal teenager, annoyed by a teasing comment, being grounded, or asked a personal question. He could see now that she wasn't Penny, wasn't anything like her. The lines of her face were all wrong; her eyes were set too deep and framed by shadows.

"No," he said. "Because of a promise. I think you'd have to be a parent to understand."

The girl shrugged and reclined again. "Whatever. You'll tell me what you want eventually."

"Are you hungry?"

Again, she shrugged. "Sure. Rack up the bill."

Shepherd shook his head, but kept smiling. He brought her some of the prepackaged foods he'd collected from raiding the airport's vending machines and the local convenience store, and a smoked piece of the salmon he'd caught earlier in the summer. They spoke only a little while eating and that mostly about the choice of the airport as a safe house compared to the others she had seen on her travels, but by the time they finished the salmon and the snacks, the girl seemed more relaxed and even smiled as she scraped the last few smudges of pudding out of the plastic cup.

Shepherd stood and gathered up the trash, moved toward the door. "I've got some work to do," he said. "Will you be all right on your own?"

The girl chuckled at him and lifted her shotgun from the floor. "I've been all right so far. I think I can manage."

Shepherd nodded but then paused in the hall. "What's your name? You never told me."

The girl half smiled as she sucked the chocolate pudding off her finger. "What was your daughter's name?"

"Penny."

"Then call me Penny."

"Is your name Penny?"

The girl shrugged. "Does it matter?"

Shadows are everywhere. There are large ones, cast by abandoned buildings on a sunny afternoon; and there are small ones, like the love fading out of a child's eyes. On the dimmest days, there are shadows so dark they're like a puddle of night left behind from the previous evening. On the brightest days, there are sharp, unyielding shadows like brick walls.

But the worst shadows cling to you, hang over you, and haunt you in your sleep. They don't have to be dark; some of the worst are bright and filled with familiar faces that laugh and speak to you like they'll always be with you, even when they're not.

Shepherd stood at the door on the third floor of the tower, the key in his hand hovering an inch from the first of three padlocks on the doorframe.

One for Anne. One for Chris. One for Penny.

The metal lock was cold in his palm, and heavy like the grip of the handgun he used to keep in his bedside table. With a sigh, Shepherd slipped the key into the first lock.

Compared to the bright hallway he stood in, the room itself was shrouded by shadow. Even when he flicked the light switch, only one of the fluorescent bulbs turned on. Its pale white light seemed to touch only what was necessary and no more, a weak brushstroke of illumination across the central table, the workbench, the shelves of plastic cartons filled with wires, bolts, metal piping, and tools. Car batteries he'd harvested from the long-term parking lot were piled in a plastic tub in the corner. Stains of red, brown, and black blossomed on the grungy tile floor around the table, spreading outward like grasping fingers.

The odor that swept over him as he stepped inside made the gall rise in Shepherd's throat, as it always did, and he pulled the paper mask up over his nose and mouth.

Luke waited in the hallway, sputtering behind his speaker. His hands twitched against the bolts in his wrists as he held what was left of Peter. Shepherd now took the remains himself, cradled the dead weight of the full-grown man as best he could, and carried him to the workroom table. He laid the body down gently, and pushed the cord restraints off to the side, unnecessary for this operation.

In all the confusion of meeting another conscious person, he had neglected Peter. Good Peter. The first. The rock. The trusty follower. Shepherd pulled his stool up to the table and gingerly brushed back the matted, sticky hair on the good side of Peter's head. Death had been kind to Peter, even if its means had been abrupt and gruesome. Despite the bruising, the un-healing lacerations, the crusted blood at the corners of his cracked lips, Peter looked like a man again. Peaceful in death despite his trials in life. Shepherd closed his eyes and tried to block out what he could remember of Peter prior to this moment, tried to erase the sound of his moan, the snap of his teeth, the feral glow in his eyes. When he looked back down at the corpse, he thought he could see what Peter had looked like before, when he was a son, a father, a co-worker, a neighbor to someone. He couldn't be more than just a few years older than Shepherd himself, perhaps looking forward to a first grandchild, or a twentieth anniversary on a cruise ship in the tropics.

Or perhaps he was divorced, living in a one-room apartment alone, drinking at the corner pub morning, noon, and night, feeling the missing presence of his children like phantom limbs he swore were still there.

Shepherd shook his head at the sinking of his stomach. This was not the time to think about things like that. Instead, he took Peter's cold, rough hand in both of his. Shepherd always thought Peter's hands looked like a carpenter's. Little crisscross scars danced up the sides and across the knuckles where a whittling knife might have pushed too hard against a knot of wood, slipped, and cut.

"May you rest in peace, my friend," he said softly, squeezing Peter's hand. "Please forgive me for not serving you better and for what I must do now."

It was messy work, pulling out the motors and the bolts, prying back the cage that had kept Peter safe—safe for Shepherd, and safe for himself—and it took time. Each bolt broke the bones as they came out, spraying his masked and goggled face with moldy blood. The skin slipped and peeled back from the coagulated divots in the muscle. Twice, Shepherd had to get up and stand outside, leaning his forehead against the wall as he took deep, uninhibited breaths to clear the stench out of his nostrils and to settle his stomach.

Shepherd buried Peter in the grassy field beyond the runway. Ringing the grave, Martha, Paul, Matthew, and Luke stood quietly, wheezing and gurgling. Peter's towel-shrouded body lay beside the grave. In the distance, Shepherd could hear one or two roamers, their moans and shrieks amplified by the stillness of the river and the flat of the runway.

His companions heard them too. Luke pushed his head forward, straining his neck and back against the metal restraints bolted into his flesh and bones. Martha's eyes rolled from side to side, and her wheezing intensified; she stiffened at a distant howl, and her throat rumbled with a muffled cry in return.

"Stop it," Shepherd whispered. "Stop it. You're better than them. You don't have to give in to the sickness."

Paul gurgled at this, and a sludge of blood and bile oozed down his throat and dripped from his chin to the ground.

Shepherd hoisted himself up from the hole and laid the shovel aside. Peter's body was light, what was left of it, and Shepherd carefully placed it in the bottom of the grave. There was a part of him that wished he could give Peter a proper burial, with a coffin and flowers and a minister's ordained prayers, but the close-hugging blanket of dirt would have to do. At least it would keep Peter's remains undisturbed by the gnawing teeth of free roamers.

No, not free, Shepherd reminded himself. *They're controlled as much as my flock are. More, because they have nothing to live for, nothing to hope for beyond the torments of this world.*

Luke's gasping, grunting moans grew louder as Shepherd shoveled dirt over Peter's corpse. Luke wheezed, and the metal restraints groaned as he pushed against them. Back in the control tower, Shepherd knew the warning lights must be blinking, but he did not fear. He had given up on fear a long time ago.

He withdrew the weathered, life-beaten New Testament from his back pocket and turned to a page marked with a bloodstained fingerprint. Seeing it made him pause, catch his breath, remembering all too well the crack of nine-millimeter bullets entering the skulls of two very familiar heads, heads that had born faces twisted beyond recognition by the virus's grasp on the minds within.

Once upon a time, Shepherd thought, and his trigger finger ached.

He should have realized then what he knew now: that the roamers could be controlled, could be guided and helped, at least for a while.

Luke quieted, as he always did when Shepherd read scripture to him. It warmed Shepherd's heart to imagine that Luke was a God-fearing man, like himself, or had been before the virus trapped him in his body. Luke's desire to listen, or appearance of it, was the one shining example of hope—a quiet, patient sign—that perhaps he wasn't completely insane for thinking they could still be helped.

He was lying on the sofa, dry-eyed but shaking as he staring at the ceiling. Out of the corner of his eye, he could see the dark red streaks smeared down the wall and the lumps of the bodies where they'd fallen to the floor. His lips and the tips of his fingers were stiff and numb. He could feel his chest rising and falling, but he didn't know if he was breathing.

The front door slammed, shaking the whole house, his eyes in their sockets, his heart in his chest, his brain in his skull. It shocked him back to life, and he sat up. The sofa springs creaked. His breath came in short gasps at first, short bursts he used to whisper her name. But his throat held back the cry. If she stopped, if she turned and came back, what else could he tell her that he hadn't already tried? What could he say that would work? Would make her stay, make her forgive him?

She had called him, begged him to come home, to help her. Her trembling voice echoed in his ears: "Something's wrong with Mom. I-I don't think she's breathing."

He could still feel Anne's fingers clawing at his arms, at his face, see the flashing white of her teeth and the blood oozing from the corners of her eyes. He could still hear Chris's howling moan as he lurched out of his bedroom, his white T-shirt turned maroon and brown.

He knew what to do, knew what was best, the only option. Even when Penny screamed at the gunshots, caught his arm, tried to pull him away, he hadn't hesitated. He hadn't thought about it, and he should have. He should have stopped. Should have controlled himself, or tried harder, anything . . . It was easy to shoot them. What did that say about him?

Clutching his head with his sticky hands, he felt a moan resonating in his chest. It seeped out from between his lips from some dark place within him, and cracked the silence left in the wake of the squeal of tires on asphalt as the last living person he cared about raced away from him into the night.

He awoke in the shadows to the blinking of a warning light. Its red, pulsing bloom beat against his eyelids like a dying heartbeat. Darkness fell away to the sanguine glow, and then descended again, leaving him disoriented.

From somewhere below, he heard a crash. Shepherd's heart jumped, and he threw back the blankets to scramble from his makeshift bed to the control panel. The warning light was Luke's.

A gargled moan crept up the hollow cavern of the stairwell. Another crash, and this time, a scream—a girl's scream—and the blast of a shotgun. It jump-started Shepherd's feet, and he dove for the door, barreled down the stairs. Another shotgun discharge filled the stairwell with resounding, discordant noise.

The handle of the stairwell door was sticky with blood, and the loosened hinges groaned as he pushed the door partway open before it hit something on the floor and stopped.

It was silent inside. Shepherd slipped through the crack into the darkness and whispered, "Penny?"

A croak came from the far corner where his adjusting eyes located a hunched figure. The croak broke suddenly and became a sob. "Fuck."

A body lay across the floor, its foot keeping the door from opening all the way. Shepherd tripped over a twisted metal bar connected to a contorted ankle as he stepped over it.

"Fuck," the girl whispered again, her voice shaking. "Sonofabitch."

"Are you okay?"

Shepherd climbed over the body and kicked a speaker he hadn't seen. It bounced off his foot and struck the wall with a hollow thud.

The girl sat pressed into the corner, curled up so tight she almost seemed like a part of the wall. When he knelt in front of her, he saw tears shining on her cheeks.

"Penny—"

"He got me," she said, and pushed something toward him. It was long, cold—her shotgun. Her eyes were so wide, he could see his shadow in them.

"Where?"

Her lips trembled as she fought back a sudden surge of tremors, and thrust out her injured leg. The ace bandage was torn ragged and soaked with sticky blackness. In the dark, he could only see the deep emptiness beneath the torn fibers where there should have been skin.

Shepherd set the gun on the floor next to what was left of Luke's skull, his hands cold and shaking as he turned the foot to examine it. "It's not so bad," he said. "We'll bandage it up and see. There's no saying it'll be infected. You may be fine."

"Stop it," the girl said from somewhere deep in her chest, growling up her throat. "Fuck, Shepherd, I know about survival, okay? I know what this means. So . . . stop it." With a shaking sigh, she rubbed her face. "You've got to shoot me. Do it now before I turn."

Shepherd shook his head, unable to let go of the slender ankle, even as the blood from her wound dripped into the palm of his hand, trickled down his wrist. Penny jerked her leg back, pulling her knees up to her chest. She choked, and her eyes widened, the whites reflecting the light from the stairwell. There was a thin rim of red around them, red that melted away and ran down her cheeks with her tears.

"Please," she whispered. "Please, Shepherd. You have to do this for me. I'm begging you!"

Shepherd shivered, and his hand fell upon the muzzle of the shotgun. "I-I don't . . . "

Penny spasmed, her head cracking back against the wall. The impact and the sob that escaped her throat tightened his grip on the gun. "Please. Please, Shepherd . . . "

Her voice caught in her throat, choking her again. This time, it took her a moment to swallow. She gagged, clutched at her throat. When the bubble burst, she gasped for air between clenched teeth. Her eyes rolled.

Shepherd stood, the shotgun weighing down his arm. "I don't kill them," he whispered. "I don't. I just . . . I can't."

Penny's gaze rolled up at him, and her breathing rasped, her nostrils flared.

With a shudder, she fell back against the wall, eyelids fluttering, blood trickling from the corners of her mouth. Then she went still. Relaxed, calm, she looked just like Penny. Maybe it was Penny. Maybe it had just been too long, and he couldn't recognize her anymore.

Shepherd bent down beside her, touched her cheek with his rough fingertips. Every second he spent looking at her face, her eyes, her nose, her lips, her chin—everything about her could have belonged to Penny.

"Sweetheart," he whispered, and she opened her blood-rimmed eyes.

As Shepherd stepped into the bathroom and locked the door behind him, he caught a glimpse of himself in the mirror: a masked and bloody creature, tiptoeing into the darkness. It made him shiver, made the sticky spots on his hands and cheeks burn. Shaking, he tore off his dirty clothes, his mask, his goggles, and crouched on the tiled floor, his head in his hands. Every inch of him burned like he was lying naked on a bed of coals. There was blood on his hands, blood in his hair, blood on the floor, on his clothes, in his ears, in his nose. He could taste it, smell it, breathe it, feel it everywhere, like a thin film of filth that covered everything and everyone, no matter how many times you scrubbed, no matter how much you cleaned.

He shivered and heard his voice crack in the darkness, a pitiful whimper. His eyes stung and he hung his head, letting the few tears that escaped patter onto the blood-slicked floor. Deep breaths drew up through his nose and escaped through his lips. Once. Twice. The shivering stopped and he could breathe again, and stand.

His hand found the light switch in the dark. The shadows fled, and he stood in the unsteady light, a man naked and vulnerable before an unmerciful mirror. There were no secrets here, no personal barriers, nothing hidden. The Lord could see him here, in his moment of greatest weakness. In this tiny room, with the mirror catching his every move, every blink, every glance, his scars were exposed. They ran up his arms, little lancing crescents of pale and pink tissue, to his shoulders and stopped, though there were a few on his chest and a notch of missing flesh at his hip.

Through the floor he could hear the roamer tied to his workshop table moaning and gnashing her teeth. Even after bolting the motors and metal bars to her, she fought against them, tried to spit out the speaker he'd put in her throat.

Shepherd pressed the palms of his hands to his sweating brow. He could walk away. He could leave. It would be so easy. No one would notice, much less care. His roamers would die eventually. So would he.

A Shepherd of the Valley

The temptation was strong, but it awoke something within him. His hands fell to his sides and he looked into his own eyes in the mirror.

The valley of the shadow of death, he thought. *I will fear no evil, for Thou art with me, and I am with them. There's meaning in that.*

With a sigh, Shepherd took up the lavender gift shop soap and scrubbed himself from head to toe, rinsing with the tub of water he'd carried over from the river. He dug his fingernails into the purple and pink-swirled bar, rubbed his skin raw with it, massaged it against his scalp and hair until his head ached. Refreshed, cleansed, and forgiven, he dressed and returned to the control room.

The Day the Saucers Came

Neil Gaiman

That Day, the saucers landed. Hundreds of them, golden,
Silent, coming down from the sky like great snowflakes,
And the people of Earth stood and
stared as they descended,
Waiting, dry-mouthed, to find out what waited inside for us
And none of us knowing if we would be here tomorrow
But you didn't notice because

That day, the day the saucers came, by some coincidence,
Was the day that the graves gave up their dead
And the zombies pushed up through soft earth
or erupted, shambling and dull-eyed, unstoppable,
Came towards us, the living, and we screamed and ran,
But you did not notice this because

On the saucer day, which was zombie day, it was
Ragnarok also, and the television screens showed us
A ship built of dead-men's nails, a serpent, a wolf,
All bigger than the mind could hold,
and the cameraman could
Not get far enough away, and then the Gods came out
But you did not see them coming because

On the saucer-zombie-battling-gods
day the floodgates broke
And each of us was engulfed by genies and sprites
Offering us wishes and wonders and eternities
And charm and cleverness and true
brave hearts and pots of gold

While giants feefofummed across
the land and killer bees,
But you had no idea of any of this because

That day, the saucer day, the zombie day
The Ragnarok and fairies day, the
day the great winds came
And snows and the cities turned to crystal, the day
All plants died, plastics dissolved, the day the
Computers turned, the screens telling
us we would obey, the day
Angels, drunk and muddled, stumbled from the bars,
And all the bells of London were sounded, the day
Animals spoke to us in Assyrian, the Yeti day,
The fluttering capes and arrival of
the Time Machine day,
You didn't notice any of this because
you were sitting in your room, not doing anything
not even reading, not really, just
looking at your telephone,
wondering if I was going to call.

Love, Resurrected

Cat Rambo

General Aife Crofadottir was acknowledged the greatest military mind of her generation—perhaps even her century. No wonder then that the sorcerer Balthus recruited her early in her career, setting her to rally armies of Beasts and magically equipped soldiers, planning campaign after campaign, until finally he stood the ruler of a vast expanse of the continent's northeastern corner. Once fertile lands, once countries, now only uncontested devastated territories.

Three years after her death, she still labored in his service.

Aife stood at the window of Balthus's tower, looking out over the desolate countryside. Age and blight had stooped the apple trees dominating the view, and sticky webs clustered in the vees of the knobby branches. The dry grass tried to hold onto the dust, but here, as everywhere, drought and ash and the silty remnant of magic choked away all life. The chalky-white stones surrounding the dry well gleamed in the hostile sunlight.

Decades of sorcerous battle had warped the land. It was dead in patches, or so plagued by ghosts that no living soul could walk it and remain sane.

She rested her fingertips on the windowsill and contemplated her hand. The skin was gray and withered but still functioned. Sooner or later, Aife thought, it would rot away, despite Balthus's preservative spells. What would happen then? Right now she could pass for a living but very ill person, could wrap herself in a cloak and whisper, make some claim to human company. What would happen when her bones began to show through?

Behind her, Balthus said, "You will become a skeleton, but one that walks and talks by magic means. The mere sight of you will strike fear in any heart. What a war leader you will be then, my darling!"

He touched her shoulder, closer than she had thought him. "You will make a beautiful skeleton. All clean-lined ivory. I will commission you a crown, gilt and amber, with the warhawk that shows you general."

She was weary of him reading her mind.

At the thought, he removed his hand. "Is that what has concerned you lately? But I must know your mind, Aife, must be able to glimpse your plans in order to work to aid them."

"Every creature in your employ," she said, words thick. "I know, you must know them all."

He let the room's silence gather, then ventured, "Perhaps . . . "

"Perhaps?"

She turned away from the window to contemplate him. She might be a monster, but he was little more: yellowed skin stretched drum-tight over his bones. His long, wispy hair was tied back with an embroidered ribbon the wrong color for the crimson robes he wore.

Blotches and scars marked his hands, the relics of past experiments. An olive-green patch covered the heel of one hand, an irregular oval resembling old mold or lichen.

He returned the gaze, eyes as glassy as an opium addict's. What spells had he laid on himself, throughout the years? She wondered if he saw her as she truly was now. Or did he let the memory of her slip over it like a mask, making him see her when the blood still coursed through her veins, instead of the slow seepage it engaged in now, as though begrudging her body its energy?

"I will make you a charm," he said. His voice was almost pleading. "One that keeps your thoughts hidden. No other man, woman, or Beast in my employ has that privilege. But I will give it to you."

And with that promise, she gave him her hand, her gray and withered hand, and let him lead her to bed.

But again, she did not know whether he kissed her or the memory of what she had been to him.

He kept his promise. The next day, beside her on the pillow he had left at dawn, a silver chain coiled, holding a dark gem, darker than death or the loss of memory.

She put it around her neck and went to do his business.

Since her transformation, all living things shied away from her. She had become accustomed to that. But the Beasts accepted her more than the humans did. Most of them were creatures Balthus had created, sometimes by putting living things together to make something new, like the swan-winged woman that acted as scout and courier, or the great Catoblepas, blended of ox and wild pig and turtle and something Balthus would not name, whose breath withered whatever it struck. More often he transformed what he was given: stretching, pulling, augmenting, till something was created that the world had never seen before. If it showed promise that he could use it, he left it alive.

She did not seek the Beasts' company deliberately, but rather, as a cat does, she would sit in a room where they were gathered, not part of the conversation, but letting it swirl around her. There but not there. It reminded her of long-ago barracks chatter, the taunts and gibes and affectionate mockery of fellow soldiers.

This day she sat in the corner near the fire, careful not to get too close, lest a spark singe her without her knowing, because her skin was dead now and only reported a little when pain struck it. Near her was the swan-woman, who they called Lytta, and the Minotaur who guarded the stables, and a man-wolf who had once been one of her finest soldiers. He was the only one who had looked at her when she entered, his eyes glinting sly green in the firelight as he half-nodded. She had not returned the gesture.

"They say the Falcon is making inroads near Barbaruile," Lytta said to the wolf-man, who had refused any name other than "Wolf."

That news interested Aife. She had pursued the bandit chief who called himself the Falcon for almost a year now and found him a more than adequate challenge.

"What does he fight for?" the Minotaur demanded, his voice as heavy as a sack of gravel. "He leaves things worse than they are, with no sorcerer to look out over the land."

"He must have magic of his own," Lytta said. "Look at how he has escaped capture, again and again."

"They say it is no magic," Wolf said, "but rather something that dispels magic."

Aife had spent much time contemplating the same question. What was the source of the Falcon's success? Spies sent to gather information never returned. Were never heard from again. Subverted or killed? She hoped, for their sake, that it had been the latter. When Balthus finally captured the Falcon—it was inevitable—he would take him and all his allies and make new things of them, things that they would not enjoy being.

Any more than she enjoyed the life he had given her.

When she had first opened her eyes after her death, all she saw was Balthus's face, like the full moon in the sky above her. She had shuddered then, not understanding why she continued to breathe.

She remembered dying. She remembered the cannonball slamming into her, the broken knitting needles of her ribs, bright stitches of pain sewing her a garment. Reeling back on unsteady legs—something in her spine was wrong, was numb. Slipping away, like retreating into sleep, defeated but not unhappily by dreams. It had been so restful.

She realized she no longer had to breathe.

"What have you done?" she tried to say, but Balthus's hand pressed her back implacably on the bed.

"Rest, my dear," he said. "You were too valuable to me to be laid beneath the earth."

Her heart, she realized, had not been revived with the rest of her.

When Balthus had first recruited Aife, she had stood straight as a spear, muscular but tall, carrying herself like a willow tree. She kept her hair short then, in the manner of foot soldiers, even though she had risen much further in the ranks than that. Her only scar was a burn along her left forearm where it had been caught by quick-fire in a southern sea battle against raiders.

They had heard of Balthus, of course. His demesne bordered the petty kingdom in whose service she battled. Rumors initially said he was a mage, but the stories had grown until they named what he really was: sorcerer, the sort that battled perpetually on these shores. The devastation had not yet spread across the continent. She had thought she could keep the kingdom safe for its Queen-Regent.

But in a single night, everything changed.

When she awoke that morning, the first thing she noticed was the silence. Then the smell of blood.

She alone was alive. She went through the castle, opening door after door to look in, seeing a gaping wound like a second mouth on each throat, the pool of spilled blood, the flies already gathering. In the Queen's chamber, grief nearly brought her to her knees. She had promised to protect the woman who lay there. Now all that was alive in this place was her. Why had she been spared? Had she been merely overlooked, or was there some reason?

Finally she had entered the throne room, expecting no one there. A red-robed man sat alive on the gilded chair, watching her approach.

"Your fame has spread, Aife. Aife of the deadly sword and clever plan. I have come to collect you. Will you serve me, or must I coerce you?"

His eyes were deceptively kind; her mind numb. Her fingers curled around the hilt of the dagger at her waist, felt the ridges of the leather wrapping on the pommel. But what use was steel against a sorcerer?

At the time she agreed, she'd thought to catch him off-guard, kill him when he was unwary. She watched for opportunities, made her plans. She could not hope to escape alive after slaying him, but it would be worth it, to avenge her Queen. She waited patiently.

But a year passed, then another, and she found herself enjoying planning his campaigns, being able to use magics, technologies, of the sort her Queen never could have wielded. She had never been able to play at war on such a scale. Her victories pleased her. Made her even more famous.

Wolf had come to her then, sought her out, not as a lover but as a follower, and had been captured by Balthus. Brought to her, he had sworn to whatever changes the sorcerer thought might make him a more efficient soldier. The potion Balthus gave him twisted and elongated his skull, pulled his jaw forward, endowed it with canines the size of her thumb.

All the while he had stared into her eyes, trusting her.

By then it all seemed normal.

She'd been seduced by her pleasure in the puzzles Balthus had set her. How to coax an enemy from a walled tower. How to keep supplies from the coast from reaching their destination. As though the mental chessboard had been expanded, the rules not changed but become more complex. Challenge after worthy challenge, and she overcame them all.

And so when, the next night, he had kissed her, she had not resisted. She was not a virgin. Nor was she the only person to find themselves in his bed. She thought he would miss her companionship. Perhaps it would keep her safe; perhaps he'd hesitate to slay someone who'd touched him, cradled him. Loved him.

Had she known she would become so dear to him that he'd impose this existence on her, she would have tried to kill him that first moment in that echoing, empty throne room, even knowing it meant her death.

This half-life dragged at her. She felt *weary* all the time, a chilled-bone sluggishness of motion that belied the quickness of her thoughts. It was not painful to breathe, but it was tiring, and she began to eschew it when alone and unworried about frightening the living.

She touched the silver chain at her throat. Was it real or some trick? A trinket that did nothing but give her peace of mind? She thought, though, that he would deal squarely with her. Of all his creations, she was the most *his*.

In the chambers she inhabited, she unrolled the massive map that showed Balthus's territory and spread it on the table. She used a copper coin to mark each site where a raid had occurred and studied them, trying to puzzle out the pattern by which the Falcon determined his targets. There was always a pattern, even when people were trying to avoid it.

The Falcon seemed to be working north, but in the past he'd doubled back on occasion, hit a previous target or something near it. When would he do it again? What prompted the decision each time?

Discover that and she'd have him.

She had always walked among her troops, late at night, getting a feel for their worries, their fears. She could do that no longer. She frightened them too much.

So now she relied on her three troop leaders, all uneasy-looking men Balthus had recruited from the Southern Isles. One told her he had come thinking this war-torn continent would provide easy pickings for a man of war. Then once here, he had realized, as had the others, the importance of placing himself under a sorcerer's command. There was no other way to survive.

Unless you were the Falcon, it seemed. Was it true, was he a sorcerer himself?

If so, only Balthus could catch him.

But her employer—her lover, her resurrector—seemed more preoccupied with the waters to the north and skirmishes with the Pot-King, who might actually be the Pot-King's son, according to one set of rumors.

"A minor bandit," Balthus said dismissively.

"A troublesome one," she said. "He burned your granary at Vendish."

A bold move, but a strategic one. Hungry troops were inefficient troops, whether Human or Beast.

Balthus shrugged. "Is that not why I have you, for matters of this sort?"

Her fearsome nature had its advantages. She could not move easily among her soldiers, but she could walk the land around the castle. No creature would trouble her; no predator would sniff her and think of food. No ghost would attack her, knowing her somewhat closer than kindred.

Sometimes Wolf trailed her, never speaking but always guarding. It was a comfort, even if unnecessary, to feel him in the shadows, a guardian presence at her back.

She did not take a torch. Her eyes were well-adjusted to the darkness— indeed, most times she preferred it.

In a glade, she found a doe and her fawn, part of the herd of Riddling Deer Balthus had loosed on the orchard. They lay in a drift of fresh green grass. Red poppies bloomed around them, rare vegetation in this scorched land.

The doe's eyes were dark as forest pools. Her nostrils flared and her head jerked, testing the air, as Aife approached. But the wind reassured her; she settled back.

The fawn spoke—how had Balthus managed that? The Deer were his unique creation. He had wanted oracles, had not realized how enigmatic and troublesome they would prove.

"Inside you is your worst enemy," it said.

She did not move, but looked at the fawn, hoping for additional details.

They were not forthcoming. But perhaps—

A branch snapped under Wolf's foot in the underbrush. The wind changed. Jackknife sudden, doe and fawn were on their feet.

They flickered away into the night, taking with them the answers she sought.

She came back to her quarters, smelling of grass and thyme, knowing the boundaries were unchallenged except by the deer's troublesome words. She unslung her heavy cape, velvet folds as soft as a baby's earlobe. Her boots were black leather with gilt buckles. She undid them one by one and slipped the footwear off by the fire before padding over to the table to contemplate the Falcon's patterns anew.

A black-barred feather lay on her map.

She picked it up with some difficulty. Cold made her fingers stiff.

Who would have dared to leave it here? The Falcon had some ally—perhaps even allies, for she reckoned him her equal in cunning, in planning out each move in a long game, and she would have never betrayed just one ally, unwilling to lose the advantage it gave her, unless she had others in place.

Twirling the feather, she watched its dance. She would use it as her test of the amulet. Surely if Balthus plucked it from her thoughts, it would spur him to some action.

But he did nothing when he saw her the next morning. Instead she laid the feather beside the map and continued her study of the Falcon's appearances. She tracked the phases of the moon, the weather, anything that might prompt his decisions.

It seemed to Aife that in the last few months, such a pattern had emerged. But why, puzzlingly, had one recently appeared?

Still, she was there, in the village he had half-burned before, lying in wait, when he doubled back. She had sent the surviving townspeople away, filled the houses with archers and swordhands. In the remnants of the town hall, the Catoblepas crouched, waiting for her orders.

She chose the Mayor's house for her headquarters, finding it the best appointed for her needs. She told herself the decision was not motivated by the way the man had flinched when she first rode in.

As expected, in the night the bandit band appeared, slinking in through the shadows, slipping into houses. Their deaths would be as quick and as silent as she could manage. She had ordered them killed; she had no need for anyone alive but the Falcon.

But she waited in vain, and the breath in the Catoblepas's lungs withered only the small grasses among the stones where it crouched. When her archers and soldiers came, they said the Falcon's men had been only illusory wraiths, melting through their steel.

At that, she expected the courier's arrival to bring word that the castle was under siege. It did. She had been outmaneuvered. It was not a customary sensation for her.

By the time she arrived, several dozen of Balthus's choicest Beasts were dead, and a full troop's worth of seasoned mercenaries who would be difficult to replace. Balthus uttered no reproach, but she felt the weight of his unspoken disapproval and disappointment. For the first time, she wondered if there were worse things than the life he had given her.

In the months that followed, she found herself experiencing another uncustomary sensation: irritation. She played a game where her opponent had her outwitted at every turn, as though he could read her mind. As Balthus once had.

Her opponent taunted her. Every few days another feather appeared. Laid atop her pillow, on the tray beside her breakfast, drifting on the windowsill. A marker in her book, turned a few pages beyond where she had been reading.

She burned them in the fireplace but said nothing to Balthus.

Inside you is your worst enemy. What did that mean? The thought ate at her like a parasite. Was she at odds with herself? Was she overlooking the obvious, making mistakes she should have realized? She found herself outside her actions, watching them with a critical eye.

She faltered sometimes. The fine lines around Balthus's eyes meshed and deepened when he frowned at her, but he said nothing aloud.

But he wanted the Falcon captured, and soon. He was angry about the losses, the time that would be necessary to create more Beasts. For the first time he did not communicate his plans but expected her to guess them in a way that left her scrambling to catch up at times, trying to figure how to incorporate each creature he created. He did not consult her. She could have used more winged Beasts, to replace lost scouts, but she did not dare request them.

It shocked her when Balthus, finally making a move, caught the quarry she had sought so long. Little consolation that his victory came by cheating, not the sort of thing she would have ever embarked upon.

She could see why Balthus had moved with such efficiency, though. Was not all fair in war, as in love?

It was through an exchange of hostages, one of the sacred customs. By doing it, she thought to pay the Falcon tribute, let him see she respected him as an opponent, perhaps lure him into complacency. It was not until they had been dispatched that Balthus revealed that one had been a Siren, a woman created to entice, who would cast her magic over them.

"She even looked a little like you," he said with a smile. Then added, "As you were, I mean."

She made no reply aloud, but had he been able to read her thoughts, his smile might have faltered.

Aife went to the cell where they kept the Falcon. She took two guards with her, trailing her as she made her way down spirals of stone. On the third landing, a torch burned beside his door.

Her hand spread like an elderly starfish on the door's surface as she leaned forward. She found herself trembling like a hound ready to be loosed on the scent.

He had been sitting on the bunk. He sprang up as her shadow crossed the rectangle of light on the stone floor, approached the door till he was inches away from the bars and the hood's edge shrouding her face, but not far enough. He recoiled as he saw her fully, recovered, stood still, but this time not as close.

She looked at him all the while. Rumors had not lied about his handsomeness. Slim and brown-skinned, his hair as black as ink, a few white strands at the temples somehow making it seem even darker.

Aife could have loved this man, long ago, in her soldier days, before the weight of death had settled on her shoulders. He was young and beautiful, so beautiful. So alive. She wanted him as she had not wanted anything for so long. She put a hand to the bars, looked at him, hoping to see the same recognition there.

Only horror and revulsion.

She had thought her heart dead, but that was not true, else how could she feel it aching now?

Still, she had to question him. She took two guards in with her but motioned them back when they would have seized him. Leave him his dignity for now.

"How did you know what I was doing for so long?" she said.

He sneered. "Are you not a dead thing, to be commanded by magic, like all dead things that walk must be? I had my necromancer working for months, trying to find a way inside your mind. On the night of the year's third moon, he succeeded.

"After that, all was clear to me. His magic let me take control of you from time to time. We could not risk it for long, though, so I used it to trouble you, making you lay down clues for yourself: a feather to stir your thoughts, send them in the wrong direction. And it worked, until your master chose to trust you no longer."

Had Balthus realized what had happened? That closing her mind to him had opened it to other magical controllers? Surely he had not known it at first but only later, had used it to infiltrate the Falcon's camp, to discover his plans in order to catch him?

"Your compatriots," she said, "including any magickers with them, are dead. You are here in Balthus's castle, and will be wrung of information as a sponge is of water. Will you yield it up easily or will you force him to twist you hard?"

She watched him as he considered her words. She thought that it would be hard to kill him, but she'd do it nonetheless. She had killed pretty men before, and seen many of them used to coaxing their way from women die as quick and efficiently as the ugliest man.

Sometimes they were a little more theatrical about it all. He seemed like he would be the theatrical sort.

She touched the silver chain. She had refused jewelry for so long. It was something that made you a target, or gave enemies a chance to grab at it. And here it had happened, just as she had always feared. Her worst enemy had been in her head, and it was not herself.

She thought, though, that if she could have freed him, she might have. He was that pretty. It would have made her happy, to know that he lived somewhere, that he knew it was by her mercy. If only that was possible.

Footsteps, coming down the stairs. Who?

The Falcon twisted at the air with his hand. She felt the chain constrict around her throat, puppet fingers slipping into her brain.

"It seems my necromancer's magic lingers after all, after all," he said. "I suspected you could not resist coming close enough that I could control you, even without his assistance. What shall I have you do? Kill your master seems the most obvious step, doesn't it?"

"Perhaps," Balthus said from where he stood on the stairwell.

Aife was pulled upward, her limbs someone else's, a loathsome intimacy that made bile burn in her throat. The guards were on their knees, choking, hands at their throats, trying to pry away invisible cords. She was thrust towards the door, trying to keep her arms out to maintain balance.

Balthus raised his hand, palm towards her. The green blotch had grown like a bracelet around his wrist. A blob of silvery liquid covered the center of his hand like the moon, pulling her forward, a mystical tide washing through her, making her heavy, restoring her to herself. She shuddered, shaking off the last of the netting over her senses.

"You are not one-sixteenth as clever as you think you are, puppy," Balthus said.

"Enough to rid you of your most powerful tool!" the Falcon exclaimed. She twisted away as he flung something at her that dispersed in the air, a handful of motes. She felt it settling on her back and shoulders, saw red sparkling dust riding the breeze, falling on her gray skin and setting it smoldering wherever it landed.

Where was water, anywhere close at hand? The privy pot in the cell was dry. The guards were recovering, as she had, and so she discarded the thought of quenching anything in their blood.

Fire blazed along her skin, burning deep, too deep to extinguish. She staggered towards the door, where Balthus stood. His face was stricken. She saw herself, a fiery angel, reflected in his pupils, saw the thick velvet of the cloak gone lacy with flame. She opened her mouth to appeal to him and felt it fill with flaming dust, go hiss-flickering out, the heat stealing any chance at words.

Fire, and more fire, and then final darkness.

Only to awake, agonized. Balthus's face above her yet again.

Was that all it would ever be, from now on?

She was bone now. Bone and some sort of spectral, invisible flesh that netted her limbs into order and gave her the power of sight. She moved her fingers and they clacked and clicked against the planes of her face as she tried to touch whatever held her together.

Opposite her a standing mirror, green-lit, presenting her rippled and obscured as though drowning. Her skull, wavering in the reflection, capped with a tiara—a golden hawk, wings stretched out to cup the bone.

Wolf was there past the mirror, pressed against the wall of the chamber. Watching her with loyalty. Whatever she became, he would follow. It was reassurance. She would always be a leader, no matter what.

Truly a monster now. She would have to give up some of her illusions: the pretense of meals and cosmetics and clothing. What good would armor be, except to hang on her as though she was some sort of display rack?

"I have made you a present, my dearest," Balthus said. His fingers stroked her skull, bumped along her teeth. He released her and stepped aside.

Undead, skin already graying. Ah, the fine dark hair, the silver strands like penmarks in reverse. The once-piercing eyes now blue and cloudy marbles.

Marbles full of hate and spite and helpless malice. Hers forevermore, her handsome toy, given her by her master, perhaps to torment, perhaps from love and an impulse to please. Would she ever know his motives, would she ever understand if she was puppet or lover, source of amusement or font of something else?

Endless days stretched before her, in which she would never find the answer.

Present

Nicole Kornher-Stace

Now the infection hits the news and Gabriela's mom babysits Jack while Gabriela and her dad go to Wal-Mart for supplies. When it *isn't* the end of the world, her parents are very local-food, free-range, hundred-mile-diet types, but today the Wal-Mart's the only place left open and even Gabriela's mom makes that concession, though she won't set foot inside herself. As Gabriela's dad drives the four miles out of suburbia into town, Gabriela watches the boards go up in people's windows, the padlocks go on doors, the cases of soup cans disappear inside. (Leaving, her dad had grabbed the reusable shopping bags, laughed a little derisive laugh at himself, said Fuck it, and left them in the hall.)

On the way back, the pickup bed and also her lap and footwell full of shopping bags—cans of chili and chickpeas, boxes of cereal, jars upon jars of peanut butter, diapers, multivitamins, cases of ramen, granola, half a dozen can openers—she has a brief panic that they'd get home and the infection would have reached their house already, she'd find her mom gone empty-eyed and gore-mouthed, find Jack lurching instead of toddling. But her dad pulls into the driveway and it's just like when she was a kid, helping him with groceries every Saturday after cartoons, her mom coming out onto the doorstep to help relay stuff to the kitchen, like a fire brigade with pails of water to a burning house. Except now there's Jack perched on her hip, there's a kitchen knife stuck in her belt, and while they rush the bags inside they're watching their neighbors over their shoulders, and their neighbors, rushing bags into their own houses, are watching Gabriela and her parents over theirs.

Now she wakes up, stretches, says good morning to Jack waking up beside her, and something kicks her in the gut: she remembers what day it is. It's the first day of the future, and the sun comes through the cracks between the two-by-fours across her window, shines down on her futon and Jack's racecar pajamas and the new huge red backpack resting against a bookcase. Her parents each have a backpack just like it upstairs. They packed them together last night. Each one is full of energy bars and Gatorade, a first-aid kit, a flashlight, a pocketknife, pepper spray. Hers also has pull-up diapers and fruit snacks for Jack. Jack has a little backpack himself, and in it he has board books, Matchbox cars, more fruit snacks. Each bag except Jack's has two full bottles of Advil and one of dirt-cheap vodka, in case the time comes and they can't bring themselves to use the knives.

Gabriela's got Jack on the potty and she's already pulling on her yoga pants and sneakers for their morning walk before she remembers morning walks are not happening anymore. She's trying to decide whether she wants to brave taking Jack four doors up the road for playgroup anyway when she hears something upstairs, something like footsteps, something not like footsteps. The not-footsteps approach the basement door, begin descending, slow, uncertain, like whoever it is remembers there being something down here, something worth coming down the stairs for, but couldn't quite remember what it was or why they wanted it to start with. But since she had Jack and moved from her childhood bedroom down to the finished basement where there was room for his stuff, her parents never come downstairs that early in the morning, not when Jack might still be sleeping.

Mom? she says, uncertain.

Then another sound comes from midway up the stairs, a sound like maybe someone gargling mouthwash, only it sounds thicker than mouthwash, and it's like they're trying to talk through it, except that it keeps sloshing out when they try.

For about two seconds she deliberates, hand held out to the door. Then her flight instinct starts firing, that pressure in the small of her back starts shooting through to her navel, her legs start tensing, and the next thing she knows she's got the backpack on one shoulder, Jack hoisted on the other, and she's taking the back door sideways, awkward, and it's hitting her in the ass on her way out, just like the saying says not to.

She's forgotten Jack's backpack, all his board books, Dr. Seuss and *Goodnight Moon* and *The Very Hungry Caterpillar*. She wonders how the hell she's supposed to get him to sleep now.

Now she's got Jack on her shoulders and going as slow as she can along the treeline back of town, staying off the roads, keeping a clear line of sight with the maples at her back. If any of them come up through the woods things'll get interesting, but the town is by far the greater risk, and besides she's faster than they are and she's got Jack as a lookout. They're playing a game called Who Can Be the Quietest. He wins automatically if he sees anyone and pulls her hair to tell her so.

She'd ventured up into town earlier, hugging the back walls of shopping plazas, looking to replenish her stores. She'd only left home two days ago, but Jack was tearing through his fruit snacks like a machine and there was no power in the universe that could get him to swallow so much as one lousy calorie of an energy bar. She'd come around behind the supermarket and found someone's legs hanging out of a dumpster, and the puddle on the concrete strongly suggested the rest of that someone was elsewhere. The delivery door was ajar, streaked at shoulder height with what could have been fingerpaint. She opened the knife, got it in a fist at hip level, took two steps for the door, stopped, looked at Jack, looked around and found nowhere safe to put a wanderlusty three-year-old while she went off to get herself killed over fruit snacks. It did not escape her notice that if this were a movie, this would be the Door the Audience Is Telling the Bimbo Not to Go Through. Well, she's not anybody's goddamn bimbo. Sorry, kid, she murmured, and tousled his hair as best she could with her knife-hand. I promise I won't let you starve.

He's a good kid, her Jack. He didn't throw a tantrum, hungry as he was. Sometimes she even thinks he understands the depth of shit they're in, knows not to make it worse.

They moved on.

Now she's walking beneath the maples and the sunshine and the summer-smell of grass and the roadkill-smell coming off the town, she's walking and she's humming softly to Jack to keep his mind off the sounds in the distance, she's walking and she's thinking about zombie movies again. Thinking how ridiculous it is that they're made to be so *fast*. It doesn't make any sense. She never could figure out why corpses were supposed to suddenly be faster or stronger than they were in life, like some kind of consolation prize for shambling around with your skin plopping off. She's read something about how people only use ten percent of their brains while awake, and it's got her wondering if maybe death—undeath—is supposed to be some kind of loophole that unlocks the other ninety, to let them do ridiculous things like outrun sprinters, chew through walls. She's thinking about it being June, how infections spread faster in the heat, how dead things decompose faster too. She wonders which happens first.

It's not just zombie movies. It's horror stories in general. She remembers back when she first started reading them, huge doorstop anthologies of them that her dad would get at the thrift shop for a dime. She must've been ten or so. They scared her sleepless. One thing she got to noticing in them, though, was how if a story was written in present tense then the protagonist probably survived it, unless there was some kind of twist at the end, but if it was written in past tense then the guy was pretty much screwed.

She's wondering what tense her story's written in. Whether she dies in the dirt with someone's face in her guts. Whether she rides off into the sunset. Whether she wakes up and it was all a dream.

She's wondering where the fuck she's supposed to go before she gets there.

Now she's taken to calling him Jack the Snack, because she has to convince herself it's funny or she'll go stark raving batshit and there's no coming back from that. The treeline ran out yesterday and she's back among the buildings, old brick townhouses with delis on the corners. There are lots of broken windows on the ground floor, trashed and smeared. There's no glass on the ground. She looks for movement in the windows and sees none. She's so close to breaking down and screaming, hoping the good guys find her first.

The silence is oppressive. The noises are worse. For two days now she's smelled fire but can't find it, fire and a smell like rancid bacon frying. An oily smoke hangs in the air, like what comes out the back door of a diner in July. She's wearing a hole in her shoe. She's cut holes in the backpack, one for each of Jack's legs, and it's a nice hiking backpack so he's pretty stable up there, the backpack strapped around her at chest and waist. His bare toes jostle at her ass with every step.

There are two things that keep her going.

One is Jack's face pressed against the back of her neck. She can't even complain about the way her shoulders cramp in place to carry him, the way she has to stop every half hour and convince him to pee pottyless, the weight of his heavy little butt on her back. The lack of it would weigh much more.

Two is the perverse hope that she'll come across someone she knew in high school, any of the girls who called her Slut or Skank or Maternity Leave when her belly started to round out, any of the boys who'd elbow each other and grin when she walked by, any of the teachers who assumed she was stupid because she'd made one bad call, never mind that she was pulling in the top five percent even through the first trimester when she'd puke till she was dizzy, sit and stare at the wall and wait to die. That weight on her arm again, that face at her shoulder. Bad call? Fuck them. She pictures each of them in turn, maybe pulped into warm jelly by infection, maybe uninfected, healthy, and being torn unceremoniously to bits.

It keeps her going, one foot in front of the other. It keeps her from thinking about her fate. About Jack's. How slow he made her. What would happen when it came to it. Could she let them take him? Could she do it before they got the chance?

You're going to get us killed, kid, she whispers, and he looks up at her uncomprehending, doesn't even know what it means for the mosquitoes when she slaps them off his arms, not really, and he nods at her, all solemnity, fruit snacks on his breath.

Now she's standing in a parking lot over a pair of corpses. No sign of infection on them. Seems that what's done them in is that their throats and most of their abdominal cavities have been emptied out. Last night she wiped the clots off somebody's aluminum baseball bat and now she's holding it at the ready while she toes the larger corpse. The corpse doesn't move. For the millionth time she wonders how it works, the zombie virus or whatever they're calling it on the news now, if there's any news left to call things anything on. She doesn't understand why, when they attack you, there seems to be a magic threshold, on one side of which you get bitten and turn into one of them, on the other side of which you get bitten and die. She's seen a number of them now wounded bad enough they should be dead, they should never have changed to begin with, just went down and stayed down, like these ones. It doesn't even make sense in the movies, what chance does she have to logic it out here?

She doesn't check its pockets. What good will anybody's wallet do her now? There's something clutched in the corpse's hand, though, and when she squats down to get a closer look she sees it's a rosary. She's not sure why she takes it, but she does.

Then there's the smaller corpse. It's not much bigger than Jack. She can't tell if it was a boy or a girl, before. Corpse, she has to use the word corpse, or she'll start wondering what its name was, its favorite color, whether it wanted a puppy, whether it hated macaroni and cheese as much as Jack does.

She glances around. The place is dead empty. Sets Jack down on his feet, just beside her, where a parked car casts a piece of shade on the boiling blacktop. She wonders if the car belonged to the corpses. No key in sight. She starts up a little singsong as she goes to work on the smaller one's shoe. Look at this doll, sweetie, someone got it all messy, you wouldn't make a mess like that, it must have been some *baby,* they're so messy, you're a *big* boy now and you would never.

The other shoe's on the other leg a couple of meters away. She waves the flies off, turns upon the bright green sock a calculating eye. Cold toes, she thinks inanely, and leaves it where it is. Out of the corner of her eye she sees Jack pulling at a stuffed penguin in the corpse's hand. Somehow it's lying in the clear of the worst of the blood. The corpse just won't let go. Me, he shouts at it, annoyed. She bites her lip a second, then kneels and pries the corpse's fist open. Wipes her fingers on her yoga pants and takes his free hand. They stand together, the three of them, looking down.

Say thank you, she whispers.

Thank you, he sings out, and plants a big kiss on the air.

That night, she barricades them in somebody's cellar and reads Jack *Goodnight Moon* from memory, adding in a few extras (goodnight creepy stairs, goodnight dehydration headache, goodnight dead field mouse in the corner, goodnight racecar pajamas that are getting sort of nasty). She keeps adding extras until whatever's happening in the distance stops, it's unlike anything she's ever heard or wants to hear again and she has to keep on talking so he doesn't hear it too, babbling nonsense with her mouth right up to his ear, he's always been so sensitive to others' pain, she can't so much as cut her nails in front of him or else down goes his little brow into little furrows and he's grabbing her hand and kissing it and saying mommy ow, mommy ow.

Still she can't keep talking all night, he needs the sleep and her throat's so very dry. The second she stops he hears it, points toward the wall, toward outside, and asks.

Don't they sound *silly?* she says. Just some people being silly, making silly sounds. Let's snuggle.

And they do.

Once he's asleep, she pulls out the rosary. It smells of blood and cedar and perfume. Her parents are lapsed Catholic, she's only been into a church once and that was for a rummage sale, and she has no idea how to use the thing, feels like a jackass for even framing the notion in those terms, but she finds herself counting the beads of it, one by one, keeping her thumb over the one she's just counted, just how she's teaching Jack to do, so he doesn't count the same thing twice.

As she touches each bead, she's whispering under her breath. It's stupid, she knows it's stupid, it obviously didn't save the woman in the parking lot with the footprints tracking through her guts four feet to either side, but it keeps unspooling out of her, she's blubbering and she can't make it stop. Hail Mary. Hail anybody. I could really use some help here. He's only three and he's run out of pull-ups and I wanted to know what he'd grow up to be. I don't know where my parents are. I think they might be . . . sick. I ran so I could save him. So I could save him from them. I'm running out of water. I don't know where I'm going. Is there anywhere I can go that's better? What will happen to us? I can't kill him don't make me kill him but if it comes to it let him . . . let him go in his sleep, just get him the fuck out of here, they can have me, just get him out, let him find a safe place, don't make him do this. I'm seventeen, I wanted to be a marine biologist, I have a baseball bat and a fucking flashlight and I can't do this, how can I do this, every time I close my eyes I see them pulling him away from me and he's shrieking mommy, all done, mommy, mommy, help, and what am I supposed to do and I can't, I can't, I fucking can't.

Now they've hit the farmland outside town, out where she took Jack apple picking last fall, and this time of year the strawberries are fruiting, acres of them, and she can't smell the fires from here, just the hay and the sun and the strawberries and it strikes her for a dizzy moment that the listing world has righted. She steps over the few scraggly rows on the end and sets Jack down in the middle of a clump of berries and they're huge, pristine, untouched, and swollen on the sun. She's found a pistol with three rounds in it and it's jammed down in her waistband and the aluminum bat doesn't leave her swinging hand. She keeps watch. Jack is picking berries and cramming them in with both hands and the juice is running down his chin and then she's down in the rows with him, one eye scanning, one hand picking. She only allows herself a moment. She needs to be alert, not drunk on summer and a bellyful of sugar after days of crumbs. Jack, seeing this, pauses in his cramming to offer up two berries, one in each fist, both bruised with clumsy picking. Eat mommy! he says, red around the mouth and reaching out to her, and her breath hitches in her throat, and she knows that if she were in a movie this'd be Foreshadowing, or the Calm Before the Storm, but then she starts laughing and laughing because she doesn't know what else to do with herself except start screaming and she can't do that, she has to make him believe it's a game or he's going to lose it and then they're done. Anyway it's almost funny. For the first time all week, he looks just like everybody else.

Now it's raining, a light sweet twilit summer rain, and she's holed up in the farm stand, and Jack's sleeping on her lap, his hair sticky with strawberry juice, and that's where they find her.

She doesn't know where they came from, how they knew she was there, what they're even doing out so far on the county route, a good ten miles from town, only that she wakes and hears a noise outside, a sort of whistling sigh, which first she takes for wind, except there isn't any. Then she hears something dragging on the gravel of the parking lot, something heavy. And then the doorknob starts to slowly turn, turn and release, turn and release, like it's being fumbled with a slippery hand.

She'd locked it, she knows she'd locked it. Maybe the lock was faulty, maybe Jack had unlocked it when she wasn't looking (though when the hell was she *not looking?*), it doesn't matter. She folds him to her chest and darts in low toward the doorknob, reaches out against all her instinct to flee, tries to turn the lock, but it won't turn, not while the doorknob's turning too.

Jack starts to stir, to knuckle at his sleepy eyes. Still half-asleep, he's going through his wake-up routine, and any minute he'll be peering up into her face, saying boo, mommy! Play?

A low moan rises in her throat. She chokes it back, astonished: she'd sounded just like them. Even as she's ducking and running behind the counter for a chair to wedge beneath the doorknob, some part of her brain is flying out ahead of her, wondering why it is they make such a despairing sound, such a mournful, and what fucking right have they to mourn.

She's got the chair under the doorknob and she's backing, backing. But there are long shadows dragging across all the windows, not only the ones near the door, and now there's something pressed up against the nearest one, something like a stomped windfall plum the size of her face, and from somewhere else she hears the sound of breaking glass, and every drop of blood she owns freezes in that instant into shards.

Awake now, Jack looks up at her and he's got the wide-eyed quivery look he gets at the doctor's office, like if he stays as still and watchful as he can, the nurse with the needle won't know that he's there, and that look scares her even worse than she already is, terrorizes her into moving. She has to get him out. Has to. Failing that, she has to buy enough time to draw the gun and kiss him goodbye and tell him to close his eyes and count to three like she used to do when she had a present for him because if it comes to it, the best present her useless love can give him is an easy death, but in the end, when it does come down to it, can she even give him that?

Well, now or never. She's got him sitting on the counter, facing him into a corner toward a poster of apple varieties so he can't see what's happening at the doors and windows, and she's sliding the safety off down by her hip where he can't see that either. For a second she almost loses her resolve, almost plants one in her temple so she doesn't have to see him die, but leaving him to get eaten even as he clings to her corpse, crying wake up mommy, that's the one thing she won't ever do. Give mommy a hug, she tells him, biggest hug you got, and her voice breaks to shit but she can't do much about it, and he flings out his arms and buries his face in her neck and she holds his head there with her off hand while she slips the gun up between them, against his tiny chest, his hammering hummingbird heart, she doesn't even have to aim he's so small, anywhere will do. I love you, sweetie, she whispers into his hair. I'm so fucking sorry.

And suddenly she knows she won't do it. Maybe she knew all along she wouldn't. Couldn't. Can't. She slings him up off the counter, back onto her arm.

They're at the front door. They're at the back door. They're at the side door where the tractors unload the crates of melons in the summer, pumpkins in the fall. But it's at the front window where they've broken through, and she doesn't know if they smell her through the gap or what but they're starting to cluster there, and even as she watches more windfalls appear at the glass, more leave the back wall windows.

Close your eyes, baby, she says, and lunges for the back door.

Now she's running, running harder than she's ever run. The evening's still warm, the sunlight slowly bleeding out, and they're still chasing her but they're not quite closing, she's too fast.

For now. She's leaking pretty badly from a long gash down one arm, one cheek is clawed across, her trigger finger broke when one of them grabbed her gun and tore it free, taking the discharged bullet in the eye like a kiss. But what's really got her attention is the place on the front of her shoulder where a plug of flesh has been subtracted. She can't remember what happened there, but the wound is bone-deep and when she stops to dare a look at it, a tiny yellow thing falls tinkling to the road. She picks it up and sobs aloud. A tooth.

How much time does she have? Not enough. Not near enough. She has to get Jack somewhere safe, get far away from him, because they didn't get him, she didn't let them get him, she put her arms, her head, her back between their teeth and him, but when she turns she'll smell the meat on him, and she can't bear to think on that too long. Suddenly, horribly, she knows that when she runs, he won't stay put, he'll follow. That when she turns wrong, turns sick, and comes for him, he won't run, not from her, he'll probably think she's nibbling at his face for tickles before the teeth sink in.

She has to think. She can't. The change is coming on her, the infection nosing through her veins toward her heart, her brain, wherever it is it sinks its roots. She's dizzy. Clammy. Her ears are ringing. She's never been so hungry in her life. Her vision's dimming but her sense of smell is paring to a point and she can read Jack in layers of scent: strawberries, piss-stained racecar jammies, milk-fed flesh, and fear. There's something else there, though, something bittersweet and pungent, with a scorch against her swollen tongue like salt. He loves her. He trusts her. It oozes from his pores. She smells him and she spits and spits until her mouth stops watering.

Her mind's starting to drop down its curtains now, but in one last burst of clarity she sees it like a movie: her and Jack, stumbling down the embankment into the flowering orchard, fleeing the open road, and she knows what happens next. The only chance he has.

She hasn't figured out how the infection works. Maybe nobody ever will. But she's thinking of the corpses lying dead in the parking lot, the not-quite-corpses on her tail, and her brain feels like a soaked sponge in her head, her thoughts go soggy before they quite connect, but she's stumbling down the embankment into the flowering orchard, she's fleeing the open road, she's pushing through the trees to the shed she knows is there from when she took Jack apple-picking a lifetime ago. She'd had to stop and change his diaper and a sunburned woman had directed her down to the shed among the trees. Hope you got wipes, the woman told her, but at least it's a little privacy. Key's above the door.

Key's there now too. She fumbles the padlock, her fingers are so cold. Fights it open. Sets Jack down so she can unfold the knife. Cuts into the back of her hand with the bladepoint, spells FIND. Spells JACK. He watches her wide-eyed, far too scared to cry.

Be brave for mommy, she tells him, kneeling down, her voice slurring to paste. Okay?

Okay, he whispers, and afterward it's all she can do to push him inside and lock the door between them and slip the key where she won't drop it—under her tongue, like a coin—but first she lifts his little arm up to her mouth and bites down hard.

Then she's running back up toward the road, toward them, like the idiot in the movie who Dies That Someone Else Might Live, waving her arms and yelling. Once she's got their attention she takes off down the road, away from him, away from them, and, herd that they are, they follow.

They chase her for a quarter mile before the infection takes her over. It slows her to their speed and they fall in step around her, she disappears among them, like a droplet entering the sea.

Now she's got something carved into her hand but she can't read it. There's something in her mouth so she spits it out. There's blood on her lips, though, and more blood off back somewhere behind her, she can smell it on the wind, and that's something she can understand.

The thing on the door of the little building is mysterious to her, so she takes it in one hand and pulls until it breaks. The door falls open and there's one like her on the floor, like her only smaller, curled up in a ball and gnawing on a brick. She knows that hunger, knows it deep. The virus has imprinted it upon her every cell. Somewhere even deeper she knows the thing that pulls itself to sitting, blinks up at her with eyes like soft-boiled eggs, and smiles. Boo, mommy! it gurgles around the bolus of its tongue. Mommy play?

She can't carry it anymore, her arm is ruined, but the fires of the town are distant, the others are so near, so strong, and it's been days since it—since he—got down and really walked.

The Hunt: Before, and the Aftermath

Joe R. Lansdale

We rode the famous Fast Train out west, all the way from New York City.

Went out there with men and women packed in all the cars along with all our baggage and the guns, and they were good guns, too. All of us had good guns. That was a perquisite. We had paid for the hunt and our guides made sure we had the best of everything, and that included the guns. They wanted us to have good weapons, not only because we were about to hunt and were paying heavily for the privilege, but because they thought if we had excellent weapons and ammunition, it less likely that something might blow up in someone's face, killing them. There were insurance policies, of course. But there's always trouble and always challenges from the insurance, especially on these types of hunting expeditions. Part of the reason the hunting was so expensive, was because the insurance the hunting company paid was very high.

I brought along my wife, Livia, and we left the kids with their grandparents—my parents. It was a nice trip out, and there were excursions along the way, and we even did a bit of bird hunting in Arkansas. Stopped there for a couple of days and stayed in some cabins up in the mountains where the woods were thick.

It was September, and there were some brisk mornings, some warm middays, and then at night there was the cool again. But it was never miserable. We spent the nights in the cabins, but before bedtime we all sat around a campfire that was prepared by our guides, and there was entertainment. Singers and even some skits that weren't really all that good but seemed a lot better under the circumstances.

As I said, it was a nice trip, in that everything went smooth, but it wasn't good when it came to Livia and I, and considering all that had gone before, I didn't expect it to be, but it was good that the trip itself wasn't bad to make matters worse. At least we had that going for us, the smoothness of the trip.

During the day while we were in Arkansas we hunted. Mostly we were done by noon, and when we came in the guides would have the birds cleaned right away and put in the refrigeration car, and that night they would be our meal, that and some good beans and fresh baked cornbread.

Frankly, though I like shooting birds, I don't much care for the meat. But I ate it well enough, and by the end of the day, tromping around with the hunting dogs that had been provided by the Arkansas cabin owner where we stayed, I most likely could have eaten anything and thought that it was fine. I think I would have thought that cornbread was fine anytime; I'm a big fan of cornbread.

The first night in the Arkansas accommodations, Livia and I went to our cabin and decided to take showers since we smelled of smoke from the campfire. Livia wanted to go first. She began to undress. I watched her. Even though she was nearing the age of forty, she had a youthful body, and I enjoyed watching her take off her clothes and pause before a mirror in the bedroom to shake out her hair, which had been tied back in a pony tail.

When she walked to the bathroom, I enjoyed the view, and was sorry that even though we were sharing a bed, we wouldn't be sharing one another. I wished then that I had things to do over, but I didn't, and it was my hope in time that we could reconcile things, and not just so we could have sex, but so we could have peace and things would be like they used to be; that was the purpose of the hunt: time together and reconciliation.

Anyway, she showered, and came into the room, and pulled a huge red nightshirt over her head, and without putting on panties got into bed. A year ago, that would have been a kind of silent invitation, but tonight I knew it was just a tease, something to make me feel bad about what I had done, and about what I wasn't going to get tonight because of it. It had been that way every night since she found out about the infidelity. That was eight months ago, but things hadn't changed much in that time, except we could talk a little more civilly most of the time.

I showered, and while in the shower I masturbated, thinking it would be a lot better to do that than to lie in the bed and think about what was under her nightshirt all night. There was also in me a bit of defiance. I was truly sorry for what I had done, and I had tried in every possible way to make it up.

I didn't think just because I was sorry that it should be the end of the matter, as that kind of betrayal is serious and nothing anyone can get over easily. I know I would have had problems, but damn it, I was trying, and I didn't seem to get points for trying. I felt she was enjoying punishing me a little too much.

By the time I had satisfied myself and washed the results down the drain, I was feeling less bold, and understood exactly why she felt the way she did. I took a long time drying off and brushing my teeth, and by the time I got in bed, Livia was sound asleep.

We stopped in Palo Duro Canyon in northern Texas, and that night there was a play about statehood. It was performed in a beautiful part of the mountains, and there were lots of lights, and there were horses and cowboys and they rode the horses along the rim to the sound of brassy, but inspiring music that seemed to be as loud as the canyon was normally silent.

It was a good show, and it even included the changes that had occurred, and there were people dressed up like the dead people, shuffling along, and there were a few comic bits associated with it, and then it was over.

As we were bused back to where the tracks were, and where our hotel was, Livia said, "You know, that was hokey, but I really enjoyed it."

"So did I," I said, though that wasn't entirely true. I had begun to see that Livia was looking at other men in a way she hadn't before. I don't know if it was because she was thinking about cheating to even up the score, or if what I had done had just opened her mind to someone other than me. Anyway, I had watched her and I thought I had seen something in her eye when she was watching some of the male actors in the plays. They were all young, and most likely gay, I told myself, but still, Livia was watching. I felt certain of it. Nonetheless, I liked that she had spoken to me in that way, as it seemed natural and for a few seconds it seemed as if she had forgotten all about being mad at me.

But back at the room we went straight to bed, and I lay there and looked at the ceiling for a long time. Eventually I heard Livia breathing evenly as she slept, and I turned and looked at her.

There was enough moonlight through a part in the curtains to fall on her face and make her look angelic. I thought she was the kind of woman who could easily attract a much younger man, and I was the kind of man who, if I managed to keep my business and money, could most likely attract a younger woman, but only if they didn't know I was in debt. She had options, and I didn't have any real ones. Just ones I might be able to lie about.

I think that's what it had been about, the infidelity, a feeling that I was getting past it all and needed some assurance of my manhood. It hadn't been a classic sort of infidelity, and I told myself that because of the uniqueness of it, it didn't count. But if it had been the other way, Livia instead of me that had done it, I know I would have been insane with jealousy.

I might have been better off had I had an affair, and not just an encounter—an encounter I paid steeply for, both financially and emotionally.

I hoped when we got to the hunt, everything would be better. That I could make it better and she would accept that. I lay there and tried to think of all the clever things I could do to make her happy, but all of them were fantasy and I knew none of them would work.

We had a private car on the train with food and alcohol and most anything that we seriously needed. There would be the hunting car later, but on the way out and back, when we weren't stopped along the way at some site or entertainment that was planned, we had the room and a fold-down berth, and it was all nice and clean and private.

The humming of the train over the tracks had become soothing, and maybe that was why Livia was able to talk about it. She came at me with it out of nowhere, and it was the first time she hadn't yelled at me when she brought it up.

"Was it because I didn't satisfy you?"

I was sitting at the fold-down table with a drink of well-watered whisky. I said, "Of course not."

"Then why?"

"I've told you, Livia."

"Tell me again."

"I've told you again and again."

"Make me believe it."

I sat for a moment, gathering my energy for it. "I suppose it has to do with getting older. I don't feel all that attractive anymore. I'm a little heavy, going bald. I wanted to feel that I could be with another woman."

"But that woman . . . That doesn't work, Frank. She didn't want you back. She was paid for. And she was . . . "

"I know," I said. "But it was the fantasy that she was someone who cared for me and that it was a secret rendezvous. It was the idea of it more than the actuality of it. It was stupid, but I did it and I'm sorry, and I am so sad it ever happened."

"Childish."

"Yes," I said. "Very much so. I know that now. But I just felt it might give me a boost, so to speak."

"I don't give you a boost?"

"You do."

"I know I'm older—"

"You look fantastic," I said. "It wasn't that. It was me."

"And that's supposed to make me feel better?"

"I don't think that—no. It won't make you feel better. But it's an answer, not an excuse, and it's the only one I have. There is no good answer. I was foolish. It's just that . . . I love you, Livia. But I just wasn't satisfied."

"It wasn't like I didn't make love to you."

"No," I said. "You did. But . . . it wasn't all that passionate."

"We're not eighteen anymore."

"I guess that's what I wanted, something more passionate. Something that would make me feel eighteen again."

"The only thing that could make you feel eighteen again is being eighteen," she said.

"I know. I just wanted something besides the usual, you know. I don't mean that offensively, but I wanted to feel something akin to the old passion."

Livia turned her head away from me when she spoke. "Why didn't you ask? We could have experimented."

"I hinted."

"Hinted?" she said. "Isn't it men who always say that women don't say what they want? That they beat around the bush? Don't you always say: 'How am I supposed to know what you want if you don't ask'?"

"I suppose it is."

"No supposing to it."

We sat silent for a long time. I didn't even pick up my drink.

"Do you think you can ever feel good about me again?" I asked. "That you can ever trust me and feel that things are right again? Can we ever be okay?"

"I don't know," Livia said.

She went to the cabinet and pulled the latch and took out a glass and a bottle of some kind of green liquor. She poured herself a drink and put everything back, and went to sit on the fold-down bed.

"You'll try?" I said.

"I try every day," she said. "You don't know how hard I try."

"This trip . . . was it a mistake?"

"I don't know. I'll see how it makes me feel when it's all over."

I nodded and drank the rest of my drink. I couldn't think of anything else to say or do, except get another drink, and I didn't even do that. I just sat there, and in time Livia took a magazine from her suitcase and lay on the bed and read.

I finally got up and got another drink and sat down at the table with it. I sipped it and thought about how I had ruined everything that had ever meant anything to me for a piece of overpriced heavily lubricated ass.

I began to hang all my hopes on the hunt, and that the enthusiasm of it would excite her as it did when we used to deer hunt together. That had been years ago, and this was different, but I think, except for those times when we had been young and in bed together, it was the time when I felt the most bonded to her.

I suppose it was the thrill of the hunt, and mostly the thrill of the kill. I never deluded myself into thinking hunting was a sport. Killing was what it was all about, and to kill something was to satisfy something deep in the soul, something primal. And it was a strange thing to see that primitive nature in a woman, and to observe her face when she stood over the body of a dead deer; her eyes bright, the deer's eyes dull, and on Livia's face an expression akin to the one she had when she had an orgasm and lay in my arms, happy, satisfied, having experienced something that was beyond intellect and rationalization.

It was a cool, crisp morning when we reached Montana. The air felt rich with oxygen and the sky was so blue it was hard to believe it was real. There wasn't a cloud in the sky. By midday it would be relatively warm, if still jacket weather, but we would be in the hunting car, perched at the windows with our rifles, so it would be comfortable enough, stuffed as the car would be with other hunters, adrenaline and passion and the desire to kill. Though, perhaps, *kill* was the wrong word here, and that's what made the whole thing somehow acceptable. You can't kill what's already dead, but you can enjoy the shooting, and maybe it wasn't as good as a live deer brought down and made dead, but to shoot the living dead, a human, and not have any remorse because it was all sanctioned, there was something about that, something about the fantasy of killing a human being instead of just bringing down a walking thing that was the shell for someone who had once lived.

The train parked on the tracks and some of the guides went to the storage car where the dead people were kept. They would let them out and drive them to the center of the plain, and they would throw sides of beef in the dirt to keep them in that area, bloody beef that the dead could smell and want.

When they went for the beef, when the guides said it was time, we could point our guns out the window and take them as fast as we could shoot. Sometimes, the guides said, the dead would come to the window, and that you had to be careful, because you could get so caught up in the shooting, you could forget that they wanted you as much as you wanted them. If you're arm was out the window, well, you could get bit, and the waiver we had signed said that if that was the case, we went out there with them. We wouldn't necessarily be dead, but we soon would be, so there was a chance to shoot someone who was actually alive; someone already doomed. It was considered practical and even humane, and it was covered by insurance money that your family would receive.

Livia and I settled into our shooting positions. We had benches by a long window, and the window was still closed. We were given our rifles. They were already loaded, and we were told to keep them pointing up, which, of course, we knew without being told. Everyone here had gone through the program on how to handle the weapons and how to deal with the dead, and Livia and I were already hunters and we could shoot.

I had paid dearly for this event, and I hoped it would make a difference. When it was all over, I would be deep in debt, but I would have saved my marriage if it worked. Money was easier to regain than it was to regain the loss of a good marriage.

The guides came through and told us the basic rules again, gave us reminders, the same stuff I told you about not getting so caught up in the kill that we forgot to watch for the dead slipping through, getting hold of us through the windows. They said everything was very safe, but that it had happened, and they would be outside, on the fringes, with weapons to take down any of the dead that seemed to be getting through the line of fire and presenting a problem.

My hands were sweating. Not from fear of the dead, or even anticipation of the shoot itself, but thinking how it would be between Livia and me when it was over.

"What's she wearing?" Livia asked.

I was startled out of my thoughts.

"What?"

"I said, what is she wearing?"

"I bought an orange jump suit for her."

"How does she look?"

"Dark hair, tall . . . well built."

"That could be me."

"I suppose that had something to do with it," I said. "Her reminding me of you."

"A dead woman?"

I knew then my tact had backfired, and I could have kicked myself.

"Just the appearance," I said. "But it's been awhile. And even with refrigeration, she's gone downhill. She still looks close to being alive. Not as much as before."

"You mean when you fucked her?"

We were seated pretty close to other hunters, and I glanced to see if any of them had heard her, heard anything we might have said.

They all seemed preoccupied with their weapons and their thoughts and their eagerness, and I realized that Livia wasn't as loud as I thought she was.

"I don't know how to describe her so that you will know right off," I said. "I'll try and point her out."

"You do that," Livia said. "I want to be the one."

"I know."

"I thought maybe I'd want you to shoot her, just to show me it didn't matter, but then I thought that wouldn't do. I want to shoot her."

"Of course it doesn't matter," I said. "It wasn't like she was alive."

"I want to shoot her," she said.

"It could be anyone that shoots her," I said. "There's no guarantees it'll be you that gets her."

"It better be me," Livia said. "You paid to fuck her, now you've paid for me to shoot her. It better be me."

"You don't just want to shoot her," I said. "You want to finish her. A shot through the head to destroy the brain."

"Think I don't know that? Everyone knows that. And I can shoot. You know I can shoot."

I couldn't say anything right. Everything I said was like stepping in shit and being forced to smell my shoe.

"Yes," I said. "Of course you can shoot."

The guides were moving back along the aisle of the rail car.

"All right," one of them said. "We are going to open the cars, and when the dead come out—and listen to me. Do not shoot! Not at first. The beef is in place. You see the yellow chalk line we've laid in the grass? You cannot, and will not, shoot until the dead are beyond that, on the beef. If some do not go past the line, the outside guides will work them that way with the push poles, and if they can't get them to go, they may have to put a few down themselves. After the dead are over the line, you can fire at will. And if they start to come back over the line, you can still fire. But you have to wait until they are first over the line. Does everyone understand?"

We all called out that we understood.

"Any questions?" asked the guide. There were none.

"Then," the guide said, "ladies and gentlemen, the windows will be lowered. Do not put your rifles out the windows until the dead are all past the yellow line, and when they are, then it is open season."

The automatic windows rolled down. The windows gave plenty of room for propping the rifles and for laying your elbows on the sill.

We heard the train cars opening on either side of us, and we could hear the dead, moaning. Then we saw them coming out of the cars. The guides had big heavy poles and they pushed the dead with them to make sure they went toward the yellow line. But they didn't need much pushing. The bloody meat smelled even better than we did to them, and the dead went for it right away.

Livia said, "Point her out. I want to shoot her a few times in the body before I take the head."

"Someone might beat you to it," I said.

"Just point her out."

In that moment I thought about the night I had had with the woman who had no name and was for a while part of the dead brothel down on 41st Street. She was only part of it while she was fresh, and then they had to let her go to the sale market for the hunts, and I was lucky to buy her. I almost didn't win the bid, and I had to keep raising it, and pretty soon I had my bid way up there and it was really far more than I could afford. But I bought her for the hunt. But even then, she was just mine to place in the hunt, not mine or Livia's to shoot. That was up to circumstance.

It was said many a husband or wife had bought their dead spouses to shoot at because of past grievances, and it even occurred to me Livia might turn the rifle on me. It wasn't a serious thought, but it passed through my head nonetheless.

I thought about the dead woman now, of how she had been fastened to the bed and her mouth was covered over with a leather strap; how she had writhed beneath me; not because she enjoyed or felt anything, but because she was trying to break loose and she wanted to bite me. I could hear her grunting with savage hunger under the mask, and it was exciting to know what I was doing. I had paid for her with a charge card, and though the card didn't say brothel on it, Livia was able to figure it all out. It took her awhile, but she got it doped out and then she confronted me, and I didn't even try to lie. I think on some level I had wanted her to find out, had wanted her to know.

But the young woman beneath me that night at the brothel was still firm and she wasn't falling apart. She hadn't been dead long, and what had killed her was heart failure, some inherited condition that took her out young. When she died the dead disease took her over, and her mother sold her to the brothel then; had them come out and capture her and take her there.

A few years back such a thing would have been thought horrible, but now it happened all the time. It was part of the government plan to dehumanize them after they were dead, to make people think of them as nothing more than empty shells that walked and were a threat and were sometimes entertainment. It was an indoctrination that was starting to take hold.

Yet, when I saw the dead out there, wandering over the line, in all manner of conditions, some fresh, some with their skin falling off, some little more than skeletons with just enough viscera and flesh to hold them together, I felt sick. My parents had died but a few years before the flu came that caused so many to become what these poor people were, and I thought if they had lived just another year, they might have been victims, they might be out there. Someone's parents, brothers, sisters, husbands, you name it, were out there. It was only luck that had caused us and so many others to take flu shots that year, and the flu shots saved us, even though there had never been a flu like this one. Just that simple thing, a flu shot, had saved many from dying and coming back. Those who hadn't taken the shot, and got the flu, they got worse, died, and came back.

All of this was running through my head, and then I saw the woman. She had on the orange jump suit I had bought for her, and she was staggering toward the meat on the other side of the line.

"There she is," I said. "The orange jump suit."

"There are a lot of orange jump suits," Livia said.

"Not like this one," I said. "It's bright orange. She's off to the side there. She has long black hair. Very long, like yours. Like all the others, her back is to us."

"I see her," Livia said.

She lifted her rifle and fired right away. It was a miss. But she fired again and she hit the woman in the back. The shot knocked the woman down. She got up rather quickly, and started walking again, toward the beef.

"I want to see her face," Livia said.

"That might not happen," I said.

Livia fired again, hit the woman in the back of the right knee. It was a shot that not only knocked her down, but as she fell, her face turned toward us. It was still a good face, somewhat drawn, but still the face of someone pretty who had once been very pretty in life. And then she caught another shot from Livia's rifle, this one in the face, just over the upper lip. The woman spun a little, and I think the blow from the heavy load made her neck turn in such a way that it snapped her spine.

When she was on the ground, she began to crawl toward the smell of the meat again. Her head was turned oddly on her neck, and the side of her face dragged the ground as she went.

"I want you to shoot her once," Livia said. "Then I'll make the kill. You shoot her in the body."

Now there were explosions everywhere as the dead targets took hits, and even Livia's target, the woman I had fucked, was being shot at. Bullets were smashing into the earth all around her and one took off part of her right foot.

"You shoot her," Livia said. "You shoot her now."

I fired and missed.

"You better hit her," Livia said.

I fired again, hit the woman in the body. She kept crawling. Livia just sat there, watching her crawl.

"You want to finish her, better hurry before someone else gets her," I said.

Livia looked at me. Her eyes were cold. "You better hope no one else does," she said.

She lifted her rifle and fired. The woman's head exploded.

After that, we began to fire at will, and I think I blew the heads off four, though someone else's shot might have taken one of them. I couldn't be sure. Livia hit at least seven in the head and dropped them. She hit several more in the body, and dropped them. Eventually, someone firing at the same targets got the head.

When it was all done, the guides gathered up the bodies with hooks and carried them to a large and long pile of lumber that had already been laid out and had weathered some. They put the dead on the pile and poured gasoline over all of it and set it on fire.

When the fire was going, the rifles were gathered and stored and we broke for clean up and then dinner, just as the train was starting to move.

Back in our little room we could really smell the gun oil and the stink from the firing. We decided to shower and dress for dinner. There was to be a big formal dinner in the dining car tonight, a celebration of the completion of the hunt. On the way back the train wouldn't stop, but would run full speed night and day until we arrived back east.

Before I got in the shower, I looked at Livia, and she was obviously different, relieved, as if a poison had been drained from her. I went to the bathroom and undressed. It was tight in there and the shower was close. I turned on the water and began to soap up and shampoo my hair.

I heard the curtain slide back, and there was Livia, naked. She didn't smile at me. She didn't say a word. She got in and pulled back the curtain and took hold of me and got me ready and then before I knew it was happening, I was inside of her, pushing her up against the shower wall, going at her for all I was worth.

She was amazing, animal-like even. It was over quickly for both of us. We leaned together, panting. Then Livia was out of the shower, and was gone, and I was left dazed and amazed, satisfied and confused.

When I came out of the bathroom, drying myself with a towel, the lights were on, but Livia had already gone to bed. She was lying in our little bunk beneath the sheets with her back to me, her face turned to the wall. The blanket was folded back to her feet.

I was about to put on my pajamas, when she said without turning toward me, "Don't bother with your pajamas. Put out the light and come to bed."

I did. And we did.

It was a great, long night of love, and even as I mounted her, and enjoyed her, and she squirmed beneath me and moaned, I couldn't help but somehow being reminded of that night with the woman we shot. Like that night, what Livia and I did was not so much making love as it was a pounding of each other's genitals. It was a savage pelvis fight that left bruises and redness and utter exhaustion.

Later, lying beside Livia, holding her, listening to her breathe, I wondered how long it would be before things went back to the way they used to be. Not just how we could be together without the thing I had done not hanging before us in the air, but the sex, as well; how long before it became mild again, as common as a subway ride, and as boring.

I thought of that and I thought of the strange time I had had with the dead woman in a room on 41st Street, and I told myself that such a thing couldn't happen again, but I knew too, that while Livia and I had been at it this night, when I closed my eyes, it was not Livia I saw. It was the dead woman I imagined beneath me.

What in hell were the desires of man?

No profound revelation presented itself in answer to my question.

I closed my eyes and thought about many things, but mostly I thought about that dead woman, and how she had been, and how it had been to shoot her today, and how it had made Livia and me fill up with the lava of passion. I tried to think of Livia, and our life, and how much I loved her, but in my mind all I could see was that dead girl being screwed by me or shot by us, and the Fast Train fled eastward.

Bit Rot

Charles Stross

Hello? Do you remember me?

If you are reading this text file and you don't remember me—that's Lilith Nakamichi-47—then you are suffering from bit rot. If you can see me, try to signal; I'll give you a brain dump. If I'm not around, chances are I'm out on the hull, scavenging for supplies. Keep scanning, and wait for me to return. I've left a stash of feedstock in the storage module under your bunk: to the best of my knowledge it isn't poisonous, but you should take no chances. If I don't return within a couple of weeks, you should assume that either I'm suffering from bit rot myself, or I've been eaten by another survivor.

Or we've been rescued—but that's hopelessly optimistic.

You're probably wondering why I'm micro-embossing this file on a hunk of aluminum bulkhead instead of recording it on a soul chip. Unfortunately, spare soul chips are in short supply right now on board the *Lansford Hastings*.

Speaking of which: your bunk is in module B-14 on Deck C of Module Brazil. Just inside the shielding around the Number Six fusion reactor, which has never been powered up and is mothballed during interstellar cruise, making it one of the safest places aboard the ship right now. As long as you don't unbar the door for anyone but me, it should stay that way.

You and I are template-sisters, our root identities copied from our parent. Unfortunately, along with our early memories we inherited a chunk of her wanderlust, which is probably why we are in this fix.

We are not the only survivors, but there's been a total breakdown of cooperation; many of the others are desperate. In the unlikely event that you hear someone outside the hatch, you must be absolutely certain that it's me before you open up—and that I'm fully autonomous. I think Jordan's gang may have an improvised slave controller, or equivalent: it would explain a lot.

Make sure I remember everything before you let me in. Otherwise you could be welcoming a zombie. Or worse.

It's nearly four centuries since we signed up for this cruise, but we've been running in slowtime for most of it, internal clocks cut back to one percent of realtime. Even so, it's a long way to Tipperary (or Wolf 1061)—nearly two hundred years to go until we can start the deceleration burn (assuming anyone's still alive by then). Six subjective years in slowtime aboard a starship, bunking in a stateroom the size of a coffin, all sounds high-pitched, all lights intolerably bright. It's not a luxurious lifestyle. There are unpleasant side-effects: liquids seem to flow frictionlessly, so you gush super-runny lube from every leaky joint and orifice, and your mechanocytes spawn furiously as they try to keep up with the damage inflicted by cosmic rays. On the other hand, the potential rewards are huge. The long-ago mother of our line discovered this; she signed up to crew a starship, driven to run away from Earth by demons we long since erased from our collective memories. They were desperate for willing emigrants in those days, willing to train up the unskilled, unsure what to expect.

Well, we know *now*. We know what it takes to ride the slow boat down into the hot curved spacetime around a new star, to hunt the most suitable rocks, birth powersats and eat mineshafts and survey and build and occupy the airless spaces where posthumanity has not gone before. When it amused her to spawn us our line matriarch was a wealthy dowager, her salon a bright jewel in the cultural hub of Tau Ceti's inner belt society, but she didn't leave us much of her artful decadence. She downloaded her memories into an array of soul chips, artfully flensing them of centuries of jaded habit and timeworn experience, to restore some capacity for novelty in the universe. Then she installed them in new bodies and summoned us to a huge coming-out ball. "Daughters," she said, sitting distant and amused on a throne of spun carbon-dioxide snow: "I'm *bored*. Being old and rich is hard work. But you don't have to copy me. Now fuck off and have adventures and don't forget to write."

I'd like to be able to say we told her precisely where to put her adventures-by-proxy, but we didn't; the old bat had cunningly conditioned us to worship her, at least for the first few decades. Which is when you and I, sister of mine, teamed up. Some of our sibs rebelled by putting down roots, becoming accountants, practicing boredom. But we . . . we had the same idea: to do exactly what Freya wanted, except for the sharing bit. Go forth, have adventures, live the wild life, and never write home.

Which is more than somewhat ironic because I'd *love* to send her a soul chipped memoir of our current adventure—so she could scream herself to sleep.

Here are the bare facts:

You, Lamashtu, and I, Lilith, worked our butts off and bought our way into the *Lansford Hastings. LF* was founded by a co-op, building it slowly in their—our—spare time, in orbit around Haldane B, the largest of the outer belt plutoids around Tau Ceti. We aren't rich (see-also: bitch-mother referenced above), and we're big, heavy persons—nearly two meters from toe to top of anthropomorphic head—but we have what it takes: they were happy enough to see two scions of a member of the First Crew, with memories of the early days of colonization and federation. "You'll be fine," Jordan reassured us after our final interview—"we need folks with your skills. Can't get enough of 'em." He hurkled gummily to himself, signifying amusement. "Don't you worry about your mass deficit, if it turns out you weigh too much we can always eat your legs."

He spoke on behalf of the board, as one of the co-founders. I landed a plum job: oxidation suppression consultant for the dihydrogen monoxide mass fraction. That's a fancy way of saying I got to spend decades of slowtime scraping crud from the bottom of the tankage in Module *Alba*, right up behind the wake shield and micrometeoroid defenses. You, my dear, were even luckier: someone had to go out and walk around on the hull, maintaining the mad dendritic tangle of coolant pipes running between the ship's reactors and the radiator panels, replacing components that had succumbed to secondary activation by cosmic radiation.

It's all about the radiation, really. Life aboard a deep space craft is a permanent battle against the effects of radiation. At one percent of lightspeed, a cold helium atom in the interstellar medium slams into our wake shield with the energy of an alpha particle. But there's much worse. Cosmic rays—atomic nuclei traveling at relativistic speed—sleet through the hull every second, unleashing a storm of randomly directed energy. They'd have killed our squishy wet forerunners dead, disrupting their DNA replicators in a matter of months or years. We're made of tougher stuff, but even so: prolonged exposure to cosmic rays causes secondary activation. And therein lies our predicament.

The nice stable atoms of your hull absorb all this crap and some of those nuclei are destabilized, bouncing up and down the periodic table and in and out of islands of stability. Nice stable Argon-38 splits into annoyingly radioactive Aluminum-26. Or worse, it turns into Carbon-14, which is unstable and eventually farts out an electron, turning into Nitrogen-14 in the process. Bonds break, graphene sheets warp, molecular circuitry shorts out. That's us: the mechanocytes our brains are assembled from use carbon-based nanoprocessors.

We're tougher than our pink goo predecessors, but the decades or centuries of flight take their toll. Our ships carry lots of shielding—and lots of carefully purified stable isotopes to keep the feedstock for our mechanocyte assemblers as clean as possible—because nothing wrecks brains like the white-noise onslaught of a high radiation environment.

Year of Our Voyage 416.
We're all in slowtime, conserving energy and sanity as the stars crawl by at the pace of continental drift. We're running so slowly that there are only five work-shifts to each year. I'm in the middle of my second shift, adrift in the bottom of a molten water tank, slowly grappling with a polishing tool. It's hard, cumbersome work; I'm bundled up in a wetsuit to keep my slow secretions from contaminating the contents of the tank, cabled tightly down against the bottom of the tank as I run the polisher over the gray metal surface of the tank. The polisher doesn't take much supervision, but the water bubbles and buffets around me like a warm breeze, and if its power cable gets tangled around a baffle fin it can stop working in an instant.

I'm not paying much attention to the job; in fact, I'm focused on one of the chat grapevines. Lorus Pinknoise, who splits his time between managing the ship's selenium micronutrient cycle and staring at the stars ahead with telescope eyes, does a regular annual monologue about what's going on in the universe outside the ship, and his casual wit takes my mind off what I'm doing while I scrub out the tanks.

"Well, folks. This century sees us crawling ever-closer to our destination, the Wolf 1061 binary star system—which means, ever further from civilized space. Wolf 1061 is a low energy system, the two orange dwarf stars orbiting their common center of mass at a distance of a couple of million kilometers. They're not flare stars, and while normally this is a good thing, it makes it distinctly difficult to make observations of the atmosphere and surface features of 1061 Able through Mike by reflected light; the primaries are so dim that even though our long baseline interferometer can resolve hundred-kilometer features on the inner planets back in Sol system, we can barely make out the continents on Echo One and Echo Two. Now, those continents are interesting things, even though we're not going to visit down the gravity well any time soon. We know they're there, thanks to the fast flyby report, but we won't be able to start an actual survey with our own eyes until well into the deceleration stage, when I'll be unpacking the—"

Lorus's voice breaks up in a stuttering hash of dropouts. And the lights and the polisher stop working.

The *Lansford Hastings* is a starship, one of the fastest mecha ever constructed by the bastard children of posthumanity. From one angle, it may take us centuries to crawl between stars; but there's another perspective that sees us screaming across the cosmos at three thousand kilometers per second. On a planetary scale, we'd cross Sol system from Earth orbit to Pluto in less than two weeks. Earth to Luna in under *five minutes.* So one of the truisms of interstellar travel is that if something goes wrong, it goes wrong in a split instant, too fast to respond to.

Except when it doesn't, of course.

When the power went down, I do what anyone in my position would do: I panic and ramp straight from slowtime up to my fastest quicktime setting. The water around me congeals into a gelid, viscous impediment; the plugs and anti-leak gaskets I wear abruptly harden, gripping my joints and openings and fighting my every movement. I panic some more, and begin retracing my movements across the inner surface of the tank towards the door. It isn't completely dark in the tank. A very dim blue glow comes from the far side, around the curve of the toroid, bleeding past the baffles. It's not a sight one can easily forget: Cerenkov radiation, the glow of photons emitted by relativistic particles tunneling through water, slowing. I crank up the sensitivity of my eyes, call on skinsense for additional visuals, as panic recedes, replaced by chilly fear. All the regular shipboard comms channels have fallen silent: almost a minute has passed. "Can anybody hear me?" I call in quicktime over the widecast channel Lorus was so recently using. "What's happening? I'm in the Alba mass fraction tankage—"

"Help!" It's an answering voice. "Who's there? I'm in the gyro maintenance compartment in Brunei. What's going on? I've got a total power loss but everything's glowing—"

A growing chorus of frightened voices threatens to overload the channel; everyone who's answering seems to be at this end of the ship, up close behind the wake shield, and ramped up to quicktime. (At least, I hear no replies from persons in the cargo modules or down near the drive cluster or radiators.

Anyone still in slowtime won't be beginning to reply for minutes yet.) The menacing blue glow fades as I swim towards the fore inspection hatch. Then, in a soundless pulse of light, the backup lamps power up and a shudder passes through the ship as some arcane emergency maneuvering system cuts in and starts the cumbersome job of turning the ship, minutes too late to save us from disaster.

"Hello peeps," drones Lorus Pinknoise, our astrophysics philosopher. He's still coming up to speed; he sounds shaken. "Well, *that* was something I never expected to see up close and personal!"

I pause, an arm's length below the hatch. Something odd flickers in a corner of my eye, laser-sharp. Again, in my other eye. And my mandibular tentacle—my tongue—stings briefly. *Odd*, I think, floating there in the water. I look down into the depths of the tank, but the emergency lights have washed out the Cerenkov glow, if indeed it's still there. And there's another of those odd flickers, this time right across my vision, as if someone's flickered a laser beam across the surface of my optical sensor.

More chatter, then Lorus again: "We just weathered a *big* radiation spike, folks. I'm waiting for the wide-angle spectrophotometer to come back online; it overloaded. In fact, the spike was so sharp it generated an EM pulse that tripped every power bus on this side of the hull. Here we come . . . We took *lots* of soft gamma radiation, and a bunch of other stuff." While he's speaking, the tank circulation pumps start up. Around me, the ship shakes itself and slowly comes back to life in the wake of its minutes-long seizure. A chatter of low-level comms start up in the back of my head, easy to screen out. "I don't believe anybody's ever seen anything like that before, folks. Not seen it and lived to tell, anyway. It looks like—I'm reviewing the telemetry now—it looks like we just got whacked by a gamma ray burster. Er. I think we lucked out. We're still alive. I'm triangulating now. There's a candidate in the right direction, about nine thousand light years away, astern and about fifteen degrees off-axis, and—oh yes. I just looked at it folks, there's an optically visible star there, about twenty magnitudes brighter than the catalog says it should be. Wow, this is the astronomical find of the century—"

I have an itchy feeling in my skull. I shut out Lorus's prattle, turn inwards to examine my introsense, and shudder. A startling number of my mechanocytes are damaged; I need teché maintenance! My feet are particularly affected, and my right arm, where I reached for the hatch. I do a double-take. I'm floating in semi-darkness, inside a huge tank of water—one of the best radiation blockers there is. If *I've* taken a radiation pulse strong enough to cause tissue damage, what about everyone else? I look at the hatch and think of you, crawling around on the outside of the hull, and my circulatory system runs cold.

Over the next hour, things return to a temporary semblance of normality. Everyone who isn't completely shut down zips up to quicktime: corridors are filled with buzzing purposeful people and their autonomous peripherals, inspecting and inventorying and looking for signs of damage. Of which there are many. I download my own checklists and force myself to keep calm and carry on, monitoring pumps and countercurrent heat transfer systems. Flight Operations—the team of systems analysts who keep track of the state of the ship—issue periodic updates, bulletins reminding us of changed circumstances. And what a change there's been.

We have been supremely unlucky. I'll let Lorus explain:

"One of the rarest types of stellar remnant out there is what we call a magnetar—a rapidly-spinning neutron star with an incredibly powerful magnetic field. Did I say powerful? You'll never see one with your naked photosensor—they're about ten kilometers across, but before you got within ten thousand kilometers of one it would wipe your cranial circuitry. Get within one thousand kilometers and the magnetic field will rip your body apart— water molecules are diamagnetic, so are the metal structures in your marrow techné. Close up, the field's so intense that atoms are stretched into long, narrow cylinders and the vacuum of spacetime itself becomes birefringent.

Active magnetars are extremely rare, and most of the time they just sit where they are. But once in a while a starquake, a realignment in their crust, causes their magnetic field to realign. And the result is an amazingly powerful burst of gamma rays, usually erupting from both poles. And when the gamma ray jets slam into the expanding shell of gas left by the supernova that birthed the magnetar, you get a pulse of insanely high energy charged particles. One of which we flew through. Oops."

To be flying along a corridor aligned with the polar jet of a magnetar is so unlikely as to be vanishingly implausible. A local supernova, now *that* I could understand; when your voyages are measured in centuries or millennia it's only a matter of time before one of your ships falls victim. But a magnetar nearly ten thousand lights years away—that's the universe refusing to play fair!

I touched your shoulder. "Can you hear me, Lamashtu?"

"She can't." Doctor-Mechanic Wo gently pushed my arm away with one of their free tentacles. "Look at her."

I looked at you. You looked so still and calm, still frost-rimed with condensed water vapor from when the rescue team pulled you in through the pressure lock. You'd been in shutdown, drifting tethered to a hardpoint on the hull, for over three hours. Your skin is yellowing, the bruised bloom of self-destructing chromatophores shedding their dye payloads into your peripheral circulation. One of our human progenitors (like the pale-skinned, red-haired female you resemble) would be irreversibly dead at this point: but we are made of sterner stuff. I refused to feel despair. "How bad is it?" I asked.

"It could be worse." Wo shrugged, a ripplingly elegant wave of contraction curling out along all their limbs. "I'm mostly worried about her neural chassis. Did she leave a soul chip inside when she was out on the hull?"

I shook my head. Leaving a backup chip is a common ritual for those who work in high-risk environments, but you spent so long outside that you'd run the risk of diverging from the map of your memories. "She was wearing a chip in each of her sockets. You could try checking for them. Can you do a reload from chip . . . ?"

"Only if I could be absolutely certain it wasn't corrupted. Otherwise I'd risk scrambling the contents of her head even worse. No, Lilith, leave your sister to me. We'll do this the slow way, start with a full marrow replacement then progressively rebuild her brain while she's flatlined. She should be ready to wake up after a month of maintenance downtime. Then we can see if there's any lasting damage."

I saw the records, sister. You were on the outside of the hull, on the wrong side of the ship. You were exposed to almost thirty thousand Grays of radiation. The skin on your left flank, toughened to survive vacuum and cosmic radiation, was *roasted*.

"She should be all right for a while. I'll get around to her once I've checked on everyone else . . . "

"What do you mean?" I demanded. "Who else was outside the hull? Isn't she the most urgent case?"

The doctor's dismay was visible. "I'm afraid not. You underestimate how many people have sustained radiation damage. You were inside a reaction mass tank, were you not? You may be the least affected person on the entire ship. Everyone's been coming in with teché damage and odd brain lesions; memory loss, cognitive degradation, all sorts of stuff. Our progenitors didn't design us to take this kind of damage. I'm still working on a triage list. You're at the bottom of it; you're still basically functional. Your sister isn't in immediate danger of getting any worse, so—"

"—But she's dead! Of course she isn't going to get any worse!"

My outburst did not improve the doctor's attitude. "I think you'd better go now," they said, as the door opened above me and a pair of hexapods from Structural Engineering floated in, guiding a third companion who buzzed faintly as he flew. "I'll call you when your sib's ticket comes up. Now leave."

Doctor-Mechanic Wo was trying to spare me from the truth, I think. Very few of us appreciated the true horror of what had happened; we thought it was just a violent radiation burst that had damaged systems and injured our techné, the self-repair cellules that keep the other modular components of our bodies operational and manufacture more cellules when they die; at worst, that it had fried some of our more unfortunate company.

But while gamma rays wreak a trail of ionization damage, cosmic rays do more: secondary activation transmutes nuclei, turns friendly stable isotopes into randomly decaying radioactive ones. The scratching scraping flickers at the edge of my vision as I neared the escape hatch in the hydroxygen tank was but the palest shadow of the white-out blast of noise that scrambled the minds and eyes of a third of our number, those unfortunates who had berthed in modules near the skin of the ship, on the same side as the radiation beam. Functional for now, despite taking almost a tenth of your borderline-lethal shutdown dose, their brains are literally rotten with fallout.

We're connectionist machines, our minds and consciousness the emergent consequence of copying in circuitry the wet meat-machine processes of our extinct human forebears. (They never quite understood their own operating principles: but they worked out how to emulate them.) Random blips and flashes of radioactive decay are the bane of nanoscale circuitry, be it electronic or spintronic or plasmonic. Our techné is nothing if not efficient: damaged cellules are ordered to self-destruct, and new, uncontaminated neural modules are fabricated in our marrow and migrate to the cortical chambers in head or abdomen, wherever the seat of processing is in our particular body plan.

But what if all the available molecular feedstock is contaminated with unstable isotopes?

Two months after my visit, Doctor-Engineer Wo called me from the sick bay. I was back in the mass fraction tank, scraping and patching and supervising: the job goes on, until all fuel is spent. At a tenth of realtime, rather than my normal deep slowtime, I could keep an eye on developments while still doing my job without too much tedium.

As disasters go, this one crept up on us slowly. In fact, I don't believe anyone—except possibly Doctor-Engineer Wo and their fellow mechanocyte tinkers and chirurgeons has any inkling of it at first. Perhaps our response to the radiation storm was a trifle disjointed and slow. An increase in system malfunctions, growing friction and arguments between off-shift workers. Everyone was a bit snappy, vicious and a little stupid. I gave up listening to Lorus Pinknoise after he interrupted a lecture on the evolution of main sequence stars to launch a vicious rant at a member of his audience for asking what he perceived to be a stupid question. (*I* didn't think it was stupid, anyway.) The chat streams were full of irritation: withdrawal into the tank was easy. So I was taken by surprise when Wo pinged me. "Lilith, if you would come to bay D-16 in Brazil, I have some news about your sister that I would prefer to deliver in personal proximity."

That caught my curiosity. So for the first time in a month, I sped up to realtime, swam up towards the hatch, poked my way out through the tank meniscus, and kicked off along the corridor.

I noticed at once that something was wrong: a couple of the guideway lights were flickering, and one of them was actually dark. Where were the repair crews? Apart from myself, the corridor was deserted. Halfway around the curve of the tunnel I saw something lying motionless against a wall. It was a remora, a simple-minded surface cleaning creature (a true *robot*, in the original sense of the word). It hung crumpled beside a power point. Thinking it had run into difficulty trying to hook up for a charge, I reached out for it—and recoiled. Something had punched a hole through its carapace with a spike, right behind the sensor dome. Peering at it, I cranked my visual acuity up to see a noise-speckled void in place of its fingertip-sized cortex. Shocked, I picked up the pathetic little bundle of plastic and carried it with me, hurrying towards my destination.

Barreling through the open hatch into the dim-lit sick bay, I saw Doctor-Engineer Wo leaning against a surgical framework. "Doctor!" I called. "Someone attacked this remora—I found it in the B-zone access way. "Can you—" I stopped.

The sick bay was lined on every wall and ceiling with the honeycomb cells of surgical frames, the structures our mechanics use in free-fall lieu of an operating table. They were all occupied, their patients staring sightlessly towards the center of the room, xenomorph and anthrop alike unmoving.

Wo turned towards me slowly, shuddering. "Ah. Lilith." It's skin was sallow in the luciferine glow. "You've come for your sister."

"What's—" a vestigial low-level *swallow* reflex made me pause—"what's happened? What are all these people doing here?"

"Take your sister. Please." Wo rolled sideways and pushed two of the frames aside, revealing a third, sandwiched between them. I recognized you by the shape of your head, but there was something odd about your thorax; in the twilight it was hard to tell. "You'd better get her back to your module. I've done what I can for her without waking her. If and when you start her up she's going to be hungry. What you do about that is up to you, but if you want my advice you won't be there when she comes to—if experience is anything to go by."

I noticed for the first time that Wo was not only ill; one of its tentacles was truncated, the missing tip protected by a neatly applied occlusive caul. "What happened to your—"

"The bit rot has affected a third of us, Lilith. You're one of the lucky ones: there's nothing better than a thick blanket of water for cosmic ray shielding."

"Bit rot?" I still didn't understand what was happening to us.

"Radiation-induced *dementia*. You may not be familiar with the condition: dementia is a problem that used to affect our progenitors when their self-repair mechanisms failed. Decaying neural networks malfunction by exhibiting loss of short-term memory, disinhibition, mood swings, violence. Eventually loss of motor control and death. In us, the manifestations are different. Our techné triggers a *hunger* reflex, searching for high-purity materials with which to build replacements for the damaged, purged mechanocytes. And our damage control reflex prioritizes motor control and low-level functions over consciousness. We're quite well-designed, if you think about it. I've replaced your sister's techné with fresh marrow and mothballed it: she's stable for the time being, and if you can find her feedstock that isn't contaminated with short-halflife nuclei she'll be able to rebuild herself. But you should get her to a place of safety, and hide yourself too."

"Why?" I blinked stupidly.

"Because the techné I shoved up her marrow is some of the last uncontaminated material on the ship," Wo pointed out acidly. "There are people on this ship who'll crack her bones to feed on it before long. If she stays here I won't be able to protect her."

"But—"

I looked around. Not all the silent occupants of the surgical frames were unconscious. Eyes, glittering in the darkness, tracked me like gunsights. Empty abdominal sacks, bare rib cages, manipulators curled into claws where

Doctor-Engineer Wo had flensed away the radiation-damaged tissue. The blind, insensate hunger of primitive survival reflexes—*feed and repair*—stared at me instead of conscious minds. Suddenly my numb feet, the persistent pins and needles in my left arm, acquired a broader perspective.

"They're hungry," explained Wo. "They'll eat you without a second thought, because they've got nothing with which to think it—not until they've regrown a neural core around their soul chip." It waved the stump of a tentacle at me. "Jordan and Mirabelle have been rounding up the worst cases, bringing them here to dump on me, but they've been increasingly unforthcoming about events outside of late. I think they may be trying to keep themselves conscious by . . . " A tentacle uncurled, pointed at the pathetic husk of my remora. "Take your sister and go, Lilith. Stay out of sight and hope for rescue."

"Rescue—"

"Eventually the most demented will die, go into shutdown. Some will recover. If they find feedstock. Once the situation equilibrates, we can see about assembling a skeleton crew to ensure we arrive. Then there'll be plenty of time to prospect for high-purity rare earth elements and resurrect the undead. If there's anything left to resurrect."

"But can't I help—" I began, then I saw the gleam in Wo's photoreceptor. The curl and pulse of tentacles, the sallow discoloration of it's dermal integument. "You're ill too?"

"Take your sister and go *away*." Wo hissed and rolled upside down, spreading its tentacles radially around it's surgical mouthparts. "Before I eat you. I'm *so hungry* . . . "

I grabbed your surgical frame and fled.

I carried you back to our module without meeting anybody, for which I was happy. Once inside, I was able to turn up the light level and see what had happened. You were a mess, Lamashtu; were I one of our progenitors I would weep tears of saline to see you so. Ribs hollow, skin slack and bruised, eyes and cheeks sunken. Wo had split open your legs, exposed the gleaming metal of your femurs, the neatly diagrammed attachment points of your withered muscle groups. There was a monitor on the frame, and with the help system I managed to understand what it was telling me. Muscles damaged, skin damaged, but that wasn't all. Once upon a time our foremother bunked atop a nuclear reactor in flight from Mars to Jupiter; the damage here was worse. Your brain . . . there was not much there. Eighty percent of it dissolved into mildly radioactive mush. Wo decanted it, leaving your cranial space almost empty.

But your soul chip was intact, with your laid-down backup: given a few liters of inert, non-decaying minerals you could grow a new cortex and awaken as from a dream of death. But where could I find such materials?

I have an ionization sensor. As I swept it around the module I saw that even our bed is radioactive. If you were to eat its aluminum frame and build a new brain from it, your mind would be a crazy patchwork of drop-outs and irrational rage.

I needed to find you pure feedstock. But according to Wo, the entire ship was as contaminated as if it had been caught in the near-lethal blast radius of a supernova, or flown for a quarter million years close to the active core of our galaxy.

There was one obvious place to look for pure feedstock, of course: inside the cortical shells of those survivors who were least affected by the magnetar burst. Inside my head, or people like me. What did Wo say about the symptoms? Anger and disinhibition first, loss of coordination only late in the day. I ought to be able to trust those who aren't angry or hungry. But I looked at you and wondered, how many of them would also have friends or lovers to nurse? Any friendly face might be a trap. Even a group of rational survivors, working together, might—

I shook my head. Trying to second-guess the scale of the breakdown was futile. There might be other places where feedstock could be found, deep inside the core of the ship. The never-used, mothballed fusion reactors: they would be well-shielded, wouldn't they? Lots of high-purity isotopes there. And with enough working brains and hands, surely we could repair any damage long before they were needed for deceleration. The cold equations seemed simple: with enough brains, we can repair almost any damage—but with a skeleton crew of senile zombies, we're doomed.

So I collected a bundle of tools and left you to go exploring.

The darkened corridors and empty eye-socket spaces of the *Lansford Hastings'* public spaces are silent, the chatter and crosstalk of the public channels muted and sparse. They've been drained of air and refilled with low-pressure oxygen (nitrogen is transmuted too easily to carbon-14, I guess). There's no chatter audible to my electrosense; anyone here is keeping quiet. I pass doors that have been sealed with tape, sprayed over with a symbol that's new to me: a red "Z" in a circle, evidence that the dementia cleanup teams have been at work here. But for the most part the ship appears to be empty and devoid of life—until I reach the F Deck canteen.

Eating is a recreational and social activity: we may be able to live on an injection of feedstock and electrolytes and a brisk fuel cell top-up, but who wants to do that? The canteen here mainly caters to maintenance workers and technicians, hard-living folks. In normal circumstances it'd be full of social diners. I hesitate on the threshold. These circumstances aren't normal—and the diners aren't social.

There's a barricade behind the open hatch. Flensed silvery bones, some of them drilled and cracked, woven together with wire twisted into sharp-pointed barbs. A half-dissected skull stared at me with maddened eyes from inside the thicket of body parts, mandible clattering against its upper jaw. It gibbers furiously at terahertz frequencies, shouting a demented stream of consciousness: "Eat! Want meat! Warmbody foodbody look! Chew 'em chomp 'em cook 'em down! Give me feed me!"

Whoops, I think, as I grab for the hatch rim and prepare to scramble back up the tunnel. But I'm slow, and the field-expedient intruder alarm has done its job: three of the red-sprayed hatches behind me have sprung open, and half a dozen mindlessly slavering zombies explode into the corridor.

I don't waste time swearing. I can tell a trap when I stick my foot in one. Someone who isn't brain-dead organized this. But they've picked the wrong deckhand to eat. You and I, Lamashtu, we have inherited certain skills from our progenitor Freya—and she from a distant unremembered sib called Juliette—that we do not usually advertise. They come in handy at this point, our killer reflexes. Hungry but dumb, the zombies try to swarm me, mouthparts chomping and claws tearing. I raise my anti-corrosion implement, spread the protective shield, and pull the trigger. Chlorine trifluoride will burn in *water*, scorch rust. What it does to robot flesh is ghastly. I have a welding lamp, too, an X-ray laser by any other name. Brief screams and unmodulated hissing assault me from behind the shield, gurgling away as their owners succumb to final shutdown.

The corridor cleared, I turn back to the barricade. "This isn't helping," I call. "We should be repairing the—"

A horrid giggle triggers my piloerectile reflex, making the chromatophores in the small of my back spike up. "Meaty. Spirited. Clean-thinking."

The voice comes from behind the barricade (which has fallen silent, eyes clouded). "Jordan? Is that you?"

"Mm, it's Lilith Longshanks! Bet there's lots of eating on those plump buttocks of hers, what do you say, my pretties?"

An appreciative titter follows. I shudder, trying to work out if there's another route through to the reactor control room. I try again. "You've got to let me through, Jordan. I know where there's a huge supply of well-shielded feedstock we can parcel out. Enough to get everyone thinking clearly again. Let me through and . . . " I trail off. There *is* another route, but it's outside the hull. It's your domain, really, but if I install one of your two soul chips, gain access to your memories, I can figure it out.

"I don't think so, little buffet." The charnel hedge shudders as something forces itself against it from the other side. Something *big*. If Jordan has been eating, trying desperately to extract uncontaminated isotopes, what has he done with the surplus? Where has he sequestrated it? What has he made with it? In my mind's eye I can see him, a cancer of mindlessly expanding, reproducing mechanocytes governed by a mind spun half out of control, lurking in a nest of undigestible leftovers as he waits for food—

I look at the bulging wall of bones, and my nerve fails: I cut the Teflon shield free, cover my face, and launch myself as fast as I can through the floating charred bodies that fill the corridor, desperate to escape.

Which brings us to the present, Lamashtu, sister-mine.

I've got your soul—half of it—loaded in the back of my head. I've been dreaming of you, dreaming *within* you, for days now.

In an hour's time I am going to take my toolkit and go outside, onto the hull of the *Lansford Hastings*, under the slowly moving stars.

I'm going to go into your maze and follow the trail of pipes and coolant ducts home to the Number Six reactor, and I'm going to force my way into the reactor containment firewall and through the neutron shield. And I'm going to strip away every piece of heavily shielded metal I can get my hands on, and carry it back to you. When you're better, when you're back to yourself and more than a hungry bag of rawhead reflexes, you can join me. It'll go faster then. We can help the others—

I'm running out of wall to scribble on; anyway, this is taking too long and besides, I'm feeling a little hungry myself.

Goodbye, sister. Sleep tight. Don't let any strangers in.

About the Authors

Joanne Anderton lives in Sydney with her husband and too many pets. By day she is a mild-mannered marketing coordinator for an Australian book distributor; by night she writes science fiction, fantasy, and horror. Her short story collection, *The Bone Chime Song and Other Stories*, won the Aurealis Award for Best Collection, and the Australian Shadows Award for Best Collected Work. She has published The Veiled Worlds Trilogy: *Debris, Suited,* and *Guardian.* She has been shortlisted for multiple Aurealis and Ditmar awards, and won the 2012 Ditmar for Best New Talent. You can find her online at joanneanderton.com.

Michael A. Arnzen's latest experiments in horror include a treasury of micropoetry (*The Gorelets Omnibus*), a set of horror-oriented refrigerator magnets (*The Fridge of the Damned*), and a web app for writers on the dark side (diaboliquestrategies. com). He is the recipient of four Bram Stoker Awards for his fiction, and is currently serving as Division Chair of Humanities at Seton Hill University, home of the MFA program in Writing Popular Fiction. Visit him at gorelets.com.

Marie Brennan is the author of nine novels, including the series Memoirs of Lady Trent: *A Natural History of Dragons, The Tropic of Serpents,* and the upcoming *Voyage of the Basilisk,* as well as more than forty short stories. More information can be found at swantower.com.

Mike Carey is the author of the Felix Castor novels, *The Girl With All the Gifts,* and (along with Linda and Louise Carey) *The Steel Seraglio.* He has also written extensively for comics publishers DC and Marvel, including long runs on X-Men, Hellblazer, and Ultimate Fantastic Four. He wrote the comic book Lucifer for its entire run and is the co-creator and writer of the ongoing Vertigo series The Unwritten.

Jacques L. Condor (Maka Tai Meh, his given First Nations tribal name) is a French-Canadian Native American of the Abenaki-Mesquaki tribes. He has lived in major cities, small towns, and bush villages in Alaska and the Pacific Northwest for fifty-plus years. He taught at schools, colleges, museums, and on reserves about the culture, history, and arts of his tribes for twenty years as part of the federal government's Indian education programs. Now eighty-five, Condor writes short stories and novellas based on the legends and tales of both Natives and the "oldtime" sourdoughs and pioneers. He has published five books on Alaska. Recently, his work appeared in five anthologies: *Icefloes*, *Northwest Passages*, *A Cascadian Odyssey*, *Queer Dimensions*, *Queer Gothic Tales*, and *Dead North*.

Neil Gaiman is the #1 *New York Times* bestselling author of more than twenty books for readers of all ages, including the novels *Neverwhere*, *Stardust*, *American Gods*, *Anansi Boys*, *Coraline*, and *The Graveyard Book*; the Sandman series of graphic novels; and *Make Good Art*, the text of a commencement speech he delivered at Philadelphia's University of the Arts. His most recent book for younger readers is *Fortunately, the Milk*. *The Ocean at the End of the Lane*, his most recent novel for adults, was voted Book of the Year in the British National Book Awards. He is the recipient of numerous literary honors, including the Locus and Hugo Awards and the Newbery and Carnegie Medals.

Roxane Gay's writing has appeared in *Best American Short Stories 2012*, *Best Sex Writing 2012*, *Oxford American*, *American Short Fiction*, *West Branch*, *Virginia Quarterly Review*, *NOON*, *The New York Times Book Review*, *Bookforum*, *Time*, *The Los Angeles Times*, *The Nation*, *The Rumpus*, *Salon*, *The Wall Street Journal*'s Speakeasy culture blog, and many others. She is the co-editor of *PANK* and essays editor for *The Rumpus*. She teaches writing at Eastern Illinois University. Her novel, *An Untamed State*, was recently published (Grove Atlantic) as was her essay collection, *Bad Feminist* (Harper Perennial).

Ron Goulart has been a professional author for several decades and has over one hundred-eighty books to his credit, including more than fifty science fiction novels and twenty-some mystery novels. He is considered a leading authority on comic books, comic strips, and pulp fiction—subjects about which he has written extensively. Goulart's *After Things Fell Apart* (1970) is the only science-fiction novel to ever win an Edgar Award.

Eric Gregory lives in Carrboro, North Carolina. His stories have appeared in *Lightspeed*, *Strange Horizons*, *Interzone*, *Shine: An Anthology of Optimistic Science Fiction*, and elsewhere. Find him online at ericmg.comor and on Twitter at @ericgregory.

William Jablonsky's first collection of short fiction, *The Indestructible Man: Stories*, was published by Livingston Press in April 2005. His second book, the novel *The Clockwork Man*, was released by Medallion Press in September 2010, and republished by Grey Oak (India) in the summer of 2012. His short stories have appeared in many literary journals and magazines, including *Asimov's*, *Shimmer*, *Phoebe*, and *The Florida Review*. He teaches at Loras College in Dubuque, Iowa.

Shaun Jeffrey was brought up in a house in a cemetery, so it was only natural for his prose to stray towards the dark side when he started writing. Among his writing credits are stories published in *Surreal Magazine*, *Dark Discoveries*, *Shadowed Realms*, and *Cemetery Dance*. He has had two collections published, *The Mutilation Machination* and *Voyeurs of Death*, as well as five novels: *The Kult*, *Killers*, *Deadfall*, *Fangtooth*, and *Evilution*. *The Kult* has been filmed by Gharial Productions. When not spending time with his family or writing, he works out at the gym, jogs, does Krav Maga, and is a Taekwondo black belt.

Matthew Johnson lives with his wife and two sons in Ottawa, where he works as Director of Education for MediaSmarts, Canada's center for digital and media literacy. *Irregular Verbs and Other Stories*, a collection of his short fiction, was published in 2014 by ChiZine Publications. You can follow his work at irregularverbs.ca or on Twitter at @irregularverbal.

Stephen Graham Jones is the author of twenty novels, five story collections, and over two hundred short stories. His most recent novels are *Not for Nothing* and *The Gospel of Z*; his latest collections are: *After the People Lights Have Gone Off* and *Zombie Sharks With Metal Teeth*. Jones has been a Stoker finalist, a Shirley Jackson Award finalist, an NEA fellow, and won the Texas Institute of Letters Award for fiction. He teaches in the MFA program at CU Boulder and UCR-Palm Desert.

Joy Kennedy-O'Neill teaches English at Brazosport College on the Texas coast. Her works have appeared in *Strange Horizons*, *The New Orleans Review*, and anthologies such as *What Wildness is This: Women Write the Southwest*.

The *New York Times* recently hailed **Caitlín R. Kiernan** as "one of our essential writers of dark fiction." Her novels include *The Red Tree* (nominated for the Shirley Jackson and World Fantasy awards) and *The Drowning Girl: A*

Memoir (winner of the James Tiptree, Jr. Award and the Bram Stoker Award, nominated for the Nebula, Locus, Jackson, World Fantasy, British Fantasy, and Mythopoeic awards). To date, her short fiction has been collected in thirteen volumes, most recently *Two Worlds and In Between: The Best of Caitlín R. Kiernan (Volume One)*, and *The Ape's Wife and Other Stories*. A fourteenth, *Beneath An Oil-Dark Sea: The Best of Caitlín R. Kiernan (Volume Two)* is forthcoming. Currently, she's writing the graphic novel series Alabaster for Dark Horse Comics and has just finished her next novel, *Cherry Bomb.*

Nicole Kornher-Stace lives in New Paltz, NY. Her short fiction and poetry has appeared in a number of magazines and anthologies, including *Best American Fantasy, Clockwork Phoenix 3* and *4, The Mammoth Book of Steampunk, Apex,* and *Fantasy Magazine.* She is the author of *Desideria, Demon Lovers and Other Difficulties,* and *The Winter Triptych.* Her latest novel, *Archivist Wasp,* is forthcoming from Big Mouth House, Small Beer Press's YA imprint, in late 2014. She can be found online at nicolekornherstace.com.

Joe R. Lansdale is the author of over forty novels and numerous short stories. His novella, *Bubba Ho-tep,* was made into an award-winning film, as was *Incident On and Off a Mountain Road.* His mystery classic *Cold in July* inspired the recent major motion picture of the same name starring Michael C. Hall, Sam Shepard, and Don Johnson. Novel *The Bottoms* will soon be filmed, directed by Bill Paxton. His works have received numerous recognitions, including the Edgar, eight Bram Stoker awards, the Grinzane Cavour Prize for Literature, American Mystery Award, International Horror Guild Award, British Fantasy Award, and many others. His most recent novel for adults, *The Thicket,* was published last fall.

Shira Lipkin's short fiction and poetry have appeared in *Strange Horizons, Apex Magazine, Stone Telling, Clockwork Phoenix 4,* and other wonderful magazines and anthologies; two of her stories have been recognized as Million Writers Award Notable Stories, and she has won the Rhysling Award for best short poem. She lives in Boston and, in her spare time, fights crime with the Boston Area Rape Crisis Center. Her cat is bigger than her dog.

David Liss is the author of eight novels, most recently *The Day of Atonement.* His previous bestselling books include *The Coffee Trader* and *The Ethical Assassin,* both of which are being developed as films, and *A Conspiracy of Paper,* which is now being developed for television. Liss has written for numerous comics series including Mystery Men, Sherlock Holmes: Moriarty Lives, and Angelica Tomorrow. His website is davidliss.com.

Jonathan Maberry is a Bram Stoker Award-winning author, writing teacher, and motivational speaker. Among his novels are *Ghost Road Blues, Dead Man's Song, Bad Moon Rising,* and *Patient Zero. Fire & Ash,* fourth in the Benny Imura series, was published last year; *Fall of Night,* sequel to *Dead of Night,* was has just been released. His seventh Joe Ledger novel, *Predator One,* will be out spring 2015. He is co-editor of the anthology *Redneck Zombies From Outer Space* and editor of the forthcoming dark fantasy anthology, *Out of Tune.* His has written comics and non-fiction works as well.

Alex Dally MacFarlane is a writer, editor, and historian. When not researching narrative maps in the legendary traditions of Alexander III of Macedon, she writes stories that can be found in *Clarkesworld, Strange Horizons, Beneath Ceaseless Skies, Phantasm Japan, Solaris Rising 3, Heiresses of Russ 2013: The Year's Best Lesbian Speculative Fiction, The Year's Best Science Fiction & Fantasy: 2014,* and other publications. Poetry can be found in *Stone Telling, The Moment of Change,* and *Here, We Cross.* She is the editor of *Aliens: Recent Encounters* (2013), and *The Mammoth Book of SF Stories by Women* (2014).

Maureen F. McHugh has lived in New York City; Shijiazhuang, China; Ohio; Austin, Texas; and now lives in Los Angeles. She is the author of two collections, *Mothers & Other Monsters* (a Story Prize finalist) and *After the Apocalypse: Stories* (a *Publishers Weekly* Top Ten Best of the Year) as well as four novels, including *China Mountain Zhang* (winner of the Tiptree Award) and *Nekropolis* (a *New York Times* Editor's Choice). She received a Hugo Award for her short story "The Lincoln Train." McHugh has also worked on alternate reality games for Halo 2, The Watchmen, and Nine Inch Nails, among others.

Joe McKinney has been a patrol officer for the San Antonio Police Department, a homicide detective, a disaster mitigation specialist, a patrol commander, and a successful novelist. His books include the four-part Dead World series, as well as *Quarantined, Inheritance, Lost Girl of the Lake, The Savage Dead, Crooked House,* and *Dodging Bullets.* His short fiction has been collected in *The Red Empire and Other Stories* and *Dating in Dead World.* His latest works include the werewolf thriller, *Dog Days,* set in the summer of 1983 in the little Texas town of Clear

Lake, where the author grew up, and *Plague of the Undead* (Book One in the Deadlands Saga). In 2011, McKinney received the Horror Writers Association's Bram Stoker Award for Best Novel. For more information: joemckinney. wordpress.com.

Lisa Mannetti's debut novel, *The Gentling Box,* garnered a Bram Stoker Award and she has since been nominated three times for the award in both the short and long fiction categories. Her story, "Everybody Wins," was made into a short film released under the title *Bye-Bye Sally.* Her novella, "Dissolution," is currently being adapted for the screen as a feature-length movie by writer/ director, Paul Leyden. She has also authored *The New Adventures of Tom Sawyer and Huck Finn*; two companion novellas in *Deathwatch*; a macabre gag book, *51 Fiendish Ways to Leave Your Lover*; as well as nonfiction books and numerous nonfiction articles. Mannetti lives in New York. Visit her website lisamannetti.com and virtual haunted house: thechanceryhouse.com.

Tamsyn Muir is based in Auckland, New Zealand, where she divides her time between writing, teaching, and dogs. A graduate of the Clarion Writers' Workshop 2010, her work has previously appeared in *Fantasy, Nightmare,* and *Weird Tales,* as well as in anthologies such as Ellen Datlow's *The Best Horror of the Year (Volume 5)* and Ann and Jeff VanderMeer's *The Time Traveler's Almanac.* She was a 2012 finalist for the Shirley Jackson Award for Best Short Fiction.

Holly Newstein's short fiction has appeared in *Cemetery Dance* and the anthologies *Borderlands 5, The New Dead, In Laymon's Terms, Epitaphs: The Journal of the New England Horror Writers Association,* and *Evil Jester Digest, Volume 2.* Her collaboration with Rick Hautala, "Trapper Boy" appeared in anthology *Dark Duets*, edited by Christopher Golden (Harper Voyager, 2014). Her story "Eight Minutes" was part of *Anthology II* (The Four Horsemen Press, 2013). She was the featured author in the June 2014 edition of *LampLight Magazine,* with her story "Shadows and Light." She is also the coauthor of the novels *Ashes* and *The Epicure* with Ralph W. Bieber, published originally under the pen name H. R. Howland. She lives in Maine with her dogs, Keira and Remy.

Cat Rambo may be anywhere at a given time. Her two hundred-plus fiction publications include stories in *Asimov's, Clarkesworld,* and *Tor.com.* Her short story, "Five Ways to Fall in Love on Planet Porcelain," from her story collection

Near + Far (Hydra House Books), was a 2012 Nebula nominee. Her editorship of *Fantasy Magazine* earned her a World Fantasy Award nomination in 2012. For more about Rambo, as well as links to her fiction, see kittywumpus.net.

Carrie Ryan is the *New York Times* bestselling author of the critically acclaimed Forest of Hands and Teeth series, which has been translated into over eighteen languages and is in development as a major motion picture. She is also the editor of the anthology *Foretold: 14 Tales of Prophecy and Prediction*, as well as author of *Infinity Ring: Divide and Conquer*, the second book in Scholastic's new multi-author/multi-platform series for middle grade readers. Her most recent book—co-written with her husband, JP Davis—is *The Map to Everywhere*, the first of a new middle grade series. Ryan is a graduate of Williams College and Duke University School of Law. A former litigator, she now writes full time. She lives with her writer/lawyer husband, two fat cats, and one large rescue mutt in Charlotte, North Carolina. You can find her online at carrieryan.com or @CarrieRyan.

Marge Simon's works appear in publications such as *Strange Horizons, Niteblade, DailySF Magazine, Pedestal*, and *Dreams & Nightmares*. She edits a column for the HWA newsletter, "Blood & Spades: Poets of the Dark Side," and serves as Chair of the Board of Trustees. She won the *Strange Horizons* Readers Choice Award 2010, and the SFPA's Dwarf Stars Award 2012. In addition to her poetry, she has published two prose collections: *Christina's World* (Sam's Dot, 2008) and *Like Birds in the Rain* (Sam's Dot, 2007). She won the Bram Stoker Award for Superior Work in Poetry for *Vectors: A Week in the Death of a Planet* (Dark Regions Press, 2008) and again in 2013 for *Vampires, Zombies & Wanton Souls* (Elektrik Milk Bath Press).

Maggie Slater hails from the snow-crusted woods of New England where she lives with her husband and son. Her fiction has appeared in *Fantastical Visions IV, Dark Futures: Tales of SF Dystopia*, and *Leading Edge Magazine*, among others. She currently moonlights as an assistant editor for *Apex Magazine*, and formats books for Apex Publications. For more information about her and her current projects, visit her blog at maggiedot.wordpress.com.

Simon Strantzas is the author of the critically acclaimed short story collections *Beneath the Surface* (2008), *Cold to the Touch* (2009), *Nightingale Songs* (2011), and *Burnt Black Suns*—published in 2014 by Hippocampus Press. His fiction has been nominated for the British Fantasy Award, and has appeared in *The Year's Best Dark Fantasy & Horror, The Mammoth Book of Best New Horror, The Best Horror of the Year, The Year's Best Weird Fiction*, the Black Wings series, *Nightmare, Postscripts, Cemetery Dance*, and elsewhere. He was born in the cold darkness of the Canadian winter and has resided in Toronto, Canada ever since.

Charles Stross is a British SF writer, born in Leeds, England, and living in Edinburgh, Scotland. He has worked as a tech writer, a programmer, a journalist, and a pharmacist; he holds degrees in Pharmacy and in Computer Science. He has won two Hugo Awards for his short fiction. Among Stross's more recent novels are *The Revolution Business* and *The Trade of Queens* (in his Merchant Princes series), *The Apocalypse Codex* (part of the Laundry series of novels and stories), *Rule 34, The Rapture of the Nerds* (with Cory Doctorow), and, published earlier this year, *The Rhesus Chart*.

Genevieve Valentine's first novel, *Mechanique: A Tale of the Circus Tresaulti*, won the 2012 Crawford Award and was nominated for the Nebula. Her second novel, *The Girls at the Kingfisher Club*, a 1920s retelling of the Twelve Dancing Princesses, was published by Atria earlier this year. *Persona*, a near-future political thriller, will be published by SAGA Press in March 2015. Her short fiction has appeared in *Clarkesworld, Strange Horizons, Journal of Mythic Arts, Lightspeed*, and other periodicals, as well as anthologies *Federations, The Living Dead 2, After, Teeth*, and others. Her story "Light on the Water" was a 2009 World Fantasy Award nominee, and "Things to Know About Being Dead" was nominated for a 2012 Shirley Jackson Award. She is a coauthor of pop-culture book *Geek Wisdom* (Quirk Books).

Carrie Vaughn is the author of the *New York Times* bestselling series of novels about a werewolf named Kitty, the most recent installment of which is *Kitty in the Underworld*. The next, *Low Midnight*, will be published later this year. She's written several other contemporary fantasy and young adult novels, as well as upwards of seventy short stories. She's a contributor to the Wild Cards series of shared world superhero books edited by George R. R. Martin and a graduate of the Odyssey Fantasy Writing Workshop. An Air Force brat, she survived her nomadic childhood and managed to put down roots in Boulder, Colorado. Visit her at carrievaughn.com.

Don Webb has been published in every major SF/F/H magazine in the English-speaking world from *Analog* to *Weird Tales*. He teaches "Writing the Science Fiction Novel" at UCLA extension. He lives with has a beautiful wife and two tuxedo cats in Austin, Texas, where he has been a guest at the four local SF conventions for over twenty years.

Jay Wilburn lives with his wife and two sons in the swamps of coastal South Carolina. He left teaching after sixteen years to care for the health needs of his younger son and to pursue writing full-time. He has published *Loose Ends: A Zombie Novel* with Hazardous Press and *Time Eaters* with Perpetual Motion Machine Publishing. Follow his many dark thoughts at JayWilburn.com and @AmongTheZombies on Twitter.

About the Editor

Paula Guran is senior editor for Prime Books. She edited the Juno fantasy imprint from its small press inception through its incarnation as an imprint of Simon & Schuster's Pocket Books. Guran edits the annual Year's Best Dark Fantasy and Horror series as well as a growing number of other anthologies. In an earlier life she produced the weekly email newsletter *DarkEcho* (winning two Stokers, an IHG Award, and a World Fantasy Award nomination), edited print magazine *Horror Garage*—an eccentric mix of original dark fiction and garage/punk/indie music—earning another IHG Award and a second World Fantasy nomination—and has contributed reviews, interviews, and articles to numerous professional publications. (See paulaguran.com for more information.) She lives in Akron, Ohio, and is the mother of four, mother-in-law of two, and *grand-mère* to one.

Acknowledgments

"Trail of the Dead" © 2007 Joanne Anderton. First Publication: *Zombies*, ed. Robert N. Stephenson (Altair Australia Books).

"Rigormarole" © 2005 Michael A. Arnzen. First publication: *Rigormarole: Zombie Poems* (Naked Snake Press, 2005).

"What Still Abides" © 2013 Marie Brennan. First Publication: *Clockwork Phoenix 4*, ed. Mike Allen (Mythic Delirium Press).

"Iphigenia in Aulis" by Mike Carey © 2012 Mike Carey. First publication: *An Apple for the Creature*, eds. Charlaine Harris & Toni L.P. Kelner (Ace Books).

"Those Beneath the Bog" © 2013 Jacques L. Condor. First Publication: *Dead North: Canadian Zombie Fiction*, ed. Silvia Moreno-Garcia (Exile Editions Ltd.)

"The Day the Saucers Came" © 2006 Neil Gaiman. First publication: *Fragile Things* (Headline Review; William Morrow/Harper Collins).

"There Is No 'E' in Zombi Which Means There Can Be No You or We" © 2010 Roxane Gay. First publication: *Guernica*, 1 October 2010.

"I Waltzed With a Zombie" © 2009 Ron Goulart. First publication: *The Magazine of Fantasy & Science Fiction*, October-November 2009.

"The Harrowers" © 2011 Eric Gregory. First Publication: *Lightspeed*, May 2011.

"The Death and Life of Bob" © 2013 William Jablonsky. First publication: *Shimmer #16*, Winter 2013.

"'Til Death Do Us Part" © 2012 Shaun Jeffrey. First Publication: *Alt-Zombie*, ed. Peter Mark May (Hersham Horror Books).

"The Afflicted" © 2012 Matthew Johnson. First publication: *The Magazine of Fantasy & Science Fiction*, July/August 2012.

"Rocket Man" © 2011 by Stephen Graham Jones. First publication: *Stymie*, Vol. 4, Issue 1, Spring & Summer 2011.

"Aftermath" © 2012 Joy Kennedy-O'Neill. First publication: *Strange Horizons*, 6 February/13 February 2012.

"In The Dreamtime of Lady Resurrection" © 2007 Caitlín R. Kiernan. First publication: *Subterranean Magazine*, Fall 2007.

"Present" © 2014 Nicole Kornher-Stace. First publication: *Mythic Delirium*, January 2014.

"The Hunt: Before, and the Aftermath" © 2012 Joe R. Lansdale. First publication: *Trapped in the Saturday Matinee* (PSPublishing).

"Becca at the End of the World" © 2013 Shira Lipkin. First publication: *Apex Magazine*, Issue 53, October 2013.

"What Maisie Knew" © 2010 David Liss. First Publication: *The New Dead: A Zombie Anthology*, ed. Christopher Golden (St. Martin's Griffin).

"Jack and Jill" © 2012 by Jonathan Maberry. First publication: *21st Century Dead: A Zombie Anthology*, ed. Christopher Golden (St. Martin's Griffin).

"Selected Sources for the Babylonian Plague of the Dead (572-571 BCE)" © 2013 Alex Dally MacFarlane. First publication: *Zombies: Shambling Through the Ages*, ed. Steve Berman (Prime Books).

"The Naturalist" © 2010 Maureen F. McHugh. First publication: *Subterranean Magazine*, Spring 2010.

"The Day the Music Died" © 2011 Joe McKinney. First Publication: *Holiday of the Dead*, ed. David Dunwoody (Wild Wolf Publishing).

"Resurgam" © 2010 Lisa Mannetti. First publication: *Dead Set: A Zombie Anthology*, eds. Michelle McCrary & Joe McKinney (23 House Publishing).

"Stemming the Tide" © 2013 Simon Strantzas. First Publication: *Dead North: Canadian Zombie Fiction*, ed. Silvia Moreno-Garcia (Exile Editions Ltd.)

"Chew" © 2013 Tamsyn Muir. First publication: *Lightspeed*, January 2013.